THE LATIN STUDENT

A Novel by Denis Brault

Flowerpublish
www.flowerpublish.com
Montreal, Canada

Uxori Micheline *et filiabus* Nancy Cindy*que*

Pars Prima: Mens sana in corpore sano

The High School Years…and beyond: Cincinnati

Prologue

The hot early morning sun was already shining brightly as I walked up the stone walled hill with trepidation, but mostly with the excitement one feels when approaching the office that will welcome you as a first-year professor. I, Holden Hainsworth, was the new Assistant Professor of Classical Studies at the Université de Montréal. I had been told that the department secretary – the only person available to welcome me as everyone else was still on summer break – would take special care of me as I was a young American embarking on a career in a francophone university. I entered the building at the top of the hill, and quickly made my way to the elevator. A few students (I assumed they were students since they appeared even younger than I was – I had recently celebrated my twenty-eighth birthday and was still quite boyish-looking!) and a security guard entered the elevator, all greeting me with a pleasant *"Bonjour!"*. The students got out on the fourth floor, and I continued to the ninth floor - the entire floor being the home of the Classics Department. The security guard seemed impressed with my choice of floors and wished me *"Bonne journée"*! as the doors closed. I presumed he would get off on the next floor - the top one – and would make his rounds going down one floor at a time. The department office was to the left of the elevator at the end of the corridor. Upon entering, I was greeted by the secretary, Mme. Sylvain. She seemed to be fiftyish, which explained her grayish hair neatly tied up in a bun. She wore a white blouse buttoned to the neck. I was quite relieved by her prudish appearance, having frequently heard accounts in graduate school of secretaries who were eager to please professors beyond the call of duty!

- *Bonjour, Professeur* "Ainswort"! Welcome to the Université of Montréal!

Her enthusiastic welcome - in English - was a noble one, even with its heavy French accent.

- *Venez!* I will show you your office.

As I followed her down the corridor to the right, I couldn't help notice that her tight-fitting black skirt was not the length of someone content with being over fifty. We entered my office, and I immediately sat down in a plush leather chair. As Mme Sylvain left with *"À bientôt!"*, I immediately swivelled the chair towards the large window which afforded a magnificent view of the city down below.

I slowly closed my eyes to contemplate the moment.

Chapter 1

- Hainsworth, decline *dies* in the singular.

- *Dies, diei, diei, diem, dies, die.*

- And what inspiring expression contains that word for "day"?

- *Carpe diem!*

- Remember that boys, and make it one of your life's goals to always seize the moment! Does anyone have another inspiring expression? Go for it, Hainsworth!

- Father McNeil, I try to live up to the ideal of *mens sana in corpore sano.*

- Very good! A suitable motto for you, Hainsworth. After all, you're an excellent Latin student, and you are our school's quarterback – the best football player we've had in the last twenty years! One couldn't ask for a healthier mind in a healthier body! Well, boys, the bell is about to ring. Don't forget next Friday's assignment – translation of the first twenty lines of the *Aeneid.*

- *Arma virumque cano, Troiae qui primus ab oris* ...

- I'm sure you could go on, Hainsworth, but there's no time. You'll soon get your chance to "sing about arms and the man who set out from the shores of Troy"! Don't forget you're serving Mass at assembly today. Aren't you glad you can now understand those Latin prayers you merely recited by rote memory when you started at St. Xavier High a few years ago?

- *Pater noster, qui es in caelis....*

- Again, there's no time. Save the "Our Father" for game time. And you might even need a "Hail Mary" play to win! See you boys at Mass. And don't forget the big game against Coryville High after school. If we don't win, Hainsworth here will have a jug! And for the umpteenth time, boys, the "jug" detention doesn't stand for "Jesuits unduly gruesome"

Chapter 2

- Thanks, Oldie! I got completely confused on the hand-off and went the wrong way. You made it look like a planned play for a quarterback keeper, and your touchdown run saved my bacon!

- You mean I saved St. X's bacon! Tommy, I think you sometimes concentrate too much on our cheerleaders from Sacred Heart. Don't you know you have plenty of time for the girls after games and practices – especially since you don't spend much time on your Latin homework.

- Oldie, I don't get how you can be so into Latin - especially since you're such a good athlete.

- Where's the mystery? *Mens sana in corpore sano*! Latin helps me understand so many complicated words in English. And it really helped me learn French. My Mom was so happy when I chose French as my complementary course.

- Your Mom is really sweet, but too cultured for me. I know you get your love of languages from her, but how come your parents saddled you with a moniker like Holden – it's almost as bad as your sister's name, Phoebe?

- Actually, my Dad named Feeb and me after the brother and sister in his favorite novel – *Catcher in the Rye* by J.D.Salinger.

- Wow! Remember how old Father Mitchell's face turned really red when we asked if our American Lit class could read that novel? But that book was written after you were born, so how come...

- My father let me read his copy. The book was published in 1951 but was written a few years before that. My Dad's English teacher at college knew J.D. Salinger, and had read the early drafts, which he talked about to his English Lit students. My Dad's class read a short story featuring Holden Caulfield that was published in the 1940's. It was called "Slight Rebellion off Madison". But I sure hope I don't become a rebel like Salinger's Holden Caulfield! My mother gave me my middle name – Denys – after the Greek god Dionysos. That's why she calls me Den, and not because it's the last syllable in Holden. As my mom says, no nickname for Holden could be better than Oldie!

- Gosh! I said your mom was sweet! But I've heard your Dad call you Bus.

- That's short for Phoebus – the male version of Feeb's name.

- You mean the god Apollo - the handsome one!

- Doesn't apply to me, Dad says.

- Go on! All the girls are chasing you - good thing you're a fast runner! Or is it?

Father McNeil briefly had me interested in Latin when he said it led to Romance languages. When I realized he didn't mean turning girls on, I started to sour on Latin. But look at you – charming all the Jesuits at St. Xavier with your skill in Latin! And being the head altar boy doesn't hurt! Old Padre McNeil sees you as a future Jesuit - probably replacing him as Latin teacher here at St. Xavier. He calls me "Doubting" Thomas – but somehow I don't think the connection with one of the Apostles is his way of saying I would be a good religion teacher. And I hang around too many girls to be a good Jesuit prospect! But I know you Oldie! You have a funny look on your face whenever those Sacred Heart cheerleaders start dancing around us. You've got the hoots for one of them, haven't you?

- I 'm not saying no, Tommy, but right now I've got to get home and change. Then I'm off to Pizza Pete's for my evening shift.

Chapter 3

- Hi ya, Holy! As usual, right on time to shove the pizzas in the oven! Did you bring any quarters for our jukebox? I got some new Doo Wop songs put in for you.

- Sure, I brought some coins. Some job – I pay and play! And I'm not holy!

- And I'm no saint! But what's in a name? You bring in the Catholics, Holy. My name's not Pete, but it helps me sell "Petezas"! Get it? By the way, I heard how your winning touchdown knocked off Coryville today. You're the star every game. The university scouts must be on your tail. I bet the UC Bearcats would love to have you. You could help put Cincinnati back on the NCAA map. And when the national anthem is sung before their games they'll sing it with pride, especially that bit "say, can UC"! Now, what's that song you like? "In the Still of the Night"? Good song to play for your girlfriend. You must have a girlfriend, good-looking guy like you - and a top jock to boot!

- I don't really have time for a girlfriend, Pete. Between my shifts here and my caddying at Indian Hills Country Club, I barely have time to keep up with my studies. And I want to major in Classics. It's a demanding programme that wouldn't leave me much time for football.

- What do you mean? Classics? Are you talking about songs by Sinatra and his black dude friend Sammy Davis? I thought you'd be going to university to get a good job. God knows you're already a hard worker. With the right diploma, you could make a lotta money.

- Classics is the fascinating study of the ancient Greeks and Romans, and their languages, Ancient Greek and Latin. Right now, Latin is my favorite subject at St. Xavier High and Father McNeil is encouraging me to study Latin at university. By the way, Sammy Davis is an Afro-American – not what you called him!

- Oh yeah, I forgot you was with the Jesuits. Civil rights and all that. All that talk about Romans. Just remember that pizza was invented here in the good ol' U.S. of A! Well, if my daughter ever showed up at the house with a black fella I 'd … I'd, I don't know, but for black and white folk to go out together isn't natural. Now you go serve those two guys. And don't forget – the pizza dough for black Afro-American customers is on the bottom shelf.

Chapter 4

- I've corrected the Vergil assignments, boys. Nice work, Hainsworth! Nelson, after reading your translation, I believe you are not the only "doubting" Thomas – I'm beginning to have my own doubts! Nonetheless, St. Francis Xavier and St. Ignatius of Loyola may grant you a miracle and help you pass the course, but the first line of the *Aeneid* is not about a man and his dog! But don't give up, Nelson. St. Ignatius himself didn't learn Latin until he was 33 – he returned to elementary school just to learn this beautiful language! By the way, boys, as you are aware, the National Latin Exam is being written next month. St. Xavier High has always done well on the exam, and many of you will no doubt keep up our tradition. But I have never had a student with a perfect paper and I haven't many years left here as St. X's senior Latin teacher. It would be nice if one of you could ace the exam this year, wouldn't it, Hainsworth?

- The preparation won't be easy, Father, but I'll do my best. *Per ardua ad astra*! And I remember you telling us that when St. Ignatius gazed upon the stars, it gave him the greatest consolation. Or was that the greatest "constellation"?

- You certainly have a way with words, Hainsworth – in English and in Latin! Now let's dissect the verb *vinco*. Since it is a third conjugation verb, the infinitive is *vincere*. Don't confuse it with the fourth conjugation verb *vincire*, or you will find yourself in a bind!

- Nice one, Father! Don't you love his puns, Tommy?

 - I would if I could understand them, Oldie.

 - *Vincire* means "to bind"!

 - Sorry, Father – I guess I got "tied up" in my verb meanings!

- A little humor is always welcome, Nelson. So keep trying! Now let's translate *vincere*, a verb that can not refer to Nelson's relationship to Latin verbs! Yes, boys, it means "to conquer". A famous Roman general used this verb in an expression after one of his many victories. And let's not overlook the derivation of the word "victory" from the verb *vincere*. Can anyone give us the quote as well as the context of those famous lines? How about you, Hainsworth?

- *Veni, vidi, vici*. These are the first person singular perfect indicative active forms of the verbs *venire, videre,* and our verb *vincere*. I believe Julius Caesar uttered the words "I came, I saw, I conquered" after his conquest of Gaul.

- Excellent on the Latin, Hainsworth, but Caesar actually used those words in a letter to the Roman Senate to report his victory over Pharnaces of Pontus in 47 B.C. But don't be embarrassed, it's a common mistake to associate those words with his commentary on his great conquest of Gaul. Some of you may remember reading snippets from Caesar's *De Bello Gallico* at the end of your sophomore year.

- *Gallia est omnis divisa in partes tres*! I think Caesar meant to give the Romans a geography lesson when he said that all of Gaul was divided into three parts. Father McNeil, my mother bought me some hard-covered cartoon books about a character named Astérix who leads a small village in Gaul against the Romans. They are successful thanks to a magic potion concocted by their Druid. They are published in France, and Mom thought reading them would be a great way to increase my French vocabulary. Of course, guys, they've been translated into English for us Americans. My Dad even bought me one of the books that has been translated into Latin. Funny, it's the closest he has come to showing an interest in my Latin studies. He is constantly saying that I should be more realistic in preparing for a financially rewarding future. Hard to believe he and Pizza Pete are on the same page about what goals I should pursue in life! But Dad shows up at all my football games. And he did get me lined up as the Pro's caddy at Indian Hills through his business contacts. Fortunately, my Mom is super supportive of my Latin studies, often saying her college studies in French, Spanish and Italian would have been much easier if she had studied Latin in high school.

- Yes, Asterix is a real star. You recall the word *astrum*, boys? And that other word for star - *stella*? As you know, I'm expecting a stellar performance from all of you on the Christmas exam! And, boys, it is true that if you persist in your Latin studies, as I truly hope some of you will, you are bound to encounter perplexity, sarcasm and other negative reactions – all in the name of a false relevance which no longer recognizes the benefits of Latin for linguistic, intellectual and cultural enrichment. To all those who will tell you Latin and Roman history are in the past and have no practical value, Cicero had the best reply when he said that not to know what came before you is forever to remain a child. Besides, the great Yogi Berra once said that the future isn't what it used to be! So if you decide to enhance your knowledge of Latin and the Romans, even to the point of pursuing a university degree in the subject, follow that dream and it will ultimately become meaningful and useful. That background will in no way be detrimental to the pursuit of gainful employment and a rewarding and successful life. Now back to our verb *vincere*. If I ask you to translate *Urbs victa* and to parse *victa* what will you say? That *victa* is the perfect participle passive of *vincere*, and as a participle, agrees in case, number and gender since it is a verbal adjective expressing a past action – with the nominative, feminine, singular noun *Urbs*. A city that has been conquered. Of course, in a sentence we may be saying "because the city has been conquered" or "when the city has been conquered" or "although the city has been conquered" or "if the city has been conquered" or simply "the city which has been conquered". All right, then. Who can label each of the circumstances illustrated by those different translations of *Urbs victa*? Yes, Hainsworth?

- Causal, temporal, concessive, conditional, and relative. And, Father, you wrote *Urbs* with a capital letter, so you are saying "conquered Rome".

- *Optime!* And you're quite right about *Urbs*, young man! We know that Rome with all her military force was never really conquered before the fall of the Empire – although she had some scares with the wars against Hannibal and Spartacus that we talked about. However, we know from the poet Horace that on an artistic and intellectual level Rome was, in fact, conquered. Can Master Hainsworth recall that verse?

- *Graecia capta ferum victorem cepit*. That's one of the best examples of historical irony I know, Father. The culture of Greece really impressed her Roman rulers – so much, in fact, that we might say that Greece sort of "captured" Rome!

- Right you are! We can't forget about the ancient Greeks, even in a Latin course especially since both the Greek and Latin languages have a common source. But we haven't finished with the verb *vincere*. Look at the expression *urbs vincenda* - not Rome this time.

This form of the verb is called a gerundive, and it indicates an obligation or a necessity. We are now talking about a city that must be conquered. For next week please review the formation and basic uses of the gerundives on page 280 of your textbook. We will then tackle that amusing construction known as the gerundive construction. Speaking of tackling, I imagine that our football team will be practicing hard after school for the championship game next week against Roger Bacon. We have to beat those Franciscans – but don't tell Father President I said that. He's afraid anything that sounds like a religious squabble will reach the higher Church authorities. He forgets that I taught Latin to the Archbishop of Cincinnati himself. He was a very good student – but not as good as you, Hainsworth. And he was rubbish at football! Finally, it's Nelson's birthday tomorrow. *Ad multos annos*, Nelson!

Chapter 5

- That was quite a workout! A couple more hard practices like that and we'll be really ready for the championship game against Bacon next Friday. The way you mix the plays and run the ball, Oldie, November 22, 1963 will go down in the history of high school football! Say, you'll be at my birthday party tomorrow, right? Our team cheerleaders will be there - you know they are all sweet on you!

- I don't know if Pizza Pete will let me switch shifts. Besides it's your "sweet sixteen" party, not mine. Since all those girls will be there, you're sure to have fun without me.

- You have to come, Oldie! I sorta hinted that you might be there.

- What exactly did you say, Tommy?

- "Holden will be at the party". Oh, and can you bring your guitar? I know you can play, even though you hardly ever bring your guitar anywhere.

- Well, my Mom suggested I learn how to play the guitar. My Dad encouraged me, too. Interesting that he was "in tune" with Mom on this one. And of course Phoebe had already begun piano lessons. Our parents feel it's necessary to develop an artistic side. So I strum a little and write down poems I pretend are songs.

- Wow! *Mens sana in corpore sano* - football player and singing Latin brain! But for the girls Holden Hainsworth is *mens bella in corpore bello* – a handsome dude with a beautiful mind! Too bad I didn't play the guitar too. We could have been "Strummer and Dumber"!

- Don't put yourself down, Tommy – our football opponents will do that for you! Say Tommy, this party you're planning with all those cheerleaders sort of reminds me of a movie I went to see with my sister a couple of weeks ago. The name of the movie is *13 Frightened Girls*! The film is about a group of students in a private girls' school who are all daughters of diplomats from different countries. The winner of a Latin competition – the American girl – got to drive the school bus. From that point – like the bus – the story went downhill for me – although Feeb liked it. Just think of Walt Disney, as if he were trying to produce a spy thriller like he was Alfred Hitchcock! But it wasn't a Walt Disney movie because there was no loveable mouse in it! And how come Ralph Kramden got to drive a bus in "The Honeymooners" without taking Latin? I read in the newspaper critique of the movie that there had been a real contest in all those countries to select the different girls, and the bus scene was shot with all of the girls in turn so that they could make the movie popular in those countries! They should make a movie all about a Latin competition – maybe call it the "Caesar Contest"! Or to make it popular with guys like you, Tommy, a contest on Roman history! The winner could be declared "Emperor"! Although, if you were in the contest, you'd probably find a way to cheat!

- Nice "sewer humor", Ed Norton!

***

- Sorry I'm a bit late, Tommy. Pete only let me leave after the evening rush. I barely had time to listen to one tune on the juke-box – "Jimmy Mack" by Martha Reeves and the Vandellas. You know we've got six Motown songs on our box. But I brought my guitar with me.

- You're really into that black music, Oldie. Oh well, I guess nobody's perfect! But I'm glad you're here – some of the girls were showing signs of leaving. Holden is here – he's my best friend, girls! Now we can play that popular party game - Movie Star for a Magic Moment – hey, Oldie, "This Magic Moment" - one of your favorite tunes! Well, since Holden – my best friend! – has probably never played this game, I'll explain to everybody how it works. The guys pick a movie star. The gals, in turn, choose one of the movie stars by name and sit blindfolded as the chosen star kisses her. She then has to guess who the star really is. So Connie's choice is Paul Newman. Do your thing, Paul! Carol has also chosen Paul Newman. Okay, Paul, go to it! Paula has chosen – no surprise there – Paul! But Paul Newman is not obliged to sing "Hey, hey Paula, I want to marry you" – just kiss her. Gosh, Paul Newman is getting all puckered out, so let's give him a rest. Oh, Debbie has chosen Elvis Presley, who will be more than happy to press his sweet lips to hers! Well girls, while you're all trying to figure out who kissed you, let's all mingle and enjoy the refreshments.

***

- What's the big idea, Oldie? Kissing all the girls. Who'd have thought Paul Newman was so popular with the female population, what with James Dean and Tab Hunter on the prowl? Oh, and Debbie admitted she picked Elvis because she was sure you had chosen that star. But you can make it up to me by grabbing your guitar and accompanying me as I serenade the girls. Ladies, Elvis is not only here for your kissing pleasure, but will grace you with his golden voice. "Are you lonesome tonight, do you miss me tonight?"

- You keep singing like that, Tommy, and you're going to be lonesome for a long time!

- Very funny! I said I had a golden voice – not a Holden voice! Say, you fit in pretty well for a guy who doesn't get to many parties. But you didn't seem to be warming up to any of the

15

cheerleaders. When I recently asked you if you were interested in one of them, you didn't say no. You don't believe all that rubbish Pizza Pete keeps feeding you about girls being nothing but trouble? That joke he told you about the guy being held up and warned "your money or your life" was pretty funny. When the bandit asked the guy why he was hesitating, the reply was "I thought you said WIFE, so I was thinking about it"! You remember what Father Peterson said in Religion class - it's not a sin to date girls? And I think Chaplain Brown was trying to be funny when he said it's what you do on dates that can be tricky.

- Tommy, I don't think Pete's joke will seem so funny when we're married. Sometimes I wonder about girls and their sincerity. Tonight they were interested in what they referred to as my Hollywood looks. For football cheerleaders, they didn't seem to know much about the game, and not one of them knew or cared about Latin. Salinger's Holden didn't care for phonies, and I guess I don't either. By the way, not all the cheerleaders were here.

- Yes, they were! Except for that black one. She's only on the squad because she can dance – but you didn't expect any blacks to be mingling here with us? Wait a minute! She's the one your interested in, isn't she? Holden Hainsworth, I never thought you'd... you're St. Xavier's all-American boy. You could have any girl you wanted. Now I get it – all that Doo Wop and Motown. But I gotta tell you – 'cause I still consider you my best friend – you're going after a whole lot of trouble. You are going to lose a bunch of friends. And don't you know that a lot of people around here are not too keen on mixed dating.

 - First of all, Tommy, I don't even know her. I've never even had the chance to say hello to her. Don't know much about her, except that she's got a beautiful smile. I know all about the problems of racial tension from the discussions in history and civics classes. And Pizza Pete, who's really a nice guy, and treats me really well - he calls me his "classy son" – is living proof of bad blood between white people and Afro-Americans - although he calls them something else. But for the rest of the weekend, I've got to concentrate on gerundives.

Chapter 6

- Barker, can you tell the class whether a gerundive is a verb or an adjective?

- Since it's declined, Father, the gerundive is an adjective.

- Something to say, Hainsworth?

- Well, Father, the gerundive is a verbal adjective. So Barker is sort of right – it's an adjectival form but with a passive verbal meaning. So *amandus* means " to be loved, ought to be loved".

- *Lingua Latina amanda est*! Very good, Hainsworth. Now, boys, pay careful attention to what follows. *Cupidus urbem videndi.* This means "wanting to see the city". As we've SEEN, *videndi* is a gerund. But look at the phrase *cupidus urbis videndae*. What has happened? Any thoughts – Barker, Warner, Hainsworth?

 I mean about this Latin phrase, Nelson!

- Father, the direct object of the gerund *videndi* was changed to the case of the gerund, here the genitive after *cupidus*, and the gerund changes to the gerundive adjective form, and therefore agrees with the new form of the noun *urbis* in case, number and gender, now being genitive, singular, feminine. This is called the gerundive construction.

- I couldn't have put it better myself, Hainsworth. There's also the passive periphrastic construction which we'll soon be looking at. But right now I would like us to focus on some aspects of Roman history. Boys, take fifteen minutes to choose a famous person from Roman history - he doesn't have to have been a Roman himself – and write down why you think he is important to us today. You may have noticed I referred to men only. Why is that?

- Because we're a boys' school?

- No, Nelson! Anybody else? Yes, Hainsworth?

- Father, in Ancient Rome women had no public role. We basically have no female writers of note – women are named rather as objects of affection by various love poets. Of course, some women were very powerful during the Roman Empire, like Livia, the wife of Augustus, and Nero's mother Agrippina, as well as Messalina, the wife of Emperor Claudius – but they exercised control behind the scenes. It seems to me, though, that the most famous woman in Roman history wasn't Roman, but the Queen - or female Pharaoh, I guess – of Egypt.

Everyone has heard of Cleopatra, but not everyone knows she wasn't Egyptian, but Greek! Unlike her predecessors, the Ptolemies, who ruled Egypt after the death of Alexander the Great, she at least learned to speak Egyptian! She also has a starring role in one of those Astérix books my mother buys me.

- A keen perception of women in Ancient Rome, Hainsworth. And I've heard through the grapevine that you have quite mature reflections on contemporary women, or rather, girls. It's apparently a quality not shared by all of you – am I right, Nelson? Okay, gentlemen, fifteen minutes. Yes, Nelson, I think we all know you have chosen Julius Caesar, but try to enlighten us on Caesar's importance even today.

***

- Well, Father, thanks to Julius Caesar we can all be entertained at Caesar's Palace and dine on Caesar's salad. Just a little humor, Father. Actually, the great general and conqueror was also quite the orator and writer. I guess you could say he was the Roman version of Holden Hainsworth, who keeps winning the School's public speaking and essay contests! We've already looked at Caesar's *De Bello Gallico*. But he also wrote an account of the civil war again Pompey called *De Bello Civili*. When he crossed the Rubicon river, he had gone too far to change his decision. That's why we say "crossing the Rubicon" when there's no turning back. Fellas, don't you think that "Rubicon" would make a swell name for a vehicle that could cross any terrain or swamp? But Caesar used another expression to indicate that he could no longer change his mind when he uttered *alea iacta est* – "the die is cast". That refers to the roll of the dice, guys, which was a popular gambling game among Roman soldiers. By the way, Father McNeil, I wasn't one of those students caught playing cards for money in the cafeteria last week. None of us Latin students were involved. In fact, Father, the only cards we "deal" are your Latin vocabulary cards! I know you're interested in etymology, Father, so we all should take note that the words Czar and Kaiser are derived from the name Caesar. Remember, guys, when we discussed those titles in Mr. Smith's World History class? But Julius Caesar was a little full of himself. That's why he forced the pirates who had captured him to increase their ransom demands. That's why he admitted being so ashamed at not having accomplished at his age what Alexander the Great had done at such a young age. That's why he thought he was so popular he would rule for many years to come and never be harmed. The assassination of Julius Caesar by Brutus and company ought to warn us that we should keep both feet on the ground if we don't want to find them all of a sudden under the ground! I thought I'd finish with some humor, Father!

- *De gustibus non disputandum est*, Nelson – I can't dispute your style. You said you would finish with some humor. Well, we're all waiting! You might have informed us that a "Caesar salad" is prepared by adding twenty knives! No, seriously, Nelson, I am impressed by your singular synopsis in highlighting key facts in the life and legacy of Julius Caesar. You've obviously digested that chapter in our book on Roman history. And, as well, if you will allow me the irresistible pun, you have given us some food for thought! We will now hear the other choices in the following order: Barker, Harris, Warner, Mittenkamp, Santos, Duke, Stewart and Hainsworth.

- I have chosen to speak about Romulus. Now, I know there probably never was a real historical figure named Romulus, but ancient Rome must have been under the leadership of some kind of king early in her history, and we might as well call him Romulus, even if his name was likely made up because of the City's name, and not the other way round. I think the Romulus-king was important because he organized the state that would become a powerful and influential force among the peoples of that region, such as the Sabines and the Etruscans. He developed the military strength of Rome very early in her history. The farmers became soldiers as well out of necessity, and to demonstrate superiority in the game of conquest. Rome's military strength and her sense of organization and governance enabled her to eventually master all of what is now Italy, and then lands beyond Italy, and then – well the rest, as they say, Father, is history! The fact that Mars, the Roman god of war, was originally a god of agriculture seems to confirm the dual role of Rome's first citizens as farmers and soldiers. He was, so to speak, the "god of the fields" – farm fields and battlefields! The Romulus figure also lends himself quite appropriately, I believe, to a Roman mythology which is based on the story of the origins of a future mighty empire. After all, Romulus was said to be the son of the god Mars. He killed his brother Remus to get what he wanted, although in a self-righteous way, claiming the kingship on the religious basis of having seen more birds - that is, more divine signs - than his brother. There's a Hitchcock movie that would have really excited him - that's my attempt at humor, Father! It seems that brothers were always killing brothers.

There are stories in Greek literature and the Old Testament about these fratricides. There's my contribution to Latin derivatives – *frater* means "brother" and the verb *occidere* means "to kill". Oh yes, it's a third conjugation verb, Father – a short "e". Say, Holden, aren't we lucky we only have sisters? So I chose to speak about Romulus because, in many ways, he's the starting point for any discussion on the beginnings of Ancient Rome.

- Father, I wanted to say my choice of an important figure in Roman history is ironic following Barker's calling Romulus the first character in the story of Rome so I could score Latin derivative points for the word irony. But I remember you telling us that the Latin word *ironia* is itself derived from a Greek word. So I'll use a real Latin derivative and call it a coincidence from the Latin prefix *co-* meaning at the same time or together – like *cum* – right, Father - and *incidere* - another third conjugation verb with short "e" – meaning "to happen". As it happens – trying to be funny, Father! – my choice, Vergil, was actually responsible for the story about the beginning of Rome. His famous poem the *Aeneid* narrates the legend of the Trojan prince Aeneas who escapes from Troy as that city is being burned by the victorious Greeks. He courageously makes his way to the shores of Italy with his son Ascanius.This son, who is also called Iulus, founds a city where later on a Vestal Virgin named Rhea Silvia gives birth to twin boys named Romulus and Remus. Supposedly, their father was the god Mars. So Rome's story begins before the arrival of Romulus. But the mother of Aeneas was Venus, the goddess of love. Now that I have Nelson's attention, I can make a connection with his Julius Caesar by pointing out that Iulus was the ancestor of the Julian clan to which Julius Caesar belonged, and so that made him a descendant of the goddess of love, Venus. I'm sure that he mentioned that fact to Cleopatra when he met her! The *Aeneid* is an epic poem about a man who travels a great distance and overcomes many dangers and wins an ultimate battle in a new land. As Hainsworth is fond of telling us, the poem begins with *Arma virumque cano* – "I sing about the arms of war and about a man". I think Nelson had assumed the story involved a dog, but *cano* is a verb, not the noun *canis*! Although I remember that Aeneas was called *pius*- that is, faithful to his duty. And we all know how faithful dogs are! Vergil was a great writer, yet some people say he just copied Homer. But I think he was clever. Homer took twenty-four books to write about a war in the *Iliad* and twenty-four books to write about the adventures of a hero in the *Odyssey*. Vergil only took twelve books to write about his hero who overcame both monsters and human foes, and then won the war in Italy! The common thread in the works of both writers is Troy. Actually, we don't really know if there was a Homer, but there definitely was a Vergil. And since I've mentioned Troy, I'd like to remind the class about the connection between Troy and our fair city of Cincinnati that we learned in our Classical Civilization course last year. It seems that Carl Blegen excavated the probable site of the Troy of Homer's Trojan War while he was an archaeology professor at the University of Cincinnati. He put UC's Classics Department on the map! Finally, a little anecdote, guys - and I know the word anecdote is Greek, not Latin – so no bonus points. Vergil had decided to have his work destroyed, since he had not been able to check and revise it. But who checks his work – right, Nelson? Anyhow, copies were made, and we have this great poem today.

- My great figure in Roman history wasn't Roman, but he was central to Rome's military history, and I can even connect him to the Roman poet Vergil that Harris just talked about. One of the greatest generals in the history of the world was Hannibal of Carthage. He is famous for having led his army and elephants across the Alps. He invaded Italy, and his great victories at Cannae and at Lake Trasimene basically had the Romans on their knees. He never actually attacked Rome, and eventually returned to Carthage in Africa, where he was defeated by a great Roman general, Scipio, who got the name "*Africanus*" because of this victory at Zama. Hannibal was not helped by the fact that jealous opponents in Carthage failed to support his efforts against the Romans. But Hannibal was a clever strategist, and his own troops never deserted him, even during the hardships crossing the Alps. Even Caesar's legionaries sometimes mutinied, Nelson! In fact, Rome fought three wars against Carthage called Punic Wars. Remember, guys, when Father McNeil explained how the word Punic came from the word Phoenicia by removing the aspiration – the "h" sound – right - since the Phoenicians were the founders of the colony on the shores of North Africa which became the powerful maritime city of Carthage? Rome finally destroyed Carthage in the third Punic War because a famous Roman named Cato kept warning the Romans after the war against Hannibal to destroy Carthage. His expression was *Karthago delenda est* – Carthage must be destroyed. Extra points, right, Father, for using the gerundive? You knew, guys, that the Romans spelled Carthage with a "k", even though that letter was not part of their alphabet, but used only in foreign words like *kalends*, the Greek word used for the first day of Roman months, and which gave us the word for calendar? And by the way– you knew there would be a "by the way", guys – I can't help it if I'm a fountain of knowledge about Roman history and Latin expressions! Although I admit if I'm a fountain, Hainsworth is an ocean of knowledge about Ancient Rome and the Latin language! Now here's the connection with Vergil, who Harris talked about. Vergil wrote about the wanderings of the hero Aeneas before he arrived on the shores of Italy. Well, before he reached his destination, Aeneas was shipwrecked on the shores of a new city founded by Queen Dido, who had fled an evil tyrant in Phoenicia. She fell in love with Aeneas, who appreciated her help, but was determined to follow his destiny. When she learned that Aeneas had abandoned her, Dido committed suicide. The Latin words *sui* – self - and *occidere* – have given us this word, which means "to kill oneself". But before she died, Dido cursed Aeneas and his future city – that is, Rome – and declared that Carthage and this city would become bitter enemies. Of course, Vergil put this episode in his poem to narrate what actually happened in history, and made it appear as a prediction of the great wars between Rome and Carthage. But as you always say, Father, the easiest predictions are those about events after they happen. You taught us the term *post diem* – "the day after". Hannibal no doubt swore to always hate Rome from the time he was a boy, because he was inspired by legends of the hatred between Rome and Carthage. Just like Hainsworth has probably sworn an oath to always love Latin!

- I want to talk about an interesting figure in Roman history, who, like Hannibal, was not a Roman, and who also was victorious for a time against Rome's mighty legions. Spartacus was the gladiator who led a slave revolt against the Romans. Father, I want to get my Latin derivative points right off the bat by mentioning the fact that the word "gladiator" comes from the Latin word *gladius* which means sword. So a gladiator was a swordsman. But we know that gladiators didn't only fight with swords, but also with nets and tridents and spears. Gladiators were the entertainers of Ancient Rome. Some individual gladiators became very popular because of their many victories in the arena. We know that Roman emperors believed that keeping the people fed and entertained would maintain a loyal and non-complaining population. The Latin expression was *panem et circenses* – bread and circuses. While some gladiators did gain their freedom, most remained the property of the gladiator school owners, who were called *lanistae*. Gladiators were mostly prisoners captured in wars, or citizens who joined the schools because they couldn't pay their debts. Spartacus was a Greek from Thrace in northern Greece, and I remember learning in our Classical Civilization course that the Thracians were fierce fighters. Many slaves joined the rebellion of the gladiators under Spartacus, until he had a sizeable army. They managed to defeat Roman armies, and many of them hoped to gain freedom by fleeing from Italy. Spartacus seemed bent on reaching Sicily, but he was betrayed and eventually defeated and captured by Marcus Crassus, who was said to be the richest man in Rome. Did you know, guys, that he used to have buildings set on fire, and then buy them from desperate owners for a ridiculously low price. He would then have the fires put out by his own fire brigade and sell the buildings at a huge profit. Stewart, whose father is in real estate, is probably thinking that there is something terribly wrong with this man! He was the same Crassus who ruled it over Rome with Julius Caesar and Pompey the Great – *Magnus* in Latin, guys! - in what is known as the First Triumvirate – a word meaning "three men," right, Father? Gladiators used to salute the Emperor before their combats with the words *Ave Caesar, morituri te salutant*. This means " Hail Caesar"- the first emperors were Caesars - "those who are about to die, salute you". I should point out that the full expression could have been *qui morituri sunt te salutant* - this is known as the active periphrastic and is used to express an impending action or an intention. Guys, do you remember that poem we read in English class "To An Athlete Dying Young"? I think the poet A.E Housman could have had a full time job at the Colisseum reciting his poem after the gladiatoral combats! Father McNeil told us that the word periphrastic comes from the Greek words *peri* meaning "around" and *phrasis* meaning "speech". Of course the future participle by itself used here expresses the same idea, but I want the bonus points for my grammatical clarification. And not to sound too much like Hainsworth, the word circumlocution is a Latin derivative from *circum* and *loqui,* meaning "around" and "to speak", that has the same meaning as "periphrasis". Spartacus was crucified together with six thousand other captured slaves. To quote Holden Hainsworth's remark in our Classical Civilisation course – Crassus must have been very cross with Spartacus! We all know that crucifixion is a Latin word, and we all remember the many discussions about that redeeming death on the cross with Father Peterson in Religion class. What a terrible sight that must have been – six thousand crosses along the Appian Way. That was the most famous of the Roman roads - built, I guess under the supervision of a Roman magistrate named Appius. All roads in Italy actually did lead to Rome – like our interstates, right, Father? The war against Spartacus was the first major rebellion of slaves in Italy. There had been others in Sicily, and I guess that's why Spartacus wanted to go there. These wars were called Servile Wars from the Latin word *servus* meaning "slave". The word "serf", used to describe peasants in the Middle Ages, comes from the same word. So servile can be used to describe work worthy of a slave. It's also the word used by Nelson to describe homework! Finally, I want to mention that great movie starring Kirk Douglas as Spartacus, which we saw in our Classical Civilization course.

- I chose to speak about the historian Livy. Let's face it, guys, without his great account of the history of Rome from her beginnings called *Ab Urbe Condita* - meaning "from the founding of the City" – another example of a perfect passive participle – we wouldn't have been able to have presentations on Romulus or Hannibal or Spartacus. Even though a large part of his original history is lost, he no doubt served as a main source for other ancient historians. He gave us both facts and legends which led to the creation of a sort of heroic mythology of Ancient Rome based in part on real people and real events. Livy tells us about the period of the Roman kings from the beginning to their overthrow by liberators led by Brutus. This involved the story of Lucretia – yes, guys, the same Lucretia in the poem by William Shakespeare we studied in English Lit class. This Brutus was the ancestor of the Brutus who believed he had to liberate Rome from Julius Caesar. He was the tragic hero in Shakespeare's Julius Caesar. Father, we saw the movie Julius Caesar with Marlon Brando – he was great as Mark Antony! It's amazing how many of Shakespeare's plays are based on Ancient Greece and Rome! He even studied Latin but wasn't as good as Hainsworth! Livy's work certainly inspired other historians who wrote about the second period in Roman history – the Republic. His approach to history even had an influence on later writers who gave us accounts about the third period of Rome's history that we call the Roman Empire. It's true that Livy's work was meant to glorify Rome and her past. But Vergil was doing that too. This didn't prevent them from producing great works in Latin, one in prose and one in poetry. And they both gave us Latin texts we could translate before we graduated from high school!

- I will present Augustus, the first Roman emperor. He made it possible for the great writers like Vergil and Livy, as well as Horace and others, to produce their literary masterpieces by providing them with the financial resources to live off of writing – apparently not so easy to do, even today! – and a theme to start them off, namely, the glory of Rome – past, present, and future. At first, Augustus was not a nice person. He was known as Octavian, and when still a teenager was thrust into power by being named as his successor by Julius Caesar in his will before he was assassinated. Caesar had adopted Octavian as his son. And so Octavian joined with Mark Antony and Lepidus to form the Second Triumvirate in order to defeat Brutus and Cassius. But then he had to face down the older and more experienced Mark Antony who was now allied with Cleopatra and counting on Roman forces in the East. Octavian had cruelly disposed of Romans who had seemed dangerous to him while he was still on good terms with Mark Antony, but now it was a two-man struggle for control of Rome and her possessions. This was a struggle between East and West. Because he had the loyalty of the legions that had fought for Julius Caesar, and because he was a good military strategist, Octavian defeated Mark Antony and Cleopatra, who both committed suicide. Shakespeare himself couldn't have written a better ending! Octavian seemed to want to preserve the traditional elements in Roman republican government, but the Roman people and Senate – symbolized by the S.P.Q.R. - *Senatus populusque Romanus* – that we see on buildings and in the movies! – gave him supreme powers, even giving him the title "Augustus", a special title of dignity which consecrated him as being sort of sacred. This reverence possibly contributed to his being ultimately proclaimed a god. The supreme power given to Augustus was called *imperium* in Latin. It's from this word that we get our words "empire" and "imperial". In some ways, Father, Augustus was like our President. For example, he was supreme commander of Rome's armed forces, was in charge of foreign affairs, and had strong influence and veto power over governing bodies. In a way he even had authority over the judicial bodies since he could grant pardons. Of course, the President of the United States is elected to his position and can only serve two four year terms – Augustus was emperor for forty-one years! Nor is the President the head of a State religion as Augustus was. For my bonus points I would like to explain the word "veto". *Veto* is a first person singular present indicative active verb meaning "I forbid". This was the verb used by the representative of that class of citizens known as plebeians, who had few rights and were at the mercy of the rich and powerful patricians. As the plebeians – the word comes from the Latin word *plebs* which just means the masses of common, ordinary people - right, Father? - began to have more rights, they were protected by a tribune who sat in on senate meetings and would veto any laws that would be harmful to the plebeians. He would say *veto* – I forbid it! As we all know, the patricians got their name from *pater*, the Latin word for "father". The *patres* were the early leaders of Roman society and government. They were also called *patres conscripti* – another perfect participle passive, guys from the verb *conscribere* meaning "to enroll". These became the first senators, a word from the Latin *senex* meaning "old man". Isn't it interesting that we also refer to the "Founding Fathers" of our country, just like the Romans. Even Canada refers to her "Fathers of Confederation". It's not surprising that America's early history has parallels in Ancient Rome and not just with the eagle as our national symbol, or with the Senate. That's because our Founding Fathers admired great Romans and the republican government. It's why we have a political party called the Republicans. The term comes from the Latin expression *res publica* which means the "common good" or "property". *Res* is one of those fifth declension nouns we were looking at a few weeks ago - right, Father? Our other political party is called Democrats because of a derivation from the Greek words *demos* meaning "people" and *kratos* meaning "power". Augustus actually referred to himself as "first citizen" or *Princeps* – from the Latin word for "first" – *primus.* Obviously, the word prince is derived from this term – thank you bonus points! So, the Roman Empire was, in fact, a Principate. Augustus was quite successful in his rule as Emperor, or *Princeps.* As we saw, he arranged to have great writers produce great works. His domestic and foreign policies stabilized Rome. He insisted on proper morals in terms of family and social values. But we know that he didn't practice what he preached! He beautified Rome by restoring and building temples. Augustus said that he had found it a city of stone and left it a city of marble. But with all that devotion to Roman state religion and all that power Augustus may have begun to consider himself divine - he was considered the son of a god since the State had deified his father, Julius Caesar. In fact, after his death, Augustus was deified, and the cult of Emperor worship became an official State religion. We spent some time in Religion class discussing how this became a serious problem for the early Christians. Finally, he did bring about *pax Romana*, "peace in the Roman world".

- I'm lucky to be able to speak about Cicero, since he's my favorite Roman. He did it all, guys! He was a statesman – or, as we would say, a politician - even though that word is from the Greek word *polis* which means "city-state". The Latin word for huge cities like Rome was *urbs* - yes, giving us the word "urban"! The Romans used the word *oppidum* for smaller towns. Cicero was also a lawyer, a philosopher, an orator, and a provincial governor. He did military service, but wasn't really into the military life, and I can relate to that! No offense, Nelson! He didn't come from Roman nobility, but from the class of citizens known as equestrians. In fact, his basic principles drove him to strive for harmony among the three classes, or orders, of citizens – patricians, *equites*, who were sometimes referred to as equestrians, since their name comes from the Latin word for horse – *equus*, and plebeians. This agreement among the three groups of citizens was known as the *concordia ordinum*. But it couldn't have been easy, since we often come across the expression "struggle of the orders"! Cicero was able to pursue his political goals by moving through the *cursus honorum*, that is the "race for honors". That meant he managed to get elected to each government office, leading to the highest position in the state. These magistracies were quaestor, aedile, praetor and finally, consul. The Romans had instituted a dual consulship as a control mechanism to ensure that no one person would have complete power over the State like a king. *Rex* was a title that no politician was willing to accept – even Julius Caesar – although he was probably tempted – after what had happened to Tarquin the Proud, the Etruscan who had been the last king of Rome. Do I get bonus points, Father McNeil, for saying that the king's name in Latin was *Tarquinius Superbus*? My cousin told me that Cicero's legal speeches are often read in university courses, but he said that his favorite work by Cicero was the *Ad Familiares*, the "Letters to his Friends". I would personally like to read his *De natura deorum*, his book on the nature of the gods. He wrote books on Greek philosophy, on oratory - one of which was called *Brutus*!, on superstition, and on the Latin language. As a politician, his political speeches enthralled the Romans as much as they captivate us. As consul, he wrote speeches against Catiline, whom he accused of treason against Rome. As a measure against this conspiracy, Cicero introduced a *senatus consultum ultimum*, which was the Roman version of martial law. We Americans would bring in the National Guard! By the way, the word "martial" comes from Mars, the Roman god of war – I need my bonus points for Latin derivatives, Father! For saving Rome against the conspirators Cicero was called *pater patriae* - the father of his country. He also wrote a number of speeches against Mark Antony, which ultimately cost Cicero his life. He called these speeches "Philippics", because he modelled them after the famous speeches that the Greek orator Demosthenes wrote against Philip, the father of Alexander the Great. Cicero wasn't perfect, but he seemed genuinely interested in saving the Roman Republic – even though he acted mostly in the interests of the Establishment, that is, the patricians and the *optimates* – the aristocratic party of the "best", as opposed to the plebeians and the *populares* – the party of the people - which Julius Caesar had championed. I would like to close with what some of you might consider trivial. Here's another "by the way" - the word trivial comes from the Latin *tres viae,* or "three roads". People would often chat when meeting where three – or more – roads crossed. This "crossroad gossip" was often unimportant or trivial. Well, it seems that the Latin word *cicer* meant "chick pea". So maybe one of Cicero's ancestors had a pimple on his face. But that's not the way I want to remember Marcus Tullius Cicero!

- Father, Cicero's a hard act to follow. But let me elaborate on one detail about the man Stewart so ably presented to us. The fact that he was the first member of his family line to become consul made him a *novus homo*. This means "a new man". In some ways, it's like the rags to riches tale of a Walt Disney. I chose the Roman Cincinnatus as the subject of my presentation. There are a few reasons for my choice, not the least of which is the fact that our fair city is named after him. But getting back to self-made men in the image of Cicero, I believe that Bob Rogers, the son of my boss Pizza Pete, is a genuine *novus homo*. Even though Pete - and that's not even his real name – never finished high school, Bob Rogers went to university and then to medical school. After a short career in municipal politics here in Cincinnati and in Springfield, Illinois, Dr. Rogers is now in the running to become Governor of Illinois. He is in a gubernatorial race. I'm claiming my derivative points for the Latin word *gubernator*, which means "steersman", and gives us the word "governor". The Governor "steers the ship of state", as they say! And speaking of service to the State, Cincinnatus would be the poster boy - or rather, man – for Rome in the early republic. He was the ideal citizen – a hard- working farmer who took up arms when necessary. Twice he was called upon to save the city from danger and conflict. To carry out this demanding mission, he was appointed Dictator. This was a position in the early constitution which suspended the dual leadership of the two consuls, and placed all authority in the hands of one man until the crisis was over. He wasn't a king – his *imperium* was limited to a maximum of six months. Cincinnatus took on the duty of saving the Republic without hesitation, and just as quickly gave up the title of "dictator" when he had defeated Rome's enemies. The actions of Cincinnatus are all the more remarkable when we consider what other men did after taking on the role of dictator – men like Marius and Sulla and Julius Caesar. They did not give up the position of Dictator until they had eliminated personal enemies and enriched themselves to the detriment of Roman citizens. Caesar, in fact, had declared himself "Dictator for life" – much like those we studied about in our World History course, such as Mussolini in Italy and Franco in Spain. Unfortunately for Julius Caesar, he got his wish when he was assassinated on the Ides of March! We already heard that the *Kalends* were the first day of the month in the Roman calendar. The *Ides* were the thirteenth or fifteenth day of the month – in March it was the fifteenth day. The other day with a name was the *Nones*, which fell on the seventh or ninth day of the month. The other days of the month were counted back from these days. Caesar should have taken Shakespeare's advice to "beware the Ides of March"! So the term "dictator", which is from a Latin verb *dictare*, meaning "to say" or "tell" like the verb we usually use – *dicere* - means the person who "tells" people what to do. And for us, then, has a pejorative meaning. The comparative form of the adjective *malus* meaning "bad" is *peius* – that is, "worse". Nobody likes a pessimist, and in Latin he would be *pessimus* – the worst. So, today, a dictator is not a nice person! Livy gives us many examples of courageous behavior, like Horatius at the bridge. But I think Cincinnatus was a true model for all Romans because he not only was brave, but also did not try to lord it over others, even when given absolute authority. I believe Augustus wanted the Romans to return to the admiration for and practice of virtue. That is why he encouraged Livy and Vergil and others to write about virtuous men and women. The ultimate virtue for women was modesty, in the sense of fidelity to a husband, as we saw with Lucretia. The Latin word for this is *pudicitia* – which I found in my Latin dictionary, Father. The word "virtue" comes, of course, from the Latin *virtus*. This Latin word actually denotes "manly virtue", which for the Romans was courage. There is probably a connection between the word *virtus* and *vir*, the word for "man". I think our first President was a American "Cincinnatus". George Washington freely gave up control of the Continental Army. After two terms as President, he retired and returned to his farm at Mount Vernon. The story of Cincinnatus makes me proud to be living in Cincinnati, Father, and proud to be an American!

- And I'm proud of you boys for doing such a great job on presenting famous figures from Roman history. And I'm really gratified you were all able to work in specific grammatical notions, as well as rather profound words derived from Latin. Hainsworth, I don't know who is more interesting, your Pizza Pete, or his son, Dr. Rogers. And I'm going to award you full points for the derivatives "governor" and "gubernatorial", even though the Latin word *gubernator* is itself derived from the Greek word *kubernetes*. Not that you need the points since you have a commanding lead in the race for this year's bonus prize – a series of books on the Latin language. We all know you are an avid reader, and Nelson here tells me you were reading Encyclopedia Britannica before you finished grade school. That's probably why you learned that the great French World War II hero and later President of France, Charles De Gaulle, as well as Alfred Hichcock, and the great writers James Joyce and Sir Arthur Conan Doyle, graduated from Jesuit schools. But did you know that the creator of Sherlock Holmes also had the name Ignatius? I suppose reading is an interest you inherited from your maternal grandmother. How do I know Hainsworth's maternal grandmother? When I was a young undergraduate at Xavier University – yes, boys, as hard as it is to believe, I was once young! – Miss Lansdowne was a young librarian in the university library. I guess books are part of your family tradition, Hainsworth! Before we end class, I want to mention a famous Roman general – *Pompeius Magnus*, who non-Latinists call Pompey the Great. During his time, pirates roamed the Mediterranean, causing havoc. The *piratae* so loved the Roman Republic you could hear the "R" loud and clear across the *Mare nostrum*, which was what the Romans called the Mediterranean, since it really was "in the middle of their land" – "our sea", they said with pride! Pompey brought about the "pirate repulsion", which brought him good "PR", until his defeat at the hands of Julius Caesar during the civil war. But you baseball fans know that there are still Pirates in Pittsburgh! Now, boys, while we are talking about pride, I expect to see all of you at the championship game against Roger Bacon on Friday. You see how I've circled Friday, November 22 on our calendar. I don't mind that classes have been cancelled, even though we usually have Latin class and our weekly quiz on Fridays. Since the game is being played at the University of Cincinnati's Nippert Stadium, there will be room for everyone. And I expect to hear even more noise than when the Bearcats are playing. I'm sure our very own quarterback Hainsworth and running back Nelson will do us proud. Kick-off is at ten o'clock. See you there!

Chapter 7

- That first half was tough, Oldie, but thanks to you we're sitting on a 14-3 lead. Your 85-yard TD run after a double fake on our first possession got the crowd going and allowed our beautiful cheerleaders to swing into action. My dumb fumble on our 30 yard-line was responsible for them being able to kick a field goal. But you gotta be proud of how we clicked together for our second score. After you gave me the hand-off for the end sweep, I didn't have any holes opened for me, so I'm glad you stayed open for the optional return swing pass, and were able to scamper the fifteen yards into the end-zone for the touchdown. Hey, I can see Father McNeil sitting up in the stands with Father Mitchell and Chaplain Brown, and a bunch of other teachers. I haven't seen that many Jesuits sitting together since the Mass for the Jesuit Martyrs. And isn't that your Dad up behind them, and your Mom sitting with him? There's a cute girl sitting beside your Mom. Oh, it's your sister Phoebe! I heard the Sacred Heart girls would be here – and not just our cheerleaders. The coaches told us to relax, but it's hard to relax with all this excitement. How do you stay so calm, Oldie?

- I'm more numb than calm, Tommie. I got hit hard a couple of times. Anyways, it's impossible to relax with you chattering the whole time. But you're right – we pulled off our "secret play" just the way we practiced it. The timing was perfect, and we needed a second touchdown before the half. Coach has been letting me call all the plays. I guess he's happy with our play mix so far. I'm really glad my folks are here. Dad can take time off from work without any problem, and I guess Mom 's not teaching today. And Phoebe's not just here to be with her friends from Sacred Heart. She actually likes football and has always supported me. We get along pretty good as far as brothers and sisters go. My aunts and uncles call us Phoebe and Phoebus, or more often – Feeb and Bus. Now that I think about it, with my mother usually calling me Den and you calling me Oldie, and our teachers calling me Hainsworth, I'm hardly ever called Holden. Feeb calls me Apollo to tease me, since Apollo is the more popular name for Phoebus. And because she likes the name Oldie that you use, she sometimes calls me Older or Old, because I'm her older brother. I have to admit I sometimes tease her by calling her Feeble. But my Dad came up with the hardest name to live up to. When I became an altar boy, he started calling me Holy! And when Pizza Pete found out, he started calling me by that name, saying that when the Jesuits worked their magic on me, that's what I would become! If I had a girlfriend, I wonder what she would call me.

- Only one way to find out, Oldie. Hey, there's Pizza Pete waiving to you. And he has that ever-present cigar of his in his other hand. He probably has money on this game. And I recognize Donnie Johnson, the Club pro that you caddy for at Indian Hills Country Club. Well, you won't see my folks here. They don't go out much since my brother Marty got killed in 'Nam. Gee, five minutes to the second half kickoff. I'd love to run it all the way back for the six points. Maybe then Father McNeil would give me a homework exemption, or a free pass out of Jug. I hate those Wednesday afternoon detentions.

- Did you know, Tommy, that Jesuits give jugs, not because it stands for "justice under God", but to apply the disciplinary tactic of harnessing bad energy and channeling it into productive energy. You see, the term "jug" comes from the Latin word *iugum*, which is a yoke used to harness oxen in order to get them to plough a field.

- Well, then, I guess the yoke's on me! Hey, here we are talking about Latin during the biggest football game of our lives!

- Weird, I know Tommy, but there's something about Latin… Say, isn't that Father President down at the field announcer's booth with Coach Mason? And I recognize Mr. Walters, the Commissioner of the Greater Cincinnati High School Football Federation, since I got to shake his hand once. They're talking to the Head Coach of the Roger Bacon team, and I think the person in the Franciscan Friar's brown robe with him could be somebody important at Roger Bacon High. I wonder what they're talking about.

- Ladies and Gentlemen, fellow Americans, it is my sad duty to inform you that our President, John Fitzgerald Kennedy, has just been shot and killed in Dallas, Texas. As a sign of respect for our fallen leader, the coaches and officials of the two teams playing today, both outstanding Catholic schools, have agreed to cancel the second half of today's game and invite all of you to say a prayer for President Kennedy, who was himself a great Catholic, to pray for his widow, Jacqueline Bouvier Kennedy, for his children, Caroline and John Jr., and for our great nation. We ask you to remove your hats and remain standing for two minutes in silent tribute to President Kennedy. We ask the players of both teams to line up on either side of center field with helmets removed. Would the cheerleaders for both teams please line up along your respective sidelines. Father President McManus of St. Xavier High School will lead us in prayer, and then the Roger Bacon Marching Band will conclude our tribute by playing The Star-Spangled Banner for the second time today. Thank you. And God bless America!

***

- I'm sorry, Coach Mason, but I can't stop crying. How can this happen in America? He was a good President. I admired him so much for what he did, and was trying to do.

- It's all right, son. All of us are crying right now. I believe the whole free world is shedding a tear at this very moment. You played a great game today, and I'm sure that if the President had been here watching, he would be admiring you. The School Chaplain wants to speak to you.

- Nice game, Holden! A young man like you shouldn't have to be caught in the middle of such a tragedy. I know you will find the strength to carry on the good fight in order to honor the man who I know was your idol. I recall the essay you wrote on a composition exam last month. Your teacher had you read your essay during our tribute assembly. The title of your composition was "In Search of an Answer". You mentioned that it was a tribute to President Kennedy. Well, Holden, not finding an answer wouldn't necessarily be a failure, but giving up the search would. President Kennedy would have been the first to tell you that. We all know that he was searching for a way to have peace here in our country and in the world. I guess he was the one who inspired you to enter the International Peace Essay Contest. Well, I hadn't had the chance to return your essay. It came back yesterday after being passed on through the various regional and state committees. You didn't win the twenty-five thousand dollar prize – a young lady from Sweden won that. But your twenty-five page essay called "Peace in our Time" was selected as the best essay in the Mid-West Region. In fact, a local TV station wants to interview you in its "young leaders" segment. It appears that you were the youngest person in the country to submit an essay! Oh, and a check for five hundred dollars was in the envelope with your essay. But I think that you will agree that the biggest prize you received is the note written on the last page of your essay. I had intended to return your essay under happier circumstances, but, well, here it is. I'll let you read it.

- "Holden, I was deeply moved and heartily encouraged by the suggestions for world peace that you presented in this essay. You are obviously a young man with a head on his shoulders, but also a compassionate and caring person. Congratulations on this fine essay. I understand that while I'm riding through the streets of Dallas you'll be on the gridiron trying to win a football championship. Young man, you epitomize what I dream for all Americans – a healthy mind in a healthy body – *mens sana in corpore sano.* Best of luck! John F. Kennedy, President."

- I don't know what to say, Father. I think I'm going to cry again.

- You do know that it's okay for a young man to cry. No man should feel shame at shedding tears. As your Chaplain, I am there to help you through difficulties in any way I can. When I graduated from high school, one of my teachers gave me this little book of meditations and prayers. I read from it every day and went on to other books for spiritual reading. No matter what happens to me or the people I encounter each day, I can always find consolation and happiness in these little books.

- Thank you, Father. See you on Monday!

Chapter 8

- A real beautiful dog you have there, Holden!

- Yeah, he sure is, thanks. You know my name!

 - Of course! I spent a lot of time this term cheering for you on the football field.

- Now I recognize you. You're one of our cheerleaders from Sacred Heart. Your name's Maxine, isn't it? I've noticed you at practices because you're the best dancer on the squad, and …and you've got a beautiful smile!

- Oh, you're sweet! Yes, I'm Maxine Davis – and you have a nice smile too! I've never been this close to you.

- Did you know that "smiles" is the longest word in the dictionary? That's because there is a "mile" between the two s's!

- Aren't you the funny one! Do you walk your dog often here in Burnet Woods? What's his name?

- This is Vergil Cane. I named him after the Roman poet Vergil and the Latin word for dog *canis*. I've had him for almost two years, and we come for a daily run here around the artificial lake. We usually make it all the way to the UC campus, but seeing you here, I think I'd run a mile for that smile! I live over on Ludlow Avenue, so this park is real convenient. But I've never seen you walking in Burnet Woods before.

- Wow! Latin! We have Latin at Sacred Heart, but I take Spanish instead. Though I'm sure Latin could be fun. I actually don't live far from here either. I live just over on Clifton. Funny how we haven't bumped into each other before. Of course, I usually go everywhere by bus. But I decided to walk through the park to go watch my brother practice basketball at UC He plays for the Bearcats.

- Clifton Avenue is close by. Maybe I could convince Vergil Cane to run along Clifton now and then. I'm always headed up the other way. I work part-time at Pizza Pete's over on Vine Avenue. But a good-looking girl like you probably wouldn't be caught dead in a greasy spoon like Pete's.

- Well, Holden Hainsworth, aren't you full of compliments! And speaking of good-looking, all the girls say you would be quite a catch – and they're not talking about football! However, for your information, my brother sometimes brings me to Dan's Diner on McMillan. We also attend Mass at St. Joseph's on McMillan. But my brother and his friends don't really like to hang out at Pizza Pete's.

- I can understand why. Pete can be a little racist – well, actually a lot racist. He usually lets me serve our Afro-American customers, which is fine by me. But Pete treats me okay and the money comes in handy – not to mention the free food. He treats the guys to free beer on Saturday nights after closing. The other guys can really put those Budweisers away, but don't tell anybody. I only have a couple so I can hang out with the gang. Since I'm under age, I don't want to get Pete - or me - in trouble. And here's another secret you can't tell anybody. Pete's not his real name! Say, maybe you've seen me at St. Joe's – I'm an altar boy there. I think I'm the only altar boy who actually understands the Latin we have to recite during the Mass. Don't you find Father Brendan's sermons real cool? You know, he rides a motorcycle!

- Actually, my family attends the masses celebrated by the other priests. I don't think my parents accept priests on motorcycles. Your little secrets are safe with me, Holden. My brother gets to drink 3-2 beer because he's eighteen. I don't think my father approves, though. He's always been kind of over-protective, especially of me. I get the Afro-American thing. I believe that's the main reason my father thinks he has to look out for me. My brother is the same way. Fortunately, my mother and my Mamie, who is my father's mother, both encourage me to live life to the fullest, and not worry about people with the wrong attitude. Even the other girls on the cheerleading team aren't comfortable hanging out with me. The only thing we have in common is that we all think you're real cute, and the very best football player! But I do have friends at Sacred Heart – white and black friends. I was really shaken when they announced that President Kennedy had been killed. And your team must have been shattered - with the game being cancelled and all. I saw you talking to a priest. But I couldn't stop crying.

- That was our School Chaplain, Father Brown. He was able to comfort me. Do you know that President Kennedy actually wrote me a note on my essay for peace? I hope you didn't see me crying.

- There's nothing wrong with crying Holden. Even my father cried when he watched the news report of the President's death. He said that we lost a man who saw beyond color, and who was doing hs best to unite our country.

- Just like Martin Luther King. It will take great men to unite a country divided over color. But I think that most of all it's going to take ordinary people, the younger generation like you and I, Maxine, to overcome prejudice and create a better America, and a better world.

- Dr. King said just that – "we shall overcome"! I guess we both share his dream.

- I don't usually hear him referred to as Dr. King.

 - Well, Dr. King attended university with my uncle, and earned a doctorate degree. Our whole family calls him Dr. King. That's how I addressed him when he was at our house last summer.

- Wow! President Kennedy wrote me a note, and Martin Luther King was at your house! I guess it makes sense to call him doctor, since he is trying to heal the wounds of American society! Martin Luther King has a doctorate – that's pretty cool! We learned in history class that Edward Alexander Bouchet was the first Afro-American to earn a doctorate degree and he got it at Yale! I remember all that because it was in 1876 – our great nation's centennial year! Well, got to run. So does Vergil Cane! Say, are you going to be at the Bearcats game at UC tomorrow?

- Of course! My parents and I attend all of my brother's home games.

- I'll see you there. I really enjoyed talking to you.

- So did I, Holden. Maybe see you in awhile!

- And bring that smile!

***

- Three seconds until the buzzer - Charlie Davis wins it for UC!

Mommy and Daddy, this is Holden Hainsworth. He's St. Xavier High's quarterback. He's an altar boy at St. Joseph's .

- I've heard about your prowess on the football field, young man, but I can't recall seeing you serve Mass. Have you, dear?

- Oh, Jim, he probably serves Mass for that young priest – you know – the one that rides a motorcycle. We usually go to the Mass that's officiated at by Father McIntyre – he's more traditional. It's nice to meet you, Holden.

- It's an honor to meet you both. Your daughter is our best cheerleader.

- We understand that you live over on Ludlow – we're practically neighbors! I'm sure Maxine would love to have you over at the house sometime. She told me you two had an interesting conversation yesterday in Burnet Woods. Her father and I don't really like her going through that park alone, but I guess it was fine since she met a nice young gentleman like yourself. And a handsome one at that! Maxine also got to meet your beautiful golden retriever. Imagine – Golden and Holden on the same day!

- You're embarrassing the poor boy, dear. Please excuse her, son. Maxine's mother thinks she's funny.

- Nonsense, Jim! Besides, Holden is an athlete, like our Charlie. They'd have lots to talk about. Why don't you come for dinner next Sunday, Holden? Did you know that Maxine is an excellent cook?

- Mommy, now you're embarrassing ME! Besides, maybe he has other plans.

 - I'd love to join you all for dinner, Mrs. Davis.

 - Oh, Charlie, over here. Great game, son. Your father and I are so proud of you.

This is Holden Hainsworth. He's a friend of your sister's, and he will be our dinner guest next Sunday.

- He will?

Chapter 9

- Boys, only a few weeks until Christmas break. We need volunteers to help out with Christmas baskets on Saturday. In preparation for your Christmas exam, let's look at some grammatical constructions. Copy these sentences – *Duce interfecto, milites oppidum ceperunt. Hostibus victis, legio ad castra revertit. Matre visa, puella cantare incipit. Magistro volente, discipuli libros legent.* Who can tell us straightaway what these sentences have in common? Remember, boys, we are talking syntax here.

- There are participles in all the sentences, Father.

- No, Nelson. You have merely identified common forms. There are also nouns and verbs in all the sentences. But you're on the right track by identifying participles. Yes, Hainsworth?

- All these sentences contain the ablative absolute construction, Father. That is, a combination of a participle - thank you, Nelson - and a noun or pronoun, which are grammatically independent – I think that's what they mean by "absolute". This means the phrase in the ablative case is not grammatically related to the subject or object of the verb. The ablative absolute is composed of a noun and pronoun or even of two nouns, like *Caesare et Bibulo consulibus* meaning "when Caesar and Bibulus were consuls" or "during the consulship of Caesar and Bibulus". Father, I read in our Roman history book that Caesar was such a dominant figure the running joke among Romans was to use the expression *Iulio et Caesare consulibus* – "during the consulship of Julius and Caesar"!

- As usual, nicely done, Hainsworth, with your signature addition of an interesting digression on the influence of Julius Caesar. Now let's translate these sentences, recalling that different circumstances can be rendered by the ablative absolute. Santos, Stewart, Mittenkamp and Harris - each of you translate a sentence, and be sure to give all explanations of the possible circumstances along with the different translations for the ablative absolute. "Although their general had been killed, the soldiers captured the town". The ablative absolute has a concessive force here, guys. But a temporal sense is also possible, in which case the translation would be "After" – or "when" – "their general had been killed, the soldiers captured the town". I don't think any of the other circumstances would make sense.

- In this sentence either the temporal or the causal circumstance would work. The sentence can be translated "After the enemy had been conquered, the legion returned to the camp" or "Because the enemy had been conquered, the legion returned to the camp." Father, the verb *revertit* could be present or perfect tense. So the sentence could be translated "Because the enemy has to be conquered, the legion is returning to the camp". The present tense wouldn't work well here with a temporal meaning for the ablative absolute.

- My sentence also has a verb in the present tense – *incipit* - and so has limited possibilities for translation. The only logical translation I can see is "Because her mother has been seen, the girl begins to sing". And it isn't the girl who has seen her own mother, because the subject of the main verb cannot be the subject of the action expressed by the ablative absolute. Technically, the meaning could be "Because A mother has been seen", but that just sounds weird.

- My ablative absolute construction contains a present participle. My translation is "Because the teacher wants this, the pupils will read their books". But the ablative absolute in this sentence could be indicating a condition, and could be translated "If the teacher wants this" – or "is willing" – "the pupils will read their books".

- That's very good, boys, but how can the writer be sure his readers will know which circumstance is intended, if there is more than one circumstance possible in the ablative absolute? Next query - there were Roman military camps throughout the Empire. What is the particular connection between the word *castra* and Roman Britain? Finally, we know that the word "master" comes from *magister*, the Latin word for "teacher". Does that mean I can refer to all of you as my slaves? And since The Latin word for students is *discipuli,* can I call you my "disciples"? Any brave soul willing to risk an answer?... Ah, Hainsworth, we're all ears!

- Well, Father, the ablative absolute is conveniently short, and looks kind of neat. But it can only be used with absolute clarity – pun intended, guys! To distinguish between a causal and a temporal meaning, the writer would have to use a full clause beginning with *quod* or *quia* – "because", or *post* – "after". Likewise, a concessive meaning could be rendered by a clause beginning with *quamquam,* the Latin word for "although". Even the use of the word *cum* is tricky because it can be translated as "when", "because" or "although". A condition is introduced by the word "if" – *si*, in Latin. The ablative absolute cannot be used if clarity is an issue. As for the word *castra,* we see it in the names of British cities which must have originally been Roman military camps. Names I can think of are Manchester, Lancaster, Chester, Leicester, Winchester, Colchester, Cirencester, and Exeter. You would never treat us as slaves, Father. In fact, the word *magister* meant "schoolmaster". It came into the French language as *maître*. My French teacher, Mr.Dubois, insists that we call him that. At first we thought that was because he had been the *maître d'* at Cincinnati's finest French restaurant! Or that he was just "crowing" about his "mastery" of French. He quoted that well-known line

"*Maître Corbeau sur un arbre perché*", but I know some of the students thought that this crow had fallen out of his tree! Strange that his name means "wood"! However, Maître Dubois soon had us eating out of his hand, even if at first it was "to eat crow"! The word *discipuli i*s Latin for "pupil" or "student." It comes from the verb *discere,* meaning "to learn". A pupil "learns", and what he learns is a "discipline". If the pupil has learned well, he is well trained, and he displays "good discipline." In the New Testament, those who learned from our Master, and followed His teachings, were known as His disciples. What was a bit confusing for me, Father, is the Latin word for the "master" of slaves. It was *dominus,* and came from the Latin word for house – *domus.* The "master of the household" was, of course, "master of the slaves" in the house. He was their *dominus.* But when I became an altar boy, I learned that the word for our Lord was *Dominus.* We say *Domine, non sum dignus,* meaning "Lord, I am not worthy". I've learned since then that *dominus* can mean "teacher" like *magister* and doesn't have to mean "slave master" regardless of what Nelson says! In fact, Father McNeil, since you are a priest, I can address you in Latin as *Domine!* And again, our dear Nelson would follow up with "have mercy"! As you once said Father, our teachers hold the "master key" to opening the door that will enable us to "master" necessary skills! But I think you are the "mastermind" behind the whole operation, given your masterful explanations of Latin grammar and your masterly and meaningful examples!

 - My, my, Master Hainsworth! Don't worry. When it comes to Latin, you are indeed *dignus!* Now, if I am "going to Rome", shall I say *Ad Romam eo*? And if I am "coming from Rome", do I say *Ab Roma venio*? I suppose I would say *In Roma sum* to tell people I am "in Rome". Something to say, Hainsworth?

- Definitely, Father! To express "being in Rome", one must say *Romae sum.* I know *Romae* looks like the genitive, but here it is a special case called the locative – from the Latin word *locus* meaning "place". Think "location", guys. Likewise with place names – cities, towns and small islands – not big ones like Sicily – we also drop prepositions to indicate "going to" and "coming from". So "to Rome" is simply *Romam* and "from Rome" is *Roma.* We use the accusative and ablative cases as usual, but without the prepositions. Of course, you might still see *ad Romam, a Roma* and *in Roma.* Unless they are errors on Nelson's paper, these mean "to", "from" and "in" the vicinity of Rome. The locative case is the same form as the genitive case, unless the city or island has a plural form in the nominative. Then the ablative case is used. Other nouns use the locative like *humi* – "on the ground" - *domi* – "at home", *belli* – "at war" – *vesperi* -" in the evening". That's our "vespers", or "evening prayers", guys. Even the Latin word for "yesterday" - *heri* - is a locative form, since it actually means "on the day before." And it's so close to the French word *hier.*

- Splendid, Hainsworth! You are constantly reminding us of your facility with French. You never know - that knowledge may come in handy some day! Don't forget to study for the exam. You boys have often heard *Ite* – "go" - the Mass is over! Well, *Ite*, the class is over!

Chapter 10

- I hope you enjoyed the roasted duck dinner Maxine cooked for you, Holden. Charlie will show you his basketball trophies up in his room. I'm sure you athletes will have plenty to talk about. Maxine and her father will help me with the dishes.

***

- Listen, you seem like a nice guy – for a whitey. But I don't think my sister needs the rough time she'd have if she kept seeing you. Those white girls on the cheerleader team don't even respect her. And you work at Pizza Pete's, don't you? He takes money from black folks, but he ain't too friendly to us. My mother seems to like you, but then she's a dreamer like Dr. King. My father probably doesn't approve, but he won't say too much so as not to upset Maxine. My sister has never had a boyfriend and she told me you never had a girlfriend. That's surprising since you're such a good athlete, and you'd be able to spend money on them with you working part-time jobs. Yeah, I know you also work at Indian Hills – that whitey golf club that doesn't accept black members. Well, I'm not bothered on campus, because I play for the Bearcats. Our coach is a pretty fair guy, but do you know that the white players and black players on the team don't hang out together when we're away from the court. A couple of the white guys are okay – we joke around and I call them honkies. But they don't need the aggravation, and so they don't hang out with us. Your first girlfriend is a black girl – that is a bit strange. I know my sister is the prettiest girl in town, but I don't want her getting hurt. You could get any white girl you wanted, and a lot of the black guys I know are real keen on Maxine. You with a white girlfriend, and my sister dating a black guy – that would be normal. Maxine says you refer to us as Afro-Americans. Well, I think a lot of people around here forget about the American part. Maxine says you study Latin. That makes you even weirder! And what I really can't get is how you come you like all those black Doo Wop songs and how you're really into Motown. But I kinda respect you, Holden Hainsworth, for sticking up for your principles. I think that if you were a black guy, we'd be good friends, and I'd be proud that you were dating my sister.

- Well, Charlie, I hope we still can be good friends. And you're right – Maxine is the prettiest girl I've ever met. She's not artificial, like so many other girls I know – including those cheerleaders you mentioned. And I don't share the opinions of Pizza Pete and some of the Indian Hills members. But we have to live and work and play as athletes together. It's like Martin Luther – uh, Dr. King – says – we're all Americans - we should all live the same dreams and hopes together. A great American president just gave his life for that ideal. Even some of my closest friends have already warned me that life is going to get complicated if I have a black girlfriend. But Maxine's smile somehow makes it worthwhile. My parents – and my sister Phoebe – all support me. And, yes, I'm a Latin student. Sometimes people find that stranger than having a black girlfriend! Even my own father doesn't think there's much of a future in studying Latin. But learning the language that gave us so much of our own English language – and so many other languages - is fascinating! And reading up on Roman history has helped me to understand the roots of our own American nation. Just like we had in the South, the Romans had slaves that they considered to be their property. Next year is my senior year and 'm already thinking of studying Latin at university. But I want to stay here in Cincinnati. I could keep my part-time jobs, but I really want to stay so I could be with Maxine. I'd probably attend Xavier University. And then, if I'm good enough, I could be accepted into UC's Graduate School. My Latin teacher, Fr. McNeil, has already told us how well-known the University of Cincinnati's Classics Department is. Charlie, I don't know if you will ever believe we can be "brothers", but maybe some day we will become brothers-in-law!

Chapter 11

- How were the Holidays, Oldie? Did you give Maxine a "White Christmas"?

- Not funny, Tommy! I hope I did well on my Latin exam. You know, ever since grade school, I've tried to get good marks to make my Mom proud of me. She's always there to support me. Especially now that our relatives and family friends are asking why I have an Afro-American girlfriend. And I really think I get my love for Latin from her, because of her interest in languages.

- Well, boys, most of you did quite well on the exam. Hainsworth, you again had the top mark - 98%. And it wasn't easy figuring out how I could deduct two marks! I want to remind you all that the National Latin Exam will be written at the beginning of March. As usual, there will be questions on Latin grammar, Roman history and mythology and of course questions on a Latin passage. We are still aiming for St. Xavier High's first perfect paper. I had thought that we could send a couple of you to the National Junior Classical League Conference next summer in Anaheim, California, but Hainsworth, who was nominated by our selection committee, isn't able to take time off from his summer job – or, two jobs actually – our young Latin prodigy is a busy man! Nelson, I know you had expressed interest, but that was because you thought your good friend Hainsworth would be attending, and not, as some of your not so good friends claimed, because you wanted to fulfil your dream of seeing Disneyland! It seems that Hainsworth, unlike you, will never have a longing for sunny California. Moreover, I added the 2% I took from Hainsworth to your paper. That's how you passed the exam, young man! Boys, I have exciting news about next year. Because we will be finishing the high school cursus in Latin this year, St. Xavier High, in collaboration with Xavier University, will be offering a university Latin course for the advanced placement students. I will be teaching a Latin reading course on Cicero – he and I are old friends! And as well, Xavier University will be granting university credits for this course towards recognition in the Classics Department program. But there's more! Next year, a young Jesuit scholastic – not a priest yet – but you will call him Father James just the same – will be teaching an introduction to Ancient Greek. He will include some Greek history in the course and promises some interesting stories from Greek mythology. Mr. James – Father James to you – is an Afro-American from Atlanta, Georgia, and he has a graduate degree in Classical Studies from the University of Mississippi. We had Greek courses at St. Xavier many years ago – in fact, I taught both Latin and Greek when I started here at St. X. It's hard to believe we have never before had an Afro-American teacher at St. Xavier, but we have had some excellent Afro-American students, even in Latin.

Isn't that right, Duke? The Greek course will not be compulsory – even for the AP Latin students. But I would strongly recommend it to all of you. You could benefit from it, Nelson, since Latin is sometimes "Greek to you"! I hope a couple of you will seriously consider studying Classics at university, in which case this Greek course will come in handy. But we'll talk about all that next year. Now let's finish the class with a fun quiz! Match the abbreviations in the left hand column of page one of your hand-out with the correct meaning of the abbreviations in the right hand column.

1) A.D. - *anno Domini*   a) and the rest

2) A.M. *ante meridiem*   b) around, approximately

3) ca. - *circa*   c) in the same place

4) cf. - *confer*   d) compare

5) c.v.- *curriculum vitae*   e) it was written this way

6) et al.- *et alii*   f) for example

7) etc.- *et cetera*   g) that is, in other words

8) e.g.- *exempli gratia*   h) after what has been written

9) ibid.- *ibidem*   i) before noon

10) i.e. – *id est*   j) immediately, urgent

11) N.B.- *nota bene*   k) may he or she rest in peace

12) P.M. – *post meridiem*   l)"course of life"

13) P.S. – *post scriptum*   m) after noon

14) Q.E.D.- *quod erat demonstrandum*   n) for the greater glory of God

15) R.I.P. – *requiescat in pace*   o) in the year of our Lord

16) sic – *sic est scriptum*   p) note well

17) stat.- *statim*   q) against

18) vs.- *versus*   r) and others

19)   AMDG – *Ad maiorem Dei gloriam*   s) that which was to be proven

20)   What is the significance of abbreviation 19)?

Now answer these questions.

1)   What do Aventine, Palatine and Capitoline have in common?

2)   Which Emperor blamed the Christians for a destructive fire in Rome?

3)   By what title was the head of Roman religion called?

4)   What was the name of the second Roman king?

5)   Which Roman magistrate was in charge of the treasury?

6)   Who was Roman Emperor when Jesus was crucified?

7)   Who was the Roman messenger god?

8)   What do the Latin words *servus, ancilla*, and *ianitor* have in common?

9)   What was the Latin name for the Roman province of Spain?

10)   What was the position of Roman soldiers who commanded 100 men?

Here is the hand-out with the answers. Please switch papers with your neighbour and correct.

1)o 2)i 3)b 4)d 5)l 6)r 7)a 8)f 9)c 10)g 11)p 12)m 13)h 14)s 15)k 16)e 17)j 18)q

19)n 20) *Ad maiorem Dei gloriam* is the motto of the Society of Jesus – the Jesuits

1)They are hills of Ancient Rome   2)Nero   3)'Pontifex Maximus   4)Numa

5)quaestor   6)Tiberius   7) Mercury   8) They are all words that depict slaves

9) *Hispania*   10) centurion

Did anybody get a perfect score?   … Nelson??

- Oh, sorry Father, I forgot to give Oldie – I mean Hainsworth – back his paper!

Chapter 12

- Hi there! Holden! Wow! You really skate well! Do you always skate here in Burnet Woods? I almost didn't recognize you bundled up in your woolen hat and scarf.

- Hi Maxine! This year we've had cold enough weather for this artificial lake to freeze over. Not so sure I would want to skate out into the middle of the lake though. While your brother practices his three pointers all winter, I practice ice skating – usually at the Dixie Bowl across the River, but I prefer the nice cold air here in Burnet Woods when we have long winter cold spells. I've actually played ice-hockey with Tommy Nelson and a few of his cadet buddies on the frozen pond out by Corryville. My skating helps me stickhandle past everybody and score lots of goals. We use a real puck, but sometimes there aren't enough sticks to go around, so I use a tree branch. You ought to come out and watch us some time. There are always a bunchof girls watching, and I think some of them are from Sacred Heart. But no matter which team I'm on, they always seem to be cheering for our side. Maybe because my team always wins. Do you skate, Maxine?

- No, Holden, but I do love walking in the cold, fresh air. I love snow, but we don't get much here in Cincinnati, do we? Once my family went up to Vermont for New Year's. There was so much snow – it was wonderful! Say, Holden, there's a Sadie Hawkins dance at Sacred Heart next Saturday? Would you come with me?

- Gosh, I'm glad you asked me, Maxine. I would have felt obliged to go with the first girl to invite me, seeing as it's a Sadie Hawkins dance. Your Vermont trip sounds like it was a lot of fun. I wonder what it would be like to live in a city where there was lots of snow. Let me take off my skates, and we can enjoy one of those walks you like taking. I know your brother is still not too happy that we're dating. But your mom is so nice to me. I haven't figured out where your father stands. I mean he always shakes my hand, and he often talks about football with me, but he never asks about our plans, or how we spend our time together. My parents on the other hand, are forever asking when you'll be over to the house next, and things like do we both like the Beatles, and will I be teaching you Latin – well, actually my mom has been asking, not my dad. You remember I told you he's not really a fan of Latin. Even my sister Feeb is always asking about you. But that's because she's nosy! Maybe she admires you because you are on the cheerleaders team from her school. Say, Maxine, I've put in a lot of hours lately at Pizza Pete's and I've saved some money so that I can treat you to a show. I've got two tickets to see The Four Tops at the Cincinnati Gardens next month. Would you like to go?

- Oh, Holden! How did you know The Four Tops are my favorite group? Isn't Levi Stubbs great? My brother will be so jealous! Although Charlie's more into the girl groups like The Supremes and The Marvelettes. And he saw Martha and The Vandellas in Dayton last year. The basketball team got free tickets from UC. It's so exciting! I could kiss you, Holden Hainsworth!

- Well, then, why not kiss me, Maxine Davis? … Wow! A lovely smile, and a great kisser! You know, I like the girl groups too, but you can't beat The Four Tops! I can't wait to see Duke Fakir on stage. I think he's a real classy guy. Sing with me Maxine – Reach out, I'll be there to love and cherish you…

- You're a crazy guy, Holden – and I love you!

- You are my special angel, sent from up above…!

- Hey, I've heard that song before! Well, this angel would love to learn Latin with you!

- Sure thing! We'll be Latin lovers together!

Chapter 13

- Boys, we've received the results of this year's National Latin Exam. You all passed, and four of you received certificates of distinction. But the big news is that young Hainsworth here scored a perfect paper! Congratulations, Holden! Well done! I'm allowing myself exceptionally to address you by your first name since this is an exceptional achievement. Young man, you've made an old Jesuit very proud and very happy! Before we begin an important review of the subjunctive mood, I want to let you know that I've entered our Latin class in the all-school track meet that will be held soon after spring break. Mr. Merchant, your physical education teacher, tells me we have a good chance of dominating the foot-races including the relay race. Since the running events weigh heavier in the overall tabulation – we won't do too well in the throwing events, he says – we have a chance to win the trophy. Hainsworth, you will be our pillar. You have already clocked the best times in the 100-yard dash in school history. We've seen enough of you on the football field to think this will be a piece of cake for you – especially since you won't have to straight-arm anyone to get to the finish line. You can anchor the relay team, and be joined by Duke, Harris and Nelson. I'm told you are pretty fast, Nelson. At least you're quick at finding excuses for not completing assignments! Hainsworth, you will also run the mile race, because of your stamina. How do I know about your endurance? Mr. Merchant heard from your grade school gym teacher that you entered a regional "last-man-standing" race when you were only twelve, and all the other competitors were at least fifteen years old. You boys were told to run laps around the track, and the winner would be the last runner to stop running. You were the winner! I bet you could have given that Greek Pheidippides a run for his money! Boys, Pheidippides was the Athenian messenger who ran all the way from Athens to Sparta to ask the Spartans for help against the invading Persians. Unfortunately, he had to run all the way back to Athens to tell the Athenians that the Spartans weren't coming. But, later, he ran the 14 miles from Marathon to Athens to announce the Greek victory over the Persians at the Battle of Marathon. Gentlemen, that was the origin of the 14-mile marathon race. No doubt, those who take Greek with Mr. James next year will hear more about the Persian Wars. So, Hainsworth, gold in Latin and perhaps gold at the track meet. *Mens sana in corpore sano*! Now let's look at why the subjunctive is so important in Latin. You've spent a couple of months learning all these forms in the subjunctive mood. You remember that the indicative mood is used for stating facts or for obtaining facts through direct questions, and that the imperative mood is used for giving direct commands, orders that the one giving the command expected to be carried out – such as a master to a slave or a military commander to his troops. But the Romans were superstitious by nature and didn't always believe that a preliminary gesture or word would guarantee an expected or desired result. That is why commands or questions could be expressed in an indirect way. Romans would indicate a purpose behind a given action without the assurance of succeeding in their goal or objective. Whenever they expressed a desire for something that they weren't sure of receiving, or a doubt about something or a fear that something might happen, the Romans used the subjunctive mood. Even orders given in the third person, like "let them eat cake" or exhortations in the first person plural, like "let's all go to the ball game" leave a sufficient level of doubt as to the eventual occurrence of the suggested action. These two uses of the subjunctive are called the jussive subjunctive – from the Latin verb *iubeo, iubere, iussi, iussus* "to order", and the hortatory subjunctive – from the Latin verb *hortor, hortari, hortatus sum*, "to encourage" or "urge". I hope you remember what we said about deponent verbs like *hortor,* which retain an active meaning, even though they only have passive forms, having "laid aside" – from the verb *deponere* - their active forms. As another example of the use of the subjunctive, consider this religious formula used by the Romans – *do ut des* – from the verb *dare*, "to give". This phrase – "I give so that you may give" – implied that the Romans paid homage to their gods on condition that the gods grant them favors. They "prayed with a purpose", we might say! Of course, we Catholics don't put that kind of pressure on God today! Not that we complain when He helps us out! It's like what President Kennedy famously said – "Ask not what your country can do for you, but what you can do for your country!" We lost a great man indeed. Let us conclude this review of the subjunctive with a few examples of the uses of the subjunctive by our Latin leader Holdsworth.

- *Edimus ut vivamus*. This is a purpose clause meaning "We eat in order to live". *Utinam bonus discipulus linguae Latinae sim* expresses a wish and means "If only I could be a good Latin student"! No offense, Nelson! *Tot homines Romam adveniunt ut urbs celeberrima sit.* This is a result clause that translates as "So many people come to Rome that" – as a result – "the city is very famous". I think the word "celebrate" comes from the adjective *celeber* and since Spring Break starts tomorrow, let's celebrate – hortatory subjunctive, guys!

Chapter 14

- So kid - Spring Break - but you're gonna work your regular shifts, right? And get four shrimp baskets ready. I don't know if all those hours you put in are 'cause you're a money-maker, or workin' keeps you out of trouble. You're workin' the full summer, right?

I know you'll be caddying for that pro at Indian Hills – nice place that Indian Hills. A golf club with only white folk. I know you're savin' up for college – that's good! Education is important, and you deserve a good one. Guess you'll be goin' to UC. The other guys here can barely handle high school, so I'll be mighty proud to tell everybody I got a college boy working my counter!

But, Holy, if you had a girlfriend you'd have to shell out some of your hard-earned cash, and you'd be tellin' me you couldn't work Saturday nights.

- Yeah, Pete, I've been meaning to tell you, I've been dating this girl for almost three months. I've been waiting for Spring Break to bring her here, and share a pizza with her. She's a cheerleader from Sacred Heart, and she has the prettiest smile you'll ever see! She hopes to get into UC, too, but we're both a year away from graduation.

- Well, I'll be a son of a gun! Holy Hainsworth has a girlfriend – but you know what – she's a lucky girl! What's her name?

- Maxine – Maxine Davis. Her brother plays basketball for UC.

- Of all the names her folks could have given her, why would they saddle her with a name that a lot of black girls have?

- Pete, my girlfriend is an Afro-American girl. She is so sweet, and not one bit artificial like a lot of other girls I've met. We even like the same kind of music – and I'm teaching her Latin.

- Well, if that don't take the cake! You finally hook up with a girl – and she's black! Just because you like spending your quarters on those Motown tunes! What do your folks think? And what do her folks think of their little girl dating a whitey? And, Holy, how am I going to explain that to the other guys here? But let me tell you this – you're still my best worker. The black customers seem to like you. Maybe now they'll LOVE you, although those people are not all keen on seeing one of their own dating a white guy, no matter how good an athlete he his. And you are the only guy that my window-washer talks to. I always wonder what that hillbilly Bobby Calhoun and you talk about. But listen, son, you bring your Maxine in here, and I'll treat her like a princess – just for you!

- Gee, thanks for understanding, Pete. I don't share all your opinions, but you've always treated me right. And I really do like working for you. As for my parents, they're really supportive. My Mom thinks the world of Maxine, and my sister Phoebe gets along really well with her. They both go to the same school, and I think Feeb wants Maxine to show her some cheerleader moves so she can make the squad next year. Maxine's mother is ever so nice to me – Moms are special – but her brother is not my biggest fan. He's probably just over-protective of his sister. As for her father, well he's very civil with me, and he even compliments me on my work ethic, but I just don't know. But hey – all the guys in my Latin class like my *amica pulchra* – that means pretty girlfriend, Pete. And the guys here know all about Maxine.

Mickey and Rick are okay with it. And I can totally understand Pizza Jeff's feelings – I mean with his sister being attacked by a black man, and all that.

Chapter 15

- Isn't it strange, Maxine – the Cincinnati Zoo is famous, and this is my very first visit.

- Hey, fellas, what a treat, we get to see one of the keepers walking his monkey!

 - You'd better apologize, you poor excuse for an American!

***

- You should have left it, Holden. I've heard trash like that before. And look at you – bleeding nose and cut lip. What were you thinking – three against one!

- Those guys were a disgrace – and I'm not going to let anyone insult you. Jesus says to turn the other cheek, but they messed up other parts of my face! Those poor excuses for human beings need Jesus to cure them of their "sickness", like He did for lepers. Why, people like them are so ignorant they probably don't know that it was an Afro-American chemist named Alice Ball who developed a treatment for leprosy before we had antibiotics!

- Gosh, you know more about our history than I do! Dr.King says we musn't fight prejudiced people – we have to fight prejudice itself! But you're so sweet for defending me – you're my hero!

***

- This is Maxine, Pete. We're going to split a medium cheese. Hi Mickey! Uh, hello Jeff.

- Hello, Miss. The pizza won't be as good, since my best pizza man seems to be otherwise occupied! I set a table aside for you two right beside the juke-box. Here's some quarters for you, Holy – I mean Holden – play some nice songs for the lady. By the way, what's with the face – you get attacked by a tiger at the zoo?

- Let's just say not all the animals were in cages, Pete. Thanks for the quarters.

Pete never usually sets aside tables for anyone. And it's the first time I've ever seen Mickey with his hair combed. And don't worry about Jeff turning his back to us – it's a sad story that I'll tell you some other time. Here's some songs you'll like. I'll even treat you to my version.

Earth angel, earth angel, will you be mine? – Say yes, Maxine, and I'll feel fine!

This magic moment, so different and so new – I'm so happy, Maxine that I'm here with you!

Hey, here's one by Little Anthony and the Imperials – Well I think I'm going out of my mind over you, over you – Maxine, I hope I make you crazy too!

- The Penguins, Charlie Thomas and the Drifters, Little Anthony – those were great choices, Holden. But it's the first time I've ever heard my name in their songs! Say, my brother is going to a dance next week that features all this music. Since it's a sweet sixteen dance, we'll be allowed in, but they won't serve us any alcohol. You're welcome to come along, if you don't mind being the only non Afro-American.

***

- In the still, still of the night... my favorite song, Maxine – and I get to dance it with you! Oh, they're going to play The Four Tops – Baby, I need your lovin', you know I need your lovin', got to have your lovin'...

- I just love being in your arms and dancing with you, Holden! And who'd have thought that you would know that Diana Ross, Mary Wilson and Flo Ballard are the names of The Supremes?

- Got to hand it to you, brother. You can dance. You got the moves. But when you is getting down between my man, Charlie, and his lovely sister, man, you is like an Oreo cookie!

- Thanks... I think. When I hear this music, it's like that Martha and the Vandellas song – it's a "Heat Wave"! And when I'm with Maxine, well, like Harvey and The Moonglows, I just want to tell her I love her "Sincerely"! Maxine is such a great dancer. And everybody here has been so nice to me tonight. I wish Americans of all colours could get along. The Kennedys and Martin Luther – I mean Dr. King - have the right message – we can all share that dream. Say, Maxine, I guess we should be heading home. It's been my best ever Spring Break! Just a couple of months and we're on summer vacation. We'll be able to spend lots of time together. And then our senior year! Let's talk about our college plans real soon.

Chapter 16

\-   Boy, did I ever have some tense moments on that last Latin test!

\-   Do you mean deciding whether the verb TENSE was past, present, or future, Tommy?

\-   If you are going to talk about my trouble with verbs, Oldie, I'm not in the MOOD to hear your VOICE! Say, have you chosen your books from the summer reading list?

\-   I sure have! I'll be reading *Brave New World*, *1984*, *Lost Horizon*, and *To Kill a Mockingbird*. I also have to read two novels for my French course, since I'm in the advanced programme. I've chosen *Le Petit Prince* and this French-Canadian novel about a fellow who arrives in a small town all of a sudden and changes the lives of some people there, and then he leaves. It's called *Le Survenant*. Looks like Father McNeil is ready to start class.

- Boys, there is one important Latin construction we haven't looked at for a while, and you are almost certain to encounter it on the final exam. Now translate the following sentences, and see if you recognize the Latin syntax.

1) *Caesar dixit se militem optimum esse.* 2) *Spero eum librum non perditurum esse.*

3) *Marcus patrem suum a Iulio interfectum esse credit.* What do you say, Hainsworth?

- Father, these sentences are examples of the accusative and infinitive construction used for indirect statements, which are different from indirect commands and questions which both use the subjunctive. The sentences you gave us, Father, illustrate the sequence of tenses which determine the time relation between the main verb and the verb in the indirect statement, which is in the infinitive. The subject of this verb is placed in the accusative case. So, the first sentence means "Caesar said that he was the best soldier". We know that Caesar was talking about himself since he used the reflexive pronoun *se* as the subject accusative. The use of the present infinitive *esse* indicates that he was talking about the same moment that he made the statement – even though the main verb is in the past tense.

The second sentence means "I hope that he will not lose the book". The verb *sperare* takes the future infinitive – here *perditurum esse* – in this construction. He is hoping now for something to happen later. No reflexive subject accusative here – *eum* refers to a person different from the one who is hoping. The last sentence translates as "Marcus thinks that his father was killed by Julius". Here the perfect, or past, infinitive is used to show that the action of the indirect statement happened before the action of thinking, which is happening right now. Again, we know that Marcus is talking about his own father by the use of the reflexive adjective *suum*. *Iulio* is the ablative of agent with the preposition *a* – the one who did the action expressed by the passive infinitive *interfectum esse*. By the way – I don't know if you're still giving bonus points, Father – but our word "credit" is actually the Latin verb *credit* that we have in the third sentence. So giving "credit" means the person believes or thinks he will be paid eventually. I guess that's why Pizza Pete never accepts credit. The little sign on his counter says "We no give credit – you mad, but if you no pay, we mad. Better you mad!"

-	Excellent as usual, Hainsworth! I hope you boys are all this ready for the exam.

If I thought that working for Pizza Pete actually helped with Latin, I'd have him hire all of you for the summer!

Chapter 17

- Okay, Hole – grab your clubs and we'll take a cart. This will be my final practice for the upcoming Club Pros event in Dayton. Since it's not far, you'll be able to caddy for me.

We'll go there the day before so you can walk the course and take notes on the trouble spots. As usual, you won't really need to pace the yardage, since your technique of telling me which club to hit on practically every shot has never let me down. But I still can't for the life of me figure out how you do it!

- Well, you're the one hitting the shots, Donnie. I know your game, so I can pretty well tell which club you need. I'm just glad you don't need me to read the greens. I've talked to other caddies at tournaments, and they all agree that Donnie Johnson is just about the best putter on the Club Pro Tour. If only you could keep your drives in the fairway! By the way, it was nice of you to give my classmate Ronnie Duke a job as club-washer this summer. I mean, since he's an Afro-American, and the members here aren't too keen.

- Well, Hole – say, you never said if the name Hole bothered you. I know it could sound a bit strange to folks hearing it, but I tell people it's short for "Hole-in-one" – and calling you that could bring me luck. Besides "Hole" is a pretty good nickname for Holden, and it's a lot better than being called "Bus" by your own father! And, after all, we do have a "whole" lot of fun on the golf course! I have no problem with having Ronnie work for me, but he won't have the privilege of playing the course like other employees. The Club rule of no black members is sad, but no one will tell me who to hire for my shop! Our country has a terrible problem – we fought a civil war because of it – but some day America will get it right. And I hope we fix that problem sooner than later. I mean it's not right for you and your girl Maxine to endure racist taunts - and more. So what are you and Maxine doing this summer?

- The first thing we're going to do is visit the Cincinnati Fine Arts Museum. There's an exhibition from the Metropolitan Museum in New York on Ancient Rome, and we'll get a chance to see some famous Roman statues, and also some Greek vases. I've been teaching Maxine some Latin, and she can already decline nouns in the first three declensions – the third is the most complicated of the five declensions. She can also conjugate verbs from all four conjugations in the present and imperfect tenses of the indicative. I'll be able to do my school reading list while Maxine is away with her family. Mr. Davis is a successful businessman, and they'll be visiting his company branch in California. I've been reading books about priests, like Graham Greene's *The Power and the Glory*. It's about a renegade

Catholic priest in Mexico who is fighting the corrupt Mexican government as well as his own demons. It has something to do with the liberal theology in Latin America that we talked about in our Religion class. Father Peterson says that we will probably have a Latin American pope one day.

Another book I read was *Nor Scrip nor Shoes* – about a missionary priest in China. There's something about priests lately. I've even watched two really good films on TV about priests – *Going My Way* with Bing Crosby and *Boys Town* with Spencer Tracy. Those two actors make the life of a priest kind of appealing, but I'm sure it isn't the magic life they make it out to be.

Oh, and in *Going My Way*, there is a funny seen where Bing Crosby takes the old priest played by Barry Fitzgerald to play golf, and the old priest says it's the first time he ever held a "caddy" in his hand! No reference to me being your "hired hand" I'm sure! Besides, one golf ball "in your hand" is better than "two in the bush" that I'd have to look for! One sad element in the story happens when we realize that the old pastor will be put out to pasture! I'm going to try to read Caesar's *Commentary on the Gallic War* in Latin. The rest of the time I'll be splitting my work shifts between here and Pizza Pete's. Maxine will be back a couple of weeks before school starts, so we'll be able to go for long walks and listen to music like we love to do.

-       Good for you, Hole! Reading all those books - and I spend my time reading greens! I've see those movies, too. But are those Jesuit teachers of yours trying to reel you in? And you're still studying Latin? But I won't bad-mouth Latin! One of our Club President's daughters studies Latin at Penn State. Of course, she will help their golf team – she hits the ball a mile! See if you can outdrive me on this hole.

-    Maybe not, but my drive will be straighter!... If I was your caddy for your next shot, I'd tell you to play a slice around that tree. That's it, Donnie – get your left foot back and open the club head – just like you showed me so many times. I hope that's a five iron you have in your hands! And you're right – only Jack Nicklaus spends more time reading greens than you do! I know you admire the "big three" – Palmer, Nicklaus and Player. You refer to them as the "three kings" of golf – the "lions of golf"! I call them the "three Magi" or the "three magicians" of golf! I guess nobody will ever invade their "kingdom" on the PGA circuit!

-       Never say never, Hole! There could be a tiger lurking, ready to be the next world champion.

-       Where my Dad often hits his ball, he could be a "tiger in the woods"!

Chapter 18

-     Well, Tommy, our final year at St. Xavier High — hard to believe! Latin has become so important in my life. I mean I want to major in Classics at university. And this year's Greek course is going to help. But I can't blame you for opting for that new military history course - you being an Army cadet and all that. I just hope my Dad will finally get on board. He didn't seem to mind that Feeb will be taking Latin this year at Sacred Heart. We had our first French class in the new enriched programme that includes units on French Canada with *Maître* — or *Monsieur* - Dubois — he's more flexible this year! Did you know that he's from Montreal, Canada. That's why his accent is different. Last year, we first thought his name was pronounced "duboys" like the Dubois clothes outlet on McMillan. But he corrected us real quick — his name is pronounced "dubwa". He told us that he studied at UC, and married a girl from Cincinnati. That's not all! He went to a Jesuit high school in Montreal, and studied Latin. He told us how French is just one of the very modern forms of Latin. And he's read all the Astérix books!

His Latin teacher in Montreal was Father Brault. And get this — that name isn't pronounced "Brawlt" like our Ault Park, but "bro". Imagine that — his Latin teacher was a "Bro"! He told us that in our course this year he would talk a lot about Montreal and about Quebec City, which he said was the most beautiful city in Canada, and where you only hear people speaking in French.

He'll also be playing songs in French. Father McNeil is ready to start class. We'll talk about your college plans later. I know you are already thinking about that Four Freshmen song — "Graduation Day"!

-     *Salvete, discipuli.* No, boys, we won't be talking only in Latin this year, although that would be fun. I simply wanted to begin by saying "hello, students!" It's nice to see all your smiling faces again — that is a smile, right, Nelson? You have all come a long way in Latin, but I know you are already thinking about next year at university. So you should all be keen to face the challenge of this year's Latin class, since we will be following the freshman curriculum of Xavier University's Classics Department. You see — a Jesuit connection isn't such a bad thing!

And I'm glad that many of you will be taking the Greek course with Mr. James, who is a fine young man. But remember to call him Father James. It shouldn't be hard — he'll be wearing a cassock, just like me. Now before I distribute the textbooks, I want you to copy this sentence.

Si quid est in me ingenii, iudices, quod sentio quam sit exiguum, aut si qua exercitatio dicendi, in qua me non infitior mediocriter esse versatum, aut si huiusce rei ratio aliqua ab optimarum artium studiis ac disciplina profecta, a qua ego nullum confiteor aetatis meae tempus abhoruisse, earum rerum omnium vel in primis hic A. Licinius fructum a me repetere prope suo iure debet. I was observing you as you all waited desperately for me to place a period. Well, boys, welcome to Marcus Tullius Cicero. You've just copied the first sentence of Cicero's speech called the *Pro Archia* – in defence of Archias. This sentence, which goes on and on, is called a periodic sentence – or, as I prefer, a Ciceronian sentence, since he was such a master in its construction. If you were out of breath reading it, imagine Cicero's audience listening to it! But he was able to allow us to follow his argument by a clever use of relative pronouns, which held everything together, and which referred – or "related" - all the parts to the central idea, as the word "relative", coming from the Latin verb *referre* suggests. Boys, let me illustrate the impact of a Ciceronian sentence with a little story. It seems that one day a Roman senator was fifteen minutes late for a meeting in which Cicero was to address the Senate. Upon arriving, he took his seat and asked the senator seated next to him what Cicero had been talking about, and the other senator replied that he didn't know since Cicero had not yet reached the verb! Before class ends, I'm going to write an English translation of our first sentence on the board. Copy it down, and before next class, try to work out how this particular syntax works, using your dictionary and your Latin grammar books from last year.

"If there is anything of natural ability in me, gentlemen of the jury, and how limited it is I do know, or if there is any successful practice in speaking, in which I do not deny that I am moderately experienced, or if there is any theoretical knowledge of this skill in me, derived from the study of and training in the best arts, from which, I confess, at no time of my life have I shrunk, of all of these, indeed among the first, this Aulus Licinius ought to claim the profit from me almost as his."

Chapter 19

- Good morning to you all! I'm FatherJames – that is, according to Father President, how you are to address me. But I'm not old enough to be your father! Forgive me, guys, I'm just trying to be funny, but I can't master humour like Father McNeil. As you can see, I'm an Afro-American, which for some people makes me different, or even inferior – I got a lot of that growing up in the South. Strange, though, that our Jesuit leader, our Superior General, as we call him, is sometimes referred to as the "Black Pope"! I wouldn't be surprised if one day a Jesuit actually did become Pope. I'm from Atlanta - that's right – like Reverend Martin Luther King. Did you know that his name was actually Michael before he changed it to Martin? I graduated from the University of Tennessee, where I studied Latin and Greek. There is something different about me – unlike your other teachers, I'll be calling you by your first names. I've been a scholastic for two years, which means that, technically, I'm still going to school. You know the word school comes from a Greek word – *schole* - which meant "free or leisure time". So you were privileged, even lucky, to be able to go to school. You didn't spend all that free time by not going to school – like Huckleberry Finn! The French use the word *école* and the Italians use the word *scuola*. The word *escuela* is found in Spanish. So you see, just like Latin, Greek has given many words to English, and to other languages. In this course, which is actually Ancient, or Classical, Greek, since Greeks still speak and write a modern form of the Greek language, we will study and learn together – a wise old Jesuit once told me that the best way to learn is to teach - the Greek alphabet and the basics of Greek grammar. In fact, the famous philosopher Socrates believed that one should devote his life to learning and not just teaching. You'll hear a lot about him in this course, since scholars throughout the ages have claimed that he was a "Christ" before Jesus. By the way, "Christ" is simply the anglicized form, as well as the French form, of the Greek word *Christos,* meaning "the Annointed One". But we won't be reading any writings by Socrates, because like Jesus, he didn't seem to have written anything, and like Jesus, even though he saw his death coming, he didn't try to avoid it. And you won't be reading the *Iliad* or the *Odyssey* or the plays of Sophocles or Aristotle's *Metaphysics* in this course. Hopefully, some of you will read them in university, along with Plato and Aristophanes and Aeschylus and Euripides and Herodotus and Thucydides. But we will talk about those writers and important events in Ancient Greek history. We shall also take a look at daily life in ancient Athens. By way of example – technically, not a "by the way" – an Athenian taylor bumps into one of his customers on the street and greets him, but is not sure of his name: "Euripides?". To which the customer replies: "Eumenides?"! This course will provide you with a morass of information on Greek civilization! So – in a nutshell – this course will take you from "elision to Elysion" or, for those of you averse to the drudgery of language mechanics – from "Hell to Heaven"! By the way – don't you just love the way we Jesuits are always saying "by the way" – we will also be looking at the Greek version of the New Testament. It was written in what is known as Koine Greek, a common form that came out of the classical dialects in Ancient Greece. By the way – I did it again – the Greeks never called themselves by that name, but rather Hellenes, from one of their founding heroes, Hellenus. That's Hellenus with two l's, not Helen of Troy, although I'm sure you boys will be happy to know that we will be looking at her – well not actually at HER, but at her story. Why the sad faces, guys? Or, as Alexander the Great said to his horse Bucephalus, after retiring him from the battlefield – "why the long face?"! Even today, Greece to the Greeks is known as Hellas. The Romans gave the name Greeks to that great people, and there were so many Greeks in Southern Italy, that they called that territory *Magna Graecia*. We will hear more about the Greeks and Romans later on this year. Perhaps you already know that the Roman Empire in the East, where Greek became the predominant language, outlasted the Roman Empire in the West by about a thousand years! In fact you could say the Roman Empire had been cut in two with a pair of Caesars! Now we can look at our Greek textbook. You will see that the Greek alphabet has twenty-four letters. There are lower case and capital letters. Many of those capitals look like English letters, but you won't see them often, because they're only used in proper names and to begin paragraphs. The names of the letters are there for you as well as the corresponding pronunciation in English. Those of you who have glanced at the book will have noticed that Greek words have accents – three types, as in French. Those of you who take French with Mr.Dubois – his name doesn't end with "boys", guys – will discover that a different accent means a different pronunciation. In Greek that's only partially true. For us, the accents will be extremely valuable in putting the vocal stress on the right syllable. So if the Romans and other peoples needed accents to help them read Greek, imagine the problems we would have without them! What about all those Greek words in the English language? Well, think back to your second year here at St. Xavier. After your freshman year, you thought you were pretty smart. After all, you were sophomores! Well that word "sophomore" comes from two Greek words, *sophos* and *moron*, which mean "a wise fool". And I'm sure there were seniors who made you feel like a moron! Another word formed from moron is oxymoron, which means a contradiction. An example would be "that hated love of Greek which consumed him". Say, boys, two morons were sitting on top of the Empire State Building – a big moron and a little moron. How come only the big moron fell off? No, not because the other one was smarter. It was because he was a "little more on"! Just before the bell goes, who can tell us the origin of the word "alphabet"?

-      Yes,Holden?

-        Sir – I mean Father – James - the word "alphabet" is just the names of the first two Greek letters joined together – *alpha* and *beta*.

Chapter 20

\-   So how was your first week back at Sacred Heart, Maxine? And you never told me what your California vacation was like. Did you get to swim in the Pacific?

\-   I really missed you when I was in Los Angeles – it's so far away! We saw the Pacific Ocean up close, but we didn't go into the water. Mommy and I did some shopping, and Charlie and Daddy went to visit the UCLA campus. Charlie was hoping to see the basketball team working out. I think they're called the Bruins. The L.A. Lakers are his favorite team in the NBA.

And Daddy really likes the Dodgers baseball team. Of course his favorite team are the Reds, and he sometimes brings Charlie and me to games – he often gets free tickets. Mommy prefers the theater. She brings Daddy along. She's seen *A View from the Bridge*, *A Streetcar Named Desire*, and *Death of a Salesman*, but her favorite is the musical *Porgy and Bess*. You know, Holden, they have great plays here during the summer in the Playhouse in the Park. We ought to go see one next summer. Oh, and we drove by some real nice golf courses in L.A. – you would have loved them. I've got some nice teachers this year at Sacred Heart, especially my Spanish teacher. She's from California, and she graduated from UCLA. Can you believe it? Miss Perez says that knowing Spanish would be useful in Los Angeles. The city's name means "the angels".

Since you often call me "angel", I guess the city had one more "angel" for a few weeks! You are always "serenading" me with that song by The Crests – "The Angels Listened In"! Our Orientation Counsellor had an assembly for the senior classes and told us to start thinking about university applications. But what about your week, Holden? How is your university level Latin course? And your Ancient Greek class?

\-   Wow – all those connections with UCLA! The Latin course is going to require a lot of work, but I was able to figure out all the grammar at the beginning of the speech by Cicero that we are going to be reading this year. You can't beat old Father McNeil, but I don't know if I like Latin so much because of him, or I like him because of Latin. And my Greek class is going to be really interesting. We have this young Jesuit teacher who is an Afro-American. And he has a great sense of humour. My French class is really advanced this year. Our teacher is from the French part of Canada. Football practice has already started. I hope you're going to be one of our cheerleaders again this year. I'll be sending in my university applications too. Of course I'm going to stay here in Cincinnati. But I'm probably going to attend Xavier University. I'll have Latin credits already. They have a really good undergraduate programme in Classics. My plan is to go on to Graduate School in Classics at UC. Their department is tops, and if I'm accepted, I'll get a scholarship, and what they call a fellowship – I'll get paid to go to school! The UC Classics Department has money that goes back to the time of President Taft. Seems like his niece married a professor who became Department Chairman, and her fortune now pays all the graduate students with the Louise Semple Fellowships. Her father also gave huge amounts of money to UC. I'm kind of proud that President Taft was born here in Cincinnati, Maxine, since he was the first President to throw the inaugural pitch at a major league baseball game. I guess this city produces "natural" ball players! The President's son eventually was an owner of the Philadelphia Phillies and the Chicago Cubs, but, sadly, not of the Cincinnati Reds. It would be neat if I were accepted at UC, but I would probably have to give up my job at Pizza Pete's. But with you going to UC – are you still going to major in American history? - we can be together a lot – just like now!

-       Oh, I'd love for that to happen, Holden - both of us at university here in Cincinnati! Yes, I want to study the history of race relations in America, and the lives of great men like Dr. King. But my brother Charlie seems to want to major in basketball! That's all he talks about – that and… well, he keeps asking me if we are going to break up. I wish he could like you just as Mommy does. If you're at Xavier U., you'll still be with the Jesuits. You aren't thinking of joining them, are you Holden – like your Greek teacher?

-       Funny you should ask that, Maxine. Father Brown, our Chaplain, had a long talk with me after our first day back – he got me out of football practice! He described the process of becoming a Jesuit, being a novice and then a scholastic. Maybe even teaching Latin and Greek in a Jesuit school. And Father Brendan has talked to me a couple of times about becoming a priest when I served Mass for him at St. Joseph's. He said I wouldn't have to ride a motorcycle!

Being a Jesuit and teaching Latin would be kind of nice. But nothing would be better than being with you for the rest of my life, Maxine Davis! And I could still teach Latin!

-       And I want to be with you, Holden – no matter what my brother thinks. And I want you to keep on being my Latin teacher!

-       My family understands how we feel about each other. And I caught my Dad listening to The Platters albums you lent me! Like me, he's come to the conclusion that Black music matters! You know, he's finally accepted that I can make a living with a Classics degree.

He loves the poet Robert Frost as much as I do, and he has probably realized that, like Frost, I have chosen to "take the road less-travelled"! I think it was all the coaxing by my Mom, and the fact that one of the senior vice-presidents at his company has an undergraduate degree in Classics. He has talked to me, though, about applying to attend university out of state – for the experience. But I told him I loved Cincinnati and wanted to stay here. That I could keep on working at Pizza Pete's and for Donnie Johnson at Indian Hills. Yet I could tell he knew the real reason I don't want to leave. But I told him I would apply to some other universities. To tell the truth, I'm kind of curious to find out if I would be accepted. And it's a question of pride.

-       I know you would be accepted everywhere, Holden Hainsworth! You're the best Latin student – and the best football player! But you're so sweet to give all that up to be with me! We do have fun together, don't we? All those walks in Burnet Woods, and along Clifton Avenue. The crazy way you dance – and sing! You even know the words to all the Motown songs. The way you serenade me with your guitar. Your sweet kisses when we say good-night. And, Holden, you treat me with so much respect. Even Charlie has to admit that.

Black music matters! Charlie would love that expression! And it sounds so prophetic.

Chapter 21

-        Damn, Oldie, we're only five points behind. We score a touchdown on our next possession and we win. But with time running out, we may only get one play. Everybody said Corryville High would kill us, but thanks to your three touchdowns we're still alive.

But I don't get how you stay so humble, Oldie. You never showboat after your TD's. Why, you don't even spike the ball – you just politely toss it to the referee. You know, you look pretty beat up. I mean Corryville is always rough, but who'd have thought they would take four roughing penalties against you. Coach Mason is fit to be tied.

-        I know, Tommy. I feel a little dizzy, but winning this game would put us in the All-State final. It looks like we're going to get the ball on their twenty. And you're right – only one play. So we'll have to try that play we used in practice. They'll be expecting you to do the end sweep, or me to fake the hand-off and run the keeper. So you know what to do, Tommy.

Take the hand-off and after a couple of seconds turn and throw the ball back to me. If we manage to fool them, I can run the twenty yards into the end-zone.

***

-        It's all right, son, you played your heart out for us today. If it hadn't have been for you, the game would have been over before the second half. In fact, you're the only reason we made it to the semis. Based on your play all season, there's no way they won't give you the MVP award.

-        But, Coach, I was going to score the winning touchdown. I mean, the crowd was screaming, and my vision was a bit blurry. But I saw the ref out of the corner of my eye, so I tossed him the ball. When I saw him move away, I looked up and realized that I had crossed the five-yard line and not the goal-line. But their safety chasing me pounced on the ball, and it was all over.

-        Holden, it wasn't meant to be. I'm proud of the way you and the team played today. You can hold your head high, even though it must be a bit sore right now. And you can be sure I'm going to file a complaint with the league over those head shots you suffered. Right now, there's folks who want to see you.

-        That was quite a show you put on for us today, Hainsworth! All your Latin classmates and I are so proud of you. This old Jesuit has seen many players come and go, but you are by far the best. And you are the best Latin student I've ever taught. *Mens sana in corpore sano*! Oh, there's a young lady who wants to see you.

-       Oh, Holden, are you okay. I'm sorry I'm crying, but I was so afraid for you, seeing you hit so hard and so often. I was really scared when I heard these gentlemen talking in the row behind our cheerleader squad at half-time. One of them, who was a doctor, was saying he couldn't believe they weren't removing you from the game with all those head hits you had absorbed.

-       Gee, Maxine, I feel like I've let you down as well as St. X. I think that hurts more than my physical pain. Funny, I set a St. Xavier record for most touchdowns in a season and with last year, I hold the all-time league rushing record for a quarterback, but I think I'll mostly be remembered as the guy who threw the ball away while running for the winning touchdown! It's kind of ironic that they just opened the Pro Hall of of Football here in Ohio last year in Canton, but my football career is probably finished!

Chapter 22

\- So, guys, just to review some peculiar features of Ancient Greek syntax.

Remember that plural subjects take a singular verb if they happen to be neuter gender. What else? Ah, yes, there is no indefinite article. But, then, in Latin, there are no indefinite or definite articles. There is a special use of the accusative case, which we saw briefly in naming people. For example, in the sentence "There was a young man, Holden by name," the noun "name" would be placed in the accusative case. This is called the accusative of respect – in this example, "Holden, with respect to his name". The Romans sometimes used this construction, in which case it is referred to as the "Greek accusative" since "with respect to" in Latin is normally expressed by the ablative case. And you all know that there is no ablative case in Greek. Of course, we have to mention the contract verbs. You recall that the combination of an *alpha, epsilon* or *omicron* stem ending combined with the regular verb endings creates, as it were, new endings. You have to be constantly reviewing the verb endings for the present tense. Before the end of the year, we will also look at the future and imperfect tenses, as well as the simple past tense, which is called the aorist tense. You should also be studying the paradigms for the three declensions of nouns. As in Latin, the third declension is the tricky one. Before I comment on your mythology projects, I want to mention a couple of well-known expressions, and speak about some ordinary Greek words that have a special meaning in a Christian context. We spoke last time about the Greek oracle at Delphi, which often gave ambiguous answers to those consulting it. In this way, the Oracle was never wrong, since there was always an alternative explanation to the prediction it made – how often have you fellas fallen for "heads I win, tails you lose!"? There are a couple of sayings attributed to the Oracle at Delphi which can be valuable guidelines in life. *Meden agan* means "nothing in excess". We know that moderation in all things is a key to healthy living. The other expression is *gnothi seauton*, meaning "know yourself". In our terms, this means knowing and accepting your strengths and limitations. Powerful stuff - right, guys? You all use the words Bible and Eucharist – The Lord's Supper – on a regular basis. Well the Greek word *biblos* came to mean "book", since it had been the word for papyrus, that is, paper. Until Gutenberg came along in 1453 with his printing press, we had to make do with papyri, or parchment, scrolls. The city in Lebanon called Byblos – "city of paper", if you will, was so-named because it was the port to which the paper was delivered, and later on for the shipping of trees, which we all know became the source of paper. Some scholars claim that Byblos is the oldest continuously inhabited city. So you all - I hope – read "the Book" - or, as it's called – "the Good Book". When you partake of the Eucharist, that is, the Lord's Supper, you are "giving thanks", since the Greek origin of that word is *eucharistos,* which means "grateful". That word, in turn, comes from *charis,* which translates as "grace" or "favour". Naturally, you recognize the English derivative "charity"! If ever you travel to Greece, remember the word *eucharisto*, which means "thank you" in Modern Greek. What is the Greek word for "fish"? For those of you who can't remember it, the word is *ichthus.* Look at the elements in the word: i—ch—th—u—s. Each of the letters stood for a word, and the whole expression became a kind of password among the early Christians. The words translated as "Jesus Christ, Son of God, Saviour – *Iesus Christos, Theou Uios, Soter*! You recall how fish are ever present in the New Testament – and in those Biblical movies we watch at Easter! You have learned the word for time – *chronos.* Hence "chronology", "chronometer", "chronic". There is another Greek word for time, which refers to the right time, or for Greek farmers or sailors – the right season. But for Christians following the New Testament, the word *kairos* has a special significance. For us, the favorable moment expressed by the word *kairos* is the time for the fulfillment of God's divine plan – the coming of Christ. Now you understand why we give the name Kairos to our senior retreats here at St. Xavier. And I'm happy to say that I will be one of your moderators at next week's Kairos. Now for your projects. It seems Billy Harris has gone into business with the Greek gods, and they have put a number of products on the market. Speaking again of fish, I suppose a Poseidon aquarium would make a good home for household fish. I would certainly buy Zeus light bulbs – I like your slogan – "for proper 'lightning' in the dark". But I don't think I will be needing any Aphrodite love potion! I did find Warren Barker's greeting cards based on Greek mythology very clever – let's read some of them together. How about this one where Jason thanks Medea for helping him to secure the ram's Golden Fleece – "I love EWE!". Or for those who hate complainers, Zeus to Prometheus – "What's eating you?". And this card where Daedalus responds to his whining son Icarus – "Who ruffled your feathers?". Then there's Herakles after slaying the nine-headed Hydra - "Better contact the NECKS of kin!". But I guess for the hero, this labour was "water under the bridge"! Guys, the word "hydra" comes from the Greek word *hudor*, which means "water"! Mercury's Messenger Service – Free Delivery to Mountain-tops, One Obol Charge to Underground Bunkers! I'm not so sure I can rely on that company – I've heard Mercury's been having his ups and downs! Here's an interesting one – Persephone's Pomegranate Pizza Pies – Heat up in less than a minute! Their card says "Very popular down under"! Somehow I don't think they're talking about Australia! We'll have to have Holden, our pizza expert, investigate. Who knows when he'll get another chance to meet an Australian! Personally, I'd jump at the chance to see a kangaroo! Speaking of Holden, he has written a poem, which, while not on the scale of Homer, certainly has epic proportions. I think you will all enjoy hearing it, so Holden, if you will…

- Ahem... "On Studying the Greek Gods"... by Holden Hainsworth

They will never believe I was there,

Describing it won't help.

Yet I feel I must reveal it all –

There may be some that care.

In Ancient Greece men sought hard to know

What makes all things happen.

Their answer they found above the clouds –

There where I was to go.

The Greeks believed that gods do exist,

And this belief is true,

For I saw their gods above the clouds –

More real than any list.

It happened two weeks ago tonight

(Time has been still since then).

I recall the loud roar of thunder,

And that bright flash of light.

I was thinking about the one called

"Father of gods and men",

And toasting with wine the rebel god

Who kept women enthralled.

The sudden noise disrupted my toast,

And the light broke my thoughts.

Then he appeared with wings on his boots –

That one to be my host.

It wasn't a dream, nor shadow thereof –

The figure spoke to me.

His eyes gleamed as he beckoned me on

"To those", he said, "above".

High over the white clouds he swept me,

And there no darkness crept,

For I saw so plainly those big halls,

And all things there to see.

My wingèd host guided me inside;

I then surveyed the place.

All those there observed curiously,

While I stared, all wide-eyed.

An old man was sitting at table,

His meal set before him.

"Sweet nectar is it, and ambrosia",

Said my host, "not fable".

He must be Zeus, father of gods and men –

The mere thought frightened me.

The gods of the Greeks must all be real –

Just as real now as then.

I dared not speak to god so mighty,

I turned then to a girl.

So pretty she looked, so innocent –

She was Aphrodite.

Somehow I resisted all desire,

And moved away from her.

But she continued to smile at me,

As sweetly sang the lyre.

The music attracted me quickly;

A young man sat playing.

This I knew was the fair Apollo –

But what message for me?

A god had really been at Delphi,

Preaching laws and the rest.

All that talk of superstitious dreams

Was, in fact, the real lie.

My host and guide had spoken no more;

His wings I knew – Hermes.

But didn't he only lead dead people

To that land called folklore?

I remembered my toast to Bacchus –

I wasn't at all dead.

And there he was dancing to the lyre –

The god Dionysos.

I wondered what all the others thought

To have him among them.

One young girl frowned at him –Artemis.

I knew she'd be distraught.

A woman called the old man harshly,

And Father Zeus trembled.

He was king, and yet he had his queen

Hera was boss I could see.

I was eager to watch the quarrel,

Like the stories I'd read.

But there was no fight, and he just smiled –

The young man in laurel.

I'd never believed there were such gods –

Now I would doubt no more.

And I even saw lame Hephaistos,

He who built lightning rods.

Hermes led me next around their home;

One by one I met them.

Hades, up from the shades, and Kore

Who through earth's fields did roam.

The terrible earth-shaker was there,

On visit from the sea.

Poseidon looked at me long and hard –

No words, only a stare.

Two warriors were there, male and female -

Ares and Athena.

The one was fierce, but she smiled kindly –

She would help without fail.

Other kind women I also saw –

The quiet Hestia,

And that venerable goddess too –

Demeter, green earth's law.

Hermes remained with me, not to speak –

He seemed to understand

That fear also shared my deepest cares

Now my home I must seek.

Suddenly a huge figure appeared,

Hero as no hero,

It was he – that god-man Herakles,

Loved by some, by all feared.

He wore the lion's coat, by his side

He carried the big club.

A loud welcome he shouted to me,

    That swelled me with bold pride.

As to fellow-man in this strange land,

    Forgetting he was god,

I ran to grasp him – it's the custom –

    But no flesh touched my hand.

The Greeks had described their gods as men –

    As men they'd seemed to me.

Now the boundary between man and god

    Was like earth and heaven.

The gods are not like any of us –

    This I accept as fact.

But will a skeptical world believe

    I'd discovered them thus?

Herakles, that ghostly god, withdrew;

    Now I stood before Zeus.

My host and guide was still beside me,

    Now I would learn my due.

All the gods and goddess approached

To hold solemn council.

Zeus explained that upon their secrets

I had indeed encroached.

My plea was one of just innocence –

The trickster had brought me.

The herald of the gods only laughed,

Never blamed for events.

No worship today do they receive –

Those gods of Ancient Greece.

Yet they control the fate of mankind -

Men who do not believe.

Zeus in the heavens is still supreme,

But decisions he shares

With all the other immortals there

So to me it does seem.

Poseidon and Hades were opposed –

I was not to reveal

The truth of all reason and concern –

My knowledge to be closed.

Ares, too, would not have me return

To preach the news to earth.

But no one would accept my story.

"Truth", I said, "men will spurn".

Then Athena to her father spoke

Kind words in my behalf.

And Apollo offered that no harm

Would come of Hermes' joke.

All the others sided with Phoebus –

Zeus agreed to free me.

Hermes my host led me back to earth,

To toast Dionysos.

\-   Boys, I wonder if you were able to detect the "abca" riming scheme. Or the 9-6 syllabic beat throughout Holden's poem. You don't have a copy of the poem in front of you, but I can tell you there are 160 verses divided into 40 stanzas of 4 verses each. Well done, Holden! If we didn't know the names of the Greek gods before, we certainly know them now! I'm almost afraid to ask, but do you have a special connection with Dionysos?

\-   Yes, Father James, my mother, who is a French teacher, gave me my French middle name Denys, which comes from the name of the Greek god Dionysos.

Chapter 23

- Dear Den, I hope you will be able to cherish these special days on your Kairos retreat. Know that your family misses you even when you are away for one day. I bought you a book, *Les Miserables* by Victor Hugo. It's quite long, but it will give you something to read in French over the Christmas holidays. Don't worry about Vergil Cane – Phoebe will be walking him each day. We'll be praying for you, as I know you will be praying for us. Your father is already checking the mail every day for letters from the universities you applied to. I'm glad he accepts your goal of studying Classics. I've always told him you have to follow your heart and pursue your dreams. It's not like you're looking for Shangri-La like that fellow in the movie *Lost Horizon* that we watched on TV. But he never gave up, and I know you won't either.

God bless you son! Love you! Mom

- Hi Older! Miss you – although it's a pleasant change not to hear you complaining about how much time I spend in the bathroom! To tease me, you play that record by the Jive Five – "What Time Is It"! Just think – when you're back home we'll be preparing for Thanksgiving. When I told my Latin teacher that Latin phrase you gave me - *Semper ubi sub* ubi – "always - where - under – where", she laughed, and claimed that she was *iocorum expers.* I thought she was claiming to be an "expert in jokes" like you, but I learned that *expers* is one of those false cognates we've been studying, and actually means "being ignorant of something". Mom calls those pairs *"faux amis"*! I thought Maxine would be with us for our traditional turkey dinner, but she told me her family will be in Los Angeles. I guess they'll be having an outdoor barbecue! Remember when Sacred Heart and St. Xavier organized that hay ride and barbecue? You and Maxine made a great couple trying to do the square dance. Sorry there was no Doo Wop music for you! I see Maxine a lot at school. I'm so grateful she helped me to make the cheerleader team. It bothers her that she isn't accepted by all the girls here. Even some of her "Black Sisters Sorority" tease her about having a white boyfriend. She says her parents are a little concerned about it. And you already know that her brother Charlie doesn't believe in mixed dating. But Maxine is head over heels in love with you, and that's what really counts. See you soon! Be good (but I guess you have no choice on Kairos – Ha! Ha!)! Your Sis.

- Miss you so much, Holden! I keep playing "In the Still of the Night" over and over! Also The Supremes, The Marvelettes, The Four Tops, The Temptations, Martha and the Vandellas, Little Anthony and the Imperials, the Chiffons, Chuck Berry – remember how much fun we have dancing to his songs? – and those Doo Wop songs by Johnny Maestro and the Crests. Did you know that The Crests are a mixed racial group? And the other day WSAI played this far out song by The Diamonds called "Little Darlin'". I hope I'm your little darlin', Holden! I was so hoping to spend Thanksgiving with you, but Daddy is taking the family out to L.A. He says everybody travels over Thanksgiving weekend, but I didn't expect to be going so far.

I said a special prayer for you at Mass on Sunday. I know the Kairos retreat is really important to you. Your sister Phoebe and I have become good friends. I wish it was the same for you and Charlie. Don't forget to call me as soon as you get back home! Love you so much! Maxine.

-       Hi there Bus! Hope you're enjoying Kairos. Do they talk Latin or Greek there? – just kidding! But I want you to know that I'm very proud of you, son – proud of what you've accomplished and of all your plans for the future. I'm glad you decided to play baseball for St. X this year. Your speed will be a real asset when you're patrolling center-field. And I bet you'll get your share of stolen bases. "Stealing" bases is not a sin, big guy! And I'm looking forward to playing a few rounds of golf with you this summer. It'll be match play – if you give me a few strokes – and a few mulligans! I have to warn you – sometimes when I'm stymied behind a tree, I use my "foot wedge"! Take care, son! Dad

- Well, boys, I guess you have all had a chance to read your letters wishing you well here at Kairos. If you are not in the Greek class, you don't know me. I'm Father James – or, actually, Mr. James. But you can call me what you want – just don't call me late for dinner!

Seriously, gentlemen, this retreat will help you not only to get closer to God, but also to each other, and even to yourselves. There will be time for silent meditation and prayer as well as group reflections. There will be small group encounters as well. I'm happy to say that Monsieur Dubois will be representing the lay staff on this retreat, and will lead one group meeting in a French prayer session. Fathers Peterson, Brown, and McManus will be celebrating the Masses.

As you know, despite the cassock and collar I wear, I cannot celebrate Mass. So I will be a server along with Holden Hainsworth, whom you all know. Holden not only knows the Latin responses but also the Greek responses at the *Kyrie eleison* – "Lord have mercy". Finally, Father McNeil, who is a little under the weather, sends his prayers and best wishes to you all, with a special *salvete* to his Latin students. Have a great Kairos, guys!

Chapter 24

\-   I hope you all enjoyed Thanksgiving, boys. *Gratias semper agamus* – let us always give thanks – *parentibus, amicis, et Deo* – to our parents, to our friends, and to God. Oh, *et magistris* - and to our teachers! We have seen so far how Cicero has portrayed his client Aulus Licinius Archias as a brilliant and distinguished man. Cicero has demonstrated in his arguments that Archias was a Roman citizen, even though he was born to a noble Greek family in Syria. Being from a rich family, he was able to pursue studies at the highest level, and became a celebrated poet and scholar. So you can see why Cicero would be eager to defend him. It was normal, then, for Archias to come to southern Italy, where the Greeks had for a long time established cities in what became known as *Magna Graecia* – Great Greece. We would say "greater Greece" – an extension of the territory beyond the main limits or border. For example, we speak of Greater Cincinnati, and don't you think it strange that the Greater Cincinnati Airport is in Kentucky? Archias had been granted citizenship in at least one of these allied cities, and benefitted from the patronage of the noble Luculli family. The clan name of this family was Licinius. Remember our discussion on the Roman *gens*?

Caesar, for example, belonged to the Julian *gens*. Archias took the praenomen Aulus and the *nomen gentilicum* Licinius. Therefore, as a Roman citizen, he was known as Aulus Licinius Archias. Those of you in the Greek class have no doubt talked about the word archon which goes back to a Greek verb meaning "to begin" or "to rule", that is, to be the first, or head, in a state government. You recall that Greek cities were independent states – until they became a part of Alexander the Great's empire, and later a Roman province. So the name Archias was pretty prestigious in its own right.

We see that notion of beginnings or ruling in our words "archaeology", "archaic", "monarchy", "anarchy", and many more. Years ago I had a pretty good Latin student whose name was Archie – we called him Archias! He didn't want us to call him by his official name, Archibald, because that name made him nervous, since his father – also named Archibald – didn't have much hair, and young "Archias" dreaded the possibility of one day having to put up with "Archie's bald"!

Cicero's Archias received benefits and protection from his patrons – but as we saw in our discussion of patrons and clients in Roman political and social life – Archias also benefitted his patrons by his association with them. You recall that Cicero has already mentioned that he was speaking *pro summo poeta atque eruditissimo homine* – "in defense of a very distinguished poet and a very learned man". I pointed out at that time that *poeta* was another of those first declension nouns that are masculine gender, like *agricola, nauta* and *pirata* – since only men were farmers, sailors and pirates – and poets! We are going to continue with the text at the point where Cicero will plead that even if Archias had not been a Roman citizen, he would deserve to be one. Cicero begins by praising literature. Now you know, boys, why I am so fond of Cicero! As you are aware, the upcoming Christmas exam will consist mainly in the translation of passages from the part of the *Pro Archia* that we have seen, and in answering some syntax questions on those passages. There will also be a short sight passage from another of Cicero's works of comparable difficulty. Of course you will be allowed the use of your dictionary – will you be bringing your big Lewis and Short, Hainsworth? – good for the muscles! But no other reference materials, such as a grammar book – or an English translation of the *Pro Archia*, Nelson! - will be permitted. Archias Hainsworth has a good ring to it, so lead us, then, not into temptation, but in translation of this sentence, and then analyze it for us. *Ego vero fateor me his studiis esse deditum.*

-        Well, Father, I translate this sentence as "In truth, I confess that I have devoted myself to these studies". I confess, guys, - no pun intended, Father – unless I'd get bonus points for it! - that I had a little trouble in finding the word for "myself", since *me* is the subject accusative in the indirect statement introduced by the deponent verb *fateor.* And *deditum esse* is the perfect infinitive passive of *dedere,* "to devote" or "offer". My Lewis and Short gave me the solution with the reflexive sense of this passive verb form. So *me* is subject of *deditum esse* and the "understood" direct object of this reflexive sense of the verb. It makes more sense to say "I devoted myself to" than "I was offered", or "handed over to" these studies.

The perfect infinitive is used because he had already devoted himself to these studies before confessing to this – which he is doing now. The noun *studiis* is in the dative after *dedere.*

-        Brilliant, Hainsworth! You sounded just like Cicero arguing to prove a point! Prepare to do well on the exam, boys, in order to enjoy your Christmas Break. To get you all in the mood for Christmas, let me tell you why Santa's helpers enjoy studying Latin. It's because they are all subordinate clauses! Here's a final reminder from Cicero on the benefits of studying literature – certainly an endeavor worth thinking about! *Haec studia adolescentiam acuunt, senectutem ablectant, secundas res ornant, adversis perfugium ac solacium praebent.* "These studies sharpen youth, delight old age, enrich our prosperity, and give us refuge and comfort in adverse situations".

Chapter 25

\-   Wasn't it nice of the Student Councils of both our schools to organize this social before the Christmas Break, Maxine? It's a perfect time to find a date for the June Grad. Of course that's not our problem – but I'll bet you are looking for your dress already! Well, it's official. I was accepted at Xavier, and I'm getting the Xavier Classics Department Scholarship – provided I don't blow my June exams. Father McNeil and Mr. James – he had to use Mr. – wrote my reference letters. Notre Dame, Miami of Ohio and UC offered me football scholarships, but my football days are over. I want to devote a lot of time to my studies, and eventually be accepted into grad school. I'll still work a bit at Pizza Pete's and for Donnie at Indian Hills – just because I like those guys. You were accepted at UC, weren't you?

\-   Uh, why yes, I was accepted at UC. Oh, Holden, the Senior Grad Ball is going to be very special for me – and I hope for you. Can you believe it – three of Charlie's friends asked me to be their date! You do know I love you, don't you? I'll come by your place tomorrow. You can try to teach me how to skate on the frozen lake in Burnet Woods.

\-   Are you crying, Maxine? Sure, some of your friends will be going out of state to university, some of mine too. But we're together - to start this new chapter in our lives. And I'm going to continue teaching you Latin.

***

\-   Maxine, Maxine! I came by to surprise you. I brought you Feeb's skates to try on. But I don't understand. Why is your house for sale? Are you moving to another part of the city? Is it Walnut Hills? It's pretty nice there? Are you going to live on one of those private streets? It's okay – Mittenkamp lives on one, and once the security patrol get to know you, they don't bother you whenever you call on friends. And guess what – Pizza Pete lives on a private street – and there's no one more down to earth than him. Anyways, I know you'll never look down on anybody, Maxine Davis.

\-   Oh, Holden, I've been wanting to tell you, but I didn't know how. Daddy is going to work at the company office in Los Angeles. The whole family will be moving. Charlie is transferring to UCLA, and will play for the Bruins basketball team. I didn't know this, but when we went to L.A. at Thanksgiving, Daddy handed in an application form for me to attend UCLA. I was accepted, but I really don't want to go. Charlie is really happy, and Daddy says it's for the best. But how can it be? Mommy says it's a real good opportunity for my father and for

85

Charlie, and she doesn't want to stand in their way. She says you're a fine boy and a strong boy and that you'll make your way in life. She's been trying to comfort me, telling me you can't always tell where life will bring you. She didn't say it, but I just know that she and Daddy are happy to be getting away from those folks around here who haven't been nice to us – especially those who have said unkind things to me. You and I have both been insulted since we've been dating, and you were assaulted. But we love each other. People are mean – and so is life!

-        Oh, Maxine – what has happened to that beautiful smile I fell in love with? I never expected this - but you know it sort of explains why your father was so distant with me. He saw a white boy dating his daughter as a problem, a threat to your happiness. In a way, I can't blame him for wanting to protect his daughter. But life is so unfair. I mean we're like Romeo and Juliet – except that we're real people! But I don't think moving away is a solution. I mean – all of America has a problem – not just Cincinnati. Kind of ironic – I chose to go to Xavier U so we could be together. Well I guess you're here until the summer – and I want to spend every possible moment with you.

Chapter 26

- Gosh, Billy, I'm really grateful that you and Freddy were able to arrange it so I could get this Peace Corps experience over Spring Break. I know Tommy Nelson would have loved to come and spend a week here at Stinking Creek, but he's committed to his Army Cadet Corps training. Sorry I bailed on you guys, and walked across that rope bridge. But I'm glad you got the car safely across. Were you driving with your eyes closed, Billy? I've already met the two ladies who run the Lend-A-Hand Mission. The one I call the Boss Lady told me it would be my turn on the first night to sleep outside since there are not enough bunks inside for everybody.

But I didn't bring a sleeping bag – I hope I don't freeze. I hear it gets pretty cold at night here in the Appalachians, even though were in southern Kentucky – practically in Tennesee!

***

- Well, guys, I didn't get a wink of sleep last night. I was so cold my teeth were chattering, and I kept praying for the morning sun to show its face. But now I'm warmed up, and ready to work. Good thing too! The Boss Lady gave me some sort of hatchet and told me I have to cut down all those stray tumbleweeds in the field behind the farmhouse. Then I have to put in new posts around the pig sty. It seems that Momma Sow needs a new fence to protect her young'uns! Say, guys, do you like the way I've picked up the lingo here? I've talked to a few fellows who seemed to be around our age. There are not many families here in Stinking Creek, but they all seem to be related. I was wondering how they all have real short hair – even shorter than Tommy's when he goes off to army camp! But then I seen – just talking like them, guys! – I seen the bowls sitting on the shelves in their little shacks. Those fellows were really nice and polite, but kind of shy. They basically have a two-word vocabulary – Yup and Nope! Oh, and those rifles they carry – they're for shooting possum and rabbits – not the do-gooders like us.

That's what they call us – do-gooders! I was told there were more families like the ones here up in Brown's Hollow, but their shacks are even more crowded because they keep their pigs inside with them! I guess nobody wants to sweat over picket posts like I have!

***

- Sorry, guys, but thanks for waiting after you drove back across the rope fence.

87

I chickened out again and walked across when I saw you safely on the other side. I know all those cars in the creek didn't fall in, but were pushed in when they broke down. No garages around here to fix cars. And no schools, no hospitals, and no electricity. And we're in the U.S. of A.! Thank God the Sweet Lady is a nurse and takes care of those folks as best she can. By the way, how did you two manage to be assigned to indoor chores with the Sweet Lady, while I had to do the heavy work outside for the Boss Lady? But you have to admit that the best part of this experience was reading fairy-tales to the families. There were seven children in the family I read to. The whole family – dressed in rags – sat politely on their beaten-up sofa and on wicker baskets. One of the little boys was actually hiding in a basket before we found him peeping out! The story I read was "The Three Little Pigs" – I'm glad I wasn't reading to a family in Brown's Hollow! Those folks are so simple and honest. I wonder if Bobby Calhoun, who washes windows for Pizza Pete, came from a family like that. I hate when the guys play tricks on him, like placing a quarter on the floor after burning it in the pizza oven, and having Bobby pick it up, or freezing his little transistor radio in the storage freezer, and giving it to him while he still has his washing gloves on and him putting it to his ear as he always does! I'm sure that little radio is his prize possession. Well, I think that Boss Lady and Sweet Lady are real saints to be helping those mountain people. I hope they continue to find do-gooders to help out. And I don't think I'll ever forget Stinking Creek!

Chapter 27

Well, boys, your last Latin class at St. Xavier High. I am proud of all of you. I wanted to say that now before I correct your final exam! But I do know that you'll all go on to successful and fulfilling lives. And never forget our Jesuit motto – "Men for Others"! You know that you will be given a couple of passages from the second half of the *Pro Archia* on your final, as well as a sight passage. I've corrected your essays on Cicero. Very interesting, Hainsworth, that your title was "Cicero – A Man for Others"! Boys, I'm anxious to see you on stage in your hoods and gowns at our commencement exercises. But I know you are all thinking about tomorrow's Senior Prom! As you face new challenges, try to remember what the wise old 'possum always said: "I can do it!" I am happy to see that you all recognized that *possum* is the Latin verb meaning "I can"!

***

- Maxine, you look so beautiful in your dress. I guess this will be the last dance we attend together. I wanted to say that you are going to light up the UCLA campus, and that whenever I'm in my Latin classes, translating some prose passage, or maybe some Latin poet's verses, I'll be thinking of you – you were always struggling to figure out all those relative clauses with the different cases of the relative pronouns and their antecedents! I've already put in my request for a dedication song – you guessed it – "In the Still of the Night". Did you know, Maxine, that Fred Parris and the Satins actually recorded that song in a Catholic Church!

- I asked for that song, too, Holden! I wonder if they will play it twice. My Daddy says that attending UCLA will be great for my future. He says people in California have a better idea of freedom than people in Cincinnati. I'm not sure – there is a kind of different culture out there, but I know they've had racial trouble in L.A.

- Well, I've heard about those hippie movements in San Francisco and all that. But I'm not about to "drop out", although I'm starting to "tune into" their music. I actually like The Mamas and the Papas. With you in L.A., I guess I'll be "California Dreamin'" too! And I like The Doors and the Lovin'Spoonful and The Byrds, and The Highwaymen with their song "Michael".

Maybe I'll try to play some of the folk songs on my guitar – I'll be a "solo" Kingston Trio! – I'm going to miss strumming along with you, Maxine. Gee, I don't know if whites treat Afro-Americans any better in California, even if there's less of a difference in skin color with those super California tans! Now that your folks sold your house, I know you are leaving Cincinnati right after your grad ceremony. And Maxine, I just know I won't be able to say good-by without breaking down. I keep thinking of that Flamingos song "Lovers Never Say Goodbye"! So I want these moments tonight to be our last together, since we always were happiest when we were dancing together. Listen, they're playing our song – "In the still, still of the night…"

Chapter 28

\-   We were so proud of you, Den, at the grad ceremony. You know your father had a tear
in his eye when you were awarded the St. Xavier Silver Medal for the highest marks in Latin.
We could tell Father McNeil was a little overcome with emotion. He told us after the ceremony
that the Classics programme at Xavier University was outstanding, and that you will continue
to be a star in Latin, and also in Greek. But he says you're so humble you'll just refer to
yourself simply as a Latin student! When Mr. James presented the Greek prize to you, I had a
little thought for Maxine, since... well...since your Greek teacher is Afro-American. You know I
spoke to Maxine's mother a short while ago. She was singing your praises. She's very
religious – in fact we used to see the Davis family at Sunday Mass long before you started
seeing Maxine.

She told me that she believes that your destinies were meant to take different paths, that
God's plan didn't involve your being together. But, like me, she is sure that your time together
enriched your lives and made you better persons. And I got to talk to your French teacher –
en français, of course. But I have to admit his Canadian French wasn't always easy to follow,
since he spoke rather quickly. But he's a gentleman! He said we should visit Quebec
someday. I eventually realized he was talking about the Province of Quebec, not the city.
They have ten provinces in Canada.

\-   I know, Mother. Monsieur Dubois taught us a lot about Quebec and Canada, and about
the city of Montreal. It actually does sound like a nice city to visit. He even taught us the motto
of Canada – *a mari usque ad mare* – "from sea to sea". They mean the Atlantic and Pacific
Oceans. But we have a nice motto too – *e pluribus unum*. It means "one out of many". It's
sad, though, because our motto seems to be saying that we are united, even though we have
many differences. But the reality is we are not so united. I mean we are "united" states, but
not a "united" people. Wouldn't it be great – wouldn't America be great – if we could achieve
that?

\-   Congratulations, Apollo! You're my hero! When you were walking over to the food table,
some important-looking people said "there goes the Latin student" because you won the Latin
medal! When I graduate, I probably won't win any prizes like you. I know you tease me a lot,
but right now it feels good to be Holden Hainsworth's sister!

91

-       Don't worry about awards, Feeb, just be yourself! Being yourself is why I like you, okay,why I love you, little sis! Now that you're taking Latin at Sacred Heart you can be the Latin student! Oh, there's Father McNeil – I want to go and thank him for all he's done for me.

-       Young master Hainsworth! I was very pleased to present the St. Xavier Latin medal to you. There never was a more deserving student. You will be starting a new chapter in your studies. But as you begin university, remember, son, that it's not just about Latin – it's about life! There's a certain freedom that you didn't have in high school. You must be really disciplined, and make good decisions. And I'm sure you will. You have never let the wrong people influence you, and I'm confident this won't change. Finally, I just wanted to let you know that you can come by the school if ever you feel the need to talk. I think you could have made a good Jesuit, but God works in mysterious ways, and maybe the good you will do in life won't be as a priest. And I wanted to give you this. It's a little book by Thomas à Kempis called *Imitation of Christ*. It was given to me when I was around your age. It was the first spiritual reading I had ever done. Oh, and the original was written in Latin – maybe you'll find a copy one day. I think your father wants his turn at congratulating you. Best of luck, boy!

-       So proud of you today, Bus! And real proud of who you are! I hadn't realized Latin was so important at St. X – or anywhere! But wow! – a silver medal! I went and bought you a very appropriate graduation gift. And what do you give a Latin student who has everything? I mean your mother told me you already had the best Latin dictionary. The answer is to give him a Greek dictionary! The biggest and best that money can buy! In fact, Father McNeil wrote down a little Latin phrase – *Liber non vilis est.* He says it could mean "the book is not cheap" or "being free – freedom - is not cheap"! Latin is complicated, but this book definitely didn't come free! Son, you are now the owner of the Liddell and Scott Greek dictionary. It's even bigger than your Lewis and Short Latin dictionary – which means carrying them around will be like going to the gym! Phoebe said something about – I have it here, I'll just read it – *mens sana in corpore sano*. I know you are still a little down over Maxine. And I'm not saying this to be harsh, son, but she has moved away and you have to move on! Well, no rest for the wicked - right, son? You have to be off early tomorrow for that golf tournament up in Cleveland. And you say your man Donnie Johnson has a chance to win. Well, with a caddy like you, how can he miss? And even though you have that scholarship at Xavier U, I have to go along with you and your plans to work regular shifts at Pizza Pete's all summer in order to put some money away for the future. I know you want to get your driver's license this summer – so you might want to buy yourself some wheels one day.

-       Wow – A Greek dictionary! Thanks, Dad. It's the first book you've bought me since the Astérix book - and that Sam Snead golf book two years ago. I can't forget Maxine, but you're right, I've got to move forward. And you know, I hope Dr. King's dream comes true! Yeah, my summer is pretty well planned out. I've got a few good books to read – including that other book J.D. Salinger wrote, you know – *Franny and Zooey*. But I know *Catcher in the Rye* is still your favorite, Dad. I still like listening to Doo Wop and Motown, but now I also like folk music, and that new wave of songs from England – they call it the British Invasion! Mark August 15 on your calendar, Dad. I have an appointment at Xavier to meet with the Department Head of Classics. Xavier University here I come!

Chapter 29

\-   That's a nice golden retriever you got there. You're Holden, aren't you?

\-   Better to be Holden than beholden, as my Dad always says. But how do you know my name?

\-   It's cool, bro! My name is Aaron – Aaron Davis. I'm Maxine's cousin! I'm from not far away – Louisville, just across the river.

\-   Still a pretty long run, though!

\-   Maxine said you had a sense of humour! No, I'm wearing this UC track suit because I just joined the UC track team. I wanted to be part of the UCLA sports programme like my cousin Charlie, but UC offered the sports scholarship, UCLA didn't. Oh well – their loss!

 While I was out visiting the UCLA campus, I got a chance to talk with Maxine and Charlie. It seems she and you were the real thing for a while. Charlie told me that for a white guy, you really were okay, actually a lot nicer than some of the brothers. Unfortunately, he said that not enough of his and Maxine's crowd thought the same way. He told me to tell you he just didn't want his sister to get hurt. Maxine told me that, since I would be jogging through Burnet Woods every day as part of my training programme, I would probably run into you or, rather, by you – see I have a sense of humour too! She told me you would be walking a beautiful dog, and probably listening to a transistor radio. My cousin told me she really misses you, but that you and she were star-crossed lovers – then she mentioned that Shakespeare dude. She said you were a great football player. I was wondering how she would know talent, but then Charlie said the same thing. Maxine told me you studied Latin, like really into it, and that you were someone really special. Back at school in Louisville, we had a name for the whiteys taking Latin – there weren't no brothers in the Latin class – but it wasn't "special"! But then Maxine said something about you that really made me want to meet you, Holden. She said that you were a genuine person, who didn't let the color of someone's skin determine how you would treat a person. That you understood Dr. King's dream – that you shared it! I just want to shake your hand and hug you!

\-   Well, Aaron, I miss Maxine too. Her moving away and all that was real sudden, and then it was like we were in two different worlds – she was that far away! But it is true that I shared – I still share – the world that Martin Luther King, - uh, Dr. King - dreams about for all Afro-Americans – and for all Americans! America has to make progress – not economic or scientific progress – but social progress. And I believe that Americans together will overcome – I like that word Dr. King uses – truly overcome our differences. And what's more, Aaron, I think that having an Afro-American President one day will help, and I truly believe that will happen.

-       Man, Holden, you has got to be a bigger dreamer than our Dr. King! Oh, and I was kinda sure you were Holden, because, bro, no other whitey would be listening on his radio to Little Anthony singing "Shimme Shimme Ko Ko Bop"!

Chapter 30

-      Good afternoon, Mr Hainsworth. So nice to meet this year's scholarship winner. As you were probably informed by the Department secretary, Mrs. McGregor, I'm Father Sloan, and I'm currently serving as Department Chair. As you are a first-year student in our Honors programme, I shall be your academic advisor this year. We have a four-year programme leading to the A.B. degree. You received glowing letters of recommendation from Father McNeil and Mr. James. But I must tell you that I've been aware of your achievements in Latin for some time, since I see Father McNeil – and your other Jesuit teachers at St. Xavier High School – on a daily basis. For the Jesuits at the high school and at the university share the same Jesuit residence.

In fact, Father McNeil and I go back a long way together – from our seminary days through graduate studies in Classics. Father McNeil actually spent time at the Pontifical Institute in Rome. I don't know if you are aware that he is a native of Cincinnati, and earned his PhD at Harvard. For years we tried to get him to come here and teach at the University, but he declined, preferring, he says, "to mold young minds". This is the programme Xavier and the Classics Department are offering you. I think you will find it challenging and very stimulating.

I will also be making my personal recommendations as your advisor, but, of course, some choices will ultimately be your decision. I assume you had a preliminary look at the course offerings for freshmen here at Xavier. In fact, based on your strong high school programme – we wouldn't have expected anything less from St. Xavier High – you will be able to forego some introductory and intermediate level courses, and enroll in courses with sophomore and perhaps even junior level students. All students at Xavier take a Classics course in their freshman year – most of them naturally opting for our general Classics in Translation course. As an Honors student, you will be reading some of those Greek and Latin authors in the original. Because you have already earned credits for a Cicero course on your transcript – fulfilling a Latin prose requirement – you will be enrolled in the Vergil course, which I myself will be teaching. Father McNeil – who, I repeat, thinks very highly of you, Mr.Hainsworth – has told me you named your dog after Vergil! Unfortunately, he will not be allowed to audit the course! Oh, I assume that by now, you're immune to Jesuit humour! As an Honors student, it would be ideal if you also took a Greek course in your first year. Technically, the limit on the number of courses freshmen are allowed to take would preclude taking a Greek course, but I was successful in prevailing upon the good graces of the Director of Freshmen Academics to allow you to take a Greek course. This is largely possible, I believe, due to the fact that having already completed the equivalent of introductory Ancient Greek in high school – and it was truly a blessing that St. Xavier High and that bright Mr. James introduced that course last year – you are eligible for the New Testament Greek course being piloted jointly by the Theology and Classics departments. And I know the Chair of the Theology Department is anxious to ensure the required minimum number of students for the course. You are also permitted one other departmental option course. You have to choose between Ancient History of the Greco-Roman World and Introduction to Classical Mythology. If I may be permitted a suggestion. All freshmen must take an English Literature course. One of the choices being offered this September is "Classical Influences from the Greco-Roman World on English Literature". Consequently, taking this particular English course would allow you to explore the world of Classical Mythology and select the Ancient History course as your option. An added bonus is the fact that Professor Taylor, Visiting Professor from Brown University, will be teaching this course, and will no doubt be using his acclaimed book on Ancient History as the course text. All freshmen at Xavier must also enroll in a Philosophy course. The course I recommend is Ancient Greek Philosophers. Finally, as an Arts student, you must choose one non-departmental course from a list of Social Sciences, Fine Arts or Languages.

- The program you've described, Father Sloan, does sound exciting. I will follow your advice, and opt for the Ancient History course. In fact, we did study Greek mythology with Father – er, Mr. James – in our Ancient Greek course. And the Greek and Roman influences on the literature of today interests me a great deal. I will be taking a French course as my non-Classics elective. My mother is a high school French teacher, and I studied French throughout high school. I'll be taking a course on the classic French tragedian, Jean Racine. I was pleased to see in the course syllabus that we will be reading *La Thébaide*, *Andromache*, and *Phèdre* – three plays based on Greek tragedy. I'm still in touch with my French teacher from St. X, Monsieur Dubois. He's from Montreal, but fell in love with a young lady from Cincinnati. After they got married, he settled here and became a high school teacher.

- Ah, why do fools fall in love? Well, because love is a many-splendored thing!

- Father Sloan, you just referred to a song by Frankie Lymon and The Teenagers! And I think "Love is a Many-Splendored Thing" is also a song title, but I'm not sure who sings it.

- That song was recorded by The Four Aces. You see, Mr. Hainsworth, I'm somewhat of an aficionado when it comes to popular songs. In the Jesuit residence, I'm known as the "Music Man" – which is a little ironic, considering I don't play any musical instruments. But Mr.

James tells me that you are quite knowledgeable about Doo Wop music – and that you play the guitar.

-       I do love music, Father, but I wouldn't say I was an expert. My sister Phoebe thinks I am, because I know that Gene Chandler, who sings "Duke of Earl", is from Chicago, and that Little Anthony's last name is Gourdine. But I'm starting to appreciate other types of music. And I've always liked pop artists like Pat Boone, Paul Anka, Ricky Nelson, and of course, the King! My mother always has the radio on, and she has quite a collection of '45's. So I've been exposed to popular songs for a long time.

-       I'm sure we'll have occasion to talk about great musical artists at our Department socials. I'm looking forward to having you in our programme, and to seeing you again in our first Vergil class in a couple of weeks. If you should have any questions in the meantime, don't hesitate to contact me. I'm sure you'll experience many magic moments here at Xavier University. Did you catch that name of a Perry Como song? Term starts on August 28. As The Classics song goes – "Till Then"! Of course, I'm referring to the singing group, not our Department! By the way, the memorable opening to that song is the voice of Al Contrera, who - like Ralph Kramden and Ed Norton of "The Honeymooners" – is from Bensonhurst in New York! He recorded the hit song "Hushabye" with The Mystics.

-       Father Sloan, your musical knowledge is truly "mystical"!

Chapter 31

-       Great approach shot, Bus! I guess you used your trusty eight iron. You should make that short birdie putt. From what I've seen, son, you've had a pretty good summer.You've made a few bucks caddying for the Pro, and a few by winning all of our matches! It would be different if I could correct that slice. I try putting my right foot further back and closing the club face a little like you said, but I guess my follow through still needs work. I think it's my hip and shoulder movement. And you've made quite a bit of money working all those night shifts at Pizza Pete's. You've now got your driver's license - you'll be able to borrow the family car, and pick up my beer at the grocer's! Your mother told me that you've bought new clothes to start the semester at Xavier. Nothing like new clothes to impress the ladies! But I hope you didn't buy a toga! Will any of your Latin friends be joining you at Xavier?

-       Dad, all you have to do is allow for your slice and aim a little to the left. And I'm not out to impress any ladies. Father McNeil once taught us the expression *vestis virum facit* – "clothes make the man". I think a medieval philosopher said it. But remember, Dad, don't judge a book by its cover! Monsieur Dubois taught us the French version – *l'habit ne fait pas le moine*. In other words, wearing a monk's frock doesn't actually make you a monk! Besides, not having a girlfriend meant I could work every night. Harris and Mittenkamp enrolled at Xavier, and they will fulfil their Classics requirement by taking the Latin course with me. But they won't be majoring in Classics.

Tommy Nelson is majoring in sociology at UC. I told him he would be able to do a case study about himself! But you know, Dad, he's really serious about the Army. I think he's going to enlist. He and I don't agree on the Vietnam War, but he's still my best friend and I can understand his belief in patriotism. Besides, I think he feels he owes his older brother who was killed over there.

-       Yes, son, that war in Vietnam is a tough one. But are we sacrificing our American boys because world peace and freedom are threatened, or does the Government have another agenda? I mean there is so much to do here in America.

Young men and women like you, Holden, can perhaps make a difference for the future of America by helping out right here. Hearing about that time you spent in Stinking Creek really blew my mind! I know you're not going on to university to avoid the draft, son. But now that I mention it, what is your game plan for the future? A colleague of mine told me that the Jesuits are more persistent recruiters than the American Armed Forces! He says their unofficial motto is "St. Ignatius needs you!" And with you studying all that Latin…

- Not to worry, Dad. I mean Father Brown talked to me about becoming a Jesuit, and Father McNeil sort of hinted at it. Even Father Brendan at St. Joe's asked me to consider the priesthood. But I think I've always wanted a family of my own – just like ours. And even through the hard times with Maxine – but I mostly remember the good times! – I knew I would like to get married someday. Of course I want to be able to support my family. My goal is to pursue my Latin studies – to eventually go on to graduate studies in Classics – probably at UC – and get my PhD. Then, hopefully, I could become a professor at university. Maybe I could teach in Dayton, or at Miami University in Oxford, which is really not far away.That is, if they forgive me for turning down the football scholarship they offered me! The salary for university professors is not too bad, and I could always increase my income by teaching extra courses in the summer, and by joining the group of professors who go on lecture tours. Who knows, I could perhaps write books. I think I would like to write a novel someday. Speaking of money, I'm six up with five holes to play – you owe me another "George Washington"!

- Bus, you had me completely buffaloed during today's round, so at the 19th hole you can "buy, son"!

- Dad, you weren't inspired today by the film *How GREEN Was My Valley*! I've seen you EAT more greens than you HIT today! You played more like a novice "green fee" player! Still you always admired that film, since it won five Oscars, and was nominated for five others. Once you've paid me, I'll have seen a lot more "green" than you today! Maybe you should have hired Al Green as a caddy, or listened to the song "Green Green" by The New Christy Minstrels!

- Bus, are you saying I looked a little green around the edges since I only hit the ball to the edges of the green?

- You had the green light to go for the pin, Dad, so what hapPINed?

Chapter 32

\-   Good-day, ladies and gentlemen! I trust you all followed my suggestion of reading the entire *Aeneid* in English over the Christmas holidays. You all did extremely well in the first semester. The passionate story of the lovelorn Dido in Book Four was truly moving, was it not? And to quote a Jesuit friend of mine – our St. Xavier High boys will know who I'm referring to – the description of Aeneas' visit to the Underworld recounted in Book Six was out of this world! During this second semester let us turn – or "Turnus", if I may! - our attention to the final books of Vergil's *Aeneid,* specifically to books ten and twelve. Right now I would like to return your first-term essays. Some were quite insightful, but a few of the essays lacked depth and clarity. Please read the comments carefully. They are meant to be constructive, but I am known to sometimes be a little blunt – but only with students who are less than sharp! Ah, Jesuit humour – hard to live with it, hard to live without it! A couple of you questioned the necessity of assigning an essay in a Latin reading course. Well, here in the Xavier Classics Department, we are very demanding. I would like to give public praise to one of you, whose essay comparing the parting of Dido and Aeneas to that of Calypso and Odysseus in Homer's *Odyssey* and Aeneas' visit to the Underworld to that of Odysseus' visit in Book Eleven of the *Odyssey*, pointing out similarities and differences was superb! Well done, Mr. Hainsworth - you even managed to include the name for Homer's account of the trip to the Underworld, the *Nekyia*! For those of you keen on the study of words, this Greek word gives the English language words such as "necromancy" and "necrology", the second part of those words being of Greek origin as well. The one difference you didn't mention was that Vergil's account was written in Latin, while Homer's was in Greek! It's all right, ladies and gentlemen – Mr.Hainsworth is used to Jesuit teasing! Did I say teasing – I meant teaching! Consider now lines 490 to 509 in Book Ten, where Turnus confronts the Trojan Pallas.

Quem Turnus super adsistens Arcades, haec inquit memores mea dicta referte Evandro qualem meruit Pallanta remitto.

Quisquis honos tumuli quidquid solamen humandi est largior. Haud illi stabunt Aeneia parvo hospitia. Et laevo pressit pede talia fatus exanimem rapiens immania pondera baltei impressumque nefas una sub nocte iugali caesa manus iuvenum foede thalamique cruenti quae Clonus Eurytides multo caelaverat auro quo nunc Turnus ovat spolio gaudetque potitus.

Nescia mens hominum fati sortisque futurae Et servare modum rebus sublata secundis! Turno tempus erit magno cum optaverit emptum intactum Pallanta et cum spolia ista diemque oderit. At socii multo gemitu lacrimisque impositum scuto referunt Pallanta frequentes. O dolor atque decus magnum rediture parenti haec te prima dies bello dedit haec eadem aufert cum tamen ingentes Rutulorum linquis acervos!'

Now will the twelve of you form teams of three to work on transLating the passage, using of course your dictionaries and the notes on Vergilian syntax I provided you with.

***

\-   Mr. Hainsworth, I see that you and your cohorts are beaming with confidence. Why don't you share your team's translation of the passage with the whole class?

\-   Certainly, Father Sloan. "Then Turnus, standing near this one said 'Arcadians, remembering my words, bring them back to Evander: I return Pallas such as he deserved. Whatever the honor of a tomb is, whatever the consolation of burial is, I grant it. His hospitality to Aeneas will not at all be of little cost to him'. After saying such things, he pressed him, lifeless, with his left foot, seizing the huge weight of the belt and the crime impressed on it: in one wedding night the band of youths, killed horribly, and the bloodied bedrooms, which Clonus, the son of Eurytus, had engraved with much gold.

Turnus now gloats at this spoil and rejoices at having gained possession of it.

The mind of humans is ignorant of fate and destiny, and of how to maintain moderation when lifted up by favorable things. There will be a time for Turnus when he will have wished that Pallas had been bought at a great cost unharmed. And when he will have hated those spoils and that day. But his allies, crowded together, with much groaning and tears, carry back Pallas, placed on a shield. Oh grief and great glory, you about to return to your father! This first day gave you to war, this same day carries you off, although you leave behind huge heaps of Rutulians."

\-   If the other teams accept this translation – and I see no reason why they shouldn't – and if there are no questions , class is adjourned for today. Don't forget the Department social on Friday. All you majors and honors programme students should drop by and talk to the professors, as well as to our Secretary, Mrs. McGregor. You'll be able to compliment her on the beautiful bulletin board she maintains. Who knows, you may spot some announcements that command your attention. She updates all the latest news from the classical associations as well as upcoming conferences and special lectures here in Cincinnati. For your information, APA refers to the American Philological Association, ANS refers to the American Numismatic Society, whose headquarters are in New York, AIA refers to the Archaeological

Institute of America – we have a chapter here in Cincinnati – ACL refers to the American Classical League, and CAMWS refers to the Classical Association of the Mid-West States. Mrs. McGregor also occasionally posts information from the classical associations in Britain, as well as from the CAC, which is the Classical Association of Canada. Finally, there are the summer study programmes and the scholarship programmes in other American universities as well as in universities abroad. Of course, we don't want to lose any of you!

Chapter 33

\- Hi there! My name's Holden. It's my first year here at Xavier. I've seen you in my Philosophy course. You raise interesting questions.

\- Steve here. You're the first person to talk to me tonight – other than Father Sloan and Mrs. McGregor – but then that's kind of their job, isn't it? I know you – you're the scholarship student, and I can see why by your comments on the Platonic Dialogues. But you seem pretty down to earth – you don't have your nose in the air, if you know what I mean.

I've seen you say hello to janitors and security guards. Don't my long hair and beard turn you off? Like, you're so clean-cut.

\- You seem to prefer the hippie look, but that's okay with me. I'd never have my summer jobs, though, at the golf club or at Pizza Pete's if I had long hair. Once a guy came in for a hoagie, and he had long red hair. Pete made this nasty comment, as he sometimes does.

Something like "he don't look human, but better serve him anyways". So you're a Classics major? I was wondering why you're not in the Vergil class. And by the way, where are you from?

\- Well, Holden, I was a psychology major when I came here. But I became really fascinated by how Freud based his Oedipus-complex theory on the Greek story of King Oedipus killing his father and marrying his mother. Then I read this book by E.R. Dodds called *The Greeks and the Irrational*. I thought it would be neat to learn Ancient Greek, and so here I am.

But I never had much Latin – one year in high school. So I've had to take Intermediate Latin and Beginners Greek. Oh, and I'm from Chicago. Say, Holden, there's no booze here – Xavier policy, but in case you haven't noticed, I've been making frequent trips to the washroom. The reason is this little silver flask in my jacket pocket. You're welcome to some, if you like.

\- No, I'm good, thanks. But, say, Steve, Chicago has some top-notch universities. Why come to Cincinnati?

\- Okay, Holden, since it seems like you're the only guy I'm going to have any connection with at xenophobic Xavier, let me tell you about myself. I didn't come here so much, but was rather sent here – by my father. I hope you'll continue to call me Steve, but my full name is Stephen Cartwright III. My father is one of the top executives at Sears Roebuck.

He sent me to lots of private schools in Chicago, but I was always either expelled or I dropped out. I finally graduated from a posh private school, but their graduation requirements must have been pretty liberal – or maybe their new auditorium sponsored by Sears Roebuck wasn't a coincidence. My father got the impression I was the worst thing to walk the streets of Chicago since Al Capone! So he sent me to "safe Cincinnati". But my appearance and my counter-culture lifestyle haven't been accepted here either. It seems there are a fair number of rednecks in these parts of the woods.

-	I've heard a lot about making love, not war – in fact, I wish my buddy Tommy Nelson was more of a believer in that philosophy, because I'm afraid he's going to end up in Vietnam. I'm not judging you, Steve, but I'm afraid the only "counter-culture" I know is serving pizzas over the counter at Pizza Pete's! But my Dad is coming to pick me up soon. Would you like a ride home?

-	Ha! Pizza counter! You're pretty funny for a smart guy! Thanks for the offer of a ride, but I go everywhere on foot with my trusty walking stick. Besides, we're probably going in opposite directions.

-	Suit yourself, and easy on that flask. See you in Philosophy class.

***

-	Ah, Mr. Hainsworth! Nice to see you chatting with Mr. Cartwright. He's a bit of an outsider. It doesn't help that he's of humble spirit, while his father is, as they say, "rich like Croesus". I'm sure Professor Taylor has mentioned Croesus, that king of Lydia who was the first to mint coins. Your History professor has a detailed account in his book of numismatic evidence as an important primary source of ancient history. And you've mingled well with the others. You seem to be popular with our female students. I suspect that is due, in part, to your own humble spirit, and perhaps to the fact that, as our scholarship student, you will be a genuine resource in preparing for the final Latin exam! Strange, though, one young lady told me that you reminded her of Paul Newman! She obviously hasn't seen him in that less than outstanding movie *The Silver Chalice*! I would see you more as a Kirk Douglas as Spartacus or a Marlon Brando as Mark Antony, or even a Charlton Heston as Ben Hur! Your professors all speak highly of you, especially your New Testament Greek instructor. I suspect he would like to steal you to the Theology Department, but having seen your performance in the Vergil course, I certainly won't be letting you go! And Mrs. McGregor thinks you're simply a dear! She was tickled pink when you praised her bulletin board display. She started humming that David Whitfield song "Cara Mia"! But maybe, Mr. Hainsworth, you know the recent version of that song by Jay and the Americans. I say Jay, but Jay Black, who recorded that song, was really David Blatt. The original "Jay" was Jay Traynor, who went on to sing with another Jay – Jay Siegel, who sang "The Lion Sleeps Tonight" with The Tokens. And speaking of Jay and the Americans, one of my favorite singers was an original member of that group – Kenny Vance, who now sings Doo Wop songs and helps new singers to form groups. If you are ever in Brooklyn, and you hear an echo, look up his group – The Planotones – he's fond of saying that's where they are from! - and in their song they are "Looking for an Echo"! As I mentioned at our first meeting, Mr. Hainsworth, in addition to my passion for the anthology of Latin verse, I am a keen student of the anthology of American song! Speaking of the Bulletin Board, were there any lectures or conferences that caught your attention?

- Professor Sloan, there is so much information on that board – I'm glad I've come by a few times to look at it. I see that Emily Vermuele, William Arrowsmith and Hugh Lloyd- Jones from Oxford will all be giving lectures at UC, and they are open to the general public. Also, the CAMWS annual conference is being held this year at Miami University in Oxford. I hope to attend all three days, since it's at the end of term. And every time I've looked at the board, this invitation to study Classics at McGill University in Montreal, Canada keeps leaping out. It's kind of scary since I've pretty well planned to do all my studies here in Cincinnati, and have never even thought about leaving home! And although I've saved up some money, it would be expensive to live away from home.

- Well, Mr. Hainsworth, I hope that it's just curiosity that is drawing you to that programme, but studying abroad, especially in Canada, is not the worst idea I've ever heard! It is true that it's more common among graduate students, but some undergraduates make their way to our northern neighbour to study in a different context. As I told the Vergil class, we don't want to lose any of you, certainly not someone of your ability and potential, Mr. Hainsworth! But, nonetheless, I feel obliged to tell you what I know of the Classics Department at McGill University. I met the Department Chairman, Professor Watson, at a CAC conference in Toronto a few years ago. He's a pleasant fellow. He's a Cambridge graduate from Ireland, and you'd love his accent! He's a specialist in Roman religion, and we've corresponded on a regular basis. That's probably why the McGill announcements end up on our Bulletin Board. They also have a specialist in the Latin language in the Department. He's actually from Switzerland – the University of Geneva – so his first language is French. You realize that Montreal is a French city.

But not to worry – McGill is a well-established English university. In fact, the undergraduate Classics programme is very reputable. And they have a very strong Master's programme. I guess I should mention their Archaeology Professor. He earned his PhD here in Cincinnati at

UC. He studied under Carl Blegen, and no doubt gives courses on Troy. He's A Canadian, though, from the western part of the country I believe. You spoke of intimidating costs. I don't want to get your hopes up needlessly, but you did notice, did you not, that a scholarship is available for the Classics undergraduate programme? Mr. Hainsworth, you probably haven't heard of Winston Parker Jr. He was a young man from New Haven, Connecticut, who had a wealthy aunt living in Toronto, Canada. She donated a great deal of money towards the promotion of culture.

Well, she invited her nephew to come and study Classics in the graduate programme at the University of Toronto. He went on to earn a doctorate in Classics, but then returned to New Haven. He apparently did not want to remain, as he put it, "a Connecticut Yankee in King Arthur's Court". This was a semi-mocking reference to the fact that the Queen of England is the titular Head of State in Canada. Well, long story short, Winston Parker inherited his aunt's fortune, and as a tribute to her and in recognition of his cherished experience at a Canadian university, he created the Helen and Winston Parker Endowment Fund which provides grants for American students studying Classics in a Canadian university.

-        New Haven, Connecticut! Wow! That's where Fred Parris and the Satins are from! Are you suggesting that I apply to McGill, Professor?

-        I think you owe it to yourself to think about it, Mr. Hainsworth, and to discuss it with your family. Your mastery of French would certainly facilitate living in Montreal. You never know – this could be a case of *carpe diem*! But if this opportunity does, in fact, present itself, will you decide to seize it?

-        Professor Sloan, there's a Lovin' Spoonful song that keeps playing in my head. I'm sure you know it - "Did You Ever Have To Make Up Your Mind"!

Chapter 34

-       Oh, Holden, I've just read the terrible news in *The Cincinnati Enquirer* about the Xavier student murdered last night, only a mile away from campus. He wasn't robbed, and the police suspect he was a victim of what they called "social violence".

-       Mom, Dad and I saw it on the news when we got home. It was Steve – Stephen Cartwright III. He is – was – a Classics major. Mom, he was at the party with me last night.

I offered him a ride with Dad, but he refused. The "social violence" the police referred to was the senseless killing of someone with long hair by a group of homophobic rednecks – that was the term Steve used – homophobic! His body will be returned to his family in Chicago.

But this time they won't send him away! *Requiescat in pace*, Steve, Rest in Peace! -

-       Den, our country needs help. America needs to be strong and faithful to God's

commandments. But I am confident that, as history has shown us, good will triumph over evil. And you must remain confident in yourself and in your future. You and all those brave young Americans can make your future bright – just like a glow worm. Do you remember that song by The Mills Brothers I used to sing to you when you were little?

-       Yeah, Mom, I remember it. "Shine little glow-worm, glimmer, glimmer. Shine little glow-worm, glimmer, glimmer..."

-       Son, tell me how your courses are going? I'm so glad you're taking a French course. I think *Monsieur* Dubois would be proud of you, too. And reading the New Testament in Greek! How wonderful!

-       You know, Mom, reading Biblical Greek – especially the Gospels – is not so hard, since I had all the basic grammar with Mr. James last year. The grammar of Koine – that's what they call this form of Greek – is actually simpler than classical Attic Greek. We've been reading excerpts from the Gospels of Matthew, Mark and John, and from the Letters of St. Paul to the Corinthians. We haven't looked at the Gospel of St. Luke yet, which is ironic, since his Gospel was originally written in Greek. As we read and translate the Scriptures, I'm often under the impression that I'm listening to Father Brendan's homilies at St. Joe's!

I've learned some interesting facts about Biblical terminology as well. For instance, the term Synoptic is applied to the Gospels of Matthew, Mark and Luke because their accounts are similar, expressing the same point of view. The word comes from the Greek words *syn,* meaning "together" and *opsis*, meaning an "appearance" or "view". That word is actually from the Greek verb "to see" – *orao.* If you're wondering about the connection of those two words, Mom, since they sound different, it has to do with irregular forms of the verb. It's a bit complicated, but kind of fascinating. Our word "synopsis" comes from the same roots.

You remember how Father Brendan sometimes refers to the Old Testament as The Septuagint? Well that word is simply the Latin word for seventy – *septuaginta* - and refers to the tradition that seventy scholars – well, sometimes they say seventy-two – translated the Old Testament into Greek on the island of Pharos in seventy-two days. Father McNeil once gave me a little book of spiritual reading, and I promised him – and myself – that I would read something spiritual every day. I'm almost finished a small book of reflections written in French.

What I'm going to do next is read a Latin translation of the Bible, and then a Greek translation. I think I will have enough spiritual reading for a long time! You'd love my French course, Mom! I love it because reading Racine's plays is like taking a course on Greek tragedy. We've already read and discussed *La Thébaïde*, which basically tells the story of "The Seven Against Thebes", in which the sons of Oedipus kill each other. We've just about finished our discussion of the *Andromache,* who was the wife of the Trojan prince Hector. But that play started with the story of Orestes, and the revenge killing of his own mother, Clytemnestra. I've begun reading our last play – *Phèdre*. Listen to these lines, Mother, where Phaedra – she's the wife of King Theseus who falls in love with her step-son Hippolytus – realizes she is a prisoner of her passion and not fit to be Queen:

'Moi, régner! Moi, ranger un État sous ma loi,

Quand ma faible raison ne règne plus sur moi!

Lorsque j'ai de mes sens abandonné l'empire!'

And these lines where she invites Theseus to encounter another monster – herself. He had once slain the Minotaur monster in the Labyrinth in the palace on the island of Crete.

'Et Phèdre au Labyrinthe avec vous descendue

Se serait avec vous retrouvée, ou perdue.'

Great stuff, eh Mom? Racine's characters are always guilt-ridden, and it's this sense of culpability that will lead Phaedra to her tragic end. Of course, King Theseus is a tragic figure, since he loses both his wife and his son. That story in the Bible about Joseph and the wife of the Egyptian King Potiphar is like the story of Phaedra, Mom, which is based on Euripides' play *Hippolytus.* My background reading in Greek literature has made me one of the "stars" in our discussions, but the real "star" of the class is Myriam, an exchange-student from France.

Nobody masters those alexandrine verses like she does.

I enjoy talking to her after class in French, but I've heard her speak English with a charming accent. And she knows Latin! When I mentioned that it was too bad she wasn't staying at Xavier to study Latin, she shrugged her shoulders and said "*C'est Livy*"! You know, Mom, "*C'est la vie*"! Like Frank Sinatra sings – "That's Life"! She's already read sections of Livy's history of Rome! We might correspond when she goes back to Lyon, where she lives. That city was a Roman town called *Lugdunum.* I told her I was going to read Racine's *Britannicus,* and she said she had seen that play staged in Paris.

- Hey, Old, are you and mom talking about your life at university? How about telling me what it's like? I bet you're glad you don't have to take math and physics anymore. I guess you got to pick courses you enjoy more. Are you still the best Latin student?

- What's with all the questions, Feeble? I should let you find out about university life yourself when you go on to university in a couple of years. But, okay, I'll tell you how I'm finding it. They talk about the freedom you don't get in high school. In a way, it's more difficult, since they don't keep reminding you about assignments and exams. You really have to discipline yourself to study on a regular basis and to keep up with short-term and long-term assignments.

It's all about time management, Feeb. But you're right about course selection. That's the real freedom in university – choosing courses that interest you. So, yeah, no more math for me. The closest I get to numbers is listening to that new song by Len Barry called "1-2-3"! Did you know – of course you didn't – his real name is Len Borisoff, who sang "The Bristol Stomp" with The Dovells – you know, that dance we goof off with! And my ordinal numbers are tested by that song "Step by Step" by that mixed racial group, The Crests. What a singer Johnny Maestro is! But in my Greek Philosophers course we were told that Plato put a lot of emphasis on mathematics in his Academy. And Aristotle wrote those books on science like *Physics* and *Metaphysics* – which just means "after physics". If I were walking through Burnet Woods, trying to fathom all those scientific notions, a "walk in the park" would be no walk in the park! Aristotle would enjoy the stroll, however, since he followed the practice of walking around while teaching his students at his school, the Lyceum. That's why we call them Peripatetics – from the Greek verb *peripatein* for "walking around". You must remember Mom telling us that *lycée* is the French word for high school. Now you understand why Sacred Heart calls their lecture hall the Lyceum! Apparently, Aristotle's school was just outside Athens near the temple of Apollo Lykaios. The Greek word for wolf is *lukos*, and in my Ancient History course we heard about the festival to Lycaean Jupiter and the Lupercalia, which derives from the Latin word for wolf – *lupus*. You know the story, Feeb, of the wolf protecting and nourishing Romulus and Remus. The Lupercalia was a Roman festival dedicated to health and prosperity. Apollo, besides being the god of learning, was also a god of medicine and healing. I believe society should never lose sight of the connection between learning – or science – and health! Apollo was, so to speak, a "lord of the wolves". That might remind you, little sister, of the William Golding novel *Lord of the Flies*, that you are studying in your English Lit class. Wolves – if left alone – won't necessarily be a threat to humans, whereas a single fly can prove to be quite a nuissance! In fact wolves prove that one shouldn't try to be a "lone wolf", as they "socialize" in packs! I bet you're thinking of the song "Leader of the Pack" – I know it's a sad story! It seems that "the boy she met at the candy store" was ironically a "sheep in wolf's clothing"! Of course, outside of their element, wolves can become dangerous, as did the boys in Golding's novel! At the risk of sounding pompous, Feeb, I want to mention the Greek word *luke*, which means "light". You can probably see the connection with the Latin word *lux*. Apollo is also the "lord of light". As such, he truly is the "beacon of learning" lighting up the world! I hope you are "wolfing down" all this knowledge! I prefer reading about Socrates! But then, the Pre-Socratics, who were the first philosophers, were really scientists. We call them natural philosophers. We talked quite a bit about the relation between nature – *physis* in Greek – and law – *nomos* in Greek. Pretty heavy stuff, little sis! We have Professor Taylor for Ancient History – he's well-known in the world of classical scholarship. He's really good at pointing out how aspects of Greek and Roman society have survived throughout history, and even influence us today. He says we have Greco-Roman roots in our DNA! He also compared America to the Roman Empire, pointing out the many influences Roman history had on the Founding Fathers.

He said something about not betraying the eagle, if we didn't want America to fall like the Roman Empire did. Oh, and my Latin course is still my favorite class. We go into a lot of detail in translating and analyzing the *Aeneid*. We also have to read it in the hexameter meter it was written in. This means there are six feet – that is, syllables – consisting of dactyls – a long syllable followed by two short syllables, and spondees, which are composed of two long syllables. But the last foot can be composed of a long syllable followed by a short. Listen to these lines from Book Six, Feeb, and try to hear the musical rhythm as I read it in dactylic hexameter. These are lines 319 and 320 that I know by heart from reading them so often:

'Quidve petunt animae? Vel quo discrimine ripas Hae linquunt, illae remis vada livida verrunt?'

Before you ask, it means "Or what do the souls seek? Or by what distinction do these leave the shores, while those sweep over the dark blue shallows with oars?". Beautiful, isn't it, Feeb?

Now you'll really want to continue studying Latin! I had good marks in the first term, and Father Sloan – he's the Department Head – calls on me quite often, but not as often as Father McNeil used to. There are some really good Latin students in my class, and they've been studying Latin at Xavier a couple of years longer than I have. Oh, and university students have lots of parties – I just have to stay away from the wild ones!

-       You'd never be wild, Old, you're *mens sana in corpore sano*! Gosh, your musical tastes have really evolved - Doo Wop to Motown to Folk and now Latin verse! Dad just came in. Maybe you can dazzle him too with your fancy Latin duck tails! As usual, he's probably as hungry as a wolf!

-       That's dactyls! Hi Dad! The Classics Department will be holding a vigil for Steve. Look at this Latin saying – *carpe diem*. It's been on my mind for a few days. Do you want to know why?

-       Hey there, Bus – or now that you are in university, should I give you the full treatment and call you Phoebus? After all, your sister Phoebe has always had the full treatment.

Again, really sorry about your fellow Classics student. It's a nice gesture by the Classics Department. Pity they weren't so nice to him when he was around. *Carpe diem* – fish of the day? Is it some kind of Latin proverb?

-       Phoebus? You'll be calling me Apollo when I graduate. By the way, Apollo is the only Greek Olympian god whose name the Romans didn't change – I guess he was too Greek!

No, Dad, *carpe* is a Latin verb meaning "to grab hold of, to seize". The expression means "to seize the day – to take advantage of an opportunity".

-       And what opportunity would that be, son?

-       Well, Dad, at Xavier they were announcing undergraduate study in Classics at McGill University in Montreal, Canada. It's funny how staying here in Cincinnati was something I didn't have to think about, but this programme at McGill sounds exciting. Father Sloan, my Latin Professor – he's a Jesuit and the Head of the Classics Department – gave me some information about Classics at McGill, and suggested I talk it over with you guys. I don't think

Mom will be too happy – she just called me her little glow worm! And who would walk Vergil Cane? He may not have three heads like that guard dog of the underworld, Cerberus, but he's always protected me whenever bad dudes tried to intimidate me in Burnet Woods. When I have Vergil Cane by my side, it's *cave canem* all the way! That means "beware of the dog", Dad!

\-   I've heard of McGill – it's in that big Canadian city Montreal which is located in their French province, Quebec. But, heck, you speak French – so no problem there. And Phoebe could walk the dog. I'd hate to get on the wrong side of those two together! Yes, your mother would miss you – we all would! But, you know, we could visit – it's less than a day's drive. I know, because Bob Darnell and I drove to Montreal three years ago for an international business conference. You know with this year at Xavier U you'll be eighteen if you go to Canada next year. That gives you adult drinking privileges up there. And those people in Montreal can really put the beers away! Bob and I found that out at the business conference social hours.

I wouldn't want you to learn that the hard way, since you haven't really had beer, you being under-age here in Ohio. But I hope this year at Xavier has been worthwhile, no matter what happens next year. At least you don't have a girlfriend here holding you back – or do you?

\-   Dad, it's so difficult to decide. No, I don't have a girlfriend. It seems like, if I really have feelings for someone, she moves away. First Maxine, and now Myriam - she's from France, and she's in my French class – but she's moving back to France. Sometimes I think I'm paying for the sins of those ancient heroes like Theseus who abandoned Ariadne and Aeneas who sailed off leaving Dido behind. Now the shoe – make that sandal – is on the other foot! No, this year at Xavier has been great – except for Steve's murder. My courses are all interesting, and you would probably enjoy my Literature course, which explores modern literary themes based on Greek and Roman mythology. We examined the history of Greek tragedies presented in Britain from the seventeenth century to the present. It was like taking a course on Aeschylus, Sophocles and Euripides, except we read excerpts from English-language productions, and not the Greek originals presented during ancient Greek festivals. Next we studied the influence of the Roman poet Ovid and the borrowing in modern times from the myths he recounted in his poem, the *Metamorphoses.* That is a Greek word, Dad, meaning "transformations", and the characters in Ovid's stories end up being changed into trees and bears and all kinds of things.

My favorite example is the story of Pygmalion, who falls in love with a statue he made, and the statue comes to life. I wish I could write a story about Greek statues coming to life!

George Bernard Shaw wrote his play *Pygmalion* based on that story. And, get this, the movie *My Fair Lady* was originally a Broadway play based on the theme of the Pygmalion story. I know how you and Mom enjoyed that movie, and you couldn't stop talking about Audrey Hepburn, Dad!

Now we're reading poems with mythological themes, like W.H. Auden's "Atlantis", James Dickey's "Orpheus Before Hades", and Tennyson's "Ulysses". But right now I kind of feel like I'm "*pius Aeneas*". I have the obligation to go off to a new city, no matter what difficulties that might present. And, Dad, I have a small confession to make. I really didn't spend all the time cleaning up after Pizza Pete closed up on Saturday nights. Pete would bring in some Buds for the guys, and we'd drink and joke around. But I never had more than a couple, and I mostly stayed around so that I could play my favorite songs on the juke-box for free. You know, after a couple of beers I'd be singing "Blueberry Hill" like Fats Domino – and that song wasn't even on the juke-box!

-       Well, Bus, I mean Phoebus, I already knew you were pious, serving Mass every Sunday at St. Joseph's. And I'm kind of glad Pizza Pete initiated you into drinking beer – he saved me a few bucks! It sounds like you're leaning towards that *carpe diem*. Tell you what, let's all drive up to Montreal during Spring Break, and we – or rather you – can make a decision then.

In the meantime, I'll talk to your mother about it. You are also going to have to figure out if you can afford living and going to school away from home, even with all the money you've managed to save.

-       Dad, I was using the Latin word *pius*, not the English word "pious" – although it is derived from the Latin word. Vergil called Aeneas *pius* because the hero pursued his destiny faithfully as a duty. Perhaps he believed that his gods were insisting that he discover this mission, and perhaps were even helping him to carry it out. Funny thing, though, Pete calls me "Holy" – even when he hasn't had a few beers! And Professor Sloan mentioned scholarships and financial grants. If I were to be awarded that money, it would go a long way towards helping me make my decision. But no matter what happens, thanks for being so supportive, Dad.

Chapter 35

\-   Father McNeil, I called the Jesuit Residence to talk to you and I was told that you were here in the hospital. One of the nurses told me it was pretty serious.

\-   No, Hainsworth, being in the hospital is like a sabbatical for a Jesuit! Father Sloan told me you are doing very well in the Vergil course, but then I'm not surprised. However, I suspect you have something on your mind.

\-   Actually, I do, Father. My family and I were up in Canada – in Montreal – over the Break, and we visited the McGill University campus and the neighborhood around the campus, which is – as my Mom put it - "quite charming" – but much smaller than UC's campus.

We found the building where the Classics department is. It's called the Leacock Building, and we were told by the Classics Department secretary, who is much younger than Mrs. McGregor at Xavier, that it's named after a Canadian humorist. That made me think of you! Their programme was posted on their Bulletin Board, and I have to admit that it's quite attractive. But in the section for Graduate programmes, the University of Cincinnati's poster was quite visible. I felt a lump in my throat! So, Father, I'm wondering…

\-   *Carpe diem*, Hainsworth! It sounds like you would be doubly blessed – an attractive programme and an attractive secretary! And if you think you'd be escaping the Jesuits, the Society of Jesus has French and English Jesuits in Montreal! Father Sloan had mentioned you were toying with the idea of going to study at McGill University. I hope the studies you've done here at St. Xavier High and Xavier U. will impress them, and your knowledge of French will make life in Montreal quite pleasant, I'm sure. *Monsieur* Dubois could tell you the places to visit – you have to pay a visit to St. Joseph's Oratory! He could probably tell you as well some places to avoid. I think that, like Aeneas, a greater destiny awaits you, and you must take that voyage. But remember, Hainsworth, to maintain a *mens sana in corpore sano*. It's just like the poet Juvenal says in his Tenth Satire: *orandum est ut sit mens sana in corpore sano* – "you should pray for a healthy mind in a healthy body"! And I hope you will continue with your spiritual readings. I'm glad to have known and taught a fine young man like you, Hainsworth.

It's comforting, as I prepare for my own journey.

-       I will be praying for you, Father. I'm glad you haven't lost your sense of humour nor your uncanny ability to quote Latin verse. In my Ancient Greek Philosophers course we learned that Thales had said that a happy man is one who has a healthy body, a resourceful mind, and a docile nature. I will keep on reading inspirational spiritual texts, Father McNeil, including the Bible. And I'm going to seize the day! I actually looked up the reference in Horace's First Ode – *Carpe diem, quam minimum credula postero* – "seize the day, putting little trust in what will come". But I have a more optimistic reason for taking advantage of this opportunity than that which Horace suggests. I now truly believe this is the right path for me, and that it will help determine my future, which I choose to define as bright!

-       Here is a favorite prayer of mine, Hainsworth, which St. Ignatius placed at the beginning of his Spiritual Exercises. Who knows, perhaps he even composed the prayer himself. I do hope you will do the Exercises one day. This is the Latin text of the *Anima Christi*. For old times' sake would you read it and translate as the true Latin student that you are!

- Of course, Father. This prayer – The Soul of Christ – is well-known!

Anima Christi, sanctifica me. Soul of Christ, sanctify me.

Corpus Christi, salva me.   Body of Christ, save me.

Sanguis Christi, inebria me.   Blood of Christ, inebriate me.

Aqua lateris Christi, lava me. Water from the side of Christ, wash me.

Passio Christi, conforta me.   Passion of Christ, strengthen me.

O bone Iesu, exaudi me.   O good Jesus, hear me.

Intra tua vulnera absconde me. Within Your wounds, hide me.

Ne permittas me separari a te.   Do not allow me to be separated from You.

Ab hoste maligno defende me.   From the malignant enemy, defend me.

In hora mortis meae voca me.   At the hour of my death, call me.

Et iube me venire ad te.   And order me to come to You.

Ut cum Sanctis tuis laudem te   So that I may praise You with Your Saints

In saecula saeculorum.   Forever and ever.

Amen   Amen

Father, do I get bonus points for identifying *laudem* as the subjunctive mood in a purpose clause?

-    Young Hainsworth, you yourself have always been a *bonus* – a good person!

Chapter 36

\-   Again, ladies and gentlemen, I have been truly impressed by the essays you submitted this term. Mr. Hainsworth, your theory of the role of Aeneas as a precursor to the great generals in Roman history and their victories in expanding Roman dominion is laudable, and indeed plausible. Your suggestion that the great Julius Caesar himself was for the Romans a "modern Aeneas" is tenable, especially since you connected the two through their common descent from Venus. Now, if you would, Mr. Hainsworth, please read the passage that you were all asked to translate for today's class – in proper hexameter of course – and then give us your rendering of these lines 887 to 927 from Book Twelve.

Aeneas instat contra telumque coruscate

ingens arboretum, et saevo sic pectore fatur:

Quae nunc deinde mora est?

Aut quid iam, Turne, retractas?

Non cursu, saevis certandum est comminus armis.

Verte omnes tete infacies et contrahe quidquid

sive animis sive arte vales; opta ardua pennis

astra sequi clausumque cava te condere terra.

Ille caput quassans: Non me tua fervida terrent

dicta ferox; di me terrent et Iuppiter hostis.

Nec plura effatus saxum circumspicit ingens

saxum antiquum ingens campo quod forte iacebat

limes agro positus litem ut discerneret arvis.

Vix illum lecti bis sex cervice subirent

qualia nunc hominum producit corpora tellus;

ille manu raptum trepida torquebat in hostem

118

altior insurgens et cursu concitus heros.

Sed neque currentem se nec cognoscit euntem

tollentemve manu saxumve immane moventem;

genua labent gelidus concrevit frigore sanguis.

Tum lapis ipse viri vacuum per inane volutus

nec spatium evasit totum neque pertulit ictum.

Ac velut in somnis oculos ubi languida pressit

nocte quies nequiquam avidos extendere cursus

velle videmur et in mediis conatibus aegri

succidimus; non lingua valet non corpore notae

sufficiunt vires nec vox aut verba sequuntur

sic Turno quacumque viam virtute petivit

successum dea dira negat. Tum pectore sensus

vertuntur varii; Rutulos aspectat et urbem

cunctaturque metu letumque instare tremescit

nec quo se eripiat nec qua vi tendat in hostem

nec currus usquam videt aurigamve sororem.

Cunctanti telum Aeneas fatale coruscat

sortitus fortunam oculis et corpore toto

eminus intorquet. Murali concita numquam

tormento sic saxa fremunt nec fulmine tanti

dissultant crepitus. Volat atri turbinis instar

exitium dirum hasta ferens orasque recludit

loricae et clipei extremos septemplicis orbes;

per medium stridens transit femur. Incidit ictus

ingens ad terram duplicato poplite Turnus.

"Aeneas presses on in opposition, and shakes a huge tree-like spear, and from his cruel heart he speaks in this way: "What now then is your hesitation? Or why do you draw back now, Turnus? We must fight not by running, but hand to hand with savage weapons. Turn yourself into all forms, and bring together whatever you are able by courage or by skill; choose to follow the lofty stars with wings or to hide yourself enclosed by the hollow earth." But that one, shaking his head: " Your fiery words do not frighten me, fierce one; the gods frighten me, and Jupiter the enemy." And speaking no more, he looks around for a huge rock, a huge ancient rock, which by chance was lying on the plain, a boundary-marker placed in the field to decide any dispute concerning the ploughed fields. Twice six chosen men would barely support it on their neck, such are the bodies of men the earth now produces; against his enemy, that hero hurled it, snatched up with trembling hand, rising up higher and stirred up by running. But he doesn't recognize himself running nor going forth nor lifting and moving the large rock with his hand; his knees buckle, his blood, icy with cold, has frozen. Then the man's stone, spinning through the empty space, neither passed over the space nor carried out the blow. And just as in sleep, when dull quiet has pressed our eyes during the night, we seem in vain to want to extend our eager running, and wearied in the middle of our attempts, we fall; the tongue is weak, the reputed strength in the body does not suffice, and neither voice nor words follow: and so to Turnus, with whatever courage he sought his way, the dreadful goddess denies success. Then different sensations turn in his breast; he looks at the Rutulians and the city, and hesitates out of fear, and he trembles at death that is approaching, nor is there anywhere he might snatch himself away, nor strength with which he might reach the enemy, nor does he see his chariots anywhere , or his charioteer sister. Having obtained this good fortune with his eyes, Aeneas waves his fatal spear at the one hesitating, and with his whole body he takes aim from far. Never in this way do rocks directed at a wall with a military engine resonate, nor do such clattering sounds burst from a thunderbolt. The spear flies like a black whirlwind, bringing terrible destruction, and reveals the edges of the leather cuirass and the outermost circles of the seven-layered shield; hissing, it pierces the middle of his thigh. Having been struck, huge Turnus falls to the ground with bent knee."

\-   Very good translation, Mr. Hainsworth. You were quite literal, which is always wise in undergraduate translations. However, one can overkill – deliberate pun, ladies and gentlemen, we are talking about someone being killed here! "Having obtained this good fortune with his eyes" in line 920, I think you will all agree, can and should be translated merely as "having seen this good fortune". In line 905 one could perhaps say that the blood has "congealed" rather than "frozen". But in the same line I very much like your rendering of *genua labant* as "knees buckle". And in the following line, I like your translation of *volutus* as "spinning". In line 909 you chose to translate *nocte* as an ablative of time, which is fine, but one could also, I believe, justify *nocte* as an ablative of means – so, "during the night", or "with the night". And if ever you find yourself translating Vergil at an APA conference, I'm sure, Mr. Hainsworth, that you will probably endeavor to render your translation in English hexameter! But, in truth, most professors don't attempt it. I hope you all noticed the simile in line 908, introduced by *velut*. Well, the approaching death of Turnus signals that this year's course on Vergil's *Aeneid* is drawing to a close. I'm sorry to say that our three St. Xavier High boys will not be returning next year. Mr. Harris and Mr. Mittenkamp are not continuing in Classics. And we wish continued success to Mr. Hainsworth as he heads north to Canada to study Classics at McGill University. But who can blame him – he has been awarded a full McGill Classics Department Scholarship as well as a generous grant from the Helen and Winston Parker Endowment Fund? Accordingly, we will allow Mr. Hainsworth a few minutes to comment on the passage he has just translated.

\-   Thank you , Professor Sloan! My reflections will be tempered by discussions that have taken place in my Anient History course with Professor Taylor. Upon pondering the phrases *lapis…vacuum per inane volutus* – "as the stone spinning through the empty space" - perhaps "turning" because hurled by TURNus! – and *volat atri turbinis instar…hasta* – "the spear flies through a black whirlwind", I can't help "turning" to the tale of turbulence that marked Roman history, especially at the end of the Republic. Rome's Republican "Revolution" became a vitriolic vortex of venomous devastation! Rome was destined to be *vincens et victa* – "victorious and vanquished"!

\-   Mr. Hainsworth, as Harry Belafonte sings in his most popular song - "my head is spinning around"! Your prophetic portrait of patrician and plebeian politics – not to mention the hallucinating alliteration which is an astounding attribute of yours – plunges us into a pessimistic perspective of a perplexed and perplexing people!

\-   Professor, the number five signified by "*V*" – as my voluminous and perhaps "vicious" – you would say virulent - use of the letter "v" was meant to suggest - is a subtle reference to the five major military disasters in Roman history – namely, the Battle of Cannae in 216 B.C., the Battle of Carrhae in 53 B.C., the Battle of the Teutonburg Forest in AD 9, the Battle of Adrianople in AD 378, and the sack of Rome by Alaric in AD 410.

-        Mr. Hainsworth has certainly read Professor Taylor's book quite diligently, but hopefully the rest of you have not been overly perturbed by all this playful verbal interplay. Although it may have proved very vexing! Our Mr. H has proven himself, if not virtuous, certainly a virile virtuoso of vocabulary! He has demonstrated the vigour and vitality to face the occasional vicissitudes of the challenging course of studies in Classics. Even though one can never claim total victory, nor vociferate the *Vae victis* of the ancient Romans, perhaps he should apply to the I-"V" League schools! What say you, Mr. Hainsworth?

-        Very problematic to say the least, Professor Sloan, in that I have been clearly bested in this contest of communication! Nevertheless, I am grateful that you did not choose to vilify or vilipend me!

-        I will only claim a "Pyrrhic victory", since, through your vivid and vehement vindications, you remain the VIP in this class – a "very" ingenious "punster" indeed! Our persistent volley of a "p" and a ''v" shall remain for me a "pet peeve"! You will undoubtedly learn German at one point, so without further voodoo – sorry, I meant "ado"- *Auf Wiedersehn*!

That, Mr. Hainsworth, was a final "v" before you vanish – I'm too polite to say "vamoose" – to vent and rage like Vesuvius in the Roman Age!

Chapter 37

-       Guys, Pete, what a surprise! Pete, you devil! You said you needed someone to help you close up. And you're all here – Mickey, Rick, Jeff, and hey - Bobby Calhoun!

-       You're leavin', aren't you? That's something to celebrate! You notice we didn't wait for you to get here – Jeff's already on his third beer! Get some beers down you, Holy – we want to hear you sing Blueberry Hill! The juke-box is all yours, but if you play any of your Motown songs, the party's over.

-       Don't worry, Holden. You remember my brother Dick, who used to work here before you became a regular? We were a great team – Dicky and Mickey!

-       More like Dicky and Dickhead! Or was it Ducky? Yeah - that was it – Donald Duck and Mickey Mouse!

-       That would make you Goofy, Jeff! Well, anyways, Holden, my brother just got married last month so he can't have fun no more. Tonight he's taking the missus to all-night bowling. But since tonight's a special occasion and all, Cheryl – that's Dick's wife - is letting him stop by after bowling to say hello – or I guess - good-by. But he's going to drive us all home in his truck. So you won't have to walk home, Holden.

-       He won't be able to walk home! Now drink up, you Latin loony. So nice that Cheryl didn't settle for any old dick!

-       Just drink your beer, Jeff. Any more talk like that and I'll put you on morning shift tomorrow.

-       But Pete, we're not open tomorrow morning – it's Sunday.

-       I know that, Rick, but I want it to really hurt! Say, did you get Bobby his glass of wine?

-       I didn't know Bobby Calhoun drank wine, Pete.

-       He doesn't, Holy. We just filled his glass with grape juice and poured a little vinegar in it. That should get him talking – even if it's only to swear at us! This is way past his bed-time, but he just had to say good-by to you. You about ready for another Bud? Someone else is supposed to show up – oh, there he is.

-       Tommy? Tommy Nelson! Geez, it's good to see you! What have you been up to? I haven't seen you since your term ended at UC. Are you working this summer?

-       If you want to know what I've been up to, Oldie, play that song on the juke-box by The Shirelles – it's the third one on the right.

-       Oh my God, Tommy – "Soldier Boy"!

-       I thought my haircut would give it away. So I am working this summer, Oldie, - for Uncle Sam! This time next year I'll probably be in Vietnam. So I hear you're heading for Canada. Might meet some draft-dodgers up there. But I respect you, Oldie. You've got a brain – no sense getting it blown out in some fire-fight. Sticking with Latin – boy that makes you tougher than most of the guys in my unit! Naw, I was afraid that old Father McNeil would enlist you in the Jesuits. You're going to make some girl happy someday. You'll serve America in another way, and probably better than me. But me – well it's just 'Nam for Sam! I've even got a Latin motto – *Cogito, ergo sum pro* Sam! "I think, therefore I am - for Sam"!

- I'll have to cogitate that one! I respect you, Tommy. And I'll pray for you. In a way, I feel bad leaving America. But I guess I'll be back some day. I still remember all the laughs we had together in Latin class! Like the first test you got back from Father McNeil – it was marked C, and you thought it meant you had aced it with a grade of 100 in Roman numeral C !

We started calling you Perry Como – you know – "Mr. C"! Father began calling you little Vulcan - not because he thought you were ugly – but now that I look at you! – no, it was when you told the class that Juno "erupted" in anger and threw her son to the ground when she saw how deformed he was, and so Jupiter named him Vulcan! Some of the guys went over the top, I thought, when they nicknamed you "Volcanic ass"! Besides, you were always making "lame" excuses for not doing homework! To cap it off, you claimed that Vulcan always hoped to go back to Mount "O - lame – pus"! My favorite moment was when you asked Father McNeil why, if the wars against Carthage were so important, the Romans called them the "Puny Wars"! But the more I thought about studying Latin at McGill, the more I was drawn to it. I had to go for it. It was *carpe diem.*

-       I've seen that expression, but I gotta tell you – yesterday I had a "crap *diem*"! My girlfriend told me that she wouldn't wait for me. But I guess it's okay – now I don't have to feel sorry for you, Oldie! Well, I gotta shove off. I hope you'll still consider me your best buddy.

-       Always, Tommy! Thanks for coming, and good luck! You take care of yourself!

- Don't worry, Oldie. You may have given me crash courses before Latin exams, and I managed to crash a few parties organized by guys too stuck-up to invite me, but I'm not planning on crashing any 'copters!

- Hey, Holy, did you just insult my old fries? I thought I heard you refer to my "codger-'tates"! You know that my fries enjoy that Sinatra song – "Fry Me To the Moon"! Bobby's leaving. He knows that if he stays, he's the guy who's going to hafta clean up. And the way Jeff's putting them away, there's going to be a lotta cleaning up to do! But you need another Budweiser in you.You gotta practice, boy. I heard those Frenchies up in Montreal drink 'til they drop. I see your soldier friend is leaving. Jeff here has thought of enlisting.

- As long as he doesn't have to engage in a battle of wits – he'd be unarmed!

- Hey, Holden, down another one, will you? Rick and Jeff are waiting for you to sing. And no matter how bad you are, Jeff's going to applaud – he's stoned!

- I found my thrills…at Indian Hills!

- Cheap thrills – chasing around after a golf ball! Say, Holdie, I bet you'd rather get a hole-in-one than one in the hole!

- Are you talking about the hole in your head, dumb ass? Leave Holden alone, Jeff. It's his freakin' party!

- It's okay, Mickey. Jeff's actually less offensive when he's drunk. But I feel like playing a Motown song to piss Pete off!

- Did somebody say I needed to piss? Play something on the juke-box, Holy. I feel like dancing, but all you ladies are too ugly!

- "Ooo, Baby, Baby"… You guys like that song by The Miracles with my man Smokey Robinson? If not, there's another Miracles song on the box called "Mickey's Monkey".

- Mickey's "monkey" is slouched over that table – his name is Jeff! Say, we should have invited the Fat Broad - she has the hots for Holden. You know how she comes in and orders a pizza just so she can give you the eye, Holden. I mean she always looks like she just finished one off! One time she came in with another girl. When they left, I told Jeff she gave him a dirty look. He asked who gave him the dirty look, and I said "Mother Nature"!

- No, no, fellas. When I'm here she always orders a fish basket. When she comes in and I ask F.B.?, she says yes. Now, do I mean Fish Basket or Fat Broad?

- Pete, you and the guys are pretty mean. Her name is Faye Barlow.

- That's what we're sayin' – F.B.

- She just needs a little TLC, guys!

- That would be tomato, lettuce and cucumber! Drink up, boys - last call!

- Remember Jeff's last call that one time from a jail cell? Say, Pete, did you just fart?

- No, Rick, was I supposed to? Come on, everybody, let's give Holy his gift. Bring out the pizza and the little box.

- You mean my favorite – pepperoni? Say what's this - you guys have arranged the pepperoni to spell out a message. Let me see – it says "Find your thrill at McGill". Guys, I'm amazed!

- So you didn't think we could actually arrange the pepperoni to spell out a message?

- No, I didn't think you guys could spell McGill!

- And here's a gift that we all shelled out for, Holy. It has those funny numbers on it.

- Oh my God! A watch – a watch with Roman numerals! You shouldn't have, guys!

- You see – we shouldn't have! I had to work two whole shifts to pay my share of the cost. And I was the messenger who had to go and pick it up.

- Put a sock in it, Jeff. If ever there was a time to "shoot the messenger" - you forgot to have it engraved "for the good times"! Just when I get a brainstorm, you have a brain fart! You're no messenger – you're a "messynger" – always making a mess of things! Now give Holy his card. We all signed it, son. The X is Bobby's signature. We had to make the card ourselves 'cause they don't sell 'em that big.

- Say, all these pictures taken of us. I'll cherish these memories forever. What does this message say? Let me read it. "Roses are red, violets are blue. But flowers are for squares, not guys like you"! Gee, thanks… I think.

- You see Holden, we're poets, but we don't know it!

- And you sure don't show it! I really had fun working here with all you guys. And sharing those Buds together – that makes us total "buddies"! You've treated me really well, Pete. This has been a whole different world from Latin class and university courses, and a part of me will always belong here.

-    I know, Holy – your apron – and I want it back!

The University Years: Montreal and Quebec (and Europe)

Chapter 38

-        Good-day, Mr. Hainsworth. We've all been eagerly awaiting your arrival. You are the first ever American undergraduate in the Department, although we have American students in our graduate programme from time to time, and you will no doubt meet other Americans here on campus, not to mention the many tourists in our beautiful city. As you can tell by my accent, I'm very Irish. But you'll encounter other accents in our Department – British, Greek, Swiss French, Italian, and that strange one from western Canada! Of course you'll come across many accents in your Greek class! Since you spent a year with my good friend, Professor Sloan, I imagine you appreciate a touch of humour. He spoke highly of you, and I see that you have a strong background in Latin. You have also studied Ancient Greek, which is rare for students starting in our programme. I say Ancient Greek because our Department also offers courses in Modern Greek. Coming from Cincinnati, you may have heard of the endowed programme in Modern Greek at the University of Cincinnati – they even have their own library!

So you may be wondering if you can bypass the first year here at McGill. Unfortunately, the Faculty of Arts and Sciences has freshmen requirements you have to complete. And between you and me, Mr. Hainsworth, you are on a full renewable scholarship – why not profit from the extra year of studies? And your American grant allows for summer study abroad. *Carpe diem*, young man! Let me now outline your programme, specifically indicating your course load for year one. You must take one English literature course. You may want to consider the "Introduction to Canadian Literature" course. If that is your choice, you will read works by Hugh MacLennan and Stephen Leacock, the one a novelist and the latter a writer of humorous short stories. They both taught at McGill, and we are in the Leacock Building. Our graduate library – where I hope you will spend a fair amount of time, since a student of your Latin pedigree will not want to limit himself to our undergraduate library! – is called the MacLennan Library. You must take at least two French courses in the bachelor's programme. In your letter, you mentioned the French courses you have taken, so why not enroll in the course on Quebec literature. It will be a useful immersion for you both in language and in culture. You must also choose a course from the following – mathematics, history, and sociology. Not to influence you unduly, the history course is entitled "Social and Political Issues in Canada and Quebec". If you are wondering why Quebec, which is a part of Canada, is mentioned separately, take this course! Finally, Greek and Latin courses. We, or rather I – I am the Department Chair! - have placed you in the Latin elegy course. This course is primarily on Catullus. You will love this course - yes, another play on words I'm afraid - you will be reading love poets! Professor Manfredi, who teaches this course, grew up in Rome, and he won't let you forget it. His Italian accent is delightful, and he selects the best wines for our Department socials. As a Classics student, you will have to become accustomed to drinking wine. By a twist of fate, the year you spent at Xavier University means you are starting with us at the age of eighteen, the legal drinking age.

You will be the only freshman at our wine and cheese parties – or I should say, Professor Manfredi's parties – he is our self-proclaimed social convener. Your Greek course will be the *Apology of Socrates* with the venerable Professor Underhill. He's very British, even though he's been teaching at McGill for almost forty years. He's an Oxford graduate, whereas I'm a Cambridge man. We sometimes end up giving a new context to the "Battle of Britain". In any event, you will be exposed to a good deal of "Oxbridge" here in the Department. In your sophomore year you will complete your French course requirement and take a compulsory philosophy course. I would recommend Professor Underhill's course on Socrates, since it is cross-listed with the Philosophy Department. He has been teaching this course for years. We jokingly attribute his vast knowledge of Socrates to the fact that he must have been present at the Philosopher's trial! Since you have already taken general courses in ancient history and classical mythology, you will be able to enroll in the "Introduction to Classical Archaeology" course given by our resident archaeologist, Professor Peters. He has the distinction of being the youngest member in the Department – he's the only one who regularly uses the stairs to come up here to the sixth floor. That is, besides our Department Secretary, Miss Templeton. I guess you've met her already. She's been with us two years, but prior to her secretarial training, she obtained a degree in Classics, no less. She is 26 years old, in case you are wondering – no need to blush, Mr. Hainsworth. I merely mention this because, although she is eight years older than you are, she is often mistaken for a student – sometimes by Professor Underhill! So she is four years younger than Jack Peters, who is the only Department member with a doctorate from an American university – from your hometown of Cincinnati! Naturally, you will complete your course load with Greek and Latin courses. In your third year, you will be able to take three language courses along with my introductory course on Greek religion. I was delighted to read in your letter that you have a special interest in Roman religion – which happens to be the subject of my research. You will be able to take my introductory course on Roman religion in your final year – but I have plans for Roman Religion here at McGill. You will again have three Reading courses in your senior year. With your predilection for the Latin language – Professor Sloan mentioned an interesting anecdote in his letter, that apparently, in some circles, you were known as "The Latin Student"! – you will probably take four Latin courses and two Greek courses in those last two years. But you will have had enough Greek to easily fulfil any requirements for acceptance into a graduate programme in Classics. Due to your advanced standing, you will be in the advanced Greek reading courses. You will probably find yourself in Latin and Greek courses with our graduate students! And speaking of graduate studies, your programme must be completed by two courses in your final two years. These two electives must be chosen outside the Department, which is fortunate, because, quite frankly, Mr. Hainsworth, we would have no Classics courses to offer you, other than to have you take courses you've already had, like Vergil's *Aeneid* and Ancient History. If I may make a suggestion, the PhD in Classics presently requires proficiency in two foreign languages, namely French and German.

You may find it strange to hear French called a foreign language here in Quebec, but this requirement is based on the fact that the three principal languages of classical scholarship are English, German and French. Your successful completion of advanced level French courses will automatically fulfil the French proficiency requirement. If you were to select German language courses for your two electives, you would also complete the German language proficiency requirement. I'm not trying to dictate choices you are free to make, Mr.Hainsworth, I'm merely trying to be practical – well, as practical as a classicist can be! Finally, and you have been sitting there very patiently and very politely – I wish my colleagues would do so during Department meetings – I want to enquire about your living quarters. In your letter, you mentioned that during your family visit to Montreal last Spring, you made arrangements to rent an apartment near campus. Most rental stipulations call for occupancy – and payment - on the first of the month – on the *Kalends* as you and I would say! So you have one week before you can settle into your "Montreal manoir". Therefore, Mrs. Watson and I would be delighted to have you as our house-guest – our *xenos,* if you will! We live in Westmount, that bastion of English wealth!

Alas, it is not my Classics professor's salary that allows for this patrician lifestyle, but my wife's inheritance from her deceased father, who had been a very successful businessman. But I must warn you – since you listed American music as one of your hobbies – for Mrs. Watson, it's a passion! By the way, she is a librarian at the MacLennan – so you will be able to say hello to her on your frequent visits to the library! One more thing – here in the Classics Department, we have a monthly social tea gathering on the first Friday of the month for Graduate students – I know, it's very British, very Oxbridge! Since you are our Classics Scholarship student, you are invited to these gatherings. Besides, you'll probably have classes with some of our graduate students. And you may want to talk with our graduate teaching assistants. Two of them assist in our large Classical Mythology and Classics in Translation classes, but Miss Talbot teaches a first-year Latin class. She's French-Canadian, so you may find it interesting to talk to her. It's also an excellent occasion to get to know all the professors in the Department, and perhaps to ask your own professors questions you wouldn't dare ask in class. Nor are you being graded at our Social Teas!

-	I've been sitting politely, Professor Watson, because I've been so overwhelmed by how comprehensive and how appealing the programme you have outlined sounds. I am truly anxious to begin. And I thank you for the invitation to the Social Tea gatherings. I already have the first Fridays marked on my calendar, since I attend Mass then. Your offer of accommodations is more than generous. I'll come back at the end of the day. Judy - that is, Miss Templeton - is keeping my suitcase in her office until then.

Chapter 39

-       Ah, Mr. Hainsworth, welcome. Let me make a general introduction, so that everyone knows who you are, and then you can mingle. Ladies and gentlemen, this young man is not a young Greek god come to visit us – is he blushing, folks? No – with his strong portfolio in Latin, he would have to be a Roman god! This is Mr. Holden Hainsworth, this year's Classics Scholarship recipient. He's an American from Cincinnati – take note Professor Peters! Some of you asked why a Department tape-recorder has been brought into the room. Ladies and gentlemen, if our "new kid on the block" was slightly embarrassed when I introduced him, he will certainly be surprised to learn that I have arranged for him to introduce HIMSELF by way of a cassette-tape sent to me from Xavier University by my good friend, Professor Sloan. This was a promotional endeavour to introduce prospective students to the world of Classics via Classical Mythology. You will see that our young student's charm is not limited to appearance, but can be vocalized with a velvet voice! The alliteration is my own contribution to this afternoon's entertainment! You are all about to hear young Mr. Hainsworth sing the Frankie Avalon song "Venus"! Thanks to Mrs. Watson, I know quite a bit about Frankie Avalon! This "modern-day Pygmalion" asks Venus to send him a girl he can thrill. Young man – you are sure to find plenty here at McGill! Some of you will have the pleasure of counting him among your students.

Although he is a freshman, he will be enrolled in upper level classes. He did one year of Classics at Xavier University before deciding to pursue his studies here at McGill. Mr. Hainsworth is fluent in French, and so, Miss Talbot and Professor Jolivet, feel free to converse with him In the language of Molière! Now, once we have enjoyed this musical moment, please indulge yourselves with tea and crumpets. Remember, classes and advisor meetings begin next week.

Because of his interest in Roman religion, I will be Mr. Hainsworth's advisor.

***

-       Welcome to McGill, Master Hainsworth. Indeed, welcome to Montreal and to Canada! I'm Professor Underhill, and I believe you will be one of my students in Greek class.

You sang beautifully, although I admit to imagining an apparition of the Greek Aphrodite as you sang of the charms of Venus. This is jolly good news! An American in Paris! That is to say, Montreal is considered a second Paris. The night life here would certainly entitle this city to be likewise called the "City of Lights". Although I must say I haven't seen much of Montreal's night life in a number of years, aside from a few trips to the theater. Advancing age, you know. But, even though you are a young man, you must manage to enjoy this night life in moderation.

Success in your studies will depend on a good measure of self-discipline. There will be times when you will have to resist temptation. Try to seek out positive influences, but most of all, if I may express myself poetically, to thine own self be true! I shall be calling you H.H. in class. I try to maintain this tradition with all my students whose first and last names begin with the same letter. It started with my own Greek professor who referred to me one day as U.U. The name is Ulysses Underhill! But I started signing my papers with W. When he enquired why, I simply informed him that he also called me "double U"! Of course a C.C. and a L.L. are fine, but Selwyn Stone's name didn't lend itself to this practice, and made our Jewish students particularly uncomfortable. Calling Peter Parsons by his initials created a bit of embarrassment from the start. And I was most saddened to learn that A.A. – Alan Addison - had a drinking problem! But your initial H will be prominent in our Greek class since it is formed from the rough and smooth breathings over initial vowels.

-       It's nice to meet you, Professor Underhill. We had an American president whose name was Ulysses – Ulysses S. Grant. He was from my home state of Ohio. Your comments on my initials are very interesting. My high school Latin teacher once told me that my success in football was due to the fact my initials are the exact replica of football goal posts. I'm looking forward to reading Plato's *Apology*!

-       Did I just hear you talking about football? Hi there, Holden. Jack Peters. Great job on that song! I believe you know that I got my PhD from UC. I really liked Cincinnati, although I also spent a great deal of time in Greece. But I used to go and watch the Bearcats at old Nippert Stadium. And I often attend the professional games here in Montreal. Canadian football is pretty exciting. But then I'm a little biased. I'm from Edmonton out West. I remember watching our Eskimos defeat the Montreal team – they're called the Alouettes – three times in a row in our national championship – the Grey Cup game. But I have to say, the best players I ever saw play were two Americans who played for the Als, as they're often called. They are also known as the Larks, since they are named after a bird, and their French-speaking fans call them *Les Oiseaux*. Well, Sam Etcheverry was the quarterback and was known as "the Rifle" – and for good reason. His passes to Hal Patterson, and that player's catches and his speed were exciting to watch. We'll have go to a game some time. They play right here at our own McGill Stadium.

So you got to meet Professor Underhill. I guess he called you H.H. Well professor "Over- the-hill", as I affectionately refer to him, is determined to continue mentoring young minds, much like his hero, Socrates. But I think the old codger just likes being able to wink at Miss Templeton every morning! What do you think of these social tea parties? Personally, I'd rather just crack open a beer! Well, enjoy your stay here. Hope we can talk about Cincinnati some time.

- Yes, I'd like that very much, Professor Peters, and I'd like to hear about your work in Greece. I was a quarterback in high school, but I've decided that it would be too time – consuming to play university football. But I'll probably attend some of the McGill Redmen games. *Bonjour*, Professor Jolivet.

- How do you do, *Monsieur* Hainsworth? And *bienvenue* to McGill. Professor Watson spoke to me briefly about you. It seems you are passionate about Latin. Or is it really Venus that draws you to Roman studies! Permit me some gentle teasing, but you seem the ideal candidate to be the "voice" of Classics! Perhaps you will one day read my book, *La langue latine*. It traces the history of Latin from its early development to its influence on contemporary language. And you speak French – I am impressed! In fact, I teach one of my courses in French. Very few students can enroll in this course, either because their level of French is not advanced enough or their level of Latin is not advanced enough. So I hope you will choose this course the next time it is offered. I guess you don't know the other professors. The one wildly waving his arms is Professor Manfredi. Like myself, he teaches Latin. I believe you will be reading Catullus with him this year. Standing by the table pouring herself some tea is Professor Wilkinson. She comes to us by way of McMaster University in Hamilton, Ontario, where she earned her PhD. She teaches Greek and Latin literature. Next to her is Professor Wilson. He is actually an American like yourself, but he did his graduate work at the University of Toronto. He also teaches Greek literature. The dark-haired woman talking to Miss Templeton is Professor Mavroidakis. She is our professor of Modern Greek. So, only two women professors, but our three Teaching Assistants are young ladies. Oh, here I'll introduce you to one of them.

Mademoiselle Talbot, *voici Monsieur* Hainsworth.

- Thank you, Professor Jolivet, for identifying the Department's professors for me.

And I will definitely read your book. Nice to meet you, Miss Talbot.

- A pleasure to meet you! Oh, and please call me Claire. Your French is very good – as is your singing! I am not really the Venus type, but I've heard you are a keen student of Latin.

Perhaps you would like to visit the "Beginners Latin" class I teach. I use the standard text by Wheelock. Have you found a place to stay?

- 	Well. Miss Talbot - I mean Claire - I would like to visit your class if my schedule works out. I think Xavier University was gambling a bit on the chance that my rendition of the song "Venus" would attract students to Classics. On the other hand, since Venus is the goddess of "luck", maybe it will pay off. Have you heard of the "Venus throw"? My high school Latin teacher once brought to class a replica of the knucklebones game the Romans used to play. There were four rectangular bones – they were called *tali* - with the numbers *I,III,IV,* and *VI*. When they "talleyed" up the points, if you had all four numbers in the same roll, the total was 14 – the perfect score. Something like getting a hand of four aces in cards, I guess. You know, Claire, since Venus is the goddess of love, I suppose we can say that falling in love brings "good luck"! I don't gamble, so maybe not being "lucky at cards" could mean I'll be "lucky in love"! Just like Frank Sinatra sings in his song "Luck Be A Lady"! Perhaps Julius Caesar had that gut feeling when he "rolled the dice" in crossing the Rubicon, counting on his family tree that he traced back to Venus! I have been staying at Professor Watson's home this week, but tomorrow I will be moving into my apartment on Milton Avenue.

- 	So close – how nice! Well, if you need help finding food stores, or if you would like to see the City, I could take you on a tour this weekend.

- 	That would be great. *Merci beaucoup*! You'll probably conduct your tour with the Petula Clark songs "Downtown"and "I Know a Place"!

Chapter 40

- I hope this letter finds you well, Den. I was so relieved when you called to let us know that you had arrived safely. That was quite a long bus ride! Now that you have settled into your apartment we can ship the big trunk to you with your extra clothes, your big dictionaries, and of course, your records! I'm glad you found an inexpensive radio and record player. That girl who took you shopping sounds nice. And you talk to each other in French – how wonderful! Let me know how your courses are going. Phoebe has been dutifully walking Vergil Cane every day. But she's never alone. She met this boy – Danny – at one of the Sacred Heart dances. He's very nice, and goes to St. Xavier High. Imagine – he takes Latin! Your father has been playing golf at Indian Hills. Donnie Johnson says hello. With you no longer on his bag, he says he often doesn't know which club to hit. Last night a young man came round and gave us a pepperoni pizza! He told us he was a friend of yours. His name is Jeff, and he told us to be sure to let you know he paid for it himself. Some sad news - *Monsieur* Dubois called us two days ago to inform us that Father McNeil had passed away. I hope you're eating healthy, Den. Write soon! Love, Mom

- Reading a letter from home?

- Yes, Professor Peters. My Mom and I will be writing twice a week. For me it'll be like writing a diary, and my mother will keep me informed of everything going on in Cincinnati. I'll be going home for the Christmas holidays.

- So I guess you'll be attending the joint APA-AIA annual convention. It's always held between Christmas and New Year's, and this year it's being held in downtown Cincy – that's how I refer to Cincinnati, by the way. I'm presenting a paper, and it will be good to visit UC and renew with my old professors. And I do mean old – some of them must be near retirement. Say, I bet that grant you have would pay for air travel to the conference. You wouldn't have to bus it – that's for plebeians!

- Thanks. I'll look into it. Got to run. I don't want to be late for my first class with Professor Manfredi.

***

- *Volare…Cantare…ooh ooh ooh ooh…* Do you recognize that tune, *discipuli discipulaeque* – my dear students? Yes, *Maestro* Hainsworth?

-        I remember hearing Dean Martin singing that song in Italian, and then Bobby Rydell sang it in English – "Your love has given me wings".

-        Ah, yes, but I am singing the original song by that Italian crooner Domenico Modugno. He made all Italians proud when he sang that song on the Ed Sullivan Show. The only Italian more popular was Topo Gigio! Everyone loves a talking mouse. Walt Disney proved that! -
        True, Professor, but Dean Martin and Bobby Rydell were Italo-Americans. Their real names were Dino Crocetti and Bobby Ridarelli.

-        Ah, the American knows his *musica*. You will love these words in the song – *trapunto di stelle* – "spangled with stars" – just like your American flag! But why am I singing this song, Mr. Hainsworth?

-        I imagine that the song expresses the energizing happiness that Catullus felt when he was with his beloved Lesbia.

-        Exactly! Let us look at the expression of that love.

Vivamus, mea Lesbia, atque amemus,

rumoresque senum severiorum

omnes unius aestimemus assis!

soles occidere et redire possunt :

nobis cum semel occidit brevis lux,

nox est perpetua una dormienda.

da mi basia mille, deinde centum,

dein mille altera, dein secunda centum,

deinde usque altera mille, deinde centum.

dein, cum milia multa fecerimus,

conturbabimus illa, ne sciamus,

aut ne quis malus invidere possit,

cum tantum sciat esse basiorum.

Has anyone prepared a translation to share with us? Yes, our music man?

-       "Let us live and love, my Lesbia, and consider as worth one penny the murmurings of nasty old men! Suns can fall and rise again: but when the brief light has shone once and for all, an eternal night must be slept by us. Give me a thousand kisses, then a hundred, then another thousand, then a second hundred, then all the way to another thousand, then a hundred. Then, when we have given many thousands, we will mix them up, so that we don't know how many, or so no evil person can bewitch us because he knows the number of kisses is so large." I'm just wondering if they were "kisses sweeter than wine", like Jimmy Rogers sang in his song!

-       *Bravissimo*, Mr. Hainsworth! Perhaps, like your Jimmy Rogers, Catullus will refer to his loved one as "Honeycomb"! And can you identify a theme in the poet's urgent invitation to Lesbia, and why call her Lesbia?

-       The name Lesbia was probably inspired by the name Lesbos, the island where the celebrated Greek love poetess Sappho lived. And I think that the enthusiasm of Catullus is an example of *carpe diem*!

Chapter 41

\-   Hi Holden! I heard that Professor Manfredi did his song and dance to start off the Catullus course. I always enjoy my classes with him. He probably put your knowledge of popular music to the test! How was your first Greek class with Professor Underhill - or Professor W, as he likes his students to call him?

\-   Professor Under - uh, Professor W - is very knowledgeable. But he spent a great deal of time talking about Socrates, and about the seminar course he teaches about Socrates. It seems that the Dean wants to eliminate the course because too many students from the Philosophy Department are taking his course rather than the course on Socrates in that Department. Professor W said he was afraid democracy might sin against philosophy a third time! This apparently was a reference to Aristotle's reason for retiring from Athens after the death of Alexander the Great - so that Athens wouldn't sin twice against philosophy by putting Alexander's former tutor to death. But our good old Greek professor said he would fight rather than retire. He mentioned that the Dean was in a pickle since he had once been Professor W's student! I guess that would have made Dean Owen Oberson O.O.! I couldn't help noticing that Plato's *Apology* starts off much like Cicero's *Pro Archia* – in both trials the speech for the defense begins with a humble admission of a lack of talent and limited ability, although Socrates is more "in denial" than is Cicero. My English Lit and French Lit courses are really helping me to get to know Montreal and Quebec society. This whole concept of two solitudes – two distinct societies – is strange to me, since in the United States everyone pulls together under the Stars and Stripes flag. Everyone speaks English, or if you can't, you don't speak, except in your home. Of course, we do have a deep division in American society, and it's based on color. Here it's based on language, not on color. It's kind of hard for me to understand the problem since I speak English and French, and I wasn't even born here! Professor Jolivet told me there are four official languages in Switzerland, and that whole country is smaller than Quebec!

I keep hearing about the Quiet Revolution. Apparently, it refers to the changes to improve the lives of the French-speaking majority, but bombs have destroyed property, and someone was even killed - so not so quiet! We've been reading a play about bombing in the name of liberty. It's called *Hier les enfants dansaient*. *Yesterday the children were dancing* is the title of the English translation. It's pretty powerful stuff! In Ancient Rome revolution led to civil war. During the French Revolution people lost their heads – literally! In American history we talk about a revolution that was anything but quiet - it led to the creation of our country. And I keep hearing that the so-called Quiet Revolution is aiming for the same thing – a separate country. I wouldn't be surprised if the Beatles, who are into social and political issues, came out with a song called "Revolution"! Boy, talk about your two solitudes! Hugh MacLennan, who taught at McGill, wasn't born here either, but he recognized this division when he came to Montreal. My History teacher hasn't been too kind in his remarks about the Catholic Church, either. But the churches here are so beautiful – you'd think people would want to attend Mass. Mark Twain was right – there are churches everywhere! This revolution is bringing about changes as well in the philosophy and organization of education. Professor Morin also told us that they want to remove Latin from the schools – can you imagine? He said Latin was for the elites. When I asked him if he considered himself elitist, he said that he certainly did not. When I asked him if he had studied Latin, he answered in the affirmative! When I then pointed out that even the poor and uneducated, as well as slaves, spoke Latin in Ancient Rome, I discovered that my History professor doesn't have a sense of humour! We've started discussing a novel with Professor Jobin in my French Lit class called *Bonheur d'Occasion*, written by Gabrielle Roy. It's ironic that the English translation – *The Tin Flute* – won the major literary award in Canada before the French original. That was because the national award for French Literature in Canada wasn't introduced until a couple of years after the French original was published. It's a sad story that takes place in a part of Montreal called St-Henri. I've noticed there are saints' names on streets everywhere. I was riding the bus the other day, and as the driver called out the stops, this old man sitting in the back kept saying "pray for us"! While I was boarding with the Watsons, we drove down to this part of the city, which Professor Watson amusingly called Lower Westmount! I remarked that it made me think of that song currently on the charts – "Poor Side of Town". Mrs. Watson immediately reacted, saying "Oh yes, that new song by Johnny Rivers!"

But, Claire, I can't figure out why Florentine would even contemplate going out with that inconsiderate, egotistical Jean Lévesque - a real "creep *diem*"!

-        She was looking for love, Holden! She was looking for love!

Chapter 42

-        Hi Mom, I hope everyone is okay. I miss you – but your letters help a lot. I'm really enjoying my Latin and Greek classes. I understand now why my Greek Professor is so wise. The more we read how Socrates is pleading his case, the more we discover how wise he really is – just like the Oracle said! I think Socrates is the *alter ego* of Professor W – we call him that – it's a long story! My Latin course on Catullus is fascinating. Professor Manfredi has been teaching us the different elegiac meters. The first poem we did – which I got to translate – was in hendecasyllables (from a Greek word meaning eleven, Mom). We also read a sad poem about the death of Lesbia's sparrow. Lesbia is the girl Catullus is in love with. Professor Manfredi shared his interpretation of what her "bird" symbolized, but I don't want to get into it. All I will say is all the girls were blushing – and a few of the boys! I later found out that it was an example of our good Professor's penile humour! We read a short poem that starts off with *odi et amo.*

Ask Feeb if she can figure out what that means. If she can't, ask her if she has ever hated and loved the same thing – or the same person! Has Dad's golf game improved? Donnie was nice to play some rounds with him. At least, if Dad can't play LIKE a pro, he can play WITH a pro! I've been getting around Montreal quite a bit. Mostly because Claire has been gracious enough to accompany me. We usually travel on the metro – that's the subway that just opened here in Montreal. It's much cleaner than the New York subway! Dad once told me about tunnels dug in Cincinnati to build a subway, but the project never got off the ground – or "under the ground"!

Montreal has a real "underground city" with all those shops! A bit like the "catacombs" – but without the praying! There are presently three "color lines" to indicate direction – green, orange, and the yellow line, which will allow people to get to St. Helen's Island for Expo 67, and to the South Shore. The St. Helen's Island stop is so popular, I wouldn't be surprised to find its name changed one day in honor of Jean Drapeau, the Mayor of Montreal who was the force behind getting this year's universal exposition for the City. I've spotted SPQR on the wall mosaic of the yellow line. I'm disappointed that there is no subway line with my favorite color, blue! But Claire said there are plans for extending a couple of the lines, and that since students at her *alma mater*, Université de Montréal, would love to travel to school on the metro, a new line will probably eventually be built, and could be "blue"! But I love hearing the conductors "speak Latin" when they say *terminus* at the end of the line. Yes, Mom, I know the word is also used in English and French! I'm still dreaming – seems like I'm often dreaming –

142

day-dreaming, that is (another way of "seizing the day?) – of owning a two-tone blue Buick like the one Pizza Pete owned. Bobby Vinton's songs "Blue on Blue" and "Blue Velvet" create an accurate image of the light and dark blue and the velvet seats of my "dream chariot"! Blue is me, Mom! Call me "Mr. Blue" like The Fleetwoods song, but a "happy Mr. Blue"! I don't ever get "the blues" – not even on Monday! Ah, "Monday, Monday"! The Mamas and Papas, Mom – not you and Dad! I consider myself loyal to my friends – "true blue"! But did you know that the color blue is also associated with wisdom and intelligence? Maybe I'm "pale" blue! With all the anti-Monarchy sentiment here in Quebec, I wouldn't want to be "royal blue"! If I'm being honest, I've always liked blue because it's the color worn by our Blessed Virgin Mary. And how about this – blue is the color of the Province of Quebec – I'm in "blue heaven" without being in heaven (best of both worlds?)! You're probably thinking –"why isn't he into "blues" music! Well, I like Rhythm & Blues! And I know about some "blues" singers, like McKinley Morganfield. Got you, Mom!

He's Muddy Waters, whose song "Rollin' Stone" inspired Mick Jagger and Keith Richards in choosing the Rolling Stones as their band name. Sounds better than being called "Catfish Blues" (another one of his songs). Claire and I have been to St. Joseph's Oratory twice. Hard to believe about all those people who were cured there. The person responsible for this magnificent shrine was a humble little porter for a religious order. Brother André is known as the "Wonder Man of Mount Royal". I wouldn't be surprised if the Church made him a saint someday. I had been going to Mass in English at St. Patrick's Cathedral, and in French to this beautiful church on Dorchester Boulevard – one of the main streets in Montreal. I'm surprised such an important street has an English name. But I suppose if this Quiet Revolution movement becomes more intense, the name could be replaced by a French name. The Church is called Marie Reine du Monde, which means Mary Queen of the World. The large French university that Claire attended is not far from the Oratory. She gave me a tour of the campus, and we visited the Classics Department. The professors all remembered Claire, since she did her *premier cycle* there. They were very nice to me, asking what my special interests were, and where I would do my graduate studies. They seemed impressed with my French, and asked if I would return to the U.S. – everybody in Montreal refers to America that way! – or did I think I would like to teach in a Canadian university some day, or even here in Quebec. My favorite spots in Montreal - other than the MacLennan Library! - are St. Catherine Street – or as Claire and I call it since we always speak French to each other - la Ste-Catherine (we leave out the word *rue* because this street is so popular!) and Old Montreal – le *Vieux Montréal*. It's near the City's Old Port, and there are vestiges of Montreal's first settlements here. Did you know that the first name for this settlement was an Indian name – *Hochelaga*? It then became *Ville Marie* – now they have a skyscraper called Place Ville Marie

– it's the tallest building in Montreal. There's a Chinatown nearby – I've never seen so many Chinese people – but then, I've never visited Chinatown in New York or San Francisco! My favorite place in Old Montreal is the Notre Dame Basilica. Claire and I walked piously up the aisles, but there were loads of tourists snapping pictures. Claire confided that if she ever got married, she would want to get married here. Then she lit a candle! She's very religious and comes from a devout Catholic family. One of her sisters became a nun, and her oldest brother is a priest. She told me that he was the one who first taught her Latin – Church Latin, as she calls it. Claire goes to Mass during the week at the Newman Center. It's very convenient – right on Campus. So I join her sometimes. There are not that many students at the Masses. There's some kind of anti-Church and anti-clergy movement here in Quebec. Claire told me that it's all part of the Quiet Revolution. The people here seem to have a hate-love relationship with religion (like Catullus' *odi et amo*!). I'm going to try to visit one of Claire's Latin classes this week. She swears my presence won't make her nervous, but that maybe some of the girls won't be able to concentrate! Go figure! You know, Mom, Claire actually skipped two years of elementary school, and that's besides the fact she started young because of the date of her birthday. She also accelerated a year in the private high school she attended. Although this is her first year of Grad School, she is actually only six months older than I am! I told her that since she was much younger than I thought, I don't owe her so much respect – even though she was such a brain! She just laughed – in a funny kind of way.

Take care Mom! Love you all! Your son, H.H. (that's what the Greek Professor calls me!)

Chapter 43

-       Ladies and gentlemen, I believe, that as we begin 1967, we should toast Canada in this centennial year, and congratulate our nation for being older than Professor Underhill! Seriously, Montreal is already buzzing with excitement over the big event that will take place this summer – Expo 67. Imagine, if we were still following the calendar of the ancient Romans, we would be in the year 2720, since the Roman "year 1" corresponds to our year 753 B.C. I wonder if classicists will still be reading my books in 2720? I know Mr. Hainsworth is reading them AT 2720 – since that is his address on Milton Avenue! Most likely, archaeologists will be digging up my bones! I hope you will all join me in ensuring that the Classics Department remains a visible part of the celebrations that will be taking place at McGill over the next eight months. Professor Manfredi has purchased some fine wines for this occasion, so don't be shy!

-       Well, Holden, Watson kept it short and sweet. So you must have been happy to see your family over Christmas. Did you enjoy the Conference? What did you think of my paper?

-       To tell you the truth, Professor Peters, I found the Conference overwhelming. So many presentations in simultaneous sessions. I didn't get to attend all the sessions I would have liked to, but I'm glad I heard all the papers on the Latin language and on Roman Religion. I also managed to attend a couple of sessions on Latin literature. Your paper on the current excavations at Pylos was very informative. So archaeologists are still examining pottery sherds to determine the different occupants of the Palace of Nestor at the time of the Trojan War?

With King Nestor away at Troy, I wonder who was literally "minding the fort". You know, although I had often seen his name written down, I had only heard the name Blegen out loud once – mispronounced as it now seems – when it was mentioned by a fellow-student in a high school presentation. So I appreciated your anecdote on the correct pronunciation of his name – "Blegen like pagan"!

-       Glad you liked the presentation. Maybe you can join us one summer to helpclean all those pieces of pottery. Here's a young lady who seems anxious to talk to you. He's all yours, Claire!

-       How did you find my Latin class, Holden?

-       Simple - I just followed your instructions to go up to the eighth floor, and go down the corridor to the large seminar room.

-       No, silly! Were my grammatical explanations clear? What did you think of the sentence translations by the students? That is, aside from the translations of the two girls sitting in the front – I think they were trying too hard in order to impress you.

-       Your explanations were excellent, Claire. You always had the right example to illustrate the syntax. But you know, I wonder about merely translating sentences out of context. Does that really help vocabulary retention? For that matter, where is the interest in going from one sentence to the next. We read Caesar and Cicero and Vergil as the continuous texts that they are. Couldn't we – shouldn't we – prepare students to read complete stories and essays and poems from their very first contact with Latin, and thereby give them a foreshadowing of the joy to be had later in reading authentic Latin literature?

-       But I learned Latin this way, by figuring out the grammar and then looking up words in the dictionary for each sentence.

-       I did too, Claire. Well, I attended Professor Jolivet's reception in his beautiful home just before Christmas – I was told he hosts this party every year. You weren't there, but let me tell you, the wine was flowing. I'm still not used to drinking wine. Fortunately, Professor Underhill was there to rescue me when Madame Jolivet kept offering to fill my glass. He really is like Socrates when it comes to drinking! Talk about your last man standing! Professor Peters kept insisting that I call him Jack. And he kept referring to Madame Jolivet as Madame Jolie, until the end of the evening when he actually addressed her as Jolie Madame! Professor Watson was also enjoying the evening symposium. During his toast of gratitude to the Jolivets, he alluded to the fact that Switzerland was a wealthy country, but that his native country, Ireland, was the richest country in the world. Why? Because its capital was always Dublin! Professor Wilson, whom I don't really know, obviously has a daring sense of humour. At one point, Professor Watson was commenting on how adept Professor Wilson was at opening the wine bottles. Professor Wilson raised a glass, and said "Elementary, my dear Watson"! Well, Professor Jolivet – and I'm proud to say that I spoke to him and his wife all evening in French! – told me he had some Latin manuals for me that had been written by a colleague of his in Geneva. Claire, they are a collection of books narrating the trials and tribulations of a Roman boy from early childhood through adolescence – including experiences at school – until he pursues a career as a teacher and writer. He, of course, knows Livy and Vergil, and in the final volumes of this series – there are five altogether - we get to read from the works of his friends. The series is called *Lingua Romanorum*. But – I hope you're ready for this – Madame

Jolivet offered to accompany me to the study to find the books. When we entered, she didn't turn on the light, but grabbed me in her arms and kissed me! As I tried to pull away, she started to unbutton her blouse. I managed to flip the light on, just as we heard Professor Jolivet coming down the stairs. His wife said she had trouble locating the books. Professor Jolivet took them off the top shelf and handed them to me. I thanked him and hoped that he would attribute the bewildered expression on my face to the wine. As I was leaving the party, I learned that Madame Jolivet's first name is Hélène! I felt like Aeneas – I had just escaped from Troy! But just like he brought his household gods – his *penates* – to his new home, I wistfully carried the books back to my apartment. We can look at them together sometime, Claire.

-      I'd like that. And don't worry about Madame Jolivet – she doesn't correct your exams! You probably hadn't been warned that she is referred to by some graduate students as the "Helvetian Harlot"- and, as you have realized, not just because the Romans called Switzerland *Helvetia*!

-      More like the "lady from Hell-vetia"!

-      You're a handsome young man, Holden. Girls – and married women – will come on to you.

-      YOU don't!

Chapter 44

- My friends, before we listen to today's reading and translation, I would like to review some of the poetic devices used by Catullus - in fact, the artistic skills that are a gift found in all the Latin poets. In poem V we saw examples of hyperbole – the exaggerated number of kisses. In that same poem, we have an example of alliteration. Notice the repetition of the "s" sound in *senum severiorum.* My dear students, you will discover that Latin poetry is truly a sublime symphony of sounds! Another form of repetition called assonance - vowels often at the end of words - is found with the "a" in the very first line – *mea Lesbia.* The repetition of the same word at the beginning of phrases is illustrated by the word nec in poem XLIII. This is known as anaphora. Asyndeton is the omission of a conjunction between words or phrases. We have an example of this at the beginning of poem LXXXVI – *candida, longa, recta.*

Poets like Catullus often compare one thing to another by implication. This technique is known as metaphor, and a perfect example of this is also found in poem V. The "eternal night"- *nox perpetua* – which Catullus is referring to is really death. Irony is often present in poetry. Catullus uses it in poem LXX to express Lesbia's words of sarcasm – or perhaps even ridicule - towards poor Catullus - when she says she would prefer no husband to him, not even Jupiter! - *Nulli se dicit mulier mea nubere malle*

Quam mihi, non si se Iuppiter ipse petat.

Finally, I wish to mention metonymy. With this literary device the poet wishes to convey a meaning by using another word that would suggest the actual word that is meant. In poem LI, Catullus uses the word "lights" – *lumina* - when it is obvious he means "eyes".

I wonder, when you were young children, and your parents said "lights out", were they inviting you to simply "close your eyes"? Or, Mr. Hainsworth, were they about to sing that Doo Wop song from the '50's by The Five Keys? Excuse me, ladies and gentlemen, but Professor Manfredi's musical knowledge must never be bested by a student! And, of course, someone who threatens to "punch your lights out" is not talking about damaging your electrical outlets! Most of the words for the literary techniques we have looked at are Greek. You can ask Professor Wilson or Professor Wilkinson about their etymology! I think that we – like Catullus – have had enough of Lesbia. But you can never get too much humour, even with your Professor Manfredi! That is why I selected Poem 13 to end the course. But I do hope you all enjoyed the interludes with Tibullus and Propertius. And since we have come full circle, as you read and translated our opening Catullus poem in September, Mr. Hainsworth, would you read and render in English this final poem? And before you read it metrically, please identify the meter.

\-   Certainly, Professor! It's actually in hendecasyllables – like the first poem I read.

Cenabis bene, mi Fabulle, apud me

paucis, si tibi di favent, diebus,

si tecum attuleris bonam atque magnam

cenam, non sine candida puella

et vino et sale et omnibus cachinnis.

haec si, inquam, attuleris, venuste noster,

cenabis bene; nam tui Catulli

plenus sacculus est aranearum.

sed contra accipies meros amores

seu quid suavius elegantiusve est :

nam unguentum dabo, quod meae puellae

donarunt Veneres Cupidinesque,

quod tu cum olfacies, deos rogabis,

totum ut te faciant, Fabulle, nasum.

"You will dine well at my house – in French, "*chez moi*"- in a few days, Fabullus, if the gods favor you, and if you bring with you a large tasty meal, not without a beautiful girl" – I've translated *candida* as beautiful, but the first meaning of this word is "white", as in *toga candidata*, the whitish toga worn by candidates for public office in Ancient Rome. But I can't say if political candidates are always candid! However, we do know that white skin was praised in Ancient Rome – dark slaves were considered exotic. Back to the translation –"and not without wine and wit and all sorts of laughter". The Latin word *sal* means salt, but we speak of salty wit, a pungent kind of wit. We also use the expression "with a grain of salt" – *cum grano salis* - to advise someone that something is being said in jest, not to be taken seriously or literally. Of course, Catullus may simply be reminding Fabullus to bring some salt for his French fries! By the way, why do you specify here that the fries are French? Back home we just say fries! We're in Quebec – the fries have to be French! Yes, Professor - translation! "if, I say, you bring these things, my charming fellow, you will dine well". The word *venuste* probably suggests "with the charm of Venus". The deities Venus and Cupid are mentioned later, in the plural form, probably because the gods of love and the force of love are all around us! Just like The Troggs sing in that newly released song "Love is all around us"! Continuing with the translation, "my money-purse is full of cobwebs. But in return you will receive nothing but love – or if there happens to be anything more pleasant or more elegant."My rendering of *meros* by "nothing but" is an attempt to acknowledge that *merus* is usually used to describe wine – "unmixed with water", or "nothing but wine"! Well, to conclude – "I shall give you the ointment which Venus and all her Cupids gave to my girl" – here *puella,* is not "little girl" like a daughter, but a "girlfriend" – "my girl" as in The Temptations song! "Fabullus, once you smell it, you will ask the gods to make you all nose!"

- Well, Mr.Hainsworth certainly KNOWS his Catullus! Your commentary, as you translated, is a sign of confidence, and that, my dear students, is always an objective in a translation exercise. Your points were well taken, although your views on French Fries should perhaps be taken *cum grano salis*. Poor Catullus! Alas, he'll never hear Lesbia playing the Mary Wells song, "My Guy", for him! And I have indeed heard of The Troggs – your "Catullan cantor" is no "Trog-lodyte"! In conclusion to Mr. Hainsworth's excellent translation, and the not so excellent banter between your Professor and his music-loving student, I would like to point out examples of two poetic devices. Hyperbaton is the separation of words that belong together. There are examples of this in the second line – *paucis…diebus* – and in the last line – *totum…nasum*. The separation of those words in this poem serves to accentuate the humour. The other rhetorical figure is found in line five, where we see an unnecessary repetition of connectives – *et…et…et.* The effect is to underline the numerous items that Fabullus must bring to dinner. This is known as polysyndeton – again, my friends, Greek words. I hope to see you all next year in a Latin Literature course. Same professor perhaps, but a different Roman poet! As an added attraction, you will probably be graced by the presence of our American valourous visionary of vocabulary, our marvel of metaphor, our wizard of word play, our pundit of puns, our artist of alliteration. I could go on displaying my own alliterative acumen, but the face of our Latin prodigy is visibly vermilion!

 And speaking of colors, class, what is black and white, and "read" all over? Why, a newspaper, of course! Oh, Mr. Hainsworth, a word if I may. Professor Watson wishes to speak to you about a proposal. Since it follows on a suggestion that I myself made, one piece of advice – *carpe diem*, young man!

Chapter 45

-       Wow! I am so sorry, Claire! I'm still not able to handle too much wine. I just wanted to celebrate the end of my first year at McGill. I remember showing you those Latin books, and we did some role-playing to test that immersion method of learning Latin. I was the student and you were the teacher – although in a real class, we wouldn't have been sharing a bottle of wine. Maybe they did in Ancient Rome, though. I recall going into the bedroom, and I guess I must have passed out. But waking up and seeing you beside me – I mean I'm ashamed and embarrassed! I mean this is real awkward, Claire. Please know that I totally respect you.

What must you think of me? After all, intoxication doesn't justify intimacy!

- I have the same opinion of you now as when I met you in September, Holden.

You are a sweet, considerate, gentle person who loves Latin like I do, and probably even more.

I've always looked forward to spending time with you – showing you the city, going to movies and plays, contradicting your suggestions on how to teach my Latin class, and, oh yes, attending Mass at the Newman Center together. Holden, have you noticed? We're both still fully dressed!

After a few minutes, I went into your room to see if you were okay. You had started to talk about the summer before you went to your room. I sat on the bed beside you because you were sleeping. I sat there for a few minutes looking at you. Holden, your inner beauty is reflected in your outer beauty! You're like the god Apollo! Well, I'm not the world's best wine drinker either.

I fell asleep beside you – and here we are! And don't worry about what my parents will think. I often sleep over with Joan and Marlene – you know, the other two teaching assistants. They share an apartment in N.D.G. So we can have breakfast, and you can tell me about your summer plans. I guess you're going home to Cincinnati. I'm going on a two-week retreat given by a nun from my sister's congregation. I'll be in Montreal most of the summer, though, teaching Latin to a group of *Opus Dei* members. As the name suggests, they are very religious, and very strict observers of Catholic teachings and practices – something not so popular in Quebec's new cultural identity. So I hope I'll get to see you for part of the summer – we can visit Expo together.

-       Gee, I'm still embarrassed! I mean what kind of host falls asleep in front of his guest? Actually, Claire, Professor Watson called me into his office, and informed me that I could spend the summer in Rome at the American Academy. Even though I am an undergraduate, Professor Manfredi's contacts would be able to secure a place for me in one of their summer seminars. Professor Watson, with his legendary tact and taste for the practical, had already selected the seminar for me. He pointed out that, since I would be taking a French course on the history of Quebec films next year, I could spend the summer watching films on Ancient Greece and Rome. I would have to do a research paper on the seminar topic. But the rest of my time would be spent in visits organized by the Academy to Florence, Milan, Venice, and the Vatican. All my expenses would be paid for by the Parker Endowment. My Mom will be disappointed and I miss my dog, Vergil Cane. But, in the words of Professor Watson, this is "a golden opportunity". But to tell you the truth, Claire, I had hoped to spend part of my summer here in Montreal with you. I mean, you still get around Montreal much better than I do.

-       I'm sure we can still spend a couple of days visiting Expo 67, before you leave.

I'll be able to spend more time on my Master's thesis, which is a study of how the Latin language reflects particular characteristics of Roman character and society. For example, the fact that there are so many different words for slaves in Latin, emphasizes the importance of slavery in the Roman world. And the constant use of the subjunctive reminds us of the tendency of the Romans to negotiate, often in an indirect fashion, and to remain superstitious with respect to the outcome of their endeavours. My thesis director is Professor Jolivet. But don't worry – he is much less likely to "launch a thousand ships" than is his wife Hélène! But let's celebrate your acceptance to the American Academy in Rome! Maybe without wine!

-       Your thesis subject sounds really interesting! Anytime you would like suggestions that you can contradict, let me know! Well, I'd like to see the American Pavilion at Expo. I hear it was designed by Buckminster Fuller. It's still kind of ironic that my mother gave me the name Denys, from Dionysos, the god of wine! She calls me Den for short. My sister once called me Dion for short – but not for long, when she heard me sing his song "I'm a Wanderer"!

She muttered something about being a "wonderer" with respect to my singing. Nor would our visits to Belmont Park prompt The Belmonts to rejoin this "Dion"! Maybe I'll tame wine one day. And about Apollo – you can call me Phoebus – my father does!

Chapter 46

- Gee, Older, what a surprise it was to see you at my high school graduation! Mom told me of your session in Rome, and so you wouldn't be home for the summer. Well, that was an easy *carpe diem!* But it's great to be in Montreal with you for a couple of days before you leave. And Danny and Vergil Cane get along really well, so it's no problem for his family to take care of your beautiful dog while we're gone. I'm going to major in political science at UC. I think I'd like to become a lawyer someday.

- Then you'd better read Cicero, Feeb! One day you'll come across the word "innuendo". This "gerund form" of the Latin verb *innuere* is used in legal jargon to mean "to wit, that is to say". In classical Latin, the verb "signified" "to give a sign" - you did notice the clever way I explained its "signification"? Do I perceive you are about to "insinuate" that I am acting like a pompous pest? True, in Medieval Latin the word came to mean "to hint at" in a pejorative sense! You probably learned in your classical civ courses at Sacred Heart that the word "politics" comes from the Greek word *polis* which means "city". The Athenians were all interested in the affairs of state, or "politics". The Ancient Greeks were political animals! Aristotle said it, not me!

You know I wouldn't miss your graduation, little sister! When I found out you guys were coming to Montreal for a visit, I just booked a one-way flight to Cincinnati, knowing I could drive back with all of you – and that Dad would appreciate a second driver, even if you take pretty well the same interstate all the way to Montreal. What did you think of Expo, Mom? How about the American Pavilion, and the French Pavilion, where they showed a continuous film of Edith Piaf singing? I know how much you like her. And I couldn't tell which one, you or Phoebe, enjoyed the rides at La Ronde more. Dad seemed to enjoy the meal we had at the Canadian Pavilion restaurant, and what he called "Quebec hospitality" from the sharply dressed hostesses.

- It's built on a great site. You said they actually filled in part of the river, and built an artificial island! Just amazing! And I'm so impressed with their subway system – you call it the metro. Ste. Helen's Island is so beautiful. You told us it was named after the wife of the French colonizer Samuel de Champlain – you're really up on your Canadian history, Den! I guess that bridge was named after him – and the bridge above the island was named for the French explorer, Jacques Cartier. Claire seems very nice, and I think she's a pretty young lady. But who was that well-dressed man beaming with confidence and striding around with a certain self-importance? He could have been Shakespeare's Julius Caesar!

-        That was the mayor of Montreal, Jean Drapeau. He was the person basically responsible for bringing the world's fair to Montreal. He does remind me of a figure from ancient history, but not Caesar. He makes me think of the great Athenian statesman, Pericles. Like Pericles, Mayor Drapeau is a great speaker. Pericles managed to convince the Athenians to embark on an ambitious and costly building programme, despite the burden of financing a war against Sparta. Well, they lost the war, but the buildings are still there on the Acropolis! Jean Drapeau has his fierce opponents, as did Pericles. But Pericles was – and Mayor Drapeau is - constantly re-elected to office. Hard to believe in this day and age, but the Mayor seems to have the same control over Montreal as Pericles had over Athens! Jean Drapeau's ultimate goal is to make this city the cultural center of North America – just as the Athens of Pericles was in Ancient Greece. He wants to bring major league baseball and NFL football to Montreal. That would make my stay here in Montreal even more exciting! His projects include state of the art restaurants and conference centers, and he wants to build a stadium and bring the summer Olympics to Montreal. All of this will apparently burden Montreal and all Quebec tax payers, but if he accomplishes all this, he will be remembered for this legacy long after his death – as was Pericles! By the way, Mom, they seem to make a distinction here between the history of Canada and the history of Quebec – in fact, both the province and the country figure in the name of their compulsory high school history course. Expo 67 celebrates Canada's centennial – just like America will celebrate its bicentennial in 1976. And Montreal hopes to host the Olympics that year. My history professor pointed out that although we speak of the Fathers of Confederation, Canada was not a confederation, but a federation. But gee, my Latin teacher could have pointed that out by referring to the prefix *con-* as a union of federations, or federal states, which the original provinces of Canada were definitely not. I like Claire a lot, Mom, and I spend a great deal of time with her, when I'm not in class or at the library, or hanging out with Jeremy. But I think she has this idea that we're in the perfect platonic relationship! I read all the news about Quebec and Canada in newspapers – and Claire explains it to me! Every day, I go to the MacLennan Library to prepare my courses, and to read *The Gazette, Le Devoir,* and *La Presse.*

It's amazing how the editorials in those three papers alone have divergent views on what is happening here! And I get to read *The Cincinnati Enquirer,* since they receive the Saturday edition here. So I'm keeping abreast (Pizza Pete would add "of chicken"!) of what's happening in good old Cincy! I also have fun talking to Mrs. Watson at the Library. She's into popular music from the past, like I am. When she mentions British music - she's from England – can

you believe it – from Liverpool! - she doesn't just talk about the Beatles and Rolling Stones.
She names all kinds of groups – The Dave Clark Five, The Zombies, Herman's Hermits, Peter
and Gordon, The Troggs, Manfred Mann, Gerry and the Pacemakers, The Animals, The
Moody Blues, the Kinks, The Mindbenders, The Yardbirds, The Searchers – and so many
more! But I really like Procol Harum – not just because their name is sort of formed from Latin
words, but their song – "A Whiter Shade of Pale" - is a kind of haunting lament that really
grabs you with its mysterious lyrics and the ever-present organ sound. Professor Watson is
an excellent resource person for my interest in Roman religion, and he does his best to be
funny, but his wife is so knowledgeable about oldies music and about current hits! She told
me about two female singers that I often listen to now – Petula Clark and Dusty Springfield. I
first heard about Tom Jones and Englebert Humperdinck from Mrs. Watson. She told me their
real names were Tom Woodward and George Dorsey. I get the catchy name changes, and
they are fantastic singers! But thanks to me, Mrs. Watson listens to Lou Christie - she loves
his song "Lightnin' Strikes" ! Of course he changed his name, too, from Lugee Sacco. I bet
Jupiter likes that song even more! Now she knows Neil Sedaka, Frankie Valli and the Four
Seasons and Wilson Pickett. She said I should listen to the cool disc jockeys on CFCFand
CKGM radio stations – which I do. But I also listen to a French station, CJMS, which plays
American hits as well as French songs. Do you remember that I told you about the French
course I will be taking in September on Quebec songs and films? So Dad, are you going to be
okay sleeping on the couch? I'll be in a sleeping bag I borrowed, so Mom and Feeb can sleep
in my room.

-       Sounds good, Bus! You're obviously keeping your mind healthy, but what are you doing
to maintain a healthy body? Have you made many friends here, son?

-       Almost all the majors in Classics are my friends, although there is this one Latin student
who is always reciting Latin poetry by heart to impress the girls. The odd thing is, they find
him obnoxious, so he doesn't impress anybody! But my closest friends are Claire, who you
guys have all met, and Jeremy, who has a special interest in Ancient Greek religion. Since
McGill concentrates more on Roman religion, he's thinking of going to the University of
Toronto for graduate studies. Dad, my *corpus sanum* – the "healthy body" you're talking about
- is mostly the result of daily jogging up on the mountain with Claire. But I played hockey this
winter in a league formed by McGill students. Thank God my skating was okay, but some of
those guys were pretty good players. Maybe Dorothy wasn't in Kansas, but I certainly wasn't
on a frozen pond in Cincinnati! Thanks to Jeremy I got into the McGill Touch Football League.

It's pretty competitive, but I ended up being chosen an All-Star at the quarterback position.
Jeremy said I was a "superstar", but when I protested I was kind of ordinary, he insisted that ,

at any rate, as a Latin student I was no "ordinary superstar"! Jeremy lives on the South Shore, across the river, in a town called Greenfield Park. He says it's a football-crazy town, so he felt compelled to play for a team that was based on our Pop Warner programme. When I asked him what position he played, he said guard – of the water bucket! – and end – of the bench! Jeremy has quite the sense of humour, but watching him play in our touch league, I kind of got the impression he wasn't lying! He said he still got to hang out with the cheerleaders, though! Jeremy is more into girls than I am. He always tells me "I'm playing the field, Hold On" – that's what he calls me – "and I'm not talking football!" Jeremy once tried to impress Claire, who he knows is very religious. He boasted of observing Ash Wednesday – only he said "Ass" Wednesday. He sure knows how to ASSert himself! Always thinking of girls, that Jeremy! Claire told him to speak to me about Lent, and he just shrugged and said that I had already "lent" him ten dollars! He has warned me not to avoid girls or I would become a loner. I quickly retorted with the fact that, frequently having to lend him money, I already was a "loaner"! And guess what? Jeremy spends his summers caddying for a pro at a golf club – the Country Club of Montreal. Dad would like to play there – that is where the mulligan was invented! Jeremy also plays golf as a junior member – not as the Pro's caddy like me –and he hangs out a lot with the Club waitresses! He once dated a waitress who was attending secretarial college, but she dumped him. I told him she probably didn't think he was her type! He even became the caddy-master, and gets a charge when some members call him "master". He told me he was glad his last name wasn't Bates! Actually, it's Bain – I sometimes call him "Bain the Pain"! True, Jeremy is a bit psycho – but, of course, not like Norman Bates in the Hitchcock film! Jeremy often hitches a ride home. I've been with him a couple of times, and we hitch-hiked across Victoria Bridge – named after that famous queen of England. Jeremy said she is known for saying "I am not amused". Just like me, I told him, when he tries telling jokes! He brought me to some different clubs and bars on the South Shore and downtown – nice places, Dad, and pretty safe! It's kind of neat to know you can walk around Montreal, and not worry about finishing up like Steve back in Cincinnati! Once, though, Jeremy – "the Pain"! - insulted a French guy in a bar by calling him ugly. The guy laughed and said Jeremy should see his twin! When he said Jeremy was drunk, Jeremy replied "Yeah, but I'll be sober in the morning!" Fortunately, the guy just laughed again.

You know, Dad, these Québécois – that's what they're called – are pretty good-natured. Well, a lot of them. My French teacher said they sometimes feel, though, that they are the "white Afro-Americans of North America" - except that he used that word that Pizza Pete often used! I'm really glad you guys were able to spend some time with me here in Montreal!

Chapter 47

- Nice to see you're back, Holden, but do I have to look at the rest of you?

- Don't tell me my sense of humour is rubbing off, even on you, Claire!

- Seriously, how was your summer in Rome? Did you see Pope Paul in St. Peter's Square?

- It was amazing, Claire! Some Jesuits dropped by the Academy, and introduced me to the Jesuit Superior General. He was really impressed by the fact that I was a Latin student. And, believe it or not, the Archbishop of Cincinnati was in Rome, and arranged for me to be part of a small group of Americans who got to have an audience with the Pope. I got to kiss Pope Paul's ring! I also met Father Reginald Foster. Some people claim he is the best Latin teacher in the world! I was humbled, but when I explained how I was at the American Academy, he wished me well and said *carpe diem*! Visiting museums in Milan and Florence and all those archaeological sites in Rome was quite the experience. I can't wait to tell Professor Peters! But, Claire, I had the strangest dream the night after I came back from Venice. I was in a boat, hauling children into it. But it didn't look like Venice, and it certainly wasn't a gondola! Speaking of dreams, Claire, do you ever dream about where you want to go in life, and think about where you might end up in life? I once read a novel by James Hilton called *Lost Horizon*. They made a movie based on the book – back in 1937! But I've seen the movie on TV a couple of times. It's about a British diplomat, Robert Conroy, who is kidnapped in China with a few other people, and brought to a strange paradise in the Himalayas, where people live for a couple of hundred years, and have no health problems, nor any other worries. This place, called Shangri-la, seems to represent Conroy's dream of a better world. He meets a girl there who wants him to share this mysterious world with her. He plans on doing so, but feels obliged to accompany his brother and a woman, who wish to leave Shangri-la. Those two die on the treacherous trek back in the snow- covered Himalayas. Conroy himself almost dies, but is rescued. He is determined to return, and the film ends with his arrival back at Shangri-la. One member of the diplomatic circle is asked if he believed Shangri-la existed, and he replied that he did because he wanted to believe it! I think that the two people died because they refused to believe in that dream. It reminded me of Thomas More's *Utopia,* which I read in Italy. I hope to read the Latin original someday. These utopic states are what dreams are made of! We shouldn't have to fear that our future will be dystopic like those I read about in George Orwell's *1984* and Aldous Huxley's *Brave New World*.

157

By the way, did you know that there was a song by The Four Coins back in the '50's called "Shangri-la"? The Four Coins were all Greek– Americans, so obviously they could sing! And there was even a female singing group called The Shangri-las! Do you want to fulfil a dream someday, Claire?

- Oh Holden, you're all about songs – and Latin! That movie *The Sound of Music* could be your biography! Did you know that one of the stars in the movie, Christopher Plummer, grew up here in Montreal? Yes, Holden, I'm starting to get a clearer picture of where my life's dream is heading. You won't believe this, but I had a dream this summer in which I also was in a boat pulling in children. How strange is that? But I bet your "boat" was meant to be a school, and you were pulling in students, just like a teacher – which you might become someday.

- So, you could be pulling in students, too! Except that you already do that. Maybe, since we both had the same dream, the boat was a bed, and we were pulling in our future children! I guess, like The Everly Brothers – that's Don and Phil - sang, "All I have to do is dream"! "Dream, dream, dream …" But let me tell you about my project - "Films about Ancient Greece and Rome". I watched a number of films that were set in various historic periods in Greece and Rome, and analyzed them for historical accuracy. But you know, Claire, many of the films were not aiming at the absolute truth, but rather at telling a story, much like ancient historians and poets. Homer and Herodotus, and Vergil and Livy were the entertainers of their day, and they could capture their audience's attention, like the movie directors and producers of today. I examined the following films on ancient Greece – *Hercules* – made in 1958, *Atlantis, the Lost Continent* -1960, *The 300 Spartans* -1962, *Jason and the Argonauts* – 1963. For Ancient Rome, I sometimes chose to watch multiple versions of the same story for comparative purposes. Consequently, I made observations on *Ben- Hur* – the silent film of 1925 – and the 1959 version, *Cleopatra* - 1934 and 1963, *The Last Days of Pompeii* - 1935, 1949 and 1960, *The Sign of the Cross* - 1932, *Quo Vadis* -1951, *Spartacus* - 1960, *The Fall of the Roman Empire* - 1964, and, finally, a completely different film – *A Funny Thing Happened on the Way to the Forum* - that just came out last year. I also pointed out the films based on novels, like *Ben-Hur, The Last Days of Pompeii*, and *Quo Vadis*. My seminar leaders all agreed that my project was well-presented, and believed that my topic could one day be the basis for in-depth study in books, and even university courses! Well, got to run, Claire, and, unlike Martha and the Vandellas, who sang "Nowhere to Run", I do have a place to go to – the MacLennan! I can hardly wait to start my course on Horace tomorrow with Professor Manfredi.

Chapter 48

-       Welcome, my friends, to this course on Horace. Sadly, for most of you, this will be your last Latin course as a McGill undergraduate. A few of you may be considering staying on in our Master's programme. And then there is our dear American friend, Mr. Hainsworth, who is only starting his second year in the honors programme. But not to worry, young *maestro* – we have many course offerings, and so you will not have to repeat the same course. I've given you all a hand-out with the various lyric meters used by Horace. The poem I shall read is known as the fifth – or greater – Asclepiadean meter. Please make an effort to follow the long and short syllables as I read today's poem, which contains the well-known phrase that I often use in giving students advice, known to some of you as the "Manfredi message"! Students, I appreciate you calling me "the man", but I know it's an allusion to Manfred Mann. Just remember, "Do Wah Diddy" – your Manfredi's a lot more pretty!

This poem is Ode 1.11. Following my reading, I shall offer a translation of the poem.

Tu ne quaesieris, scire nefas, quem mihi, quem tibi

finem di dederint, Leuconoe, nec Babylonios

temptaris numeros. ut melius, quidquid erit, pati!

seu pluris hiemes, seu tribuit Iuppiter ultimam,

quae nunc oppositis debilitat pumicibus mare

Tyrrrhenum : sapias, vina liques et spatio brevi

spem longam reseces. dum loquimur, fugerit invida

aetas : carpe diem, quam minimum credula postero.

'' Do not ask – it's not right to know – what end the gods have given to me, to you, Leuconoe, and don't try Babylonian numbers. How much better it is to endure whatever will be!

Whether Jupiter grants many winters, or the one which now cripples the Tuscan Sea with its exposed pumice-stones: be wise, strain the wine, and because of the short span of time, curtail any lengthy hope. As we speak, the envious time of life will have fled: seize the day, trusting as little as possible in the one that follows." Let us review the figures of speech we saw in the course on Catullus. Who can identify the figures in lines 1, 5 and 6, as well as 7 and 8? Go ahead, Mr. Hainsworth.

-       *quem mihi, quem tibi* is an example of asyndeton, the omission of connectives.

The *quem…quem* combination is an example of repetition at the beginning of a phrase, that is, anaphora, but is also, because of the omission of the verb *est*, an example of ellipsis. Tyrrhenum, going with mare in the preceding line is an illustration of enjambement - from the French verb for "straddling", or, literally, "placing a leg over"– thus, running over from one line to the next. In line 6, *sapias, vina liques* is another example of asyndeton, just as *aetas* in line 8 is another example of enjambement. In fact, *invida aetas* – attributing a human characteristic to an inanimate object – is an instance of personification. Finally, the implied comparison of hope for a long time of life in *spem longam* is an example of metaphor.

-       Nicely done, Mr. Hainsworth! The perfect "lie" – locate, identify, explain!

Horace is possibly espousing the Epicurean philosophy here, or simply trying to entice Leuconoe to take advantage of their time together. The famous phrase is, of course, *carpe diem.* Horace is contrasting what we can control with that which we cannot. Is it not true that no one can predict the future? We can, though, enjoy the present. Epicurus, and Lucretius after him, would have said don't risk putting off enjoyment that is not certain to last – and, most of all, let tomorrow take care of itself. Even if the poet is being self-serving here, implying that Leuconoe should not risk waiting for a future lover – one could argue that *postero* at the end of the poem is to be understood with the unexpressed *viro* rather than with the assumed dative *diei*, after the accusative *diem* – the *carpe diem* invitation is still valid. You are all aware by now of Mr. Hainsworth's penchant, his particular propensity for play on words - not to mention an amourous addiction to alliteration! So, here are some examples of clever lines in Horace. In one of his odes we read *Amphora coepit institui currente rota cur urceus exit.* The poet asks why what started out as an amphora – a large Greek jar – after turning on the Roman potter's wheel – comes out as a little pitcher! My friends, he is saying that the Romans can only be a lesser imitation of Greek art. The large Greek amphora "turns" into a little "urn" – an *urceus!*

And this line from the *Ars poetica* – *ac ne quis modici transiliat munera Liberi* . The line means "let no one abuse the modest gifts of Bacchus". To appreciate "Horace's humour" here - as our own H.H. surely does – one has to consider that with the verb *transiliat* we normally see the word *moenia* - walls! Consequently we "jump" from the image of transgressing walls to that of "gifts"- *munera*. Even though the adjective *modici* agrees in the genitive with *Liberi*, we know that Bacchus is never "temperate", but rather here his gifts are "modest"! I assume you all noticed the ironic alliteration in the line – *CURrente rota CUR URCeus!* Just before class ends, I should like to ask our resident music authority, Mr. Hainsworth, if he can tell us the name of the popular song that, like Horace, preaches a blissful acceptance of the fact that we cannot predict the future.

- With pleasure, Professor – no allusion to Epicureanism! Doris Day sang the song "Que sera, sera" in the Alfred Hitchcock film *The Man Who Knew Too Much.*

- Ah, yes! "Whatever will be, will be, the future's not ours to see, *que sera, sera...*" Fate did decree, though, that the delightful actress would bear the name found in *carpe diem*! Since you are now all in a daze over my "Day" allusion, class dismissed!

Chapter 49

-      Hi Mom! Well, it's back to the deep snow in Montreal. My friend Jeremy has been asking me if someone has ever spotted an "abominable snowman"! I keep answering "not Yeti"! But I do enjoy my walks – and running – on the mountain. Seeing the snow on the trees reminded me of that Robert Frost poem "Stopping by woods on a snowy evening". I remember watching him on TV as he paid tribute to President Kennedy at the inauguration. He had composed a poem called "Dedication", which he couldn't finish reading because of the bright sun! So he recited from memory his poem "The Gift Outright". I know there was a mutual admiration between the two men – after all, they were both from New England! I think eveyone hoped that President Kennedy would be that "bright sun" that would continue to shine upon our country! Frost was a Poet Laureate, and the first to present a tribute at a presidential inauguration. I firmly believe, though, that poets will be important participants at future inaugurations – "advocates of the people", as it were! This is what happened in Ancient Rome, when Vergil "inaugurated" the Augustan Age with his poem the *Aeneid*! Robert Frost is my favorite poet – after Virgil and Horace and Ovid! Your wonderful meals during the Christmas holidays reminded me of how much I miss home cooking! All the food they served at the Sugar Shack that I went to with Claire last spring couldn't make me forget that when it comes to good old "motherhood and apple pie", you are far and away tops in both categories! But I still remember the song "Sugar Shack" by Jimmy Gilmer and The Fireballs! The French name for sugar shack is *cabane à sucre*, which you'll recognize as a literal translation, Mom. However, you may not figure out why "shepherd's pie" is *pâté chinois* – "Chinese pie" - here in Quebec. Well, it seems the Asian workers mix all that meat and potaoes along with corn, and have made it a staple in their diet! Professor Watson once boasted about how delicious the Irish version of the dish is! If Dad's mouth is watering, just mention that I still have porridge for breakfast every day, now with "Brown Sugar:" – the Stones' song, not the sweetener! I sometimes go to this restaurant not too far from McGill – well, actually a half-hour walk – but it's good exercise – *corpus sanum* and all that! It's on Rachel Street, reminds me a bit of Pizza Pete's. And get this – the waitress who serves me is named Rachel! She says she's a student, but she's always there whenever I am. And speaking of Pizza Pete, it was great to see him again. And the rest of the guys – Mickey, Rick, and yeah, Jeff! Pete is basically a very patriotic American, but maybe not to the point of being "Patriotic Pete"! And he'll certainly never become "Poetic Pete"! He once asked me about the poet "Lori Ett", that he kept hearing about. I finally figured out that he was talking about a poet laureate – which of course, means a poet that has earned honorary "laurels"! The only "poem" of Pete's I ever saw was the note on the door leading to the back room where Pete and the boys could watch his little television set – it said "When football is on the box/ you come in, but you no talks"! There's a new guy, Timmy, and Pete told me he's now the guy who keeps the juke-box warm! I don't know if he'll get a nickname like mine – the "Juke of Earl"! They have some new songs, and I was glad to listen to " A Whiter Shade of Pale". Mom, I never mentioned this to you, but I think that Pizza Pete had once planned on taking me under his wing – to eventually take over "Pizza Pete's". That was before he realized I was so serious about Latin. He once told me that my knack for mixing pizza dough just right could enable me to make a lot of dough one day! He said that "The Pizza Prince" would make a good name for a pizza joint! But honestly, my lack of a nose for business – as well as my heart not being in it – would make me end up being both the "Prince" and the "Pauper" of that novel by Mark Twain!

I certainly didn't have the ambition to become The Prince described by Macchiavelli! Did you know, Mom, that there is a book written by that Italian Renaissance writer called *Discourses on Livy*, but it is filled with so much contemporary commentary on Livy's account of Rome, that it would hardly be a suitable source book for the student of Roman history! I was always amused when Pete, mildly angry at Mickey, would belt out "for the love of Mike" – Mickey's real name was Michael!. Likewise, when he sometimes complained that Jeff's pizzas were like his ideas – half-baked – he would throw his hands up in the air and cry out "for Pete's sake"! At least that kept him from taking the Lord's name in vain! It was nice to meet Feeb's boyfriend Danny. When I asked him if he had heard of Danny and The Juniors, he asked if I meant the guys who sing "At the Hop". Wow! He's okay! I really enjoyed running through Burnet Woods again with Vergil Cane. My short visit to Xavier U was fun – Father Sloan was in his office – some Jesuits don't take holidays! He was glad to hear I was enjoying McGill. I told him about the "singing Professor Manfredi" and about "W" - Professor Underhill, and his obsession with Socrates. Our course is about distinguishing what is Socrates and what is Plato in the Platonic Dialogues, but, to be honest, I sometimes can't distinguish between Socrates and Professor Underhill – he's the wisest man I know! This study is called the "Socratic question" - but, actually, all those questions that the Athenian philosopher asked were "Socratic questions"! We've been looking at some sources on Socrates, like Aristophanes' play *The Clouds* and *The Apology of Socrates* by the historian and soldier Xenophon. I actually read his *Anabasis*, that account of his march through Asia Minor with ten thousand mercenaries. It's pretty easy Greek, but I was wondering if he was referring to his march back, or a march up country since the Greek preposition *ana-* can mean both "upwards" and "back". You can tell Dad I was blown away by the hockey game I saw at the Montreal Forum. The Canadiens were playing their arch- rivals – the "Big Bad Bruins", and so there were a lot of fans from Boston who had made the trip to Montreal. My friend Jeremy, who got the tickets for us, said we might meet up with some of them after the game at some bar he was taking me to, and so my American accent would come in handy! I really admire the Montreal captain, Jean Béliveau. What a graceful player – he directs the plays with his accurate passes just like a quarterback! And he scored three goals! It's called a hat-trick – I found that out when everyone started throwing their hats onto the ice! Didn't they know it would be cold outside after the game without their hats on! But Boston had this young defenseman, Bobby Orr, who was quite good, and he scored two goals. I think he's going to be a star in the league.

Interesting – his number 4 is the same as the Montreal captain's! I'm glad the Habs – that's what the Montreal team is sometimes called, short for the French word *habitants* - won the game, because Jeremy told me that the fans can become unruly when the team loses. He told me that their hero, Rocket Richard, was once suspended for all the playoffs. This "rocket"may not have been "NASA", but the crowd got "NASty". He had to come on the radio to tell the people to call off the riot! Jeremy says people believe that was the start of the Quiet Revolution! I try to imagine what would happen in Cincinnati if a star player for the Reds like Pete Rose ever got suspended. The Montreal team is sometimes referred to as *La Sainte Flanelle*, a reference to the wool used to make their sweaters. So they actually do worship the team! Jeremy says no doubt about it, hockey is a religion in Quebec. But I think they do more praying in the Forum than in church! There was even a fan at the game holding a sign that read "Jesus saves, but the Canadiens score on the rebound! And I like that name Forum – just like in Ancient Rome! There is also an arena in Quebec City called the Colosseum – well, the Colisée! But hockey is the entertainment now, not gladiators – except when they have these fights! There were two in the game I saw! The Montreal Canadiens have lots of other names too – *Bleu-Blanc-Rouge*, which are the colors of their sweaters, *le Tricolore* – same reason - *les Glorieux*, because they've won the Stanley Cup more than any other team – wouldn't the Reds be "glorious" if they always won the World Series?, and – get this – the "Flying Frenchmen"! The fact that they have so many French-Canadians on the team is another reason they're so popular! Actually, almost all the players in the league are Canadian – hockey is Canada's national sport after all! But I think that someday there will be more American players. If I can play hockey a little, imagine those guys in the American universities up North! And there are no black players! There was one, Willie O'Ree, who played a couple of years for Boston – maybe they liked his Irish-sounding name! But Jeremy says all kids play hockey in Quebec, including black kids, so it's just a matter of time before more black athletes make it into the National Hockey League. I remember Dad telling me the story of Jackie Robinson breaking the color barrier in baseball. And he did it here in Montreal! He played for the Montreal Royals back in 1947, before going on to play with the Dodgers. Pittsburgh

Pirates great Roberto Clemente also played in Montreal. The Royals played their last season at old Delormier Stadium in 1960. I discovered that the actor Chuck Connors played for the Royals before going on to the majors. He also played basketball in the NBA! I wonder if he was their "trigger-man" before becoming "The Rifleman" in that television show that Dad liked! Speaking of the Dodgers, you must remember that Dad and I both liked the pitcher Sandy Koufax, since he had played for the University of Cincinnati. I wonder if he studied in the Arts faculty – he could have been "the artful dodger"! I know you get that Charles Dickens reference, Mom! Actually, in Montreal they don't seem to pay that much attention to color – just to the language you speak. It seems that Montreal is divided by this street called St. Laurent Boulevard – that's the same Saint Lawrence for whom the river is named! All those to the east of it speak only French, but west of it, you can hear a lot of English. And on the street itself, you will hear Italian, Spanish, even Yiddish! They don't have the "melting pot" of the good old U.S.of A.! In Canada, they talk about a "cultural mosaic"! Mom, I'm still doing my spiritual reading. I've started reading my Latin Bible, so I'm doing a *lectio divina* every day! Say hi to Dad and Feeb for me. Write soon! Love, Holden.

Chapter 50

\-   Hi Claire! Another year almost over! So, I guess you've finished your thesis.

Will I be invited to your convocation next September, so I can see you in your M.A. gown? I've never seen you dressed up - you don't seem bothered about always wearing the same outfit – as if it were a nun's habit!

\-   Only if you promise to sit in the first row! And look who's talking, Mr. "jeans and T-shirt"! So tell me how your classes went this year – I know you want to!

\-   Just so you know, Claire, I sometimes "dress up" with a turtleneck sweater! Jeremy says that doesn't make me "Mr. Dressup" – apparently he's the star of a new TV show for kids that Jeremy's young cousins watch. Jeremy doesn't wear turtlenecks because, as he says, he's already "out of his shell"! I remember Pizza Pete joking about going to the dentist, and saying to his molar : "You'd better get dressed up – doc's taking you out tonight"! Well, my Homer class was with Professor Wilson – I don't think you've had classes with him. He's pretty funny for an American – just joking! We read some books in the Greek hexameter from both the *Iliad* and the *Odyssey*. I'm not going to forget about the "anger of Achilles" or the "much-travelled" Odysseus – or was it "very clever" – *polytropos* – take your pick! He had us read the entire poems in English for discussion purposes. On his suggestion, I read the translation of the *Odyssey* written in prose by Lawrence of Arabia. Professor Wilson pointed out that both T. E. Lawrence – he used the name T.E. Shaw, after George Bernard Shaw, for his translation – and Odysseus set out for foreign lands in search of adventure, even though that meant fighting wars. But one was "conqueror of the seas", while the other was "master of the sands"! Did you know that T.E. Shaw read the proofs of Robert Graves' novel *Claudius the God* – I know you read that novel along with *I, Claudius*? Graves and Lawrence/Shaw must have been good friends, since Graves wrote "an intimate biography" of the adventurer called *Lawrence and the Arabs*. Lawrence's career in Arabia reminded me of the '50's song "Band of Gold", where Don Cherry sings of people who "sail to Arabie"! He's the second "Don" I know of who was a professional golfer – the other being Donnie Johnson, who I caddied for in Cincinnati. Why are you rolling your eyes, Claire? Anyhow, in class we had a discussion about Odysseus and the women and goddesses in the *Odyssey*. Was he a victim, or a profiteer? Professor Wilson said he took advantage of women to make his journey back home. But it seems to me that Calypso and Circe wanted him more than he wanted them. And he didn't take advantage of the maiden Nausicaa, when warrior-kings of his time would

166

have. He was driven by a longing to return to his home and his wife Penelope, but also to a previous happier period – twenty years before - when he was king of Ithaca – so nostalgia in both senses of the term – place and time. By the way, all those accounts of the heroes returning to their homes are called *Nostoi* – Greek for "The Returns".

That word and the Greek *algos* combined to give us "nostalgia" – suffering caused by a longing to return to a better place - home – or a better time in the past. My opinion was that, if anything, Odysseus took advantage of his men. After all, he risked their lives by insisting on confrontation with the giant Cyclops, Polyphemus. Here Professor Wilson interjected with his unique brand of humour by agreeing that Odysseus and Polyphemus did not "see eye to eye"! Of course, Polyphemus was to find out that with Odysseus there was more than what "meet's the eye"! The wily Odysseus also put his men in danger when he ordered them, with wax in their ears, to sail near the Sirens. If the wax had fallen from their ears, they would no longer have been "waxing poetic"! He also sacrificed some of his men when he ordered one of his ships to sail through the clutches of the monster Scylla as a distraction, so that he could sneak by with his own ship. And he neglected to supervise his men, with the result that they ate the cattle of the sun. Not one of his men made it safely back home with their leader. Coincidence? I think not! Professor Wilson's commentaries are always interspersed with clever conundrums. For example, he asked the class how the Greeks reported the succes of the Trojan Horse to the Greek homeland so quickly. While some of us were trying to figure out how the beacon signals might work, our "witty Wilson" interjected with the following reponse "by pony express"! So much for " not looking a gift horse in the mouth", I muttered. Professor Manfredi's course on Horace was great, but let me tell you about archaeology. I had gotten to know Professor Peters already, and I think he believes that we have this special "Cincinnati connection". So he feels he can share "Department secrets" about people and all that. And the things he says when he's had a couple of drinks! But he's a really good teacher, and he certainly knows his stuff. The class learned about archaeological methods, and about the history of classical archaeology.The stories about Heinrich Schliemann at Troy and Mycenae and Sir Arthur Evans on the island of Crete, and not to forget the excavations of Carl Blegen and the University of Cincinnati at Troy and Pylos, are fascinating! Professor Peters also spoke about major digs in Italy and Greece, but especially about his own work at Pylos with a team from Cincinnati as well as Greek archaeologists. He also showed us Greek art – vase painting, sculpture, and temple architecture – thanks to his enormous collection of slides. But the big news, Claire, is that he invited me to be part of the student team that will do some post-dig work at Pylos this summer. He also said that the team gets to visit other sites in Greece. I can't wait to climb the Acropolis, and to visit Delphi!

-        That's fantastic, Holden! No wasted moments for you! You seem to be living your dream – a classicist's dream! But did you enjoy your French course on Quebec film and music? Or need I ask?

-        As you know, Claire, since I've been in Montreal, I have been watching lots of movies on TV. I like many of the movies that were produced by Metro-Goldwyn-Mayer – that's the MGM studios. I get a kick out of seeing the roaring lion at the beginning of the movie. But I would be "lyin'" if I didn't mention the real reason – just another example of my funny wordplay, Claire – I think a pun is always fun! In any event, I appreciate seeing that Latin expression over the Lion – *Ars Gratia Artis* - "art for the sake of art". It reminds me of my high school class when a fellow student of mine named Arthur Morris was a little averse to learning Latin, my Jesuit teacher, Father McNeil, would repeat that he would nevertheless continue to teach the art of Latin for "Art's sake"! I've seen some great MGM movies over the years. Maybe you have seen some of them, Claire – *The Wizard of Oz*, *Gone With the Wind*, *Boys Town*, *An American in Paris*, *The Philadelphia Story*, *The Yearling*, *Julius Caesar*, *National Velvet*, *Lassie Come Home*, *A Night at the Opera*, *Ben-Hur*, *Goodbye, Mr. Chips*, *Cat on a Hot Tin Roof*, *Doctor Zhivago*, and, of course, *The Cincinnati Kid*! You probably have come across the expression *ars longa, vita brevis*, translated as "art is long, life is short". That saying used to puzzle me until I came across the entire quote - *occasio praeceps, experimentum periculosum, iudicium difficile!*

This means " opportunity is fleeting, experiment is dangerous, judgment is difficult". Well, Claire, I was even more intrigued until I discovered that the expression was actually a Latin translation of a saying of the Greek "Father of Medicine", Hippocrates. It appears that *ars* must refer to the Greek *techne,* which means "skill". So applied to medicine, that expression makes a lot of sense, since there is relatively little time to acquire medical knowledge and to perfect the practical skills of medicine during a lifetime. By the way, Claire, if you hear Jeremy "swearing the hypocritical oath", it refers to his take on some people, and not confusion with the "Hippocratic oath"!

-        I guess the "*septième art*" was mentioned in your course, Holden. It was coined by the 19th century French poet and literary critic, Théophile Gautier, to describe the art of cinema.

-        As a matter of fact, Claire, I remember that my Professor mentioned him. Who could forget a name that means "loving God" or "loved by God" – either way, a great name! We briefly discussed the six traditional arts – music, poetry, dance, architecture, sculpture and painting. My Professor also spoke about the eighth and ninth "arts" – television and comics, that is those BD's like *Astérix* and *Tintin* – which I accept as true art! At the risk of confusing you with the wisdom of Confucius, Claire, I read up on the Six Chinese Arts, which purport to develop the full person. They are Rites, Music, Archery, Chariotry, Calligraphy,and Mathematics – so a mixture of the artistic and the practical! Some of them have obviously become "lost arts"! This course opened up a whole new world for me, Claire. I now feel like I'm part Québécois! The part of the course on film also featured some popular television series. The earliest films we discussed were based on a 1933 book by Claude-Henri Grignon called *Un Homme et son péché*. His "sin" was avarice – a greed that consumed him, and led to the death of his young wife, Donalda. Séraphin was the name of the character who was so despicable that people stopped giving that name to children. The story tells of life in the Laurentians. It's beautiful up there – I travelled through some of the towns once with Jeremy. That's why the TV series was called "Les Belles Histoires des pays d'en haut". We saw two films based on this story – *Un homme et son péché* made in 1949, and *Séraphin* from 1950 . But I've got a feeling that this captivating story is sure to be brought back to the big screen in the future, and maybe even to TV. Viewers seem to be drawn to villains! We saw another film from 1949 called *Le Gros Bill.* It portrayed typical rural life in Quebec – it made me think of Vergil's *Bucolics* and his *Georgics*. Vergil himself grew up on a farm! The main character was a big lovable guy. I guess that's why I heard some fans refer to Jean Béliveau as "Le Gros Bill" when I went to the hockey game with Jeremy. Then we saw a film from 1953 called *Tit-Coq*. It featured Gratien Gélinas, and I remembered that name because we read his play *Hier, les enfants dansaient* in our French Lit class last year. *Tit-Coq* – I guess this little rooster thought he was king of the roost! – is the story of an orphaned soldier who goes off to war, and his fiancée marries another man. We studied a couple of other films based on novels I had read in my French Lit class – *Poussière sur la Ville*, about a doctor who takes up practice in a small town, and his wife gets bored, and Le Survenant - my favorite story – about a free spirit who has a deep effect on the villagers when he arrives. That novel, which I had read back in Cincinnati, was written by Germaine Guèvremont and also became a TV series. And speaking of doctors, Claire, did I ever tell you that my old boss, Pizza Pete, had a son who became a doctor.

When I asked Pete where his son was going to practice, he said his son was already very good, so he didn't have to practice! Sad to say, I think Pete was serious! We saw two more recent films – *La vie heureuse de Leopold Z*, which came out in 1965, and tells the story of a man whose job was ploughing snow - I guess you can have a happy life doing that – maybe he listened to " A WHITER Shade of Pale" all day! – and a 1967 film, *Entre la mer et l'eau douce*, which follows a singer who leaves his home up North, and comes to Montreal, where he eventually sings at Place des Arts. And the class went to the cinema to see the film *Le Viol d'une jeune fille douce*. The film is about the trials and tribulations of a young girl who has a baby out of wed-lock. She makes up a description of the father, and when her brothers go looking for him they pick up a young girl who is hitch-hiking, and rape her. So she's the sweet young girl in the film's title who gets raped. Boy, I don't think I'll hitch-hike with Jeremy anymore! You know, Claire, almost all the Quebec novels I've read, and the films I've seen, are about unhappy people! I guess it's true that misery loves company! I remember my History professor saying that the guilt-complex that people feel here is the fault of the Catholic Church, and her control over their lives. But how can they miss the message of hope and love that the Church preaches? As you might guess, my favorite part of this course was listening to all those French songs – made in Quebec! We got to see many of the singers on documentary film, often taped from television shows. It seems that Quebec had its own version of "American Bandstand"! But even though there is heavy censorship for films, they didn't need an Alan Freed to play unpopular music. American Rock and Roll was fine - they even imitate it here, and do French versions of the songs! Although, apparently the Archbishop of Montreal succeeded in having Elvis Presley banned from giving a concert in Montreal! But then, Ed Sullivan also exercised some censorship when the King was a guest on his show. First we studied the songs composed and sung by the *chansonniers*. Many of these artists were poets before they started singing in coffee shops and "*boîtes- à-chansons*". Félix Leclerc is a legend! And when Gilles Vigneault sings ''*Gens du Pays*" and ''*Mon pays ce n'est pas un pays, c'est l'hiver*'', you get the feeling he's singing some sort of Quebec national anthem.

Georges Dor sings "*La Manic*", a haunting lament about lonely life working on the dams in the Far North. There are quite a few others – Claude Léveillée, Pauline Julien, Monique Leyrac, Louise Forestier, and a real popular singer – Jean-Pierre Ferland. Many of their songs have social messages like those of America's folk singers. And like some American folk singers, some Québécois singers have cross-over hits that make it to the pop charts, like Renée Claude and Claude Dubois – the name of my high school French teacher, who was from Montreal! It's interesting how some names in French can be first or last names, as in English – Sonny James and James Dean. But some first names are given to males and females. There is a female singer, for example, whose first name is also Claude – Claude Valade. But we also get that in America with names like Bobbie. The song "Ode to Billie Joe" was sung by Bobbie Gentry, a female country singer. Billie Joe was a guy, but Billie Jean would have been a girl. I guess my favorite from this group is Robert Charlebois, who sometimes seems bigger than life – but that could be because of his hair! Talk about your Québécois Afro! He teamed up with Louise Forestier to sing one of my all-time favorite songs – "Lindberg". It's a bit weird – like "A Whiter Shade of Pale".

But it talks of flying on different airlines, so I guess that's where the name of the aviator Charles Lindbergh comes in. The invasion of British groups gave rise to a plethora of Québécois groups, all vying for popularity by having far-out names or costumes. So we heard *Les Habits Jaunes, Les Gants Noirs, Les Gendarmes* – who had a great lead singer who sang a French version of Neil Sedaka's song, "Oh Carol"! - *Les Bel Canto, Les Excentriques, Les Sultans* – I really liked their lead singer, Bruce Huard, when I listened to "*La Poupée Qui Fait Non*"! - and a super group called *Les Classels*, all dressed in white and sporting white hair! They had hits with songs like "*Ton amour a changé ma vie*" and *''Et maintenant''*. I won't embarrass you – or myself - by singing them to you, Claire! Actually, I had heard the English version of that second song sung by Sonny and Cher, but I learned that it was indeed a French song, written and recorded by the French singer, Gilbert Bécaud. In fact I bought a 45 by Bécaud called "*Vivre*". Listening to that song can put real zest into living! "*Que c'est bon de vivre – Comme un oiseau libre – Comme un bateau ivre*"! Ah, what images – "free as a bird" and "drunk like a boat" – not like a sailor – that would be more like my friend Jeremy! Professor Manseau mentioned some singers from France, like Bécaud, Charles Aznavour, Johnny Hallyday - the French Elvis! - Adamo, Dick Rivers, Joe Dassin and a few others, but we didn't actually listen to their songs. A group called *Les Hou-Lops* sang a catchy tune called "*Blue Jeans sur la plage*" – I still have the image in my mind! The song reminded me of Jimmy Clanton's hit "Venus in Blue Jeans". They also sang "*Vendredi m'obsede*", which is a version of "Friday on my Mind" by The Easybeats. Our Professor mentioned the conflict that arose when the group had dyed their hair white and were called *Les Têtes Blanches*. But the "dyed in the wool" star group *Les Classels*, who were "white" from head to toe protested – a clear case of two "whites" making a wrong, Claire! Oh, I love your laugh! Well, *The Hou-Lops* went back to their natural colour – "hair today, gone tomorrow", I guess! A trio called *Les Baronets* put out some records that were French versions of Beatle songs – "*Twiste et Chante*" and "Lady Madona". Another group, *Les Sinners*, did the Beatles song "Penny Lane" in French. A group called *Les Surfs* sang "*Reviens Sloopy*". The original by The McCoys - "Hang on Sloopy" – is kind of special for me, because it became the official state rock song of Ohio! A female group, *Les Milady's*, recorded French versions of the Nancy Sinatra song "Sugar Town" and The Sandpipers hit "Guantanamera". But it should come as no surprise to you, Claire, that my favorite group is *César et ses Romains* – dressed as Romans, no less! One of their hits was the Bobby Darin song, "Splish-Splash". There was an American group from Los Angeles who were called Little Caesar & The Romans! They sometimes wore togas, and their hit song was "Those Oldies But Goodies (Remind Me Of You)". I hope that song will remind you of me! I don't think the song on the flip side – "She Don't Wanna Dance (No More)" will make you think of me! The group split up because two members argued over who should be

"Little Caesar"! At least there was no bloodshed as happened during the Roman Empire when there were arguments among the Julio-Claudians as to who would be Caesar, that is, Emperor! To think "Little Caesar" is now a pizza chain based in Detroit. I guess Pizza Pete didn't realize that his "Latin student" employee could have been a "Little Caesar" distant "cousin"! The founders of Little Caesar's own the hockey team in Detroit – the Red Wings. They play at the Olympia, so I imagine they are counting on the help of the gods, although they have their own hero, the legendary Gordie Howe, leading them on their quest for the "Golden Fleece"! I know, Claire, that you realize I am referring to the Stanley Cup! No " friendly MEDEA" to encourage them – only a "friendly MEDIA"! I suppose that even if the BUCK doesn't stop here, the owners are counting on the PUCK to stop here! Quebec has its crooners – Michel Louvain, Fernand Gignac, Robert Demontigny, Raymond Berthiaume – a great voice! - Paolo Noël, Marc Gélinas, who sang a song about going to La Ronde, and Tony Massarelli, to name a few. Johnny Farago is a young singer who sings Elvis songs in French. Some of the popular singers we listened to were Pierre Senécal and Donald Lautrec, who sang the English and French versions of the Expo 67 theme song – "Hey Friend, Say Friend" and *Un Jour, Un Jour*". Joël Denis is probably Quebec's answer to Jackie Wilson, since he dances as well as sings. He sang a catchy dance tune called "Ya Ya", as well as the French version of a Tom Jones song, *Quoi de neuf, Pussycat*"? Tony Roman sang the Manfred Mann song in French – "Do wah diddy diddy". He teamed up with Nanette Workman, an American girl who came to make a career in French in Quebec, to form a sort of Sonny and Cher duo. Other well-known female singers are Michèle Richard, who also sings country because her father, Ti-Blanc Richard, is a country fiddler, Jenny Rock – who is kind of sexy in her own way - Ginette Reno, who has quite a voice - I could see her singing the national anthem before Montreal Canadiens games, and who sings the French version of a Dionne Warwick song – *Le chemin pour San Jose*", Chantal Pary, Margot Lefebvre, whose songs include *C'est la faute au bossa nova*", the Eydie Gorme hit, and Renée Martel, who is really cute, which made her the perfect choice to sing the Shelley Fabares song, "Johnny Angel". I first heard the original song when Donna Reed's "TV daughter" sang it on "The Donna Reed Show". Renée Martel also sings Quebec country and western songs, because her father is a country singer. She sang the French version of a Nancy Sinatra song – *Ces bottes sont faites pour marcher*" – "These Boots were made for Walking". And speaking of cute, a young singer named Claire Lepage recorded the French version of The Sonny and Cher hit "Bang Bang" – with the same title! So having the name Claire seems to guarantee being pretty! Often, though, the French versions tell a completely different story from the English original. By far the most popular singer in Quebec – especially with the young ladies – is Pierre Lalonde. Imagine a Dick Clark who can sing! He is fluently bilingual – again, imagine me if I could sing. I know that you believe I'm a great singer! He actually went to high school in the United States and hosted a TV show there with an English name – Peter Martin. He is called the French Frank Sinatra! He hosts a popular TV show, where you get to see all the current singing stars in Quebec. And of course he sings his hit songs, many of which are French versions of American or British songs. Like the American shows, his show features girl dancers, one of whom is Candy Greene. I've never met a girl named "Candy", and I don't know if I ever will, but as Jeremy keeps reminding me – you never know what life has in store for you! I guess you could say that about a box of chocolates! I hope that one day my "store" will turn out to be a "Miracle"- Mart! You know, Claire, our Professor never actually referred to the English versions of the songs by all these Quebec artists, and I don't think too many of the students were aware that those songs were originally recorded in English, mostly by American singers. But hearing the tune allowed me to make the connection with those original versions. So, some of the Pierre Lalonde hits are "*Le Sourire de mon Amour*" – "The Shadow of your Smile", sung in the movie "The Sandpiper", and which won a Grammy for Tony Bennett, "Gina" – originally recorded by the singer with the REAL velvet voice, Johnny Mathis, "*Ces mots Stupides*" – "Something Stupid", recorded by Nancy Sinatra, "*Je croyais*" – which is the Beatles' song, "Yesterday", "*Donne-moi ta bouche*" – that's "There's a Kind of Hush" by Herman's Hermits – there is no Herman – their singer is Peter Noone, so a "British Pierre"! "*Petit Gonzales*" – the Pat Boone song, "Speedy Gonzales" – and Pierre Lalonde does project the clean-cut Pat Boone image - and "*Je les aime tant*" – The Troggs song, "With a Girl Like You". The theme song on Pierre Lalonde's TV show, "*Jeunesse d'Aujourd'hui*", is "*C'est le temps des vacances*". Claire, I couldn't have said it any better myself!

Chapter 51

\-   Hi Claire, I might arrive back in Montreal before this letter does, but I wanted to tell you about my summer in Greece. As you know, I was working with Professor Peters and his team of graduate students at the Pylos dig. There were no formal lectures, but Professor Peters – some students actually do call him Jack when they're in Greece! – was never at a loss for stories around the meal table – more often a dirt mound, since we always ate outside. It's like you're in a completely different world, and you forget home, family ties, and the rest! Now I know how Odysseus – and Aeneas, for that matter – felt! And that's before the wine starts flowing! I mean literally flowing, Claire! Once, we were in a park, and wine barrels were everywhere – and the wine was left running! But try to find a bottle of water! As I said – a different world! I was feeling kind of proud of myself, since I never let the wine inebriate me – unlike Professor Peters! But one day, some of the Greek crew – rather old labourers – offered me a harmless-looking drink called *ouzo* – they seemed to be drinking it like water. So how did it affect me? Well, let's just say that for a while I was fighting the Minotaur! So, Professor Peters talked about Blegen and his work at Troy, and especially at Pylos. Did you know he's still alive - but pretty old? Well, not as old as Father Perrault in *Lost Horizon*. But both men lived their dreams! We heard a lot about the Linear B tablets found at Pylos. And we heard the fascinating story of their decipherment by Michael Ventris. It turns out they were in Greek and contained the names of gods. I was surprised to hear that the name Dionysos appeared on the tablets, indicating that he wasn't a "new" god, but had been worshipped from Bronze Age times! That made me even prouder to have the name Denys that my mother gave me in honor of that god! Some of the moments I'm less proud of, Claire, were encounters with Greek females that made that night with Madame Jolivet pale in comparison. We were being given a tour of a museum by an employee of the Greek Ministry of Culture – I think she was with the Greek part of the team working with Professor Peters, and she was kind of attractive. Well, she spoke pretty good English, but at one point she said something in Greek to the museum staff, and they went off to another part of the museum with the other students who were with us. She invited me to accompany her to a room where she said Linear B tablets were stored. I followed her – I'd like to say with a pure academic interest in ancient documents, but, if I'm being honest, I was a little – well, a lot – mesmerized by this beautiful woman! Once inside the room, she closed the door, and before I could blink, she had completely removed her dress.

Honestly, Claire, I thought I was staring at Aphrodite! A real Venus de Milo - with arms! And all her charms! She put her arms around me, and I guess she expected me to kiss her. But I hadn't been drinking wine, nor – heaven forbid! – *ouzo*. I pulled away, saying I didn't want to take advantage of her. As if! – but she understood my heart wasn't in it! The other situation was more serious. I often took walks, or jogged, into the village named Pyla, which was not far from the excavation site. I came across a young girl there one day, and she knew all about our excavation team, and the fact that many of the male grad students were with their wives and girlfriends. I was probably the only male member of our team who was unattached – which she was able to find out from me. Her name was Ekaterina. I saw her often on my almost daily excursions. She brought me into the small hills a couple of times, and showed me a couple of Greek shrines. I thought she was merely showing me the area in order to satisfy my curiosity. She spoke some English, but sometimes I had to guess what she was trying to tell me. I found myself often answering her with "yes" – one of the few Modern Greek words I know! She seemed to know quite a bit about our excavation work, and seemed genuinely interested in archaeology, considering she was only sixteen years old. One day, she brought me to her home, where I met her parents. They were pretty friendly, although her father kept looking at me like a parent who wanted his daughter home before eleven! Ekaterina had to interpret for me, since her parents didn't speak English. Her father set a glass of *ouzo* on the table for me, which I felt obliged to drink. The three of them were wrapped up in a sometimes emotional discussion. I learned that Ekaterina had three older sisters that had all married and left the village. Long before eleven o'clock, after her father shook hands with me – rather warmly, I was happy to note – I set out for the excavation team house. A couple of days later, Professor Peters, who knew people in all the neighbouring villages, came up to me, and shook my hand to congratulate me. When I asked why, he said "for being engaged to a young girl in Pyla!" He laughed and allayed my anxiety by telling me he had explained the misunderstanding to Ekaterina's father. It appears that Ekaterina genuinely saw me as a ticket out of the village, and her father was looking forward to bragging rights with the other villagers for having a daughter married to a young man from "across the seas"! Holy moly! Holy – that's me – Holden, and moly - the magic substance that saved Odysseus from the witch Circe – that was Professor Peters! Two close calls in "sandy Pylos" – that was Homer's description of the place! I felt that I had narrowly escaped the clutches of Circe and Calypso! But, Claire, now I won't be able to listen to the Johnny Maestro song "Sixteen Candles" or Neil Sedaka's "Happy Birthday Sweet Sixteen" without thinking about a sixteen-year-old village girl! Honestly, I am going to have to learn Modern Greek before I wake up one morning and discover I'm married! But I did enjoy the archaeological experience in Greece, and the visits to Athens, and some important historic sites.

Hope you are well, Claire! See you soon! Holden P.S. Can't wait to applaud as the Dean hands you your M.A. diploma!

Chapter 52

-      My dearest Holden, now that you're back in Montreal, and reading this letter, please
don't be angry with me – and don't feel sad! You have no doubt learned that I am no longer in
Montreal, and so will not be attending the McGill convocation. For a time I thought I was
falling in love with you, and was hoping you were more than just being nice to me. But, on
attending a second retreat with the sisters from La Congrégation de Notre Dame, I became
finally convinced that I had a vocation to become a nun - not the Flying Nun, like the TV show
you joked about, nor the Singing Nun, whose song "Dominique" you liked to play on your
guitar! But if you remember me by her French name, *Soeur Sourire*, that would be super,
since the lasting image I will have of you is that of a sweet and handsome young man who is
always smiling, and who has a dream, and has the courage to follow it! And I hope you will
understand, Holden, that now that I have found my dream, I must follow it too. In terms you
will surely appreciate, do you recall that song "Come Go With Me" you once played for me on
your record player? – I truly believe that record player is your most prized possession after
your Latin Bible and your Latin dictionary! I don't remember the name of the group that sang
it, but you mentioned that it was a Doo Wop song by a mixed racial group, and that you
played it for the Afro-American girl – her name was Maxine, wasn't it? - when you wanted to
go steady with her.

Well, I know now that the Blessed Virgin Mary has asked me to "come go with her"! So I am
presently in a convent in France as I undergo my initiation to religious life. We are both devout
Catholics, but I know that I have to live my *vita Christiana* as a nun, whereas you will probably
"pass on the fruits of contemplation" one day to your children as a happily married man –
contemplata aliis tradere, as the Dominicans say! I have kept the Latin book you showed me -
Lingua Romanorum - for I will forever remember you, dearest Holden, as "the Latin student"!

God keep you safe! Never hesitate to *carpe diem*! Claire

P.S. I left a little Latin prayer book for you at the Classics Department office. It's addressed to
the "Latin Labyrinth" – because you are so a-MAZE-ing!

Chapter 53

-      Well, well, Holden. Still single are you?

If you want to stay that way, keep away from Greek villages! I've noticed you have been faithfully attending these monthly Department tea socials. Is it because your advisor is the Department Chair? Or do you have your eye on one of our Graduate T.A.s? We lost a good one when Miss Talbot left! It's funny, isn't it, how the T.A. Selection Committee, the noble Professors Underhill and Manfredi, keep choosing females as Department Teaching Assistants! Naturally, you're in Jolivet's Cicero course, which he always teaches in French. Maybe Madame Jolivet put in a good word for you! You know, Holden, I regret not taking French immersion when I was growing up in Edmonton. At least I can read all those French excavation reports! Another year with Wilson, the Demosthenes course, is it?

Does he know your middle name is Denys, so, technically, you could become Mr. Wilson's "Dennis the Menace" – just like Demosthenes tried to convince the Athenians that Philip of Macedon was a menace to Greek freedom! And how do you like BMW?

-      BMW, Professor Peters?

-      Baroness Marianne Wilkinson! Oh, she's not a real Baroness – she just acts like she is! True, she is the only Department member who teaches advanced literature courses in both Greek and Latin. Watson could as well, but he is too busy being a department chairman, and writing his third book on Roman Religion. Play your cards right, Mr. Hainsworth, and you could become a foot-note in that book!

-      Professor Watson has talked to me about being a T.A. for a new Roman Religion course he is planning. But more of a research assistant, he told me. I am taking his Greek Religion course this year. My friend Jeremy is in the course. He wants to specialize in Greek personal religion, and if things work out for him, he'll do a PhD at the U. of T. I'm hoping to do my major paper in the religion course on the mystery rites at Eleusis. I really enjoyed our visit to Eleusis last summer, Professor Peters. Maybe I'll make you a foot-note in my paper! I can see Professor Wilkinson acting like a baroness – the theater is her life! We're reading Plautus' play, *Amphytrio.* That is also the play she intends to present with her MLTT – McGill Latin Theater Troupe. You have to admit, Professor Peters – an amateur group of students putting on a play in Latin is quite an achievement! I'm hoping to land a role in the play. It's being taped, so I would send a copy to my sister in Cincinnati.

-       I wouldn't mind delivering it for you, Holden – any excuse to visit Cincinnati again. Yes, I have to admit Professor Wilkinson has done U.B.C. proud. That's University of British Columbia, Holden, where she did her undergraduate studies. Apparently there is a professor who puts on plays in Greek at Laval University. Nice campus out there in Quebec City, and a great Classics Department – they have a Professor of Roman archaeology on staff! You should visit it sometime, a bilingual guy like you! Say, the CAC is holding their annual meeting there in two years. Mark your calendar!

Chapter 54

-       Hi Mom, Hope everyone is okay at home. Is Feeb taking good care of Vergil Cane? I still get to Mass at the Newman Center during the week, but it feels a bit strange without Claire. When she mentioned that Del-Viking song "Come Go With Me" to talk about her vocation it reminded me of that Bing Crosby movie *Going My Way* - you know - the one where he plays a priest who gave up a romance with an opera singer to follow his vocation. Claire actually made reference to that TV show, "The Flying Nun", which stars Sally Field, who played in the show "Gidget" that Feeb used to watch. I was especially moved by a film I saw on TV called *Come to the Stable*, and which starred Loretta Young. Remember her show "The Loretta Young Show" that you and Dad used to watch? The movie tells the true story of nuns from France who build a hospital in the small town of Bethlehem in New England – "O Little Town of Bethlehem"! That song has me thinking of Christmas – and, of course, your birthday! I was easily able to follow the French dialogue that was featured in the film. Then there was another film called *Trouble With Angels* about a private boarding school for girls run by nuns. The girls weren't all "angels"! A sequel to that movie came out not that long ago, which also starred Rosalind Russell as Mother Superior. It's called *Where Angels Go, Trouble Follows*, and again, not all the girls were "angels"! This movie was about a bus ride across the country to attend a student rally. I also learned that there had been contests in different states to select "the girls".

Mary Jo Begley was chosen from Ohio. Did you ever teach her, Mom? I can easily picture Claire being a devoted teaching nun! I know she won't be another "singing nun". But then, I'm no "singing student" either – after all, just as one swallow doesn't make a spring, one cassette doesn't make a career! Not like those "singing cowboys" you listen to, Mom! I remember Tex Ritter who sang that Oscar-winning song "Do Not Forsake Me Oh My Darlin'" in the movie *High Noon*, Roy Rogers and his horse Trigger, and Gene Autry and his horse Champion – a regular "rodeo on radio". Here's one for Dad – What do my records have in common with horses? They're all "herd"! Actually, I've started watching "made-for-TV" movies. I think they will become more and more popular. Some of them have been sponsored by Procter&Gamble – still making Cincinnati proud (even though Dad no longer works for them)! But you know, Mom, since the Vatican Council removed the traditional Latin Masses a couple of years ago, there are not many Masses in Latin here in Montreal. And I discovered that McGill has also removed the Latin prerequisite for acceptance into their advanced Arts programmes. Professor Watson told me the future of classical studies will definitely take a turn for the worse! I always thought of the Latin Mass as an uplifting celebration. It's like listening to opera

– you don't understand the words, but you enjoy listening to it! I've always considered the Mass to be a continuous conversation with God – and He definitely understands Latin! I think that for most people the "mystery" of Latin should remind them of the mystery of God! Of course not knowing Latin could pose a potential breakdown in communication. I remember Father Brendan telling me once about a parishioner named Dominic who offered to pass the collection plate at Mass one Sunday. After Mass, when Father Brendan asked him why he had gone around with the collection plate four times, he said he kept hearing Father Brendan say "Dominic, go frisk 'em!" I guess *Dominus vobiscum* did sound like that, but with Father Brendan, you never know if his stories are true! Just the same, "the Lord be with you" is a message Dominic would appreciate!

Claire's vocation reinforced my "vocation". I guess I'm hoping for a "career" as a Classics professor, but I really feel that I am "living for Latin" – it's a "calling", so "vocation", Mom. Kind of ironic that we had that *Living Latin* book at St. X. I played golf a couple of times this fall at the Country Club with Jeremy. He's a junior member – and a pretty good golfer. Since he used to caddy for the Pro, we got to play with him once – and I beat him! The Pro shot 71 and I shot 70! The fairways are quite narrow, so the fact that I can keep the ball pretty straight helped. And the course is much shorter than Indian Hills. Jeremy shot 76, so he paid for the beers – I only had one, Mom – and it was a ginger beer! And speaking of beer, I remember Dad telling me about those German beer companies that are all over Cincinnati. So he'll be happy to learn that I'm taking a German course. It's really to help me eventually read important books on Roman and Greek history and literature. Professor Watson has already referred to Martin Nilsson's two-volume *Geschichte der griechischen Religion* – that means the "History of Greek Religion", Mom! Thank God he didn't write it in his native Swedish! I guess knowing German will also help me enjoy Oktoberfest a little more! My Professor's name is Werner Goethe, which is intriguing, because the German Cultural Center here is called the Goethe Center! I'm hoping to get a role in the Latin play directed by my Latin teacher, Professor Wilkinson. I have a course with her on Roman Comedy, and we're reading plays by Plautus and Terence. My other Latin course is on Cicero, and Professor Jolivet always teaches it in French, so that the McGill Classics Department will have "an international reputation of being bilingual"! It's usually entirely selections from the *Ad Familiares* – Cicero's letters to his friends, but this year we are also reading the *De natura deorum,* Cicero's book on the nature of the gods. Professor Peters thinks that Professor Watson persuaded Professor Jolivet to modify the content to get me to take the course. There are only two other students - two girls finishing their Masters' degree. No other graduate student has enough proficiency in French, and the couple of francophone undergraduates haven't reached that level of Latin. I'm glad I'll be able to get home at Christmas, since, as I told you, I'll be in

Rome again next summer. This time it was Professor Watson's connections that got me accepted at the British School in Rome. Professor Manfredi congratulated me with his usual *carpe diem*! Wish Phoebe good luck for me in her political science programme, and tell Dad to try and break 80 instead of his clubs! Love you, Mom! Your "Den".

Chapter 55

\-   Good day, class. Today we will be continuing with our reading of Plautus' play, *Amphytrio*. Let us look at the plot of this Plautine play! And Professor Peters says I have no sense of word play! You will remember that Jupiter has taken the form of Amphytrion while the soldier is at war, thus fooling Amphytrion's wife, Alcmena. Mercury assumes the identity of Sosia, an absent slave. Following this deceit on the part of the two gods, Alcmena is at a loss to defend herself against her husband's accusations, until Jupiter finally reveals the truth of his intrigues. This story is based on the legend in Greek mythology of the birth of Herakles, wherein Alcmene gives birth to the hero-god with Zeus as the father. Another example in the ancient world on the theme of divine intervention in human birth! This story of the birth of Herakles is sometimes featured in those Hercules movies that are popular with the more plebeian elements of the movie-going public. The theme of mistaken identity is cleverly produced in Shakespeare's play, *Comedy of Errors*, which was adapted in the Broadway play, *A Funny Thing Happened on the Way to the Forum*, and which, in turn, was adapted into a movie. But the master of the mistaken identity motif in film was Alfred Hitchcock. I recommend that you try to see the film *North by Northwest*. Of course it's more dramatic than the comic relief aimed at by Plautus.

We are at Act IV, Scene 2. Some of you have indicated an interest in auditioning for the staging of this same play. Now, Mr. Hainsworth, Holden dear, we'll start with you. And you do have that Cary Grant leading-man look - read the Latin text as I do a preliminary evaluation of your voice projection. But since this is a Latin course, please follow with a translation of the passage.

Mercurius: Quis ad fores est?

Amphytrio: Ego sum.

M.: Quid ego sum?

A.: Ita loquor.

M.: Tibi Iuppiter dique omnes irati certo sunt, qui sic frangas fores.

A.: Quo modo?

M. : Eo modo, ut profecto vivas aetatem miser.

A.: Sosia.

M.: Ita, sum Sosia, nisi me esse oblitum existimas. quid nunc vis?

A.: Sceleste, et etiam quid velim id tu me rogas.

M. : Ita, rogo, paene effregisti, fatue, foribus cardines an foris censebas nobis publicitus praeberier? quid me aspectas, stolide? quid nunc vis tibi? aut quid tu es homo?

A. : Verbero, etiam quis ego sim me rogitas, ulmorum Acheruns?

quem pol ego hodie ab istaec dicta faciam ferventem flagris.

"Mercury: Who's at the door?

Amphytrion: I am. M.: What "I"?

A.: I who am speaking just so!

M.: Well Jupiter and all the gods are certainly angry with you, who are breaking down the door in this way?

A.: In what way?

M.: In this way – that you will certainly live your whole life as a miserable man.

A.: Sosia!

M.: Yes, I am Sosia, unless you think I have forgotten! What do you want?

A.: Scoundrel, you are even asking me what I want!

M.: Yes, you idiot, I am asking that – you almost broke the hinges off the door, or did you think I was given them at public expense? Look at me, you fool! Now what do you want? And which man are you?

A.: I'll beat you, you who are still asking me who I am, you underworld of elm-rods, whom I'll certainly make hot today with scourges because of your words."

- Nicely done, Holden! But it seemed at the end that you were translating *verbero* as the verb "to beat", when it is in fact the vocative of the noun *verbero* – "scoundrel". So yes, Amphytrion is threatening to beat the pseudo-Sosia, but is also using yet another word to insult him, even after calling him *scelestus!* Of course, there is a little bit of *quid pro quo* going on here since Mercury has insulted Amphytrion with *stolidus* and *fatuus*. Your intonation was pretty good. You can come for the audition at seven o'clock this evening.

Since it's after dinner-hour, just come over to my apartment at 922 Sherbrooke Street. It's apartment 312. We'll see if you can play the role of a scoundrel!

Chapter 56

- *Guten Tag*, Jeremy! *Wie geht's?*

- What's that, Holden, you want to play tag by the gates? What gates? McGill's Roddick Gates?

- No, *dummkopf*! I'm practicing my German. I said hello, and asked you how you were.

- Well, I'm not so sure now that you called me *dummkopf*! It sounds a lot like "dummy"!

- Well, if the shoe fits! Or in this case – the hat! At least I didn't call you an *umlaut*! No, that's not German for "omelette" – although I have seen you with "egg on your face" a few times! Just think two dots, as in diaeresis and trema! Maybe I should make you an honorary German and call you "Jerry". I know that some students have nicknamed you "Gerry-mander" because of all the arguments you present to professors to get an extension for term paper deadlines! But I'll never call you "*Kraut*", in spite of your sometime "sour" disposition – get it? And you can't claim to be an "*Arminius*" – you know – Hermann the German, who destroyed a whole Roman legion in the Teutonburg Forest! My final test – when you hear "*burger*" do you think German villager or McDonalds? I already know that when you hear the "William Tell Overture", you think "The Lone Ranger"! Like that cowboy of justice and Zorro – the Spanish "Caped Crusader"– maybe you should wear a mask in public! Seriously, Jeremy, pollution and germs – not Germans – could become a serious problem. Remember the plague in Ancient Athens and the Black Death? We might all have to wear masks one day! Imagine all the ventriloquists that will be out of jobs! I know that even a Hellenist as yourself is aware that the word is formed from Latin *venter* – belly – and *loqui* – to speak. My high school speech teacher used to exhort us to "speak from the diaphragm"! Just think of those occasions when you start talking a lot – when you become "loquacious" - and I implore you to just move your lips! I've mentioned that when you start chirping, you remind me of Buddy Holly and The Crickets! When you once asked if it was because you could sing like them, I replied "That'll Be The Day"! Professor Watson is quite proud of his knowledge of the game of cricket, and so it wouldn't "be cricket" to tell him that in knowledge of pop music he is "batting zero"! Especially when he publicly acknowledged that my performance in and out of class made me a "cornerstone" of the Classics Department! Your claim of occasionally being on a corner "stoned" is better left without comment! And before you make a snide remark about the high ratio of girls in the class, I'm taking the German class to fulfil a foreign language requirement for doctoral studies in Classics, not because there are fourteen girls and only three males in the class! Actually, one of the males is just auditing. He's quite old – I think he's an important McGill benefactor. He doesn't say much, but mostly sits there in the back, sometimes making embarrassing noises. The rest of us call him Baron Sitzenfartz! But my Professor, who is from Austria, is very engaging. When he learned of my interest in the ancient gods, he asked if we should equate Zeus/Jupiter with the Germanic god Odin, the Norse "father of the gods", or with his son Thor, the god of thunder. When I replied that I hadn't studied comparative mythology "THORoughly" enough, and that it was a "THOR spot" with scholars, I discovered that *Herr* Goethe had a sense of humour, and in a contest for power, he hoped none of the gods would prove to be a "THOR loser"! Isn't Professor Watson's course on Greek religion captivating? You must be lapping it up! Do the discussions on those katachthonic deities remind you of Montreal's "underground" transportation system? The bus-driver dropping you off at the stations could be a modern "Hermes" – the *psychopompos* conducting you to the entrance to Hades! And just like the Ancient Greeks, you have to pay to get in! Yeah, I know, the obol has seen a lot of inflation since then! But wait until I tell you about my audition with Professor Wilkinson! I mean Professor Peters sort of warned me about her, but he didn't tell me the half of it! You know about the Latin play, and how I'd like to obtain a role. Well, by some strange twist of fate I was scheduled for the last audition. The last few were scheduled at Professor Wilkinson's apartment, which was okay since she only lives fifteen minutes away from McGill. As I arrived, Penny Smith was just leaving. Obviously, she's trying out for the role of Alcmena. She'll probably get it, since she has a background in Theater Arts. Penny told me Professor Wilkinson had really been busy – she was still wearing her business suit that she had on in class. Well, when she finally answered her apartment door and let me in, BMW – don't ask, that's what Professor Peters calls her – was wearing a loose-fitting, low-cut white dress, as if she were going to some fancy ball! And, my God, there was an open bottle of red wine on her living-room table with two glasses already filled! You see where I'm going with this, Jeremy! Professor Peters had told me she had been married to an archaeologist, but was divorced. He actually knew her former husband from meetings of the AIA. He didn't tell me she was the original "gay divorcee"!

-      Oh my God, Hold On! My mother forced me to watch that movie with her one time. This woman is divorced from her husband who was a geologist. I guess her marriage was on the rocks! Ha! Ha! This young man – a dancer - falls in love with her. Say, in the movie his name was Holden! Guy Holden. It starred Fred Astaire and Ginger Rogers. My mother swooned over Fred Astaire's dance moves. You could say she got "astairical"! You see, Holden, I'm almost as funny as you are! Wait a minute, you're not going to tell me you danced with her!

-       More like she danced with me! She told me to loosen up for the audition and not be nervous. Jeremy, I was getting more and more nervous by the minute! She obliged me to drink some wine before the reading. My voice was firm, she told me, and said she liked when men were firm! Jeremy do not go there – I know what you're thinking! She danced very, very close. I got really uncomfortable when she started unbuttoning my shirt. She noticed me squirming, and said she was merely about to suggest I read the text in Roman costume. I panicked, and asked her if she had ever taught Claire Talbot. That sort of brought her back to the reality of being a Professor with her student. And I think she was aware that Claire and I had been close. Claire must have been praying for me somewhere, because Professor Wilkinson took back my copy of the text, and said I could have the role of Mercury, if I wanted it. She also said there wouldn't be any private rehearsals. I think I must have reinforced her choice of Mercury for me when I hurried out of her apartment, as if I had wings on my feet! But as I left the building, I couldn't help thinking about the Leonard Cohen song "So Long, Marianne"!

-       Gosh, Hold On – I hope you didn't blow your chances of getting an A in her course! But don't tell me you're still carrying a torch for Claire – for God sakes, she's a nun! You must realize now that those "heart to heart" moments you shared with her on top of Mount Royal were actually Claire's "Sermon on the Mount"! Don't you get it - J.C. – "Jesus and Claire"!

You know what you need, Mr. Latin student? You need to get laid! Well, maybe not by one of our professors! But look at you – good-looking and all, I mean what a waste Fourteen girls in your German class, and you treat them all as if they were Heidi! Wholesome Holden! H.H. – Hey, all of a sudden I'm Professor Underhill! No, you could be your own 4-H Club – Handsome Wholesome Holden Hainsworth at your service! Just don't ask me to service you, ladies! You may be one of the best STUDENTS ever, but we sure couldn't call you STUD for short – at least not for long! Aw, but I like you, Holden, even if I can't BE like you! How about this tribute to old Professor W? I wish I had a way with women like you have a way with words! You see, I'm inheriting your L.L. – your "linguistic legacy", but – for better or for worse – not your M.M. – your "magnificent morals". Still - we are both keen on ancient religions! And that's nothing to sneeze at!

-       That would bring on a *Gesundheit*! But oh my gosh – I've created a mimeographing monster!

\-   No you haven't, Dr. Holdenstein! You're not C.C. – the "Cincinnati Creator". Just A.A. - the "American Advocate", who is always in my corner!

\-   Jeremy, you realize that you know at least one German word – kindergarten! It's from the word for "garden" – *garten*.

\-   That's right. And since it is a "garden" for children, one has to be "kinder".

\-   That's "kind - er" correct! "From the mouth of babes" – it's gotta be true! But tell me, Jeremy, what do you say to a German barber when you enter his barbershop?

\-   Since I'm not as razor-sharp as you, I don't know.

\-   Good day, *Herr* cut!

Chapter 57

-     Let me congratulate the three of you for taking this course on Cicero in French. Later
this year we will read letters that the great Roman statesman and philosopher wrote to his
friends on a variety of subjects including the political situation at the time. But we are starting
our course with Cicero's discussion on the nature of the gods. We can call his *De natura
deorum* a book on ancient Roman theology! It is a philosophical discussion in three books,
giving the Epicurean and Stoic views of the gods. Cicero attends this discussion at the house
of Cotta, the *Pontifex Maximus*, who is skeptical of both philosophical views. I appreciated
your suggestion, Mr. Hainsworth, that you each work on different sections in preparation for
the classes. You will each bring your translation to the group, and that way, we can cover a
much larger selection from this work. One of my colleagues from the Faculty of Education
informed me that this approach is called Cooperative Learning. All members of the group rely
mutually on the other members of the group to experience all the learning objectives of a
given course. He also told me that his Faculty is working on a modular programme to help
prepare future university professors for teaching. As you know, we professors present
material we have studied and researched, and we publish books and scholarly articles.
Occasionally, we present ideas and information to colleagues at conferences. We don't
consider what my friend in Education calls "learning objectives". I have on more than one
occasion listened to a presentation by noted scholars, whose books I enjoyed very much. But
I was extremely disappointed in their presentations. They were unable to communicate
verbally to a group. I can imagine the discomfort of students having to listen to them for a
whole year in a course. So if you are contemplating a university teaching career, you might
consider such a programme, where you examine the value of a good first class, the
determination of teaching and learning objectives, evaluation techniques, and other aspects a
good teacher must take into consideration. When my colleague used the term "master
teacher", I was pleased to inform him that in Latin one word expresses the notions contained
in those two words – *magister*, the Latin word for "teacher", has evolved into the word
"master"! Before we begin our reading, I would like to inform you that next year a course on
Greek tragedy will be offered in French, and will be taught by Professor Martin Marcoux of
Université Laval. He will no doubt stage a play in Ancient Greek as well. Mr. Hainsworth, we
will now hear your sections – Book One, sections 43 -49 – which present some Epicurean
notions on the nature of the gods. Please begin with the Latin text – one can never over-
estimate the value of oral reading! Just think of how all university life was conducted in Latin
in the Middle Ages – the study of Medieval Latin is quite interesting . Latin was also the

academic language during the Renaissance, even if "modern Latin", or vernacular, languages began to emerge - the so-called Roman, or Romance, languages – Italian, French, Spanish, Portuguese, and Romanian. Even when one speaks English, one has borrowed extensively from Latin. Did you know that doctoral dissertations were still composed in Latin into the twentieth century? And of course Latin is still the official language of the Vatican.

[43] Cum poetarum autem errore coniungere licet portenta magorum Aegyptiorumque in eodem genere dementiam, tum etiam vulgi opiniones, quae in maxima inconstantia, veritatis ignoratione versantur.

Ea qui consideret, quam inconsulte ac temere dicantur, venerari Epicurum et in eorum ipsorum numero, de quibus haec quaestio est, habere debeat. Solus enim vidit primum esse deos, quod in omnium animis eorum notionem impressisset ipsa natura. Quae est enim gens aut quod genus hominum, quod non habeat sine doctrina anticipationem quandam deorum, quam appellat prolepsin Epicurus, id est anteceptam animo rei quandam informationem, sine qua nec intellegi quicquam nec quaeri nec disputari potest. Cuius rationis vim atque utilitatem ex illo caelesti Epicuri de regula et iudicio volumine accepimus.

[44] Quod igitur fundamentum huius quaestionis est, id praeclare iactum videtis. Cum enim non instituto aliquo aut more aut lege sit opinio constituta maneatque ad unum omnium firma consensio, intellegi necesse est esse deos, quoniam insitas eorum vel potius innatas cognitiones habemus; de quo autem omnium natura consentit, id verum esse necesse est; esse igitur deos confitendum est. Quod quoniam fere constat inter omnes non philosophos solum, sed etiam indoctos, fatemur constare illud etiam, hanc nos habere sive anticipationem, ut ante dixi, sive praenotionem deorum (sunt enim rebus novis nova ponenda nomina, ut Epicurus ipse prolepsin appellavit, quam antea nemo eo verbo nominarat) –

[45] hanc igitur habemus, ut deos beatos et inmortales putemus. Quae enim nobis natura informationem ipsorum deorum dedit, eadem inculpsit in mentibus ut eos aeternos et beatos haberemus. Quod si ita est, vere illa sententia est ab Epicuro, quod beatum aeternumque sit, id nec habere ipsum negotii quicquam nec exhibere alteri, itaque neque ira neque gratia teneri, quod, quae talia essent, imbecilla essent omnia. Si nihil aliud quaereremus, nisi ut deos pie coleremus et ut superstitione liberaremur, satis erat dictum, nam et praestans deorum natura hominum pietate coleretur, cum et aeterna esset et beatissima (habet enim venerationem iustam, quicquid excellit), et metus omnis a vi atque ira deorum pulsus esset; intellegitur enim a beata inmortalique natura et iram et gratiam segregari; quibus remotis nullos a superis impendere metus. Sed ad hanc confirmandam opinionem anquirit animus et formam et vitam et actionem mentis atque agitationem in deo.

[46] *Ac de forma quidem partim natura nos admonet, partim ratio docet. Nam a natura habemus omnes omnium gentium speciem nullam aliam nisi humanam deorum; quae enim forma alia occurrit umquam aut vigilanti cuiquam aut dormienti? Sed ne omnia revocentur ad primas notiones ratio hoc idem ipsa declarat.*

[47] *Nam cum praestantissumam naturam, vel quia beata est vel quia sempiterna, convenire videatur eandem esse pulcherrimam, quae conpositio membrorum, quae conformatio liniamentorum, quae figura, quae species humana potest esse pulchrior? Vos quidem, Lucili, soletis (nam Cotta meus modo hoc, modo illud), cum artificium effingitis fabricamque divinam, quam sint omnia in hominis figura non modo ad usum, verum etiam ad venustatem apta, describere;*

[48] *quod si omnium animantium formam vincit hominis figura, deus autem animans est, ea figura profecto est, quae pulcherrumast omnium. Quoniamque deos beatissimos esse potest nec virtus sine ratione constat, beatus autem esse sine virtute nemo constare nec ratio usquam inesse nisi in hominis figura, hominis esse specie deos confitendum est.*

[49] *Nec tamen ea species corpus est, sed quasi corpus, nec habet sanguinem, sed quasi sanguinem. Haec quamquam et inventa sunt acutius et dicta subtilius ab Epicuro quam ut quivis ea possit agnoscere, tamen fretus intellegentia vestra dissero brevius, quam causa desiderat. Epicurus autem, qui res occultas et penitus abditas non modo videat animo, sed etiam sic tractet ut manu, docet eam esse vim et naturam deorum, ut primum non sensu, sed mente cernatur nec soliditate quadam nec ad numerum, ut ea, quae ille propter firmitatem steremnia appellat, sed imaginibus similitudine et transitione perceptis, cum infinita simillumarum imaginum species ex innumerabilibus individuis existat et ad deos adfluat, cum maximis voluptatibus in eos imagines mentem intentam infixamque nostram intellegentiam capere, quae sit et beata natura et aeterna.*

Professor Jolivet, I would like to thank you for your suggestions regarding French-language dictionaries. I am now the happy owner of the Latin-French dictionary of Felix Gaffiot and the Greek-French dictionary of Anatole Bailly. My passage is the defense of Epicurean theology by Gaius Velleius. He does at one point address Lucilius, who is the Quintus Lucilius Balbus that will propose the Stoic views of the gods. I know that Cicero will view the Stoic position as closer to the truth. I personally admire many elements in Stoic philosophy, and Seneca is my favorite prose author – but I also like his tragedies. But I would never suggest suicide as a "noble solution" - a "*beau geste*" to quote the name of the film with Gary Cooper, in which he steals a fake diamond to protect the reputation of his adoptive mother. The film is mostly about the adventures of Beau, played by Gary Cooper, and his two brothers in the French Foreign Legion.

The setting makes me think of Lawrence of Arabia. A remake of the movie came out a couple of years ago, but I haven't seen it. There had been a silent movie, but of that I shall not speak!

Just a bit of humour for the girls, Professor! But I have always admired Gary Cooper. One of my favorite films is based on the short story, "The Tin Star". In the film, called *High Noon*, Gary Cooper must face a group of brothers out for revenge. He had cleaned up the town as sheriff, but when no one in the town helped him, he rode off into the sunset with his new bride – played by Grace Kelly, who later became Princess Grace of Monaco! By the way, the French title for this film is *Le train sifflera trois fois* – a reference to the train that will arrive at noon with the murderous gang leader – at high noon! The connection with today's lesson is the stoical courage displayed by Gary Cooper's characters in those films. I do, however, owe a debt to Epicurus for inspiring *carpe diem*, which has been one of the guidelines in my life. Nonetheless, unlike Socrates, I don't think "I owe a cock to Asclepius"- though I am in good health! Now for my translation.

[43] "To the errors of the poets one can join the portents of the magi, and in the same class, the folly of the Egyptians, and then also the beliefs of the masses, which are versed in the greatest inconsistency through ignorance of the truth. Anyone who considers these things, which are said rashly and without any basis, ought to venerate Epicurus and consider him in the number of those very gods, the subject of whom is the present inquiry. For he alone first saw that the gods exist, because nature herself has impressed a notion of them in the minds of all men. For what nation or what tribe of people is there that does not possess a preconception of the gods that is without a certain learning? Epicurus calls this *prolepsis,* that is, a certain preconceived image of something in the mind, without which nothing can be understood or investigated or discussed.

We have received the force and usefulness of this reasoning from that divine book of Epicurus on rule and judgment.

[44] You see therefore that the foundation of this question – such as it is – has been clearly laid down. Since the belief has not been established by any authority or custom or law, and since the unanimous and firm consensus of all remains, it is necessary to understand that the gods exist, since we have an instinctive, or rather innate, concept of them; that about which the nature of all men agrees must necessarily be true; it must then be admitted that the gods exist. And since this is agreed upon by nearly all philosophers, as well as by the unlearned,

we must admit that we agree also that we have a preconception, as I said before, or a prior notion of the gods (for new names must be established for new things, just as Epicurus himself called *prolepsis* that which no one had ever named with this word before) –

[45] We have this, then, that we consider the gods happy and immortal. The nature which gave us this idea of the gods themselves engraved on our minds the same idea, so that we consider them eternal and happy. If this then is so, truly that belief of Epicurus that whatever is happy and eternal can neither itself have any trouble, nor give it to another, nor be held in check by anger or favour, since all such things are weak.

If we seek nothing else except to worship the gods piously, and to be free from superstition, sufficient discussion has already taken place, since the lofty nature of the gods would be worshipped by the piety of men, because it was eternal and most happy (for whatever is eminent has its just reverence), and all fear of the power and anger of the gods has been driven away, since it is understood that both anger and favour are separated from a happy and immortal nature; and because these things have been removed, no fears of those above hang over us. But the mind, in order to strengthen this belief, inquires after the form and life and action and motion in the mind of god.

[46]   And concerning the form, in part nature advises us, in part reason teaches us. For by nature all men of all races consider no other form of the gods except a human one; for what other form ever appears to anyone, whether awake or asleep? But so that everything will not be referred to first notions, reason itself declares this.

[47]   For since it seems to be agreeable that the most distinguished nature, since it is happy and eternal is also the most beautiful, what disposition of the limbs, what form of features, what shape, what figure can be more beautiful than the human one? All of you, at least, Lucilius, (for my friend Cotta says now one thing, now another), when you describe the skill and the divine craftsmanship, are wont to describe how in the human figure all things are suitable for usefulness and beauty.

[48]   But if the human figure surpasses the form of all other living beings, and god is a living being, that figure is certainly the one which is the most beautiful of all. And since it is agreed that the gods are very happy, and that no one can be happy without virtue, and that virtue does not exist without reason, and that reason is never present, except in the human form, then it must be admitted that gods are of human form.

[49]   Nor nevertheless is this form a body, but like a body; nor does it have blood, but something like blood. Although these things discovered by Epicurus are too acute and

expressed too subtly for everyone to be abl to understand them, nevertheless, relying on your intelligence, I shall discuss it more briefly than the subject demands. But Epicurus, who not only sees with his mind things that are secret and deeply hidden, but even touches them with his hand, and teaches that the force and nature of the gods are such that they are first perceived not by the senses, but by the mind, and not by substance or individually, as those things which, because of their firmness he calls *steremnia*, but by the images perceived by similarity and succession, since an infinite train of very similar images comes into existence and flows towards the gods, our mind intent and fixed on those images, with the greatest pleasures, perceives what a happy and eternal nature is."

Before I proceed with my commentary, as you requested, Professor Jolivet, I should like to point out that Epicurus used two Greek words quoted in this passage with specific meanings.

Prolepsis is a "preconception" – the Greek prefix *pro-* means "before" - a mental picture or scheme into which experience is fitted, and *steremnia* – a neuter plural form – means "solid objects". The Epicurean point of view talks of human beauty. This echoes the belief in ideal human beauty depicted by the sculptors of the archaic period, with their stereotypical *kouros*-figure, a series of Apollo look-alikes. In Cincinnati, some people called me Apollo – more humour for the young ladies present, Professor! Ultimately, Epicurus gives the gods human form, albeit on a superior scale. The Pre-Socratic religious philosopher Xenophanes would have taken exception to this automatic assumption, repeating his remark, that if - in this instance, the Epicureans – had been horses, the gods would have been perceived as horses. Epicurus calls the gods eternal – in contradiction to the traditional accounts in the Greek myths that the gods were born, as we find in Hesiod's *Theogony* – the "birth" of the gods. This would mean that the Greek gods were not eternal, as they had a beginning! They were in all accounts immortal – they did not die. In our Christian theology, God is immortal, but then so are humans, by reason of our souls. The Biblical account in *Genesis* – another word from the Greek verb *gignomai,* like *Theogony*, meaning "to come into existence" – says that "God made man in his image".

Epicurus, and the ancient Greeks in general – and the Romans, following them – seem to make "god" in man's image. But this anthropomorphic approach is found in Christian art as well.

Genesis is also the name of a rock band that has recently "come into being", with a talented lead singer, Peter Gabriel, so talented that he will probably go on to a solo career, as so often happens in these groups. But they are sure to find an equally talented replacement.

-       Thank you, Mr. Hainsworth, for your interesting comments. Your parallels with Christian theology are admirable, although it is only fair that I inform you that I am an atheist. I am pleased to see you make good use of Bailly's lexicon in defining the Greek terms used by Epicurus. Finally, your tendency to expand on your explanations by way of digressions suggests that you may someday make a good professor! Ah! "The Tin Star". Do you think that you might like to write a short story one day?

Chapter 58

\-   Hi Mom, hope this letter finds everyone well! My summer in Rome at the British School is amazing! In the first week, I went over to the Janiculum Hill. No, Mom, not because it was one of the "seven hills" of Ancient Rome – because it wasn't! Those hills were the Aventine, Caelian, Capitoline, Esquiline, Palatine, Quirinal, and Viminal. Quiz Feeb on them, when you get a chance! No, the Janiculum was outside the territory of Ancient Rome, but became important for its connection to the god Janus – yes, Mom, we get the name January from this double-faced god who looks back at the old year - and ahead to the new year! Actually, I went to see some old friends at the American Academy, which is located on the Janiculum. My year went very well. I was a little – no, a lot sad! - when Claire left, but I have come to terms with that, and I'm glad she is following her dream! At least I didn't light a lamp in my window every night like that tragic heroine in *Le Survenant*. She would look out every evening for her saviour to come back, but he only returned at the end of the story – when she had died! I think she looked upon him as some sort of angel – a kind of rural "Johnny Angel" for older folks living off the land! Maybe that was why her name was Angélina! You can tell Dad there are now two English translations of that novel, in case he would like to read it. One is called *The Monk's Tale*, and the other is *The Outlander*. I had Professor Watson for Greek Religion. He was great! I'm looking forward to the Roman Religion course with him next year.

Just think, Mom, my senior year! My last year in Montreal! And speaking of Roman religion, all my courses at the British School are on aspects of Roman religion: the gods, the priesthoods, the cults, public and private worship, and so many more! This was my second summer in Rome, so I was familiar with the places to visit, and the best restaurants – that I could also afford! I didn't get to see the Pope this time – at least not close up! Oh, and Mom, even though I am in love WITH Rome, I had no delusions about finding love IN Rome! I know you thought – or wished? – it might happen when you wrote to me about that movie *Roman Holiday*. A fairy-tale, Mother! Although a movie you could enjoy because it starred your favorite actor, Gregory Peck! And Dad liked it because he is infatuated with the co-star Audrey Hepburn – but in an innocent way! I like Gregory Peck, too. He was great as Atticus Finch in the movie version of *To Kill a Mockingbird*, and *The Keys of the Kingdom* was another of those films about priests who are heroes. In this film he plays a missionary priest in China. Remember when I played John the Baptist in our elementary school play, and Father Burns said I would make a good missionary. I admit it had me thinking, but right now I feel like I'm a missionary for Latin studies! And the lovers in *Roman Holiday* didn't find "eternal love"- even though they were in the Eternal City! A few strange things I have to tell you about, Mom.

Last winter there was a major incident at Sir George Williams University – you know, that other English university in Montreal. There is also Loyola College, owned by the Jesuits. And they also have a high school – Loyola High School. I visited the campus one day. It's small, but beautiful! I met a couple of Classics professors out there.

They were very nice, and congratulated me on being a scholarship student at McGill. Kind of "classy", seeing as the two institutions are rivals! Well, there were some accusations of racism towards black students at Sir George – yeah, racism in Montreal! One day, as a protest, these black students threw all kinds of computer cards and equipment onto the street from the Hall Building, their main building. I don't know if the situation is going to be resolved, or if it's a sign of a deeper problem. I sure hope they don't end up with a racial divide like we have back home!

And get this! I was listening to good old American music on my radio in my residence room at the British School, when this song by The Band began playing…"Virgil Caine is my name…I drive the Danville train". Can you imagine - my dog's name is in a song! The song is called "The Night They Drove Old Dixie Down". It's a song about the Civil War. No, they weren't paying tribute to Vergil and Roman poetry – or to dogs! I guess they needed a name to rime with "train". Mom, I'm going to try to play it on my guitar with my own song. "Vergil Cane is my dog… he's always with me when I jog…" Well, maybe not! And did you know that the name "Dixie" comes from a French word? In New Orleans, way back when, banknotes had the word for ten – *dix* - written on them! So next time I play golf with Dad, we'll play for "dixies"! He probably thinks the word was named after ice cream! The last thing is a bit delicate, Mom. There is a student from London in my classes here in Rome. His name is Jordan, and he's very much into Greco-Roman art, as well as Renaissance art. So we had some interesting visits to the museums, followed by discussions and gelato – not dixie cups! One day, Jordan invited me to his room to see his paintings. Some of them looked like nude Apollos. He asked me if I would like to pose nude for a painting! When I hesitated, he blurted out that we should sleep together like the ancient Greeks. I blushed, and trying to be funny, I said I was more of a Latin student! Jordan then said he was gay, and was trying to seize the moment. Again trying to be funny – because I was so nervous, I guess – I told him I'd better leave before he tried to seize something else! I can just imagine him walking into Pizza Pete's for a pizza! Pete would probably say something like "keep your peter in your pants!". I hate to think what Jeff would say! But you know, Mom, I didn't shun him away during our remaining weeks at the School. It took some effort, and I admit I'm not totally comfortable around him, but I'm trying to show Christian respect for a fellow human being. And I remember Professor Peters – well, that's his name! – telling me to be careful around male professors who invite you into their office to "talk about life"! I think he once had a bad experience. I'll be back in Montreal in a couple of days. I'll be seeing my friend Jeremy before he's off to graduate studies in Toronto. He once suggested that I should think of going there after I graduate from McGill. Sometimes when he sees me he does his – awful – imitation of John Wayne by saying "Howdy Pilgrim" because of my "peregrinations" in Europe! Mom, the Latin verb *peregrinari* - a deponent verb – means "to travel in foreign lands"! Jeremy is going to tell me all about his experience at Woodstock – you know, that big music festival that was held a couple of weeks ago in upper New York State. We'll be going to that little restaurant I told you about, where that nice waitress, Rachel, works. I say nice, but she's also kind of mysterious! I miss you all. Will write again soon! Love, Holden.

Chapter 59

- I think you'll like the menu in this restaurant, Jeremy – real nice simple food! I hope Rachel is working today. So, tell me about Woodstock.

- First you tell me about your summer in Rome. That's two summers there now.

You become an "Italian stallion" yet? No, of course not!

But it was the summer of '69, Hold On! 69 – get it? Negative, again! No hot times in the city, like in that Lovin' Spoonful song, "Summer in the City"? I tell you, your love of music is rubbing off on me. Like when you apparently played that song "See you in September" by The Happenings for that Rachel chick. But with this restaurant being on Rachel Street – wouldn't you like to be on Rachel? Walking over here you told me about this weird experience with an artist – a guy! – in Rome. It's like I always say, Holden my friend, you keep turning away the girls, then the guys start hitting on you! But I'm glad you handled it okay. I probably would have shoved his paintings where the sun don't shine – and there aren't too many places in Rome where the sun don't shine!

- The British School is a great place. Just think, all those books you've been reading on Greek religion, Jeremy - well I read quite a few on Roman religion. I read two books in French – Georges Dumézil's book on Roman archaic religion and Cumont's book on the Oriental religions in Roman paganism. I read an interesting article in the Journal of Roman Studies by H.J. Rose, in which he noted important books and articles on Roman religion written between 1910 and 1960. It brings me within ten years of being up to date! I also read Rose's book, Ancient Roman Religion. I read Martin Nilsson's book, *The Dionysiac Mysteries of the Hellenistic and Roman Age*, as well as a fascinating essay he wrote called "Religion as Man's Protest against the Meaninglessness of Events" - you should read it. You'll probably be reading a lot of his books on Greek religion. I also read a recent article in the Journal of Religious History by H.D. Jocelyn entitled "The Roman nobility and the religion of the Republican state". And some really good books – you know how much I like to read! There was Marthe Wilson Hoffman Lewis – I know you would get tired just reading the author's name. Well, her book is *The Official Priests of Rome under the Julio-Claudians* – the title is also a bit long for you, Jeremy! I read the books *Religion and Philosophy in the Histories of Tacitus* by Russell Scott and *Phases in the Religion of Ancient Rome* by C. Bailey. And I was lucky enough to get hold of a book by R.M. Ogilvie that just came out. It's called *The Romans and their Gods in the Age of Augustus*. In that book, there is a clever claim that "gods, like dogs, only answer to their names"! I think he may have been quoting Pliny the Elder, who wrote about dogs and dog collars! The experience with my Vergil Cane bears that out for dogs, but I haven't called upon the Roman gods – so far! There are some classic books on Roman religion written by German scholars, but I'll need at least one more German course before I can read them. The books are Kurte Latte's *Römische Religionsgeschichte*, which means "the history of Roman religion", and the "oldie but goodie" – sorry! – *Religion und Kultus* - "religion and culture" by Georg Wissowa. Professor Watson says many more books will be written on the subject of Roman religion over the next few years, some based on research being done now at his alma mater, Cambridge. That University did indeed "nourish him like a mother", he's fond of saying! He gave me this strange look as if to say, "Aren't you going to write one, Mr.Hainsworth?". Of course I have my own copy of his two books, *The Roman Cults and their Greek Origins* and *The Roman Worship of the Greek Gods*. He hasn't got a title for his third book yet, but he's apparently working on some kind of source book for Roman religion. You know, Jeremy, I do have ambitions of writing a couple of books on Roman religion – on individual and community worship, and on foreign cults in Rome. I would also like to write a book on Seneca. I even have a title – "Seneca - The Man and his Message". I'm hoping that one day I'll have a book published on the subject of the Latin language. Again, a possible title – "The Latin Language: Evolution of Syntax and Style". It would examine archaic, classical, and Late Latin. And I'm going to share something with you, since your such a close friend, and a classicist to boot! My English teacher in high school said I had a "flair for fiction" – his exact words! While we were doing a unit on Chaucer's Canterbury Tales, I wrote a "tale" of a couple sleeping together in a strange episode of mistaken identity occurring in the dark of night. My teacher – a Jesuit! – described my story as "ribald and bawdily delightful" – again, his precise words! I've since discovered that this motif was narrated by Ovid in his account of Myrrha sleeping with her father, King Cinyras of Cyprus, who is unaware of her deceit. But my version didn't involve incest. If my books were to get published, it may take a "Myrrhacle"! Encouraged by my teacher's enthusiasm, I got this notion to write a novel. I had this inspired title – "The Nine Lives of Father Marcus". It was to tell the story of someone who survives nine near-death experiences – just like cats are said to have "nine lives". He was to grow up to become a priest, but I never got beyond the "first life" - his survival of a complicated life-threatening birth. But, Jeremy, I want to write that novel one day, to "give it life" (nice pun, right?) - and get this – in Latin. The title will be "*Novem Vitae Domini Marci*", and the "ninth life" will be surviving an attempted assassination of the now Cardinal Marcus. Yes – intrigue in Rome! But I'm sure professional writers will come up with some really intriguing plots for mystery deep in the Vatican – there are so many demons

– but also "angels" - there! And just think – if the novel ever appeared as a movie, the theme song could be The Clovers hit "Love Potion Number Nine"!

-       Golly gee willikers, Hold On! Why don't you just write a book about your own life and your love affair with Latin? You could call it "The Latin Guy" – or maybe "The Latin Guru"! If you write all those books, you won't be "The Latin Student" – you'll be "The Latin Legend"! Don't wait until you're old and retired, and have to write a book called "Life after Latin"!

-       Yes, I guess writing a story about the life and loves of a Latin student would be a "novel" idea for a novel! But if I become a "legend", it won't be in my own time – just in your mind! Perhaps I will encounter my writing "Muse" one day – hopefully without having to climb Mt. Helicon in Greece. Besides, with the nine Muses up there, there wouldn't be any room for me! Or maybe I could go over to Mt. Parnassus at Delphi, where they also hang out! "Climbing Mt. Parnassus" could be my initiation into the world of the arts that blossomed in Ancient Greece! I would be receiving inspiration from my two "namesakes" – Apollo and Dionysos – since those two gods received a shared worship at Delphi. The musician Orpheus had a following at Delphi, so it was natural for "Dionysiac dance"to be practiced as well. It was an inevitable case of "Dance to the Music" – you know – that song by Sly and The Family Stone! You're always referring to my moves on the dance floor as "Denysiac dance" – I should never have told you that my middle name was Denys! Interacting with the gods has always fascinated mankind, hasn't it , Jeremy? Let me tell you about a couple of films on that theme. Actually, the second movie was a sequel to the first one, which was called *Here Comes Mr. Jordan*. In that film, a prizefighter named Joe Pendlleton is killed in a plane crash, although he perhaps wasn't "scheduled" to die! The "angel" who goofed has to bring him back to earth, where Mr. Jordan – angel supervisor – arranges for Joe to assume another life. But he eventually gets back into boxing, and wins a championship. Apparently, the film was originally to be called "Heaven Can Wait" , and I'm almost certain that any remake of the movie would use that title. The sequel – *Down to Earth* – is about the Muse of the Dance, Terpsichore – I can "feel" the connection with Dionysos – who doesn't like the way a certain play has been written because it portrays the Muses as man-crazy, so – with the permission of Mr. Jordan, who seems more like "God" in this sequel - she comes down to earth as Kitty Pendleton – no relation to Joe – to get the play changed, and she falls in love with the writer. She gets a part in the play, and her agent is the same "person" as the fighter's manager in the first film! Alas, the writer is killed. Terpsichore plays a lyre in the film, and I play the guitar – so I guess you could say I'm a bit "terpsichorean"! After all, that muse's name means "delighting in the dance" – and I think my Mom's name for me – Denys – destined me for "delighting in dance" as well! I've been reading a second century AD writer named Lucian of Samostrata.

He wrote a treatise defending dancers – he calls them pantomimes! There is a Latin name for this essay – *De Saltatione* – but all his works were written in Greek. Yes, the dancers only danced – not like the Fred Astaires and Frank Sinatras of today! You would like this author, Jeremy. He wrote essays on the Homeric gods, on oratory, on Heracles, on Greek tragedy, and an interesting account of the incursion into India by the god Dionysos. The people of India were convinced he would be crushed by elephants, but greatly underestimated the power of this god. If they had read *The Bacchae* , they would have recognized "the elephant in the room"! Unlike Alexander the Great and Hannibal, who did not relegate elephants to "IVORY towers"! But, Jeremy, I think a better subject for movies would be the Titans – with those battles against the Olympians! Maybe one day! Go Titans! After all, those movies about the Titanic were "huge" successes, and I'm sure there will be more Titanic movies, which will feature "big" Hollywood stars! The theme is certainly "unsinkable", and definitely not "unthinkable"! So why not movies about monsters, and not just a monstrous boat! Of course the "boat" that caused the Romans the most grief was the KingSHIP! I'm just glad the boat that has kept our good relationship afloat is friendSHIP! I hope my puns are not forcing your lordSHIP to endure too much hardSHIP! All this reminds me of the StarSHIP Enterprise with Captain Kirk! You are really proud that the STAR of that TV show "Star Trek" is a Montrealer, William Shatner, who attended McGill! You never convinced me to become a "trekkie", but there were a few episodes that I enjoyed – for obvious reasons! You remember "Bread and Circuses", "Plato's Stepchildren", and "Who Mourns for Adonais"? Let's not forget that Spock is a Vulcan"! He doesn't walk with a limp, though – like the blacksmiths in old westerns! Maybe a building on the McGill Campus will be named after Shatner! Wouldn't it be great, instead of taking the elevator, to be able to simply say at the entrance "beam me up"! Then you'd really be beaming with pride, Jeremy! I'm just grateful for the sake of my Roman studies Augustus was able to steer the "ship of state" on a steady course! I have to admit, however, that Captain Kirk and Company performed in a more sophisticated setting than did Flash Gordon, who was attempting to save the universe from evil adversaries. Still, my Mom and Dad seemed to be entertained by watching re-runs of that (archaic?) 1930's serial. I could never understand why Flash Gordon had to move about awkwardly in space when the actor, Buster Crabbe, who was an Olympic swimmer, could easily have defeated "maritime foes", and saved the studio the fees for a stunt-man stand-in! He also played Tarzan, as did another Olympic swimmer – Johnny Weissmuller. Why have champion swimmers swinging through the trees?

Buster Crabbe also had adventures in space as Buck Rogers. Compared to those tacky "space heroes", Ed Norton's "Captain Video", instructing him to don his "space helmet", didn't seem to make everybody's favorite sewer worker – "subterranean engineer", as he called

himself - the "space cadet" that Ralph Kramden called him on "The Honeymooners"!
Nonetheless, I am sure there will be more appealing Flash Gordons in the future. The
conquest of space still enchants people today. The closest I came to seeing a "muse" was
when my Dad took me to a ballgame to watch the great Stan Musial! He played for St. Louis
and so was a "Cardinal" – just like Father Marcus! If I did have books published, I'm sure Père
Lebrun would sell them in his bookstore - if he's still alive then! He has to be over ninety
years old! You remember that bookseller I told you about who owns a little shop on St.
Alexandre Street. You know how I admire longevity, how much I respect old age. I admit that
reading Seneca has influenced me. It's rather fitting that I was "introduced" to Seneca, as it
were, by Professor Thompson at Xavier University. He was Professor Emeritus, and no longer
teaching. But I got to meet with him on occasion for discussions about Latin literature. He
called these meetings *conversationes* – conversations, and *conversiones* – friendly
exchanges of opinion. I was reminded of high school debating – although the competitions
were far from being "friendly exchanges". My partner, Harris, and I did manage to win the
Regional Championship in our senior year. Just another one of my hidden talents! In fact, I
had quite the reputation for refutation, with my "no-buts-barred" rebuttals!

My coach called me the "Count of Confrontation"! I once mentioned that Professor Emeritus to
Pizza Pete, and he blurted out "Why did 'e merit you"?! Pete was a real card. There was this
time when I was had just started to work at Pizza Pete's - he asked me if I had served that
Chinese nurse Ada. "Ada who?" I asked, and he shot back, "Oh, so you did serve Ada Hu!".

You would have liked Pizza Pete, Jeremy, except for his racial comments. But Pete did
become more open-minded while I was dating Maxine. Speaking of an open mind, once when
Jeff banged his head getting a pizza out of the oven, Pete said that Jeff would be okay. He
said that any doctor could examine Jeff's head from ear to ear, and he'd find nothing there!
Pizza Pete was proud to claim he was "unique", but the way he pronounced the word it
sounded like "eunuch"! Good times! But back to Père Lebrun. People think that his store's
name – *La Petite Alexandrie* – comes from the street name, but it is actually named after the
famous Hellenistic library in Alexandria in Egypt. Père Lebrun often talked to me about the
Greeks and Romans. He stocked these very old Latin manuals. But his store window
displayed French-Canadian novels. I think I learned more about Quebec history and culture
from him than in my course at McGill. I used to sit and listen to him in his quaint little office,
where there was very little room for us because of the piles of books – mostly book
catalogues – scattered helter-skelter. He also told me the story of his life, which is fascinating,
but sad. He isn't really a priest – I think people call him "Père" because of his age and
wisdom. He had studied Greek and Latin in the *cours classique*, and had planned on

becoming a notary. He fell in love with a Jewish girl, and converted to Judaism in order to marry her. Because of this, he was rejected by his family. I guess they were even more biased than Maman Plouffe in the novel about that family. The name of that novel was *Au pied de la pente douce* - something about being in the lower town – "at the bottom of the slope, or hill". Sadly, Père Lebrun's wife died in childbirth, and they couldn't save the baby. Despondent, he sold the house that the couple had received from his well-to-do in-laws, and opened a bookstore. Père Lebrun became a kind of hermit, completely wrapped up in the reading and selling of books. I bought a few books from him that gave me a pertinent perspective – alliteration, Jeremy! – on Quebec society. One was *Le Libraire*, about a former teacher, Hervé Jodoin, who goes to work in a bookstore where he reflects on life. He is lazy, but loveable. He discovers a room where books "on the index", that is, censored, were stored. The room was called *capharnaüm*, which meant the room was a mess – a bit like Père Lebrun's office – or your bedroom that you once showed me! That word might remind you of the town in Galilee where Jesus would be followed by people who were all over the place! Did you know that only Jerusalem is mentioned more often than that town in the Gospels? In the English translation, titled *Not For Every Eye*, which I also read, the word is translated as *sanctum sanctorum* – "the holy of holies". I guess they couldn't find an English word for *capharnaüm,* but I loved the Latin. The religious expression suggests the censorship of books by the Catholic Church, which is the theme of the book. In fact, the author, Gérard Bessette, was himself censored because of his atheism, and had to leave Quebec to find a teaching position. He ended up in Pittsburgh! I wonder if he listened to oldies songs – although at that time they would be "newies"! Another book I read was *Salut Galarneau* by Jacques Godbout. It tells the story of François Galarneau, the "King of the Hot Dog" – "*Le Roi du Hot-Dog*". Galarneau is writing a novel about his reflections on life – which is what, in reality, Godbout himself is doing! As in so many stories, the main character is, in fact, the book's author! If a "seller of hot dogs" can write a novel, then yours truly has a chance! I eventually read *Les Belles-Soeurs* by Michel Tremblay.

He's one of the most popular writers in Quebec, maybe because he is the "apostle of *joual*"! It's kind of amazing that his story about a group of women pasting "Gold Stars" would leave its "stamp" – did you catch that, Jeremy – on the collective memory of generations. Of course, the "Sisters-in-law" of the title were not really all related, but were actually a common "sisterhood" of ordinary women looking for a bit of cheeriness in their otherwise humdrum "kitchen gatherings". In contrast, in those days the men would get together in the living-room – the parlour, as it was more often called. Two worlds apart, or so it seems! I enjoy listening to Père Lebrun speak about the "French fact" in Quebec, especially here in Montreal. I've heard about "La Grande Noirceur" under Premier Maurice Duplessis, and "Le Refus Global", which was a document signed by a group of painters and writers in 1948 seeking greater freedom for intellectuals from what they considered a stranglehold on artistic expression through the censorship by the Government and the Catholic Church. Père Lebrun pointed out that the current separatist movement was initiated by the intellectuals of Quebec society before becoming a grass-roots populist cause. I've heard you use the term "Frenchie", Jeremy, which seems innocent enough, but Père Lebrun explained the origin of some of the other terms I've heard used by English and French speakers in reference to one another. The word "bloke" is an ordinary word used by British folks in the same way you and I would use the word "guy".

However, when French-Canadians use it, "*bloke*" takes on a derogatory meaning. Even more offensive is *tête-carrée*, which Père Lebrun said came from the square-headed nails used in the wheels of horse-drawn carriages driven by the English. He may have been a little tongue-in-cheek, because I've see that term used in reference to the square-designed houses belonging to the English population. Either way, nobody likes to be called a "square"! And where would you find a tuque to fit a "square" head? The English, in turn, could be very offensive when they referred to French-Canadians as "frogs", a term that originated during the 18th century conflicts between France and England, and reflected the fondness of the French for frogs' legs! It gives me a different reading of the Aristophanes play! And I am a bit sensitive when it comes to that word, since I starred in my elementary school's play, *The Frog Prince*! I wish I had known the Robert Charlebois song that goes "I'm a frog, you're a frog – kiss me". The applause for my performance might have been louder! Likewise, here in Quebec, the habit of drinking Pepsi and eating pea soup led to the pejorative monikers "pea soups" and "peppers". Maybe you really are what you eat! I still think that this backlash against the Church is a case of throwing out the baby with the bath water – or should I say baptismal water?! By the way, I don't mind being called "Yankee", except when it's followed by "go home"!

\-   Your talents are not hidden at all, pal of mine – you're the original T.G.I.F.! Talented, gifted, incredible, fantastic! And not only on Fridays! But honestly, Hold On, your puns can be more taxing than the government! I should start calling you "Hold Off"! It's like you sometimes had bats in your belfry! I'd like to be able to take a page from Caesar, and proclaim, in victory over your word mastery "*Veni, vidi*, vaccinated!". But I do appreciate you're being so benevolent towards me, and your wishing well makes me wish I had a wishing well to repay your kindness! Did I come close to a clever "Holdenism"? I'm sure I have some hidden talents, but they're so well hidden that I can't find them! And I'm not like Robinson Crusoe - I get behind in my assignments, so my work is never done by "Friday"! Well, I guess I do have a talent for the odd joke!

-        Very odd indeed! So my love of music rubbing off on you took you to Woodstock!

-        Well, the music and the wild adventure of rubbing noses – and maybe something else! with hundreds of girls seemed very appealing! There were so many great groups and individual singers – it was like a who's who of your record collection, Holden! I can't name all the songs because we'd be here all night – and besides, I wouldn't be able to remember them all. Some groups I didn't even see – I got kinda distracted – if you know what I mean! The artists sang so many songs - I think The Who sang at least twenty! But I remember the Sha Na Na songs, because they basically did a medley of some of your favorite oldies you play all the time at your so-called Latin parties. The music was almost as bad as listening to Warren Thompson reciting Latin poetry from memory, although I think the girls preferred the music! Anyways, Warren's a royal pain! They sang "Come Go With Me", which I know makes you think of Claire, "Get a Job", which might make you think of me, "Silhouettes", "Teen Angel", "Wipe Out", "Book of Love", "Teenager in Love", "Little Darlin' ", "At the Hop", and your favorite, "Duke of Earl". Crosby, Stills and Nash sang "Marrakesh Express", and then were joined by Neil Young – he's from Toronto, and his father's a sports writer – talk about falling far, far from the tree! One of the songs they sang was "Mr. Soul". Richie Havens opened the Festival with "Freedom" and "From the Prison", and Jimi Hendrix closed the show with "Foxy Lady", "Purple Haze", and this crazy guitar solo where he played "The Star-Spangled Banner" with his mouth! In between I got to see Tim Hardin sing "If I were a Carpenter" – you probably like the Bobby Darin version. And Arlo Guthrie sang "Amazing Grace", while Joan Baez sang "Oh Happy Day" and "We Shall Overcome" – which made me think of you and Maxine – you ever hear from her? Joe Cocker sang "Feelin' Alright" and "With a Little Help from my Friends". The Who sang "Pinball Wizard" and "Summertime Blues". Jefferson Airplane - well mostly Grace Slick – sang "Somebody to Love" and "White Rabbit", Janis Joplin – loved her – sang "Piece of my Heart", which is what she got from me! The crowd was yelling "Pearl" while she sang. Santana sang "Evil Ways", John Sebastian of The Lovin' Spoonful sang "Darlin' Be Home Soon" and "I Had a Dream" – again, I thought of you! I tell you, Hold On, there were some great acts. The Grateful Dead sang "High Time", Canned Heat sang "Going up the Country", and one of your all-time favorite groups, Creedence Clearwater Revival, took the stage. CCR sang "Green River", "Proud Mary", and "Suzy Q", and maybe one other song! The Band sang "The Weight", but I was a few beers too gone to get the meaning of their song. And Sly and the Family Stone did this medley that I had seen them do on The Ed Sullivan Show – "Everyday People", "Listen to the Music" and "I Want to Take You Higher". But somehow it didn't seem the same – different crowd I guess. You know, Holden, people are saying that if you really lived the Sixties, you won't remember them! But I don't think I'll ever forget Woodstock! And they filmed it, so it's probably going to turn up on TV as a documentary in about fifty years! You'll be able to watch it – if you can tear yourself away from Vergil and Horace! See if you can spot me – I'm the only one with my shirt on – but the camera better not have panned down! Say, Hold On, you should make the scene if another hippie-like music festival rolls around. Just think, you are all for "peace and love" – well, at least peace! But if push comes to shove, I know you would rather make love, not war! I love – can't avoid that word, pal – but I really dig that name you gave yourself. A *"Paxifist Romanus"*- can't beat that! You are forever "The Latin Student"!

-       Wow! I'm glad you had a great time, Jeremy. Imagine – going straight to Woodstock – and coming back "straight"! No lifestyle changes for you! But, Jeremy, no long hair for me! I support local barbers – with a thought in mind for the great crooner Perry Como, who had been a barber. He went from cutting hair to cutting records! I don't know if I'll ever go to San Francisco, but I certainly wouldn't be "wearing flowers in my hair", as Scott McKenzie suggests in his song! But seriously, Jeremy, don't do drugs! You recall that time near the Forum, when someone offered us a joint, and you said we go into joints – we don't smoke them! Well, I remember this one joint we "went into", and my immediate reaction reminded me of The Animals song "We Gotta Get Out Of This Place"! I've always done my own thing – obviously, since I have continued to pursue clssical studies! Again, The Animals sum it up with their song "It's My Life"'! Say, there's Rachel – oh, but she's not coming over. She seems to be blushing.

-       That girl is Rachel! Holden, buddy, I'm sorry to rain on your parade, but she's a PTP! She is most definitely not your type!

-       What do you mean - PTP?

-       Holden, she's a part-time prostitute!

You can probably guess how I know. You see, you not only look good – you live good! But yours truly, J.J. – Jeremy the Jerk - can't be the clean-cut guy you not only look like, but actually are.

-       No, Jeremy, you're J.J. all right – "just Jeremy"! You've been a good friend! You've shown me around Montreal, even taking me to those taverns. I know how hard that was for you – drinking in a bar that doesn't admit women. Those places would be empty in Cincinnati, but here they're always full! When we did venture out to clubs, I recall you worrying that I would cramp your style, but I protested that I was very "stylistic" – like the singing group!

You finally had to admit I was a good "wing-man", since girls did accept to talk to you when I was along. You were always thinking you were Montreal's answer to James Bond – just because you have the same initials! But, J.B., every girl you asked to dance with became a "Dr.No"! I really used to get a kick out of you saying "eeny meeny miny mo" – which girl gets to dance with Jeremy the Pro? When the "lucky girl" invariably refused, I would taunt you with "I guess she was 'MEANY'! And I enjoyed visiting your hang-outs on the South Shore and meeting your family. Funny, you weren't as uptight as most older brothers would be when you introduced me to your sister! And didn't we have fun playing golf at the Country Club? But I don't get it. Rachel is always so pleasant with me, and shows an interest in my studies – she even asks questions about Roman religion. She said she was in a completely different programme at university, but there never seemed to be enough time to ask her about it. Even when we spent that day at La Ronde, we were having too much fun to talk about school!

- So she never did tell you what she studies – or even where she studies. I only met her the once, Holden, but she struck me as being one of those poor girls who is hard up for money. I bet she never talked to you about her family, or if she did, it was made up. Is her name really Rachel? I mean, is it a coincidence that we're in a greasy spoon on Rachel Street? And if that slimy-looking guy behind the counter is her boss, I can figure out how she got to work here .

"A job for a job" – non-negotiable! I feel sorry for her - I really do! Especially since she met you! Why – because you were her knight in shining armour! You are probably the only guy who ever treated her right – talked to her nicely, respected her for what she was, and not for what you could get from her. I think you're going to have to move on, Holden, not all the way to Toronto like me, but maybe find another place to eat. She's probably going to be too embarrassed to even look at you, much less serve you! To describe her in terms you'll understand, just think about that Frank Sinatra song – "The Lady is a Tramp"! Well, maybe in her case, not quite – but you know what I mean!

 Perhaps you're right, Jeremy. It's kind of sad, though. Well, all the best in Toronto! At least the NHL built the Hockey Hall of Fame in Toronto so people in that city would get to see the Stanley Cup!

Chapter 60

\-   Welcome to the world of Ovid, and let me point out that Ovid's world is not restricted to Ancient Rome, nor to the Age of Augustus! Publius Ovidius Naso wrote a great many works, but the theme of his works, with the exception of the *Fasti* and the works written in exile, is love. Perhaps Sergio Mendes & Brasil '66 describe Ovid's poetry best in their song "The Look of Love"! I realize, Maestro Hainsworth, that your "Ovidian ostentation" cries out for the Dusty Springfield version of that song! And, as those of you who have taken courses with me before well know, when you say love you say Manfredi! The *Fasti* are incomplete. That is to say, we have six books on the origins of the Roman calendar, but Ovid claims to have written twelve – one for each month. However, scholars are sometimes given to doubting what Ovid said about himself. The *Fasti* are though, like the *Metamorphoses* we will be reading, an excellent source of Roman – and Greek – mythology. Ovid wrote the *Amores*, a collection of love poems, the *Heroides,* a series of letters from mythological heroines to the lovers who had deserted them, the *Ars Amatoria*, a manual on the art of loving – although I must say, a bit tongue-in-cheek – pun intended, Mr. Hainsworth!, *De Medicamine Faciei*, advice on how to use make-up, *Remedia Amoris*, poems on how to resist love, Tristia, and *Epistulae ex Ponto*. The *Metamorphoses,* a Greek word meaning "transformations" - and this itself, a Latin word - consists of ten books of mythological stories. I trust that in addition to preparing the passage from book ten – the delightful tale of Pygmalion – you have all undertaken to read the entire poem in English. Mr. Hainsworth here has informed me that while in Rome this past summer, he had occasion to read all of Ovid's works in English. And what better place to read about love! I realize that this is your final year as an undergraduate at McGill, Mr. Hainsworth, even though you may feel at times like a graduate student, since most of your courses in the last two years have been with our M.A. students. Ovid claims to have been sent into exile by Augustus because of a poem – *carmen* - and an indiscretion – *error.* His "error" may have been an involvement with Julia, Augustus' daughter, or he may have been a threat to the wife of Augustus, Livia. Ovid endured rather bitterly his exile, but his attempts to return from Tomis, a remote and uncultured town on the Black Sea, were refused by Augustus, and later, by Tiberius. Think of being exiled to Siberia today by an Emperor we'll call "Siberius"! Ovid lived an exile much like Dante, and this was but one aspect of his influence on the genius behind *The Divine Comedy*! Sadly, Dante had to leave his beloved Florence, never to return. Otherwise, he would have been burned at the stake! A burning steak on the barbecue pales in comparison, doesn't it? And since Dante was a founder of the modern Italian language, all Italians can claim a debt to Ovid – as I certainly do.

Incidentally, his name – Naso - could suggest someone "nosy" enough to witness affairs of the Imperial family he should have avoided! When speaking of Ovid's influence down through the ages, one must mention of course Shakespeare's Midsummer Night's Dream and its stories from the *Metamorphoses*. But we may also think of T.S. Eliot, James Joyce, and the poet Hilda Doolittle – you may know her as H.D. To make specific mention of today's selection on Pygmalion, the play *Pygmalion* by George Bernard Shaw comes to mind. You may be more familiar with the delightful story of Professor Higgins and Eliza Doolittle - or is "Heliza" H.D.? – from Lerner and Loewe's Broadway musical, *My Fair Lady*, that starred Rex Harrison and Julie Andrews, and the movie version, also with Rex Harrison, but with the better-known Audrey Hepburn – who couldn't sing like Miss Andrews. And it was Julie Andrews who became a star with roles in *Mary Poppins* and *The Sound of Music*, even winning an Oscar! You may still hear on the radio the great songs from the *My Fair Lady* productions – "I could have danced all night", "On the street where you live", "Wouldn't it be lovely", "Get me to the church on time", "With a little bit of luck", and "I've grown accustomed to her face". And indeed our Pygmalion "grew accustomed" to the face of his statue Galatea! So, in this way, we owe a debt to Ovid for such marvelous contemporary theater and music! Mr. Hainsworth, now that I have excited you with all those musical references, would you please read, in their hexameters, lines 270 to 297 from book ten? You will then share with us your translation.

-       Yes, Professor Manfredi. Statues coming to life! I'm actually working on a short story on that theme.

Festa dies Veneris tota celeberrima Cypro

venerat, et pandis inductae, cornibus aurum

conciderant ictae nivea cervice iuvencae,

turaque fumabant, cum munere functus ad aras

constitit et timide "si, di, dare cuncta potestis,

sit coniunx, opto," non ausus "eburnea virgo"

dicere Pygmalion "similis mea" dixit "eburnae".

sensit, ut ipsa suis aderat Venus aurea festis,

vota quid illa velint et, amici numinis omen,

flamma ter accensa est apicemque per aera duxit.

ut rediit, simulacra suae petit ille puellae

incumbensque toro dedit oscula : visa tepere est;

admovet os iterum, manibus quoque pectora temptat :

temptatum mollescit ebur positoque rigore

subsidit digitis ceditque, ut Hymettia sole

cera remollescit tractataque pollice multas

flectitur in facies ipsoque fit utilis usu.

dum stupet et dubie gaudet fallique veretur,

rursus amans rursusque manu sua vota retractat.

corpus erat! saliunt temptatae pollice venae.

tum vero Paphius plenissima concipit heros

verba, quibus Veneri grates agat, oraque tandem

ore suo non falsa premit dataque oscula virgo

sensit et erubuit timidumque ad lumina lumen

attollens pariter cum caelo vidit amantem.

coniugio, quod fecit, adest dea, iamque coactis

cornibus in plenum noviens lunaribus orbem

illa Paphon genuit, de qua tenet insula nomen.

Some examples of literary devices are: alliteration – the "c" sound in *conciderant ictae nivea cervice iuvencae*; the *co*-syllable – assonance – in *coniugio… coactis cornibus* and "u" and "a"sounds – *rursus amans rursusque manu sua vota retractat*; litotes – that is, asserting something by denying its opposite, as when I proclaim that Professor Manfredi is no slouch when it comes to musical expertise! The example in our passage is *oraque tandem ore suo non falsa premit*. There are other literary figures as well in this passage, but here is my translation:

"The most celebrated festival day of Venus in the whole of Cyprus had come, and with their wide horns spreading gold, heifers had fallen, struck on their snowy neck, and incense was smoking, when, having performed the rites with his gift at the altar, Pygmalion stood and timidly said 'if you gods are able to give everything, I hope my wife may be, not daring to say the ivory maiden, like the ivory maiden'. As golden Venus herself was present at her own festival, she sensed what those prayers wanted, and, as a sign of her benevolent divine power, the flame burned three times, and led its point through the air. As he returned, he seeks the statue of his girl, and lying on the bed, gave it kisses: it appeared to grow warm; he moves his mouth to her again, and feels her breast with his hands: the touched ivory softens, and with the firmness laid aside, it gives way and yields to his fingers, just as Hymettian wax softens under the sun, handled by the thumb, it bends into many forms and becomes useful by use itself.

While he wonders and rejoices doubtfully and is afraid of being deceived, again and again he touches his wishes with his hand. It was a body! The touched veins jump under his thumb" – at this point, Professor Manfredi, I can't help thinking of the Rolling Stones song "Under my Thumb"! – "Then indeed the Paphian hero takes hold of the fullest words, with which he may give thanks to Venus, and finally presses the not false mouth with his own mouth, and the maiden perceived the given kisses, and blushed, and raising her timid eye to his eyes, she saw her lover at the same time as the sky. The goddess is present at the marriage which she made, and after the lunar horns had been gathered together in a full circle nine times" – which I know means after nine months, Professor – "that woman bore Paphos, from whom the island has its name."

- Well done, Mr. Hainsworth! Would you say that Pygmalion was a "Dream Lover"? I know you are a Bobby Darin fan! And since Ovid was banished to the shores of the Black Sea, why not reflect on the songs "Black is Black" by Los Bravos and "*La Mer*" – the sea – by Charles Trenet, sung in the English version – "Beyond the Sea" – by none other than Bobby Darin! So you are quite right to say that your Professor Manfredi is no slouch when it comes to music!

Chapter 61

\-   Mom, your last letter brought me great sadness! Imagine Tommy Nelson being killed in Vietnam! In memory of my departed soldier friend, I played the Pete Seeger song "Where Have All the Flowers Gone" on my guitar. As with all that great balladeer's songs, many artists recorded this one, but I have the Peter, Paul and Mary record. That trio's name sounds like they are straight from biblical times! Paul conveniently uses his middle name, since his first name is Noel. That's the French word for Christmas – hey, your birthday, Mom! Maybe he should use that name on their Christmas albums! Tommy always found a way to make me laugh.

We sometimes watched those music shows on TV – you know "Hullabaloo" and Murray the K. I know, Mom, you told me the K stood for Kaufman, and that he was known as the "fifth Beatle", because of his friendship with the Fab Four! Anyhow, it's what was happening in music back then! Tommy used to get excited watching the go-go girls dancing, and said they would fall for him if were dancing on the set. I always enjoyed telling him they would rather be "go…go…gone"! I found out that the band leader on Murray the K's show was Bobby Vinton! I guess after he kept asking to sing, he came out with the record "There I've Said It Again"! Here in Montreal I'm reminded of Tommy when I watch music shows like "A Go-Go '66" and "It's Happening". In fact, people here refer to events as "happenings". By the way, The Supremes recently released a song called "The Happening"! Father McNeil liked to tease Tommy, but I think he had a soft spot for his "Nelson". When Tommy had trouble seeing the board, Father McNeil had him sit up front. I think our wise old Jesuit also wanted to "keep an eye" on him! One day Tommy sat at the back of the class. When Father McNeil informed him he had to sit in front, Tommy protested, saying he now had contacts. Well, Father replied that he didn't care who Tommy knew, he still had to sit in the front! When I think of how Tommy felt the duty to go to Vietnam because his brother had died there for our country! In our Greek Tragedy course we have been reading the play *Seven Against Thebes* by Aeschylus, in which two brothers, Eteocles and Polyneices – the sons of Oedipus – kill each other. It reminds me of the Roman story of Romulus killing his brother Remus. Even the Bible was not spared a similar tragic murder with the story of Cain and Abel. But Tommy's brother didn't kill him, even though in a way, Tommy died because of his brother! We will be reading *Antigone*, by Sophocles, which tells of the burial of her brother Polyneices despite the King's proclamation forbidding it. I've seen the play *Antigone* and Euripides' *Medea* staged here in Montreal in English. The name of the theater is interesting – it's called the Centaur Theater – so I guess they won't shy away from presenting the Greek classics! The English theater-going public seem to enjoy stories about heroines. The French plays I've seen are about kings – *Oedipus the King* by Sophocles and the *Agamemnon* by Aeschylus. And did you know that Bobby Kennedy quoted Aeschylus' *Agamemnon* in the speech he delivered after Martin Luther King's assassination? He said "And even in our sleep, pain, which cannot forget, falls drop by drop, until in our own despair, against our will, comes wisdom through the awful grace of God". Like Dr. King, Robert Kennedy spoke against hatred and division. And – just like in a Greek tragedy – Bobby Kennedy was himself assassinated! Mom, even though those tragic events happened almost two years ago, my soul is suffering as if they had occurred yesterday! The last play we will study is the *Hippolytus* by Euripides. It's my favorite play, even though it ends with a horrific death. It's ironic that the name "Hippolytus" comes from the Greek word *hippos*, meaning "horse" and he is dragged to his death by horses! So Uncle Phil's full name – Philip – means "lover of horses". By the way, does he still bet on them at the racetrack in Kentucky? In fact, Professor Marcoux from Laval University in Quebec City is teaching the course in French. He is also staging the play here at McGill in the original Ancient Greek, and I have landed the role of Hippolytus, largely on the recommendation of Professor Wilkinson, who directs the Latin plays at McGill. She may have recognized "a bit of Hippolytus" in me, but I'm not going to tell you why! Or maybe I was chosen simply because my name starts with "H"! Professor Marcoux grew up in the city of Sherbrooke, and is really fun to talk to – of course he doesn't have Professor Jolivet's European accent! Under his guidance, I'm working on a paper about religious sentiment in the Hippolytus play! He also convinced me to join *SEGELQ – La société des études grecques et Latines du Québec*. It's the Quebec association of classicists, and Professor Marcoux is Vice-President. For some reason I kind of trust him more than America's Vice -President, Spiro Agnew. And I have a funny feeling about President Nixon as well! But maybe that's just me! It may sound strange, but the saddest news you sent me was that Vergil Cane had to be put down. If a dog is man's best friend, he would be my *alter ego*! That dog was such a free spirit! He never complained, and always seemed to enjoy the moment on our daily runs! You were always about *carpe diem*, my best buddy! Here at McGill, Professor Underhill passed away just before the beginning of term. He had been told by the University that he would have to retire. I think that it was the ultimate example of Socratic irony that our venerable Professor W died at age seventy, like Socrates, and like the philosopher, he taught until the very end. I think that the idea of being forbidden to teach the young of Athens is what drove Socrates to accept the fate of death, and I believe that the thought of no longer teaching snatched away our Greek Professor's will to live! In his honor, the students decided to name our seminar room the W Classics Room. I think the irony was lost on them, given that the room is next to the stairwell with the men's washroom, and given Professor Underhill's penchant for first letter abbreviations, that this room will probably eventually be called the W.C.! But some good news! I've been too busy to tell you up to now, but I participated in a radio contest last month on Motown songs. Sure, the guys back home at Pizza Pete's would have said "if it's Motown, for Holden it's no contest!" Anyhow, parts of three Motown songs were played every morning – fortunately before I left for class – and callers had to identify song title and artist. At the end of the week, the two people with the most correct answers would win a weekend trip to the Motown Tenth Anniversary Concert in Detroit! Well, without appearing hubristic – *hubris* is a Greek word, Mom, meaning overstepping the boundaries with the gods – I really believed all of Montreal would be competing for second place! True, I don't think Professor Manfredi or Professor Watson's wife knew about the contest! Well, I correctly identified every song and singer! And the station tried to stump listeners by sometimes playing three songs by the same group! This happened with songs by The Supremes – "Stop in the Name of Love", "Back in My Arms Again", and "I Hear a Symphony" – as well as "Tears of a Clown", "The Tracks of my Tears", and "Shop Around" by Smokey Robinson and the Miracles. The other songs I correctly identified were "Get Ready" by the Temptations, "Dancing in the Street" by Martha and the Vandellas, "Please Mr. Postman" by the Marvelettes – I think of that song every time I check my mailbox, hoping to find a letter from home! – "What Becomes of the Brokenhearted" by Jimmy Ruffin, whose brother David sings with The Temptations – now I'm just bragging! – "Shotgun" by Junior Walker and the All-Stars, "I Was Made to Love Her" by Stevie Wonder, "Ain't No Mountain High Enough", sung by Tammi Terrell and Marvin Gaye, and another Marvin Gaye song, "I Heard it through the Grapevine" – but I prefer the CCR version! The last song was "Reach Out, I'll Be There" by The Four Tops. Five Days, fifteen songs, and it was off to the concert for the winner of "Montreal's Motown Monopoly"! On the plane I sat next to Corina, the girl who came second with an amazing total of twelve songs and eight artists! She's German, and so I got to practice my sixteen months of German classes with her. She works for the Goethe Center, which is the German Cultural Center, so I promised I'd drop by when I got the chance. We both enjoyed the fantastic concert, and we got to go backstage. I shook hands with Levi Stubbs and Duke Fakir – my two favorite Tops! Couldn't "top" that! And Corina spent a couple of minutes talking to Marvin Gaye. The really good news, Mom, is that I'll be home soon for Christmas! Despite the political tensions here, Montreal is still a great place to be! I don't feel at all in exile like Ovid! Your loving son, Den.

Chapter 62

\-   Don't you just love it up here on Mount Royal, Holden? And you run up here or

cycle! Pretty good for a Latin student! Quite the *mens sana in corpore sano!*

\-   I definitely like being up here with you, Corina! You know, when I finally went to the
Goethe Center, I didn't know you were the Assistant Director – I mean you're only a year
older than I am! And Latin students are allowed to like physical activity – even those like me,
who spend a lot of time reading and writing! You're quite the jogger yourself, and the two
years of Latin you had at the *gymnasion* in Germany gives you a certain sophisticated
demeanour! Besides, culture is in your German blood! I really appreciated the drive we had
into the Eastern Townships, or *Estrie*, as they called it. I also heard it referred to as *Les
Cantons de l'est*. I guess it all depends on whether you're speaking to the English population
or the French people. I was happy to visit Sherbrooke, where Professor Marcoux grew up. I
can see where he gets his friendly nature. And the air is so pure out there! You know you
really impressed me, Corina, when you did some horseback riding in that little town of
Bromont. You said that in Germany you fell off horses a few times, but you looked really
elegant on the horse this time. I've never fallen off a horse, but then I've never been on one! I
felt embarrassed when you said "easy there, handsome". I didn't realize you were talking to
the horse, and not me! Wishful thinking, I guess! As they say, beauty is in the eye of the
beholder, and I once read a book – *Black Beauty*, where "Beauty" was a horse! And I don't
even want to think about *Beauty and the Beast* – because naturally yours truly would be the
"beast"! The sign said *Equitation*. Even without the picture of the horse, I would have figured
out that it had something to do with horses because of the Latin word *equus*, meaning horse.
But I learned in my French Literature and Culture course that the plebeian word for horse,
caballus, gave us the French word *cheval,* from which came the word for the "street-French"
dialect, j*oual.* So speaking "like a horse", - and not elegantly like Horace! After all, horses are
found on streets, and not in theaters or university lecture halls! By the way, I hear somebody
is writing a play to be called *Equus.* It will be a gruesome tale about a young man who blinds
horses! So much sadder than simply putting "blinders" on them!

\-   You have such a command of word play, Holden! I was happy to drive out into the
country with you! And I guess it came as no surprise that I drive a Volkswagen – the "people's
car"! You Americans would call it a car for "plain folks"! One thing is puzzling me.

Whenever we are rushing together downtown in my car, we always get green lights! I'm looking forward to driving with you to Cincinnati at Christmas. I know it's a city with a certain German heritage. Speaking of which, your German is coming along just fine! You've brought your guitar today – are you going to play for me?

-        Well, thanks to that radio contest I know you like music – and not just Bach, Mozart, and Beethoven! There's a little of Chuck Berry's "Roll over Beethoven" in you, Corina! I'll let you in on a little secret. Whenever I see you stressed over time while we are in traffic, I say a little prayer to the Blessed Virgin to guide us to green lights, because I know She would never ever get caught in a red-light district! I guess it's a bit like Dionne Warwick singing "I Say A Little Prayer For You"! You're a bit of a mystery too, like that German woman, whose picture was on a table in one of the back rooms in the Goethe Center. I didn't get a chance to read the caption, which looked like it was put together from newspaper articles.

- That was Gerda Munsinger. She was an East German call-girl who dazzled some high-ranking Canadian government ministers in the late fifties and early sixties, and caused the fall of the Conservative government. She remained a mystery, as she seemed to disappear from the public view. It had been feared that she was privy to state secrets, and was spying for the Soviets. This was never proven, however. You who appreciate clever play on words, Holden, will smile when you hear that this episode in Canadian history is sometimes referred to as the "Mudslinger Affair"! You told me that you were reading Tacitus in one of your Latin courses. I believe you are reading selections from the *Annals* and the *Histories*, along with sections of Livy's "History of Rome". I wish my Latin had been at a level to allow me to read the works of Tacitus. I would have enjoyed reading his *Germania*, an essay on the history and geography of *Germania*. I do not say Germany, since the territory of *Germania* in Roman imperial times was larger than the Germany of today. However, his treatise is all about my origins!

- Yes, I'm taking that course with Professor Jolivet, who is teaching in English this time. My other Latin course is on the poet Ovid, who sometimes addresses his beloved, a girl named Corinna! Unlike other elegiac poets such as Tibullus and Propertius, and of course, Catullus, who used pseudonyms that concealed the actual names of their objects of affection, Ovid may be naming Corinna merely to bring his poetry to life, much like one of his characters, the craftsman Pygmalion, brought his statue to life through his love for her. After all, this name could be a pun on the Greek word for girl, *Kore*. So your name means "girl". Ray Peterson's song "Corinna, Corinna" could be about you! And so could all those "girl" songs, like "Go Away Little Girl", so popular it was sung by Steve Lawrence, The Happenings, and Bobby Vee, and "Young Girl" by Gary Puckett and the Union Gap. But, honestly, Corina, the song that really describes you is "Oh Pretty Woman", by Roy Orbison. He happens to be one of my all-time favorite singers – not just because of his enchanting voice, but because he often sings songs about dreams. Songs like "In Dreams I Walk With you", "Beautiful Dream", "Big as I Can Dream", "Daydream", "Dream You", "Dream Baby", and, as The Everly Brothers sang – "All I have to do is dream"! One message that the Pygmalion story in Ovid gives us is that dreams can come true. Walt Disney's Jiminy Cricket told Pinocchio as much when he said that dreams can come true, when you wish upon a star! And aren't the stars bright tonight up here, Corina? By the way, did you know that the name Jiminy Cricket was originally a euphemism for Jesus Christ – same initials - J.C. – I know those initials are often used to shorten the name Jean-Claude here, but Jean-Claude Cricket somehow doesn't sound right! I guess that's why my old boss Pizza Pete was always screaming Jiminy Cricket when he was mad at us! But if that little cricket was Pinocchio's conscience, then the name sure makes sense!

- I don't know if you're making sense, you dreamer! But let me tell you about some German songs you may have heard! I don't know if you saw the notice at the Goethe Center about the film *Stadt ohne Mitleid*. It means "Town Without Pity", and features the title song by Gene Pitney. The story is sad – about four American soldiers – you call them G.I.'s – I think it means General Infantry – who are on trial for raping a girl. My father used to joke that the best general in the American Army was the General Infantry. My uncle Hans always claimed the two best American generals were General Motors and General Electric! However, these soldiers were convicted, in spite of a good defense lawyer played by Kirk Douglas. I know you like that actor because he was Spartacus – remember in the film when he said "I am Spartacus". But then everybody else said the same thing! I guess they all wanted top billing! You have no doubt heard of *The Three-Penny Opera* by Bertolt Brecht. Professor Goethe has probably mentioned it in your German course. A feature song in that production is *Die Moritat von Mackie Messer*, or, in English, "The Ballad of Mack the Knife". And you probably enjoy listening to Bobby Darin sing "Mack the Knife"! One of the characters mentioned in the song – Lotte Lenya - was the wife of Bertolt Brecht! And if I could sing, Holden, I would sing the Wayne Newton song, *Danke Schoen* – "thank you", Holden, for giving me such sweet moments! But you can sing – and you have your guitar!

- Gee, Corina, you're pretty and you're funny! My friend Jeremy used to say that about me – that I was pretty funny! He always left out the word "and"! You call me a dreamer. Well, The Harptones sang "Life is but a Dream"! I read somewhere that John Lennon is writing a song with the title "You may say I'm a dreamer", so I guess I'm not the only one! His song will probably be released on record one day. I did want to sing a few folk ballads – "Turn, Turn, Turn", that Pete Seeger song based on verses from Ecclesiastes, and which I love hearing

The Byrds sing – the group, Corina, not those pretty little flying creatures – although band member Roger McGuinn was often "flying high" with his buddies on the West Coast! , "Blowin' in the Wind", the Bob Dylan ballad that I first heard on the Ed Sullivan Show when the Chad Mitchell Trio sang it, and that beautiful song by The Youngbloods – "Get Together". I'm also going to sing "Abraham, Martin, and John", which includes the lyric "have you seen my old friend Bobby", a tribute song by Dion to Abraham Lincoln, Martin Luther King, John F. Kennedy, and Bobby Kennedy - four brave men who gave their lives to help make and keep America great! And I've been composing my own version of Pete Seeger's "If I had a Hammer". Everybody sings it, but nobody sings it better than Trini Lopez! However, you won't see me singing in coffee houses on the West Coast or in Greenwich Village, or on college campuses across America – you need real talent for those performances! Well, here goes!

 "If I had a dollar,

I'd spend it in the morning

I'd spend it in the evening

All over this town!

It's a dollar for breakfast

Two eggs 'cause I need 'em!

One coin for love from the madams and the misters…"

It still needs work – I haven't "hammered" it all out yet! I guess we should be heading back,

Corina. I found my thrill… on Mount Royal Hill…!

Chapter 63

\-   I'm glad you have all had a certain facility in reading Livy's account of the war against Hannibal. We will be forging ahead with perhaps the greatest historian of all time – certainly, in my opinion, the best of the Roman historians-Tacitus. But his Latin, from the Silver Age of Latin Literature, will be more challenging! Today's passage from the *Annals* is about a son only a mother could love and the only mother a son could hate! We are speaking of course of Nero's attempt to assassinate his mother, Agrippina. Mr. Hainsworth, you will read the passage from *Annals* XIV, 5, and translate please.

\-   *Noctem sideribus illustrem et placido mari quietem quasi convincendum ad scelus di praebuere. nec multum erat progressa navis, duobus e numero familiarium Agrippinam comitantibus, ex quis Crepereius Gallus haud procul gubernaculis adstabat, Acerronia super pedes cubitantis reclinis paenitentiam fiii et reciperatam matris gratiam per gaudium memorabat, cum dato signo ruere tectum loci multo plumbo grave, pressusque Crepereius et statim exanimatus est. Agrippina et Acerronia eminentibus lecti parietibus ac forte validioribus, quam ut oneri cederent, protectae sunt. nec dissolutio navigii sequebatur, turbatis omnibus et quod plerique ignari etiam conscios impediebant. visum dehinc remigibus unum in latus inclinare atque ita navem submergere: sed neque ipsis promptus in rem subitam consensus, etalii contra nitentes dedere facultatem lenioris in mare iactus. verum Acerronia, imprudentia dum se Agrippinam esse subveniretur matri principis clamitat, contis et remis et quae fors obtulerat navalibus telis conficitur : Agrippina silens eoque minus agnita (unum tamen vulnus umero excepit) nando, deinde Lucrinum occursu lenunculorum in lacum vecta villae suae infertur.*

\-   "The gods provided a quiet night, lit by stars and a calm sea, as if to reveal the crime. The ship had not set out too far, while two from the number of her friends were accompanying Agrippina, one of whom, Crepereius Gallus, was standing not far from the rudder, and Acerronia, leaning over the feet of Agrippina as she lay there, recounting with joy the remorse of her son and the recovered favour of the mother, when, after a signal had been given, the roof fell to the ground under a good deal of heavy lead, and, being crushed, Crepereius died immediately. Agrippina and Acerronia were protected by the projecting sides of the couch, which fortunately were too strong to give way to the weight. Nor did a breaking up of the ship follow, and, with everyone in confusion, the many who were ignorant of this plot hampered those who knew about it. It seemed like a good idea to the rowers to lean towards one side, and in this way submerge the ship: but there was no ready consensus among them for this sudden plan, and others, leaning in the opposite direction, provided an opportunity for a gentler slide into the sea. Indeed, Acerronia, in her imprudence, while she calls out that she was Agrippina in order that aid be brought to the mother of the Emperor, was killed by poles and oars and whatever naval gear chance had provided: Agrippina, remaining silent, and for that reason, not recognized (nevertheless she received a wound in her shoulder), by swimming and an encounter with some fishing-boats, and after being carried to the Lucrine lake, was brought to her villa."

-        Thank you, Mr. Hainsworth! Five of you are finishing your Master's programme this year, and so must schedule an appointment with Professor Watson to discuss your plans for next year. As you know, we do not presently have a doctoral programme here at McGill, but some professors, like Dr.Watson, do collaborate in supervising PhD candidates in other universities. So those of you continuing on to the doctorate must apply elsewhere. In any event, there is much merit in doing graduate studies in more than one university. Mr. Hainsworth, may I have a word? Unlike the others, you will only be starting a Master's programme. You may have been considering going back to the U.S. for graduate studies. And I know how attractive those Semple grants are at the University of Cincinnati. But Odysseus was away from home for ten years, and Aeneas never did go back home – true he no longer had one to go back to! The point is, your Professors would love to have you stay and do an M.A. here at McGill. You are by far the most promising student we have had in my years in the Department, and you are able to take the courses we offer in French! *Je prêche pour ma paroisse*, as Professor Manfredi would say! But you do have your advanced standing in course selection, which will give you some flexibility in your choices. Above all, given your interest in Roman religion, why not take advantage of the expertise of Professor Watson in this field? To again quote my colleague Manfredi *carpe diem*! So think about it, and let our Department Chair know your decision before he falls off it!

Chapter 64

-        Good-day, Mr. Hainsworth! I am so pleased you will be staying with us for another two years. Was it Professor Jolivet's attempt at humour with his remark about my falling off my chair that convinced you! Well, I actually did fall off my chair once, while interviewing Miss Templeton for the position of Department secretary. I think the poor girl was more embarrassed than I was! No wonder I haven't been named to a "Chair" at McGill! But you certainly can aspire to the prestige of being appointed to one of those endowed positions some day! Miss Templeton was by far the best qualified candidate, so the only requirement I imposed on her before she was hired was that she not tell Jack Peters how I "fell for her"! I didn't want him making it his favorite anecdote at AIA/APA meetings! And speaking of Professor Peters, now that you will be a legitimate attendee at our monthly Department tea socials for staff and grad students, our unflappable Professor of Archaeology will continue to grace us with his presence, because for some reason, you are the only person he talks to at these gatherings. Could be the Cincinnati connection, or the fact that he saved you from being a farmer in Greece for the rest of your life, although I'm sure he has exaggerated the details of that story! I am truly delighted to be your M.A. thesis director. Your intention to explore the Dionysus-Liber/Bacchus connection is admirable, especially since I did not delve in great detail into that aspect of Greco- Roman religion in my books. You know my reputation for organizing and planning - not only Department budgets and Faculty teaching assignments – but also graduate student course loads! So this is what your programme will look like – it is based in part on discussions we have had in the past. First of all, I am happy to offer you the position of teaching assistant for the new Roman Religion course we will introduce next September. And to prepare this course, I am "prepared" to bring you to Cambridge this summer. Did you notice my anaphoric repetition?

Maybe you were not "prepared" for it! You see, even I will stoop to faint attempts at humour to keep you here! While in England, we will spend some time at Oxford and at the British Museum.

Cambridge is offering a summer course on "Valerius Maximus and Roman Religion", which you will certainly want to take. Oh, and you will be staying with Mrs. Watson and myself, as you did four years ago, but this time for a slightly longer period. She is delighted you will be joining us, and keeps referring to a counter-British Invasion – whatever that means. It may have something to do with the passion for music that you both share, but beyond the Beatles and the Rolling Stones, I'm afraid that I am still at the "undergraduate level" in musical knowledge! My dear wife - God bless her – did suggest, no doubt tongue-in-cheek, that prior to beginning Department meetings, I play a song by a group called The Limeliters entitled "There's a Meetin' Here Tonight". Like myself, Mr. Hainsworth, you've probably never heard of that group.

In addition to M.A. Thesis supervision, we will work together in a Latin Prose Composition Tutorial. You see, Mr. Hainsworth, I do indeed read requests made by students in the Department suggestion box. And although the suggestions are unsigned, I suspected that this particular one came from you. The other anonymous request whose author I was able to identify was the one for beer at our tea socials! And I spoke to a certain professor about that!

You will be enrolled in two Latin courses – "The Tragedies of Seneca" and "Roman Satire: Juvenal and Martial". You will have a Greek reading course on Plato and Aristotle – you may be the only student in this course! You have indicated an interest in studying Modern Greek, and Professor Mavroidakis is eager to have you join the group. This course still counts as a Classics course, and so you may enroll in one other course outside the Department. After a couple of summers in Italy, you may want to study that language formally, and earn what is commonly called in the jargon of some of our undergraduates "easy credits"! If you are continuing in Modern Greek during your second year, Professor Mavroidakis will want to send you on a scholarship to the Balkan Institute in Thessaloniki during the summer following your first year in the Master's programme. And speaking of scholarships, the glowing letters of recommendation by Professors Manfredi and Jolivet are sure to earn you a McGill University Graduate Scholarship. As well, your Parker Endowment is renewable! Maybe you should consider moving to an apartment on Park Avenue! We don't have a "Parker" Avenue! Just kidding! One of the personal traits I respect about you is your humility – even though your fellow students refer to you as "THE Latin Student"! I also admire your sense of humour, and yes, your vast knowledge of music. Anyone who can go head to head with Professor Manfredi certainly has my unconditional admiration! In your second year, you will probably want to continue with Italian – usually two years of study in these modern languages gives a solid base of understanding and communication, as was the case with German. Your Greek course will be Herodotus and Thucydides, and your two Latin courses in the programme will be the prose works of Seneca and the *De rerum natura* of Lucretius. So Stoics and Epicureans will go head to head! It works out well that you will have a second course on Seneca, since you have selected him as your major author. Professor Jolivet, who will be teaching the course, has a soft spot for Nero's tutor as well! All that sounds a little overwhelming, I'm sure, but *carpe diem!*

- 	Overwhelming, yes, but I am not, as Little Anthony and The Imperials sing, "Going Out of My Mind"! Actually, I have heard of The Limeliters. As a matter of fact, I was intrigued to hear them sing a song recorded in 1964 by Phil Ochs called "The Power and The Glory". That's the name of the Graham Greene novel I read a few years ago. The song is not based on the story in the book, but, in a sense they are connected, since they both praise God's glory – the novel's title refers to the kingdom of God in the Doxology prayer, and the song praises God's glory in the splendid beauty of nature! The title of Canadian singer Robert Goulet's song "Sunrise, Sunset" likewise suggests praise for the natural wonders of God's universe! By the way, thanks to Claire Talbot, my favorite drink is spruce beer – my tribute to nature!

Chapter 65

\-   So how was your summer in England, Holden? Did you meet the Queen? Did you get to see the Beatles in the flesh? Stop looking at me that way! You know what I mean – as opposed to seeing them only on television.

\-   I'm only teasing you, Corina! No, I didn't see the Beatles – except on some posters. But thanks to Mrs. Watson, I did have a memorable musical experience – even if it wasn't exactly a magical mystery tour! She had procured two tickets to a concert that featured some of the biggest names in British pop music. Prince Charles was in attendance – along with some well-dressed bodyguards! Wayne Fontana sang "Groovy Kind of Love", Peter and Gordon sang "A World Without Love", Petula Clark belted out "My Love", followed by The Tremeloes with "Here Comes my Baby". Then Manfred Mann – really Paul Jones – sang "Do Wah Diddy".

Gerry and the Pacemakers sang "Ferry Cross the Mersey", and Lulu sang "To Sir With Love" – I've seen the movie. Then my favorite British singer took the stage. The one and only Dusty Springfield sang two songs – "Son of a Preacher Man" and "You Don't Have To Say You Love Me". I was already in British heaven when the final act came on stage – Procol Harum singing "A Whiter Shade of Pale"! Mrs. Watson had been eager to find out where the Rolling Stones were staying, since they were in town, but she was unsuccessful. I mentioned to her that it was a pity that Professor Peters hadn't come to England, since as an archaeologist, he would have left no "stone"unturned in the search! She laughed, but wondered if by "stone" I meant Mick Jagger! We have a lot in common – humour, music, and an admiration for Professor Watson! So it wasn't all work and no play! But I spent a great deal of time in the Cambridge University libraries looking up literary texts in Latin on the subject of Roman religion. I discovered that the British have a particular sense of humour, despite the dour image they present. And many Brits have a more than passing grasp of Latin. I was about to enter one of those quaint British pubs – this one was called "All's Well When Ale's Well"! – when a fellow asked If I could lend him a "quid". A "what" I asked him, and he replied "that's right – one will do"! Pursuing the Latin exchange, and wanting to ascertain his reason for needing money, I rejoined with *cur*. He took this "why" as an insult, shouting that he was no scoundrel, no lowly cur of a dog! He stormed off muttering *quid nunc*, and I never learned if he had insisted on receiving the "*quid*" right away, or he was calling me nosy – as in "what now", Corina! So I DOUBT they are all as "doughty" as they make out! I also spent some time at Oxford musing over material that touched on the Roman god Liber. There I had a mind-blowing experience. While I was reading some Valerius Maximus for my Cambridge course, the distinguished

Regius Professor of Greek, Hugh Lloyd-Jones, approached me, welcomed me to the hallowed grounds of Oxford, and said "Young man, I believe we have met – in the United States". Corina, I attended his lecture in Cincinnati five years ago! And yes, I had asked him a question from the audience. But for him to recognize and remember me - was it some kind of divine intervention? Professor Lloyd-Jones has written a book about Zeus! My visit to the British Museum – thanks to Professor Watson, I had full access - inspired me to finish a short story I had been working on. I actually wrote it in French, but will probably translate it into English. It's called "*Les statues grecques*". Maybe you can translate it into German one day! It's about an old teacher who takes his students on an outing to the Montreal Museum of Fine Arts to see an exhibition of Greek statues. Long story short - no pun intended! – the statues seem to come to life, but at the end of the story, we're not quite sure. I think Professor Manfredi will enjoy reading it, since it's partly inspired by Ovid's story of Pygmalion. I had been toying with an idea for some time, but when I sat down to begin writing, the words started to flow – some readers might say "overflow"! – but I just went with the flow!

Interestingly enough, water does begin to flow at one point in the story! By the way, Valerius Maximus seemed more interested in examining morality in Rome, and the way people behaved in accordance with religious precepts, rather than in the systematic organization of Roman religion *per se*. But what about you, Corina? How have you been? Did you find it lonely on Mount Royal without me this summer? And what's new with Goethe – the Cultural Center, not my Professor!

-       I'm glad you got to profit from your time in England, Holden. The Museum, Cambridge, Oxford, a great concert, and a professor with a fantastic memory! But then you're not so easy to forget, as I'm sure I'll soon find out. You see, Holden, I'm returning to Germany, to Munich, to be exact. I have accepted a position as Coordinator of all Goethe Center activities throughout Bavaria. I have grown to love Montreal, and the people here - some more than others, Holden! But my parents are still in Germany, and they are not getting any younger.

I wrestled with this decision for a while, but ultimately it is a professional opportunity that is difficult to turn down. I think I have feelings for you, and great admiration for "my Latin student", who so much epitomizes *mens sana in corpore sano*, and who has a mind for musical appreciation! But it's *carpe diem* for me now, as I'm sure it was for you when you left Cincinnati four years ago. I'll be leaving next week, and be in Munich in time for the famous Oktoberfest. And my first *prosit* will be for you, Holden!

-       Corina, Corina! In dreams, I'll think of you!

Chapter 66

-    Hi Mom, hope this letter finds you all preparing for my visit home next month at Christmas. It was so nice that you all made it to Montreal last June for my graduation. And thank you for being so understanding about my decision to stay on at McGill for my Master's degree. I think back on those times when all four of us used to watch "Father Knows Best" on TV. Although Jim Anderson was the ideal father, married to the ideal wife and mother, you and Dad always topped them, since you two were the real deal – not reading from a TV script!

Moreover you were one Mom who "knows Father best"! That nice German girl you met has gone back to Germany. She asked me to say good-by to my folks, but I had to say good-by to her Volks! Now I'm back to getting around by BMW! Before everybody back home gets too excited, I mean "Bus, Metro, Walk"! As you can see, I'm a little more stoical when girls I have feelings for leave. It must be all the Seneca I'm reading. I was so sorry to hear that Pizza Pete had died.

When you said his widow was selling Pizza Pete's, I was a little upset. But then I realized the place could never be the same without Pete. He did so much for me, and was a real character!

Professor Peters would have gotten on well with him. How about that – they shared a name – Pete and Peters! You know, Mom, Montreal isn't so nice a place to be as it was when you visited last summer. Last month, all Hades broke loose! A group of terrorists kidnapped a British diplomat named James Cross. He was eventually freed, but another group kidnapped the Labor Minister, Pierre Laporte, and killed him! So another "Pete" died! The Prime Minister of Canada – a very bilingual and very flamboyant leader – whose name is also Pierre – Pierre Trudeau – sent in the Army, and the soldiers patrolled Montreal, arresting hundreds of people, so-called political dissidents. It reminded me of the Berrigan brothers, you know the priests who led the anti-Vietnam protests with the Catonsville Nine and the Harrisburg Seven. Except Vietnam wasn't in America, but this War Measures Act was martial law – you know, martial as in Mars, the Roman god of war! – here on Canadian soil! It was like a civil war was breaking out on account of language! They're calling it the October Crisis, but, honestly, it's more than that.

Many French-speaking people feel they are being treated like second-class citizens by the English-speaking minority. It's a bit like the racial problems back home. But there's no Martin Luther King here leading the cause of social justice for the down-trodden. Some groups want

227

a political solution, while others prone violence. Even the Prime Minister – whose first name means "stone" – was pelted with stones at a St-Jean Baptist parade! So some of those "gentle and easy-going folks", as you call them, Mom, can get nasty! It's the "two solitudes" that Hugh MacLennan wrote about. If you're bilingual, and comfortable with the two cultures, as one of the characters in his novel was, you don't feel the *angst* of the less-privileged group. I'm comfortable with both languages, and I appreciate the French-Canadian culture, like the music and films and plays much more than my McGill classmates do. And I'm from America, where the language and culture of the majority trumps all others – *e pluribus unum*! But this resentment is relegated to one part of the country – Quebec. So, if you speak of the whole country, the majority language is English. But the French-speaking population claims founders' rights – they were here before the British! There is now a separatist movement that wants Quebec to leave Canada. There is a political party that wants to make Quebec independent. It's called the *Parti Québécois*, and its leader is pretty charismatic as far as politicians go. His name is René Lévesque. Kind of ironic that his name means "bishop", and he has the confidence of the Quebec "flock", rather than the actual Church bishops! At least he's not egotistical like the Jean Lévesque in the novel *Bonheur d'occasion*! It's a bit like if California wanted to separate from America because a lot of people speak Spanish as their first language. I recently came across a poem by Leonard Cohen called "French and English". Cohen is a Montreal poet and singer who became famous and then sort of disappeared. He had actually been a student at McGill. I don't think we have heard the last of him, though. He has the kind of talent that is timeless, and he's sure to return to the international scene. Well, that poem of his inspired me to write a poem on the same theme – that language should not be an obstacle to social harmony – as a tribute to him. Here it is, Mom. It's called "Language".

I think you are clever to speak French.

It reminds me of Latin.

French is a sacred language –

it helps you find God.

When you eat in French you dine with class.

It's very romantic of you to speak French.

I can feel your sensitivity and your sensuality.

When you speak French

I am aroused by your emotions.

I listen and I understand that *je ne sais quoi*!

I think you are clever to speak English.

You are able to tell me everything I want to know.

No subject is taboo for you.

After all, everybody speaks your language.

I know you like to sound intelligent.

But when you sing in English,

You speak so sweetly!

I hear you speak in English and I feel strong.

When you speak English, I listen - and I think I know you.

French invented English, and English invented French.

Vive la différence!

I don't dream with you in English.

I don't dream with you in French.

I make love to you –

but not in French and not in English!

I'm happy with you!

But I'm not happy in English and I'm not happy in French.

I read to you in English the poetry of Leonard Cohen,

And you read his poems back to me in French!

I think I'd like to write more poems, Mom, and maybe sing them while strumming my guitar. You know the Latin word *carmen* means both poem and song. So if everybody here sang in both English and French they would be able to live in perfect "carmeny"! I'll never change, Mom! But I think that people are disgruntled for other reasons as well. The Montreal Canadiens didn't make the play-offs last year – for Montreal and the whole province of Quebec that's tantamount to a national disaster! But I think they'll bounce back this year – probably even win the Stanley Cup. There are rumours that this will be Jean Béliveau's last year, and he's such a classy guy, he's sure to go out on a winning note! And speaking of winning, Dad was sure glad to see the Reds beat the Montreal Expos went we went to the game at Jarry Park during your visit last June. So the people here are missing *circenses*, the Roman "circuses" – chariot races and gladiator contests – that prevented social unrest in ancient Rome. They need their Stanley Cup parade! As for the *panem*, I think many people have lost their "spiritual bread". I mean, they don't go to church anymore. Especially young people my age. For sure, there's never been anything like the Campus Crusade we see on university campuses back home. Remember when in elementary school Sister Agnes had me join the Crusaders? We had prayer meetings, but I especially liked wearing the blue beret and red kerchief "uniform". And of course the Crusader badge! And then at St. Xavier High we had "Christ's Crusaders"! Right now, though, I feel more like a Crusader for Classics! But most people here are Catholics like us, Mom. They just need something – or someone – charismatic to bring a renewed practice into their lives! I guess I spend time reflecting on this because of my research on ancient Roman religion - only now it's Roman Catholicism! I still hear lots of people – including youngsters – using terms from Catholic religion, including sacraments and the Mass, but not as terms of devotion, but rather as cuss words! It just goes to show you the power and influence of language! But not everything is doom and gloom here, Mom. Montreal is still a vibrant city. Mount Royal – you know that name is just another version of Montreal! – is still a beautiful spot! I'm certainly not BORED, even if I spend most of my time studying Latin, and reading, and listening to my collection of oldies records, Dad! True, not everyone is on BOARD with me! On the other hand, while we were in England last summer, Professor Watson's wife started calling me "Mr. Oldies"! Can't use the Greek *men...ge* here, since I didn't start with "on the one hand"! Good old Tommy Nelson – wish he were still here - called me that, but not always in such a polite way. Mrs. Watson got me watching this British TV soap called "Coronation Street". The show celebrated its tenth anniversary last year, but it's so popular, I can see it going on for another fifty years – maybe forever! Most of the action takes place in an English pub called The Rover's Return. I just love the different British accents, and my favorite character is Ken Barlow, a young teacher. With his intellectual demeanour, he doesn't seem to fit in with the "plebeian publicans" – how's that for Latin alliteration, Feeb? Yet, he's the only character who has been there since the first show, and I see him just getting older as the show continues! Watching the show I learned the expression "to take the mick", which means to tease someone. I wish I had known that expression when I was working with Mickey at Pizza Pete's! One of my most enjoyable moments here up north in Quebec is watching the geese fly south for the winter – something I myself usually do at Christmas as well – but in a plane (otherwise, my arms would be very tired)! Their honking in unison – like the honking that saved Rome from the attacking Gauls! – and their flight in V-formation is magnificent to watch! And they follow the one leader – they have their own Cicero, or Julius Caesar or Augustus Caesar! Watching them always reminds me of old Didace Beauchemin in my favorite Quebec novel, *Le Survenant*, as he prepares to go hunting. In fact, "Beauchemin" means "beautiful road", a bit like the main character who has this *Wanderlust* – now I'm thinking of Corina! – and must continuously "hit the road"! He's like Jack Kerouac in his book *On the Road*, which I recently read. That Ray Charles song that you and Dad like – "Hit the Road, Jack" – actually pays tribute to him - no reference to him, though, in the Dion song "I'm a Wanderer"! I know Dad enjoys reading the accounts of the Beat Generation members like Allen Ginsberg and Neal Cassady. I guess the beatniks were kind of romantic hippies. Pizza Pete created his own "Beat Generation" when he was always telling the same group of high school truants to "beat it"! He called them "deadbeats"! Although I find some attraction to the free-spirited and artistic Beatnik lifestyle, I'm too much of a conservative "establishment man" to adopt a life outside the mainstream. I've got too much Cicero and Seneca in me! I mean, sometimes it would be great to be a wild stallion, but I see myself as a Clydesdale pulling the Budweiser beer wagon! But then again – a handsome horse with all that beer – life could be worse - right, Dad? After seeing the movie *Ben Hur*, I certainly wouldn't want to be one of the horses pulling the chariots in the Circus Maximus in Ancient Rome! Yet I could have been a participant in the Roman games – the *ludi Romani*! It's not such a "ludicrous" idea – I have the sports background for the *ludi circenses* and the theatrical experience for the *ludi scenici*! As well, I have the necessary "religious fervor", inasmuch as these games were first and foremost religious festivals. Dad, you could even have come as a spectator in your underwear, since "boxers" were quite prominent at the games, as were yours when you sat on the sofa Saturday nights watching T.V.! Admit it, dear parents – I'm too good! All that talk about roads reminds me of two things – first, the famous Roman roads like the Appian Way. And all roads really did lead to Rome! The Romans had a gift for practical genius, like the development of this important system of communication and transportation throughout Italy, and eventually throughout their Empire. The roadways of the ancient Romans were truly the airways of today! And, in a funny way, I'm reminded of all those "Road movies" with Bing Crosby and Bob Hope, and oh yes, Dad, Dorothy Lamour! But watching them didn't make you a "Roads Scholar", Dad! Let me see, there was *Road to Zanzibar*, *Road to Morocco*, *Road to Bali*, *Road to Hong Kong*, *Road to Singapore*, *Road to Rio*, and *Road to Utopia*. These were exotic places – like *National Geographic* for people who didn't like to read! Or, for kids growing up like me, who loved those *Tintin* books in French that you used to buy me, Mom. I only found out later that the author's name, Hergé, was really formed from placing some letters from his real name, Georges Remi, backwards! You know, the explanation for the word utopia, that unattainable land of perfection, is the etymology from the Greek words *ou* and *topos* – "no place". Sort of like when Odysseus told the giant Polyphemus his name was *ou tis* – "nobody", and the rest is, as they say, "history" – or, in this case, ancient literature! By the way, the word "history", meaning "investigation", was coined by the Greek historian Herodotus. I'll be taking a course on him next year. I guess if he had had some famous women to write about, I would be taking a "herstory"course! But the *Road to Utopia* movie was about striking gold in the Klondike, and becoming rich. I've just read a book about the gold rush in the Klondike by Pierre Burton, a well-known Canadian writer. Well, if you take the Latin words *ut*, which Vergil uses to mean "where", and *ops*, which means "power", especially that power that wealth and resources give you, you could put together the word "utopia"! It's called playing with words, Mom! Writers like Robert Graves did it all the time. But I did enjoy reading his books *The Greek Myths* and *The White Goddess*, just like I enjoyed J.G. Frazer's *The Golden Bough*. But my favorite Bing Crosby movie is still *Going My Way*. And I really liked Spencer Tracy in that true story *Boys Town*. They are heart-moving stories of priests who made a difference! I guess it's my Jesuit upbringing! A little Oscar trivia, Mom. After Spencer Tracy donated his Best Actor Oscar, the replacement trophy was mistakenly engraved DICK Tracy! I guess the error was "detected" after a little "detective" work! Mickey Rooney didn't win Best Supporting Actor for this movie – I guess you could say he "came up short"! Just some dark humour, Mom! But for a little guy, he sure got to marry a lot of beautiful women! Wow, this is a long letter, isn't it? And you probably want to hear about my courses. Well, as expected, my Latin courses are extremely interesting.

My Greek course on Plato and Aristotle with Professor Wilson meets on a flexible schedule, since I'm the only student. I also got to choose the texts. So we are reading some selections from Plato's *Republic* and the entire *Symposium*. This Dialogue is on the theme of love – and could have the title "Love Is All Around"! That song was recorded by The Troggs, and written by their lead singer Reg Presley. Mrs. Watson told me his real name was Reginald Ball. I guess being renamed after a "King" didn't hurt – after all, it worked for Henry, Charles and Richard! They weren't exactly your Tom, Dick and Harry – unless you consider that some "Richards" are called Dick! I'm not sure British kings were called Hank and Chuck! We will also be reading from Aristotle's *Nichomachean Ethics* and *his Art of Rhetoric*. Those topics are more interesting to me than the scientific works such as his *Physics* and *Metaphysics,* which just means "after physics".

But I am determined to read all the works in English of both Plato and Aristotle for discussions with Professor Wilson, who is now our resident philosopher since the passing of Professor Underhill. Modern Greek is not too difficult so far. My Professor introduced me to her daughter Maria at the Department's Open House Wine and Cheese. Professor Mavroidakis has already suggested I attend the Balkan Institute in Greece next summer! I'm taking an intermediate level Italian course, but it's not too difficult. My Professor is Mona Martucci, but I have nicknamed her Mona Lisa because of her enigmatic smile and, well, because she's Italian! But no, I don't sing Nat King Cole's "Mona Lisa" to her! See you all soon! *Ciao* everybody! Your son, "Holdoni"!

Chapter 67

\-   Well, Mr. Hainsworth, this new version of my Roman Religion course is proving quite popular, and after the first class, in which you introduced yourself as T.A., who would manage all information sessions and consultation on essay topics, more students enrolled, mostly of the female persuasion. Though not exhaustive, the list and texts of ancient sources you compiled last summer was fairly comprehensive. As we had agreed, since the course deals only with so-called pagan cults, beliefs and practices, we eliminated Christian apologists from your list, such as Minucius Felix, and Firmicus Maternus, although I agree that their works may have been useful for comparative purposes. I am grateful to you for supplying the Latin texts, and in the case of Dionysius of Halicarnassus and Plutarch, the Greek texts, along with the English translations. That way, if this course should evolve into a graduate seminar, students will be able to consult and refer to the original texts of the primary sources. I am glad I left you the responsibility of explaining and commenting on these sources as your share of our lectures.

Comparing Dionysius' account of the foundation myths in his *Roman Antiquities* with that of Livy in the first book of his *Ab Urbe Condita* was an excellent choice of topics for your first lecture. As was the discussion of Cicero's beliefs in your second lecture when you quoted extensively from *De Divinatione* and *De Natura Deorum*, which I know you read with Professor Jolivet. Your third lecture in which you compared Plutarch's essay on Isis and Osiris with the account in Book 11 of Apuleius' *Metamorphoses* – I couldn't help but notice the laughter when you referred to the latter's other title, *The Golden Ass* – was well-received, but in hindsight, I'm wondering if there is too much Egyptian content for the scope of our course – did you notice, I referred to this course as "our course"? No matter, for McGill, which pays individual salaries, Roman Religion is still my course! I'm looking forward to hearing your lectures on religious thought in Vergil, Ovid, and Valerius Maximus, as well as your final lecture on the *Roman Questions* of Plutarch which deal with religious matters. Some day you and I will have to discuss how much Latin he really knew, considering that he only wrote in Greek about the Romans! I must admit that I was in a quandary on how to avoid duplication in essay topic selection due to the unexpected increase in course enrolment, when you came up with the brilliant suggestion of two-person teams for each topic. Hopefully, but I can honestly say, probably, the partners will share the work responsibly. Well, I guess that's what T.A.s are for!

Did that idea come from the modular course you are following on university teaching? Your log of student consultations shows that some students are quite keen, booking appointments as often as three times! Again, it seems the young ladies taking this course are the keenest! But please do not increase your stated availability time to answer what I suspect is not so much an infatuation with Roman Religion – of the sort I have long been a victim – but rather with the Roman Religion teacher! And this time yours truly is not the victim! Well, so much for Roman Religion. Now, let's move on to the Prose Composition segment of this meeting. It is so fortunate to be able to schedule these meetings at our convenience, as you do with Professor Wilson in your Greek course! You have been doing well in sentence translation that highlighted different grammatical constructions. Let's see how you did in your first attempt to translate a continuous passage into Latin. So far, your English-Latin dictionary has been an adequate tool.

Sometimes, though, I may clarify your translation with some idiomatic refinement. I'll just quickly read over the English text before you proceed with your Latin translation. It is Livy's account of Horatio at the Bridge. "There is no one who hasn't heard how bravely Horatius Cocles defended the bridge on which Rome's enemies hoped to enter the city. At first with two comrades, and then alone, he resisted all the attacks against him, and prevented the enemy from crossing; nor is there any doubt that he was the salvation of the Roman state. Although the enemy attacked again and again, they were always driven back with the greatest losses. Finally, when the bridge was almost broken by the Romans, while his fellow citizens cried out for him to return, after praying to the god of the river, he jumped into the water. His friends were afraid he would drown, but against expectations, both of his own men and of the enemy, he safely reached the other bank".

-       As you know, Professor Watson, I read some Livy last year with Professor Jolivet, but we didn't read all the accounts of early Roman heroes. However, I've certainly heard of this story, along with others about the courageous family of the Horatii. I translated as follows:

Nemo est quin audierat quam fortiter pontem quo hostes Romanorum se urbem intraturos sperarent Horatius Cocles – "Cocles meaning one-eyed" – defenderit. Primum cum comitibus duobus, deinde solus omnem in se factum impetum sustinens hostes prohibebat transire; neque dubium est quin saluti reipublicae Romanae fuerit. Identidem agressi hostes semper multis amissis repulsi sunt. Tandem cum haud multum abesset quin pons ab Romanis rescinderetur, civibus ut rediret exclamantibus, deum fluvii precatus in aquam se proiecit.

Amici ne submergatur verentur, sed praeter opinionem et suorum et hostium tutus in alteram ripam evadit.

-       Very good, Mr. Hainsworth! I'm glad you picked up on the double dative with *saluti reipublicae*. The phrase "with great losses' could also have been rendered by *magna strage*, *strages* being a word meaning "military slaughter", as opposed to a defeat *per se*.

When we meet next time, I'll try to find a passage from an author you are less familiar with!

We'll also discuss your thesis research on the Roman god Liber/Bacchus. It is curious that you admit having the image of Horatius diving heroically into the river engraved in your mind!

Chapter 68

- Good morning, class! Before we begin today's reading in the *Phaedra,* just a WORD on wordplay in Seneca – nice introduction to the topic, if I do say so myself! In the *Agamemnon,* the arrival of the king's herald Eurybates is announced with the words *vasto concitus miles gradu* -"a soldier approaching fiercely with a wide step". The herald's name is Eurybates – a Greek name meaning "wide step"! Obviously Seneca was "playing" to a bilingual audience who would appreciate the Greek and Latin interplay. No doubt our bilingual Mr. Hainsworth – an unequivocal fan of Seneca's - is also revelling in this instance of Senecan wit!

In Seneca's *Phaedra* thus far, we have seen a heroic Hippolytus, who gives orders to his companions concerning the hunt. He presents himself as very masculine, but disinclined to interact with women – so, ladies, not a male chauvinist pig! Please excuse my "misandric" description, gentlemen! I have invented the word, meaning "man-hater", as a contrast with the word "misogynist". You have all had enough Greek to recognize the etymology of both words.

Hippolytus does indeed cherish one female – the goddess Diana. We will continue to explore the merits and faults of both Hippolytus and Phaedra as we read the play. Certainly, Seneca seems to lay blame – where blame needs to be laid – strictly on the temperament and character of the individuals, rather than on divine intervention or interference, since the gods, or rather, goddesses, do not figure as characters in Seneca's version, as they do in Euripides' play. I am pleased to see members of our Latin Play Troupe in the class, including a couple of students who performed last year in Professor Marcoux's Ancient Greek presentation of Euripides' *Hippolytus*.

Mr. Hainsworth, you were excellent in the role of Hippolytus, and I hope we can count on you to reprise the role in our Latin presentation of Seneca's *Phaedra*. In fact, I would like you to read and translate our first passage today. Do you have any preliminary remarks before you read the passage from Act II, Scene 2, lines 566 to 573. And, obviously, you and Miss Smith would be exempt from individual auditions, since I am well aware of the talent you both have. No need to blush upon receiving a well-deserved compliment, Mr. Hainsworth. For what it's worth – slight play on words, class – your name and that of our Greek protagonist both begin with the letter H, the symbol in Ancient Greek for correct breathings, and we all know that proper breathing is important in acting!

- Yes, I would like to be the Latin "Hippolytus" in this year's production. I guess Paul Anka is not the only one in love with Diana! I'm sure everyone knows the song, since he's

Canadian. Personally, I think Hippolytus' hatred of women is a defense mechanism in his efforts to ward off unwelcome advances of older women! He goes from hunter to "hunted", from masculine hero – as the son of Theseus, it's in his genes – to chaste virgin! So he's being "chaste" and being "chased"! Just some of my own play on words, everyone! Be that as it may, here is the passage, which I will read in my best Hippolytus voice! It follows the nurse's line, in which she asks *Cur omnium fit culpa paucarum scelus*? "Why does the crime of a few become the guilt of all?"

Detestor omnis, horreo fugio execror

sit ratio, sit natura, sit dirus furor:

odisse placuit. Ignibus iunges aquas

et amica ratibus ante promittet vada

incerta Syrtis, ante ab extremo sinu

Hesperia Tethys lucidum attollet diem

et ora dammis blanda praebebunt lupi,

quam victus animum feminae mitem geram.

"I hate them all, I abhor them, I flee from them, I curse them!

Be it reason, be it nature, be it cruel fury, it is pleasing to hate them!

You will join water to fire, and beforehand the unstable Syrtis will promise friendly waters to ships, beforehand the western sea will raise the shining day from its deepest chasm, and wolves will offer caressing mouths to young deer, will I, won over, bear a friendly disposition towards the woman." Like my old boss Pizza Pete used to say, "I'll let you pay on credit when hell freezes over!"

- Very good translation, Mr.Hainsworth.

Once more, class, you are witness to what our Department Chair has dubbed "Hainsworth Humour"! Surely that phenomenon would have provided our memorable Professor Underhill with another H.H. for his repertoire! I'll let you know when rehearsals begin. Ah yes - Paul Anka. He had another hit with the song "Puppy Love". Quite different from Patti Page's "How Much is that Doggy in the Window?" I guess every dog has its day! And before we dismiss, I shall recite for you a little poem I composed for my dog Bambie.

You little brown bundle of beauty,

With the cutest black muzzle and fluffy tail.

How can I not hug and kiss you

As I celebrate the little dog you are.

You came to me, a rescued pup from the street.

Could your former master have been so cruel?

A dog's instinct told you I was kind,

And that you would be happy in your new home.

To see you eager for your daily walk,

And show your delight at every treat,

Makes my life a constant hope

For good and love and joy.

Your jumping about like a deer

Gave me your name – Bambie!

You care for me and protect me

In your animal way.

The time I spend away from home

Is hard on me and hard on you,

But the affection you show me on my return

Makes you so very special, truly a little gift!

- That is so beautiful, Professor Wilkinson. I'm reminded of the dog I once had – Vergil Cane!

Chapter 69

\-   Hi Holden, how's my favorite Latin student doing? I'm glad to be there – or here In Toronto! – for you! I'm still trying to take in all the news you sent me. Our Methodology Professor would say "I'm trying to process it!" I can see why you wouldn't want to share this with your Mom! Did you really mean it when you said you could tell me anything, that it was like being in a confessional? You may seem immortal with all your success at McGill, but here I am nothing but mortal…sin! Actually I've reformed a little. *Noblesse oblige*! I've gone from hardly working to working hard! The U. of T. is great for Classics, even though Toronto is kind of dull.

Did you know that hockey fans here are still gloating about the 1967 Stanley Cup victory over the Canadiens? Although Expo 67 was a watershed moment for Montreal, not only did the Leafs "rain on Montreal's parade", they literally robbed the City of a parade that the population had become accustomed to, following Stanley Cup victories! You should think of coming here – you'd be a good fit! I mean in the PhD programme, not in boring Toronto! I saw the news about that monster snowstorm – the storm of the century they're calling it! My folks in Greenfield Park were stranded in their house, but they survived – mostly because my Dad had three cases of beer on reserve! I wonder what would happen if they ever got hit with something like an ice-storm. I don't follow football much anymore, and I know you're only interested in the Super Bowl because of the Roman numerals for each year of the championship game. So the Canadiens had to cancel a game because of the snow – too bad the Leafs didn't have that excuse! Were you still able to get to church? You call it devotion, and I call it your "Mass hysteria"! I'm working on my puns, but I know I'm not in the championship category like you - or like this girl I met. When I mentioned that Toronto didn't get enough snow to get excited – only six inches - she said she got six inches the night before and was quite excited! As I've always told you, Hold On, it's a game of inches! And so you've "made up" with Professor Wilkinson – without kissing! She probably realizes she dodged a bullet – I've heard of professors losing their jobs by coming on to students – especially male professors who come on to students! Say, you're not going to show this letter to anyone, right? But I'm glad you're continuing your acting "career", and that Professor Wilkinson has learned to appreciate your assets rather than your ass! So she realized that putting you in her plays didn't make you her "playmate"! Speaking of which, unbelievable! So you were tutoring Professor Watson's wealthy neighbour, Mrs. R. You say you had figured she had a family name that was difficult to pronounce, or that using just an initial was cool for this attractive widow, or she had been a student of Professor Underhill! Now if I've got this straight, you showed up one day for the Latin lesson, and she answered the door in her bathrobe, and when you followed her into the living room, she was lying on the sofa in the buff! Too bad the lesson wasn't on those statues of Venus – you wouldn't have needed any slides! But what really blew my mind – unfortunately that's all that's getting blown these days! – is when you asked her what her full name was, she said, "Why, it's Mrs. Robinson"! I can imagine the "sound of silence" that followed! I know you saw the movie *The Graduate* because you like Simon and Garfunkel. I like them, too – we both like the same songs – "Homeward Bound" and "A Hazy Shade of Winter". Well, when that last song isn't hinting at giant snow-storms! And you like Smokey Robinson – but there was no "Miracle" here! And his Mrs. Robinson can sing! What's her name – Claudette Robinson? And you told me her cousin, Bobby Rogers, is also a member of the group. I guess your Mrs. Robinson is not about to start bragging to the Watsons about her "graduate student" giving her a miss. If you were marking her pass/fail, I guess we have to say her pass at you failed! So what's with you and older women? Madame Jolivet, Mrs. Robinson, Professor Wilkinson! Are you Hippolytus reincarnated? These women are old enough to be your mother! That would put you in a weird Oedipus-complex scenario – but let's not go there! Fortunately, unlike those fated figures in Greek tragedy, you somehow managed to get out of a tight squeeze. So "Hail, Squeezer"! At least Mrs. Watson didn't come on to you in England. You mentioned that you actually admired the Watson couple, and that Professor Watson is inspiring you to contemplate a university teaching career. I think you would be a great professor. If you had a class full of girls, you wouldn't even have to prepare lectures – you could just stand there and let them look at you!

But then what else could THE Latin student do for a living? Oh yeah, become a gigolo! Your relations with girls your own age are a little more normal – even though you kiss a girl good-night and consider it sex! I was really intrigued when you said you've gone dancing with a couple of university girls. So Professor Mavroidakis – I know she's the Modern Greek professor – had you chatting with her daughter at an event at the Montreal Hellenic Community Center. Don't mess up your chance of getting an "A"! And you met an attractive T.A. from the Italian Department at a reception hosted by the *Istituto Italiano di Cultura*. I remember that the Italian Cultural Institute is just down the street from McGill. So you could drink loads of wine and walk back to school! What really got my attention about your new-found love life – just yankin' your chain, buddy! – is that both girls are named Maria! I can see you now serenading them with the West Side Story song "Maria"! "I just met two girls named Maria"! Of course you can't sing like Johnny Mathis! But what you told me next was a real remedy for my boredom. Your story was better than the ones I read in those pricey magazines! So the Italian girl is also called Gina by her close friends. Then you just sing that other Johnny Mathis song, "Gina", to her. You know that song was a tribute to the Italian actress Gina Lollobrigida. She's a real hooker – I mean looker! But I know you prefer Sophia Loren because she starred in the movie *Fall of the Roman Empire.*

Or you could sing the French version of "Gina" by Pierre Lalonde – I saw him on TV a couple of times. My sister referred to him as "that good-looking French guy"! Sad to say – so did my Mom!

You did mention that the Italian Maria was trilingual. You remember the phrase Professor Manfredi used – *Tria corda habeo quia tres linguas loqui scio* – "I have three hearts because I can speak three languages". I believe the poet Quintus Ennius was referring to his ability to speak Greek and Oscan and Latin. So, my dear polyglot, by this reckoning you have seven hearts!

Count them – English, French, Latin, Ancient Greek, German, Italian and Modern Greek – although you maintain that Greek is the same language from ancient times to the present. Let's see how many girls have broken your heart - or "hearts"! There was Maxine and Myriam and Claire and Corina, and now we can possibly add for future reference – sorry, man! - Maria and Maria. You're running out of hearts! Now, pretending I'm Professor Underhill, with all those names I'm picturing M.C.! But you were never up for "entertaining" them as "Master of Ceremonies"! Yet I guess they were content with their "Master of Classics"! Oh, what the "heck – atomb"! Six "fallen maidens" for you is like a hundred fallen warriors in the Trojan War (or "Troyjen" War, as it sounds with Professor Watson's accent!) – that's right - a real hecatomb!

But the clincher in your scandal report – and this is juicier than the plot in that old movie *Roman Scandals,* since that movie was not about Caligula or Nero, so no sex! - is the inside info on Gina, the Italian Maria. You wrote that she actually admitted to you that she was bisexual! Think of the possibilities – a real *ménage à trois*! How's my French now? She's trilingual and bisexual – how do you "figure" her out? I still need to work on my word play! Remember how you used to call it POW, because you held me "prisoner of your words"! You added that some day, as a professor, this slogan would be your trademark for "pedagogy of wisdom". Well then, Holden, - a "word to the wise"! You were wondering if you were taking advantage of these girls because they all helped you to practice the languages you are studying. You all speak the same language- the language of love! And especially you, Hold On, when you consider that music is international – it's the language of love! Like the story of Odysseus – these women just showed up – all of them with the hots for you. So play it cool, you hot guy! My advice to you, dear friend is to " *carpe* the freakin' *diem* "! I know you are happy just to be greeted by so many girls with those three little words – "The Latin Student"!

Hey, I still envy you! Finally, being the great golfers that we are – okay, that you are - you must have been impressed by your American astronaut, Alan Shepard, who hit a couple of six-iron shots on the moon! I wonder if, before putting, he had to remove the flag planted two years earlier by Neil Armstrong! With all those holes – er, craters – on the moon, it must have been an easy course – unless he hit the ball out of bounds towards Mars! Speaking of Armstrong – now a professor at the University of Cincinnati - when you played football on the astroturf in their stadium, are you sure it wasn't "astronaut turf"? Your friend – the "classy" – make that the Classics – student!

Chapter 70

-        So what did you think of the concert, Holden? Isn't the food here delicious?

-        This Greek food is great! And such a lovely restaurant! You obviously have good taste – in food and décor and in the company you keep! Well, two out of three isn't bad! It was so nice of your mother to give us those tickets. Nana Mouskouri is a lovely singer, but with those horn-rimmed glasses she could easily pass for a university professor. I loved the song "White Rose of Athens", and all those other international hits she sang. And she sings in English, French, Greek, and German – she could pass the PhD foreign language requirements for Classics! Place des Arts is a magnificent venue - a really classy place!

-        Actually, my mother was supposed to attend the concert with me, but thought it would be a nice opportunity for us to spend some time together. You may have noticed that she has given us theater tickets, gift certificates for lavish restaurants, movie passes, tickets to the Cat Stevens concert at the Forum, and flyers announcing – her words – "stimulating conferences". I do enjoy your company, Holden, but I have a confession to make. I believe I can trust you to be discreet. For two years I've been in love with Nicky – actually his name is Nicholas. My parents, especially my mother, do not approve. Why? Because Nicky never attended university and works in a restaurant. He knows all about you, and our "cultural outings"! And he respects you! Actually, he feels grateful to you, since now my parents haven't been asking me questions about him. But all this matchmaking on the part of my mother – your Professor Mavroidakis - is not fair on Nicky or me – or you!

-        Gosh, Maria, I see a bit of Romeo and Juliet here. Or maybe a Greek tragedy! Of course I won't be talking to your mother about your love life – not until I've secured my "A"! Just kidding! You know back home in Cincinnati I worked in a restaurant – although I guess you couldn't really call Pizza Pete's a restaurant as such – more of a greasy spoon. And believe me there is a big difference between greasy food and this fine food from Greece! Now that I think about it, all that food I ate for free at Pizza Pete's may have caused the kidney stone attack I suffered last August. And I do mean suffered! I had just returned home from England the previous week, when all of a sudden I felt this excruciating pain on my side. I thought I had appendicitis, and Professor Watson, who happened to be with me in his office, had me rushed to the McGill University Health Facilities. That's where I was told I had a kidney stone. They gave me a shot of morphine to ease the pain, and some pills. I was released from the hospital the next day, and was able to pass the stone at home two days later – in time for the start of classes! I never told my Mom about it, because I didn't want her to worry. So you see, you're not the only one who has secrets!

-        Well, Holden, I'm glad you're better. You are a beautiful physical specimen, and it's hard to imagine you ever being ill. All my Greek girlfriends who have met you say you're like Apollo, or maybe Dionysos – I think they'd love to be your maenads! But Nicky is no Hephaistos either! I was amused when you told me about the village girl in Pylos. I don't want you to think that this city girl has designs on you – in spite of my mother's scheming! But do be careful when you attend the Balkan Institute in Salonika this summer!

-        Actually my middle name is Denys, a derivative of Dionysos. I appreciate your frankness, Maria, and your love of music. You're a naturally good dancer – but not in the "maenad style"! I kind of like this new disco music – it's great for dancing! And those songs – "Mr. Big Stuff" by Jean Knight, "She's a Lady" by Tom Jones, "Temptation Eyes" by The Grass Roots, another version of "Proud Mary" by Ike and Tina Turner, "Sweet City Woman" by The Stampeders, and how about "Venus" by Shocking Blue. Actually, just like the "goddess" Venus can be, that song is "shocking", compared to the innocent Frankie Avalon song that yours truly has been known to sing! And I have to admit I really enjoyed our slow dances together – although now I realize you were probably thinking of Nicky during those moments. It's even a little embarrassing when I think of some of the song titles like "Make it With You" by Bread and "'Take Time to Know Her" by Percy Sledge! I really appreciate talking about music with you, since you're so knowledgeable. And talking about Greece! You've been to Greece so many times! We've talked about the Acropolis and the Plaka, and the islands and Greek wine and baklava! And Greek singers like Demi Roussos and Georges Moustaki, who I know wasn't Greek-born, but if you're born in Alexandria that makes you an "international" Greek! Just like Cat Stevens, who was born in England. I love his song "Wild World"! After all, there is a part of Greece in the British Museum – those Elgin Marbles. Some of the songs you like, I like too. Especially "Mercy, Mercy Me" by the great Marvin Gaye. I think Carole King is very talented – very "poetic" in her song "I Feel the Earth Move". We both like "Riders on the Storm" by the Doors. I like The Bee Gees, who sing "How Can You Mend a Broken Heart". Such great voices – I think they are going to have many more hits! A song I'd like to learn to play on my guitar is "My Sweet Lord" by George Harrison. But you're really into contemporary pop, Maria, while I have more eclectic tastes – I like Doo Wop, '50's Pop, '60's Pop, Rhythm and Blues, Soul – including Philadelphia Soul, Folk, Folk Rock, the Motown Sound, British Pop – thanks to Mrs. Watson – some Country music, California Beach music like The Beach Boys and Jan and Dean, and now Disco. Have you heard of Pookie Hudson and The Spaniels, who sing "Goodnite, Sweetheart, Goodnite"? …Well, it's time to go… And I guess it is time for us to go, Maria! I wouldn't mind meeting Nicky someday.

-       You can meet him now, Holden. He works in this restaurant!

Chapter 71

\-   Good afternoon, everybody! As we continue our reading of Lucretius, we marvel at his poetic skill in defending the principles espoused by Epicurus. It is ironic that Epicurus himself did not really trust poets to present philosophical notions and truths, but saw poetry as a form of entertainment. Therefore, as we explore the nature of the universe, let us also enjoy the entertainment provided by reading Lucretius! Mr. Hainsworth, please read in Lucretian hexameter today's passage from Book Three, lines 323 to 336, followed by your translation.

Haec igitur natura tenetur corpore ab omni

ipsaque corporis est custos et causa salutis;

se radicibus haerent nam communibus inter se

nec sine pernicie divelli posse videntur.

Quod genus e thuris glaebis evellere odorem

haud facile est quin intereat natura quoque eius.

Sic animi atque animae naturam corpore toto

extrahere haud facile est quin omnia dissoluantur.

Implexis ita principiis ab origine prima

inter se fiunt consorti praedita vita

nec sibi quaeque sine alterius vi posse videtur

corporis atque animi sorsum sentire potestas,

sed communibus inter eas conflatur utrimque

motibus accensus nobis per viscera sensus.

\-   "This nature, then, is held together by the whole body, and is itself the guardian of the body and the cause of its health; for they cling between themselves to common roots, nor are they seen to be able to be torn apart without disaster.

Insofar as it is easy to tear away the scent from lumps of incense without its nature also being destroyed, so it is easy to draw away from the whole body the nature of the mind and the soul without everything being destroyed. With their first principles" – here Lucretius means atoms, Professor Jolivet – "intertwined from their very beginning between themselves, they are endowed with a common life, nor is the power of the body and the mind to sense separately, each for itself, seen to be possible without the force of the other, but a sensation is kindled in our flesh, enflamed on both sides by common motions between them."

-       So Lucretius, in contrast to Christian teaching, proposes the inseparability of the soul!

Chapter 72

\-   Mr. Hainsworth, I have been granted a six-month sabbatical to work on the completion of my book. Consequently Mrs. Watson and I will be in England from September to February. Professor Jolivet will be acting Department Chair during that time, and has pledged to continue the monthly tea socials. Mrs. R. will be looking after our house. I was surprised to hear you were no longer tutoring her in Latin, but it's just as well, since you will be a very busy young man next year. If you are wondering what will happen to the Roman Religion course, I have already solved that problem. You, Mr. Holden Hainsworth, will teach the course! You will be given a contract as a sessional lecturer. You are the ideal replacement, since you are very familiar with the course. But you will not have a teaching assistant. You've already committed to teaching introductory Latin at Loyola College, and I understand you will use the reading approach with *Lingua Romanorum*. Your Latin courses will be challenging, but the Greek course on historians should be less time-consuming than this year's course on the philosophers.

I assume your second year of Modern Greek and Italian won't be too taxing. The fact that you will again be participating in the Latin Play may cause havoc with your social life – unless, of course, you consider your role in Terence's *Phormio* your social life! I trust you have made the necessary preparations for your summer in Greece at the International Balkan Institute in Thessaloniki. Your thesis research seems to be going well, and we can discuss your theories for a few minutes now, and of course during the last months of term. I will be able to supervise the final draft upon my return in February of next year. You will have to submit your thesis at the beginning of April, and if all goes well – as I'm sure it will – you will be awarded the Master's Degree in June of next year. That means we shall also have to discuss your plans for doctoral studies, which will probably be a four-year programme, culminating in the submission of a dissertation. The title of your Master's thesis is "The Roman Dionysus – Bacchus or Liber?". I know you have evidence associating the Greek god Dionysos with the Roman counterpart of *enthousiasmos* and *ekstasis*, Bacchus, as well as with the agricultural deity Liber. You will be attempting to ascertain a dual nature in the adoption of Dionysos by the Romans. Will you find a merging of this dual nature in the Roman cult, or the worship of completely separate gods?

Chapter 73

-     I'm having a great time dancing with you, Holden! But I have to admit I didn't think you would feel comfortable around me after I revealed my sexual orientation. Actually, I'm feeling more and more lesbian than heterosexual. And I can't tell my parents, you know, since they're old-country Italians – very Catholic and ultraconservative. They wouldn't even understand who I really am, much less accept the real me. So if you do come for supper on Sunday, please don't act strange. My sister knows, but my brothers don't. They wouldn't understand either! But my parents might think we are a dating couple. I just don't want you to think I'm using you. You are so clean-cut, a real straight arrow! My Papa is going to feel proud of his little girl. Little girl! I'm 23 years old and teaching at university! And you're so good- looking, my Mamma is going to adore you! You know, if we were a couple, they could make a TV show about us! We could be a new version of that show "He and She", but our show would last more than a year!

-     No problem for Sunday. It's not too much to pay for a home-cooked meal – especially an Italian one! Bring on the lasagna! I'm having fun dancing with you tonight – you're such a good dancer! And I don't think they will be playing too many slow songs at this discotheque! As for being the designated "lover", it's okay! I don't have time for a real girlfriend, and if my friends at McGill think I am dating someone, they'll get off my case. Besides, you probably have a better chance of meeting the right girl than I do! Too soon? It's just that I often use humour to relieve tension. And hopefully your father won't send a "Mafia hit man" after me! Besides, you're okay – you know a lot about hockey. Like me, you think *Les Canadiens* will win the Stanley Cup this spring, and like me, you think Canada will beat Russia in the Super Series next year. But not in four straight games that you're predicting – I think it will go down to the wire! But it is cool talking to you in Italian. It's really interesting to visit Little Italy, considering I've been to "Big Italy" a couple of times. In my Quebec history course, we talked about the tension in St. Leonard over language issues. I think if the separatist party comes to power there could be big trouble – a bit like the race riots back home! I remember passing through this big city on the way to the Laurentians with Jeremy. It's called Laval, and apparently there are many Italo-Canadians in that city. Interesting that it has the same name as the university in Quebec City. I've learned that in French I just have to say Québec when I'm talking about the city, and *Le Québec* when I'm talking about the province – pretty convenient! I'll be at Laval University in May to read my paper at the annual Classical Association of Canada conference. I'll be staying at the Château Frontenac, which I've heard so much about.

-        All that travelling, Holden! You lead a charmed life! But then you yourself are a charming person! Everyone says you are a perfect gentleman.

-        I thought the last perfect gentleman was Phileas Fogg! He travelled a lot too! I really enjoyed that Jules Verne novel *Around the World in 80 Days*! Such a romantic story! And that Passepartout - such a kid at heart! Say – that would be a great name for a children's television show! They need a show here in Quebec to rival our Captain Kangaroo! But sometimes I would just like to be another Robinson Crusoe, living a peaceful life on his island. Then he had "Friday" on his mind! The Easybeats song could have been a theme song for that movie! Of course, if I become a university professor, I would like to have contact with the community – no ivory tower for me! I'd gladly participate in an outreach programme. Say, now that they have another French university in Montreal - everybody just calls it UQAM – you can think of a teaching career. I know you're working on your doctorate on the subject of Dante's *Divine Comedy*, and your teaching experience as a T.A. at McGill should help.

-        Actually, Holden, there is a provincial network called Université du Québec with campuses in different regions. We have the biggest one here in Montreal – Université du Québec à Montréal. But the prize teaching job in Montreal would be at the Université de Montréal. Hey, they're playing some good dance tunes. Let's get up on the floor!

-        You were right – Maria –or should I call you Gina? It was fun dancing to those Dawn songs "Candida" and "Knock Three Times", and those great songs by Chicago – "Make Me Smile"and "25 or 6 to 4". You know that song by Steam, "Na Na Hey Hey Kiss Him Goodbye", would make a great song at hockey games, if the crowd sang it to the losing team! I like all songs by The Supremes, so it was great to dance to "Stoned Love" and "Where Did Our Love Go"!

It's interesting – they played "Band of Gold" by Freda Payne. There was a song by Don Cherry in the '50's with the same title. But it wasn't the same song, and we couldn't have danced to it like we did to this one. "Get Ready" - the Rare Earth version - and "Travelin' Band" by Creedence Clearwater Revival were awesome! And there was that new Cat Stevens song, "Peace Train", and "Give Me Just a Little More Time" by Chairman of the Board. I wonder if the name was chosen because that great singer Frank Sinatra was called that! And "Old Blue Eyes" has Italian roots, Gina! My friend Jeremy has a professor in Toronto, whose lectures are quite dull, so he calls him "Chairman of the Bored"! I'll have to play that song for Professor Watson if I don't finish my thesis on time! And I was wrong – they did play a slow song. I actually liked dancing with you to "Hey There Lonely Girl". What a voice that Eddie Holman has!

-       I know, Holden, and one day Montreal will accept two girls dancing to that song, so that there will be fewer lonely girls!

Chapter 74

\-   Hi Mom, hope this letter finds you all well. A bit of sad news to begin with. There is a graduate student – Matthew – who is severely diabetic. His condition worsened, bringing on blindness. I have been visiting him in hospital, and the experience is unsettling. First of all, there is a television in his room, and he invariably asks me to switch it on. He always says I'll watch, and he'll listen! To top it off, each time I leave, he says "See you"! Professor Watson said I would be busy, and he wasn't kidding! When you received those cassettes, you probably got an idea of just how busy. Your phone call to express your pride and joy at hearing my "singing voice" again like on the Xavier tape brought tears to my eyes, Mom! I have to tell you that recording Frankie Avalon's "Venus" in French and Italian was the brainstorm of Professor Manfredi, and involved McGill's Music Faculty, as well as the French and Modern Language Departments. It was neat how the French translation worked out "Venus if you will... *Vénus si tu veux...*O Venus, goddess of love that you are...*O Vénus, déesse de l'amour que tu es...* Surely the things I ask... Can't be too great a task...*Sûrement les choses que je demande...Ne peuvent être une tâche trop grande...*I'll give her all the love I have to give...As long as we both shall live...*Je lui donnerai tout l'amour que j'ai à donner...Tant que nous deux vivrons*"! But keep checking the mail because – guess what – I've also taped German and Greek versions! Currently, we are preparing versions of Sam Cooke's song "Cupid". Renée Martel, whom I really like as a singer, recorded a French version. However, a really brilliant student in McGill's Music Faculty is re- writing the words for our Classics "promo". Here's a brief sample – "Cupid draw back your bow...Let go your lovely darts...Straight to my students' hearts... Cupid please hear my plea...They'll love Classics with me"! In one of his songs, Sam Cooke sings about not knowing much about history or biology. It would be nice if he impressed his "girl" with Greek and Latin – what a "Wonderful World" that would be! He wouldn't be a Roman slave – he wouldn't be working on a "Chain Gang"! I know you recognize all those Sam Cooke song titles, Mom! When the French and English "Cupid" tapes are ready, I'll send you copies. In fact, with the new technology at McGill, we are going to produce videocassettes! The downside is that my fellow-students are forever teasing me by calling me the "Classics Crooner"! I hope listening to me singing "Cupid" doesn't make you think of the Connie Francis song "Stupid Cupid"! If it does, I'll regret sending you the tapes, and have to listen to her song "Who's Sorry Now"! When my good friend Jeremy heard about the tapes, he telephoned me, asking if he could form a singing duo with me, saying we could become a "mythical" act – "Cupid and Sidekick"! I replied that his new take on myth would be a "myth-take"! Besides, I was a "straight arrow", and he was, well,

Jeremy! I explained to him that the recording was meant to be an "attraction" to Classics, not a "distraction" from Classics! Hearing this, he informed me that any collaboration in the future would be as the duo "Bad and Jeremy"! I countered that I would prefer to work as "Glad and Jeremy", but for now we were relegated to "Sad and Jeremy"! Poor Jeremy thought we could become the "new" Righteous Brothers, but, sadly, he was just being "self-righteous"! He was so desperate for us to "perform" together that he quoted Shakespeare's "all the world's a stage", to which I replied that I didn't want to get "booted off" it when the audience began chanting "get off the stage"! But to be fair, Shakespeare could be very "contemporary". You recall watching that Canadian comic duo of Johnny Wayne and Frank Shuster on The Ed Sullivan Show, Mom? They are from Toronto, and made a record 67 appearances on his show - and for good reason! Their Julius Caesar sketch was great, but I especially liked the "Shakespearean Baseball" skit, which they called "A Comedy of Errors, Hits and Runs"! It was full of references to the Stratford Bard, such as Macduff and in assigning the bases, Richard the third! Baseball players alluded to were Sandy (Koufax), Rocky (Colavito), Pete (Rose), manager Leo "the Lip" Durocher, Rusty (Staub), and Joe (DiMaggio). When I talked to Jeremy about the great MM associated with The Yankee Clipper, he didn't mention Mickey Mantle – the "Commerce Comet" – but Marilyn Monroe! Of course, although she never stole any bases, she did steal "Joltin'Joe"'s heart! Then Jeremy muttered something about not getting beyond first base with girls. But believe me, he wasn't a "hit" on the diamond either! All the same, I'm proud that Dad keeps that baseball autographed by "Muscles" Mickey on our mantle! Speaking of muscles, I'm still eating spinach.

Do you remember when I was very little, you encouraged me to eat spinach so I would be like Popeye? You meant having his muscles, and I thought you meant looking like him, and so I was very reluctant. I have become a "sailor man" in a manner of speaking, since I've gone to Greece, the land of olives, but - fortunately – did not meet Olive Oyl. However, I wouldn't have minded sharing a hamburger with Wimpy! I don't know if Alice the Goon was that scary, since *gune* is simply the Greek word for woman! I did enjoy watching them in cartoons, even though they all were a little challenged in the beauty department! Jeremy did think that we could be another Wayne and Shuster, when we entered McGill's Comedy Festival. But when I tell you our best lines, you'll know that was never going to happen! Picture this – I'm an airline pilot and he's a disgruntled passenger. I announce that an engine has malfunctioned and we will be in the air an hour longer. Shortly after, I announce that our other engine has broken down. He quips: "Great – now we will be up here all day!" A fellow passenger (me), who is listening to his transistor radio, tells him to be quiet because Sam is singing. "Sam who?" he asks, to which I reply "Samwhere over the Rainbow!" Boy, I'm sure glad I have Latin to fall back on! My courses in Latin and Greek are as interesting as ever. We've been reading Herodotus'

History of the Persian Wars. It's in Ionic Greek, but it's not too different from the Attic Greek of the other prose authors I've been reading. Right now we're reading Book Two on Egypt. Fascinating! After Christmas – and I'll be seeing you all then! – we'll be reading the *History of the Peloponnesian War* – the war between Athens and Sparta – written by Thucydides. Professor Jolivet had said that Tacitus was the greatest historian. Professor Wilson, being a Hellenist, claims that Thucydides is the greatest historian. Greek versus Roman. Why not compromise and choose Polybius, who wrote in Greek for the Romans! My Italian and Modern Greek courses are more demanding, but speaking those languages with the two girls I go dancing with really helps. Both of them are named Maria. Tell Dad not to get too excited, we only go dancing! I actually enjoy that change of pace from my studies and reading – and thesis writing. It beats going to the tavern for beers, like I used to do with Jeremy! Silly Jeremy once teased me by suggesting that my favourite teaching assistant was T.A. Verne! I stumped him when I asked if she was related to Jules Verne! One Maria has a boyfriend, and the other Maria has a girlfriend. Don't ask – I don't want to go into it! You say *Ave Maria,* Mom, I say *Oy vey,* Maria! And speaking of different dialects of Greek, at McGill we learn *katharevousa,* a "purist" form of Modern Greek, but at the Balkan Institute in northern Greece we were studying *demotiki,* the standard "language of the people". I think even the University of Athens will eventually accept this version as the official language of Greece. Did you know, Mom, that university education is free in Greece, but places are limited, and the competition is nerve-racking! Apparently there are more Greeks attending university in Italy than in Greece! We had to be in class every morning at 8 am for a Greek dancing class! Then we had courses on Greek History and Greek Literature, followed by our Greek language course, with a really energetic teacher! I took an extra course, since they were offering an Ancient Greek course on Lucian of Samostrata. We read his satirical work called *A True Story* – it was anything but! It is supposed to be the first work of science fiction. True (a pun, Mom!), it kind of reminded me of Jules Verne's *From the Earth to the Moon* – Professor Watson once referred to this novel as *Journey to the Moon.* Do you remember the movie we saw based on another Jules Verne novel – *Twenty Thousand Leagues under the Sea*? I do, because it starred Kirk Douglas! Speaking of movies, I recently saw the film *Love Story.* I was eager to see it because it was based on the novel written by a Classics professor from Princeton, Erich Segal. It seems that the novel was written with the movie in mind. But such a sad story! If I ever wrote a novel, and especially if it was adapted as a movie, I would want it to have a happy ending. And I wouldn't say apologetically "I'm sorry"! As I told you in a previous letter, Professor Watson is away for six months, and I am teaching his – now our! – Roman Religion course. The good news is that the enrolment is up significantly. The Department and the University are happy, but they had to give me a bigger room. The bad news is that I have many more papers and exams to correct – with no T.A.! Also, our Secretary, Miss Templeton, is being swamped with requests for student appointments by what she called "smitten women", and she warned me about some of them whom she would categorize as *femmes fatales*! I've encountered a bit of the same success - or distress – with the Latin course I teach at Loyola College. It's a beautiful campus – a twenty-five minute ride by metro and bus from McGill. Professor Jones, the Department Chair, has been very helpful. He noted an increase in the number of students for this course, and wondered "out loud" if this gain in popularity was due to the new method I was using or to the new professor using it! The Department secretary – Paula - she insists that I call her that – has offered to stay late if I needed typing done for the course. Mom, she looks even younger than Miss Templeton at McGill! So she won't be hearing me say "Hey Paula" – I'd be afraid she'd say "Hey, Hey Paul"! You know – like the song! If ever that happened, she'd be looking at one pale Paul! I've been applying some of the principles I learned in the "Methods in University Teaching" modular course I followed at McGill. Module number one emphasized the importance of the first contact with the students. I decided to write a poem about Latin to begin the course. What do you think of this poem, Mom? It's called "Why Study Latin?".

Latin isn't only the subjunctive and the ablative case –

It's the story of the Romans, once a mighty race.

The language survived many changes and opinions,

The tool it was of many – majesty and minions.

Latin is more than the stories of Caesar and Vergil.

From this language many tongues have come full circle.

The builders of Western society still live because of Latin.

They communicate now in words as refined as silk and satin.

So pay heed to the accusative and infinitive construction.

Save language and history from awful destruction!

When I finished reading it, one female student yelled out – "so cute!" My pride soon dissipated when I realized she was talking about me and not the poem – do you see me blushing, Mom? But the group is working very hard. They were intrigued when I confessed that I was "polyamorous". When I pointed out that *amor* is "Rome" spelled backwards, I added that by the end of the course they should all be "in love with Rome" – and with Latin! I told them the word meant that I liked them all, and then explained the Greek and Latin etymology of the word. I asked if a student in the class could give another word with the prefix *poly-*, and one young man offered "Polly wants a cracker"! Not to be outdone by this whippersnapper, I retorted with "thanks for the wisecracker, but *poly-* indicates "many". He had an instant rejoinder – "then Polly wants many crackers"! Mom, I've got competition! At the request of McGill's interim Chair of Classics, Professor Jolivet, I gave a talk sponsored by the McGill Graduate Students Society on the relevance of Classical Studies. I started off by playing the song "Spooky" – you can tell Dad, it wasn't to "spook" them! In a mini capsule of that game show "Jeopardy" which you and Dad always watch, I prompted the audience with "we are the group that sang the song you just heard". Surprisingly – or perhaps not – a few people shouted out "Who are Classics IV? "For everybody!", I answered. Well, they were hooked! Hopefully, on more than just "a feeling", like B.J. Thomas in his song! Of course I didn't dazzle them with the fact that drummer – and eventually frontman – Dennis Yost named the group after the Classics drums that he played, nor that I shared his first name with the name Denys that you gave me, Mom! Nor did I overdo the Roman numeral in the group's name. All of that trivia would have been irrelevant, unlike the Classics that I was promoting. I suspected that Professor Jolivet was hoping I could "drum up" some business – even though most of the audience and myself were "beating to a different drum"! One young lady politely – or perhaps shyly – asked "why study Latin?" I reassured her that the same question has been asked down through the ages – beginning with the Romans themselves! My answer was "communication and expression". Knowing Latin well – think Cicero, Catullus and yes, Julius Caesar – enabled the Romans to disseminate information and to render their feelings in the best possible way. Likewise, even today, a comprehensive grasp of Latin roots provides speakers and writers of several languages with adequate tools for truly accurate, and yet stimulating, verbal and written exchanges. I read my paper on religious sentiment in the *Hippolytus* of Euripides at the conference hosted by Laval University. My conclusions on the nature of piety expressed through the character of Hippolytus were well received, and Professor Marcoux and the other Laval professors went out of their way to make me feel welcome. Mom, I am seriously considering doing my doctoral studies at Laval.

But the real scoop is this. I was talking to a doctoral student from France who had presented a paper on Greek philosophy. He invited me to join him and his wife for dinner that evening.

Was I surprised when I met her! It was Myriam - the exchange student in my French course at Xavier University! Another weird coincidence was the movie I saw last week in Montreal's *Quartier Latin* – imagine, a district named in honor of Latin! And the main street is St. Denis! Your Denys! I'm in the heart of Latin territory – and Latin is in my heart! Are you crying, Mom? The movie is called *Deliverance,* and is about four men on an adventure trip in the Appalachians. They are taken prisoner by a couple of mean mountain men and maltreated. Burt Reynolds, one of the four men, ends up being the hero. That film reminded me in an eerie kind of way of Stinking Creek. To tell you the truth, Mom, I sometimes feel like I'm immersed in a mixture of emotions! Sort of like being in a soap opera – yeah, like Coronation Street, but without the British accents! More like French accents instead – sharp ones! *Accent aigu,* Mom – fortunately I can still laugh at – make that WITH - life! Will Feeb be going on to Law School? Love you! Den

Chapter 75

\-   Good morning, everyone. It is always a good morning when we begin our day with Martial's art! No, I'm not talking about the art of war – I am not referring to the god Mars. There will be no physical fighting here – that would be martial arts! But the name of our poet – Marcus Valerius Martialis – may suggest that he sometimes pens "fighting words"! That is the nature of satire, which the Romans claim to have invented. You recall the statement made by the rhetorician and educator Quintilian: *satira tota Romana est*? The Greeks had been more graceful, perfecting epic and lyric poetry. To elaborate on Martial's "biting" satire, I wish to share some thoughts on a poem which was adressed to a dinner-host named Mancinus. It is poem 43 in Book One. The wild boar - *aper* – which he had placed on the table, was too small to satisfy the appetite of the guests, and so it is suggested that the host should be placed in front of the boar like Charidemus – *sed tu ponaris cui Charidemus apro*. Explanations are in order!

Apparently, a certain Charidemus, whose Greek name suggests "pleasing to the crowd", was slaughtered in the arena by a wild boar during the reign of Domitian. The host could therefore "entertain" his guests! Moreover, with a bit of imagination, we could read that Greek name with Latin "components" - *caro*, meaning "flesh" and *edere*, meaning "to eat". A "fatted calf", perhaps, to replace the "puny pig"! The guests would not be "bored" by the boar on the "board" (the table), but entertained by the host "boared" by the boar! So much for ''Martialian meaty meters"! We will also be reading selections from the satires of the "master" – Juvenal.

But Horace, whom some of you read with me in a previous course, also wrote satires. So we could say the later satirists "ode" him a debt! Yes, Mr. Hainsworth, let the games begin! *Ego qui semper jocor, te saluto*! Since you are the prime target of my "joking" and "saluting", Mr. Hainsworth, you may read and translate today's poem – number 11 from Book 2. The meter is a scazon, an iambic trimeter whose final iambic element is replaced by two longs, and so it causes the line to drag or "limp" close, because it finishes with three long syllables in a row. Read it as a "limping iamb" – or as a choliambus.

\-   I will proceed with your command, Professor Manfredi, since I am only a "deputy Martial"!

Quod fronte Selium nubile vides, Rufe,

quod ambulator porticum terit seram,

lugubre quiddam quod tacet piger vultus,

quod paene terram nasus indecens tangit,

quod dextra pectus pulsat et comam vellit :

non ille amici fata luget aut fratris,

uterque natus vivit et precor vivat,

salva est et uxor sarcinaeque servique,

nihil colonus vilicusque decoxit.

maeroris igitur causa quae? domi cenat.

"As to the fact, Rufus, that you see Selius with a gloomy expression,

That this stroller roams by the colonnade so late,

That his grim face holds silent something sad,

That his ugly nose almost touches the ground,

That his right hand strikes his chest and tears his hair:

It's not that he's mourning the death of a friend or brother,

Each of his two sons is alive, and I pray may live long,

His wife is safe, as are his belongings and his slaves,

His tenant-farmer and his overseer have squandered nothing.

What is the cause of his grief? He dines at home!"

-      Very accurate translation, Mr.Hainsworth. Well, ladies and gentlemen, fortunately, you don't have to dine at home! Professor Jolivet has asked me to remind you of the Department tea social coming up this Friday, and the highlight will be the reading of a poem by our own Mr. Hainsworth. I suspect, like Johnny Tillotson's song, it will be "Poetry in Motion"!

-      Well, Professor Manfredi, my poem does contain the line "moving on"! But I suspect the "motion" will be that of everyone heading for the exit when I begin reading!

Chapter 76

-    How are you, Jeremy? Hope your PhD work is going well. When you obtain it you'll have one of only two good things coming out of Toronto. The other one is the 401 highway leading to Montreal! I've been ever so busy here in Montreal. When Professor Watson told me I'd have no time for "lollygagging", I admitted that I had never heard that word before. He smiled and said it meant "being idle and goofing off"! So maybe YOU have heard the word!

Like you always say when singing that Trashmen song "Surfin'Bird"– "the bird Is the word"! I've been anxiously waiting to have some time to bring you up to speed – not to bring you UP "with" speed! – on my summer in Greece! The courses were great, as were the visits to monuments, museums, places – like Mount Athos, where monks are carried up in baskets – like Socrates in Aristophanes' *Clouds*! Talk about your "birds-eye view"! Makes me think of another Aristophanes play – *The Birds*! Come to think of it, you wouldn't have been out of place, since you are already a basket case! How would you like to go from unorthodox to Orthodox…priest!

But some of my extracurricular activities were a little dicey! I spent almost all my time with this Australian guy from Dubbo, named Malcolm – but we called him Mackie. He may not have been Aboriginal, but he certainly was original! He tried to impress me with the Latin phrase *cygnis insignis*. I was already admiring the poetic alliteration when he pointed out that the swan had symbolic status in Western Australia. I burst his bubble by suggesting that if swans were associated with the land down under, he must be their "ugly duckling"! That eventually put an end to his "swan song"! Mackie was forever searching for sexual escapades as well as other "adventures". And if you're asking if I am blaming "Mack the Knife" for our "thrill-seeking", I totally am! On the very first day of our "exploratory" outings he challenged me to a foot-race – which I won handily! He crowned me with some "laurel", and we became a team – the "dynamic duo", as the other students called us! What we actually were, if truth be told, was an adventurous version of "Laurel" and Hardy! We could conceivably end up in the French Foreign Legion, like those two nincompoops in the film *The Flying Deuces*! Like two clowns caught in comedy capers, Mackie's ideas were often half-baked – just like those pies you would offer me at your place! Even though you weren't able to feed me, at least you offered me good feed-back during our discussions on ancient religion! The American students referred to us as the "Bobbsey Twins" or as the "Hardy Boys"! Having read many of those books when I was younger, I was almost flattered, but Malcolm didn't have a clue about those adventure stories. I told him that we didn't solve mysteries like the Hardy brothers, but probably created some! We were considered "twins" because we were always together – like brother and sister Bobbsey. It had nothing to do with looking alike. Good thing, Mackie retorted, because if his dog looked like me, he would shave its behind and make it walk backwards! Being good-natured as I am, I took that remark in stride – but forward strides! I was used to being the "butt" of his jokes! Based on our antics, they could have made another Bing Crosby – Bob Hope "Road" movie - "Road to Salonika"! On the subject of movies, I sometimes called Malcolm "Francis", and told him about the movie with "the talking mule". I guess I could have been the star Donald O'Connor – given my dancing dexterity! How about that, I've hung around with an "ass" and a "mule"! I suppose you want me to bury my "burro" humour – unless you would like to "borrow" it! We were always last to have lights out, and the first to be up and ready for the day's activities. The very first day I knocked on his door – of course, his room was next to mine! – he was slow in answering, and told me that until he found some girls he had to take matters into his own hands! Only he would imitate Bugs Bunny's "What's up, Doc?" with a literal, but dirty, thought in mind. As you could guess, his image of Woody Woodpecker was for the birds! I suppose I was a real "Daffy" Duck to always tail along with him. It was hardly a case of birds flocking together, but that first night, he had us sneak up onto the roof of our male residence. For a minute – but only for a minute – The Drifters song "Up on the Roof" came to mind! He had binoculars with him, and - believe it or not! – we actually spied through the windows of the Greek girls in the residence next door! In fact, all our "outings" could have been taken from the pages of Ripley's *Believe it or Not*! When the supervisor was doing his rounds, we hid behind the curtains near the roof door. I saw myself spending a few years in a Greek jail, with nothing to drink except *ouzo*! Mackie remarked that most of the girls had their curtains open for our convenience. I quickly set him straight by pointing out that they weren't expecting peeping perverts acting like "Fiddlers on the Roof"! At one point, I was sure I was staring at a beautiful bronze reproduction of an Aphrodite sculpture – until it, or rather she, moved! O Pygmalion, where art thou? Mackie tried to bolster my enthusiasm by saying we had a free show, since it was ON the house! I replied that the show was IN the house next door, and so we had better not be seen AROUND that house by the supervisor – whom I called "Castro" because he always wore a uniform that looked like the one worn by the Cuban dictator! Not to be outdone, Mackie said he was reminded more of an "infidel"! Nevertheless, I feared that, if caught, we would end up being buried UNDER the house! A few days later, Mackie had the urge to go and talk to some girls in the residence, and so set up a rendez-vous with me AT the house.

Mackie's Greek was quite good – in fact I could understand him more easily when he spoke Greek, than when he spoke English with his Australian accent! Did you know that the biggest number of Greeks living outside of Greece live in Australia? Well, he had the idea of posing as television repairmen to get past the restriction barring males access to the building. Now I thought we were becoming Abbott and Costello! But the receptionist bought the story – or maybe she took a shine to Abbott – that was me! We got to talk to some girls in the lobby, including "Aphrodite". Mackie said that if we played our cards right, all the girls would show up, and so we would have a "full house"! With him, I always knew I could count on a "wild card"! I was starting to feel comfortable, since I was sure they hadn't noticed"Batman and Robin", who had been on the roof three nights in a row! But suddenly the residence matron entered screaming that there was no television in the building. She had that Medusa effect on me – even without the snakes! We scrambled to leave, and as we did so, "Aphrodite" smiled at me, and said she admired the fact that I wasn't afraid of heights! I never saw Mackie reading, but he seemed to know every trick in the book! He told me how he would feign illness at the private school he had attended in order to be sent to the school nurse. He had this mischievous gleam in his eye when he recounted how "well-treated" he was by her. I was a liitle dismayed when he said the Brits would call it the "full English"! I suspected it involved the "full monty"! There was no sense quoting that football expression Tommy Nelson often used – "the whole nine yards"! Even less so, when Pizza Pete referred to an all-dressed pizza as "the whole shebang"! I cleverly remarked that by "masking" his real health condition, his "trick" secured him a "treat"! I asked if by chance he had pulled that stunt on October 31! I'm sure glad I wasn't with him in Australia to be his fall guy – no not the season! – but a remnant of the October Horse – you know, the ancient Roman sacrifice to Mars! I'm glad the *religio romana* mostly featured bloodless sacrifice, and proud that the god Liber – you would continue to call him Dionysos, Jeremy, the "guru" of Greek religion that you are sure to become! – introduced offerings of incense, barley and even of wine! All that reminds me of the Christian offerings of "bread and wine", accompanied by incense on certain occasions! Interesting, isn't it, that we have a "bloodless" sacrifice in which we consume wine that is "really" the Blood of Christ – in addition to a "modern" form of barley represented by the Host – the Body of Christ! So we Christians consume a sacrificial Victim without any ritual slaying, and consume "Blood" in a "bloodless" sacrifice! This "mystery" of the Eucharist – a "symbolic" commemoration of a "human sacrifice" - would no doubt have boggled the minds of the ancient Romans! To paraphrase a well-known saying, for us Christians – and I count you as one of us, Jeremy, since I know that in spite of your laudable study of Ancient Greek Religion, you are not a polytheistic pagan – "believing is seeing", as it were! I guess the Apostle Thomas invented the saying "seeing is believing" – *videre est credere*! We talked about him in my high school religion classes. Since his name in Hebrew – or if you are being picky, in Aramaic – means "twin", he was sometimes called by the Greek name Didymus. There are accounts that say he was Jesus' twin, but I rather think that there was probably a ressemblance between the two! Still, when Thomas did get to see Jesus, it turned out to be a very "touching" moment! There are texts called "The Acts of Thomas" and "The Gospel of Thomas", but they are from the 3rd century after Our Lord – so "Doubting" Thomas would have been truly dead and buried! Those texts became part of the "apocryphal Scriptures". Since you are a Hellenist in the making, you will recognize the origin of that term in the Greek verb *apokruptein* - "to hide away". Apparently, these texts would have been too sacred for the uninitiated to read! This term reminds me of the "spurious" texts that our professors warn us about. Please don't accuse me of "linguistic lunacy", but I researched the etymology of this word, and it goes all the way back to Etruscan! The word meant "city, state, or people". The expression *tular spural* referred to "city boundaries". I assume the sense of *spural* was "outside of what was proper or legitimate" – you know – *publicus* and *populus,* the "common people"! The Latin word *spureus* means "base, impure". This led to the word *spurius*, meaning "illegitimate, as in an "illegitimate child". And guess what – "spurious" is *spurio* in Italian and *espurio* in Spanish! But for you, Jeremy, back to Greek! The opposite of "spurious" is "authentic", which comes into English and French from the Medieval Latin word *authenticus,* but is an "authentic" Greek word – *authentikos* – meaning "genuine, original". That word, in turn, can be traced to *authentes*, which means "acting on one's own", which had a "kaleidoscope" of senses. I am perhaps using this last word incorrectly, but I know you recognize it as a Greek word, and besides, I wanted to "add a little color" to my description! So, please, no "off-color" remarks! That word – from *autos* – "self" and the participle of "to be"- *hentes* - can refer to an actual murderer, even of oneself – so a suicide – or an absolute ruler! True, in ancient Greece, many rulers had people killed! There is also the Greek word for "tools,weapons", or "instruments" – *entea*. Therefore, you have "acting with your own – authentic! – stuff"! I hope you don't mind me chasing down the roots of all these words, but for me it's a reflex – "automatic", you might say! Well what do you know – and they call this English! But I hope you won't stop "rooting" for me, Jeremy! Mentioning horses always makes me think of my Uncle Phil. The October races - which were kinder to horses than those Roman religious sacrifices – were the Shadwell Turf Mile, the Breeders' Futurity, and the Jockey Club Gold Cup. I wonder if my high school Latin classmate, Tommy Nelson, was always horsing around because he had worked as a gas "jockey"! Maybe too many fumes! Thanks to Uncle Phil, I know about the "Grand Slam" of horse-racing! There's the Triple Crown – gosh so many baseball terms! Uncle Phil always attended the Kentucky Derby, and then they had the Preakness Stakes and the Belmont Stakes. The fourth race in the Grand Slam was either the Travers Stakes or the Breeders' Cup Classic – the closest my uncle came to appreciating "Classics"! He always seemed to lean towards high stakes – unlike his brother – my Dad – who preferred barbecue steaks, lean or otherwise! Because of his fondness for Shakespeare, Dad knew about the "lean and hungry look" of Cassius in the play *Julius Caesar*, as that leader of the assassins contemplated what was "at stake" for the Roman Republic! As for me, a bit like Brutus, I don't love the writings of Julius Caesar less, but I love the works of Seneca more! I guess watching all those westerns made my Dad fond of "stake-outs"! Don't you think I deserve a "Grand Slam" crown for wordplay, Jeremy? I know you cautioned me that there will come a day when I will wonder where the words went, or why they went, or who they went with – a welcome warning, to be sure! Uncle Phil never lost his shirt at the track – don't ask how I knew he wore Fruit of the Loom underwear! – but I don't think his horse ever came in.

My cousin Annie was fit to be tied when, one day, Uncle Phil told her he was leaving her his fortune, and it turned out that his "fortune" was his cocker spaniel, Fortune! I once hit a grand slam home-run playing for Xavier University, but given that sweeping serve, tennis deserves the true title of Grand Slam victories. However, I never took up that sport - I guess it wasn't my racket! I wonder if that "racketeer" Mackie ever played tennis. True, his idea of an "Australian Open"was an Australian "open to suggestions" on how to procure female entertainment!

Maybe he complained of "tennis elbow" in order to be sent to the school nurse! I know I'm getting off track - Uncle Phil wouldn't be pleased – but I can't resist mentioning the Grand Slam of Golf! We've often talked about the PGA Championship, the U.S. Open, the British Open – I know, simply called The Open Championship by the British – even though American Lee Trevino has won it the last couple of years! I proudly point out his LATIN-American roots! And my favorite - The Master's – it has to be - it's played at Augusta National with it's AMEN Corner. That tournament is won with skill AND a prayer! But did you know that Bobby Jones was the only player to win the Grand Slam in the same year? We both love Arnie, but lately you mentioned that Gary was your favorite Player! Wise guy, eh? He may be the "Black Knight" but you might be "black-listed" one day, Jeremy! You were always scrambling when we played golf, and you probably find me rambling in this letter. That's probably the effect of listening to Nat King Cole sing "Ramblin' Rose" so often! I wonder if he ever drove a rose-colored Rambler? Maybe just a pink Cadillac! Remember when you had that black-out playing football at McGill, and the team dubbed you "Mr. Hydro"? Of course basketball with its "SLAM dunk" could lay claim to "Grand Slam" honours. In America that sport causes more "March Madness" than the March 15 assassination of Julius Caesar did in ancient Rome! But basketball never caused me any HOOPla, perhaps since a certain star on the court didn't appreciate the fact that I began to "court" his sister – I told you about Maxine. Again, I don't think my "friend" Mackie plays basketball, but I wouldn't be surprised if he ended up in the "slammer" one day! Not surprising, his favorite Elvis song is "Jailhouse Rock"! I've mentioned my sister Feeb's courtship to you, and I think she plans on ending up in court some day – as a lawyer! I don't know if there is a "Grand Slam" in bowling, but I have a gut feeling there should be – or is that a "gutter" feeling? All that info on sports brings me back to Mackie, who happened to sport a beard! In fact, he was a little hirsute in appearance, so I referred to him as that "wild and woolly guy"! In point of fact, he actually was very apt at "pulling the wool" over the eyes of unsuspecting victims. He confided in me about even his most outrageous capers. I have to tell you, Jeremy, that we often came across stray dogs in the streets, and even near our residence. They made me think of my Vergil Cane, but this "wily Odysseus" succeeded in infiltrating a small residence for Greek girls with a couple of the dogs. He told the girls his name was "Nobody", which they obviously wouldn't understand. He was able to smooch with them for an hour or so, and left before the supervisor arrived. She, however, did understand English, and after asking who had let the dogs in – that was the phrase she used, in Greek of course – was told "Nobody"! Mackie then claimed she must have assumed that the dogs had gotten in on their own! He bragged about being a "dog whisperer", since he had succeeded in getting the dogs to heel. I appealed to him to utter "not a whisper" of dubious deeds to the other students to avoid being considered a heel! At this point, I began to nervously contemplate that Mackie would prove to be my "Achilles heel"! But I refused to listen to more intimate details, since it was "Nobody's" business! As far as I was concerned, he was "in the dog-house"! Honestly, Jeremy, to use an expression I learned in England, he would sometimes "be doing my head in"! My American roots had me thinking of the song recorded by Little Anthony and The Imperials – "Goin' Out of My Head"! We continued to care for the strays we would meet, even feeding them. We certainly weren't about to perform a *supplicia canum* on them! At the mention of this term, Mackie suddenly became interested in my Latin studies. When I pointed out that this "punishment" of dogs in Ancient Rome was by crucifixion, he listened attentively as I acted a bit like a "hot dog" in sharing my "canine knowledge" of the Romans. The Republican period had ended up in a "dog eat dog" world, but sadly, some religious sacrifices involved a "man eat dog" practice. This time I wasn't talking "hot dogs", which, by the way, Jeremy, the Romans probably would have called *pastillum botello fartum*! This sacrifice was not due to the fact that "dog"is "god" spelled backwards, but to the capture of the Roman citadel by the Gauls in 390 B.C. when the watch-dogs had failed to warn the Romans. I suppose it was at this point the dogs started to realize that "their goose was cooked"! Fortunately, the geese did save Rome with their cackling that finally alerted the Romans! However, the dog did eventually become the Roman man's "best friend". This was inevitable when one considers that the wolf – the *canis lupus* – had nurtured Rome's founders!

In fact, some Romans named their dogs "Rome" - not for Romulus, but after the Greek word *rhome*, which means strength, as exhibited by the wolf. Other Romans would have opted for the name "*Celer*" because that was the Latin word for "swift". "*Rex*" – "King"- might have been a popular name until 509 B.C.! I suggested that the "god of dogs" would have been Cerberus – the hound from hell – and not least of all because his three heads would correspond to the Capitoline Triad of Jupiter, Juno and Minerva. When Mackie remarked that it was strange that two of the deities were female, I referred to an archaic Triad composed of Jupiter, Mars and Quirinus, adding that the Romans were called *Quirites* in their early history. As today, the ancient Romans would have used dogs for hunting – *canis venaticus* – and as watch-dogs for livestock – canis pastoralis. But if we think about the myths of Diana – including the one where poor Actaeon is slain by his hounds for seeing the goddess naked - and I'm glad we didn't have dogs with us when we were chatting up "Aphrodite" and friends – naturally the Romans would breed dogs for hunting. It appears that one of the most popular species was a predecessor of our greyhounds! So, Jeremy, since I wasn't able to listen to Nat King Cole singing "Those Lazy-Hazy-Crazy Days of Summer", I mostly spent those "dog days of summer" in Thessaloniki with Mackie! Did you know that this expression – which our Québécois friends call *la canicule* – comes from the fact that at that time of the year, the sun occupies the same region of the sky as the constellation *Canis Major* – "the Greater Dog" - as I explained to Mackie? The brightest star – Sirius – is also seen in that part of the sky! That reminds me of the French novel *La Planète des Singes* by Pierre Boulle. You liked the Hollywood version with Charleton Heston, but in the novel, astronaut Ulysse Mérou has a child with the "savage" woman Nova, and the baby is named Sirius, which probably is meant to foretell a "bright" future for him - and the "new" human race! Jeremy, I am being SERIOUS! The asronaut Ulysse ends up being a "traveller" – like Odysseus/Ulysses – not in space, but in time! *Nova* - Latin for "new"- probably suggests a "new beginning" for civilization, and actually would make a great name for a television show on discoveries in our modern world! After my "lecture", Mackie, with dogged determination, suggested we go see the movie *Straw Dogs*, but I declined the invitation, having read – in a Greek newspaper! – how violent that film was. Fortunately, Mack the Knife was more bark than bite, and stopped hounding me. It seems that in the film Dustin Hoffman's character had an even scarier time during his "walk in the Cornish countryside of Wales" than he had had in Mrs. Robinson's boudoir! Mackie boasted of being an awesome Aussie, though I corrected him by suggesting that he was more of a "kooky kiwi"! But let me tell you about the "last straw"! Mackie often wanted to explore the different parts of the city – interestingly enough, those areas where the tour guides didn't bring us! We stopped into a bar – I wished we had "stopped into a church" like the Mamas and Papas sang in "California Dreaming"- and before long a bevy of girls were sitting with us –

actually wanting us to pay for bevvies! They were suggesting things – and although none of
their vocabulary was in my Greek dictionary – what they were saying brought back images of
"scenes I'd seen" – I know you were waiting for that one, Jeremy! – on Greek vases! Jeremy,
to paraphrase something you once said, they were FTP's – full-time prostitutes! Fortunately
we didn't have enough drachmas to purchase their "souvenirs" – I was glad not to be "rich like
Croesus"! Mackie wanted to come back – actually, some of the non-human scenery was quite
charming. He said that since there was free entry into museums on Sundays, maybe he could
pick up a bargain "hetaira" as well! Having seen that delightful Greek movie with Melina
Mercouri, *Never on Sunday*, I decided to go along. Neither of us knew that the other hadn't
brought any money. Mackie generously invited me to lunch at this exquisite restaurant, where
the patrons were served on a beautiful terrace surrounded by well-trimmed hedges. The meal
was "fit for the gods" – I had the impression there was "Diony- SAUCE" on my steak! After
finishing the meal that was expensive - even for "Croesus" – Mackie confessed that he had no
money with him. What to do? Mackie always had a solution – when the waiter entered the
restaurant to get the bill, we would jump the hedge and run. As I ran – even faster than during
that first foot-race with "Mack the Knife" – I kept praying we wouldn't see spears flying in the
air! I was back at Thermopylae - in a real tight squeeze – and not because the "Hot Gates"
had relegated the Spartans to a very narrow space! I mean, look what the Greeks had done to
Socrates – and we weren't even philosophers! I found myself praying to "DionyS.O.S."!
Mackie pointed out that since we had escaped unscathed, "all's swell that ends swell" - again
proving that he didn't read much – not even Shakespeare! He insisted that I was fortunate to
have such a treasure as a friend. I protested that if he pursued his daredevil deeds he would
end up as a "buried treasure"! There were a lot of my countrymen – you know – Americans -
at the Balkan Institute. A young professor from Columbia University – who taught Ancient
Greek! – advised me not to follow "that Aussie" so blindly, since I wasn't privy to truth like the
"blind Teiresias"! He said our jaunts around northern Greece might end up being a veritable
"Gullible's" Travels for me! Quite the sense of humour! Maybe all Americans are funny when
they leave America! One American student, a bearded, long-haired "spiritual" from Chicago,
was always dressed in a flowing white garment. The rumour circulated one day that he had
run through the city in the nude – you know, totally in the buff! Talk about a crazy "streak"!

You can probably barely stop laughing – but it's the naked truth! Gosh – he could have used a
barrel! But nobody was yelling "*eureka*". More like "you freaka"! I had thought that if he hadn't
spent much time at the beach, nobody would notice he was naked, but still "all in white"! I
recall being so tanned at Pylos that some of the villagers thought I was Greek – especially
since my hair had grown quite long! We never saw him again – maybe they thought HE was a
philosopher! Another American had me do something crazy – this one was on me – no blame

for Mackie this time. This guy, who was from Milwaukee, had the hots for a girl from France, and she seemed to have a little fire going too! Like most Americans, he only spoke English, and unlike the French who leave native soil, she didn't speak English! Love is blind, as they say – but not deaf. Consequently, I served as their interpreter, including when they hatched a plot to smuggle her into our male residence. Now I was Zero Mostel in *A Funny Thing Happened on the Way to the Forum* – or, I guess this time, to the Agora! All good things come to an end, and we were in good spirits – lots of spirits! - at the closing party. Girls say that I'm a good dancer, but it's not that easy when you're on a table, as part of a "dancing chorus" with your Greek teacher! Boy did she look different without her glasses, and with her hair untied! Kind of like Dionysos and one maenad! Can you imagine Gladys Knight and one Pip? Of course I don't dance with the sweet style of Sammy Strain, who is one of Little Anthony's "Imperials"!

Mackie kept trying to get me to do slow dances with different girls – mostly because they had turned him down – seems his reputation had preceded him! We all got to "unWINEd", but things were WINEding down when a girl approached and asked me to dance. She was a redhead from Romania. Hey, "redhead from Romania" – sounds like a country song-title! She had this round face, and when talking with Mackie I always referred to her as "Moon" (as in "moon- faced", Jeremy). Mackie called her Ruby. She was a quiet girl, but I figured this Ruby was planning on "taking her love to town"! If you don't get the reference, Jeremy, look up Kenny Rogers songs. Well, we were dancing cheek to cheek, I was humming "Moon River" in her ear – I wouldn't be able to actually sing that song like Jerry Butler or Andy Williams, but maybe like Audrey Hepburn in *Breakfast at Tiffany's* - and Moon was telling me how she had studied Latin.

Of course, since the Romans had conquered the land of Dacia, I was picturing Trajan's Column – don't even equate that with what is in your dirty mind! Besides, the Romanian language was derived from Latin! They must have a soft spot for the Romans though, since you can't sound more "Roman" than "Romania"! Suddenly I felt her hand in my pants. No, it wasn't a *carpe diem* moment! She was trying to steal my money! The cheek – and this time not in a dancing way! I wasn't about to report her. I'm not bloodthirsty – I'm no Dracula, but this Transylvanian she- devil sure hoped to COUNT my money! Funny how the Roman Empire became a Roman vampire! She discreetly left the party. Somehow I felt like I was witnessing an "eclipse" of the "Moon"! She kind of puts the "bad moon" in CCR's "Bad Moon Rising"! Since I am the "soul of discretion" – you once called me the "dean" of discretion – I didn't mention anything – even to Mackie, who had been oblivious to the whole affair. Do you remember Professor Watson claiming to use his discretionary powers to use "discretionary funds" to purchase fine wines for Department socials? The next day, we all parted ways. But not before I "loaned" some Canadian cash to Mackie for his flight home – apparently he had made a couple of visits to our FTP "friends"! We both knew he wouldn't pay it back, but he tried to rationalize our one-way transaction by saying my money and his money all eventually ended up in the Queen's pocket!

He mumbled something about Canada and Australia, and claimed that my money and his money were a "common wealth"! I could actually imagine Mackie counterfeiting money by printing two dollar bills with the picture of two male deer and calling it "two bucks"! So much for Greece! I did have a very positive experience in Quebec at the CAC conference. People applauded after I read my paper, but then, they're kind of obliged! But a special moment came when I was eating lunch in this restaurant called Marie Antoinette. And although some people there were actually eating cake, I was enjoying a juicy hamburger! Since the place was so crowded, this girl – she was under twenty-five, so I'll call her a girl – asked if she could sit at my table. Being a true gentleman, I said yes. But again, there was kind of an obligation here. We had a nice conversation. She was very good-looking, I mean really attractive! I tried not to stare. I told her I was an American, and she said that I probably found Quebec so French that I imagined I was an "American in Paris". Can you believe it – she knew about movies and music and about my favorite dancer, Gene Kelly! We talked about pop music, and she seemed to know which songs I was talking about, without knowing the actual song titles. Eventually, she had to leave, since she had been on her lunch break and was returning to the Federal Government building where she worked as a secretary for the Department of Veterans Affairs. Why are secretaries always so young and pretty? She said she occasionally came to Montreal for government business – at least I knew she was not a Gerda Munsinger! So we exchanged phone numbers. I told her I was leaning more and more to coming to Laval University to do my PhD. I know what you're thinking, Jeremy! But, yeah, there was this twinkle in her eye! Her name is Manon Plouffe.

Because I had been so kind, she offered to pay for my lunch. I don't know if it was because I was just a student, or she was a super liberated woman. But when I said "*mais non*, Manon!" she couldn't stop laughing. On the way home, I couldn't stop thinking about her. I've had feelings for other girls before, but there's something about Manon! I finally remembered why her family name sounded so familiar. In my French course on Quebec music and film, we watched some episodes of a TV series called "La Famille Plouffe", and it had been based on a novel by Roger Lemelin about a family in Quebec City. I recalled one of the characters being named Ovide – like the Roman poet! But there was also one of his brothers, Guillaume, who was so good at baseball that a Protestant minister, who was engaged to an American girl studying at Laval, and who was also a scout for – get this – the Cincinnati Reds, offered to get him a try-out with the Reds. But the presence of a Protestant minister caused some *angst* for Guillaume's very Catholic family.

The oldest brother, who "managed" his brother's "career", acted like a general, and was very aptly named Napoleon! I don't think that the brothers knew that the Cincinnati Reds were the first professional baseball team and were initially called the Red Stockings. They probably changed names because that name sounded too much like what you hang up for Santa Clause to fill with goodies! The Plouffe Family story is so good, they will probably make a movie about it some day. And I remember we listened to a song during one of our classes by Donald Lautrec called "Manon, viens danser le Ska". I wonder if someday I'll get to invite Manon to dance! Take care! The Latin Guy

-     Well, then, Holden, not too many of these tea socials left for you. Some guys have all the luck! But seriously, I'll miss our chats during these get-togethers. You've been here almost six years, and you have never ceased to amaze me. You've achieved so much! Not only two degrees in Classics - I know the M.A. is not official yet, but really! - but teaching here and at Loyola, and acquiring proficiency in Modern Greek, German, and Italian! You've written poetry and a short story, which is about to be published. When can we expect your novel? The paper you read at the CAC is being published, and you have made valuable contacts at the British, American and French Schools in Athens and Rome. You are so organized – I think Professor Watson has had a profound effect on you! The villagers near Pylos still talk about you – in a nice way! For what it's worth, you were the only student invited to Miss Templeton's wedding. I sometimes think she got married in order to stop dreaming about you! Don't blush – now I can stop dreaming about HER! It was a beautiful wedding, though, at St. Patrick's Cathedral. The reception was great – all that beer! So I hear you have been officially accepted into the doctoral programme at Laval. I think you made a wise choice. They have an excellent faculty. Professor Marois has an international reputation in Roman Religion – much like our own dear Watson. They may even collaborate in directing your research. Professor Marcoux, whom you know, has just been named Department Chair, so that's a plus for you! I suspect he will co-opt you onto the *Conseil* of *SEGELQ*. But that will have its perks! What is really exciting about Classics at Laval is their Roman Archaeology programme. Professor Picard is doing field work at Pompeii in collaboration with an American consortium. Your bilingualism will certainly be an asset, if you work on the site, and I don't see why you shouldn't, given the religious connections with Pompeii – the House of the Mysteries, for example. Just be careful around the village girls! Sorry, Holden, but I'll never let that go! And only because you have a great sense of humour! I can see you becoming a fine professor some day! You'd be very popular at Bryn Mawr – since it's a women's college! Now I'm really testing your stoic humour! But Tenney Frank and Richmond Lattimore taught there! Who knows? Maybe you will pursue a career this side of the border? And I'm really impressed by how you can span centuries of artistic excellence in your knowledge of poets and singers from Homer and Vergil to Bob Dylan and Stevie Wonder! I've seen Professor Manfredi returning to his office after a class with you, singing your praises – which is a welcome change from everything else he sings!

-     I've enjoyed talking with you too, Professor Peters, especially about Cincinnati! You have been a connection with home that I would otherwise have missed. You don't mind being called "the missing link", do you, Professor? And yes, in Pylos you saved my life – or perhaps a would-be wife! I'm sure we're both grateful! You see, your sense of humour is second to none! I will miss Montreal, even though Quebec is not far. I will miss my apartment on Milton. It will be from now on Milton's "paradise lost"! I will miss the Faculty and students in the Department, many of whom I have known for almost six years. True, I will miss Mrs. Larsen – until last month, Miss Templeton. But I'm ready for new challenges, and the final chapter in the life of "the Latin student". So far, I have been fortunate in being able to seize and enjoy every opportunity that presented itself. But when I get to Quebec and settle in, there is a phone number I could call. No, that I will call! *Carpe diem*! I see Professor Jolivet is beckoning me to the podium. Wish me luck, Professor Peters!

-       Knock them dead, Holden!

-       Hello, everybody. I say "hello", you say "good-bye" – just a little Beatles reminiscence before I read a poem I wrote for my modular teaching course. It followed an interesting visit I had to an inner-city high school, where I gave a talk on Classical mythology. The students were keenly interested, and asked many questions. I felt sorry that they had no opportunity to study Latin. I will be moving on, as is mentioned in my poem. But I'll only be two hundred and fifty miles away – a Greek messenger ran further than that in one day! – I guess he missed the inter-city bus! So our paths are sure to cross – I'd rather cross paths than cross Professor Manfredi!

The poem is entitled "On Teaching".

 Did you know, young man,

That Socrates walked barefoot

to be one with nature?

Does the word "*physis*" mean anything to you?

Are you reminded of physical

and physics, our own study of nature?

And did you know that "*nomos*" meant law?

You've removed your shoes again

in our classroom, an anomaly for sure!

Moving on...

You wrote in your journal, young man,

That your family visited Disney World

 and that you enjoyed that vacation very much.

How far is Disney World?

Which direction did you take

When you all set off in the family van?

Moving on...

You're not concentrating on your history test.

There's something on your mind, young man,

that I've noticed by that sad expression you bear.

I'm free at lunch hour.

You can drop by if you'd like to talk,

and maybe discuss re-writing your test.

Moving on...

Atticus Finch was a courageous man.

You shouldn't kill an innocent mocking-bird,

 or any other bird for that matter.

Vultures and buzzards aren't innocent, you say,

Since they are like the evil-minded bigots

waiting for Lawyer Finch's black man to die.

Moving on…

You are going to examine

Society's conviction of an innocent man

in Plato's *Apology* and Harper Lee's *To Kill a Mockingbird*.

Take a look at the map of North America.

 Situate Florida in relation to your home,

which is somewhat to the north.

But I especially want to know, young man,

If you are happy, and can I help?

-       Very touching, Mr. Hainsworth! Very moving – this last pun in tribute to you for the
many pleasant moments you have brought to this Department – inside and outside of class!

-       Thank you, Professor Jolivet!

Chapter 78

- Welcome to another class on the moral lessons of Seneca. As we have seen, this Stoic philosopher's advice, admonitions and accolades – notice I have given Seneca an "A" for his content, all the while using assonance – lower case "a"! – remain wisdom for the ages! We have already noticed a significant difference between the style of Cicero and that of Seneca. Whereas the philosopher and statesman of the Roman Republic favored a style in which one did not express one's ideas in a few words when one could expand the message into numerous sentences, Nero's tutor delivered his thoughts in what is known as the pointed style, that is a very succinct and terse expression of thought. Seneca said that "great artists enclose all things in a small space" – *magni artificis est clusisse totum in exiguo*. We shall have occasion to examine the life and works of Seneca throughout our course, paying particular attention to his Stoic creed.Today we shall read and translate his thirty-fourth letter to his friend Lucilius, in which he expresses elation at the latter's success, himself a follower of Seneca. I remind you that Seneca wrote 124 moral epistles. Now, Mr. Hainsworth, you have on occasion mentioned to me the practice you have of writing letters home on a regular basis, and also to our mutual friend in Toronto. It is fitting, then, that you present today's letter to the class.

- Certainly, Professor Jolivet! And I hope you will be as proud of me as Seneca was of Lucilius! *Seneca Lucilio Suo Salutem Cresco et exulto et discussa senectute recalesco quotiens ex iis quae agis ac scribis intellego quantum te ipse – nam turbam olim reliqueras superieceris. Si agricolam arbor ad fructum perducta delectat, si pastor ex fetu gregis sui capit voluptatem, si alumnum suum nemo aliter intuetur quam ut adulescentiam illius suam iudicet, quid evenire credis iis qui ingenia educaverunt et quae tenera formaverunt adulta subito vident? Adsero te mihi; meum opus es. Ego cum vidissem indolem tuam, inieci manum, exhortatus sum, addidi stimulus nec lente ire passus sum sed subinde incitavi; et nunc idem facio, sed iam currentem hortor et invicem hortantem. "Quid illud?" inquis "adhuc volo.". In hoc plurimum est, non sic quomodo principia totius operis dimidium occupare dicuntur. Ista res animo constat; itaque pars magna bonitatis est velle fieri bonum. Scis quem bonum dicam? Perfectum, absolutum, quem malum facere nulla vis, nulla necessitas possit. Hunc te prospicio, si perseveraveris et incubueris et id egeris ut omnia facta dictaque tua inter se congruant ac respondeant sibi et una forma percussa sint. Non est huius animus in recto cuius acta discordant. Vale.*

"Seneca sends greetings to his friend Lucilius.

I spring forth and rejoice, and with my old age shaken off, I glow whenever I understand from what you do and write how much you have outdone yourself – since you left the crowd behind long ago. If the tree brought to fruition pleases the farmer, if the shepherd takes pleasure from the offspring of his flock, if no one looks upon his pupil other than he judges his own youth, what do you believe happens to those who have educated minds and they see the young they have shaped suddenly grown up? I claim you for myself; you are my finished work. When I had seen your natural ability, I placed my hand on you, I exhorted you, I supplied stimuli, and did not permit you to go slowly, but encouraged you continually; I do the same thing even now, but I am encouraging one who is already running and encouraging me. 'What else, then?' you say, 'I'm still willing'. In this situation, it is quite considerable, and not as they say - the beginning of a task occupies the half of it. For this matter here depends on the soul; therefore the larger part of goodness is to be willing to become good. Do you know what I mean by a good man? A perfect, complete man, whom no force, no necessity is able to make bad. I see this man as you, if you persevere and devote yourself and pay attention so that all your deeds and words are in harmony with themselves and correspond to each other and are stamped with a single form. The soul of one whose acts are in conflict is not on the right path. Farewell."

- Good translation, Mr. Hainsworth! I should point out that the words *inieci manum* refer to the procedure wherein a Roman claimed possession of something belonging to him, without having sought a legal pronouncement. This often happened in the case of runaway slaves. So a talent scout today would take complete control over a singer and become his uncompromising manager. Think of Colonel Parker and Elvis Presley! And the notion of "a job begun is half done", obviously applies to manual tasks and not to the "business of the soul". Do you have any comments on your translation, Mr. Hainsworth, before we adjourn?

- True, I have known students who swear by Cicero, but also those who swear AT Cicero, as they sweat over seething Ciceronian *sententiae*! Whereas the style of Seneca, which you just described, Professor, allows him to get right to the point! It's too bad The King didn't sing "Don't be Cruel" to Colonel Parker! To paraphrase Seneca, I did a good translation, because I "was willing" to do one! I suppose Seneca would subscribe to the belief that "where there's a will, there's a way"! As they say in French – vouloir c'est pouvoir! The beginning of the letter suggests that you can remove the *senectus* from Seneca, but I don't think you can remove the Seneca from the *senectus*, that is, his preoccupation with "old age"! But this passage is another proof that – with apologies to Sam and Dave – Seneca was a real "Soul Man"!

Chapter 79

-       I hope you enjoyed your sabbatical in England, Professor Watson. Were you able to read my thesis draft?

-       England was very nice. London, being London, was a little wet at times. Mrs. Watson was often singing "Raindrops Keep Falling on My Head", which she told me was a song recorded by one B.J.Thomas. I think Mrs. Watson would have appreciated having you there to compare notes on the new songs she heard on the radio. An amusing incident occurred when Mrs. W. announced she was going to see "The Animals". I protested that the zoo wasn't open at this time of the year, but she sighed and said "Do you mean to say you've never heard of "The House of the Rising Sun"? I had assumed she was talking about a new breakfast restaurant that was opening. She finally explained that she would be attending a music concert, featuring a band called "The Animals". The niece of the Curator of the Ashmolean Museum had two tickets.

But, yes, I read your thesis twice. The first time I read it, Mrs. Watson was a bit of a distraction, as she sang "Don't Let Me Be Misunderstood" in the background! You are proposing that we should not use the Roman names for Dionysus, Bacchus and Liber, interchangeably, as is commonly done in mythology handbooks and elsewhere. The claim that Dionysos was known in Greece in Bronze Age times, contradicting the legend of the god as a newcomer, as recounted in *The Bacchae* of Euripides, can be rationalized, you say, by the fact that the name of Dionysos on Linear B tablets appears only on Crete. Therefore, you say, his eventual appearance on the mainland at a later date, would be accurate. Furthermore, you explain that the myth of Dionysos – or Bacchus, another Greek name for the god – saving Ariadne, the Cretan princess, after she had been abandoned by Theseus, was related to the god's connection with Crete, and not primarily with the god's role in the Orphic tradition as the protector of mortals. We have evidence of this role, of course, in the Orphic text which reads "Tell Persephone it was Bacchios himself who set you free". You go on to say that Dionysos did make his way into mainland Greece – as you point out, there is evidence of his presence in Greece from the sixth century. He arrived there from Thrace, or perhaps, Phrygia. You very conveniently have him arrive, after having been worshipped in both those places. You make much of this later in your thesis when you describe how the Romans likewise imported divinities from Asia Minor, which became the "oriental cults" of Rome. You also mentioned that the connection with Orpheus, whose cult was always outside mainstream religious worship in Greece, was probably due largely to the fact that the origins of Orpheus can also be traced to Thrace. Dionysos-Bacchus was the object of worship in the frenzied practices of "savage women" - maenads – who were driven to wild dancing under the influence of wine. You note, as well, that the priests of this cult, when it made its way to Rome with other eastern cults, such as those of Isis, Mithras, and *Magna Mater*, were likewise described as wild and effeminate, and given to imbibing great quantities of wine. They were no doubt eunuchs. You go on to analyze the nature of Bacchus as the inspiration for the Greek traditions of dancing and acting, which led to the "birth of tragedy", to borrow Nietzsche's expression! You explain how the association with actors and other artists was maintained in the worship of Dionysos as in some sort of international brotherhood. You trace the dance of tragedy to the even more ecstatic dance of women worshippers, magnified through wine. After all, women were not permitted to dance or act on the Greek stage. Herein lies the overlap with the Roman Liber. This deity was the god of the fields – one of many Roman nature gods – who assured fertility, hence a very masculine divine force. The followers of Dionysos were largely women, or effeminate, debauched men. Dionysos is the god of the vine, a symbol of nature. But, you suggest, perhaps this assimilation comes about from his role as the god of wine, which is the by-product of the vine fertilized by the nature god Liber – or *Liber Pater*, the "patriarchal force of fertility", who could impregnate Mother Earth, herself possibly associated with the *Magna Mater* from Phrygia – also the original home of Dionysos! You talk about the worship of Dionysus by the Etruscans - *Fufluns Bacchus* – in the city of Vulci. There is even evidence for worship in a private house. The Etruscans had contact with the Greeks, as well as origins in Asia Minor. Consequently, familiarity with the "Greek" Dionysus and the "oriental" Dionysus is no surprise. So the Romans would have "imported" this god from a variety of traditions. The superstitious Romans would have been only too eager to accept one more god.

We know of the Roman tendency to worship – or at least to accept – all divine beings and forces of nature. They also were keen to give Roman names to Greek gods – but not to other foreign gods. There was still an Isis and a Mithras. But it was a source of pride for the Romans to "Romanize" elements of Greek culture, including the names of gods. Yes, I know, Apollo was an exception – that I daresay proves the rule! Bacchus was a Greek name, to be reserved for the unconventional – or non-Roman - cult practices. You mention the banning of these exaggerated practices in the decree of 186 B.C. concerning the *Bacchanalia*. The logical choice then, to assume the Roman role of Dionysus, in his traditional association with nature, is Liber, a Roman nature god. But the wild side of Dionysus, the Roman Bacchus, was sometimes then, as it is nowadays, also attributed to Liber. Artificial freedom, the reward of Dionysiac/Bacchic worship, was confused – in the sense of "fusion" and "confusion" – with authentic freedom represented by the divine Liber. You add that Plutarch discusses this transfer of the epithet "free" to the Roman god in number 104 of his *Roman Questions*, and "wonders" if this is due to a fusion with *Dionysos Eleuthereus* – "the free one" - from the city in Boiotia near Attica. An earlier refusal by the Athenians to accept Dionysos was followed by acceptance and introduction of the Dionysia festival following a plague in Athens. The other interpretations offered by Plutarch are that *Liber Pater* was the "father of freedom" for drinkers, or that he provided the means for libations – this, of course, refers to wine. This association of Liber - or *Liber Pater* - with Bacchus/Dionysus is tantamount to blaming the vine-grower - or "wine producer" - for the drunkenness of the wine drinker! Having read Cicero's *De Natura Deorum*, you were in an excellent position to summarize that Roman's position on the attribution of Roman names to the Greek god Dionysos. You also examined other works by Cicero, and concluded that he used the name Bacchus to refer to negative aspects of the Greek god's cult in Rome, speaking specifically of excesses due to the drinking of wine – this reflects the severe measures of 186 B.C. with the *senatus consultum de Bacchanalibus*. When speaking of more civilized practices of the cult, Cicero refers to the god as Liber. You seem quite excited when you refer to the Stoic Balbus and his argument in the conversation recorded in the *De Natura Deorum*. He makes the distinction between the Liber, son of Semele – that is, the Greek Dionysos, and the Liber, son of Ceres – a "Roman" Dionysus, as it were. By the way, I commend you on consistently using the Greek spelling *-os* for the "Greek" Dionysos and the Latin ending *–us* when referring to the "Roman" Dionysus! Balbus further states that the children of Ceres were named Liber and Libera, after the practice of calling children *liberi* in Latin, hence literally "the free ones". This lack of imagination and diversity in choosing names is also seen in the Roman practice of naming children by numbers – Quintus, Sextus, Septimius, Octavius, Nonnus, Decimus! You may be even more of a Stoic than you think, Mr. Hainsworth! You answer the objection that the Romans used Bacchus when they meant the ancestral Liber with the Roman eagerness to "Greekify" – in art and literature, as well in religious practices of the State. They even, at times, made use of Greek practices in their worship – the *ritus Graecus*! You appropriately quote Horace's famous line – *Graecia capta ferum victorem cepit*: "Captured Greece captured its savage captor". The Greeks, we know, considered the Romans, like all other non-Greeks, "barbarians", a reference to their language not being Greek, and therefore incomprehensible.

Interestingly enough – and this is further proof of Horace's claim – the Romans did not consider the Greeks barbarians. Dionysos was not a universally worshipped god in Greece. An early cult on the island of Naxos – and here again we have the "thread" of the Cretan connection with the rescue of Ariadne - I noticed the pun here – but of course that won't be in your final draft! – made its way to Athens where it was only natural for festivals of Dionysos to rival those of Athena, goddess of the city of Theseus, who had abandoned Ariadne before she was rescued by Dionysos! Aside from the association with poets – tragic and comic – Dionysos remains – literally - off the beaten path, and is the object of the restricted worship of initiates in a mystery cult, involving some sort of reincarnation. Actually, when you consider that an actor puts on the mask of a deceased character in a play, he "reincarnates" - brings to life on the stage - that mythical or historico-literary figure! Likewise in Rome, as you mentioned, the worship of Bacchus was not practiced without reservations. His worship did continue, however, in spite of the suppression of the orgiastic elements of his cult practice. The Romans underwent, in different stages, strong moral sentiments that precluded any participation in a *prava religio*, but they were not about to offend any divine being. The worshipers were depraved, not the god being worshipped! They did outlaw Christ, but they did not consider Him a divine being. However, the study of the "fall and rise" of Christianity – as ironic as that phrase sounds when speaking about the Roman Empire! – is outside the subject of this thesis. You conclude with the mention that *Liber Pater* was front and center in the second century under the reign of the African Emperor, Septimius Severus! The coinage under this Emperor does exhibit some iconographical elements of "Dionysus of the vine", but the Romans were forever copying Greek art, especially when it depicted mythological elements. And thus the so-called Temple of Bacchus at Baalbek has been attributed to Bacchus/ Dionysus because of the architectural maenads on the temple. Possibly it was dedicated to *Liber Pater*. After all, a few decades later, there seemed to have been plans to build a temple in his honor under Septimius, just as an earlier temple had been built in Tripolitania, modern Libya. With this supremacy of the god *Liber Pater*, Dionysus/Bacchus is now genuinely "Romanized"!

-        Thank you for your comments, Professor Watson. I have two months left to finalize and submit my thesis. I have been investigating the dichotomy of Dionysos as an early Greek god, as attested by the Linear B tablets, and as a "newcomer", as told in the story of *The Bacchae* of Euripides. This has led me to a reference to "Diyanus" in an epic romance poem from the ancient Persian corpus called *Vamiq and 'Adhra*. It was written at the beginning of the 11th century AD by a court poet named Abu'l-Qasim 'Unsuri, and purports to be modelled on a Hellenistic Greek novel called *Metiochus and Parthenope*, since the Persian title means "The Ardent Lover and the Virgin". The Athenians, of course, had honored their goddess Athena as a "virgin" with the construction of the Parthenon! That tradition has come down to us with the "Maiden" Mother of God revered as "The Virgin Mary". Even Robin Hood had his "Maid Marian"! The Persian poem refers to the king calling upon his poet minstrel, who played an instrument similar to the lyre, to "play the songs of Diyanus and the sacred music". In the poem, Diyanus – obviously "Dionysos" – is said to be a name for the Islamic Harut – a fallen angel who knows arts forbidden to men. This is reminiscent of the story of Prometheus and of the Christian tradition surrounding Lucifer! The minstrel's name is Ifuqus – ironically similar to Ibykos, a Greek poet of the 6th century B.C. , who was at the court of the tyrant Polycrates on the island of Samos. The king's name in the Persian epic is strangely similar to Polycrates! I also learned that in Vedic mythology there is a plant called Soma that has similar effects on people to those of the "wine of Dionysos" on the maenads, such as sexual arousal and increased physical strength! The name for this intoxicating plant is also given to the god of vegetation associated with this overpowering force and the drink produced from the plant. Professor Watson, I recognize here Dionysos and the vine, as well as the wine produced from that vine! In Persian mythology there is the Haoma plant, associated with a certain "Duraosa", which translates as "beautiful man". That name was close enough to "Dionysos", and the description in *The Bacchae* of the "handsome young man", who turns out to be the god Dionysos, drove me to "follow Dionysos" further East. My "travels" brought back memories of the film *Thief of Bagdad* and a film from 1941 about the incursion of Alexander the Great into India called *Iskandar*, parts of which were shown to us in my Ancient Film course at the Academy in Rome. If I remember correctly, the elephants shared top billing with Iskandar! I've heard that there was a Bollywood remake a few years ago. I fondly remember tales from *The Arabian Nights*, such as "Aladdin's Wonderful Lamp" and "Ali Baba and the Forty Thieves". As I mentioned, Bagdad only needed one thief! I know that the official title is *One Thousand and One Nights* – that's almost as many kisses that Catullus wanted to share with his Lesbia! The Arabian Odysseus – Sinbad the Sailor - was an offshoot of those tales, and I imagine that when he runs out of American "material", Walt Disney will produce super animated features based on the Arabian tales! We have seen throughout history that merchants will arrive in new territories before soldiers and settlers – the Phoenicians proved that! So when Alexander arrived in India, the inhabitants were already familiar with Greek cultural elements, including the worship of the god Dionysos, who had been "sent by Zeus" to conquer Asia before returning to Greece. I think this explains the mystery of an "old" and a "new" Dionysos in Greek legend! In fact the god had founded a city at the top of a hill called Nysa, apparently named after the god's nurse. And we know from the worship that Dionysos shared with Apollo at Delphi that the "god of the vine" loved hilltops! Another name for the city – or perhaps there was another city – was Dionysopolis. Supposedly, out of respect for the god, Alexander did not ascend the mountain to attack the city. But I rather think that he did not want his men to see the vineyards up there and become homesick! I ended up – no not the end of my voyage – reading parts of the *Dionysiaca*. Only parts, since that Greek epic poem is over 20,000 lines, making it almost as long as the *Iliad* and the *Odyssey* combined! It was written at the end of the 4th century by Nonnus of Panopolis, a town in Egypt which seems to have an affinity with the god Pan – unless it was named as a tribute to "all" cities, just as the Roman

Pantheon was a tribute to "all the gods"! It is said to be the longest – and the last – epic poem in Ancient Greek Literature! It is considered the last great celebration of the Greek gods – a poem I wrote in high school notwithstanding! In India they swore by the sacred waters of their rivers, such as the Ganges and the Indus. However, this poem speaks of the Asian conquest by Dionysos, wherein '"wine triumphed over water"! For some reason, I'm reminded of Jesus' miracle at the wedding of Cana! The poem recounts several love affairs of Dionysos. Although my mother gave me a name in honor of that god, my occasional sentimental relationships cannot compete! By the time of Augustus, trade – and probably cultural exchanges – were well underway. But Pausanias says that Dionysos was the first to invade India. Therefore Indo- European religious beliefs as well as linguistic roots would have given the Romans more knowledge of that Greek god whom they would adopt as Bacchus and associate with their own god Liber. In his *Natural History*, Pliny the Elder claims that Alexander followed Father Liber in conquering India, and in his *Metamorphoses*, Ovid speaks of Dionysus – Liber – as the conqueror of India. I was quite pleased to see references to Bacchus leading soldiers into India in two plays of Seneca – the *Oedipus* and the *Phaedra*!

- My, my, Mr. Hainsworth! You have enough material there to submit a second thesis – perhaps to the Oriental Institute at the University of Chicago!

- Thank you, Professor, but I merely want to have all my bases covered – like the Chicago Cubs or the Chicago White Sox - to "steal" a line from baseball! As you know, thanks to you, I'll be attending the British School at Athens this summer to participate in a seminar on numismatics, perhaps to get a first-hand look at those Septimius coins! I'll also be taking a course on Pindar and the Greek lyric poets. My doctoral programme begins in September. A friend has already found me an apartment near the university campus. I will be able to power walk for twenty minutes! When it's raining heavy, I'll take the bus. My parents will be here for the convocation in June, and will probably want to join me in thanking you for all you have done for me over the past six years. Six years – that's one quarter of my life so far!

- And you've lived it to the full, Mr. Hainsworth! Almost as if *carpe diem* was your birthmark! A friend already in Quebec! You'll like life there, especially since you're so fluent in French. As you know, I am reluctant to speak French with my Irish accent, unless there is wine in the room, or I'm speaking about Department business with Professor Jolivet. But my reading knowledge is excellent, and if I were to co-direct your doctoral research, I would have no problem in reading your drafts. Some of the professors at Laval speak good English, like Professor Marois, their authority on Roman Religion, and Professor Marcoux, who was here last year. He told me he learned English by attending the summer programme for a few years at Bishop's College in Lennoxville. Apparently, quite a few Americans attend that university. I don't know if you are aware that Professor Saucier at Laval is an internationally respected authority on Seneca, and you will no doubt be taking a seminar with him. Given all the Greek and Roman authors you have read over the past seven years here and at Xavier University – yes, I've been reviewing your transcripts – you will be able to fulfil your comprehensive reading requirements with a regular course load in your first two years. You will not have to spend a year reading a plethora of Greek and Latin authors with a view to writing comprehensive exams on said authors! And you have already completed your foreign language proficiency requirements!

Chapter 80

-       Hi Manon! It was so nice of you to find a conveniently located apartment for me. Right next to the Marie Antoinette! I hope we'll be able to eat there together sometimes.

There is so much I'd like to know about you, and hopefully, you're interested in hearing more about me. This time I'm going to pay for the meal!

There are a lot of tourists here, but I was expecting that. This shopping mall – Place Laurier – is huge! So many stores, and I've seen at least two bookstores! I'll be meeting my professors at Laval next week, and I was kind of hoping we could visit Old Quebec on the weekend.

-       Yes, we could do that, Denys. I hope you don't mind me calling you that. When you told me that your mother gave you that name I found it so cute. And I must confess it's easier for me to pronounce than Holden. One of the government supervisors from Ottawa has that name – but it is his family name! Maybe your professors might like to call you Denys. Be careful if they write it down – they may spell it Denis. If we're still friends at Christmas, I'd like to meet your family when they come to visit you. You say you like dancing. Well, I usually go dancing on Saturday nights with a couple of girlfriends. You're welcome to come along. I take my mother out on Friday nights, but I don't think you'd like to come along then! Eventually, you can meet my family. You shouldn't be in a hurry to meet my father – none of the young men I've presented to him liked him. But then, my father didn't like them either! I have two brothers – Michel, who studies Social Work at Laval, and Antoine, who is in high school. I have a sister, Nicole, who is still in elementary school, and an older sister, Marguerite, who is married to Robert, an American truck-driver from Baltimore. We call him Bob, and he calls my sister Maggie. He's really nice, but he's away two days a week. If he's away on a Saturday, Marguerite comes dancing with us. He calls me Manny. Michel is Mike, and Antoine is Tony! Nicole he calls Nicky, a name she loves! He can't make Denys shorter, so don't be surprised if he finds a completely different name for you! Changing everybody's name is a little idiosyncracy he has. However, my mother's name is Mariette, and my father's name is Marcel, but Bob calls them M. and Mme. Plouffe! Papa is a retired fireman, and Maman – I call her Ma – stays home to look after everybody! She's originally from Montreal. Papa calls her Maoui, because I'm Manon! I've been working for Veterans Affairs for two years, and I'm saving up to buy a car.

-       Well, I would like to meet your family – it's bigger than the Plouffe Family in the novel! I can see why you want a car – everybody drives here. Of course, you have no metro system. So we won't hear Petula Clark's song "Don't Sleep in the Subway" played on the radio!

Maybe that's why people seem to be less in a hurry here. But I have to admit that The Supremes song "You Can't Hurry Love" has me wondering! It's nice to be able to relax and "smell the flowers" – I'm hoping to give you the chance to do just that! Do you like roses? I guess it's true that you can enjoy life more by not rushing around! *Festa lente*, as Professor Watson always says, "Take your time going fast"! You say that if your father likes me, he'll probably call me "the Latin student". I'd actually like that! I hope he doesn't have negative vibes about me and call me "*maudit Americain*". You say he never calls Bob that, but then you wouldn't call a truck-driver a nasty name, would you?

Does Bob ever sing "Maggie May" to your sister? He probably doesn't have Rod Stewart's raspy, but sexy voice! I have a song for you – "Love is a 'Manny'!- Spendoured Thing"! I'm anxious to visit St-Romuald, where you live. There seem to be more saints here in Quebec than in Montreal! My friend Jeremy lives on the South Shore of Montreal, so it's kind of ironic that you also live on the South Shore. That bridge you take, Pont du Québec, looks pretty old. But I would very much like to visit your church, *Église* St. Romuald. I'll be attending Sunday Mass near the University at *Église* Saint-Thomas -d'Aquin. It's on Louis-Jolliet Street, I guess named after the explorer who was the first white man to cross the Mississippi, along with a priest, Father Marquette. You know we have schools back home named after them. They went all over, and explored the Ohio Valley. So I'll be exploring Jolliet's native country! The district around Laval is called *Cité Universitaire*. Back home, a lot of university campuses - you know if I were using real Latin, I'd say "*campi*" – are miniature cities, but we don't call them that. However, I know the city is actually called Sainte-Foy, like that smaller shopping center next to Place Laurier. That's where I can get a bus to Montreal. The bus company here is called Voyageur – so a bus ride is like going out to explore! The American company is called Greyhound – so it's like racing off somewhere! *Festina lente*! You know, Manon, I will be renewing my Parker Grant, which pays for my tuition and living expenses, for a seventh year. I was told that I will be the first student to receive the grant for more than six years. They also pay my summer travel and tuition in Europe, so they're pretty generous. The money I made teaching I can save for a rainy day, as they say. If that's the case, Professor Watson says, I'd have to spend it all in London, if ever I spent a whole year there! Although even a "rain cloud" can have a silver lining. Maybe we can meet for breakfast at the Marie Antoinette on Saturday, Manon, and take a bus into Quebec City!

-       Sounds good, Denys, but we won't need to take the bus – I'll borrow my father's car.

Chapter 81

-       Hello, Holden. Good to see you again! You may be aware that here, we call students by their first name. McGill is a fine institution, but as much as possible, we like to be *bons vivants*! After your work on Dionysus, that should be easy for you! Instead of tea, we drink wine and beer here. But not every day! Except maybe for Professor Walter – for him each day is Oktoberfest! This habit he probably developed as a student at Tübingen University! You will like him, though, even if he's very Epicurean, and you subscribe to the Stoicism of Cicero and Seneca. I am speaking in an academic sense, of course! I know that, like me, you are a practicing Roman Catholic. You met our Secretary, Madame Larouche. She has been with the Department longer than anyone else – thirty-two years! I'm wondering if the news that a handsome young American was coming to study here helped her decide to stay at least one more year! And speaking of Madame Larouche, she noticed in one of your documents that your middle name is Denys, and asked if she could address you with that name. In fact, I'm wondering if we couldn't all call you by that name. In which case, Professor Roumelis may wish to call you Dionysos! He has an interest in numismatics, by the way, and you can talk about the subject with him, when you get the chance. Obviously, you will want to practice Modern Greek with him. You will be very interested to hear that he spent one year at the University of Cincinnati during his doctoral studies, which he completed at Princeton, following his B.A. in Athens. And you can practice German with *Herr* Walter, as well as Italian with Professor Ricard, who, because of his excavations in Italy, including Pompeii, has developed a certain proficiency. You had enquired about studying Spanish, mostly because you have been coming across interesting articles on Roman religion written in Spanish. Normally, this would not be possible, but since my wife teaches Spanish in the Modern Languages Department – you may have seen Ismelda at the McGill socials on a couple of occasions – she has agreed to let you audit her Introductory Spanish course. You won't receive credits, but you won't be taking the course to earn credits.

You will be in Professor Walter's Epigraphy class, and join Professor Saucier's Seminar on Seneca. Do you know that he is a leading authority on Seneca? You have read so many authors in your previous university courses, that the Department has been able to devise a programme that will allow you to complete your required readings within the framework of your credited Latin and Greek courses. During my year at McGill I received valuable help from Professor Watson on how to structure course loads.

Consequently, you will be able to take Professor Giguère's course on the *Letters* of Pliny. By the way, students still address Professors by title, and not by first names – even though Madame Giguère is only a few years older than you! You will be enrolled in two Greek courses – Strabo and Polybius with Professor Roumelis, and my course on Aristophanes and Menander. Oh, we are staging *The Frogs* of Aristophanes in our Greek Theater Group. I have already benefitted from your acting ability when you played Hippolytus at McGill, And I'd love to have you join. We will be reading that play in our course.

Denys – you're okay with that name? – I know you are super organized and have superior skill in time management, not to mention a certain facility in both Latin and Greek. For that reason, I am going to share some requests that have been made to our Department, one of them specifically about you. Professor Jones at Loyola was so impressed with your teaching last year, that he is hoping that you can travel to Montreal one day a week to teach two courses, namely a Latin reading course on Vergil's *Aeneid*, and a lecture course on Greek and Roman religion, which is a new course they are introducing. A certain Professor Watson recommended you! Ah, the importance of synchronized scheduling. The two courses at Loyola are scheduled on Tuesdays, and Tuesday is the one day you have no classes here at Laval! My friend, Professor Watson, helped me plan an itinerary for the day. You would take a Voyageur bus at 7 AM, and arrive in Montreal around 9:30. Both courses at Loyola last two hours – Latin at 10:30 and Greco-Roman Religion at 1:00 PM. Or, the other way round – now I have forgotten.

You would then be able to meet with Professor Watson at 4:00 at McGill to discuss Roman Religion, and a possible PhD dissertation. Supper would be included at the McGill Classics Department's expense – he promises more than tea biscuits! Finally, you would catch the Voyageur bus to Quebec at 7 PM, and be home around 9:30. Professor Watson also mentioned a new guest lecture programme, with monthly lectures at 4 PM on Tuesdays! By the way, our special lecture programme is on Fridays at noon. Now, then, Denys, Father Meloche at the Grand Séminaire du Québec has been asking us for three years to send someone from the Department to teach Ecclesiastical Latin and New Testament Greek. Would you be willing to sacrifice – perhaps "sacrifice" has too much of a religious connation for the circumstances – would you be willing to give up your Wednesday afternoons to teach those two course to seminarians? The Seminary apparently has a budget for a generous remuneration. The Diocese must be doing well! Finally - or almost – Laval sponsors a public lecture series on Thursday evenings here on campus. The Dean of the Faculty has asked the Department to prepare a four-year programme of lectures. If you accepted this assignment – for which there is a stipend – the series would be as follows : Year one – Greco-Roman

Mythology. Year two - Greco-Roman History. Year three – Greco-Roman Literature. Year four – Greco-Roman Religion. One more thing! There is a non-profit group of enthusiastic people who have formed an association to promote the study of classical languages and cultures. They are looking for someone to teach a Latin course to the general public on Monday or Wednesday evening. I thought you might like to teach such a course using *Lingua Romanorum*, that you think so highly of! Because of your busy Tuesday, I imagine you would opt for Wednesday evening. As for your schedule of classes, since the Spanish class meets on Thursday afternoons, you will have two classes a day on Mondays and Thursdays and a single class on Wednesdays and Fridays. Play rehearsals are on Friday afternoons, and will start in October. I assume you will have a bit of a social life on the weekend, which should leave you a part of the weekend for thinking about, and eventually working on, a dissertation. Actually, there's more! Ismelda is taking a group of students to Spain and Portugal for two weeks during the annual Spring Break – you know – when American students usually head for the beach! If you were willing to give a couple of lectures to the group on Roman Spain, you could go along as one of the group leaders. And finally – yes - this time, finally – through Professor Saucier's connection with *L'École française à Athènes,* you would be able to spend next summer in Athens where they are offering seminars on papyrology and the *Hellenica Oxyrhynchia.* You should know that Professor Saucier, a graduate of the Sorbonne, began his distinguished career at the Université de Lyon. I see I haven't mesmerized you! Professor Watson has told me that you find no challenge too daunting, that you are the least pusillanimous student he has ever met, that you actually prefer seeing the whole multi-faceted picture at once. I myself would probably have opted for intermittently taking your blood pressure, if for no other reason than to measure your levels of excitement! So, Denys, what do you have to say?

Carpe diem, Professor Marcoux, *carpe totum diem*! I would indeed love to introduce Latin to the general public. At the risk of appearing to profer a pretentious pronouncement, I am ready to teach Latin *"urbi et orbi"*- not as a pontifical blessing on the population, of course, but in the spirit of the universal benefits of knowing Latin. Nowadays, too many people are unaware that this beautiful language does not have to be an "arcane science". I'm not referring, Professor Marcoux, to those ancient Greek and Roman texts of magic and ritual that even the ancients themselves considered to be some sort of *arcana mundi* – "secrets of the universe", as it were.

The rudiments of Latin grammar and syntax, and the treasure-trove of Latin verse and prose do not have to remain an esoteric body of knowledge for all who are anxious, or even just curious, to learn Latin!

-	Very inspiring, Denys! Is it your education with the Jesuits that is imbibing you with such a "missionary spirit"?

-	Actually, I'm just a Latin student who wishes to share his passion!

Chapter 82

- Hi Mom, I love the pictures you sent of my graduation! That's two university convocations, and hopefully, still one to go! My courses are going really well. Being able to read inscriptions when I finish my epigraphy course will help my research tremendously. The numismatics seminar I took will also be useful. I plan to study papyrology and paleography as well. Next year I'll be able to take a Roman archaeology course, and hopefully spend the summer at Pompeii – Professor Ricard is doing excavations there. This summer I'll be in Greece, at the French School in Athens - that's where I will be studying papyrology. It will be a change from the British School in Athens, where I studied numismatics last summer and took a really heavy course on Pindar and the lyric poets – I guess the names Bacchylides and Simonides and Alcaeus and Sappho don't ring a bell! It was taught by an Oxford don who reminded me of Hugh Lloyd-Jones. Tell Dad that an Oxford don is not the same as a mafia don! I imagine Dad watched the Canada-Russia Series! I know he has heroes like Joe DiMaggio and Mickey Mantle and Oscar Robertson and Paul Hornung and Arnold Palmer and Jack Nicklaus, but now Canada has a hero – Paul Henderson! It's the first real interest I've had in hockey since Jean Béliveau retired last year along with his "gladiator sidekick", John Ferguson – but they won the Stanley Cup! As I mentioned in my last letter, I'm doing a lot of teaching – at Loyola and the Seminary – that's a lot of priests in my "bubble", since Loyola College belongs to the Jesuits (remember them?) – and the public lecture series at Laval and the Latin outreach programme which I teach in the evening at *Cégep* Ste-Foy. A *Cégep* – it's an actual word formed from the first letters of the words it stands for, so, an acronym – is a post-secondary institution for students going on to university or learning a professional trade. It's a bit like our junior colleges – in fact the "c" stands for "college" – except that it's compulsory for anyone who plans on attending university in Quebec. It's all part of a huge educational reform programme introduced a few years ago.

Actually, with my Master's degree, I could get a full-time teaching position in a *Cégep* – there's a big English one in Montreal called Dawson College. I was told that this reform was also responsible for removing Latin from the public school system – shame on them! Mom, since I can live comfortably with my Parker grant, I can save all the money I make teaching for my old age! Just kidding! I guess I've been reading too much Seneca! I'm happy I'm able to take a Spanish class – I hear a lot of tourists speaking Spanish in Old Quebec – called *Vieux Québec.* I suspect that a lot of them are from Mexico. I once saw some teenagers climbing on the canons that line the boardwalk – Place Dufferin – yelling "Alamo, Alamo"! I couldn't figure out if they were for or against Davy Crocket! But I'm looking forward to the two weeks in Spain and Portugal with the Laval University group. I'll be giving a couple of lectures on the history of Roman Spain. I may talk about Hannibal, but I certainly will talk about Seneca and Trajan and Hadrian. The lectures will be in French, not in Spanish – or Latin! I will be recommending to the students Marguerite Yourcenar's novel *Mémoires d'Hadrien*. I believe you have read that book too, Mom. Unfortunately, Hadrian's own autobiography has been lost, but in Yourcenar's book, the Spanish-born Emperor writes "advice" for Marcus Aurelius. I have read that Emperor's *Meditations,* which he wrote in Greek. I guess he inherited an appreciation of "things Greek" from Hadrian! I have also read some other works by Yourcenar. There is *Les charités d'Alcippe*, where Alcippus offers to various recipients like the Sirens his heart, body and soul. Then there is *Pindare* - a biographical essay on that poet. She rewrote the myth of Orpheus in a book called La nouvelle Eurydice. She wrote a 120-page poem on the myth of Icarus entitled *Le jardin des chimères*, and a book I really liked called *Electre, ou la chute des masques*. In this adaptation of the Electra and Orestes saga, Electra hates her mother Clytemnestra because she herself is in love with her mother's lover, Aegisthus, and Orestes kills Aegisthus in memory of the father he always admired, Agamemnon, but especially in anger against Aegisthus when he discovers that his mother's lover was in fact his real father. Unlike Oedipus, who marries his mother, Orestes kills his! Marguerite Yourcenar is especially fond of the Greek poets, and I imagine she will eventually produce her own translations of Greek poetry. Mom, she is such a good writer that I wouldn't be surprised to see her elected one day as the first woman in the *Académie française*! We'll be visiting Barcelona and Madrid – and also Cordoba, so the group doesn't think we're only there to watch soccer matches! And it will be good to see Seneca's birthplace! Since Spain is under the rule of the dictator Franco, I wonder if I'll feel like I'm in Ancient Rome at the time of Marius or Sulla or Julius Caesar! I remember how Pizza Pete used to talk about dictators. "Rotten potatoes" he called them – "dic-taters"! I won't tell you how he explained "glad-i-ater" - it's too gross! Even though his name was Rogers, we would never have called him "Mister Rogers" – Pizza Pete's was definitely not the same "neighborhood"! We won't be attending any bull-fights, which is fine by me – I had more than my share of "bull" when I used to hang out with Jeremy in Montreal! Once we had an argument about the myth of Pandora's Box – I'm going to leave out the nasty part of his explanation of her "box" - and he claimed "hope"was a good thing that would save the world, and I questioned that, when Epimetheus – "After- thought" – put "hope" in the box, he didn't realize that when Pandora kept it there, it could give mankind "false hope", that is, unrealistic aspirations! Prometheus – "Fore-thought" - had realized that mankind would need faith and charity, or love, as well, which he sought to give to people on earth. But the Devil – that vicious vulture – was making things difficult for him! Jeremy insisted that Pandora was the "Greek Eve", responsible for evil in the world. Then he played "the Catholic card" with me, saying that Mary brought hope! To which I replied that She brought faith and love to complement hope, and so avoid pointless hope. The Mother of Jesus is proof that you can't blame women for evil in the world! I had hoped Jeremy would accept my interpretation, but to no avail - I guess confirming my theory of "false hope"! It was then that I started calling him "No-thought"! During the "Hispanic Holiday" we'll spend a couple of days in Portugal – called *Lusitania* by the Romans. We will be mostly in Lisbon. It will be fun to imagine I'm sailing from the ports of Portugal under Prince Henry the Navigator to explore a New World in the West! Actually, I'll be doing just that - but in reverse! But that Procol Harum song "Conquistador" keeps ringing in my head. To think they recorded it with the Edmonton Symphony Orchestra – that must have made Professor Peters proud! But I know Gary Brooker – love his haunting voice - wrote that song as a protest against the War in Vietnam. Speaking of Spain, here's a Latin expression for Feeb – *plus ultra* – it means "further beyond", and became the motto of Spain after Christopher Columbus discovered the "New World" – new to Europe that is! Before that, Spain had been associated with the expression that appeared on the "Pillars of Hercules" in the Straits of Gibraltar - nec plus ultra. Tell Feeb that sometimes *non* or *ne* replaced *nec*. As she may figure out, this means "nothing further". That signified what the ancients considered the end of the earth! However, when Columbus proved that you wouldn't fall off the edge by sailing out into the ocean, the phrase became a sort of paradox, and so the *nec* was dropped. Actually, today, *nec plus ultra* is often used by commercial enterprises to indicate that their product is the very best – the "cat's meow", as it were! I sure hope Manon considers me her "top cat"! The notion of going the extra mile reminds me of the Ignatian *magis* -" the more"- that the Jesuits talked about so often at St. Xavier! St. Ignatius of Loyola was Spanish after all, and "ignited" his Companions with a burning fire to go "further beyond" - like Francis Xavier who went to China, and Brébeuf and his fellow martyrs who travelled to New France. Again for Feeb – *ignis* is the Latin word for "fire"! Mom, I like to associate St. Ignatius with ancient Rome, since his family name – Loyola – is derived from *Lobo-y-olla*, which means "the wolf and the kettle", and refers to the fact that the Loyola family produced enough food for themselves and the wolves. So, just as a wolf nourished the founders of Rome, Romulus and Remus, the wolves were now being nourished in gratitude! There is also another story that the Loyola family arose from birds. Even though nobody seriously believes this, I remind them that Rome began with a "sign" given by the flight of birds! Just a coincidence, I suppose, that hordes of migratory birds fly through the campus of Loyola University in Chicago every year! And as Father McNeil used to say, the Jesuits have been "roamin'" the world since their foundation!

I've got a close friend here at Laval who is also doing research on Roman religion. He's finishing his Master's degree, but he's a couple of years older than I am. He was in the seminary, where I teach "Church Latin" and "Biblical Greek". Remember when Father Brendan used to say I'd end up in the seminary one day? Well now I AM there one day – a week! My friend was planning to become a priest. He left after one year because he kept thinking of a girl he was in love with. He told me he was the new "Ovide Plouffe" of Quebec! We talked about that novel a few times, especially since I am fond of a girl named Manon Plouffe! He told me not to worry – the girl of his dreams – and in his dreams! – was Lucie Doyon. She was his "Rita Toulouse"! – but he hadn't had the courage to contact her since he left the seminary. I told him to follow his dreams – as weird as some of them seemed! Lucie was his to win or "to lose"! He knows enough English to understand my play on words with "Toulouse", the girl with whom Ovide Plouffe was besotted in the novel, causing him to leave the seminary. In fact, he's the only person here who sometimes calls me Holden! His name is Martin Provost. Mom, that name is pronounced like Provo, Utah, and not like the title of those administrators in university! That word actually comes from the Latin *praepositus*, later *propositus*, meaning "someone placed before – or, in charge of – others". Look at me, Mom – even with you I'm "a Latin student"! And Mom, I just said I was fond of Manon, but it's more than that! I haven't had feelings like this for a girl since Maxine. And since I'm older now, these feelings are even stronger. True, we don't have the hassles Maxine and I had, but Manon's father seems just as protective of his daughter as Maxine's dad was! In my seven years away from home, I've learned that love doesn't come easy (uh, kind of sounds like that new Ringo Starr song!). We haven't known each other too long, but strange as it seems, Manon seems to understand me! She was able to find an apartment for me exactly in the right place, and the type of lodgings that are just what I need. Manon is down to earth, and has a quick smile. Yet she has a certain sophistication about her that commands respect. She doesn't judge me, and doesn't feel "weird" around a Latin student! She has never studied Latin, but knows some Spanish – on hearing about my plans to visit Spain she said *Vaya con Dios* , and "God be with you" is a comforting wish for a staunch Catholic like me! - and she has read quite a bit on Classical mythology. You know, she even typed a couple of term papers for me! She's a real whiz at typing and stuff like that. She attended O'Sullivan Secretarial College, and works for the Canadian government. Remember when President Kennedy said "ask not what your country can do…."! We go dancing most Saturdays, but sometimes go to movies.

We've even been to a drive-in – with her younger brother in the back seat! We saw *Godspell* – and it cost me a small fortune for popcorn! Manon has shown me some of the better restaurants in Quebec – there are no "Pizza Pierre" joints! Would you believe my favorite restaurant is right across the street from my apartment! It's called Le Deauville, and it's the fanciest restaurant I have been in – even more posh than the dining room in the Château

Frontenac! We're happy when we're together. It's as if that song by The Turtles – "Happy Together" - could be our theme song! – I didn't think anyone could make me forget about Latin for a while and still make me happy! So, Mom, I hope you guys won't mind if I bring her home to meet you all at Christmas! Love as always! Denys – even Manon calls me Denys!

Chapter 83

-       Hi there, Denys, you're the first one here. Is it because you were anxious to see me?

-       No, Professor Giguère. I mean, it is nice to see you. It's raining quite hard, so I had to take the bus, and therefore arrived earlier. I am enjoying this course on the correspondence of Pliny on such a variety of subjects – poetry, politics, leisure, social issues, history, science, and so many more.

-       Well, Denys, if you like, I can drive you home after class. We could even do a little reading of some letters that won't be covered in the course. By the way, when the other students are not around, you can call me Ginette – or even Gigi! You know, Denys, I did my doctoral dissertation on Pliny. In fact, I will be reading a paper on Pliny's relationship with Trajan at a conference at the University of Ottawa next Saturday. I'm driving to Ottawa on Friday afternoon and coming back Sunday – so you could come along to give me moral support, and you wouldn't miss any classes. Don't worry about not having reserved a room – I'm sure my room would be big enough for both of us!

-       Thanks for the kind offer, Professor. But I'm meeting Manon's brother-in-law on Saturday. He's also an American, so I'm anxious to meet him. Is Gigi for your initials G.G.? Actually, I'm meeting Manon for supper later, but thank you for offering me a lift. Won't your husband be going to Ottawa with you?

-       No, Gigi is the first syllable of my name Ginette repeated – but your explanation is kind of cute – like you! Now you are blushing, Denys, which makes you even cuter! My husband rarely attends these conferences. Is Manon your girlfriend? – no matter, you could tell her you had already booked a room, and that this conference sounds very interesting. I promise I will bring you back to Quebec in one piece, Denys! Oh, here's Martin - and the others should be close behind. Greetings, class. We've seen already that Pliny corresponds with some important figures in Roman history, like Trajan and Tacitus. Today we have yet another letter addressed by Pliny to his friend, the historian Tacitus, to whom he wrote the greatest number of letters. Denys was the first to arrive, so I will ask him to read the letter and to translate for us. It is Letter 6 from Book One.

-       *C. Plinius CornelioTacito Suo S. Ridebis, et licet rideas. Ego, ille quem nosti, apros tres et quidem pulcherrimos cepi. "Ipse?" inquis. Ipse; non tamen ut omnino ab inertia mea et quiete discederem. Ad retia sedebam; erat in proximo non venabulum aut lancea, sed stilus et pugillares; meditabar aliquid enotabamque, ut si manus vacuas, plenas tamen ceras reportarem. Non est quod contemnas hoc studendi genus; mirum est ut animus agitatione motuque corporis excitetur; iam undique silvae et solitudo ipsumque illud silentium quod venationi datur, magna cogitationis incitamenta sunt. Proinde cum venabere, licebit auctore me ut panarium et lagunculam sic etiam pugillares feras : experieris non Dianam magis montibus quam Minervam inerrare. Vale.*

"Gaius Plinius greets his friend Cornelius Tacitus.

You will laugh – and it's okay to laugh! I, the guy whom you know, even I captured three really beautiful boars! You? You will ask. In person! Yet I didn't depart completely from my laziness and quiet life. I was sitting by my nets; but there was no hunting-spear or lance nearby, just my pen and writing-tablets; I was reflecting on something and taking notes, so that if I came back empty-handed, I would at least have wax tablets that were full. You shouldn't condemn this kind of study; it's amazing how the mind is stimulated by the activity and movement of the body; for having the woods all around and the solitude and that very silence itself which is provided by hunting, are great inducements for thinking. So, when you go hunting, you'll pardon me for advising you to bring along as well your provisions of bread and wine: because you'll find out that Diana doesn't roam through the mountainsides more than Minerva. Farewell!"

- Nice translation, Denys! I like your use of idiom and contemporary expression. I see that Martin wants to stay behind - probably to compare notes with you on your translation. So class, next time we will look at Pliny's correspondence with the Emperor Trajan concerning the Christians. As we have noted already, Pliny was governor of Bithynia at the time.

***

- You don't look too well, Holden. Are you feeling under the weather? You seem a little peckish! Have you caught that flu bug that's going around? Not another kidney-stone attack I hope!

- Martin, while Diana and Minerva are roaming in the mountains, Venus is here in our classroom! Professor Giguère just tried to seduce me! If you apply the British sense of "peckish" to Pliny's "filly", she is indeed hungry – and I am the main course! If she is about to "peck" like a bird, I'm afraid I'll end up being the "*passer*" to this "Lesbia-come-lately"! She invited me to spend the weekend with her in Ottawa! She joked about bringing me back in one piece, but I know what "piece" she's after! She is certainly not planning to leave me in peace! She didn't say she won't bite, because I think she will! Speaking of biting, since Pliny the

Elder wrote about dogs, do you think his nephew, Pliny the Younger, took an interest in bitches, or perhaps the other way around?

- So she's up to her old tricks! I guess I shouldn't say "old tricks" – she's still pretty young or – as everybody says – pretty AND young! At least you were offered a trip to Ottawa. I was a victim of the "Sillery Siren" at her home – beautiful, almost palatial, as it is, being in fashionable Sillery! Last year was my first year here, and I was still quite confused about Lucie and the Seminary. Well, Professor Giguère – she asked me to call her Gigi! – caught me while I was very vulnerable. She had invited me to her magnificent home on the pretext of helping me with some translation of Cicero' s letters. She made it sound so innocent – we would be looking at the techniques of the epistolary style. Her husband was out of town, and before I realized what was going on, she was all over me! She really is a beautiful woman, Holden, you have to admit. You can probably imagine – or maybe not, in your case – how she looks when totally naked. I don't know if I actually thought I was making love to Lucie, or if I was just giving in to this gorgeous – now I would say "gorgonesque"! – creature who had just offered herself to me. But she has never propositioned me since. I think Professor Giguère is all about conquest – and you are her next prize! Or maybe in your case she feels conquered by you! Remember what Horace said about "the captured capturing its capricious captor"! "Capricious" rather than "wild" or "savage" allows me a greater use of alliteration – let's not argue! Diana was also mentioned in the last line of today's letter. Given your tendency to rationalize the Venus- Diana conflict, as you did in your paper on religion in the *Hippolytus* of Euripides – yes, "Gigi" and I were both in the audience – you may be able to resist this "Phaedra- come- lately". On the other hand, weren't you Hippolytus in Professor Marcoux's staging of that play in Montreal?

- Well, this "horse-loving Hippolytus" is not about to do any "horsing around" with a young "Phaedra filly"! You referred to Professor Giguère as a "*gorgoneion*", Martin. It reminds me of the mosaics I was looking at in a book just the other day. They featured gorgon faces that could "hypnotize" you if you stared at the center of them long enough. I wonder if this is an example of "nature imitating art", and so stories about people being "petrified" by a monstrous creature would have been inspired by these depictions of a dreadful being! This "optical illusion" had me singing to myself Tommy Roe's song "Dizzy"! Well, if our Professor persists, this "Pliny" is going to have to write a letter to the "Emperor Trajan" of the Classics Department! But for now, whenever I arrive on campus early, I'll meet you in the library, Martin!

Chapter 84

\-   Hey, there, young man, got room for a starving stranger at your table? I'm guessing you're Holden alias Denys. You fit Manny's description, and joining you at your table worked for her. So here I am. Bob's the name, trucking's my game!

\-   Real nice to meet you, Bob, and not just because you're an American! Manon told me about your great sense of humour. But she said you'd probably have another name for me.

\-   Well, I won't call you "The Cincinnati Kid", since you don't look like a poker player. A shame, that is, 'cause I like playing cards – but then Maggie would never forgive me for taking money from a student. Maybe you can be "The Kid from Cincinnati ", or the "The Cincy Kid". You see, I like to "kid" around! Oh yes, Manny told me about how clever you are with words! No, you're going to be Dennis the Menace – and I'll be Bob the "Mean Ace"! Actually, I'm thinking of calling you Denis or Denise, depending on my mood – or your mood! You must know that Doo Wop song, "Denise", by Randy and the Rainbows. You see, Menace, I listen to music tapes all day long – or sometimes all night long – while driving my rig. Say, that would be a good name for a song title – "All night long"! I'll have to explain to Maggie and her sister that the difference between Denis and Denise is a matter of pronunciation – and of sex! But I figure someone will record the boy's version of that song and simply call it "Denis". Just like the song "Don't Walk Away Renee" by The Left Banke, wasn't addressed to a guy, least of all to René Lévesque who walked away from the Liberal Party in Quebec. But don't get me started on politics – American or Canadian! And I think The Left Banke walked away, because I never heard songs from them again!

\-   Yeah, there are so many one-hit wonders. And I think Mike Zero sang lead on that song "Denise". I guess "I got you Bob"! Or do you have a Sonny and Cher comeback for me? But I have to admit I am impressed by your knowledge of music. I brought this quote from Plato for you. "Music gives a soul to the universe, wings to the mind, flight to the imagination, and life to everything"! Manon tells me you are crazy about football. I think I heard her father refer to you as crazy too, but he didn't say about what! Could it be that your in-laws consider you an "outlaw"? Or maybe he was just talking about the song "Crazy" by Patsy Cline! But don't feel insulted – that song could inspire a movie some day – it would make a catchy title! I don't follow football so much anymore, and the French population in Quebec doesn't seem to be too much into football. Of course hockey is their panacea – a Greek word, Bob, meaning a cure for everything! I'm told it's their new religion! A lot more people go to hockey games than

301

to church! They talk about hockey all year round. My friend Martin brought me to a game at the Colisée to watch their new team, the Nordiques. Even though they play in the World Hockey Association, it's pretty exciting. The other team had Bobby Hull, who used to be a star player for Chicago in the NHL. But I think it's just a matter of time before the Quebec team joins the National Hockey League. What a rivalry that will make with the Montreal Canadiens! And that Montreal player I really liked - Jean Béliveau – was idolized when he played here in Quebec.

Now everyone worships Guy Lafleur. His "Flower Power" makes him the only "flower" more popular than the fleur de lys! They use a word here that puts the team in "Greek heaven" – *fleurdelysé*! "*Elysion*" was the Greek heaven, Bob, so my fanciful translation of "stamped with the fleur de lys" is transformed into "the flower of *Elysion*"! Fields of those flowers give us *Champs Elysées* – the "fields of *Elysion*"! You'll discover that I sometimes let my imagination run away with me!

\-   Well, "Da Do Run Run" – with or without your imagination! If I had wild ideas like you, I would be "Running Scared"! But as a Latin student, I guess you might have to "Run Through the Jungle" on occasion! And don't throw those fancy words and famous names from ancient times at me, Menace, 'cause it's all Greek to me! I knew you weren't talking about a "pan" of something to eat or Mickey Mouse's dog! You see, I keep up by reading a lot – I have no choice with the time I spend away from home. And I listen to music. Funny, according to Manny, that's what you do! When you're not at school of course! So we have a lot in common, even besides the fact that we're connected to two sisters. You are connected to Manny, aren't you?

\-   I hope so, Bob, I sure want to be! Look at you – naming songs byThe Crystals, Roy Orbison, and Creedence Clearwater Revival! So you drive through the United States? Do you ever go to Cincinnati? Have you seen the Bengals play?

\-   Well I mostly drive from New York State around the Great Lakes to Michigan. I've had to drive down to Florida, and yes, I had stopovers in Cincinnati a couple of times. Back home I used to go to the Colts games with my Dad. He loved quarterback Johnny Unitas – and would swear allegiance to the "Unitas" States of America! Dad was killed two years ago. He was in a bank, and got shot trying to stop a bank robbery – he worked as a bank guard. Dangerous places those banks – they take your money or your life! Lots of violence in America, right Menace? Not so much here in Quebec. I did see Cincinnati play against the Colts in Baltimore.

But Cincinnati's the greatest city in America! Just kidding – no offence, Menace! I hear you're taking Manny to Cincinnati to meet the family. I think they'll like her. Good girl, that Manny! And speaking of good – what a dancer! Although I hear you can trip the light fantastic yourself – in a disco kind of way! I like disco music, but on the dance floor I move like a truck – not surprising considering what I do for a living! Funny though, after a few beers my dancing gets better! But maybe you can teach me some moves.

-       I'm glad you like disco, Bob, because the Latin word *disco* means "I learn"! But the beauty of disco dancing is that all the moves are the right ones. I know that if I told you that Manon and I have often "skipped the light fandango" and "turned cartwheels 'cross the floor", you would recognize the song "A Whiter Shade of Pale" by Procol Harum. It's a song you can really enjoy if you don't try to understand it! So you drive across Quebec and Ontario, and into the U.S. It must be exciting being in that big forty-five footer, and in complete control! I'd love to experience that feeling!

-       I sometimes have a Saturday – Sunday run to Detroit or Buffalo. I cross into Detroit from Windsor and when I do, I make sure to play my Motown tapes! Say, they've just opened the Motown Museum - Hitsville USA - in Detroit, since Motown Records has moved to Los Angeles. Strange, since the Motown artists certainly don't need a California tan! The American customs officials just dance on to the next truck, barely looking at my cargo! You'd like the trip to Buffalo – I cross over at Niagara Falls! You'd be able to check that spot out for future reference! Did you ever watch "The Honeymooners" on TV? No reason to feel uncomfortable, Menace – you don't have to be married to go there! But as for the TV show, nobody could make me laugh like Ed Norton! Since you have American citizenship and a Canadian student visa, you can cross the border as easy as I can, and built like you are, you can easily pass for my helper.

Just don't go quoting Play doh, or whatever his name is! And I just might hold you to being my helper – if we unload the truck in half the time we could take in a movie! You know, I never went to college, but I love my job. You've spent years in university, but you could become a truck-driver too!

-       That would be my second choice, Bob - I 'm hoping to teach at university. But, yeah, I would like to "check out" Niagara Falls – even if it means some heavy lifting!

-       Aren't these Marie Antoinette burgers great! I'm glad Manny didn't arrange for us to meet at that fancy Deauville place across the street. I call it the "Doughville" because of all the bread you have to spend to eat there! Manny has brought Maggie and me there a couple of times. At least I got to wear the suit I bought when we got married. As you probably would have guessed, Manon was maid-of-honor for her sister, and her brother Mike – you know Michel – was my best man. It was either him or Willie Nelson! Manny has a lot of class – I'll give her that. But I prefer to eat in simpler places. Like that one time I was in your hometown of Cincinnati. I parked my rig in a shopping mall parking lot, and another driver I knew took me to a place called Pizza Pete's. Best pizza I ever had! There was a juke-box in the corner, and I played it the whole time we were there. This cigar-smoking guy serving us – and he was quite a character – told me he used to have an employee – Holy he called him – who always played the juke-box too.

-      That was me, Bob!

Chapter 85

-     Hi Jeremy, I know I haven't written to you in a while – I didn't want to disturb your studying! When you stop laughing, you can read the rest of my letter. I really like the programme at Laval University, and I'm in love with Quebec City – and someone IN Quebec City! I know what you're thinking - just more *déjà vu* - but this time I think it's for keeps! Manon is not pushy, but I think she feels the same way about me. I've had time to think about all the girls "in my life" – now I'm sounding like Willie Nelson! That could be a plus for me with Manon's brother-in-law – you might not catch that, I guess you had to be there! Maxine was my high-school sweetheart, but I'm older – and hopefully wiser! But Manon also has that easy, warm smile – and her brothers LIKE me! Myriam was only someone to talk to, since she was going back to France. Now she's married! There was always something that kept my relationship with Claire platonic – more like brother and sister. Corina left before any really deep feelings could develop, probably as much for her as for me. Maria and Maria/Gina were never going to happen for the reasons I gave you already. And Rachel – or whatever her name was – well you were right about that! Manon met my family at Christmas. They absolutely loved her. Feeb took a liking to her, and the three of us went dancing - on Vine Street at a club where Pizza Pete's used to be! At first it felt a bit weird, but it's good to know that music keeps on playing at that spot where I once took care of a "hot juke-box"! We danced to some really good songs like "Love Train" and "Backstabbers" by the O'Jays, "Long Cool Woman in a Black Dress" by the Hollies, "I'll Be Around" by The Spinners – did you know that they were also known as The Detroit Spinners and The Motown Spinners to distinguish them from a group in England called The Spinners?

Come to think of it, I spin so many records on my record player, I could be an "honorary member" of The Spinners! No room for you, Jeremy – I'm talking "spinners", not "sinners" – and there is no lack of them on this earth! Next came a couple of songs by my new favorite group the Chi-Lites, "Oh Girl" and "Have You Seen Her". Don't laugh, but their lead singer is Eugene Record – and I'll bet they're selling lots of them! Yeah, of course they're from Chicago. And I got to do slow dances with Manon and Feeb. But my favorite slow dances were with Manon when they played Al Green songs – "Let's Stay Together" and "Tired of Being Alone". I hope Manon got the message! His voice is heavenly, but then he is actually Reverend Al Green!

We got to dance to a couple of Elvis songs – "It's Now or Never" (another message for Manon?) and "Love Me Tender" (one more message!) I did my "crazy moves" with Feeb to the songs "Layla" by Derek and the Dominos" and "It's a Family Affair" by Sly and The Family Stone, but my sister said I was more like Flintstone, and started calling me Fred! I lost her when I said we could "Do the Freddie", which was a song by Freddie and the Dreamers that Mrs. Watson introduced to me when we were in England together – no wait, that sounds bad to my American ear – when I was with Mr. and Mrs. Watson in England! But Manon remembered the French version "Do le Freddie" by Les Baronets. No giant leap in translation there! Not like the "giant leap for mankind" that Neil Armstrong made on the moon back in 1969! I'll always be proud of the fact that the "small step" was made by a University of Cincinnati professor! You know, "Derek" of the Dominos is really Eric Clapton, a very talented British guitarist and singer, who was in the group Cream that produced such great songs as "Badge" and "Sunshine of Your Love". Manon and I danced the last slow song of the evening, Billy Paul's "Me and Mrs. Jones". Before you ask, yes, I had flashes of "me and Mrs. Robinson", "me and Mrs. Wilkinson", and – heaven forbid – "me and Mrs. Jones", the wife of my boss, Professor Jones, at Loyola College!

Just so you know, I have more chance of meeting SMOKEY Robinson than MRS. Robinson here in Quebec! And instead of a Miss Templeton, we have the "ancient" Madame Larouche. I'm not the one who calls her "ancient", even though she reminds me of my grandmother! And did you know Miss Templeton got married? But life is never simple, is it? So I have to tell you about Professor Giguère! Think of a younger and much prettier Professor Wilkinson! Except that Professor Giguère doesn't beat around the bush – maybe IN the bush if you give her a chance!

She propositioned me before a class and offered to take me to Ottawa for a weekend. I was able to politely refuse – I wasn't up for "capital" punishment in Ottawa! You see, I try to maintain my sense of humour, no matter what! But Professor Giguère makes our Professor Wilkinson look like Mary Poppins! Fortunately my friend Martin – he's the "new you"! – settled me down. She hasn't been a "professor behaving badly" since, and Professor Giguère does know her Pliny! Oh, don't worry – I know there will only ever be one Jeremy! And when I visited Manon's family in the little town of St. Romuald, it reminded me of Greenfield Park, only I didn't hear anyone speaking English! Manon has actually suggested that we go to Toronto sometime to visit you – which has to be proof of her love for me! She has given new meaning to *carpe diem*! Speaking of which, I started thinking of songs that would literally "make my day" – but in a good way! What do you think of "Day by Day" from the musical *Godspell*, and "Day after Day" by Badfinger, and of course,"Good Day Sunshine" by the Beatles? There is also "Our Day Will Come" by Ruby and the Romantics. Romantics – it doesn't get any better than that! I guess you're getting closer to completing your doctorate. All my courses are really interesting. You can't challenge Professor Walter on any point at all. Once a student protested that a statement he had made went contrary to nature, and our venerable Professor of Greek and Latin Epigraphy merely replied *"Das ist sehr schlecht für die Natur"*! Well, too bad for nature! Professor Saucier has me liking Seneca even more! I'm still in line for an A in Professor Giguère's class – she has even taken to asking me how Manon is doing! I never told Manon about the "Ottawa invitation" – she respects Latin, and I don't want that to change! My course on Greek Comedy is lots of laughs – no, wait a minute – I mean because of Professor Marcoux – what a sense of humour! He's even funnier here in French than he was in English when I was in his course at McGill a couple of years ago.

Even though that course was taught in French, he had a collection of one-liners in English! Some of them actually "crossed the line" – if you know what I mean! I'll be playing Dionysos in his production of *The Frogs*. I don't know if that's due to my superior acting ability or to the fact that my other Professor of Greek actually is Greek, and already calls me Dionysos, which is what everybody else calls me in French – Denys. So if you ever call the Department, don't ask for Holden! I'll be going to Spain for two weeks in March – so eat your heart out! – no forget that – it's too close to Seneca's *Thyestes*! Hope you can find a destination to "keep your body plain and your mind sane" – you haven't forgotten that I'm a poet in my leisure hours! I still think about that awesome night of poetry in Montreal in 1970 – La Nuit de la poésie! I can remember Michèle Lalonde reciting "Speak White". It was like a battle-cry for the downtrodden. That made me understand the "two solitudes" more than all the books I read and the lectures I attended on that reality. It made me think of the plight of blacks in America. After all, they were the first to be told to speak white! They called it the "Woodstock of Quebec poetry" – but I didn't get naked like you at the real Woodstock! My record collection is growing, Jeremy. I had to leave quite a few of them back home in Cincinnati. My Mom refers to my pile of Capitol records as "Capitol Hill"! My sister says that no one could come close to those records under my watch! I wonder if our State Capitol will always be as well-guarded! My Mom also calls my Stax label records my "Stacks"! My Dad had to get his two cents in, and quipped that whenever I was sorting my Decca records, it was "all hands on Decca"! I wonder if ever the legendary Casey were waiting for his turn to bat, they would play a song about him "on Decca"! I have some great songs that I can sing to Manon while playing my guitar – hopefully loud enough to drown out my voice! Oh, but she knows that at McGill I was a "singing *vedette*"! There's "American Pie" by Don McLean. The line "the day the music died" is a reference to the plane crash that killed Buddy Holly, The Big Bopper – real name – J.P.Richardson - and Ritchie Valens. Actually, "Buddy" was Charles Holley!

But "Peggy Sue", "Chantilly Lace" and "La Bamba" will never die! I bought "Heart of Gold" by Neil Young – the cool dude from Toronto! I also have "Lean on Me" by Bill Withers, which also makes me reflect in a sad way on suffering Afro-Americans! People in Quebec call them "African-Americans" – maybe because there are a number of Africans studying at Laval University. I bought a couple of slow songs to play for Manon on my "beat up" record player- "The First Time Ever I Saw Your Face" by Roberta Flack and "Precious and Few" by Climax.

The lead singer is Sonny Geraci, who sang with The Outsiders. Another record I've added to my collection is "Alone Again (Naturally)" by Gilbert O'Sullivan - is that you these days, Jeremy? I'm sure it's not! Obviously, he's using the name of the Victorian era opera composers, Gilbert and Sullivan. You know, "The Pirates of Penzance" and "The Mikado"? Maybe not! His name is O'Sullivan, though, but his first name is Raymond. I even bought a song by Mac Davis – "Baby, Don't Get Hooked On Me" – which for some reason reminds me of Manon's brother-in-law, Bob - maybe it's Bob's "country singer" look! But her sister, Marguerite, or Maggie, is truly "hooked" on him. I now own another Cat Stevens record – "Morning Has Broken", which, I have to confess, does remind me of Professor Mavroidakis' daughter, Maria. I hope she's with her Nicky!

Other records that are now part of my collection are "Summer Breeze" by Seals and Croft, and "Brandy(You're a Fine Girl)" by Looking-Glass. That name keeps reminding me of Alice in Wonderland! Manon gave me a record – "I Am Woman", by Helen Reddy! At least she didn't give me Lesley Gore's "You Don't Own Me"! And I already have the Aretha Franklin song "Respect". That song has a message all right – I hope I don't have to spell it out for you Jeremy!

I'm hoping my family will get to Montreal in June, before I leave for the French School in Athens. My Mom was thrilled to speak French with Manon. My Dad looked at her like he wished he were twenty years younger, but I think he should concentrate on twenty pounds lighter! He says he's happy for me, but he kept saying something about wild oats! Somehow I don't think he was talking about the porridge I eat every morning! Take care, Jeremy! Don't do anything I wouldn't do – which is asking a lot, I know! And don't take any wooden nickels - whatever that means – but a character said it in the movie *Lost Horizon*. Holden (now Denys)

Chapter 86

-     Good-day, everybody! We have been looking at the life of Seneca and his writings, as well as the general tenets of Stoic philosophy. Some of you with a background in Christian theology and philosophy are exploring the claims of a connection between Seneca and early Christian teaching, including his spurious correspondence with St. Paul. That is not to say that the Christian apologists did not take the writings of Seneca into consideration, and indeed we find references to him in St. Augustine and St.Thomas Aquinas, for example. This in spite of his role as "tutor to the devil", that is, Nero! Some of you have chosen to investigate Seneca's popularity during the Middle Ages and the Renaissance, which was considerable. Others are sifting through contemporary literature on Seneca. But we will hear today Denys' presentation on a subject that certainly must have been time-consuming. But this is his third course on Seneca, in addition to independent readings on the Roman philosopher, whom he has chosen as his major author. Denys has been collecting "words of wisdom" or "food for thought" from the various writings of Seneca, and will present them today for our dining pleasure! This play on words is a tribute to our American friend, since Professor Marcoux has informed me that he is very clever in his choice of words, even in his adopted language of French. Some of you have also seen in other courses, apparently, that Denys also has a wide knowledge of song and music – in English and French – which he is wont to demonstrate during class presentations! I'm afraid that I will be at a loss if the reference is not to Aznavour or Bécaud or Jacques Brel!

-     You're right, Professor Saucier, this has been a labour of love, but Seneca does preach about making the most of the time at our disposal! Accordingly, I would like to begin with a quote from Seneca's *De Brevitate Vitae – On the Shortness of Life*, in which he reminds us that any length of life is sufficient if well-lived. In ix,1 – and I will be giving the book or chapter and verse references, as I'm sure my friend Martin here will be verifying them! - Seneca advises us to "live immediately", or "in the now", as we would say. His expression is *Protinus vive*, which, in form, resembles the *carpe diem* of Horace – which was my personal mantra, as it were, during my years at McGill. It facilitated, for example, my decision to leave home and the family I love, and to spend all my summers abroad. However, whereas Horace was encouraging us to seize every opportunity to change our lives – to manage our destiny, I believe Seneca is calling on us to live our present moments correctly, and not to dwell on the past or the future. It sounds Epicurean, but it does not preclude accepting whatever life is presenting us at the moment. And speaking of the "devil", Seneca addressed his *De Clementia, On Mercy*, to the Emperor Nero, pointing out the need for the supreme ruler, the "master of the world", to show clemency, as when our American Presidents are called upon occasionally to grant pardons, or our State Governors, when they commute death sentences! In *Liber* I, xvii,1, Seneca says *nullum animal morosius est, nullum maiore arte tractandum quam homo, nulli magis parcendum.* He is saying "no creature is more fretful or should be treated with greater tact than man, nor is deserving of greater forgiveness". This could be Martin Luther King pleading for the suffering Afro-Americans! This statement could be defining Seneca as the ultimate humanitarian! It's a pity Nero didn't apply these principles to the Christians – or even to his own mother! During my research I came across a lengthy commentary on this work by the Protestant reformer John Calvin. Ultimately, though, Calvin does not accept Seneca's Stoic beliefs to the point of incorporating them into his Calvinist doctrine. I should point out that Seneca, like other writers of his day, often quoted or made allusion to Cicero and Vergil and Horace! But I must say, of all the Roman writers – and Greek, for that matter – Seneca is the one who most teaches me how to live! Of course, I must sometimes apply the proviso of *mutatis mutandis.* That is, it's necessary to consider today's context, modern situations – even my own Catholic faith – and make the "necessary adjustments" in applying Seneca's guidelines.

It is true that some find in Seneca the greatest hypocrisy. His great wealth despite his advice to be wary of accumulating riches, for instance. In fact, Seneca was not against wealth *per se,* but rather the dependence on wealth. In this, he seems to echo the teachings of Jesus Christ – "render to Caesar what is Caesar's"! Seneca is criticized for his cow-towing to Nero. I believe, though, that he genuinely hoped to control the evil that would be caused by an unbridled ruler, and when this was no longer possible, he would at least preach – through his writings – a morality and "practice of life" that would prove beneficial to others, including posterity. I, for one, am happy he continued to write, and that so many of his works have survived! That is why, a few years ago, I took to writing down his pithy statements – but really grand pronouncements on life! After all, *qui scribit bis legit*! "Writing it down, like reading it twice" – sounds so nice! – has helped me to take to heart these gems of philosophical – and sometimes practical! – meditations. I sometimes wonder who came up with that clever little proverb – perhaps a medieval scribe who was conscientious of checking the work he was copying! Even Santa Claus keeps a list to remember "who is naughty and nice" – although I find myself checking my "Senecan sayings" more than twice! Seneca wrote this as well in the first book of his *De Clementia* – in iii,2, Martin! - *qui hominem sociale animal communi bono genitum videri volumus.* Translated, this reads "we who wish man to be considered a social animal born for the common good". Of course Seneca followed the teaching of Aristotle with this notion, but his emphasis on doing good in society as opposed merely to living in society is interesting. Today, the social animal that is man often applies the principle of "survival of the fittest" and "dog eats dog" – read "man". To answer the question *cui bono,* - for whose benefit is this communal living? – man's reply is "me, myself, and I" – not *communi bono*! It is interesting that Thomas Aquinas attributes this notion to the medieval philosopher Boethius rather than to Seneca, confusing them I think because both suffered a "forced death" under a cruel ruler. Seneca illustrated his tactic of "playing safe" while revealing the inadequacies or outright wrongs of his day when he penned the satire on the deceased predecessor of Nero, Claudius. At the beginning of his "*Pumpkinification*" - *Apocolocyntosis* I ,1, - we read "one ought to be born a king or a fool" – *aut regem aut fatuum nasci oportere*. As we know, Claudius was less of a "fool" than people thought, and more of a ruler. Unlike Julius Caesar, who lost motivation, and Caligula, who "faked" the conquest, Claudius successfully brought Britain into the Roman Empire. Seneca often speaks of death or consolation following someone's death. Thus, in his letter of consolation to his friend Polybius on the death of that one's brother in *Consolatio ad Polybium*, he writes *Tota vita nihil aliud quam ad mortem iter est.* "All life is nothing but a path to death". Today we are told, in fact, that in a biological sense, death begins the moment we are born! Christian teaching tells us that the "journey" is towards eternal life, not simply death as a final step! I have to say that the word "eternal" can be problematic in its usage. We often use it in the sense "everlasting" or "immortal" – that is to say, "without end". But the root meaning of "eternal" implies also "without beginning". We live on through our "immortal" souls, but we were born, and so not "eternal", in the sense of sharing in the "eternal nature" of God.

Interestingly, in making his point that everything comes to an end, Seneca predicts the destruction of the Seven Wonders of the World. History has almost completely validated his prediction! We still have the Great Pyramid at Gizeh and fragmentary remains of the Artemision – the Temple Of Artemis – at Ephesus. We Latin students might prefer to call it by its other name – the Temple of Diana. Sadly, we have lost the Hanging Gardens of Babylon, the Statue of Zeus at Olympia – here, we must not refer to it as the Statue of Jupiter! - and also the Mausoleum of Halicarnassus – they never built one for Herodotus who was from that city! - as well as the Colossus of Rhodes and the Lighthouse of Alexandria. However, society is sure to come up with a new list eventually – of surviving monuments! I imagine the Colosseum in Rome will be included, but I am not sure about the Parthenon on the Acropolis in Athens, since there are other temples on that citadel, and a Greek temple from the ancient list – the one dedicated to Artemis – still partially exists. In any event, as technology allows the creation of newer "wonders", other lists will be produced. They may include numerous skyscrapers – but, assuredly, none will be dedicated to Zeus or Jupiter! Seneca writes as well on the unpleasant aspects of human nature in his books on anger, *De Ira*, in which he expounds on the consequences, and also the control, of anger. In Book II, xv,4, he states that "no one can rule without also being ruled"– *nemo autem regere potest nisi qui et regi*. So, a leader must be calm and in control of his emotions and his desires. In the same book, at xx,8, Seneca states *In oculis vitia aliena habemus, a tergo nostra sunt*. The translation is "We have before our eyes the vices of others, our own are behind our backs". There is a saying in English that illustrates very well this truism, namely "the pot calling the kettle black". He speaks of anger that builds up and needs an outlet, but sometimes is the result of frustration or sense of futility in Book I,iii,2 when he describes our wish "to punish the powerful" – *ad nocendum potentes sumus*. In *De Vita Beata, On the Happy Life*, I,4 Seneca writes to his brother Gallio that we shouldn't rely on others, when he warns that "everyone prefers to believe than to investigate" – *Unusquisque mavult credere quam iudicare*. We can conclude that the "happy person" is self-reliant and independent. This Gallio, by the way, was the proconsular praetor in Greece in the years 51-52 who dismissed the charges against St. Paul. Gallio later committed suicide. Seneca's other brother, the father of the epic poet Lucan, also committed suicide, as did the poet. Ultimately, Seneca himself was constrained to commit suicide – all under Nero. I don't know if four suicides in the same family was a Guinness record in Ancient Rome! Athens may have sinned against philosophy in its condemnation of Socrates, but since Seneca also wrote, Nero sinned against both philosophy and literature! There is practical advice for benefactors and those receiving benefits in Seneca's work *De Beneficiis – On Benefits*. In Book II,11 he writes *Qui dedit beneficium taceat; narret qui accepit*. This means "The one who made the act of kindness should be silent; the one who receives it should tell about it". I guess Seneca is preaching modesty here, but perhaps also genuine gratitude. In Book IV,1 he reiterates this notion when he says "the reward of honest dealings lies in the deeds themselves" – *rerum honestarum pretium in ipsis est*. In Book IV,34 our Stoic warns that *Fallaces sunt rerum species*, that is to say, "The appearances of things are deceptive". Unfortunately for the Trojans who took in the giant wooden horse, they hadn't had the opportunity to read Seneca! Perhaps one SHOULD look a gift horse in the mouth! They also missed out on Vergil's warning – *timeo Danaos et dona ferentes* – "I fear the Greeks even when they are bearing gifts"! In this next passage from Book V,15 of the *De Beneficiis*, Seneca seems to say we are saints or sinners - with no grey area in between! "He who has one vice", he writes, "has them all"! *Qui unum habet vitium, omnia habet*! Seneca addresses his *De Tranquillitate Animi – On the Peacefulness of the Soul* – to a friend, Annaeus Serenus. The family name, Annaeus, suggests that they may have been distant relatives.

Because Seneca's aim was to remove Serenus' anxiety and general disgust with life, to make him "serene", the name of the addressee may sound suspect, but, then, the *De Otio – On Leisure* – and the *De Constantia Sapientis* are also addressed to this Serenus. In xvii,10, of "serenity" Seneca says it's okay to "goof off"! *Aliquando et insanire iucundum est –* "Sometimes it is enjoyable to be insane"! He goes on to say in Book X,1 that "Necessity teaches us to bear misfortunes bravely, habit to bear them easily". The Latin quote is, *Necessitas fortiter [onera] ferre docet consuetudo facile.* In Seneca's *De Constantia Sapientis – On the firmness of a wise person –* we read in Book I,17,2 *nemo risum praebuit qui ex se cepit.* This means "no one ever became a laughing-stock who laughed at himself" – literally, "who took himself as a subject of laughter". So contrary to the popular adage, he claims that "he who laughs FIRST laughs best"!

Seneca, like all playwrights, often passes on valuable advice through the voices of his characters. Seneca's plays seemed more directed at a listener at recitals than at a spectator in a theater, so he would have been very popular on radio! But I was in a stage presentation of his *Phaedra* a few years ago! Where there's a will, there's a way, especially when Will has his way – Will Shakespeare that is! Seneca's plays were known as *fabulae crepidatae –* stories with characters in sandals – or *fabulae cothurnatae –* stories with characters in boots. In other words, he wrote tragedies based on Greek plays. I would like to present various quotes from a few of his plays, some of which would contain advice for Nero, who might quite possibly be paying attention, given his love of the theater and all that was dramatic or poetic! In his *Oedipus,* Iocasta says to Oedipus at line 1019 *nemo fit fato nocens –* "no one becomes guilty by fate". What she means is that you are not responsible for actions beyond your control. How many defense lawyers have quoted Seneca without ever having read his *Oedipus*? In his *Troades – Trojan Women –* Seneca has the Chorus say at line 397 *Post mortem nihil, ipsaque mors nihil.* The gloomy meaning of this line is "after death there is nothing, and death itself is nothing", and so we can pass over any *post-mortem* discussion! At line 1010 the Chorus says *Dulce maerenti, populus dolentum –* "It is sweet for one in grief to know that other people suffer". As we know, misery loves company!

Seneca provides fodder for the prosecuting lawyer with these lines from his *Medea,* 500-01, where Medea addresses Jason – *cui prodest scelus, is fecit –* "he who benefits from the crime is the one who committed it". So much for "innocent until proven guilty" – all one needs is a motive. In the *Thyestes –* definitely not a story of brotherly love, so I don't see this play being staged in Philadelphia, the "city of brotherly love"! – Seneca has an attendant to Atreus – *satelles –* say in lines 217-20 *nefas nocere vel malo fratri puta –* "you should consider it a crime to harm even an evil brother". And in lines 607-8 the Chorus says *vos quibus rector maris atque terrae ius dedit magnum necis atque vitae–* "you to whom the ruler over sea and land has given jurisdiction over death and life". I can imagine Seneca attempting to have Nero realize the seriousness of his position as Emperor. In the *Hercules Furens –* Hercules gone mad - Lycus, the usurper of the throne of Thebes, complains at lines 344-5 that " the throne of another is not stable" – *alieno in loco haud stabile regnum est*. The message is very clear – sovereignty over a foreign land is insecure. Even waging war in a foreign territory can be difficult, as the Americans discovered in Vietnam! In an interesting novel entitled *Vendredi ou la vie sauvage*, based on the celebrated story told by Daniel Defoe, author Michel Tournier illustrates this reality by describing a battle between grey rats which inhabited the island and black rats brought to the island from the shipwreck. The black rats were defeated since, as the author points out, an animal – and, I would add, this could be the human species of the animal race – fighting on its adversary's territory is almost always beaten! This novel also condemns racism by describing how the native "Friday" was condemned by his fellow natives because his skin was darker. And did you know that the "Robinson Crusoe" character was based on an actual shipwrecked sailor named Selkirk? But I digress! I've often seen this "native soil" phenomenon in sports contests, with home teams in baseball, football and hockey taking advantage of location and local support – especially when the Montreal Canadiens play at the Forum – even the revamped, improved building, where my idol, Jean Béliveau, scored the first goal in 1968! I suspect, though, that even the venerable Forum will bow to time with home games played elsewhere some day! Just as the Roman Forum no longer serves the same purpose for "modern" Romans! In the same play, Megara, the wife of Hercules, expresses very beautifully one of life's truths at line 437, when she says *Non est ad astra mollis e terris via* – "There is no easy way from the earth to the stars". I wonder if Neil Armstrong was thinking of this during his historic voyage in 1969. I remember that he has a fondness for the Classics, close as he is to the reputable Department of Classics at the University of Cincinnati. This phrase reminds me of that often-used motto *per ardua ad astra* – which I poetically translate by ''over the bars on our way to the stars''. This Latin phrase, possibly coined at the end of the nineteenth century, when people well-versed in Latin made up their own expressions, eventually became the motto of the British Air Force, that is, the Royal Air Force, and of the Canadian Air Force as well! However, the Canadian Air Force changed its motto a couple of years ago to *sic itur ad astra*, which is actually taken from Vergil's *Aeneid*, where in the last book Aeneas tells his son Iulus "this is how we travel to the stars". What is the motto of the American Air Force, you ask? Something about fighting and winning – or else – yes, or else death! *Aut vincere aut mors*! I've seen it expressed as the password for George Washington's troops while crossing the Delaware. Washington knew Latin of course, but the expression may go back to ancient Irish and Scottish clans. If their battles were anything like those presented in movies and documentaries, that motto would sound about right! I came across another expression, which comes from a play called *Hercules Oetaeus*, which I know not everyone accepts as a play actually written by Seneca.

But it would not be unheard of for a playwright to write more than one play with the same major characters – Euripides did it it with Hippolytus and Phaedra, as did Sophocles with Oedipus. This play refers in its title to Mt. Oeta in southern Thessaly where, in mythology, Hercules dies. In Act II, scene 1, line 444, the Nurse says to the wife of Hercules, Deianeira, *Culpa par odium exigat*, that is, "Let the guilt demand equal hatred". As we saw with other quotes from Seneca, this advice could be used in present-day law courts by both prosecutors and defense lawyers – let the punishment fit the crime! As you can imagine, the bulk of my quotes from Seneca will come from his moral letters, his *Epistulae Morales*, to his friend and pupil Lucilius, since he wrote 124 such letters, and because I took a course on these letters at McGill. But Lucilius was already an adult, slightly younger than Seneca himself, and serving as procurator of Sicily. He was a convenient vehicle to provide a sounding-board for Seneca's philosophical ideas, and I wonder if Seneca didn't consider Lucilius his *alter ego*! I could ask the same question about Cicero and Atticus, the recipient of so many of the Republican period philosopher's letters! All this talk of lawyers - I am once again reminded of "Atticus" Finch in To Kill a Mockingbird ! Of the teacher – pupil relationship, I am tempted to paraphrase the well-known saying that "old soldiers never die" with the proposition that indeed "old teachers never die", in that their teachings, lessons about life, continue to be remembered by students and posterity, and so teachers continue to teach, as it were, "from beyond the grave"! Their lessons become immortal! Well, in Letter 4,2 we read *Illi levia, hi falsa formidant, nos utraque* – "some people sweat over little things, others fear unreal things, and we are afraid of both!" So let's avoid becoming nervous wrecks! In Letter 5,9, Seneca writes *Ferae pericula quae vident fugiunt* – "Beasts flee the dangers they see", which could reinforce the advice in the previous quote, but also be an invitation to prudence. In this letter, Seneca is in fact preaching "the golden mean"! Letter 7,8 contains this reflection, which I have already begun to experience – "Men learn while they teach" – *Homines dum docent discunt*. I have truly "learned" – no pun intended, Professor - the value of *docendo discimus* – "we learn by teaching" since I started teaching courses at McGill and Loyola College, and here at the Seminary and even in courses I teach to the general public. I now consider myself a better "Latin student" ! There is the love of learning and there is just love! A simple message is given in Letter 9,6 – *Si vis amaris, ama* – "if you are looking for love, give love!" He sounds a bit like Ovid here. That saying could certainly serve as a contractual "declaration of love" for my girlfriend Manon and me! In another letter in which Seneca writes about the advantages of old age, he says in Letter 12,10 "Everywhere many short, easy paths lie open to freedom…let us thank god!" The Latin reads *Patent undique ad libertatem viae multae breves faciles…Agamus Deo gratias.*

Seneca warns us against overdoing physical exercise in Letter 15,5, but really is preaching moderation, and not condemning the rationale of *mens sana in corpore sano*, a phrase which sums up my personal lifestyle! He says *id bonum cura quod vetustate fit melius*, that is to say, "take care of the good, since it becomes better with age". And just as wine improves with age, so can a well-cared-for human being! He had already warned against exaggeration in the same letter – 15,3 – when he writes *copia ciborum subtilitas impeditur* – "accuracy" – in thinking – "is impeded by an abundance of food" – and I am aware of what over-eating is doing to American youth! This next passage may sound strange – or even hypocritical – coming from someone who today would be considered a millionaire! Today, multi-millionaires can – and do – help the less fortunate through donations, foundations, endowments. I am a case in point, as all my years of university education in Canada – including my living and travel expenses, as modest as they are – have been paid by a generous grant from the Parker Foundation! In Seneca's time, perhaps countless persons were helped – possibly only spiritually or psychologically – through his writings. Today, many books purport to produce a like benefit. In Letter 17,5 Seneca writes *si vis vacare animo, aut pauper sis oportet, aut pauperi similis* – which translates as "if you want to grow in spirit, it is fitting to be poor, or similar to a poor person". And Jesus said "Blessed be the poor in spirit"! In his letter, Seneca is explaining how a philosophical approach to riches is the best way to manage wealth and being wealthy. In Letter 22,1 Seneca says *Gladiator in arena consilium capit.* "The gladiator is formulating his plan in the arena" is an obvious *caveat* against planning things too late. Such, I guess, was the case for all those gladiators in the "sword and sandal" – or – "*peplum*" movies who were killed before the end of the film! Half-way measures often prove futile. A common belief today is that a change of scenery will solve our problems. Seneca warns against this false sense of relief in Letter 28,1, when he advises *animum debes mutare non caelum* – "you should change your attitude, not your sky". Moving away doesn't solve problems – it simply relocates them! One has to change one's way of life to have a better life. Letter 29,11 offers advice that sounds like the pronouncements of modern-day psychologists. *Multo autem ad rem magis pertinent qualis tibi videaris quam aliis.* This translates as "it is much more important what you think of yourself than what others think of you". To this I say "Amen"! All work and no play may lead to an undesirable disposition, but Seneca maintains in Letter 31 that "Work is not good... What then is good? The knowledge of things". Here he sounds almost like an encyclopedia salesman! The Latin text is *Labor bonum non est... Quid ergo est bonum? Rerum scientia.* Seneca does not condemn all work, just useless work – here he sounds like a disgruntled student! Seneca goes on to say that evil is the lack of knowledge. The arguments pertaining to knowledge and the lack thereof go all the way back to Adam and Eve! Of course we have Vergil extolling the merits of work in the *Georgics* –

Labor omnia vincit – "Hard work is a remedy for everything". But in his *Bucolics,* Vergil claims that "Love conquers all" – *Amor omnia vincit.* Well, different strokes for different folks, I guess! And then if we read *amor* in reverse, producing *Roma*, we have Rome conquering everything, which our historical records tell us is true for a significant period in the history of the world! Indeed, many Romans, such as Cicero and Cincinnatus, were guided in their actions by their "love for Rome"! Seneca praises his "pupil" Lucilius in Letter 34. In section 3 of that short letter he says *pars magna bonitas est velle fieri bonum* – "the great part of goodness is wanting to become good". How often do we hear today "you can be as good as you want to be – you can be a champion!". Had he been surrounded with a little more goodness, even Terry Malloy – the magnificent Marlon Brando in the film *On the Waterfront* – "could have been a contender"! Here we are talking about enhanced performance, but it can apply, as Seneca suggests, to moral righteousness. In Letter 35,1 Seneca sheds light on some sad facts of life. *Amicitia semper prodest, amor aliquando etiam nocet* – "Friendship always takes advantage, love sometimes harms – or fails – us". Seneca has something good to say about ambition, even reaching for the stars, in Letter 39,5. He tells us that "when once ambition has passed its natural bounds, its progress is sure to be immense". The Latin phrase is *necesse est in immensum exeat cupiditas quae naturalem modum transilit.* Lawyers should also pay heed to what Seneca says in Letter 49,12 – *veritatis simplex oratio est* – "the language of truth is simple". Seneca actually attributes this maxim to "that tragedian" – *ille tragicus*, but he means Euripides, who, in his *Phoenissae – Phoenician Women*, lines 469-472, has Polyneices pronounce these words to his mother Jocasta and brother Eteocles. These two brothers, we know, will slay each other in the story known as "The Seven Against Thebes", and their sister Antigone will die defending her right to bury her brother. What Seneca says in Letter 66,12 sounds very close to Christian theology. It reads *Ratio autem nihil aliud est quam in corpus humanum pars divini spiritus mersa* – "Reason is nothing other than a part of the divine spirit merged into the body of human beings". Seneca indeed waxes philosophical in Letter 71,3 where he states *Ignoranti quem portum petat nullus suus ventus est* – "For the one who doesn't know which port he is seeking, no wind is favorable". Seneca strikes a chord with me in Letter 82,3 when he writes *Otium sine litteris mors est et homini vivi sepultura* – "Leisure without literature is the death and burial of a living man". I wonder where I would be even now without my books, oh, and my records! I suppose Nero would have been a collector of records – perhaps by the Quebec singing group, *César et ses Romains*! Not too flattering an image, but then I wouldn't have a slave serving me grapes as I listened to record after record! Although it would be nice to have someone changing all those '45's on my record-player! I try to remember at wine and cheese gatherings what Seneca says in Letter 83,20 – *non facit ebrietas vitia, sed protrahit* – "drunkenness does not create flaws, it just shows them"! I try to put into practice the temperance that Seneca recommends. There is certainly food for thought in Letter 85,32 – *Artes serviunt vitae, sapientia imperat* – a fine example of the brief, pithy statement with a powerful message! The translation is "Arts provide a service to life, while wisdom governs it".

In section 34 of the same letter, Seneca writes *tranquillo enim ut aiunt quilibet gubernator est.* This means "any governor will do during time of peace". Such a statement reminds us of the powerful leadership of men such as Winston Churchill, Franklin Delano Roosevelt and Charles de Gaulle in time of war. If you will permit me a lighter moment amid this serious discussion on the teachings of Seneca, when the same Charles de Gaulle was making waves with his famous "*Vive le Québec libre!*" speech, security concerns arose, and Montrealers asked "Who will guard de Gaulle?" It was my first year in Montreal, and a casual acquaintance told me the answer was "de goalie"! That was my first inkling of the importance of hockey in Quebec! Of course that exchange was less serious than Juvenal's concern over the morality of women when he famously asked in his Sixth Satire *Quis custodiet ipsos custodes*? - "Who will guard the guards?" Today we ask this question with regard to world leaders. Strong leadership allowed Augustus to lay the foundations of an empire, with a *Pax Romana* – Roman peace – i.e. world peace - that lasted two hundred years! Many people take Seneca to task for this statement in Letter 87,22 – *Divitiae bonum non sunt.* Translated as "Wealth is not a good", it presents Seneca as someone who doesn't practice what he preaches. However, when *bonum* is translated as "THE good", that is, the ultimate good, we can hear Seneca warning us against becoming a slave to material goods, and ignoring the simple things in life. Reading the first line of Letter 89 makes me wish he had been my math teacher when I started high school! "It is easier to understand the parts", he states, "than to understand the whole". *Facilius per partes in cognitionem totius adducimur.* I know the burning of *Lugdunum* mentioned in Letter 91 by Seneca fills you with a certain sadness, Professor Saucier, since we are talking about your native Lyon. But in section 16 Seneca reflects on a truth we are all too aware of – "ashes make everybody equal" – *aequat omnes* cinis. The view of death – this "great equalizer" – was for Stoics like Seneca the paramount instrument of freedom. Of course, for Christians death is also a source of "freedom", since death is merely a passage to eternal life. This sentiment is echoed in St. Paul's *First Letter to the Corinthians* where he asks "Death, where is thy sting, where is thy victory?". And St. John in his Gospel claims that "the truth will set you free" - the truth of eternal life! As for all practicing Catholics – especially those who read Scriptures regularly – passages such as these are always in the back of my mind. But I am also aware of my temporal life – the secular day-to-day business of life – for me, that of being primarily a Latin student, and so the reminder that "the truth will set you free" has a definite connotation of academic freedom! I suppose all those issues went through the mind of Socrates when he accepted death as the ultimate freedom. The adage "Don't kill time – work it to death" can recall for us the sadly ironic sign posted at Auschwitz – "*Arbeit macht frei*"- "work makes you free"- which exhorted the prisoners to work themselves to death, since this was their only means to a final "liberation"! This again echoes the *Labor omnia vincit* of Vergil! Seneca continues the theme of freedom in Letter 92,33, where he reminds us that "no one is free who is a slave to the body" – *nemo liber est qui corpori servit*. Here my favorite Stoic is warning us against exaggeration in food and drink and - how shall I put it - overindulgence in the exchange of bodily fluids! Letter 101, 15 gives us a possible motto – even mantra – for life! Here Seneca says *quam bene vivas referre non quamdiu* – "it's about how well you live, not how long"! For us who have marveled at the works of Sophocles, Vergil, Lucretius, Dante, Shakespeare, Beethoven, Molière, T.S. Eliot, Hemmingway, Picasso, and so many others – I would add Smokey Robinson, but that's just me -, Seneca leaves an inspiring message in Letter 102,22 with *nullum saeculum magnis ingeniis clausum est* – "no century" – I would even venture "no generation" – "is closed to great talents". Seneca's pronouncement in Letter 106,12 may sound out of place for us students gathered around the table here. For he says *Non scholae sed vitae discimus* – "We do not learn for school but for life". But I am sure that, when looking at the big picture – in this case, of life – we can acknowledge the soundness of that statement. I suppose it's like comparing "superb instruction" with "solid education"! Seneca is referring to the "school of life", which doesn't exclude various "internships" at institutions like Université Laval! Letter 107,11 echoes in a way that majestic capsule of life stated in Letter 101. Here we learn that "destiny carries the willing man, drags the unwilling". *Fata volentem ducunt, nollentem trahunt.* Letter 114 talks about man in the context of his whole life. One should live and "go out" in style, so it seems. In section 1 we read *talibus hominibus fuit oratio qualis vita* – "such was the men's speech as was their life". I came across a reference in which Cicero is said to have attributed this saying to Socrates. Cicero has a good memory, since Socrates left nothing in writing! Therefore, it is not what one eats, but what one says that makes the man! In the very last line of the letter, Seneca says *quidquid facies, respice ad mortem* – "whatever you do, have a look out for death". My last quote from Seneca's letters is from Letter 122,3, where he says *nullus agenti dies longus est* – "no day is long for the busy person". This must explain why – put poetically - "in preparing this report, I found my days so very short"! Throughout history, Seneca has been constantly quoted, and I dare say, sometimes misquoted, or even quoted for statements he never made! But I would like to attest to the popularity of Seneca by making reference to writers who most probably were referring to the actual words, or at least to the gist of Senecan thought. In his compendium on ancient Roman religion, *Saturnalia,* at I,11,10, Macrobius seems to be following Seneca's views on slavery when he says *Non fortuna homines aestimabo, sed moribus* – "I do not estimate men by their fortune, but by their habits". Shades of Martin Luther King! In Letter 47, Seneca invites us to consider slaves as fellow human beings, but does not actually condemn slavery *per se*. Nevertheless, there are those that look for a "Christian Seneca" in this letter. In one of his *Canterbury Tales*, "The Tale of Melibeus", Chaucer often quotes Seneca – as well as Cicero – but obviously not so accurately. On the other hand, faced with a plethora of Latin sayings, to whom else would one attribute these proverbs? In fact, it can be ascertained that some of the sayings should have been attributed to one Publilius Syrus, a contemporary of Cicero, who published collections of sayings, which are known as *sententiae*. One such saying attributed to a lost – or never written – work by Seneca called *De Moribus* in Chaucer was *Bonis nocet qui malis parcit* – "He harms good people who spares bad people". The message is that what goodness discourages, evil doesn't! A Benedictan Dom of the eighteenth century, Nicola Jamin, writing his reflections on ancient authors, includes this quote attributed to Seneca – *testimonium veritati, non amicitiae reddas* – "may you give testimony to truth, not to friendship". This reference – obviously with a legal connotation – also appeared in some unpublished documents in the collection of writings by the Society of Jesus whom most people simply call the Jesuits. And I would like to mention Martin de Braga, a sixth century bishop in Portugal, who very likely relied on knowledge of Seneca in his own writings. In his work, *Formula honestae vitae* – "Guide for an honorable life"- which is quite possibly an epitome of the lost work by Seneca I just referred to – known as *De Moribus* – On habits - de Braga quotes *Qui nescit tacere, nescit loqui* – "he who knows not how to be silent, knows not how to speak". We know that "speech is silver", and Seneca wrote during the Silver Age of Roman literature, but he would not be considered a "silver-tongued orator", that expression seemingly going back to the ancient Egyptians. Seneca spoke with his pen, thus practicing a "form" of silence! His writings are therefore, like some of the music I listen to, "solid gold"! And to justify your compliment on my musical knowledge, Professor, I'll just point out that the other part of that maxim – "silence is golden" was also the title of a hit song for The Tremeloes in England, but was actually written and recorded by one of my favorite American groups, The Four Seasons. And the song "Sound of Silence", by Simon and Garfunkel, strikes at the heart of this discussion with the lyrics "people talking without speaking, people hearing without listening"! By the way, a third dimension can be added to the popular saying – namely, "print is dynamite"! Long live books! As they say, "better to be silent and thought a fool, than to speak and remove all doubt"! I cannot end on that note, so by way of conclusion I will refer to the practice of simply saying "to quote the philosopher" or "as the philosopher said" when we don't know the source of a pertinent quote – Latin or otherwise ! Gratien Gélinas has his character, Pierre Gravel, do just that in the play *Hier les enfants dansaient*. The quote is meant to finish his speech with gusto. This Pierre Gravel, offered the position of Justice Minister by Prime Minister Lester Pearson – a position he has to turn down due to the devastating circumstances in which he finds himself at the end of the play – is really the "Pierre" who is Canada's current Prime Minister, Pierre Trudeau. Trudeau is a self-proclaimed champion of social justice, and the play is a story of less than passive rebellion against social injustice. I find it extremely interesting that Prime Minister Trudeau named his son, born last year, Justin. Is he committing him to the same battle for justice? Perhaps young Justin is destined for a career in politics. Maybe one day he too will become Prime Minister of Canada! We have seen this happen in American history. John Adams was the second President of the United States, and his son, John Quincy Adams, was elected as the sixth President. And so concludes my presentation on the sayings of Seneca, which no doubt will continue to inspire American Presidents and Canadian Prime Ministers and humble Latin students such as myself!

- Thank you, Denys, for that stimulating look at the words of Seneca. But there is some time remaining. Would you like to to give us more enlightenment on Seneca, although I believe it is now safe to say that you and I are not the only ones in this room who already have a renewed respect for this celebrated Roman philosopher?

- Well, Professor, I would like to attempt to "set the record straight" concerning his relationship with the Emperor Claudius. With all due respect, Professor, since that Emperor was born in your birth city, Lyon - called *Lugdunum* in Roman times – but Claude was really a clod, albeit a deliberate one! To explain: our dear and divine Emperor imprisoned and had executed many Roman senators and prominent citizens – as well as hordes of others who were not so prominent. Deeply influenced by his wives, he proved that one could indeed be "a fool and an emperor"! Although in his pre-*Princeps* days, he seemed to favour a return to the glorious days of the Republic, he became very wary – and weary – of the Senate, and strove to curry favour with the Praetorian Guard – who, after all, had given him the job of Emperor! He did so through bribery, treachery, murder, *etc.* (and there was an "*etc.*", but I go on). Seneca had a certain following in the Senate, and would have been considered by some factions as a sort of "champion". As such, he was a threat to no less a "shaker and maker" than Messalina, the wife and therefore "power behind the throne" of Claudius. The Emperor's niece, Julia Livilla, was a reputed harlot – who wasn't, in that imperial "Peyton Place"? Messalina seems to have contrived to rid Rome of Seneca by imputing an extramarital liaison between Livilla and the potential "throne thrasher" – Seneca apparently had gifted oratorical ability. By banishing his niece for immorality, Claudius would appear as a "new Augustus", prepared to sacrifice family in the name of moral integrity. Likewise, the current Emperor would maintain the standards of the illustrious first *Princeps* (said out loud, I realize how redundant that phrase might seem!) by in turn banishing into exile a great man of letters. Seneca would be Claudius' "Ovid"! Exile, and not death, because there was no conclusive proof – in either case – of a capital crime! Obviously, both writers would seek the advantages of associating with the rich and powerful. This should not mean that they removed their togas for extracurricular pleasures! Who is our source for Seneca's libertarian lunacy? None other than... Robert Graves! In his novel *Claudius the God*, Graves has the Emperor justify his banishment of Seneca to Corsica for impropriety with Claudius' niece Lesbia. Graves cleverly gives Livilla this name because she was born on the island of Lesbos! Perhaps also with a nod to Catullus, whose "Lesbia" likewise displayed behavior that left much to be desired (but she herself was very desired!)! Permit me, ladies and gentlemen, to point out that Robert Graves was not a Roman – or even contemporary – historian, in spite of being an astute student of classical civilization! I do admire the literary genius of his work – which implies an occasional use of "poetic license". As a matter of fact, I intend to read the German translation of his great work of fiction – I use the word "fiction" deliberately! - entitled *Ich, Claudius, Kaiser und Gott*. Graves himself collaborated on this shortened version of his two novels on Claudius. But I sometimes wonder if the comma in the title was another way for Graves to claim *Ich "bin" Claudius* – I "am" Claudius – the "I" being Graves himself, and as such, allowing himself to malign Seneca in the guise of Claudius! The Stoic-minded Philosopher endured his exile much better than did Ovid. This is illustrated in his letter to his mother, *De Consolatione ad Helviam Matrem*, written in exile, and entreating his mother not to fret over his plight. Seneca may have been attempting to win favour with Claudius, when he wrote another letter of comfort while in exile, this time to Claudius' literary secretary, Polybius. In *De Consolatione ad Polybium*, Seneca consoles Polybius – always with Stoic principles – on the death of his brother. If Seneca thought that such openness with a member of the Emperor's inner circle could put an end to his exile, can you blame him? By the way, Seneca's other *consolatio, De Consolatio ad Marciam*, was a letter to a rich and influential Roman matron, who had been grieving for her son for three years. This was written before his exile, and was most probably another example of Seneca trying to remain "connected" to high society! Foundation Golf Tournaments didn't exist in those days! I shall conclude with some remarks about the "Pumpkinification" of Claudius. This Menippean Satire – so-called after a Greek writer, and written in prose, not in verse like the satires of Horace and Juvenal - has been generally attributed to Seneca. Why not – his exile gave him good cause, and in his new position as tutor and then adviser to Nero, he wished to warn the incumbent Emperor against being unjust and incompetent (Seneca really did look upon Claudius as a "fool"!). It is true that Claudius' legacy in judicial matters was seriously flawed. It's even hinted at in Graves' novel!

However, it should be noted that Petronius, a contemporary of Seneca's, also wrote a Menippean Satire – *The Satyricon* - and perhaps even his own satire on the death of *"Divus"* Claudius. Could the "Senecan novel" actually be the work of Petronius? The story of Claudius ascending to the heavens, and attempting to convince the gods to deify him owes its title to a play on words on the concept of *"apotheosis"* - declaring someone a god - which Seneca believed was too common, and not always merited. The Romans, we know, did declare the deceased Claudius *"Divus"*. The title is a Latinized form of a Greek word – *Apocolocyntosis* – derived from the Greek word for "gourd". Pumpkins are of this family, but I am not so sure that even the song by Jay and The Techniques – "Apples, Peaches, Pumpkin Pie" – would bring a smile to Claudius' face! I must admit, that I also began to have misgivings about that very popular symbol of Halloween! Robert Graves conveniently appended a translation of this satiric novel – which also features segments written in verse – to his book, *Claudius the God*. True, the account is quite comical, beginning with Claudius' plea to Hercules to secure permission to plead his claim to divinity before the gods. At first, the hero-god is distressed, thinking this task will become his "Thirteenth Labour"! To use an analogy with golf, we know that Hercules was never the most useful "club" in the bag, despite always carrying one himself! Hercules would be "the old spoon" – a two-wood – so not really necessary to have in your bag, if you can hit a decent three-wood or long iron. Speaking of which, golfers are wont to carry a one-iron in their bags, which they clutch to during lightning storms, since even God cannot hit a one-iron! The story ends with Caligula claiming that Claudius was his slave – true, the "Mad Emperor" had been accustomed to mistreating "foolish Uncle Claudius" – but Claudius is handed over to a freedman who will employ him as a keeper of records. So the Claudius we know will again have his nose buried in books! As a final note, Seneca alluded to Claudius being raised to heaven with a hook – an apparent reference to executed prisoners being dragged to the river with hooks. While it is safe to say that Seneca and Claudius never did "hook up" together, I leave the final words to Nero, commenting on the death of Claudius by empoisonment. Dio Cassius quotes Nero declaring that mushrooms were the "food of the gods", since mushrooms had allowed Claudius to become a god! Suetonius, we know, records Nero's play on words with a reference to the verbs *morior* – "to die" – and *moror* (long o) – "to be a fool"! I would add the other verb *moror* (short o), which means "to delay" or "tarry", and gives us the word "moratorium". Consequently, Claudius, in "dying", no longer had to "hang around" on earth as "a fool"! To add my own anecdote – Pizza Pete, my boss in Cincinnati, used to replace anchovies on pizzas with mushrooms for customers he didn't like! So let us declare a moratorium on slandering Seneca! In closing this *apologia* – my personal defense of Seneca - I believe it is fair to say, Professor Saulnier, that as a native son of Lyon, you have redeemed that city and the mistreatment of Seneca at the hands of the Emperor Claudius, by your life of research and teaching on the subject of our dear Seneca!

Chapter 87

\-   Thanks for inviting me to join you and Manon on your regular date night. I know how you two love dancing on Saturday nights! Is this your regular spot?

\-   Yes, Martin. When Saturday night comes along, a Dionysiac frenzy starts to take hold of me - especially since I know I'll be with my "magnificent Maenad" – Manon! So I hope you catch the "fever"! Say, wouldn't that make a great title for a film – "Saturday Night Fever"! The regulars here know us, and the waiters bring me a beer without taking my order. And they bring Manon's Bloody Caesar as well. The one drink lasts her pretty well the whole night, since we spend most of the time on the dance floor! I don't know if she has always been drinking that drink or she adopted it after I talked to her about Julius Caesar one day! Although, come to think of it, she always orders Caesar salad with her meals! Too bad they haven't come up with a "Seneca Sling". On second thought, it would probably be too strong – "suicidal" - to drink! But it would have "potential" for those who appreciate a "potent" drink – especially if they know that *potos* means "drinking contest" in ancient Greek! Thinking about those all-male taverns in Montreal, it's kind of sad to know that the Greek word *posis* meant "husband" and "drinking"! *Plus ça change...* However, my "*symposia*" with Manon and company are always "sensible"!

\-   You think about Seneca even on your night on the town! Honestly, Denys, I don't know how Manon puts up with you! So you say she's bringing a girl you've never met?

\-   That's right, Martin. Apparently, she's only been working with Manon for a couple of months. I wouldn't mention the Seminary to her. Since you are a Classics student, she probably already thinks you have two left feet! Before the girls arrive, I have to tell you the news. You know that Laval is starting its huge financial campaign. The Dean of the Faculty has asked each department to prepare a publicity poster. Wouldn't you know it, Professor Marcoux has asked Professor Giguère and me to pose for a Classics Department photo – with the caption *Mens sana in corpore sano*! – My personal motto on a publicity photo!

\-   Well, Denys, you have to admit, you can't find a body more *sano* than Professor Giguère's! And no Latin student at Laval has a mind more *sana* than yours! But tell me, will you both be wearing clothes?

- That's not funny, Martin! Besides, if they wanted nudes in the poster, they could use that replica of the Venus di Milo in the Department showcase – or maybe a statue that has arms!

- Well, if we can't see Professor Giguère's hand in the photo, we know where it will be!

- Again, Martin, not funny! Oh, here are the girls now! And none too soon – they'll be starting the disco music any minute now.

- Hi, Denys. Hello, Martin, how are you? Guys, this is –

- Lucie?

- Martin? I thought you were in the Seminary!

- I was. Now I study Classics like Denys here. What a surprise!

- Likewise! Imagine, two Classics students in the same place! And one of them is an American! Nice to meet you, Denys! Manon has told me all about you!

- Nice to meet you, Lucie! But you shouldn't believe everything you here!

- It's all good!

- Like I said – don't believe everything!

- Stop, Denys! These two obviously have some catching up to do, so let's dance

- "Let's dance" - that would make a great song title! That's "Superstitious" by Stevie Wonder. I wonder if he wrote that in honor of the Romans. After all, they were "very superstitious"! Listen now – "writing's on the wall". Is he referring to graffiti at Pompeii?

- You're still talking shop, Denys! Try being a Latin lover instead of a lover of Latin!

- You're right, Martin! I'll snap out of my Latin trance and concentrate only on the dance! Take a sip of your Bloody Caesar, Manon! - you're lucky March 15 is not until next week! Speaking of which, do you remember that song "Vehicle" by The Ides of March? I guess that group will never get to play Caesar's Palace! March 17 is also next week – the wearing of the green for St. Patrick's Day! It's a big deal in New York – and in Montreal ! The belief in having good luck when you find a four-leaf clover is understandable when you consider that they are so rare. The Irish are clever, though, in associating shamrocks with three-leaf clovers. I know the "luck of the Irish" had its origin in all that gold discovered by Irish miners during the 19th century gold rushes. That must explain the "pot of gold", which was so precious to the leprechauns! Funny, Patrice Leprohon in my Latin classes never mentions it! I am Irish on my mother's side, but back home I was never allowed to drink Irish whiskey because I was an "Irish minor"! I think it was the three-leaf clover that brought real luck to the natives when St. Patrick returned to Ireland from Gaul, that is from France, as Bishop – even though he had been a slave to the nature-worshipping tribes of Ireland. He demonstrated the HolyTrinity by using that plant, and "planted", as it were, the "seeds" of conversion. The Romans called Ireland *Hibernia,* and Patrick wrote in Latin, calling himself *Patricius* in his *Confessio,* which was his autobiography – a word meaning "one's life recounted by oneself" from three Greek word: *autos – bios – graphe.*

Personally, I would be reluctant to write an official memoir of my own life, and would probably "camouflage" my life-story in a novel! I believe this French-Irish connection explains why there are so many Franco-Irish marriages in Quebec, and why there are numerous people here with Irish names, but who can't speak English, as well as people with French names who don't speak French! There's more, folks! I believe that the fleur de lys on the Quebec flag can bring luck to this land of Quebec since, like the three-leaf clover, it has the three "points" of the Trinity, and combines the blue and white colors of the Virgin Mary! This flower, known as the lily in English, was associated in Greco-Roman mythology with a "virgin" birth, in that - according to one tradition – Juno gave birth to Mars, not by Jupiter, but by contact with the lily flower! Hence, the Québécois have chosen to associate themselves with Mars, originally a god of agriculture – synonymous with the early history and demography of Quebec. The connection with Mars, the god of war, I explain as the political battles which ultimately dominated Quebec's history! The lily is the "Easter flower" – symbol of the Resurrection of Jesus Christ. Prosperity and harmony can be part of Quebec's future, if the traditional beliefs of the faithful are, in turn, "resurrected"!

Martin, you know that in our conversatons on social injustice, we talked about individual and collective attitudes in society. You didn't disagree with my conclusion that people here are beginning to worship the wrong "trinity" – "me, myself, and I"! When coming upon the abbreviation U.I., our inclination should not be "unemployment insurance" – what's in it for me? – but "you and I"! In other words, helping each other without prejudice and seeking personal gratification. I was already putting forth those ideas in an essay I wrote in high school in searching a formula for world peace! I might as well talk about the other big day next week – the Feast of St. Joseph on March 19. Bear with me, Martin, and stop growling at me like a bear!

The Quebec faithful – those who are still fervent – have a special fondness for St. Joseph – probably because he was a real down-to-earth hard worker. In fact, he is the patron saint of fathers, of families, of labourers, of refugees – after all, he had to flea with Mary and Jesus to Egypt! He is the patron saint of people dying, since he had a "happy death" in the presence of Jesus and Mary. However, my connection with him is the fact that he is the patron of "dreamers"! That's because an angel appeared to him to let him know he had to leave for Egypt.

He also had a dream telling him to return, and a couple of other dreams as well. St. Joseph was the "silent partner" in Jesus' mission, since he never wrote anything, and no words are attributed to him in the Scriptures. He would have appreciated The Tremeloes song "Silence is Golden"! Yes, I know that the undeniable patron saint of Quebec is John the Baptist - mainly, I think, because the Québécois can relate to someone "crying in the desert" for social justice.

Interesting, though, that St. John The Baptist was celebrated here in Quebec accompanied by a lamb. Those most vociferous for change complain that the French population accepted their lot passively like sheep. This led to the negative connotation of the "flock" being guided by the Catholic clergy! People seem to have lost sight of the "Good Shepherd"! Quebec is seeking something new, and just like "new circumstances" in Latin is *novae res* – the Roman expression for "revolution" - people here are counting on change by revolution! What most people are aiming at with a "quiet revolution" is a change in attitudes and accommodations that will lead to an "authentic equality" and respect for rights – starting with the French language! When you think about it, Jesus was a "revolutionary", bringing His own *res novae* – His own "new ideas", as we read the "Good NEWS" in the NEW Testament, with its promise of a NEW life!

-       Denys, you had us mesmerized – now we're the ones in a "trance"! If we were Irish, our eyes would be "smiling" at your captivating raconteurship!

-       Thank you Martin! I'm glad I know so many song titles – I'm one of the few people in here who can actually ask the DJ for requests! Since he sees us here every week, he actually let's me give him playlists! The DJ – Fantastic Frank – I think his name is actually François – is a really nice guy! And I think he appreciates you buying him a drink every week, Manon. I can just picture him drinking beer out of a mug in a German beer garten. A regular Frank and *stein*! He says having us on the dance floor most of the night is good publicity for his music. I've heard him tell the Club manager "we have the right moves because he plays the right grooves"! It looks like Martin and Lucie are getting up to dance – I'm glad I put a few slow songs in my playlist! The song Freakin' Frank – I mean Fantastic Frank – is playing right now is for your brother-in-law, Bob, who just arrived with Maggie. It's called "Keep on Truckin' ". Frank was impressed when I told him that the singer, Eddie Kendricks, used to be in The Temptations. By the way, Frank's not insulted when I call him "Freakin' " or "Fantasy" Frank – he likes those names. But he doesn't like when Bob deliberately says his DJ name too slowly, and it comes out Fant - ass - tic Frank! All the couples will like this one – he's playing "Do You Love Me" by The Contours. Say, Bob, will you be "wearing the green" next week on St. Patrick's Day? You could be the "Jolly Green Giant", like in that song by The Kingsmen!

- No, Menace, you would be the "Green Giant", since you're both corny! And besides, I'm not always that jolly! But thanks for the song! I'd buy you a beer, but I see you've already had one!

- Thanks for looking out for me, big guy! You're all heart – where your wallet should be! Oh, Bob, Maggie, this is my friend Martin and this is Lucie, who works with Manon.

- Hi there. Denys says you're an American too, Bob. God Bless America! Nice to meet you, Maggie! How come you and your sister are so infatuated with "Stars and Stripes"?

Say, Denys, Lucie wants to know the titles of the songs the DJ played. I told her you're the University's expert on pop music, including songs from the past. She said – and she'll probably blush now – that as a Classics student you would naturally be interested in the past!

- Don't blush, Lucie – that's a "classic line"! The songs you and Martin were dancing to – and quite well, I might add – were "Ain't No Woman Like The One I Love" by The Four Tops, "Crocodile Rock" by Elton John, "Nights In White Satin" by The Moody Blues , "Brother Louie" by The Stories, "Stuck in the Middle with You" by Steeler Wheel, and "Long Train Runnin'" by The Doobie Brothers. After his break, Fantastic Frank is going to play a couple of songs by The Spinners – "Could it be I'm Falling in Love" and "One of a Kind Love Affair", as well as the Timmy Thomas song "Why Can't We Live Together". And just so you'll know, the slow songs he'll be playing right before closing are "Angie" by the Rolling Stones - Bob's favorite group, and the good news for Bob is that I have a feeling they are going to be around for a very long time! – "Killing Me Softly with his Song" by Roberta Flack and "Midnight Train to Georgia" by Gladys Knight and the Pips. Say, Bob and Martin, do you guys want to be the Pips with me?

There are three Pips that sing and dance with Gladys, and one of them is her cousin. By the way, Mr. American truck-driver, the song was originally called "Midnight Train to Houston" – would have been a longer trip for you! The last song Frank will be playing is for Lucie and Martin. It's a song by Sylvia called "Pillow Talk". When you hear it, you'll know why Reverend

Al Green refused to record it! While the others are dancing, Manon, I want to say how much I'll miss you while I'm in Athens this summer. Two months is a long time, but I'm hoping it will make your heart grow fonder of me. It's a *carpe diem* thing, Manon. I really should take advantage of those special seminars they are offering at *L' École française*. Before you ask, I've been to Greece three times so far – to Pylos for an archaeology project, to the British School at Athens for courses on numismatics and Greek poets, and to Thessaloniki in northern Greece for an international programme at the Balkan Institute. By the way, don't refer to that city by her Ottoman name, Salonika! In fact, Thessaloniki was named for a daughter of Philip II, which made her a step-sister of Alexander the Great. Her name means "victory over Thessaly", which Philip celebrated with that name! But I don't leave until the middle of June, so we have lots of dancing left, and I'll write to you even more often than I do to my Mom! And you'll have even more time to spend with your mother. One day, maybe we'll be able to visit Greece together, and Italy – we have to go to Rome. I know you'd like to travel to Spain, since we've both studied Spanish. I know you're jealous that I'll be there for two weeks next month! Another country I'd like to visit is Germany. It would be especially stimulating, because the first real modern studies on Greece and Rome were carried out there. All those names of German scholars from the past come to mind – Göethe, Nietzsche, Winckelmann, Wilamowitz-Möllendorff, Fränkel, Jacoby, Mommsen and Werner Jaeger. The tradition is being continued at Laval by Professor Walter. I should mention Heinrich Schliemann, who, although not a scholar, got the ball rolling in classical archaeology. We should visit *Lutetia* some day – it would be so romantic! I'm talking about Paris, Manon – the *Lutèce* of the Astérix books! The name "Paris" comes from the Parisii, a Celtic tribe that inhabited that territory. Naturally, going anywhere with you, Manon, would be romantic! Even our walks on the Plains of Abraham and in *Vieux Québec*, especially in *La Rue Des Trésors*, are fun. Walking along Place Dufferin gives me an appetite, so I'm always glad when you suggest a meal at *La Maison du Spaghetti*! Fortunately, I'm not neophobic, since you are always getting me to try new delicacies of French cuisine! Actually, as a student of ancient languages and civilizations, it's a wonder I don't suffer from the fear of "new things", or neophobia! Our promenade along the boardwalk near the Château Frontenac also reminds me of the song by The Drifters – "Under the Boardwalk"! Skating on that little rink near the Château as a light sprinkle of fluffy snow descended on us was really special – and you skate so well! Our visit to the Aquarium was fun, but I bet you'd love Marineland! And I'd like to go back to *Le Musée de la Civilisation* with you. There's an exhibition of statues of the Greek Gods arriving from the Louvre next year! How about that, you made Martin so happy tonight when you brought Lucie along. And you make me so happy! There's something magical about you, Manon! You remind me of that Lovin' Spoonful song –"Do You Believe in Magic?"! Not so much The Vogues song "Magic Town", which is about false dreams. In fact, the first line in the song dispels the notion of "streets paved in gold". I have to laugh when I think back on a disillusioned Jeff who asked Pizza Pete if he would ever realize the "American dream" of streets paved with gold.

Pete told him that there were streets in Cincinnati that weren't even paved – and - get this – Jeff would probably end up being one of the guys who would have to pave them! So, the only "gold" was Pete's wicked wit! That, and the "solid gold" hits on his juke-box!

- Well, Denys, if I were a real magician, you'd be my favorite rabbit!

- Or maybe just a "White Rabbit", like in The Jefferson Airplane song!

Chapter 88

\-   So your first year here at Laval is coming to an end, Denys. How do you find our programme, and how does Quebec compare to Montreal?

\-   I love Quebec City, Professor Marcoux! Life is more relaxed here than in Montreal, where everybody seems to be in a hurry. Maybe their lifestyle is determined by the subway system – the metro – which has people going everywhere so quickly! Of course, spending time with my girlfriend, Manon, makes life so enjoyable. And I really appreciated the courses I had in this first year. I'm looking forward to my summer programme in Athens – except for the fact that Manon and I will be away from each other for two months. Even my programme for next year promises to be very enriching! I get to practice German again after class since I'll be taking the Greek and Latin Palaeography course with the always interesting Professor Walter. Naturally, I'm looking forward to the Greek course on Hesiod and Apollonius of Rhodes with Professor Roumelis. I always appreciate conversations with him in Modern Greek. I have a great deal of respect for Professor Saucier, and so I am pleased to be able to take his Latin course on Apuleius and Petronius. I consider myself fortunate to be able to take Professor Ricard's Roman Archaeology course – all the more because I can practice my Italian with him. He has already mentioned that I will probably be able to participate in the summer excavation work at Pompeii at the end of next year. Obviously, the Roman Religion course with Professor Marois will be very important in guiding me towards a definitive topic for my dissertation. And I am grateful to your wife for allowing me to enroll as an auditor in her Intermediate Spanish course. She sometimes calls me Don Quixote because I have so many dreams for the future! But, honestly,I don't know if I prefer Cervantes or *Cerveza*! It will also be a pleasure to be a part of next year's Greek play production, *The Bacchae*, if you will have me.

Martin says I should naturally have the role of Dionysos – not just because of my name, but because I'm always talking about religion! I suppose he is a little sensitive since he left the Seminary. At least he seems to have found his true vocation – her name is Lucie! And as at all our wine and cheese socials, he seems to be enjoying today's "symposium". The wine may not be Falernian, but then it's not Mass wine either! Well, *nunc est bibendum*, as they say! So I'll "drink up"! Why we say that is perplexing, since the drink is going down!

\-   Of course, you'll be in *The Bacchae*, Denys. All that research on Bacchus/Dionysus and Liber you did for your Master's thesis will certainly help you "get into character"! I want to mention a bit of a strange exchange I had last month when I was at McGill University for a colloquium sponsored by *la SEGELQ*. At the reception that followed, I was speaking with Hélène Jolivet – you know, Professor Jolivet's wife. When she asked how you were, I mentioned that you would be at the French School in Athens this summer. She said that she and her husband would be in Paris, but she would prefer that Paris were in her, and that life would be so beautiful with Paris. I had never known her to be so lyrical, but I finally caught on to the Paris – Helen reference. But with kind of a wistful look, she then pointed out that because of the martyrdom of St. Denis who became patron saint of Paris, Denys and Paris are, in a way, synonymous. I still haven't figured out the reason for that reference! But speaking of *la SEGELQ*, as I had mentioned, I put forth your name for a position on the Council, and you were elected, along with another new member, Professor Giguère. By the way, the poster of you two turned out beautifully! With two attractive young classicists as our heralds, it should be clear that Classics is not only about the past, but also about the future! Let's just hope that our brazen attempt at boosting enrollment is beneficial. At least you can admit, Denys, that my alliteration was successful!

-       And Classics is also about the present, Professor Marcoux! If you will excuse me, I want to catch Professor Roumelis, while he's free.

-       So, Denys, you are making preparations for Athens. You know I spent my formative years there at the University of Athens. However, I was born on the island of Santorini. But to a Classics student like yourself it sounds more exciting if I call it Thera! I grew up hearing about all the legends of Atlantis. The story of the great maritime destruction that reached all the way to Crete is really for me what explains the lost world of Atlantis. Survivors would eventually themselves find their way to that distant Island – distant for those days — where an underworld civilization was being established – yes I'm talking about the Palace at Knossos and the underground labyrinth. I believe that subterranean network was too elaborate and too important to be the home of one measly monster! You may have read accounts in Plato, but you must remember that, although he criticized the myths of Homer and others, Plato himself was a great teller of tales, and not past inventing myths of his own, designed to explain and find acceptance for his philosophical and political ideas. Many scholars have investigated and debated the stories behind the Atlantis legend, but take it from me, we Greeks have an intuition about these things, and for those of us from Santorini – call it Thera if you will – Atlantis is part of our heritage!

-       So fascinating, Professor Roumelis! So Atlantis was not a city beneath the sea, but a thriving metropolis beneath a Cretan palace! How could Sir John Evans have missed that? But speaking of heritage, how was the year you spent in my hometown of Cincinnati?

-       I have to say that my American experience was a bit overwhelming. My only contact with Americans up to then had been with the numerous tourists in Greece. And, speaking frankly, they appeared like modern imperialists of Ancient Rome, acting like our "masters", at least in an economic sense. But even they seemed awed by the cultural vestiges of classical Greece, much like the ancient Romans! However, when I was persuaded by one of my professors to spend a year at the University of Cincinnati, known to me through the work of archaeologists such as Carl Blegen and John Caskey, I discovered a milieu very rich in resources for the study of ancient and modern Greek literature. I was doing research on the travels of Jason, as recounted in the works of Apollonius of Rhodes – I must specify, since other important writers also had that name, such as Apollonius of Perga, but as all Greek professors, I digress! – and the tragic poets. Perhaps you have seen the film *Jason and the Argonauts.* It was a great movie for students of film and film-making, less so for serious students of classical mythology!

But the story of Jason is so interesting that I'm sure other movies will be made about him, and maybe even television will turn to the various legends about him. As for the city itself, I did not get acquainted that well with Cincinnati. I tended to stick close to the campus, where professors and staff treated me very kindly. They prepared me well for my doctoral studies at Princeton. However, my English at the start was not very strong. I was – and still am – much more fluent in French. But I remember walking often through the huge park next to the campus - Burnet Woods it was called. My biggest surprise was how friendly and helpful the Americans were. Americans at home are definitely different from the American traveler! Yet there was an exception I can recall. I once accompanied a fellow-student to a rather quaint-looking pizzeria, where I had a delicious meal. But the man at the counter, obviously the owner, a man named Pete I gathered from the restaurant's name, was not that friendly. My colleague had as much trouble as I did in placing our order in clearly spoken English. Finally, Mr. Pete told us to "speak American"!

-       Professor Roumelis, I guess it really is a small world! I grew up and lived next to Burnet Woods. My family still lives there – on Ludlow Avenue. Sounds like you ate at Pizza Pete's. That man was the owner, but his name wasn't Pete. In fact he passed away a few years ago. I actually worked there – that's how I paid my private high school tuition. Pete wasn't the most diplomatic person you could meet – he sure had his prejudices! But he really did have a good heart, and always treated me well. Your experience reminds me of the stories I heard in Montreal of French-speaking people told to speak English. But I wanted to thank you for your course. What we read in Strabo actually helped me prepare the talks I gave in Spain with the travel group. I concentrated on the theme of the Romanization of Spain. Julius Caesar had claimed that all of Spain had been pacified, but Rome only completed the total conquest of *Hispania* in 19 B.C. under Augustus. So this process lasted two hundred years, whereas Julius Caesar conquered all of Gaul in ten years! This type of resistance probably explains why there are still efforts for independence in Spain even today, such as with the Basques. Strabo had said that Further Spain, that is *Hispania Ulterior* in the south, was completely Romanized. Nearer Spain – *Hispania Citerior* in the north - had not been occupied as long by the Romans. In fact, Strabo, as well as Cicero and Valerius Maximus, claimed that the inhabitants in the Iberian Peninsula were wild barbarians! So far from the erudite family of the Senecas! Excuse me I want to catch Professor Walter before he leaves.

- Professor Walter, I wanted to thank you for the Epigraphy course. Reading inscriptions will be invaluable in my research. Often they are the most reliable documents in ascertaining the veracity of literary texts. As well, our exchanges in German before and after class have helped improve my comprehension and expression in a language that I admire!

- Thank you, young man. I understand that you did a great deal of teaching in addition to carrying a full course load. I am glad they found someone to teach Latin and Greek to the seminarians. With your education in the Jesuit tradition, you would understand the importance of an educated clergy, one trained in the classics. And your contribution to popularizing the classical languages and civilizations in an outreach programme aimed at young and old is laudible. How do you feel about that experience?

- Well, Professor Walter, I've certainly been enriched by meeting and sharing with so many people outside of university circles. The Latin course taught through the immersion method of continuous reading – much different from traditional approaches of grammar and translation of sentences devoid of context – proved very popular. Indeed, next year a second-level course will be offered to students continuing in the programme, as well as the introductory course. Moreover, due to a significant demand, including from students in the Latin course, an introductory course in Ancient Greek will also be offered. Fortunately, *Cégep* Ste-Foy has graciously agreed to make a room available three nights a week. It helps, of course, that one of the founders of this outreach movement is an administrator at that Cegep! Because I will be teaching again at Loyola College in Montreal on Tuesdays, the second-level Latin course will be offered on Fridays. This did not seem to pose a problem for most of this year's beginning students – that's how keen they are! I mentioned my teaching at Loyola. I had the pleasure of teaching Vergil's *Georgics* and *Bucolics.* I must say that I prepare more as a teacher than I do as a student, since I am expected – and I demand it of myself – to know the answers to all student questions, or at least be able to direct them to a source that will provide an answer to their queries. Likewise, in the Greek and Roman Religion course, I attempted to stimulate discussion, which I had to be able to moderate, rather than simply "dictate" endless facts and terminology.

In the classroom, as in state politics, "dictator" can have a very negative connotation! Next year I will teach a course entitled *Cicero Ad Familiares*, a Latin reading course on Cicero's letters to his friends. It's like reading the noted statesman's diary! I'll also be teaching a seminar for senior students on Greek history. It will be on the life and legacy of Alexander the Great. The courses at the Seminary are very particular. The seminarians are often aware of the material we look at, but have to learn the rudiments of Ecclesiastical Latin and Biblical Greek, in order to read the texts, which were written by Church, or Patristic, Fathers. We read texts from the Vulgate Bible, including the evangelical accounts – and students are intrigued on learning basic meanings of words, such as the Greek sense of "bringers of good news" for evangelists – and we read the writings of philosophers and theologians such as Augustine, Jerome, and Ambrose, papal bulls, even prayers and canticles. Aside from the Greek and Latin, these courses are very rewarding for me, as they allow me to investigate and reflect upon my own religious traditions. In somewhat the same way, I will attempt analysis and synthesis of various aspects of Greco-Roman religion, pagan though it was. The study of Christianity is outside the scope of my doctoral research, but the courses at the Seminary allow me to explore that aspect of religious thought and practice in the Roman Empire. I appreciate, as well, the opportunity to lecture in a relaxed atmosphere in the Classical Civilization series offered to the general public. Since I am not presenting material for an exam or as part of a course syllabus, I am free to add anecdotal elements to the general information. There already was a significant motivation among students in this year's course which was on Greek and Roman mythology. I think that interest was heightened by my frequent references to contemporary illustrations of the ancient myths, in literature, art or film. My girlfriend, as well as her sister and mother, and Martin's girlfriend all attended the lectures. But I did warn Manon that she would have to write an exam if she misbehaved! Next year's course will be on Greek and Roman literature.

-        Well, Holden – I've discovered your real first name – never underestimate the depth and breadth of German scholarship! – and, as you can see, I'm also aware of your acute sense of humour! I am deeply impressed by your commitment to classical studies – as a learner and as a teacher. In the sense that true students are life-long learners, you are indeed "the Latin student"!

Chapter 89

- Hi Jeremy, I'm writing this letter to you on the plane ride home from Greece. Just something to do during my nine-hour flight! No, seriously, you know how I appreciate your reactions to my study programmes. I can't "talk shop" with my Mom and with Manon, although Manon seems to be acquiring some knowledge about the Greeks, and especially about the Romans through "osmosis". Maybe "os most" of the time were together! Which reminds me that she appreciates the new words I supply her with, like "*cosmos*", which the Greeks used to describe the well-ordered universe. That's why cosmetics can "bring order" to one's face! Manon, who doesn't use – or need – make-up, enjoys doing crosswords, and I don't interfere to avoid "cross words" between us! That way, we never have to "make-up"! Manon is becoming very adept at word play. She began referring to me as her "Classics Cosmonaut" – because I was out of this world! That would make a cute caption for Classical Studies! I wrote to my Mom often during the two months, but sometimes I was literally talking about the weather! With you it's different – it's about "whether" you've been a good boy! And you're still my number one sounding-board for puns! By the way – you know that with me there's always a "by the way" – Ralph Kramden of "The Honeymooners " would hate me! - that term for "play on words" goes back to the Latin verb *pungere*, meaning to "prick" or "pierce"! Once a Latin student, always a Latin student! From this comes *punctum*, which means "point". Do you get mine? My Italian studies taught me the word *punto* – point – which led to the diminutive for a fine point or quibble – *puntiglio*! Did you know that a pun can be called a paranomasia, which as the excellent Greek scholar that you are - no pun here, seriously! – you will recognize as meaning "a calling by a different name" or, literally "a naming besides". I hope you enjoyed that "vehement vocabulary voyage" – got to continue practicing alliteration! – my poetic "litter"!

You'll be disappointed to hear that my whole time at the French School in Athens was devoted to very serious courses on papyri and Greek history. So no older women trying to seduce me, no female – or male – professors coming on to me, no lesbians or homosexuals, no young students offering themselves as research projects, and no young village girls trying to marry me! Jeremy, you'll probably wait until you're a Professor Emeritus before spending time at one of the international academies, but I consider myself very fortunate to have spent summers in Greece, Italy, and England. The time in Spain was an extra bonus! I realized that the world is my oyster!

It could be yours too, Jeremy, if you avoid being so crabby, as you sometimes are wont to be!

There's nothing "fishy "about my advice! Actually, to paraphrase that old (fishing?) line about teaching a boy to fish, I discovered that the pleasure I derived from reading a translation of Vergil's *Aeneid* lasted the few days I spent reading, but that studying Latin seriously and continuously would enable me to enjoy Latin literature for the rest of my life! There's no time like the present! Like the Grass Roots song says – "Live for Today"! It's funny, when I heard that song a while back, it triggered something in my memory. Then it hit me - not in the same way you used to hit me! – I had heard the song in Italian when I was in Rome. It turns out that the Italian version *Piangi con me*, which translates "Cry With Me" was the original version of the song, and was recorded by a British group, The Rokes, who had relocated to Italy! Since "rokes" is a variant of "oaks", they could have recorded "Tie a Yellow Ribbon Around the Ol' Oak Tree", but then where would Tony Orlando and Dawn be? Then again, The Rokes could have called themselves "The Druids" – since those Celtic seers were sort of "oak-priests", based on the Greek word *drys* – meaning oak-tree. I guess you've heard of those wood nymphs called Dryads.

As such, they could have been the opening act at Caesar and his Romans concerts! Cover versions of songs are quite common, and often more successful than the original versions. Elvis Presley recorded the Carl Perkins song "Blue Suede Shoes", and the Beatles re-recorded songs by The Marvelettes – "Please Mr. Postman", Chuck Berry – "Roll Over Beethoven', and The Isley Brothers – "Twist and Shout". Santana put out a version of "Black Magic Woman", which had previously been recorded by Fleetwood Mac, and Jimi Hendrix sang "All Along the Watchtower" - as only he could! – a song originally done by Bob Dylan. But I didn't spend my time in Athens listening to records. I was studying, and thinking about Manon. I had her picture near my bed – don't get randy – not much you can do with a picture – unless, I guess, your name is Jeremy! It's like that song we listened to in my course at McGill – "*J'ai Ta Photo dans ma Chambre*"- translated for a guy in Toronto as "I've Got your Picture in My Room." It was sung by Johnny Farago, an Elvis wannabe! Actually most of the songs we studied in that course were covers for American and British songs! My course on papyrology was challenging, as was the course on the *Hellenica Oxyrhynchia*. You have no doubt heard about the debate on the authorship of this text, which continues the account of the Peloponnesian War in Thucydides. The main "suspects" are Theopompus, Ephorus, and Cratippus. I was kind of proud when I suggested that it was likely Cratippus, because, after my presentation, my Professor said that Cratippus had been his choice when he was doing post-doctoral research on some papyri from that period. But we will probably never know the author's name. I also took a Greek reading course on Diodorus Siculus and Dionysius of Halicarnassus – two more authors I can scratch from my required comprehensive reading list. I'm really enjoying teaching, Jeremy, and I can't wait to do it full-time! Not just teaching in university – but giving courses at all levels to students and non- students alike (yes, if I'm teaching them, they are my "students", but you know what I mean!).

People coming in the evening to learn Latin – for whatever reason! I use the book Professor Jolivet gave me. Oh, and apparently his wife, "Helen", has taken to calling me "Paris"! I won't tell you about the "ins" and "outs" of how that came about, but you can figure out even from those few words how gross the whole affair is! I wouldn't even go to Troy, New York with her! A highlight of these Latin classes is, I think, what I call SPQR – "Some Popular Quotes Retold".

Think of that next time you read about the *senatus populusque romanus* – the official seal of the "Senate and People of Rome". I simply use proverbs to illustrate grammatical notions. For example, I use *satis verborum* - "enough said" – as an example of the partitive genitive. Impersonal verbs – in this case, *licet-* I present with the phrase *non licet in bello bis peccare* – "in war it is not permitted to err twice". But it's probably not fun to err even once! As an example of the use of the emphatic adjective and pronoun, I give students the phrase *ipsa scientia potestas est* – "knowledge itself is power". The jussive subjunctive is shown by the Latin phrase *caveat emptor* – "let the buyer beware" – which also allows me to explain the use of the Latin word caveat in English! To illustrate the ablative absolute – after the students finish marveling at the name of that construction! – I use the phrase *omissis iocis* – "leaving aside joking" – something, as you know, Jeremy, I have a hard time doing – even with beginning students! Teaching Latin and Greek at the Seminary is also accompanied by stimulating conversations. Once a student brought this phrase to class – *ubi divisio peccatum ibi.* It's from the Church Father Origen of Alexandria, and means "where there is division there is sin"! This led to a discussion on Satan as the "Great Divider". In fact the word devil originates from the Greek *diabolos* – "one who scatters about", so, "divides". The word came to mean "slanderer" – Socrates could tell you much on that subject (with an "apology" to Plato!). You know, Jeremy, the verb *diaballo* – " to slander". Although Socrates had his *daimon* – his "spiritual guardian"- he was up against some really slanderous devils! The notion of *Ho Diabolos* as "The Dark Power" was picked up in other languages as well – French *diable,* Spanish *diablo,* Italian *diavolo* and *German Teufel.* Come to think about it, I could be "tempted" in all those languages! Naturally, I can't let all this talk about the devil go by without reference to some appropriate song titles. So here goes: "Devil with the Blue Dress on" by Mitch Ryder and The Detroit Wheels – I know, Jeremy, - a connection with the center of the car industry! And yes, blue is still my favorite color! And there is the song "Devil or Angel" by The Clovers. Come to think of it, if you are what you eat, I imagine angel food cake is on my menu, and you're the one eating deviled eggs! Yes, Satan is the master of "divide and conquer"! The message of "Divided we stand, united we fall" rings out from earliest times, starting with the story in Aesop of "The Four Oxen and the Lion", and echoed in the various New Testament Gospels. In fact the song "United We Stand" – it continues with the lyrics "divided we fall"- by The Brotherhood of Man – aptly named, don't you think? - is a good musical illustration of the concept. So much so, that it has been translated into French, *Nous resterons unis* – meaning "We will remain united"- into German, *In Gedanken* – meaning "In Thought" - and into Italian, *Voglio Stare con te* – "I want to be with you" – shades of Dusty Springfield's "I Only Want To Be With You"! I didn't actually bring up these songs with the seminarians, since I think they're more into Gregorian Chant! We did discuss however the sins of division which pit black against white in America and French against English here in Quebec. We also looked at historical divisions caused by confrontations between religious groups. Now that I've embraced different languages, after my presentation in "*Seigneur*" Saucier's Seneca Seminar – hey, more alliteration! - I selected one of the sayings of Seneca – do you remember when our intramural hockey team at McGill was called the Senecas, not because we were philosophical about our chances of winning, and certainly not because we were stoical in defeat, but we wanted to pretend we were somehow akin to the McGill Redmen? - and translated it into French, Spanish, Italian, German, and Greek – that is, Modern Greek, Jeremy. If it sounds like I'm boasting, it's because I am! The saying is "The wind is never favorable to those who don't know where they are going". I have to admit, I've had fair winds so far in heading off to Xavier University, and McGill, and Laval! Same goes for Italy, Britain, Greece, and Spain. By the time I finish these translations, I should be close to landing in Montreal – if the winds stay favorable!

"Le vent ne souffle jamais dans la bonne direction pour ceux qui ne savent pas où ils vont".

''Nunca hay viento favorable para el que no sabe hacia donde va''.

''Il vento non soffia mai dalla parte giusta per chi non sa dove andere''.

''Wer den Hafen nicht Kennt, in den er segeln will, für den ist Kein Wind ein günstiger''.

''O anemos den einai pote ourios yia ekeinous pou den xeroun pou kateuthunontai''.

Why am I humming Tommy Roe's song "Windy"? Why are you probably whistling that Frank Sinatra tune "Summer Wind"? I know you're "blown away" by all this, Jeremy! One final note on wind – and I'm not trying to "wind" you up – oh those words with two different pronunciations and meanings! I don't know if you ever got "wind" of the fact that in Hebrew the same word is used for "wind" and "spirit" – so the "Holy Spirit"! You often confessed to me that "the spirit was willing, but the flesh was weak"! But I trust that you are in good spirits, and not drinking too much "spirit water"! I know by now you are happy that I'm not beside you, and you would be looking for someone to "spirit" me away! So much for my "Pentecost platitude". I know you will take all this in the spirit it was meant! May the Spirit be with you! Your "spiritual advisor", Hold On!

Chapter 90

-       Denys, it's so nice to be with you again!

You can't imagine how much I missed you!

-       Actually, if it's as much as I missed you, Manon, I CAN imagine it! Here we are at Le Deauville – our restaurant for special occasions. I love Greece, but I have to be honest – I'm not high on all Greek food. Souvlaki and Greek wine, and I'm happy! So the pepper steak I ordered is going to be very welcome! And you didn't say no to the sea food platter! We're a real surf and turf couple! I remember Pizza Pete trying to pass off a meatball hoagie and fish basket as a "surf and turf special"! The Mountain Dew that went with it didn't exactly pass for fine wine either! I can recall showing Pete a "haute cuisine" menu one day, and he thought it was a note about my "hot cousin" – go figure! So it's agreed – a couple of Spanish Coffees for dessert! Since we are both studying Spanish, we deserve them. You seem to like your Spanish course. Is it that sexy Flamenco dancer who moonlights as a Spanish teacher at *Collège* Ste-Foy?

-       Are you jealous, Denys Hainsworth? At least you know he doesn't keep me in after class, since I always meet you after your Latin class down the hall. It's so nice that the two courses are on the same evening.

-    It sure is! This year, though, I'll be giving classes three nights a week, including Friday evenings. The class finishes at eight o'clock, so we'll still have plenty of time for dancing! As long as it's not Flamenco dancing! You also seemed to enjoy the Classical Mythology course taught by a certain American matinee idol!

-       No, I prefer your Mythology course! Ha!Ha! You lecture so well, and your French is so good that when I mentioned to a few students that you were American, they didn't believe me. Honestly, I sometimes had the urge to stand up and applaud! My mother and Marguerite too! We are all going to take the Classical Literature course this year. So is Lucie!

-       That's great, Manon! And don't stand up during class. That usually means you want to walk out! But you really did display self-control during the first class. Remember when I asked if there were any questions, and a young lady in the front row asked if I was married. I said no, but I could have sworn you uttered to her "not yet"! Well, it seems funny now! Say, let's have a second Spanish Coffee!.

- I did spend a lot of time with my mother, but we didn't travel. So I kept a couple of weeks of vacation for a longer period of time off in the future. I hope you won't be upset, but I have to tell you something. An old flame – well more like burnt ashes – saw me a few times with my mother. He assumed there was no man in my life. There isn't – but I have you! Sorry, Denys, it's the Spanish Coffee – and maybe the Bloody Caesar I had before the meal! Well, to make a long story short – actually, the story isn't very long – he asked me to marry him! At first he didn't believe I had a handsome American in my life. But when I told him you were a Latin student, he said I wouldn't make that up. If he hadn't believed me, my Plan B was to tell him you have a black belt in Karate! -

- I know I shouldn't leave you all summer without a bodyguard! Say, is Bob free next summer? Ah, yes, next summer! Do you want the bad news or the good news first? At least I hope it's good news.

- I'm assuming you mean bad news for me, Denys. I smell a *carpe diem* in your plans. Please don't tell me you're moving back to the States!

- I said BAD news, Manon, not terrible and awful! You are probably thinking of that song "Runaway" by Del Shannon, whose real name, by the way, is Charles Weedon Westover – a little too long for a record label! Say, a French version of that song has just been released by a singer from France known as Dave! I've discovered, though, that he is actually Dutch, and his real name is Wouter Otto Levenbach! If he were writing books on Ancient Greek or Roman religion, that name would be fine. But since he's a singer, we'll call him Dave! Like Stevie Wonder says – "You are the Sunshine of my Life"! Or that singer you like – Ginette Reno - when she sings "*Des Croissants de Soleil*"! I'm sure my first breakfast with you will be nothing but sunshine! You really do light up my life – somebody should sing a song with that message!

To tell the truth, Manon, right now I'm thinking of the Frankie Valli song "Let's Hang On" - to what we've got! This singer's real name is Frankie – well Francesco – Castellucio. I wonder if the name Valli was inspired by the name of an original pop star and teen idol, Rudy Vallee. This crooner had inspired later crooners Bing Crosby, Frank Sinatra and Perry Como – these last two being Italians like Frankie Valli. When I was in Rome, I kept hearing the song by Italo-American Julius La Rosa called "*Eh, Cumpari*". And never forget, Manon, that, just like Frankie Valli, I "Can't Take My Eyes Off You" because "my eyes adored you" the first time I saw you! Say, that would make another great song title for him! So I hope you will take Ginette Reno's advice when she sings "*Aimez-le si fort*" – since it describes the way I love you! You know I am going to be at the Pompeii excavations for three weeks next summer.

Well, Professor Walter has arranged for me to take courses at his old University at Tübingen – and I do mean old, not just former, University! I would be there for four weeks, and then spend a week travelling to some other universities. I've always wanted to visit Germany, and now my stay will be paid for by the Parker Endowment Fund! So you're right, there is some *carpe diem* there. I would be away for two months like this past summer, but we can make reservations again here at Le Deauville when I get back – if you're not married! Professor Watson at McGill always told me to have a sense of the big picture and to plan ahead. Professor Marcoux is much the same. It's amazing how the network of contacts presents so many opportunities. Professor Saucier, whom I really like, is able to reserve a place for me in a Greek and Roman Philosophy Seminar along with Greek and Latin courses that are being planned for the summer of 1975 at the Sorbonne.

EVERYBODY plans ahead, so it seems! Part of the good news is that the courses I was planning to take at the British School in Rome in the summer of 1975 are the ones I will take in Germany next summer. So I will be free for the programme in Paris. Professor Saucier knows about us, and how I spend my summers in Europe. He romantically suggested I tell you "*Sénèqu'un au revoir!*" You realize that Seneca is our common password, but I take it as a compliment that he is using a play on words! The real good news is that you can come with me to Paris if you want to!

Professor Marcoux had even suggested that I could spend a whole year at the Sorbonne, or at the Université de Lyon, but I immediately told him there were four reasons compelling me to decline. *Primo*, there were my teaching commitments, quite considerable, all things considered. *Secundo*, I didn't want to miss the courses I'm planning to take at Laval. *Tertio*, there was a chance – I should say definite risk – that my doctoral programme would be extended by twelve months if I were to study abroad for a full academic year. I have set my goal from the outset of obtaining my PhD at the end of four years – just shy of my twenty-eighth birthday. What a party that will be! I'm hoping you'll be the guest of honor, Manon! Both Professor Marcoux and Professor Saucier knew my final and most important reason – how could I leave you for a whole year, Manon? I was going to wait to talk to you about a couple of conferences that are being held at the beginning of summer in two years time. Major conferences definitely have to be planned well in advance! The University of Toronto is hosting the Classical Association of Canada Conference in May of '75. Miami University in Oxford, Ohio is hosting The American Classical League Annual Meeting a week later. The campus is only an hour's drive from my home in Cincinnati. I'm hoping you will want to attend the conferences with me, and another special event – the tenth anniversary reunion at St. Xavier High School! The ACL conference organizers have approached me about speaking on the immersion method of teaching Latin used in *Lingua Romanorum*. I may also be invited to present a paper on the same subject at the CAC Conference in one of the Pedagogy sessions. This time you would be allowed to clap! The very best part of the news is that we could leave the following week to spend ten weeks in France! I realize you would have to ask for a two-month leave of absence, since you would already have a month's vacation owed to you. I'm sure your superiors will be nice to you about this. Tell them that I'm always vaunting the efficiency of their bureaucrats. Why just the other day I was telling Martin - and his Lucie works with you, Manon - that your office workers are so fast that even though you finish at 4:30, you're all home at 4:00! This three-month adventure has to be planned in advance! Don't fret about the expenses.The Parker Foundation pays for all my summer travel and living expenses. You would be staying with me – and don't worry - the rooms in Paris are just as big as those in Ottawa! Someday I'll explain that little enigma to you! So your expenses will be the plane fare home from Cincinnati - we'll bus there from Toronto - it'll be an adventure - and the return flight fare to Paris, and transportation to Toronto. Maybe we can hitch-hike – Jeremy would appreciate that! Just kidding – I wouldn't mind taking the train.

There's a nice connection – Quebec- Montreal – Toronto. I've saved quite a bit of money teaching these last few years, and I will pay for your travel expenses, as well as the Bloody Caesars and the *cafés au lait frappé* that you imbibe while I'm in class at the Sorbonne! I kno you pay room and board at home, but if your parents wave that for the three months you will be away, maybe you won't be too much out of pocket, even if you have to forego two months of your salary. I guess it's a good thing you didn't buy that car you were looking at! But you can spend the following summer again with your mother and sister Maggie. The "Three Graces" – the *Gratiae*, or the *Charites*, for your Greek friends! Your mother is definitely the Grace of Charm, Maggie would be the Grace of Creativity, and you, Manon – well you're the Grace of Beauty!

-       Wow, that's a lot to take in, even for someone like me who is fast enough to get home half an hour before she leaves work! But I'll look into our leave of absence policy. I wonder, though, what the Grace of Charm will think. My mother and I have never been separated for three weeks, let alone three months.

Chapter 91

\-   Ladies and gentlemen, do you believe in ghosts? How about werewolves? Perhaps you began to have second thoughts about the supernatural when preparing today's readings. The ancient Romans have always been considered a superstitious people – even selecting their first king on the basis of the flight of birds! Cicero told ghost stories, and, as well, Vergil's Aeneas spoke of his wife Creusa "vanishing into thin air", after advising him to flee the burning city of Troy. Petronius used the same phrase as Vergil and other authors to describe these surrealistic occurences – *haec ubi dicta dedit* – "when he/she had spoken these words".

One can imagine a camera panning to a Lon Chaney being transformed into a werewolf in those horror movies of what now seems a distant past! The more frightening scenes I believe you will find are in Fellini's *Satyricon*, where gluttony and sexual debauchery help visualize the "satire" in Petronius' *Satyricon*. When women today sometimes refer to men as "animals" – but I'm sure that doesn't apply to the young men and women here present – they are not echoing the ancient belief of lycanthropy, that men did actually become wolves or other wild animals! And then there's the legend of Romulus and Remus being suckled by a wolf! Petronius, we know, was Nero's "judge of elegance and good taste". But not taste in food! For culinary cookery and criticism read that fourth century Roman cookbook, wrongly attributed to Apicius since that gastronomic genius lived in the time of Tiberius! I hope you are giving me "five stars" for alliteration, Denys! Perhaps the author of that book should be called "Appetitius", or something like that! No, our Petronius, if he were alive today, would be more like de Givenchy or Christian Dior, that is to say, a fashion designer! I would say that Trimalchio's dinner – although tasty or tasteless, depending on your personal delectation – is more about the dinner chatter, the stories, such as the one being told in today's reading by the freedman, Niceros, which begins at 61,6 of this novel – one of the very few that we have. It is in the pages of the historian Tacitus that we hear of Gaius Petronius Arbiter as the *arbiter elegentiae* – so you see, Denys, play on words did not originate with you!

Petronius was also in the "Who's Who" list of Nero's suicide victims. Well then, let's have our modern master of mystic messages – our wizard of words – our American anthology of alliteration – read and translate the passage for us.

\-   Thank you, O Professor of Petronian Pranks!

Cum adhuc servirem, habitabamus in vico angusto; nunc Gavillae domus est. Ibi, quomodo dii volunt, amare coepi uxorem Terentii coponis: – everybody, this is the Vulgar Latin form for *cauponis - noveratis Melissam Tarentinam, pulcherrimum bacciballum. Sed ego non mehercules corporaliter illam aut propter res venerias curavi, sed magis quod benemoria fuit. Si quid ab illa petii, numquam mihi negatum; fecit assem, semissem habui; quicquid habui in illius sinum demandavi, nec umquam fefellitus sum. Huius contubernalis ad villam supremum diem obiit. Itaque per scutum per ocream egi aginavi,quemadmodum ad illam pervenirem: scitis autem, in angustiis amici apparent. Forte dominus Capuae exierat ad scruta scita expedienda.*

Nactus ego occasionem persuadeo hospitem nostrum ut mecum ad quintum miliarium veniat.

Erat autem miles, fortis tamquam Orcus. Apoculamus nos circa gallicinia, luna lucebat tamquam meridie. Venimus inter monimenta: homo meus coepit ad stelas facere, secede ego cantabundus et stelas numero. Deinde ut respexi ad comitem, ille exuit se et omnia vestimenta secundum viam posuit. Mihi anima in naso esse, stabam tamquam mortuus. At ille circumminxit vestimenta sua, et subito lupus factus est. Nolite me iocari putare ; ut mentiar, nullius patrimonium tanti facio. Sed, quod coeperam dicere, postquam lupus factus est, ululare coepit et in silvas fugit. Ego primitus nesciebam ubi essem, deinde accessi, ut vestimenta eius tollerem : illa autem lapidea facta sunt. Qui mori timore nisi ego? Gladium tamen strinxi et – matavitatau!

- Professor, I looked for variant readings in the *apparatus criticus*, and I came across other editions which replaced this Vulgar Latin word by *in tota via* . It seems the word was used only once, so a *hapax legomenon*. The seventeenth century Swedish scholar, Johannes Scheffer, who fortunately wrote in Latin and German, since my knowledge of Swedish is limited to meatballs, justified the inclusion of *matavita tau* by references to single uses of words in Cicero. This "abracadabra" fits the context of magic and mysterious apparitions.- *umbras cecidi, donec ad villam amicae meae pervenirem. In larvam intravi, paene animam ebullivi, sudor mihi per bifurcum volabat, oculi mortui, vix umquam, refectus sum.Melissa mea mirari coepit, quod tam sero ambularem, et, "Si ante", inquit, "venisses, saltem nobis adiutasses; lupus enim villam derisit, etiam si fugit intravit et omnia pecora tamquam lanius sanguinem illis misit. Nec tamen; servus enim noster lancea collum eius traiecit." Haec ut audivi, operire oculos amplius non potui, sed luce clara raptim domum fugi tamquam copo compilatus, et postquam veni in illum locum in quo lapidea vestimenta erant facta, nihil inveni nisi sanguinem. Ut vero domum veni, iacebat miles meus in lecto tamquam bovis, et collum illius medicus curabat. Intellexi illum versipellem esse nec postea cum illo panem gustare potui, non si me occidisses. Viderint alii quid de hoc exopinissent; ego si mentior, genios vestros iratos habeam.*

"When I was still a slave, we lived in a narrow street; now it's Gavilla's home. There, as was the wish of the gods, I fell in love with the wife of the innkeeper, Terence. You knew Melissa from Tarentum, a very beautiful little pearl of a girl!" Professor Saucier, I used "pearl" to describe what is probably a reference to her shape - round like a berry, since I think *bacciballum* could come from *bacca* – so the roundness of the *margarita,* or pearl. Maybe I could say she's "berry beautiful"! or "a peach of a girl". Or maybe she was just pleasantly plump! The music aficionados among you will recall that Janis Joplin's nickname was "Pearl", and her last album was called "Pearl". Why that nickname – I honestly don't know! She wasn't pretty or especially round – but she was tiny – and a real gem to her friends! But I do know that her last album featured the song – "Me and Bobby McGee" – a real gem of a song! To continue -"But, by Hercules, I didn't long for her physically or on account of sexual cravings, but rather because of her good character. If I asked her for something, I was never refused; if she made a penny, I had half; whatever I had, I put in her pouch, and I was never cheated. Her husband met his last day at his country inn. So by shield or by greave I planned and put into action a way that I could get to her: for you know that friends appear in difficult times. By chance my master had gone to Capua to take care of some choice belongings". – I realized here, Professor, that the locative was being used for the accusative to express destination – no wonder they call it "Vulgar" Latin!

There's also a constant use of asyndeton, as if Petronius was a little "disconnected"! – "Having gotten this opportunity I persuaded one of our guests to come to the fifth milestone with me.

He was a soldier as bold as deadly Orcus. We bugger off around dawn, the moon was shining like at noon. We came to the cemetery: my friend began to do it among the tombstones, and I stand back singing and count the tombstones. Then as I looked back at my companion, he stripped down and placed all his clothes beside the road. My heart was in my nose" – maybe he could "smell" a heart attack! – "I stood there like a dead man. He made water around his clothes, and suddenly became a wolf. Don't think I'm joking; no one's inheritance is of such value that I should lie. But as I had begun to say, after he had become a wolf, he began to howl and fled into the woods. At first I didn't know where I was, but then I move forward to take away his clothes: they had turned to stone"- the black magic of Medusa, Professor! Reminds me, too, of The Four Tops song, "I'll Turn to Stone". As you can see, everybody, when doing my research, I "leave no stone unturned"! After all, "a rolling stone gathers no moss". "Like a Rolling Stone", Bob Dylan sang. Reminds me as well of The Rolling... oh, we don't have time – and Martin is looking at me as if I were stoned! So last one – "Stoned Love" by The Supremes – without Diana Ross! That's like the First and Second Triumvirates without the "lead" – Julius Caesar and Octavian Caesar! - "Who was about to die from fear but me? Nevertheless I drew my sword – and whoosh whoosh – I cut down the shades until I reached my friend's house. I entered like a ghost, I almost made my breath boil over, sweat was pouring down between my legs, my eyes were like they were dead, and I barely regained my strength. My Melissa began to wonder why I was walking around so late, and said, 'If you had come before, you could have helped us; for a wolf entered the estate and bled all the sheep like a butcher. Yet he didn't make a fool of us, even as he fled; for our slave pierced his neck with a spear'. On hearing this, I wasn't able to close my eyes again, but at dawn I fled in a hurry like a robbed innkeeper". - I think, Professor Saucier, that this alludes to Aesop's fable of a thief who robs an innkeeper after scaring him by pretending to be a wolf. I'm looking forward to the course on Aesop which I understand will be offered next year – "After I had come to that spot where the clothes had been turned to stone, I found nothing but blood. But when I got home, my soldier friend was lying in bed like an ox, and a doctor was looking after his neck. Then I realized he was a werewolf, and from then on I couldn't take even a bite of bread with him, not even if you were to kill me. Let other people decide what they think about this; if I am lying, may I answer to angry household spirits!"

-       My dear Denys, you interspersed your excellent translation with sometimes pertinent, sometimes amusing, commentary. As for your musical tastes, I shall be no Petronius - *non Petronius sum*. After all, *de gustibus non disputandum est* – "there is no accounting for taste"– especially when it comes to your sense of humour and your musical preferences. I believe you are reading Hesiod in the Greek course this year. Are you "amusing" the Muses?

Chapter 92

-    Greetings, and I must say I'm impressed by the submissions you have all made in the selection of topics we will address in this seminar on Roman Religion. I have asked Denys to present today. You are all aware, I believe, that he will be doing his doctoral dissertation on the subject of Roman Religion – the first to do so at Laval, although I have supervised a few Master's theses in this field during the eight years I have been here. I don't think Denys will object if I announce his subject. You may come across pertinent information that you could share with him. Denys will be examining personal religious beliefs and practices in the context of the official state religion during the second and first centuries B.C. He tells me it will be a literary, historical, and epigraphical study of primary sources that will look at aspects such as individual religious freedom, group cult worship, senatorial decrees and state control of religious worship, acceptance of foreign cults, and other related subjects. His dissertation will be under the joint supervision of Professor Watson of McGill University, where Denys did his M.A. It is therefore very convenient, Denys, that you get to meet with him once a week when you travel to Montreal to teach. My friend and colleague Watson informed me that Denys was known as "The Latin Student" in high school and during his years at McGill, and he shared some interesting anecdotes on our American student! Professor Marcoux also has some tales about Denys - who was known to our Chairman as Holden during the year he taught him at McGill. But I guess we will be calling Denys, "The Roman Religion Student"! Although Professor Saucier will probably continue to refer to him as "Seneca's Sidekick", because of the interest that Denys has for that author. I believe you will be teaching a course on Seneca next year in Montreal. Denys is already aware of the big change that comes into effect next September, which will especially interest those of you from Montreal. Loyola College and Sir George Williams University will be amalgamated into one institution to be known as Concordia University – a name that reflects the harmony that everyone hopes will replace the rivalry that existed between these two academic establishments. It is not known by all that Loyola, not having university status, could not officially grant degrees to its graduates, and so Loyola alumni hold a degree conferred by l'Université de Montréal. However, this changes next year. I'm sure, Denys, you will speak to your students about the *concordia ordinum* - the social and political entente among the three citizen classes that Cicero strove so hard to maintain. I mention all this because some of you will be looking for a university teaching position in a couple of years, and this may be an opportunity for those of you who are bilingual. You may want to practice English conversation with Denys, and who knows – picking up an American

350

accent may turn out to be a plus! So, Denys, what subjects are you bringing to our seminar table today?

- First of all, thank you for giving me a new nickname, Professor Marois! But I'll always be a student of Latin! And my competence in Latin will certainly be tested in my research, examining the principal Latin texts pertaining to Roman religion. The first subject I considered for today is religious experience. A few years ago I read a book called The Varieties of *Religious Experience* by William James. Therefore, I decided to look at personal religious experiences among the Romans. I recommend on this subject *The Religious Experience of the Roman People from the earliest Times to the Age of Augustus*, written by W. Warde Fowler. I gathered some of the information from authors I have read, or am presently reading, like Cicero, Valerius Maximus, Apuleius - who I'm reading this year with Professor Saucier - and Plutarch – I'll be taking a course on that author next year with Professor Roumelis. Religious experience, individually or in groups, is often inspired, or enhanced, by religious paraphernalia, such as statues, altars, sanctuaries, and even temples. This is, in a broad sense, like worship today, with churches replacing temples – although some world religions still gather in "temples" – and shrines answering the same needs as did ancient sanctuaries. The prayer books and spiritual writings of today had their ancient counterparts as well. Private religious worship by a group of workers, perhaps the equivalent of a guild or corporation – I wouldn't identify them as a syndicalist union! – is evidenced in sanctuary remains at Ostia, for example. An inscription also informs us that Mithras instructed a certain Proficentius to set up a cult site, following a religious experience by the latter. Professor Walter's epigraphy course is proving invaluable for my research! A noteworthy account on religious experience is Lucian's account of his protagonist who has set out on a journey to become an initiate of Isis. In Book 11 of his *Metamorphoses*, section 23, we read *Accessi confinium mortis et, calcato Proserpine limine, per omnia vectus elementa remeavi, nocte media vidi solem candido coruscantem lumine; deos inferos et deos superos accessi coram et adoravi de proximo*, which I translate as "I arrived at the boundary of death, and after having traversed the threshold of Proserpina, and after having travelled through all the elements, I came back. In the middle of the night I saw the sun shining with a bright light: I arrived in the presence of the gods below and above, and worshipped them from nearby". Here we must ask if the causes of the sensation are natural or divine. Groups, such as those who would attend – or tend to - the rites of Isis, or such as the First Friday worship groups or Ignatian spirituality groups of today, provide the setting for an experience, but the actual emotion or sensation depends on the individual.

Another subject to be investigated is the connection between the Dionysiac myths of the rescue of and marriage to Ariadne. This story is regularly part of the iconography on Roman *sarcophagi.*

But often we see Ariadne being greeted not by Dionysos, but by Pan, or as he was known to the Romans, Faunus. Since the female counterpart to Faunus is Fauna, who is often called Bona Dea, this led me to examine the ritual practices surrounding the cult of the Bona Dea. Everyone knows the story of the intrusion of Clodius into the house of Julius Caesar during the rites of the *Bona Dea,* rites that were supposedly forbidden to men. Caesar repudiated his wife on the grounds that she should be "above suspicion". I suppose this reason would be as good as any for getting rid of an unwanted wife! Commentators in antiquity mostly relied on the account given by Cicero in his prosecution of Clodius – who nevertheless was acquitted, but not without having his reputation severely tarnished by Ciceronian invective. However, Clodius was a political adversary of Cicero. Could Cicero have been biased in his condemnation of this "intruder"? Would Clodius have been welcome in his female dress, as a sexually non-threatening observer, much like the eunuchs who participated in oriental cults that revered female deities, if he had not been suspected of an affair with the hostess of the ceremony, Pompeia, Caesar's wife? Caesar himself, the *Pontifex Maximus*, did not seem overly concerned about the religious impropriety of Clodius' act, but rather by his wife's reputation, and, by extension, his own. The notion that men were always excluded from the *Bona Dea* is based in great part on the account that Plutarch gives of the intrusion by Clodius in his *Life of Caesar* (at 9-10), where he says: "The Romans have a goddess called *Bona*... the Romans say she was a Dryad nymph and the wife of Faunus.. the Greeks say she was a mother of Dionysos. This is why the women cover their booths with vines when they celebrate her festival, and why a sacred serpent sits by a throne alongside the goddess in accordance with the myth. It is unlawful for a man to be present at the sacred ceremonies, or even to be in the house during the ceremony.

…On the occasion I am speaking about, Pompeia was celebrating this festival, and Clodius, who was still beardless and on this account thought to pass unnoticed, dressed like a female musician and entered the house, in the appearance of a young woman. A servant-girl brought him in to wait for Pompeia….but he, losing patience, wandered around the house." This account might suggest that Clodius had gone to meet Pompeia, knowing that Caesar would be absent, and not to spy on the *Bona Dea* ceremony. On the other hand, Clodius would be aware that Pompeia would be busy hosting the ceremony. Is it possible that, on occasion, "harmless", female-like males could be admitted, in spite of Plutarch's general statement about male presence? The answer may be in this passage from the *Ars Amatoria* of Ovid at

3.633- 638, where the poet says *"Bona Dea* forbids the eyes of men in her temple, except those she welcomes there herself". There are inscriptions, as well, describing offerings made by men to so-called women's deities, such as *Bona Dea* and *Felicitas*. One example I came across reads as follows: "Felix Asinianus, public slave of the pontifices, fulfilled his vow to *Bona Dea Agrestis Felicula* willingly and with good cause, sacrificing a white heifer on account of his eyesight having been restored by the aid of the Mistress". Another subject I am bringing for discussion is prompted by information I received in Professor Ricard's course on Roman Art and Archaeology, which obviously looks in detail at Pompeii. Evidence of cultic performances that would require certain physical structures and specific features of cult practice have been found in and around the so-called Iseum, that is, the Temple of Isis, excavated at Pompeii. The religious re-enactment of Isis worship would require a cultic theater and passageway for the ritual Isiac procession, and a ritual drain – a water basin for ritual purification. There would naturally be sacrifices and banquets in honor of Isis. The Temple of Isis, it was discovered, did indeed contain a *cubiculum*, a *triclinium*, a *sacrarium*, a kitchen with an oven, and a latrine. In Book 11,23 of his *Metamorphoses,* Apuleius says that Lucius is brought to baths near the Temple before his initiation. Conveniently, there are baths in Pompeii near the Temple of Isis! The celebrations in honor of the goddess are described by Plutarch in his book on Isis and Osiris, where he talks about devotees finding and joining together the missing parts of Osiris' body, and rejoicing in a drunken orgy. The final subject I bring to your attention is the place occupied by the worship of foreign deities in Rome. Again, the cult of Isis lends itself to the study of Roman practices and beliefs. When examining the senatorial banning of temples and altars – in other words, places of worship – associated with the cult of Isis, the Roman Senate was attempting to exercise a certain control over cult ritual practice, that is, over certain behaviours considered "un-Roman".

This overt censure did not eliminate the worship of Isis. This is reminiscent of the law decreed in 186 B.C. that outlawed the cult practices associated with the worship of Bacchus. But that god continued to receive worship. These two instances of laws proclaimed in the name of religion actually had more of a political than a religious motivation. It was a question of authority and, perhaps, of "cosmetics". The Romans had always – even in the early days of Etruscan religious influence – been willing to integrate foreign elements into their own native religious system. The fact that laws were formulated to regulate practices concerning these *sacra* – the Romans were fond of legalese – gave these religious beliefs and practices a "Roman flavour"! By way of remote comparison, one can point to the Latin Mass becoming vernacular as possibly a secular concession to re-establish and maintain a traditional authority.

- Well, Denys, your agenda could conceivably occupy us for a large part of this course. You have demonstrated scholarly rigor in searching out sources – literary and epigraphical – to illustrate the problematic issues you wish to raise. We will certainly discuss the points you have introduced today in the coming weeks. In closing for today, I hope everyone took note of how Denys incorporated information for his topics gathered from other courses that he is presently following, or that he has already completed.

Chapter 93

- Hi Mom! Hope you are all fine. I've been on an emotional roller coaster lately! I was really happy to receive those pictures that Maxine had sent for me. Wow! Now's she's married! I still think of her as "Sweet Little Sixteen" – like the Chuck Berry song we used to dance to! I like the way he covers all of America with the words of that song – from Boston to 'Frisco by way of Texas. He mentions two great "music cities" in the song – Pittsburgh, where they love to play oldies, and Philadelphia where they have their own "sound" – "Philly soul"-like artists at Motown. I have also evolved into harboring a fondness for the soul sound and for rhythm and blues – R&B, Mom. I guess "soul" music is a good fit for a staunch Catholic like me!

And since I'm a Latin student, I can appreciate being a "Roman" Catholic! But Maxine is almost twenty-five – how time flies – I should say *tempus fugit*! I'm glad she married a pro basketball player – her brother is sure to like him – especially since he's Afro-American! I know she's going to visit Cincinnati, and will probably drop by to see Feeb. So I'm sending you this poem I composed for the happy couple. Can you pass it on to her?

Husband and Wife

Tender moments, shared smiles.

Anxious times stored in life's files,

A surprise meal served to her man,

A little gift he gives to her when he can.

Happy events, or a sad occurrence,

Success alone, or in our partner's presence.

Thoughts always for the other,

Life as a father, life as the mother.

Words that brighten the other's life,

355

The love of a husband, the love of a wife.

Sometimes written, sometimes spoken,

Often a deep symbol, often a visible token.

Each feeling in their hearts true sentiment.

Together, living happiness and contentment.

Time, if it is kind, keeps them as one,

Throughout life's journey of pleasure, work, grief and fun!

I don't know if it's because I'm studying a couple of poets in my Greek course – Hesiod and Apollonius of Rhodes – but I've been writing a lot of poetry lately. This next one was for a sad occasion. There was a student I had gotten to know when I first arrived in Montreal – his name is Perry, and he's Italian. He went to study in Rome for a year, and when he returned he married his high school sweetheart. Before you know it, he had two kids, so he dropped out of graduate school and went to work with his father as a barber. He reminded me of myself, since he adored his mother. I used to tease him by calling him Perry Como, and trying to sing to him those songs that you always loved – "Magic Moments", "Hot Diggity(Dog Ziggity Boom)", "Dream Along with Me", "Catch a Falling Star", "Wanted" and "It's Impossible". Kind of ironic that Perry Como was a barber before he became a singing star on TV! Oh yes – the roller coaster. When I got back from Athens, there was a message for me from Professor Manfredi, who knows Perry and his family well – and probably all the Perry Como songs! Sadly, Perry's mother had passed away from a sudden heart attack. So I missed the funeral. I recently sent him this poem.

Ode to my Mother at her Tomb

As I stand before this stone deep in thought,

Reflecting on good things in life you'd brought,

Seeing now with what great courage you'd fought,

My happiness, the goal your motherhood sought.

The youngster you would send on a mission to the store

Was the same boy you left on day one at the school door.

Taking pride in my success, yet the sadness you bore

As you shared the disappointments life had in store.

When my studies led me to a city distant,

Your frequent letters to me a companion constant,

And your mother's love my strength at every instant,

Your joy at my return to me so important.

My marriage and children made you step aside,

But you did not consider me with less pride.

Your mother's love, source of joy, you didn't hide.

Your young boy in you continued to confide.

All these thoughts in this graveyard fill my heart,

Mixed with sadness, yet a joy at the start.

Each week I'll be here although we're apart,

To talk to you with love in a poetic art.

I'm so lucky to have a great Mom like you, that I get to write to, and to see – I know, not often enough! Which is why I'm glad you and Dad and Feeb are going to be spending two weeks here in Quebec over the Christmas holidays. I'm hoping you'll get to meet Manon's family.

We'll have lunch at Le Marie Antoinette restaurant next to my apartment building, and breakfast at Le Château Frontenac. We'll have supper at least once at Le Deauville across the street from my apartment. It's funny how Manon, and her sister and brother-in-law, feel strange whenever I pay for a meal or drinks. Just because I'm a student. But the Parker grant allows me to live fairly comfortably. I'm certainly not relegated to a Spartan lifestyle. Nevertheless, this serious student is definitely not living the life of Riley! Dad's mouth must be watering as he reads about those restaurants. I had to laugh when you told me your suggestion to keep his weight down was greeted with "you'll have a long "wait"!". I've been able to save most of the money I've earned teaching. Speaking of teaching, Loyola College will become Concordia University next year, and Professor Jones has already confirmed that I will be teaching two courses. I'll still be teaching on the beautiful Loyola campus. I'm enjoying the Alexander the Great course I am teaching this year. We've talked about Alexander's campaigns against the Persians and his ambitions for a World State – just imagine – East and West in a cultural union! I showed the class the Alexander the Great film with Richard Burton. It's a little dated, and I wouldn't be surprised to see another movie made on this young Greek king who dreamed of becoming a second Achilles! We looked at Plutarch's "parallel lives" of Alexander and Julius Caesar, and noted Caesar's frustration at not having accomplished as much as Alexander at a similar stage in his life. During the last part of the course, we will examine the division of his Empire among his successors – in Egypt, for example, where the dynasty of the Ptolemies was established, the last of which was Cleopatra. A couple of the students who know Greek are reading passages from the historian Arian that I listed as an optional assignment. My own courses are going well – Latin, Greek, Spanish, Greek and Latin Palaeography, where we've looked at Latin Rustic Capitals and Uncials, among other subjects. The Roman Art and Archaeology course is fascinating. We see how Romans, many of whom were illiterate, could marvel at the great accomplishments of their leaders through iconographical accounts of great victories, such as Trajan's column. We have also looked at monuments such as the Pantheon and the Colisseum, as well as domes, vaults and aqueducts. You already know about my three weeks at Pompeii next summer, but when you are all here at Christmas, I'll talk about my five-week stay planned for Germany! Manon had told me her cousin was interested in the fallen arches in the Roman Empire. When I asked her if he was a podiatrist, she said no, he was an architect! I told her to have him read the *De architectura* by Vitruvius – in translation of course! Speaking of books, Manon gave me a series of books called *Alix*, a young boy who is the "Tintin" of Ancient Greece and Rome. She doesn't call me her "Latin student" like the folks in Cincinnati, but rather her "Latin Superstar"! Of course she is biased! I've been gradually eliminating Greek and Roman authors from my compulsory reading list. Don't worry, Mom, I attend Mass regularly on Sundays, and I

continue to read spiritual books, having received some recently from the students I teach at
the Seminary. I will be playing Dionysos in our Greek production of *The Bacchae*. I still write
to Jeremy in Toronto. You remember him! He found himself a bit "on the ropes" in his
programme at the University of Toronto when he started letting his independent reading slide.
As they say, give someone enough rope, and he'll hang himself! I chastised him for half an
hour on the phone, and he was "fit to be tied"! Fortunately, he was able to thread his way out
of a "knot" so nice predicament! (sorry, Mom!). The whole situation reminded me of that
Hitchcock film *Rope* where the piece of rope was the *pièce de conviction*! We used to pretend
to be Chad and Jeremy! Well, he didn't pretend, since he was "Jeremy". But he "pretended" to
sing their songs, as I played my guitar to tunes like "A Summer Song" and "Yesterday's
Gone". We had fun talking about the Batman TV episode where Catwoman stole Chad and
Jeremy's voices. I loved telling him she didn't have to steal Jeremy's voice, because he didn't
have one! My favorite moments are spent with Manon.

She often gets off the bus on Laurier Boulevard – when she isn't using her father's car, and
we usually have breakfast a couple of days a week at Le Marie Antoinette before she heads
off to work, and I walk - or jog – over to the Laval campus for my classes. Because I'm
teaching every night, except Tuesday, where I spend the day in Montreal, we get to have
supper together only on Fridays – a late supper after eight o'clock before we go dancing. I
always tell her we have to start with slow dances so I can digest my food! Don't laugh, Mom –
I think she swallows it! Say, that's a play on words! I guess I'm a natural! Speaking of which,
Dad would enjoy reading the novel *The Natural* by Bernard Malamud. It's about a star
baseball player whose promising career is ruined after he is shot by a woman. The story is so
good they should make a movie based on it! It could star that actor you love, Robert Redford!
Some people have found Homeric parallels for this novel, but Homer is so profound and wide
reaching in his images and themes, that one could easily find some similarities in much of
today's great literature – even if most writers are not aiming at becoming "another Homer" –
as if! Heck, I will soon have imitated the ten-year wanderings of Odysseus (Montreal, Quebec
City and Europe) since I left home, and if the fates are kind, will find a wife at the end of my
journey (Manon?)! Just the same, it is kind of neat to find parallels between ancient and
modern literature. I recall you telling me about a book you thoroughly enjoyed. It was called
Leave Her to Heaven, and I had thought at the time that it was one of those books about the
saints that you like to read. However, I recently saw on TV the film based on that book, and
realized it centered on the theme of jealousy. In the movie, a *femme fatale* is very jealous and
possessive with regards to her husband, and is responsible for the drowning of his young
brother as well as the miscarriage of their baby. Mom, she's a modern-day Medea!
Furthermore, she is obsessed with her dead father – that's a real Electra-complex, Mom – you

know - for her murdered father Agamemnon! There is a scene in the film where the woman (played by actress Gene Tierney – yes, sounds like a man's name) is riding a horse as she scatters her father's ashes. She is carrying the urn at her waist, which seems like a minor detail, but to the classicist that your son is becoming, this could very well be an allusion to the nymph Hippolyta (whose name is derived from the Greek word *hippos*, meaning horse), who received a girdle for her waist from her father. So, again, a daughter-father connection! The film has the same title as the book. I suppose that a good scriptwriter can turn a good book into a good movie! I love sitting on the Plains of Abraham talking with Manon, "holding hands and making all kinds of plans – just me and Manon Plouffe"! I know, it does sound kind of like song lyrics!

When I look out on the Plains, and think of the battle between Wolfe and Montcalm, I'm amused that both generals have a part of Roman legend in their names. Wolfe is "*lupa*", the she-wolf, who suckled Romulus and Remus. I'm reminded of a Hungarian proverb I once read – "when fleeing the wolf, you encounter the she-wolf"! In other words, while looking for safety, you will run into a greater danger! The "*mont*" in Montcalm means "hill", and there were seven hills in Ancient Rome. I also remember my Quebec history teacher at McGill telling the class that, following the French loss to England, it was still possible for Quebec - *Nouvelle France* - to remain French, if the King of France had ceded some other territory to England, and had kept New France. Maybe French and English wouldn't still be "battling it out" today. Maybe there wouldn't be so many people feeling "*maussade*". I guess you teach that word in your French class, Mom, and explain how it means basically "really irritated and down in the dumps". There was this Afro-American from New Orleans who often came into Pizza Pete's. We called him "Frenchy". He always looked grumpy in a sad kind of way, and his usual greeting was that no one was "mo' sad" than him! At which point Pete would jump in and ask if Frenchy was claiming to be a sexual deviant. I then had to correct Pete and say that he was again thinking of the Marquis de Sade! It's confirmed that both Professor Marois and Professor Watson will be the supervisors for my dissertation on personal and public religion in Ancient Rome. See you soon, Mom. Your Den.

Chapter 94

-       I trust everyone is eager to continue with this delightful novel by Apuleius. But before we begin, please take note of this ingenious example of Apuleian wordplay from the *Metamorphoses* – *invita remansit in vita* – "she remained unwillingly alive". This line was pronounced about a bride-to-be upon finding her husband-to-be murdered! Last time, Denys presented Lucius' quest for initiation into the rites of Isis, remarkable for its insights into the cult of that foreign deity. Today we will look at that delightful tale of *Amor et Psyche*, or, more precisely, *Cupid and Psyche*. I would suggest a subtitle – "Cupid finds his soul-mate" - based on the Greek name of the young heroine. It involves the jealous anger of "a queen of beauty", much like that narrated in the fairy-tale Snow White and the Seven Dwarfs. Only it is not a servant who is to carry out the evil designs of a wicked step-mother, but the son of the scheming mother. Personally, I count this story of "roundabout romance" as the most entertaining tale in the *Metamorphoses.* Denys, you will no doubt have appreciated the alliteration in that expression, and with that introduction, would you kindly lead us through the Latin text and your translation.

-       Certainly, Professor Saucier. I shall proceed directly as requested, and not in a "roundabout" fashion! As you all have noted, the text is in Book Four, beginning at chapter 28.

Erant in quadem civitate rex et regina. Hi tres numero filias forma conspicuas habuere, sed maiores quidem natu, quamvis gratissima specie, idonee tamen celebrari posse laudibus humanis credebantur, at vero puellae iunioris tam praecipua tam praeclara pulchritudo nec quidem laudari exprimi ac ne sufficienter sermonis humani penuria poterat. Multi denique civium et advenae copiosi, quos eximii spectaculi rumor studiosa celebritate congregabat, inaccessae formositatis admiratione stupidi et admoventes oribus suis dexteram primore digito in erectum pollicem residente ut ipsam prorsus deam Venerem religiosis venerabantur adorationibus. Iamque proximos civitates et attiguas regions fama pervaserat deam quam caerulum profundum pelagi peperit et ros spumantium fluctuum educavit iam numinis sui passim tributa venia in mediis conversari populi coetibus vel certe rursum novo caelestium stillarum germine non maria sed terras Venerem aliam virginali flore praeditam pullulasse.

Sic immensum procedit in dies opinio, sic insulas iam proxumas et terrae plusculum provinciasque plurimas fama porrecta pervagatur. Iam multi mortalium longis itineribus atque altissimis maris meatibus ad saeculi specimen gloriosum confluebant. Paphon nemo Cnidon nemo ac ne ipsa quidem Cythera ad conspectum deae Veneris navigabant; sacra diae

*praetereuntur, templa deformantur, pulvinaria proteruntur, caerimoniae neglegentur;
incoronata simulacra et arae viduae frigido cinere foedatae. Puellae supplicatur et in humanis
vultibus deae tantae numina placantur, et in matutino progressu virginis, victimis et epulis
Veneris absentis nomen propitiatur, iamque per plateas commeantem populi frequentes
floribus sertis et solutis adprecantur. Haec honorum caelestium ad puellae mortalis cultum
immodica translatio verae Veneris vehementer incendit animos, et impatiens indignationis
capite quassanti fremens altiussic secum disserit.*

*"En rerum naturae prisca parens, en elementorum origo initialis, en orbis totius alma Venus
quae cum mortali puella partirario maiestatis honore tractor et nomen meum caelo conditum
terrenis sordibus profanatur! Nimirum communi numinis piamento viariae venerationis
incertum sustinebo et imaginem meam circumferet puella moritura. Frustra me pastor ille
cuius iustitiam fidemque magnus comprobavit Iuppiter ob eximiam speciem tantis praetulit
deabus.*

*Sed non adeo gaudens ista, quaecumque est, meos honores usurpaverit : iam faxo eam
huius etiam ipsius inlicitae formositatis paeniteat".*

*Et vocat confestim puerum suum pinnatum illum et satis temerarium, qui malis suis moribus
contempta disciplina publica flammis et sagittis armatus per alienas domos nocte discurrens
et omnium matrimonia corrumpens impune committit tanta flagitia et nihil prorsus boni facit.*

*Hunc, quamquam genuina licentia procacem, verbis quoque insuper stimulat et perducit ad
illam civitatem et Psychen – hoc enim nomine puella nuncupabatur – coram ostendit, et tota
illa perlata de formonsitatis aemulatione fabula gemens ac fremens indignatione: "Per ego
te", inquit, "maternae caritatis foedere deprecor per tuae sagittae dulcia vulnera per flammae
istius mellitas uredines vindictam tuae parenti sed plenam tribue et in pulchritudinem
contumacem severiter vindicia idque unum et pro omnibus unicum volens effice : virgo ista
amore fraglantissimo teneatur hominis extremi, quem et dignitatis et patrimonii simul et
incolumitatis ipsius Fortuna damnavit, tamque infimi ut per totum orbem non inveniat miseriae
suae comparem".*

As soon as Martin finishes wiping the tears from his eyes, I will begin translating. Apuleius is
not talking about Lucie here, Martin! "In a certain city there lived a king and queen, and they
had three daughters who were quite prominently beautiful; but the older ones, although quite
pleasing in appearance, were thought to be suitably admired merely in terms of human praise,
yet the beauty of the younger girl was so outstanding that the poverty of human speech could
neither express nor praise it properly. Many of the citizens and numerous visitors, whom the

news of this exceptional vision had caused to assemble, dumbfounded by their admiration of this inaccessible beauty and moving their right hands to their mouths with their fingertips resting on an upright thumb" – Giving her a thumbs up, I guess! - "worshipped the goddess Venus herself in religious veneration.

Soon a rumor had crossed over to the nearest states and surrounding regions that the goddess whom the deep blue of the sea had borne and the dew of the frothing waves had raised, having given up the grace of her divine being, was moving about here and there among large numbers of the populace, or indeed once again by some new offspring of the celestial drops, a new Venus was shooting up, providing not the seas but the lands with a virginal flower. And so this belief advanced boundlessly every day, not only to the nearest islands but to a great part of the mainland, and her fame spread to many provinces. Now many men flocked after long journeys and the deepest passages of the sea to the glorious model of that time. No one sailed to Paphos or to Cnidus or even to Cythera into the presence of the goddess Venus; her sacrifices were delayed, her temples were dishonored, her sacred cushions were trampled, her sacred rites were neglected, her uncrowned statues and empty altars were disfigured with cold ashes. A girl was prayed to, and they appeased the divinity of such a great goddess bearing human features, and during the morning promenades of the young girl, the name of the absent goddess was propitiated with sacrificial victims and feasts, and crowds of people worshipped her with garlands and bundles of flowers as she passed through the streets. This immodest transfer of celestial honors to the cult of a mortal girl violently inflamed the pride of the real Venus, and losing patience, her head shaking wth indignation, muttering on high, she speaks to herself in this way. 'Behold the primal parent of nature, behold the very origin of the elements, behold Venus, nourishing mother of all the earth, I who am mistreated by the honor of my dignity being shared with a mortal girl, and my name, founded in the heavens, is profaned by base things on earth. Doubtless I shall endure the uncertainty of a vicarious worship through a common sharing of my divinity, and a girl destined to die will carry around my image!' – This is obviously said in an ironic tone of foreboding – 'In vain that shepherd, whose justice and good faith great Jupiter approved, preferred me to such great goddesses on account of my remarkable beauty. But no rejoicing in this way for that girl, whatever she is, who has usurped my honors: for I shall bring it about that she grieves on account of that illicit beauty of hers'.

She quickly calls her son, winged and quite bold, who with his evil habits and contempt for public behavior, armed with his torches and arrows, running around other people's houses at night, ruining everyone's marriages, he commits shameful acts without punishment, and does no good at all. She arouses him even more, although he is imbued with natural wantonness, and leads him to that state and to Psyche – for the girl was called by that name – and shows her to him openly, and after the tale of that one's beauty was narrated with envy, groaning and moaning with indignation, she said: 'I beseech you, by the bond of maternal love, through the sweet wounds of your arrow and the honeyed itches of that flame of yours, make her a victim of complete revenge for your parent, and inflict severe punishments on her insolent beauty, and wanting this one thing for everything, bring it about that the maiden is seized by a "burning love" – obviously not in the same sense that Elvis sang about in his song of that name! – for a man so miserable, whom Fortune has deprived of dignity, wealth, and of health itself, of the lowest rank such that she will find no one who compares to that one's misery!"

- A very moving translation, Denys. Almost as moving as your version of the song "Cupid" that you recorded at McGill University, and that, thanks to Professor Marcoux, we will now listen to! And so that Martin - and others here present - do not despair of true love, I will point out that Cupid himself abandons the wicked schemes concocted by his mother, and true love triumphs! But with Valentine's Day just around the corner, let us not "see red" in the way Venus did in this story, but the red that Cupid strikes in one's heart – including his own! Of course we shall not ignore the crimson cheeks of our "classics crooner"! Any concluding comments Denys?

-        I guess you mean other than my complete capitulation to your alliteration from "c" to "c"! Maybe Cupid got to listen to me singing "Cupid" - that is, "the made-for-Classics" version! The flowers given to Psyche by the throngs of admirers remind me of flowers I have to purchase for a certain young lady. And the ending of this story – seeds to be eaten - tells me I should probably purchase some chocolates as well! But Professor, the highlight for me in this story is the final reconciliation between Venus and Psyche. I imagine that if Cupid gives flowers to Psyche for Valentine's Day, they will not be the artificial "Paper Roses", that Anita Bryant sang about in that song! Nor will Psyche have to sing to Cupid that '50's song by Joan Regan, "Someone Else's Roses"! In addition, this tale in Apuleius also reminds us that there is always hope that one can win over one's mother-in-law!

Chapter 95

\- You are such a romantic, Denys! After chocolates and flowers, dinner and dancing for Valentine's Day! Except that we should leave early from the club – I looked outside and that snowstorm is getting pretty bad. Anyways, we got to dance to some new songs.

Fantastic Frank always seems to know what to play – even without your suggestions! And you never cease to amaze me with your knowledge of songs and singers! "Rock Me Gently" is a great song by Andy Kim. But you say his name is really Andrew Youakim – not much of a change!

\- You're right, Manon, but he's planning to change his name completely – just wait and see! I bet you didn't know those other fun songs we used to dance to were also by him – your Mr. Kim! "Baby I Love You", "How Did We Ever Get This Way", and "Sugar, Sugar" are all his songs! I really liked the songs tonight – "Show and Tell" by Al Wilson, "Rock Your Baby" by George McCrae", and "I Am a Rock" by Simon and Garfunkel. Frank wasn't kidding when he said we'd be "rockin'" tonight!

\- I really enjoyed dancing to "Love's Theme". You said it was by Love Unlimited Orchestra. Well, Denys, isn't tonight's theme all about love? And I can tell you right now, my love for you is truly unlimited!

\- Who's the romantic now, Manon? You have proven that this sentiment I have - *amor puellae* – is true in both senses! In other words, the love I have for my girl is also the love my girl has for me! But I don't want to spoil the mood by expounding on subjective and objective genitives in Latin! I think Barry White was reading my thoughts when he recorded "Never, Never Gonna Give You Up"! I hope you've noticed my new "disco moves"! And those "crazy moves" when Frank played "I Shot the Sheriff" by Eric Clapton! I'm glad we got to dance to a couple of slow songs. Don't you love "Hello, It's Me" by Todd Lundgren? My neighbours in Cincinnati were the Lundgrens, and when I was about six or seven, I often used to have to knock on their door, so they would unlock their fence and let me enter their back yard to retrieve my baseball or football. I vaguely remember always saying to old Mr. Lundgren "Hello, it's me - again"! Fortunately, he was very nice and didn't play Little Richard's "I Hear You Knockin', but you can't come in"! But the highlight of the evening was dancing to "You Make Me Feel Brand New" by my "brand new" favorite group, The Stylistics! Their lead singer, Russell Thompkins, has such a sweet voice! I bet if they ever broke up, he could be just as popular with a new group – say how does this sound – The New Stylistics?

-      Maybe the highlight so far, Denys! You know, I'm not going to make it across the bridge with this snowstorm. I don't know if you have noticed that we almost always get a lot more snow here than in Montreal. And we don't have the metro to get around.

-      You've got to stay at my place, Manon. Do you remember when I used to talk to you about Vergil's *Aeneid*, and you were always intrigued by the story of Dido and Aeneas forced into a cave by a rain-storm – and by the will of the goddess Venus? Especially now that I let you listen to the tape of my version of the song "Venus"! I can't really explain it, Manon, but nature - this snowstorm – is going to force us into my "cave" – which is what I call my apartment. And it's happening during the favorite modern festival of the goddess Venus – Valentine's Day! You know we've often talked about the right moment! I have a feeling that your parents and my parents think that moment has passed. But it has to be special, right?

***

-      Denys, it was exactly that, wasn't it – special!

-      I never imagined there would actually be music in the background when we would make love for the first time! I can still hear the songs playing when we started kissing – "This Guy's in Love With You" by Herb Alpert, "The Look of Love" by Dusty Springfield, "To Sir With Love" by Lulu – were you thinking you were making love to a teacher? – "Love is Blue" by the Paul Mauriat Orchestra, "My Love", by Paul McCartney and Wings, "Unchained Melody", by Bill Medley and Bobby Hatfield - The Righteous Brothers, and the first song, "Summer Wine" by Nancy Sinatra and Lee Hazlewood. I vaguely remember you saying that the daughter of "Old Blue Eyes" was singing while you were making love with "Young Blue Eyes"! I can't remember the other songs - just that scratching sound of the record player. Venus must be working for God these days, because you were right – the highlight of last night was not The Stylistics! Your voice is the sweetest song I'll ever hear! You had me at "relax", but I hadn't ever even dreamed of the "happy ending" to last night! Manon, I am no longer Hippolytus! But don't worry – I don't have ambitions of becoming Caligula! Your parents were relieved you didn't have to risk a trip home – even taxis weren't going to St. Romuald! Waking up to Merilee Rush singing "Angel of the Morning" was sheer bliss, my angel! But our first breakfast in bed – let's enjoy!

-      Since I'll definitely be going to Paris with you, it won't be our last, will it? But you will be spending time before then in Italy and Germany!

-      I will definitely be looking forward to many more "days of wine and roses"! Not like in that gloomy movie of the same name, but like in the Henry Mancini title song, sung so beautifully by Andy Williams. The movie did at least inspire Bill Withers to write that ballad "Ain't no sunshine". And "when you're gone", Manon, the sun ain't so bright!

Chapter 96

-        My beautiful Manon, I guess you got that frantic phone call message I left at your office to let you know I was fine following the "incident". Now I can give you all the details.

I had also called my Mom, but she hadn't seen anything on the news. I'm glad she now has all the information. I was in the bank in Rome this morning, when a young man pointed a gun at the teller. Since it was early, there were only seven people in the bank, including the employees.

The other teller pushed the alarm button. The young robber realized this and ordered everybody to group together in an empty office. He looked really scared – but then everybody else – staring at a gun - was scared too! In fact, one teller really had the "heebie-jeebies"! My Dad taught me that expression to indicate extreme nervousness, and he told me it appeared in Barney Google cartoons. You wouldn't have heard of him, Manon, nor of his "goo goo googley eyes"! But don't you find the name "Google" kind of catchy? I wouldn't be surprised to see it "catch on" again in the future! But then I don't have a crystal ball – unless I count the football I received one year for my birthday from my cousin Crystal! The police arrived pretty quickly, but didn't get too far into the bank before the guy shouted that he would shoot his hostages if they didn't leave the bank. This made us even more nervous, as the police took up a position outside the bank. The others didn't look too well, and I guess I hadn't really registered what was going on. However, I spoke to the gun-wielding robber, and convinced him that he didn't need to keep everybody as prisoners, and that he would have better control of one hostage than a whole group. Furthermore, as I told him, the police wouldn't rush him if he still had a hostage.

Surprisingly, he saw the soundness of my reasoning, and allowed the others to leave the bank. I would be his "bargaining chip" – but in some weird way he saw me as an accomplice, since I had freed him from the nerve-racking situation of watching seven people at once. He kept the gun pointed at me, and lit a cigarette. He even offered me one, but I told him I didn't smoke. He was a bit intrigued, since he realized I wasn't Italian, but was able to speak to him with no problem. I told him I had spent three weeks at the site of the Pompeii excavations, and would be leaving for Germany the next day. Well, then he started talking about Pompeii and the destruction of the city in the year 79, and of the account he had read in Pliny, and how Pliny's uncle, Pliny the Elder, in charge of evacuating the area, had perished during the volcanic eruption. When I told him I was impressed with his knowledge of the event, he said he had been a student of Roman history, and had read numerous Latin authors, but that his favorite author was Seneca. When I mentioned that Seneca was also my favorite author, he seemed to relax a little, but he didn't lower his gun. I asked him what he planned on doing with his "hostage", and – I don't know why – I mentioned the Latin word for "hostage" – *obses*, and that the word originally didn't mean "prisoner", but merely a pledge of good faith, but that there could have been a connection with the Latin word for enemy, *hostis*. He quickly told me that he didn't consider me his enemy. I noticed tears in his eyes when he started telling me he became desperate for money to pay a gambling debt. Again I don't know why, but I mentioned to him how Seneca had said we shouldn't be slaves to money. He then talked about how humane Seneca's attitude towards slavery was. It seemed to me like we had been talking for hours, but it was only a few minutes. Then he revealed to me that he had started to regret entering the bank with a gun, but felt he couldn't change his mind, that he had to go through with his plan. I asked him if he felt like Caesar when the famous general crossed the Rubicon. He replied with *alea iacta est* – Caesar's words! "The die is cast", he said, it's too late for me. The song, "It's Too Late" by Carole King came into my mind, but the moment didn't seem right to talk about music! I tried to convince him that so far his crime wasn't the worst thing he could have done, that everyone makes mistakes. Now he was sobbing. Through it all, I discovered that he had been close to finishing his Master's degree at the prestigious University of Sapienza in Rome, but had run out of money to pay tuition. His family didn't have much money - he had been accepted because of an outstanding record in high school. When he told me his name was Livio, I reminded him that he shared a name with the great historian who gave us the early history of a magnificent city.

His thesis director was Professor Micetti, who had taught one of my summer courses at the American Academy in Rome a few years ago. I was slowly discovering that we had a lot in common for two people in this awkward situation. The most surprising "bond" that we two Latin students had was your name, "Manon"! Livio had a girlfriend who had stood by him in his despair and depression. Believe it or not, her name was Maeona – from the same family of names as yours! The police had used a megaphone to tell him to free me, but then just waited. I could see them through the front doors of the bank from the small office we were sitting in.

Livio mentioned that he had taken a course with Professor Manfredi from Canada in his first year at Sapienza. He remembered him because Prof. Manfredi would break into song in the middle of his lectures. When I told him where I had studied and that I had had "musical knowledge contests" with Professor Manfredi, Livio smiled for the first time, but quickly started looking sad again. We started talking about Pompeii and about Seneca once more. When

Livio mentioned that his middle name was Lucilio, I went for broke, and said he could read Seneca's letters as if they were addressed to him – a modern-day Lucilius! I told him that with his knowledge of Pompeii he could become a tour guide, and eventually earn money to pay off his debts, which, as it turned out, were not insurmountable – less than what the Parker Foundation gave me each year! He had not actually used his weapon, and had let everybody go except me. I would be willing to testify that we had been discussing his surrender the whole time, which in a way, we had been. Livio decided to give himself up. He threw his gun across the floor towards the front door, and we slowly walked towards the exit with our hands in the air. The *carabinieri* handcuffed Livio and took him away. I gave him a thumbs-up, hoping his knowledge of Roman history would not lead him to think I was condemning him to a miserable end, since Roman emperors condemned gladiators to death with an upturned thumb, and not a downward motion, as they show in the movies! The downward thumb was a signal to lay down the sword, and so spare the defeated gladiator. There is a debate over the significance of the upturned thumb, but I think it could be the sign of victory – the raised sword – which signaled the death sentence for the defeated gladiator. Remember your admiration of my "raised sword" during that special night in my apartment? So I'm quite all right, Manon. It's "all jolly good", as one of the British archaeologists at Pompeii never stops saying! I'll live to "raise my sword" again! Do you miss me, Manon? A young Italian reporter stuck a microphone in front of me and started asking questions, and complimenting me on my sangfroid – although I had initially feared a murder in "cold blood"! She referred to me as "Goldoni" Hainsworthy! I guess Carlo Goldoni is still popular in Italy! I saw a French version of his comedy *The Venetian Twins* when I was in Montreal. They staged it in such a way so as to have the same actor play both twins! The duel scene between them involved some clever work with the stage curtain! Imagine saving a whole salary for a leading actor! An American reporter – Rome is full of them – interviewed me, and said his article would have the title "Hostage Holden in Latin Liberation"- makes you want to read the article just to find out what that crazy title means! I started being intrigued by your name, Manon. I discovered it's one of the five most popular names in France! You're going to be a hit in Paris a year from now! The French name means "of the sea" or "bitter-sweet" – the characteristics of the goddess Venus – or Aphrodite, if you prefer! In Wales, the name means "wished-for child" or "Queen" and "the most beautiful"! I guess I know how to pick them! Since we've been together, my Mom sent me a book called *Manon des Sources*, about a girl in the French countryside who detours a natural source of spring water to avenge the death of her father. Oh yes, and she marries a teacher! I discovered that the novel was actually preceded by a film in the early 1950's. Both are the work of Marcel Pagnol, who is pretty popular in France. I know of him because he translated Vergil's *Bucolics* into French. It makes sense for him to translate pastoral poetry, given the subject matter of his novels. As you know, I taught Vergil's *Georgics* and also his *Bucolics* – which means poems about "cowherds" and which are also called the *Eclogues*, meaning a "selection" – at Loyola a couple of years ago. That's not all! On one of the days off from my work at Pompeii I attended a repertoire film festival in Rome. Why?

It was a series of films on Manon Lescaut! I know you read the eighteenth century novel by Abbé Prévost and that neither you or I will be attending any of the operas based on the novel any time soon! I watched the 1940 film *Manon Lescaut*, the 1949 adaptation *Manon*, which changed the original story, the 1955 film Les Amours de Manon Lescaut, and a 1970 version, which was a rather loose adaptation of the original story, but it starred Catherine Deneuve, who looks a lot like you, so worth the price of admission! The music for this film was written by Serge Gainsbourg, you know, that cult legend in France who sang that song with his girlfriend, Jane Birkin. We used to listen to it – "*Moi je t'aime…non plus*". But Manon, I discovered the original version here in Europe. He wrote it for and sang it with my favorite French actress – Brigitte Bardot! Don't be jealous! Finally, the festival featured American, Italian, and German silent films on Manon Lescaut. I enjoyed seeing her adventures that took place in Louisiana! But I still long for more Manon! Most of the buildings at Pompeii are open to tourists, and they vastly outnumber the archaeologists and student staff members like myself. I've had the chance to visit my favorite buildings several times. You can locate them in the book on Pompeii that I gave you last Christmas. They are the House of the Faun, the House of Sallust, the House of the Tragic Poet, the House of Menander, the Villa of the Mysteries – you know we should have looked at those pictures on erotic art that night of the snowstorm – just kidding! There are also the temples of Isis, Apollo, and Jupiter. We attended a couple of lectures on the history of Pompeii, how it was originally settled by speakers of the Oscan dialect, and the Oscan word for five – *pompe* - may explain the name, perhaps referring to five villages in the original settlement. But then again, maybe it was settled by the *gens Pompeia*, hence the name! The Etruscans then settled in the area, but it was the dictator Sulla who eventually became master of the city. We read about the eruption of Vesuvius in 79, as related by Pliny the Younger. I wonder if, ignorant of their impending doom, some of the residents would have been sitting on Otis Redding's "Dock of the Bay", enjoying life in the Bay of Naples! Sadly, Otis and his band would also meet a tragic end! During the slave uprising of the early 70's B.C., Spartacus had once gone with his band up the slopes of Vesuvius to escape the Roman legions. If he had been there a hundred and fifty years later, the volcano would have "blown his cover"! The work I'm doing – mostly cleaning and recording – in restaurant hierarchy, I'd be a busboy! – is being carried out in various sites within the nine regions – *regiones,* that is, "neighbourhoods" and *insulae*, or "neighbourhood blocks" - that the Pompeii site is divided into. These aren't in your book, but they are the

House of the Europa Ship, the Garden of the Fugitives, The *Forum Boarium*, which is quite a recent investigation, the House of the Garden of Hercules, the House of Marcus Lucretius Fronto, and the ongoing excavation of the House of Marcus Fabius Rufus and the Golden Bracelet. A couple of days after our arrival in Pompeii, the students were treated to a mini film festival on Pompeii. After some silent films, we saw a 1935 adaptation. However, the film that caught my attention was the 1959 movie, *The Last Days of Pompeii*, which is based on the 1834 novel by Edward Bulwer-Lytton. The story of Pompeii is so appealing that I'm sure we'll see other movies about it in the future, maybe with special effects to enhance the eruption! The novel's author, Bulwer-Lytton,was a fascinating character! He was a British diplomat who turned down the crown of Greece! He was pretty well responsible for the founding of British Columbia, since he sent a certain Richard Clement Moody to govern that territory. I wonder if Pat Boone was paying tribute to him when he sang "Moody River"! Speaking of Pat Boone, his song "Love Letters in the Sand" makes me think of the letters I wrote to you, while sitting on the shore in the Bay of Naples. I was in the sand – not the letters! I enjoyed my short visit to the island of Capri. Tiberius was there much longer – at his *Villa Jovis*, that was destined to be the Temple of Jupiter - until his nephew Caligula ended the stay – and the life - of the reluctant successor of Augustus. But I don't think the "Madman Emperor" sang "*Capri, c'est fini*", that song by Hervé Vilard I hear often out here. Back to Bulwer-Lytton – and the town of Lytton in B.C. is named after him – he is credited with the expression "the pen is mightier than the sword" from his play *Richelieu, or The Conspiracy*, about the famous Cardinal Richelieu, who along with King Louis XIII, founded *l'Académie française*! But the message in that saying had been around ever since the phenomenon of a "war of words" began. So naturally the idea has been attributed to famous writers like Euripides and St. Paul, but I haven't actually seen this phrase in their works – unless you believe that St Paul, that great writer of *Epistles* – like my Seneca, who most likely never communicated with Saul become Paul – wrote the *Letter to the Hebrews*. Other "famous words" attributed to Bulwer-Lytton are "It was a dark and stormy night", with which he began his novel *Paul Clifford*. I hope you are finding all this interesting, Manon, but once "a Latin student", always "a Latin student"! So then, the opening words in a story are called an *incipit*, meaning "it begins", and refer to just a few words at the beginning of a text. The end of a text is called the *explicit*, from the Latin verb *explicare*, meaning "to unravel", therefore "to reveal the ending"! If you are wondering, the word "explicit", meaning "clear, specific", comes from the same Latin verb, which also means "to explain". Such extravagant and ornate words to lend a melodramatic touch to literary texts are known as purple prose, based probably on the words of Horace in his *Ars Poetica – Inceptis gravibus plerumque et magna professis purpureus, late qui splendeat, unus et alter adsuitur pannus*. Don't worry, Manon – I'll translate for you! "With heavy beginnings and utterances proclaimed for the most part in grand fashion, and one or the other purple rags, which shine afar, sewn on". Words can be "purple", I guess, but then "violets are blue" as Bobby Vinton sang in "Roses are Red (My Love)". Actually, I'm feeling "blue", since I'm not with you! In fact, the "dark and stormy night" beginning goes back to *A History of New York,* written by the American, Washington Irving, to whom we owe such classics as *Rip Van Winkle* and *The Legend of Sleepy Hollow.* I realize now that in my high school literature classes I didn't appreciate enough great writers such as Nathanael Hawthorne, Henry David Thoreau, Herman Melville, who wrote *Moby Dick*, Henry Wadsworth Longfellow, whose *Evangeline* became a Canadian icon!, and Edgar Allan Poe, the "Baltimore Bard" – my expression, Manon! You know the poem "The Raven"- it sort of fits "the dark and stormy night" image. But I think "Ravens" would make a great name some day for a Baltimore sports team! I'm wondering though, if any one would read a story that starts with "it was a bright and sunny day"! Funny, that's what the weather is like here today! I'll write to you from Germany! Denys

Chapter 97

-       I must say, *Herr* Hainsworth, that you have impressed all of us with your mastery of German. And I will be sure to inform my friend and research colleague, Professor Walter, how well you translated the passages in Quintilian that were assigned to you. Young Hainsworth, you should know, gentlemen, is a veritable polyglot, since he is fluent as well in English, French, Greek, Spanish and Italian, as well as in Latin and Ancient Greek. He tells me that this is the first class he has been in since high school that was composed uniquely of males. I assured him that this was an exceptional year, and that at Tübingen, we classicists are not misogynists! In any event, *Herr* Hainsworth, after you complete your courses here, and I know you are also taking Professor Schmidt's seminar on Oscan, Umbrian, and Etruscan, you will spend a week visiting some other German universities. If I'm not mistaken they are Berlin, Munich, Heidelberg and Freibourg. You are sure to encounter many a pretty *Fraulein* in your travels! I think we can bring closure to our discussion of Quintilian and his *Institutio Oratoria*, his rather thorough study of rhetoric in twelve volumes. *Herr* Hainsworth, as our guest, will you give us some final commentary on Quintilian before you read our first passage in Sallust.

-       Certainly, Professor Jürgens. As we've seen, Quintilian valued education – one based on the fine art of oratory, or as it can be called, public speaking. Sadly, in Montreal and Quebec, where I am pursuing my studies, the "art of oratory" for many citizens means the decorations in St. Joseph's ORATORY! Very few schools privilege the art of public speaking and debate. I once asked a fellow university student if he valued the importance of debate, and he said that it was indeed necessary – in order to catch "de fish"! Quintilian believed that good men were good speakers, and had the duty to embrace public life and public service.

In this regard, he thought very highly of Cicero. Quintilian probably admired Seneca for his skill in oratory and for his pertinent remarks on education, but considered him more of a philosopher, and not active enough in public life. But then, Seneca did spend some years in exile. It pains me to say that Quintilian would have found Seneca a little superficial. We Americans admire great leaders who were all great speakers – I suppose in the "Quintilian mode"- Abraham Lincoln, John F. Kennedy, Martin Luther King, Billy Graham. By the same token, Richard Nixon was not a particularly good speaker! Hitler was an exception to the adage of a "good speaker, hence a good man". The world should have listened more to "what" he was saying than "how" he was saying it. I shall now read the Latin text of our passage from Sallust's book on Catiline and his conspiracy. I am beginning at chapter 5. As you requested, Professor, I will then proceed with my translation.

374

L.Catilina, nobili genere natus, fuit magna vi et animi et corporis, sed ingenio malo pravoque. huic ab adulescentia bella intestina, caedes, rapinae, grata fuere, discordia, civilis ibique iuventutem suam exercuit. corpus patiens inediae, algorism, vigiliae supra quam cuiquam credibile est. animus audax subdolud varius, cuius rei lubet simulator ac dissimulator, alieni adpetens, sui profusus, ardens in cupiditatibus: satis eloquentiae, sapientiae parum. vastus animus immoderate, incredibilia, nimis alta semper cupiebat. hunc post dominationem L. Sullae lubido maxuma invaserat rei publicae capiundae, neque id quibus modis adsequeretur, dum sibi regnum pararet, quicquam pensi habebat. agitabatur magis magisque in dies animus ferox inopia rei familiaris et conscientia scelerum, quae utraque eis artibus auxerat, quas supra memoravi. incitabant praeterea conrupti civitatis mores, quos pessuma ac divorsa inter se mala, luxuria et avaritia, vexabant. res ipsa hortari videtur, quoniam de moribus civitatis tempus admonuit, supra repetere ac paucis instituta mairorum domi militiaeque, quo modo rem publicam habuerint quantamque reliquerint, ut paulatim immutata ex pulcherrima atque optuma pessuma ac flagitiosissuma facta sit, disserere.

Urbem Romam, sicuti ego accepi, condidere atque habuere initio Troiani, qui Aenea duce profugi sedibus incertis vagabantur, cumque eis Aborigines, genus hominum agreste, sine legibus, sine imperio, liberum atque solutum. hi postquam in una moenia convenere, dispari genere dissimili lingua, alii alio more viventes, incredibile memoratu est quam facile coaluerint : ita brevi multitudo dispersa atque vaga concordia civitas facta erat. sed postquam res eorum civibus moribus agris aucta satis prospera satisque pollens videbatur, sicuti pleraque mortalium habentur, invidia ex opulentia orta est. igitur reges populique finitumi bello temptare, pauci ex amicis auxilio esse : nam ceteri metu perculsi a periculis aberant. at Romani domi militiaeque intenti festinare, parare, alius alium hortari, hostibus obviam ire, libertatem patriam parentisque armis tegere. post ubi pericula virtute propulerant, sociis atque amicis auxilia portabant, magisque dandis quam accipiundis beneficiis amicitias parabant. Imperium legitumum, nomen imperi regium habebant. delecti, quibus corpus annis infirmum, ingenium sapientia validum erat, rei publicae consultabant: ei vel aetate vel curae similitudine patres appellabantur. post ubi regium imperium, quod initio conservandae libertatis atque augendae rei publicae fuerat, in superbiam dominationemque se convortit, inmutato more annua imperia binosque imperatores sibi facere : eo modo minume posse putabant per licentiam insolescere animum humanum.

Sed ea tempestate coepere sequisque magis extollere magisque ingenium in promptu habere. nam regibus boni quam mali suspectiores sunt semperque eis aliena virtus formidulosa est. sed civitas incredibile memoratu est adepta libertate quantum brevi creuerit : tanto cupido gloriae incesserat. iam primum iuventus, simula ac belli patiens erat, in castris per laborem usum militiae discebat magisque in decoris armis et militaribus equis quam in scortis atque conviviis lubidinem habebant. igitur talibus viris non labor insoliyus, non locus ullus asper aut arduus erat, non armatus hostis formidulosus : virtus omnia domuerat. sed gloriae maxumum certamen inter ipsos erat : se quisque hostem ferire, murum ascendere, conspici dum tale facinus faceret, properabat; eas divitias, eam bonam famam magnamque nobilitatem putabant. laudis avidi, pecuniae liberales erant; gloriam ingentem, divitias honestas volebant. memorare possem quibus in locis maxumas hostium copias populus Romanus parva manu fuderit, quas urbis natura munitas pugnando ceperit, ni ea res longius nos ab incepto traheret.

Here is my translation of chapters 5, 6 and 7 : "Lucius Catiline, born of a noble family, was endowed with great force in mind and body, but with an evil and depraved character. From his youth civil wars, slaughter, pillage and civil discord were pleasing to him, and in those circumstances he spent his youth. His body endured hunger, cold and lack of sleep, beyond what anyone could believe. His mind was daring, devious, fickle, pretending or hiding whatever he pleased, seeking the possessions of others, immoderate with his own possessions, passionate in his desires: he had a certain degree of eloquence, but too little wisdom. His desolate mind always sought after the exaggerated, the unbelievable, that which was beyond limits. After the domination of Lucius Sulla, a very great desire for taking control of the republic came over him, taking little thought for the means by which he would achieve this, as long as he took power for himself. His wild spirit was agitated more and more each day by the poverty of his own possessions and by his consciousness of his crimes, both of which he had increased by the methods I mentioned above. Moreover, the corrupt morals of the state stirred him on, a behaviour which evils, very bad and different from one another, luxury and avarice, had rendered worse. Since the situation itself seems to urge me on, inasmuch as the present occasion reminds us of the morals of the state, to go back and discuss the institutions of our ancestors in peace and at war, in what way they governed the republic, and such as they left it, and how gradually it was changed from the most beautiful and the best to the worst and most shameful." This is the German way, is it not, Professor Jürgens, to go back to the beginning when describing the present, even to Adam and Eve, if necessary, or in the case of the Romans, to Aeneas?

"In the beginning, as I have accepted, the city of Rome was founded and inhabited by the Trojans, who were wandering about as fugitives, with no fixed home, under the leadership of Aeneas, and with them the Aborigines, a wild race of men, without laws, without government, free and unrestrained. After they assembled within the same walls, a different race with a different language, each living with customs different from each other, it is unbelievably well-known how easily they merged: in a short time the wandering and scattered multitude became a state thanks to harmony. When their state having increased in citizens, customs and land, seemed prosperous and strong enough, as so often happens among mortals, envy arose on account of their prosperity. Therefore, neighbouring kings and neighbours attacked them in war, few friends came to their aid, for the others, driven by fear, stayed away. But the Romans, attentive to their homes and to their military forces, made haste, prepared, encouraged one another, went out to meet the enemy, and protected their freedom, fatherland and parents with arms. When afterwards they had repelled the danger through their valour, they gave help to allies and friends, and secured friendships by giving rather than receiving favours. They had a legitimate government, and as a name for this government, a monarchy. Chosen men, weak in body on account of their years, but whose minds were strenghthened through wisdom, took counsel on behalf of the state, and they were called Fathers, either because of their age or on account of the similarity of their duties. Later, when the monarchy, which in the beginning had been a source of preserving freedom and advancing the state, changed into a rule of haughtiness and domination, after changing their custom, they created annual commands and two rulers: they thought that in this way it would be least possible for the human mind to become insolent through absence of restraint. But at that time each person began to rise above others and to have his ability at the ready.

For to kings the good are more suspect than the bad, and for them the valour of another is always something dreadful. But the incredible fact is well-known, how great the state grew when liberty had been acquired: such a great desire for glory had arisen. At first, when the young were capable of enduring war they learned the exercise of military life through hard work in the camp, and they had a desire more for beautiful weapons and war horses than for prostitutes and parties. Consequently, to such men, no labour was unfamiliar, no place too rough or difficult, no armed enemy too frightening: valour had conquered everything. But the greatest struggle for glory was among themselves: for each one was in a hurry to strike an enemy, to ascend a wall, to be seen while he did such a deed; they considered as riches this great fame and outstanding nobility. They were avid of praise, generous with money; they wanted great glory, but well-earned riches. I would be able to mention in what locations the Roman people routed very large forces of the enemy with a small band, which cities, fortified by nature, they captured, if this account did not carry us too far from the narrative we began."

Fortunately, other historians have described these battles for us, but I appreciate the description of character that Sallust gives us.

-       Excellent work, *Herr* Hainsworth! Your translation was clear and to the point, almost as if you were speaking in the manner of Seneca. Consequently, we have a few minutes before class ends. Would you care to share some thoughts on the ancient Italic tongues you are studying?

-       Yes, Professor. I am fortunate to have studied epigraphy with Professor Walter, as most of the evidence for these languages comes from inscriptions. Oscan and Umbrian are indeed Indo-European, directly linked to the Italic branch of languages. Oscan was effectively the language of the Samnites, that is, of southern Italy, which was eventually colonized by the Greeks, who transformed the area into a greater Greece, almost the way we speak of "Greater New York"! Of course we wouldn't call *Magna Graecia* the "Big Apple"! Maybe the "Big Olive"! Or maybe the "Big Grape". A very witty professor who once taught me Greek history told me that Alexander of Macedon became so fond of wine that his detractors referred to him as "Alexander the Grape"! Oscan was a conservative language, retaining many old archaic forms, which disappeared in Latin. An example would be the final '-d', which was dropped in Latin phonology. The Umbrians had received their alphabet from the Etruscans, who had received it from the Greeks. It is actually closer to Oscan than to Latin. For example, Oscan and Umbrian use 'p' and 'b', where Latin uses 'qu' – understandable since 'p' and 'b' as well as 'ph' are in the same group of Greek letters, just like 't', 'd' and 'th', and 'g', 'k' and 'ch' - and the '-re' of the Latin present active infinitive is '-om' in the other two dialects. Our knowledge of Umbrian comes mostly from the Iguvine Tables found in ancient Iguvium, which is the modern town of Gubbio. What may interest everybody here is that in the novel *Der Steppenwolf,* written by Herman Hesse, the protagonist, who considers himself part wolf, is overlooking a hill in Gubbio!

This "wolf-man" reminds me of the werewolf in Petronius' *Satyricon*. The "*steppe*" are grassy fields that are home to the prairie grey wolf. I don't know too much about the word since it is of Russian origin, but I know that if you encounter this wolf, you better "watch your step"! Be prepared to go "Step by Step", as in the song by The Crests. I know American music is very popular here in Germany – I think since Elvis Presley was here! Well the steppewolf is actually the *canis lupus campestris*. I picked up the habit of ascertaining the Latin names for animals during the time I spent visiting the Redpath Museum on the McGill University campus. This Museum has many animal figures, but also an Egyptian mummy, about which I gave a talk there.

In fact, while I was doing my Master's, I participated in some readings of ancient authors at the Redpath which were offered to the general public. Although I did read some Latin and Greek, most of the text was read in English. I recall reading passages from Homer's *Odyssey,* Lucian's *A True Story*, Plato's *Apology,* Plutarch's *Parallel Lives*, Seneca's *Moral Epistles*, and Ovid's *Metamorphoses*. What interests me about *Steppenwolf* is that it is the name of a rock band, whose lead singer, John Kay, could pass for a "wolfman" with his long hair. Their songs include "Magic Carpet Ride" and "Born to be Wild", the song that became associated with so-called "heavy metal" music, but the metal was the motorcycles in the movie *Easy Rider*, about two wild and free motorcyclists, not your Blue Knights type, but not the Hell's Angels either. The song became an anthem for motorcycle lovers! The most interesting – and most powerful – people in Italy before the rise of the Romans were the Etruscans. They originally settled in southern Italy, and so came into contact with the Greeks. They also had close ties with the Phoenicians, as is evidenced from a gold tablet containing Etruscan and Punic texts.

Unfortunately, a twenty-volume history of the Etruscans written by the Emperor Claudius has not survived. I assume he was the first "Etruscologist"! Eventually, the religious influence on the Romans outlived the linguistic connection. Right now, efforts to restore knowledge and understanding of Etruscan would have to be considered "a work in progress"! We have not had the "break-through" decipherment that occurred with Michael Ventris and Greek Linear B or Champollion and hieroglyphics. The Etruscan alphabet is clearly adapted from the Greek alphabet, and Etruscan, like Latin, was an inflected language. There are many inscriptions and even Etruscan words that appear as glosses - explanatory words - in ancient authors. But I cannot gloss over the fact that Etruscan is not an Indo-European language!

-       Since you are fond of music and word play, *Herr* Hainsworth, we will see you Bach here tomorrow!

-       You know, Professor, you can shorten the formal "*Herr* Hainsworth", and call me "H.H." – as did one of my McGill professors!

-       *Sehr gut*! Very well, then! After your splendid translation of the "historian" Sallust and your "histrionics" on the subject of Alexander the Great, you shall receive the "honorary" title of "Historian Hainsworth"! Perhaps after your "heroics" with that "hysteric hostage-taker" we should call you "Heroic Hainsworth" or even "Historic Holden". No silent "H" in German "humour"!

-       Professor, the double "H" will forever remain for me "harrowing and haunting"! I am truly "humbled" – and "halted" by silence!

-       "Hallelujah"!

Chapter 98

-       I'm glad you are ready to undertake your third year with us, Denys, and if the timeline we originally established remains in effect, this will be your penultimate year. I must tell you – and all your Professors have attested to this fact – you always display a delightful combination of serious *gravitas* and down to earth interactions with everyone who is fortunate enough to cross your path! If truth be told, your magnanimous spirit has made you the heart and soul of our graduate programme. Your "*magna anima*" is indeed the image that our Department wishes to portray! For that, I am truly grateful! Your fellow students – especially Martin – never cease to remark how kind you are. Moreover, Professor Saucier says you are one of a kind! Ah, Denys where else will you find humour of this "kind"?

-       I appreciate your "kind" words, Professor Marcoux! But being a good person depends on wanting to be just such a person. As the Latin expression *bene volens* suggests, being benevolent means doing good because you want to! I don't believe there are "mean" words, but rather people acting "mean" give words an evil "meaning". We are in fact "creatures of our own creation". By that I mean – ah, that ever present word – there must really be a "golden MEAN"! - we decide to be good or bad, just as we decide to follow or not the path where life leads us. Pygmalion formed his maiden statue with grace and beauty, but Galatea "came to life" because she wanted to! Any success in my studies which I have enjoyed are the result of my wanting to succeed, blessed as I have been to have certain abilities and opportunities. I guess it comes down to "free will". As they say, where there's a will, there is a way!

-       It seems, Denys, that our "Latin student" is also a "philosophy pupil"! I know that you are maintaining a torrential schedule – did you ever read the short story "Le Torrent" by Anne Hébert – you probably discussed her novel *Kamouraska,* and maybe saw the movie in your courses on Quebec literature and film at McGill. I mention "Le Torrent" also to congratulate you on your watery heroics last week. I just got back from vacation, but Martin showed me the news clipping from *Le Soleil.* A small boat had capsized, and a young man was drowning. You happened to be picnicking along the banks of the river near the Aquarium with Manon – I know the spot. What I didn't know was that a person could battle the current – even the excellent swimmer that you obviously are! You risked your life by diving into the St. Lawrence at a spot where there have been drownings of thrill-seeking swimmers and divers, and swam to shore with the young man. Such bravery! Such physical strength and such force of character! Apparently you were cheered on by numerous onlookers who had gathered by *Le Pont du Québec,* and who witnessed bravado worthy of the Roman Horatius at the bridge! Far from seeking publicity and attention, once it was ascertained that the young man was okay, your immediate actions were to comfort Manon, who needless to say, was in a state of shock.

Depite your customary modesty, Denys, please know that the Classics Department, and indeed, Laval University, are truly proud of you, and will accordingly acknowledge this display of heroism with an appropriate ceremony. You are continuing your instruction at the Seminary as well as the Latin and Greek courses to the public. I hear you have found a way to introduce a second Greek course by alternating introductory and advanced Greek each week with an extra hour per week for each course. You are indeed "*débrouillard*", Denys. I would suggest that you will soon need an eight-day week for all your projects, but then you will mention the song of that name by the Beatles. I know about the Beatles, Denys - Professor Watson's wife was always talking about them whenever I was a dinner-guest at their home during my year at McGill! I noted that your course in the public lecture series this year is Greek and Roman Religion, which is convenient, since the overview will be helpful in developing your dissertation.

I know you will be meeting regularly with Professor Marois, and you continue to meet weekly with Professor Watson. From what Professor Jones at Concordia tells me, the afternoon meetings at McGill are the excuse you often need to end the regular line-ups of young ladies at your office door. It's good to see such a passionate revival of interest in Classical Studies! I hope you don't mind me teasing you, but the high female registration in your courses should balance your all-male experience in Germany! Oh, Professor Jürgens spoke to Professor Walter about your contributions to the courses in Germany in highly laudatory terms! You will be teaching a course on Seneca's essays, I believe. You must be "over the moon"! How often did you hear Mrs. Watson use that expression? Also a course on the Roman Empire, right? Heaven forbid they ask you to teach a course at Concordia on the role of women in the ancient world! Actually, Professor Giguère has proposed just such a course here at Laval, and had asked me if there was a possibility you could be her T.A. for the course. I suppose the Department poster of the two of you could be a drawing card, but I suspect even you could not find time for yet another commitment. In any event, by the time the Faculty Committee on New Courses approves the course – if they approve it – you will have finished your programme here! And speaking of commitment, I am glad you have accepted the demanding role of Oedipus in this year's Greek production of *Oedipus the King*. Professor Roumelis will be co-directing, and Professor Giguère has offered to help with costume and make-up. I've been able to finalize your actual course-load. You will be taking one Latin course with Professor Saucier on the historians Cornelius Nepos, Suetonius, and Ammianus Marcellinus. This course should prove useful for your Roman history course at Concordia. Professor

Giguère had wondered if you would be in her course on Cicero's letters, but taking her course would be superfluous since you taught that course yourself last year at Concordia. Now that I mention her name out loud, it strikes me as coming up often in connection with your projects. Is her offer of service to the play a question of make-up, or make out ? I jest, of course! But you will have two Greek courses – Pausanias and Plutarch with Professor Roumelis, and my course on Aesop, Hippocrates and Marcus Aurelius.

You will be the only student – unless Professor Giguère requests to audit – relax, Denys, I am joking once more! You will have figured out no doubt that my course is designed to help you complete your reading list of compulsory authors. You will be reading authors during your summer programme at the Sorbonne. The courses on the menu - I am referring to a "five-course meal"- include *The Library of Apollodorus* – light reading for you! There will be a course on Diogenes Laertius, a must read since you will be taking the prestigious Seminar on Greek and Roman Philosophy with Professor Raynault. You will also have Latin courses on the poets Statius and Claudian. I think I have whetted your appetite with that witty word wisecrack about five courses!! The alliteration is dessert! I am very happy that Manon has made arrangements to accompany you. I understand she was able to enrol in the summer Contemporary French Cinema course. Perhaps we won't mention your summer plans to Professor Giguère until after Christmas. She is eligible this year to apply for a summer grant! We wouldn't want her to pull an *Io Saturnalia* trick on you on December 17 - you know, the Roman "April Fool's Day", when masters served their slaves, giving them "nonsense gifts"! If they had been Christians, I guess these would have been considered "Christmas gifts"! I suppose you will want to avoid banks in Paris! What is this story I heard echoes of – a Latin Liberation?

-       If I gave you all the details, Professor Marcoux, you would again start talking about a ceremony! I certainly don't want the Professor "serving" the student, even though I recall Catullus in his Poem 14 complaining of having received a certain book on the *Saturnalia*, "the best of days" – *Saturnalibus optimo dierum*! But if this Latin student can avoid the clutches of "Pliny's Prostitute", he will be happily and truly "liberated", and you, Professor, our "Supreme Department Judge", will not be obliged to "throw the book at her"! I guess the CAH - the *Cambridge Ancient History* collection - would really hurt!

Chapter 99

- Oh, Professor Hainsworth, I don't have an appointment, but since no one is around, could you see me now?

- Ah, Miss Williams, sure I have fifteen minutes before my next appointment. What can I do for you?

- It's more about what I can do for you, Holden – I love that name! Fifteen minutes! That's what Bernadette Peters says to Burt Reynolds in the film *The Longest Yard*! It's playing downtown, and it's about football. Professor Jones told me you used to play football. I wouldn't mind going to see the movie again with you! Please call me Candy!

- Well, I suppose Candy is short for Candace. But the Department has a strict policy of not exchanging with students on a first-name basis. So, Miss Williams, I'm Professor Hainsworth. Since I'm only in Montreal once a week for a day – a very busy one! – I only catch the odd movie in Quebec. Did you have some questions about Seneca?

- Actually, boys call me Candy because I'm so sweet! I'd like to show you how sweet I can be – even if it's only for fifteen minutes – unless you tell the Secretary to cancel your next appointment! I could go to Quebec as well one weekend!

- I'm afraid you've let your predilection for passion get the better of you, Miss Williams. Seneca would not approve! Reason must triumph over the limitations of our physical nature.

- You are a perfect Seneca ! You have his mind in the body of a young athlete. Golden Holden! I picture you taking your shower after a football game, sweat and soap pouring down over your muscular physique. During one of your lectures in the Roman Empire course, I closed my eyes and imagined you were Caligula taking advantage of me! In class you used the expression *carpe diem*. Shouldn't we seize the moment?

- My dear Miss Williams, I think we should take advantage of the moment to avoid a regrettable situation. The fifteen minutes are up. Re-read some of the passages where Seneca gives sound advice on moral rectitude. I hope these fifteen minutes will eventually prove to have been useful to you. Don't feel embarrassed at our next class. As your Professor, I consider that this short meeting has been a teachable moment. Have a nice day!

***

- Hello, Professor. I'm Dido Salinger, and I have an appointment with you. I saw Candace Williams leaving your office. She usually doesn't take the time to see her professors outside of class. I hope you didn't pay any attention to what she was wearing. I know it's not very Christian-like to speak badly of anyone – and I am a practicing Catholic - but Candace Williams, whom I've known since high school, is one of those women that Augustus would have banished from the streets of Rome!

- Well, well, fortunately for Miss Williams, Augustus is no longer with us! I am also a practicing Catholic, and maybe that's why I didn't pay particular attention to her accoutrement. I must say, you have an intriguing name – I'm referring to both your *praenomen* and your *cognomen*.

- Well, Professor Hainsworth, my father is a distant cousin of J.D. Salinger, but he's never met him. He's a fan of Vergil, and so I was baptized Dido. So you won't be surprised to hear that I'm majoring in Classics with a minor in English Literature.

- Very few people have met the recluse author of *Catcher in the Rye*. Don't worry – there was no danger of Miss Williams becoming my "catcher in the raw"! Did you have questions about the essays of Seneca we are reading, or about the Roman history course?

- Professor, I just wanted to compliment you on how meaningful you have made the Latin reading of Seneca! When he says in *De Otio* that our leisure time can be truly devoted to the cause of humanity, I feel a burst of enthusiasm for Classical Studies! You are so young, Professor, yet you project an aura of wisdom. Please don't pass me off as another Candy Williams – but I am genuinely infatuated with you! You are the Aeneas to my Dido! But I have taken to heart the lessons Seneca has given us, and which you so brilliantly pass on. Yes, I accept that living according to nature is living according to reason. But I also believe that reason responds to the sentiments of the heart. What I am trying to say, Professor, is that beyond a physical bond which I believe is our destiny, there is fated for us a true union of our souls – two Catholic souls, so it seems! I think that the fact that I am your student is merely a circumstance. The classroom is our "fateful cave" that Dido and Aeneas shared in the *Aeneid*.

- Well now, Miss Salinger. If this weren't the actual delicate situation that it is, it could be the plea of a fair maiden in some lost Latin love elegy. Fortunately, you have invoked Seneca, and we can appeal to his invitation to practice moderation. Your "philosophical fantasy" is flattering. In the future, I hope you will recall my alliterative response to this unburdening of your soul. I am wondering, too, if you are the mystery person who removed the Laval

University poster from the Classics Bulletin Board – the one that featured my picture alongside one of the professors.

-       Yes, Professor, I have the poster in my room – that is, half of it. Even now, I find your kindness and wisdom very comforting. I see you now as a true *pius Aeneas*, whose duty as a "true Latin student" calls you to a different destiny – a PhD on another shore! You are even in our modern context a "pious professor". But you have been so understanding that I will not go the way of Dido. How long I will harbor these feelings for you, I don't know. But with your periodic reminders, Professor Hainsworth, I shall endeavor to strive for the virtues espoused by Seneca in his essay *De Constantia Sapientis*.

-       Continue to enjoy Latin and Classical Studies, Miss Salinger. Your heart is now in a good place, and I believe you will someday find your destined "soul-mate"!

Chapter 100

\-   Hello, Jeremy, my old friend – are you thinking of a Simon and Garfunkel song? Fortunately, the only "darkness" in my life at the moment is my spiritual reading of *Dark Night of the Soul* by St. John of the Cross – I'm actually reading it in the original Spanish - *La noche oscura del alma*. My "spiritual catharsis" continues with these religious readings – "sacred selections" as you once called them! Nonetheless, I do have "little crosses" to bear, about which I can't remain "silent"! Thank God I've got you to unload on! Otherwise I'd have to dig a hole in the ground like King Midas and tell all my secrets. But I don't want to wear a funny hat, so here goes. As usual, you ended your last letter with "what's new?" I wish I could say "same old, same old". You know how conservative and traditional I am! And you can't get more "same and old" than Latin! As I tell my students, one of the beautiful things about Latin is that it will never change! I mean, people talk and write English and French a little different than before. Those languages are still changing in syntax and vocabulary. Even word meanings change. A homosexual smoking a cigarette, for example – now we use the same word for both elements in that phrase! But I don't smoke, and I'm not a f.. – well you get the picture! Same goes for Greek and Italian and even German. The vulgar language and the slang in Latin – I prefer to call it idiomatic! – also won't change. I told you about the "incident" at the bank in Rome – Manon still gets mad when I refer to it as just an "incident"! But that seems like a walk in the park compared to some situations that I've had to face in the last little while! Here are some clues to my first uncomfortable moments: "Big Girls Don't Cry" by the Four Seasons – well some do, so it seems! "California Girls" by the Beach Boys – I really wish they all could be there, but a couple are a lot closer! "My Girl" by The Temptations – it's hard to convince some of them that it's not going to happen! "Brown-eyed Girl" by Van Morrison – I discovered that she can be dangerous! "Hey Little Girl" by The Syndicate of Sound – how do you convince her to back off? "You're Going To Lose That Girl" by the Beatles – I wish I could! I suppose you've guessed that I'm talking about girl troubles. Specifically, Jeremy, about a couple of my students! One girl offered herself up on a plate – she could have been a brown-eyed Rita Hayworth in the film *Salome*! She was a younger version of Professor Giguère! – who by the way is still on my tail – er, trail! This young thing - only five years younger than I am - but still! – wanted me to call her Candy. But I wouldn't even BUY her candy! The other girl was a little more problematic – could be in her genes, because she is a distant relative of J.D. Salinger – I guess with that hermit I should say "very distant". She was more sensible than "Miss Bonbon", but a lot more sensitive. Ironic, isn't it, that the French word *sensible* means "sensitive"! I talked to her as if I were Seneca, but really felt like I was giving her advice like a big brother. I'm sure glad, though, that I didn't tell her I was named for a Salinger character! Like Vergil's "Dido"- that was her name! – she would have considered that we were somehow husband and wife! I hope my "Salinger year", that is, my year with Miss Salinger, doesn't get any more complicated! This next installment of "the tumultuous life of Holden Hainsworth" is genuinely frightening, and could have turned out very badly. How badly? Well let's just say, worst-case scenario, you wouldn't have received this letter from me – nor would you be receiving any letters in the future! I saw a film in my Quebec film course at McGill called *Le Viol d'une jeune fille douce*, about two brothers who rape a young girl. A few weeks ago, I was walking home from the PEPS, the sports center at Laval University. That's where I work out. I hope I didn't lose you at the word "work", or completely turn you off with "work out"! And before you start imagining that francophones are called "pepsis" because of this building, let me set you straight. The working-class French population, and it seems that it's the large majority of the Québécois, often have a bottle of good old American coke with their lunch. But when Pepsi Cola came out with a similar drink in a bigger bottle at the same price, well, figure it out! So the Coke-drinking "bourgeois" started referring to them as "pepsis"!

But it seems to me we might have talked about that once before. So back to "Alfred Hitchcock Presents"! It was rather late, almost ten o'clock. As I passed this park area, I heard a scream from behind the high shrubs. When I ran to the area I saw two guys holding down a girl. I remember that she was wearing a silver-colored jogging suit – or rather, had been wearing one! Her bra had been ripped off, and one of the bastards was tugging at her underwear. I immediately ran and pulled him off. At this point, bastard number two pulled out a knife and lunged at me. I grabbed his arm just in time, and was able to wrestle the knife away. Bastard number one had gotten up and gave me an awful kick in the guts. They were obviously tougher when dealing with a poor helpless girl, because, with a few quick punches to the head, I had him lying semi-conscious on the ground. There was obviously no bond of loyalty between them, as the other low-life took off. At this point, a few students - on their way home from the library, I guess - heard all the ruckus and came running behind the shrubs. The would-be rapist, abandoned by his accomplice, lay on the ground as a few of these muscular students hovered around him. There were a couple of girls with them, and they started looking after the assault victim, who was still very much in shock. One student had run off to get Campus Security. It was quite late, when the police had taken the rapist away, and had questioned both me and the victim. The police had made a phone call and the jogger's husband arrived. He had been worried when she hadn't arrived home, and thanked me profusely for what he called my "heroic action".

I've been called a hero three times now in the past year, but after reading about Heracles and Theseus and Jason and Ulysses – you know – the Roman name for Odysseus - well in spite of how exciting their adventures seem, I haven't been left with a particularly good feeling after my exploits. I actually felt kind of sick. I think I would have preferred taking on the Minotaur or the Nemean Lion! The girl was still in too much shock to talk to me, but her husband was going to take her to the hospital - the CHUL is very close to the Campus. I made her husband promise to never let her jog at night again. I imagine, though, that she will make it easy for him to keep his promise! I'll have to testify eventually. Oh, and the police recovered the knife! But, Jeremy, I found some relief from the stress caused by this affair by recalling to mind that night in Montreal when, being three sheets to the wind, you boasted of saving a girl from being attacked…by controlling yourself! I also delved into my "world of Ancient Rome" and remembered that the "rape of Lucretia" was a catalyst for a new era of Roman government that proved – at least initially – more enlightened. The liberators of Rome were good "chess players", as they got rid of the king! You recall, though, don't you, that my best moves were not on the chessboard, but rather on the football field? You weren't only my mate – you were always my "checkmate"! But I can't complain that this is an *annus horribilis* for me. I have Manon to remind me that life can still be pleasant. In fact, I have to admit that these university years have pretty well been *anni mirabiles* – "wonderful years", thanks to Latin and Manon! Of course, the recollection of the "Montreal daze" we were sometimes in when we hung out together is comic relief for any trying moments I might face. As I always said, whenever you got "maudlin", it was time for me to get "meddlin" – to keep you out of "hot water"! Even at a distance you make me laugh. Like in a previous letter when you talked about having your own *"anus" horribilis*, I thought you had misspelled *annus,* but you said you were telling me you were having a "bad-ass" year! I did need Manon's soothing company after this next incident that I'm about to describe for you. You remember my good friend Martin? Yes, the ex-seminarian who rekindled his love affair with the girl who works with Manon. Well, as it turns out, he isn't as resilient as you are when it comes to life's bitter disappointments. We were at a small café in Old Quebec, which he apparently knew quite well. I was desperately trying to cheer him up, after he had had his Master's thesis rejected. When I was returning to our table from the washroom, I caught a glimpse of Martin swallowing a white substance. How do you handle a friend whom you have just discovered has been taking drugs? The words of Seneca weren't working this time. I mentioned all the good things in his life, but he had become addicted, and couldn't focus on "real life". I left him that night with his promise that he would get professional help. Two nights later I got a call from his girlfriend, Lucie. Somehow, he had kept her from finding out about his dependence. In fact, he had hidden it from all of us. He had been rushed to the hospital with a probable overdose. Fortunately – maybe even miraculously – he recovered.

He is being treated in a rehab center, and the staff there told me his prospects look good. To her credit, Lucie has stood by him. I talked to Professor Marcoux about him, or rather on behalf of him, and it was agreed that he would be on a temporary withdrawal from the master's programme for medical reasons. "Withdrawal" somehow sounds too apropos! Do you remember that one night after the hockey game we went to at the Forum, and a sleazy character offered to sell us "some stuff" near the Atwater metro? You asked "how much", and I asked "how about getting lost"! He was upset, but you laughed, and we left. I had thought about saying "you can stuff your stuff", but some of those guys can be nasty! Don't do drugs, Jeremy!

Remember what happened to Odysseus' men in the land of the *Lotophagi*, you know, the land of the Lotus-Eaters. If the Sirens had been singing their songs there, that place would have been the original Woodstock! Not sure that this time you would have been able to come back to tell me about it, Jeremy! But I want to end this letter on a high note – gosh, no pun intended – I swear – and you know that I usually try to avoid swearing! I remember saying, when I was Hippolytus in the Euripides play of the same name, "My tongue swore, but not my mind". I had been tempted to cross my fingers behind my back! When I do swear, I don't use all those Church words like the sacraments and altar objects that all the French-speaking people seem to use in Montreal and here in Quebec. I'm a proud Catholic and I don't take the Lord's name in vain, nor any of the sacred vessels! But the Québécois are Catholics, too – just not so proud I guess! I learned in my courses at McGill that a reaction against the Catholic Church was part of the Quiet Revolution. Back home, most Catholics continue to practice the faith openly in fellowship and song. I guess anything that involves songs keeps me on board! But here, because of their heritage, they still use "Church language" to express strong emotion, but instead of joy and hope and charity, they use those words to express anger, frustration or just to give the impression they are brave enough to utter words of rebellion. The poor little kids I hear muttering those words don't know what they mean, but feel they gain a sense of empowerment by shouting them out. You know, Jeremy, saying "back home" is starting to sound strange since I've been in Quebec for the past nine years. I find myself referring to "the States", like everybody else here, rather than talking about "America". I almost feel like I'm Canadian. Well, actually, no – I get the impression that I'm a Québécois! Partly because I'm immersed in the French element of Quebec society – and very comfortable in it, I might add – but that's in large part due to Manon! Yet I can understand how the majority of people in this province don't feel connected to the larger country. In America –

I'm deliberately using the name! - Americans travel all over the country, especially at Thanksgiving, and often move to different states. Yet they don't feel estranged. The citizens of Quebec rarely travel across their own country! As a matter of fact, vacation for Quebecers means a trip to Old Orchard Beach or Lake George or Florida! Those who spend winters down there are called "Snowbirds"! And a lot of Québécois have cottages in Vermont! I sometimes get the impression that they feel more like Americans than Canadians. But I think they just want to have their own little America here in Quebec. In any event, I can feel the winds of change blowing – and they're blowing stronger! Probably all the way to Toronto! I just want to say a few words about my Greek courses this year. Speaking of travelling, Pausanias provides a more interesting travel guide to Greece than all those modern travel books! You would appreciate his book as well, since he speaks of all the Greek cults. The other author we are reading in this course is Plutarch. Naturally, we are reading the *Parallel Lives*, like the comparison Plutarch draws between Alexander the Great and Julius Caesar. But we have also read sections of his *Magna Moralia*, including his "Advice to Bride and Groom". Yes, Jeremy, I'm storing it for future reference!

In my other Greek course with Professor Marcoux – remember him? – I'm reading Aesop – wonderful stories!, Hippocrates – now HIS oath is something worth swearing! - and Marcus Aurelius - his *Meditations* are quite profound, but I like his philosophical reflection that says basically "Think happy thoughts!". When I say I'm reading, I mean I'm the only student in the course. I'm taking three courses this year and two next year. With the authors I'll be reading in Paris next summer I'll have completed my compulsory reading lists, so no comprehensive exams for me! In fact, other than my non- Classics courses at McGill, I haven't written exams since I graduated from high school! My major preoccupation in these last two years is, of course, my dissertation on Roman Religion. With your dissertation on Greek Religion we could be the "Holies"! Not to be confused with the "Hollies"! That's the group that Mrs. Watson was talking about on the plane ride to England – seems so long ago now! Anyhow, they were from Manchester, just outside of "Weatherfield", the fictional town in "Coronation Street"! They had so many hit songs – "The Air I Breathe", "Carrie-Anne" , "On A Carousel", "He Ain't Heavy, He's My Brother" – I love dancing that slow song with Manon! – and "Bus Stop", which runs through my head every Tuesday when I take the Voyageur bus to Montreal! Did you know that Graham Nash from that group is the "Nash" in Crosby, Stills, Nash and Young? You might have a vague recollection of having seen them at Woodstock. True, everything you saw at Woodstock was a "vague blur"! Take care, old man – you're older than I am! By the way, I started my course on Seneca with the song "Old Man" by Neil Young – the second "good thing" coming out of Toronto! As I explained to my students, the name Seneca means "old man"! Yours, "Hold On"! Remember that name when I show up with Manon at the CAC in May

– "Hold On, I'm Coming", the song by Sam and Dave! After all, you referenced the song "I'm A Man" by The Spencer Davis Group, when I told you you about Manon and me on Valentine's Day! But it didn't beat "This Magic Moment" by The Drifters – or by Jay and The Americans, if you prefer that version! Your Friend, Hold On (yeah, like I said, "I'm coming…")

Chapter 101

\-   I don't mind eating at Le Deauville, Manon, but you say that the special occasion this time is news that Bob and Maggie have for us. I guess we'll find out when they get here. You asked how my teaching was going. Well, the seminarians are a little more advanced now, so we are reading Biblical texts in Latin and Greek, as well as treatises by the Church Fathers who wrote in those two languages. The number of students taking Latin and Greek in those public courses at *Cégep* Ste-Foy keeps increasing, especially in Latin. The students love *Lingua Romanorum*, which is good news, since I'll be presenting that method at the Conferences in May and June. I appreciate the questions students ask in the Monday evening course on Greek and Roman Religion, since they contribute to my reflection on certain questions raised in my dissertation. My Seneca course at Concordia is very stimulating for me, and I hope for the students as well. Apart from the translation, we discuss Seneca's advice in terms of our contemporary world. In the Roman Empire course, which is part lecture, part seminar presentations by the students, we have already discussed some of the causes of the so-called "Fall" of the Roman Empire. They are all under the impression that the vast hordes of savage barbarians destroyed the Empire, almost overnight. I have to point out that the demise was a longer process and that the so-called "barbarians" were often as civilized as the Romans. Many of their leaders spoke Latin, and were trained in Roman customs and warfare. I believe sickness and lack of capacity to care for the sick contributed in large part to the eroding of the power structure in place. Even in our own day and age, sickness and lack of attention to care for the elderly and the vulnerable could lead to dire circumstances. Hopefully, I am not being a prophet of doom! Plagues on an Empire-wide scale – we would call them pandemics – had a strong destructive consequence on education and learning, the arts, scientific progress, trade and the economy. I am convinced that the Roman Empire as it existed then was too weak to recover, and was forced to yield to a new socio-political dynamic. During the Antonine plague of the second century and the Plague of Justinian in the sixth century, millions upon millions of inhabitants died. Ironically, the Roman territory was taken over by peoples who had initially infested the Roman world through contact with Roman soldiers and merchants! Maybe I should have reinforced this theory by playing that old Peggy Lee song, "Fever", or perhaps the Johnny Rivers song "Rockin' Pneumonia and the Boogie Woogie Flu"!

\-   Hi you guys! I guess we're just in time, Manon. The Menace here has probably been boring you with Latin quotes and stories about the Romans.

-        As a matter of fact, Bob, Denys was talking about the Romans, but I wouldn't say he was boring me! So Marguerite, what is the exciting news you two have for us?

-        Manon, we're moving to Montreal! Bob has a job with the biggest transportation company in Quebec! He will be working the cross-town deliveries, which means he will no longer work weekends, and will not be travelling across the country, except for the occasional trip to Quebec. The best part is that his salary will be slightly higher.

-        No, Maggie, the best part is that you have been hired to work in their accounting department. I had a chance to look for houses on my Montreal run, and we have found a nice little house on Montreal's South Shore. It's in that rather big city called Longueuil – you probably know it, Menace!

-        That's not all, Manon! You know how Papa and Mama were worried by the fact that Michel will be starting his Master's degree at UQAM next September, and would be in Montreal on his own. Well, he'll be able to stay with us – at least for the first year, until he gets his bearings.

-        That's great news! Although it means we won't get to see you that often, or go dancing together.

-        And you were coming along so well with my disco lessons, Bob! But I'm glad you two will have a more normal life.

-        So Mama and Papa don't know yet?

-        We'll be telling them at supper tomorrow night. You two will be there, won't you? Antoine is starting university next year, and he's been talking to Michel about going to UQAM as well. I think he doesn't want Denys "spying" on him at Laval! If both boys leave, Mama and Papa will have heart attacks – unless…

-        What Maggie is trying to say is the whole family could move! We actually found some nice little houses they might like in St. Lambert, which is right next to Longueuil. Not too many choices, though, because most of the homes there would be too expensive. It's not Sillery, but I think the good folks there like to pretend it is!

-        I know St. Lambert. My friend Jeremy used to play golf there. And there is a nice private high school for girls that would be ideal for Nicole. Isn't she starting high school next year? But what would you do, Manon?

-      Manny could get a transfer and work in Montreal. She would still be able to hang around with her mother! After all, Menace, next year is your last year at Laval, right, meaning your last year in Quebec City. I'm only a truck driver, but it seems to me that Latin students like you have a better chance of finding a "Latin job" in Montreal than in *La Vieille Capitale*! You and Manon could still see each other on weekends. Being apart for a while is not the end of the world – just look at Maggie and me! Besides, you two have survived those long summers apart, you being a Parker-paid pupil conquering Europe! Did you hear those "p's", Menace? And when you're in Montreal, shouldn't you and Manny be looking for a church?

-      This a lot to take in, isn't it, Manon? And so as not to confuse your father, you'd better make sure he knows you're all talking about St. Lambert near Montreal, and not St. Lambert-de-Lauzon, which is only a stone's throw from where you are already living! Although moving from the South Shore of Quebec to the South Shore of Montreal may not sound all that strange to him, and isn't your mother from Montreal? Well, in case you all still want to go dancing, I brought a play-list for Fantastic Frank. What do you think of these songs, Bob?

-      Let me see that list. "The Most Beautiful Girl" by Charlie Rich. "The Way We Were" by Barbara Streisand. "Best Thing That Ever Happened To Me" by Gladys Knight and the Pips. "Nothing from Nothing" by Billy Preston. "Then Came You" by Dionne Warwick and The Spinners. "Rikki Don't Lose That Number" by Steely Dan. And "Hang on in There Baby" by Johnny Bristol. These are great songs, Menace! Even if I don't dance, I'll enjoy listening to them.

Chapter 102

-     Hello everybody! Today's class takes a look at one of the personalities from the ancient world described by Cornelius Nepos, that first century B.C. historian and biographer, whose work *De Viris Illustribus* we are reading from. I chose the *Life of Hannibal* because I suspected you would like to compare his account with that of Livy's. Denys would you kindly read the text from chapter three and give us your translation. I know your tendency is to illustrate certain passages by way of popular song, but I think some students are already aware that in talking about the crossing of the Alps, you will make mention of the song "Ain't No Mountain High Enough" by Diana Ross. I hope we haven't stolen your thunder!

-     No, Professor Saucier, that would only happen if you mentioned the song "Lightning Strikes" by Lou Christie! But since this passage makes mention of Hannibal's father, uncle and brother, I feel obliged to reference the song "Family Affair" by Sly and the Family Stone. Here then is the Latin text:

Hac igitur aetate Hannibal cum patre in Hispaniam profectus est. Cuius post obitum, Hasdrubale imperatore suffecto, equitatui omni praefuit. Hoc quoque interfecto exercitus summam imperii ad eum detulit. Id, Carthaginem delatum, publice comprobatum est. Sic Hannibal, minor V et XX annis natus imperator factus, proximo triennio omnes gentes Hispaniae bello subegit; Saguntum, foederatam civitatem, vi expugnavit; tres exercitus maximos comparavit. Ex his unum in Africam misit, alterum cum fratre Hasdrubale in Hispania reliquit, tertium in Italiam secum duxit. Saltum Pyrenaeum transiit. Quacumque iter fecit, cum omnibus incolis conflixit: neminem nisi victum dimisit. Ad Alpes posteaquam venit, quae Italiam ab Gallia seiungunt, quas nemo umquam cum exercitu ante eum praeter Herculem Graium transierat, quo facto is hodie saltus Graius appellatur, Alpicos conantes prohibere transitu concidit, loca patefecit, itinera muniit, effecit, ut ea elephantus ornatus ire posset, qua antea unus homo inermis vix poterat repere. Hac copias traduxit in Italiamque pervenit.

"So at this age Hannibal set out to Spain with his father. After this one's death, when Hasdrubal had succeeded him as commander, he was placed in command of all the cavalry. When that one was also killed, the army handed over the supreme command to him. This, having been reported to Carthage, was publicly confirmed. So Hannibal, younger than twenty-five years old, was made commander, and in a period of about three years he subdued in war all the tribes of Spain; Saguntum, an allied state, he conquered by force; he assembled three very large armies.

Of these he sent one to Africa, the second he left with his brother Hasdrubal in Spain, and the third he brought with him into Italy. He crossed a Pyrenaean pass. Whatever route he took, he came into conflict with all the inhabitants. He sent no one away who was not conquered.

Afterwards he came to the Alps, which separate Italy from Gaul. And which no one had ever crossed with an army before him, except the Greek, Hercules, from which deed it is called today the "Greek Pass"; he cut down the inhabitants of the Alps who were trying to prevent him from crossing, he laid open the region, he fortified the routes, and brought it about that an armoured elephant could go where a single unarmed man could barely crawl through before. In this way he led his forces over and brought them into Italy."

Far be it from me to correct a Roman historian, but he has introduced into his account the myth of Hercules and his tenth labor – the stealing of the cattle of Geryon, the three-headed king of Spain. Therefore, it was these cattle, and not an army, that Hercules led over the Pyrenees and the Alps. Fun fact – the "Pillars of Hercules" were set up by the Greek – later to become Roman - hero on each side of the Straits of Gibraltar to commemorate this feat! I would like to add a bit of my own pseudo-mythology by referring to the novel *The Elephant Man,* which would be an apt nickname for Hannibal! To those who protest that this story refers to a deformed man, I would point out that Hannibal was eventually "deformed" by the loss of an eye! Alexander the Great's father, Philip II, a "great" commander in his own right, also lost an eye. However, this did not prevent him from "having an eye" for women and young boys! So those two generals could be dubbed in Latin *"Cocles"* or in Greek *"Monophthalmos"*!

Consequently, the epithet may not be so dumb-O! The story of "the Elephant Man" may be brought to the silver screen one day, but as for Hannibal, I would recommend the Italian movie with Victor Mature.

Chapter 103

- Good morning, Professor Marois, I've brought my notes for today's discussion on my dissertation. I was wondering what you thought of my thesis that religious practice – and belief - was not imposed upon the masses of Republican Rome, but that it was the people who dictated, in a sense, to the governing elite the direction that state religion was to follow.

- Good day, Denys. Yes, your premise is intriguing, and you have interesting arguments. Of course, as expected, you have documented your contentions with pertinent sources. It seems that you have been collecting statements on religion from your various courses on Roman authors such as Cicero, Valerius Maximus, Dionysius of Halicarnassus, and Greek authors like Polybius and Plutarch, among others. It seems as well that in your course on epigraphy with Professor Walter you concentrated on inscriptions of a religious nature. But this quote from Karl Marx needs explanation. Let me see, ah, here it is. *"Die Religion ist Das Opium des Volkes"*.

- Yes, Professor. This much-quoted phrase – part of a longer explanation, I admit, that ''religion is the opium of the people'' summarizes very well one of my underlying suppositions, namely that, while it is true that the government in Republican Rome – the *Sanctus Senatus* - had nominal authority over state religion, and discretionary powers, which they definitely exercised, the "wise *patres* " were conscious of the need to ensure that the people had "their fill of religion". Much like the demand for *panem et circenses*, a need for "bread and circuses", the superstitious nature of individuals required "religious nourishment" presented in the most entertaining fashion possible! Hence, the "Marxian" – I do not say "Marxist", because that suggests philosophical and social leanings that I am not espousing here – contention that "man makes religion, religion does not make man" seems to apply to the relationship between "church and state" in Republican Rome. The Roman "man on the street" believed in the power of religion, in the worship of the gods. This was part of his superstitious make-up. Another part was the insistence on ensuring that this power remained a benefit for him and his family – and, by extension, for the Roman State. The individual Romans knew the "what" and the "why" – the well-known *do ut des*. "I give in order that you give", this contractual formula meant to express the belief in the gods and the recognition of the power of the gods, was an attestation of the sanctity and finality of law felt by the Romans. Polybius, that acute analyst of the Roman "system", recognized the need for government authorities to channel this deep-rooted superstitious nature into an organized form of religious worship which could be harnessed by elaborate rules of religious conduct. In the sixth book of his *Histories* he states:

"The Roman constitution seems to me to have the greatest difference for the better in its policy on religion. In fact, I believe that something that would be criticized among other peoples actually holds the Roman state together, namely its superstition. This aspect is filled with such a need for the grandiose, both in their private affairs and in the city's public affairs, that one cannot exaggerate this fact. I feel they have done this because of the masses, because they are always unthinking, full of lawless wants, unbridled passion, and violent temperament. They can only be controlled through obscure fears and pompous presentation." This elaborate cult worship would have state-imposed limits, since the Senate, the ultimate dispensers of this "opium", were determined to protect the "morality" as well as the "morale" of the "masses".

I'm hoping the alliteration of that expression will find its way into my dissertation, Professor!

The Roman Senate was aware of this facet of human nature long before Marx came along! The religious elite, government and government-appointed officials, counted on the importance of tradition to monitor the behavior of the masses of worshippers. There was no question of "censuring" the gods! The elaborate system of priesthoods was more than a stepping-stone for political advancement among the scions of society – more alliteration, Professor! The religious officials symbolized the individual and state "part of the bargain" in the age-old religious formula of the reciprocal relationship with the divine. In this way cult practices could be severely scrutinized. We only have to consider how religions have resisted change for centuries in their manner of celebration! This resistance to change did not begin or end with the Romans. The notion that "old is good, new is bad" was dramatically evidenced in the Roman Senate's reaction to the imported cult practices of the god Bacchus. The god was accepted, but worship of him had to be acceptable. In this way, morality and *pax deorum* – "peace with the gods"- could be maintained. In practice, secret ceremonies would have taken place, while tempered and restrained worship of this foreign god would probably be non-existent. How – or why – does one worship Bacchus if you take all the fun out of it? Yes, I was fortunate in Professor Walter's class to have worked on the proclamation *De Bacchanalibus* of 186 B.C. from the *Corpus Inscriptionum Latinarum*. I have it here in my notes, but I also found useful in the epigraphy course some religious formulae that I constantly come across. The following list has proven very convenient: *dedicavit* – dedicated, or gave; *de suo* – at one's own expense; *dis manibus* –   to the departed spirits (the Manes of a person); *donum/dono dedit* – gave this gift, or as a gift; *fecit* - built or made; *fieri curavit* – caused to be built or made; *Iovi Optimo Maximo* – to Jupiter Best and Greatest; *laetus libens* – happily and freely; libens or *lubens* – freely; *locus datus decreto decurionum* – land given by decree of the *decuriones* - the senators on a town council; *merito* – deservedly; *pecunia propria posuit* –

deposited at one's own expense; *pro pietate posuit* – deposited out of piety; *sacer/sacrum* – sacred; *sua pecunia* – with one's own money; *voto soluto* – in payment of a vow; *votum solvit* – one has paid the vow.

These are the pertinent sections of the proclamation made by the Senate concerning the worshippers of Bacchus – *Bacchanales:*

"That none of them should wish to hold a Bacchanal; or if there are any who claim it is necessary for them to hold a Bacchanal, that they should come to the Urban Praetor and that after a hearing our Senate should decide about these matters, provided that not less than a hundred Senators be present when this matter is discussed.

That no man should wish to approach the Bacchae, neither Roman citizen, nor anyone of Latin or Allied status, except if they have approached the Urban Praetor and he has given permission in accordance with the opinion of the Senate provided that not less than a hundred Senators be present when this matter is discussed. Decided.

That no man should be a priest, nor any man or woman be a president. And that none of them should wish to hold common funds, nor anyone wish to appoint either man or woman to a magistry or promagistry. And that they should not afterwards wish to make between them joint oaths, vows, promises, or undertakings; and that no one should wish to create a bond of loyalty between them.

And that no one should wish to perform rites in secret, nor anyone to perform rites in public or in private or outside the city, unless he has approached the Urban Praetor and that after a hearing our Senate should decide about these matters, provided that not less than a hundred Senators be present when this matter is discussed.

That not more than a total of five men and women should wish to perform rites, nor that on such occasion should more than two men or more than three women wish to attend, except in accordance with the opinion of the Urban Praetor and the Senate, as written above.

…if anyone contravenes what is written above, they have decided it is to be considered a capital offence…"

I think, Professor Marois, that Livy's account is proof of how serious this law was. He says in Book XXXIX of *Ab Urbe Condita* that "more were killed than thrown into chains – and there were many of both – men and women. Condemned women were handed over to their relatives or guardians to be dealt with in private; if there was no one to punish them, they were dealt with publicly. The consuls were charged with destroying all Bacchic cult places –

first in Rome, then in all of Italy – unless they found an ancient altar or statue consecrated there."

I assume, Professor, that being "dealt with" meant execution!

-        Most probably, Denys. But it seems that worship of foreign gods outside of Rome didn't necessarily share the same fate as that in Rome. You did some work at Pompeii.

What did you discover? And what did Cicero say about the traditional practice of religion in Rome? I believe you read his *De natura deorum* when you were at McGill.

-        Well, Professor, the worship of Isis kept coming back to Rome, and mainly due to its popularity with the masses. This brings us back again to the role of the common people in religious practice in the State! I'm reminded of the song "Everyday People" by Sly and The Family Stone – but, of course, this won't be referenced in my dissertation! The conflict over the cult of Isis is mentioned with reference to the consul Gabinius being prevented in 58 B.C. from taking the auspices because he had not allowed altars to be built for worship of Isis and Serapis.

I also have in my notes from my course on Valerius Maximus, in the "memorable words and deeds" he recorded in Book I of his *Factorum ac dictorum memorabilium*, the following incident from 50 B.C.: "When the Senate had decreed that the shrines of Isis and Serapis should be destroyed and none of the workmen dared to touch them, the consul Aemilius Paulus took off his official robe, picked up an axe and struck the doors of that temple." But the Second Triumvirate of Octavian, Marc Antony and Lepidus had voted a temple for Isis and Serapis.

However, Marc Antony joined Cleopatra and they became the enemy. Obviously, Isis would now be *dea non grata*! Nonetheless, her worship in Pompeii was very popular. I had a chance to look at the finds around the Temple of Isis in that resort town. Superstitious, "traditional" Romans might be tempted to claim that the eruption of Vesuvius was punishment for the irreverent cult practices in Pompeii. The wall-paintings in the Villa of the Mysteries could be construed as evidence of non-conformist religious practices. Cicero and Caesar were ideological foes, yet both used positions in the upper echelons of the religious hierarchy to advance their individual causes. Bibulus, consul with Caesar, tried to prevent his colleague from passing certain laws by delay tactics involving watching the heavens – tactics that proved unsuccessful.

Ironically, it seemed that Caesar, when *Pontifex Maximus*, had no great interest – or belief - in religion. Augury had no effect on him! Remember "the Ides of March"! He famously claimed that augurs must have had a good laugh when they crossed each other in the street. With this attitude, he seemed rather Epicurean. I should point out, in speaking about Caesar, that the Senate no doubt agreed to decree Caesar *Divus* while he was alive due to popular conviction and pressure. Caesar was wont to curry favour with the masses through religious appeal, but I have a feeling that the "Great One" - good term for a future hockey star – but again, not in my dissertation! - already considered himself divine! Moreover, Augustus – even that title was religious – would endeavor to legitimize his new sociopolitical order in the Principate by maintaining traditional religious practice, and thus remaining "one" with the masses, albeit "THE one"! Cicero, it seems, also had some misgivings about religion, and probably viewed the maintenance of traditional religion as being vital for his *concordia ordinum*, that is, a harmonious socio-political order. He says to his wife in *Ad Familiares* 14 that "neither the gods you have always so purely worshipped nor the men to whom I have always given service have been grateful". Cicero seemed ready to compromise his true belief about the gods in order not to upset the general population. Keeping them happy in their worship practices was important - even though he probably considered their beliefs nothing but superstition. He carefully guarded his true sentiment, so that the established religion would continue to serve the useful purpose of keeping the rabble in check. I think what Cicero says in the second book of his work *De divinatione* is very telling: "But I want to make it clear that the destruction of superstition does not mean the end of religion. For I believe it to be the function of wisdom to preserve the institution of our ancestors, by maintaining their sacred rites and ceremonies.

Moreover, the celestial order and the beauty of the universe force me to admit that there is some excellent and eternal being who deserves the respect and praise of men". We have here, Professor Marois, a philosopher and "analyst" of religion who yields to the desires of the people in spite of his own religious convictions. Further proof, I believe, that my suggestion that the masses dictated – in the general sphere – religious cult practice to the highest levels of government in the Republic, and not the other way around, inasmuch as they maintained the raison d'être for such practices! The great poem of Lucretius, *De rerum natura*, in which he preaches an Epicurean renunciation of superstition – sentiments, I repeat, no doubt shared by Julius Caesar – is another instance of "philosophy bowing to the will of the mob"! The stronghold that superstition maintained in religious matters is illustrated in this anecdote from Plutarch's *Life of Crassus*. When legal procedures failed to stop Crassus from embarking on his ill-fated Parthian campaign, the tribune met Crassus at the gates of Rome, and " burnt incense and poured libations and called curses down upon him, that were horrible and terrifying, and at the same time invoking dreadful and strange gods. The Romans claim these ancient and mysterious curses are so powerful that no one can escape them, and even he who utters them suffers evil". Crassus attacked the Parthians, and the rest, as they say, is history! The tribune also fared badly, as his career was promptly over! Further to this all-consuming preoccupation of the Romans with the gods, one must consider the practice of *evocatio*, by which Roman generals would bring the gods of defeated enemies to their side, such as they did at Carthage, and would therefore, in a sense, "capture" the gods of the enemy. These gods would then become "Roman" through the worship given to them in the process known as *devotio*.

Naturally, "captured gods" would last longer, and present a stronger symbol of victory than "captured people", who would only be enslaved for a finite period of time. This tradition dated all the way back to the Trojan War, when the gods of Troy were brought to Italia by Aeneas.

These gods would inevitably be pleased, as they became the recipients of worship by new and powerful devotees. On the state level, certainly, this acceptance of a multitude of deities was a declaration of power over defeated enemies, but in the sphere of religious practice, afforded the masses more *panem et circenses*. Thus, Roman citizens would not become restless, but would be fed and entertained with a "smorgasbord" of divinities. By the way, Professor Marois, this Swedish word reminds me of Martin P. Nilsson, whose book, *The Bacchic Mysteries in Italy*, was instrumental for my Master's thesis research on that god. Hence, instead of "all you can eat", the Roman people were afforded "all you can worship", since variety is the "spice" of life – no pun intended on the image of eating, Professor! If you will allow me an analogy, the people were the "motors" of religion in Rome, while the senators and religious officials were the "mechanics" who ensured "safety regulations", that is to say, moral standards and adherence to correct public ritual practices. Later, the Christians would be hated and feared because they refused to accept these standards. Ultimately, this collaboration between the government and the citizenry in secular and religious matters was neatly summarized by Seneca when he proposed that "one should talk among humans as though the gods were listening, and with the gods, as though men were listening"! In other words, *senatus* and *populus* were obliged – and I believe commited – to act in accordance with human and divine law. There is also another aspect of religion to consider, namely its role in determining Roman identity. For the Hellenes of Greece, "Greekness" was defined by a common language and religion.

Geography, because of widespread colonization and settlement in the East and in the West, was not a unifying factor. Likewise for the Romans, "Romanness" was determined by language – Latin – and religion. However, the Romans, bent on an ever-increasing imperial sway, had also to consider geography. A common language was no longer a given.

Nevertheless, by their behavior, and as evidenced by proclamations of several writers, notably Cicero, the Romans believed themselves to be the most religious of peoples. Consequently, religion would become the common denominator for "Roman peoples", especially since religion and politics were so inextricably joined in the Roman social order. Foreign cults, inside and outside of Rome, would display different elements, but religiosity remained the underlying factor. The practice of religion – for the Romans, religion was indeed more "doing" than "believing" - was the common bond for the masses that provided the identity that facilitated government – and even control – for Rome's rulers, who realized that "peace with the gods" – *pax deorum* - would guarantee *pax populi* – a docile citizen body.

-       You certainly have deliberated at great length over your thesis of religion as a placebo to tame the wild crowds of Rome, Denys. Your sources do indeed provide valuable testimony. I am pleased that my book *Ius sacrum et lex religiosa: Religious Law in Ancient Rome* is proving to be an invaluable point of reference for your investigation. The danger may be in attributing religious sentiment and practice as they developed throughout history to the particular context of late Republican Rome. After all, the Latin Mass, which I know you are fond of, certainly added a dimension of mystery to the cult of Christian worship, yet was withdrawn to keep the "worshipers" of an increasing vernacular society willing participants!

-       True, Professor, but then cult worship in Latin would not have been an issue in Ancient Rome! There is another aspect of Roman religion and the social reality of Republican Rome. We all know that women had no official voice or role in the state government. We have no evidence that, individually or collectively, they ever sought such prominence. However, I believe that women were more involved in the religious life of Rome than is generally accepted.

Nor do I speak only of private and domestic worship. Inscriptions – and I rely mainly on epigraphic evidence for my position – reveal dedications made by women in the public sphere at cult sites, and even the erection of temples at their proper expense. In addition to the special role as Vestals, and important obligations in cults such as *Bona Dea* and *Magna Mater*, there appear to be indications that religious worship on the part of women was not limited to devotions to female divinities. Likewise, it seems that men also took part in the traditional worship of goddesses – but I am still investigating this notion. I suggest that women, and here I am mainly speaking of wealthy women of the patrician persuasion, actively pursued greater "religious freedom". My contention is that "Senatorial women", that is, those related to Senators, and even the wives of senatorial lawmakers, would not be content with the limited religious praxis of worshipping only the "good goddess" or "the great mother". They would prevail on their male relatives to allow women an active role in a more varied sphere of religious practice. Senators, anxious for "*pax domi*"- this "household harmony", as it were – would acquiesce in these requests – or, perhaps, demands – especially since no political privileges were being accorded. Limited in their legal rights, and without political status, the only social sphere in which women could aspire to respectability on a par with men would be in the domain of religion! Thus, even though the governing religious magistrates, as always, maintained certain "management prerogatives", such as forbidding women to partipate in the worship according to the *ritus Graecus* – that is the "Greek rite" of being bareheaded, but perhaps wearing garlands - the "trade-off" of according (at least some) women permission for a certain prominence in religious rituals on a wide scale is another dimension of Roman religious practice being determined by the population, albeit in this case, a restricted element of the population. Again, Professor, your caveat regarding assimilation to Christian tradition and practice notwithstanding, even today in both eastern and western traditions of Christianity, we observe the *ritus Romanus* practice of worship with covered heads maintained by women worshipers – this "Roman rite" dating back to the kingship of Numa!

Chapter 104

-        Hi Mom, Don't you just love Quebec City in the winter? I don't ski, but Manon and I enjoy going sledding and snow-shoeing. We have authentic snow shoes that I bought from Chief Max Gros-Louis at the Huron Village! And we really have fun skating together! You saw that little rink near the Château Frontenac when you were here at Christmas. Manon and I have "romantic moonlight skates" there sometimes. There is also a big circular skating rink in Ste-Foy where I dazzle Manon with my speed skating. Well, maybe "speed" is a little exaggerated! I don't get to play hockey very much like I did at McGill, but just last week I filled in for a player on the team Manon's brother Michel plays for. It's only a pick-up league and is supposed to be just for fun. But wouldn't you know it, this "goon" started to pick on Michel, so I moved in to help him. Nobody there knew me, and I didn't know I had such a terrific right hand! I think I broke the guy's nose! Another guy on their team jumped me, and I know for sure that I broke HIS nose! I thought I was in the Montreal Forum! The players on Michel's team were slapping me on the back, and calling me "Rocket". No chance they'd call me Jean Béliveau! The game ended abruptly – but at least there was no riot! Manon's father talks to me sometimes – but always about hockey! He told me that there had been a great goaler in Montreal in the 1920's and 1930's whose name was Hainsworth! His father had been a water commissioner, so I guess it was only natural that George – that was his first name – should also have a career on water – "frozen water"! Ice - er nice – joke - right, Mom? By George, maybe hockey is in my blood! Just joking again – I'd probably end up spilling it on the ice if I played regularly – and they don't need more red lines on the ice! This great goalie had succeeded another George – maybe they came from a "farm" team since that name comes from the Greek word for "farmer"! They named the trophy for best goaltender after him – the Vezina Trophy. Georges Vézina was known as the "Chicoutimi Cucumber". I guess he was "cool as a cucumber". But since he was always wearing a tuque, he might have been "cold" as well! At least he always stopped his opponents cold! That quip just led to an "icy" stare from Papa Plouffe! When he used the word *cerbère* for goaltender, I pointed out that the word was used because in Greek mythology Cerberus was the three-headed guard dog in Hades, but he claimed not to know "what the hell" I was talking about! Telling him that they may eventually play hockey down there when "hell freezes over", didn't really soften him up, but he did admit that the "Devils" would make a good name for a hockey team. With pride he recounted how a Montreal Canadiens goaler, Jacques Plante, was the first goalie to wear a mask in an NHL game. He apparently also used to knit tuques – strange breed these goaltenders! When I said that I once wore a mask on stage – it was in *The Frogs*, Mom – he was only mildly interested. You know, when we wear a mask, it does protect us. Manon's brother Michel, who is really into environmental issues, once told me his worst fear was that all of society would one day have to wear masks for protection against diseases caused by serious bacteria in the air. But, if you think about it, masks can also conceal our real intentions – "mask" them, so to speak. The French word *mesqin* – I'm sure you know that word for "nasty" Mom – sounds like it could be connected with *masque*. Don't look up the etymology, Mom, it's just me playing with words! "No word" makes it "awkward" with Manon's father, but when I told him that I had a try-out with the Mohawks in Cincinnati – Dad remembers that I almost made that hockey team! – he beamed, and said his grandmother had been a Mohawk.

So Manon has First Nations blood in her! You and Dad didn't seem so surprised when I announced that Manon and her family were moving to Montreal to follow her sister and brother-in-law. Her brothers will be going to university in Montreal – as I did! But going from Quebec to Montreal is hardly "the giant leap" of going from Cincinnati to Montreal! Instead of a lot more snow, they'll have a lot less. Manon's department – you know – Veterans Affairs – has an opening in September at the Montreal office, and that will work out fine for her, since she has her leave of absence in July and August to be with me in Paris. The Montreal office is just down the street from St. Joseph's Oratory. I know you and Dad were impressed when you visited it. Dad seems to have more and more of a "what will happen will happen" attitude, which could make him either Epicurean or Stoic. And Mom, you have always had that "all things happen for a reason" philosophy. As you know, I've never been a "one day at a time person".

All my years as a student at McGill and Laval – including my summer sessions in Europe – have been planned over a long period. Do you realize I have been away from home for nine years? That's a third of my life! It is true that with Manon I've learned to enjoy the moment – or moments! Just like that Four Lads song – "Moments to Remember"! I also like their song "Istanbul (Not Constantinople)", since the title alludes to Late Roman history! I'm so glad Manon will be accompanying me to Toronto and Cincinnati for the conferences and the St. Xavier High reunion. And especially excited about our trip to Paris! Do you know that we'll both be students there? If you can call watching and studying films being a student! I love teasing Manon about that. And speaking of teasing, when Manon explained that her leave of absence wasn't difficult to secure because of the annual summer slowdown, I needled her by saying the government "slowdown", if it's any slower than the usual pace, must actually be a "summer standstill"! Boy am I glad she has a sense of humour! I had a nice talk with Dad in the Château Frontenac bar. I told him I was anxious to play a couple of rounds of golf with him at Indian Hills in June, and he asked if it was because I was short of money! Dad still has that

dry sense of humour! He admitted that Latin and I have come a long way, but he was
wondering where I thought I might be teaching. At least he's no longer asking me IF I thought
I might be teaching!

But you know, Mom, I can't see Manon moving to the U.S.A., or even any great distance from
her mother. Right now, I just don't know. So much for long-range planning! It was fun talking
to Feeb about her studies in Law School until I started quizzing her on all those Latin legal
terms. If I had continued, she would probably have ended up saying *habeas corpus* to you! It
means "you may have the body", Mom – she's asking you to get me out of there! You didn't
tell me she was engaged! Did she play the song "Will You Marry Me, Bill?" by Marilyn
McCoo? It seems that she is leaning towards remaining in Cincinnati. There are worse places
you could be! W.C.Fields didn't care for Philadelphia, but the music is good. I like the
"Philadelphia Sound"! Say, if Uncle Phil played the harmonica, could he form the
"Philharmonic" Orchestra? After reading that weak attempt at humour, even if there's a play
on words, I know you're hoping that this letter is coming to an end! But Mom, you started me
on the slippery slope of puns by sending me off on the path to word play! Surely you won't
ever forget that grade-four assignment I had - to compose a nursery rime inspired by a piece
of furniture. You suggested I use my imagination in a funny kind of way. I immediately thought
of Dad's old wicker chair. I still have the "rime" Miss Jacobs handed back to me with the
comment "In our Holden there's a flame burning bright with all its might"! The rime was "Jack
be nimble, Jack be quick, Jack jump over the 'wickerstick' – while I finish this rime, just in the
'wick' of time"! I'll write again soon, but we'll all be together in June. Just keep thinking of The
Supremes song – "Someday We'll Be Together"! Love you! Den

Chapter 105

-       Good day, everyone! As you know, today we are beginning our reading of selections from the writings of Suetonius. Since twenty per cent of our time in this course on Roman historians was devoted to Cornelius Nepos, and we have reserved twenty per cent of course time for Ammianus Marcellinus, we wil be able to allot sixty per cent of our time to Suetonius, by far the most popular writer of the three. Popular because of his subject matter, that is! Most likely you have all read his complete biographies of the twelve Caesars in French .

Denys, you may have read his work in English. You told me that you had read his biographies of famous poets in translation. Certainly, all of you have had courses on Livy and Tacitus. Denys has had the opportunity of taking a course on Sallust in Germany, as well as some courses on Greek historians of Rome. The rationale of reading three authors in this course is to allow you to advance in the compusory list of writers required for the doctorate. Denys, and I realize I refer to him quite often *exempli gratia*, will most likely complete the list of Greek and Latin authors without having to prepare comprehensive exams, which require courses in tutorial readings of selected authors. Don't let the family name of Suetonius – *Tranquillus* – fool you. He was very active, as his writings attest, and he was a lawyer as well, and a secretary to the emperor Hadrian. The graphic details in his description of the so called "evil" emperors have been adapted by some movie producers to present scenes of decadence on the "silver" screen – not exactly our "Silver" Latin of Seneca, wouldn't you say, Denys? So the biographies of the Caesars –Julio-Claudians and Flavians - are the depictions of the lives and deeds of Julius Caesar and the first eleven Emperors – Augustus, Tiberius, Caligula – with whom we will be beginning shortly – Claudius, Nero, Galba, Otho, Vitellius, Vespasian, Titus and Domitian. So then, Denys, without further ado, please read our sections for today, chapters 8, 9, 11 and 13. Afterwards, as is our practice, you will give us your translation.

-       Certainly, Professor Saucier. Of course Suetonius refers to Caligula officially by his real name, Gaius. In the later chapters, which I believe we will be reading next time, he gives a description of the despicable disposition of a demented dictator. Perhaps I, too, exaggerate in my use of alliteration! One can imagine Caligula parading about to the sound of Bobby Pickett's "Monster Mash"! I begin with the opening section of chapter eight, followed by the other chapters.

C.Caesar natus est pridie Kal. Sept. patre suo et C. Fonteio Capitone coss. Ubi natus sit, incertum diversitas tradentium facit. Cn. Lentulus Gaetulicus Tiburi genitum scribit, Plinius

Secundus in Treveris vico Ambitarvio supra Confluentes; addit etiam pro argumento aras ibi ostendi inscriptas ob Agrippinae puerperium . Versiculi imperante mox eo divulgati apud hibernas legiones procreatum indicant: "In castris natus, patriis nutritus in armis, iam designati principis omen erat".

9. Caligulae cognomen castrensi ioco traxit, quia manipulario habitu inter milites educabatur. Apud quos quantum praeterea per hanc nutrimentorum consuetudinem amore et gratia valuerit, maxime cognitum est, cum post excessum Augusti tumultuantis et in furorem usque praecipites solus haud dubie ex conspectu suo flexit. Non enim prius destiterunt, quam ablegari eum ob seditionis periculum et in proximam civitatem demandari animadvertissent; tum demum ad paenitentiam versi reprenso ac retento vehiculo invidiam quae sibi fieret deprecati sunt.

11. Naturam tamen saevam atque probrosam ne tunc quidem inhibere poterat, quin et animadversionibus poenisque ad supplicium datorum cupidissime interesset et ganeas atque adulteria capillamento celatus et veste longa noctibus obiret ac scaenicas saltandi canendique artes studiosissime appeteret, facile id sane Tiberio patiente, si per has mansuefieri posset ferum eius ingenium.Quod sagacissimus senex ita prorsus perspexerat, ut aliquotiens praedicaret exitio suo omniumque Gaium vivere et se natricem populo Romano, Phaethontem orbi terrarum educare.

13. Sic imperium adeptus populum Romanum, vel dicam hominum genus voti comprotem facit, exoptatissimus princeps maximae parti provincialium ac militum, quod infantem plerique cognoverant, sed et universae plebi urbanae ob memoriam Germanici patris miserationemque prope afflictae domus. Itaque ut a Miseno movit quamvis lugentis habitu et funus Tiberi prosequens, tamen inter altaria et victimas ardentisque taedas densissimo et laetissimo obviorum agmine incessit, super fausta nomina "sidus" et "pullum" et "pupum" et "alumnum" appellantium.

I suppose Caligula's theme song in "boot camp" could have been Nancy Sinatra's song "These Boots Are Made For Walking"! Here is my translation:

"Gaius Caesar was born the day before the Kalends of September" – so on the last day of the month of Augustus, and for a superstitious Roman that could be portentous! – "in the consulship of his own father" – who, as we know, was Germanicus – "and of Gaius Fonteio Capito" – it was the year AD 12 - "The variations among those reporting it make where he was born uncertain. Gnaeus Lentulus Gaeticulus writes that he was born at Tibur" – this is Tivoli today! – "Plinius Secundus" – we know him as Pliny the Younger – "says he was born among the Teveri in the village of Ambitarvium above the Confluence"; – this would be of the Rhine and Moselle Rivers - "he adds also for this claim that altars are shown inscribed 'on account of Agrippina's delivery'. Soon after he was Emperor, verses that were circulating indicate that he was born among the legions while they were in winter quarters: 'Born in the camp, nourished among the arms of his country, this was already a sign of the designated Princeps" – i.e. Emperor.

9. "The nickname of Caligula he draws from a camp joke because he was raised among the soldiers in the clothing of a private soldier. How much he was especially valued among them in love and favor through this contact with them as his care-takers is especially known since, after the death of Augustus, being in an uproar, and heading towards madness, he alone without a doubt caused them to change their minds at his sight. For they did not let up before they noticed that he was being led away because of the danger caused by their rebellion, and being brought to the nearest town; then at last becoming repentant, having grabbed and held back his carriage, they begged to be spared of the ill-will that would occur against them.

11. Even then he was not able to curb his cruel and shameful nature; he rather very eagerly took interest in the suffering of those handed over for punishment and correction, and concealed in a wig and long robe, he engaged in debauchery and adultery, and very eagerly sought out the theatrical arts of jumping and singing, and with Tiberius clearly allowing this, if he could tame his wild nature through these. Because that very wise old man had clearly perceived, as he sometimes predicted, that Gaius was living for his own ruin and that of everyone, and that he was raising a viper for the Roman people, and a Phaethon for the world." - Phaethon was, of course, the mythological son of Helios who lost control of his father's chariot – the bad "son" of the "Sun"! I wonder if that happened to other sons, and so the Johnny Rivers song "Seventh Son"!

13. "Taking up the imperial rule in this way, he caused the votive prayer of the Roman people to be fulfilled, or I might say, of the human race, a 'princeps' most eagerly chosen by a large majority of the provincials and soldiers, because very many of them had known him as a child, but also by the entire urban plebs, because of their memory of his father Germanicus and the pity they had for his nearly destroyed household. Therefore, as he went from Misenum, although in the clothing of a mourner and following the funeral of Tiberius, he came upon altars and sacrificial victims and burning torches of those meeting him with a very dense, yet very joyous throng of those calling him beyond the auspicious names 'star' and 'little chick' and 'little boy' and 'nursling'."

-        Nice translation, Denys, and thank you for the pertinent information you gave us during your translation. I hope you all are patient enough to wait for next class when we will read the salacious sequences that will follow. Nice alliteration, don't you think, Denys?

-        Definitely, Professor! But just to be sure, are we talking about Suetonius' salacious sequences or Saucier's salacious sequences? And if everyone is really patient, I understand that Penthouse Magazine is starting to film their production of *Caligula*, which should be in theaters next year. But I don't imagine that Penthouse will be added to our compulsory reading list!

Chapter 106

\- Aren't you excited about the dance contest tonight, Manon? Fantastic Frank is bringing his two DJ buddies from Montreal, and that New York guy who organizes dance contests south of the border. I guess that's why the prize is a weekend in New York City! Those three guys will be the judges.

\- I can understand your enthusiasm, Denys, but I'm a little nervous, and I probably won't even have heard of half of those dances, and have danced to even fewer of them. It would be nice to win, since I've never been to New York. The closest I've been is watching Ed Sullivan on TV. My parents always watched that show until it went off the air a few years ago. My father couldn't name the President of The United States, but he could name the singers that appeared on that show! That's also why I know a lot of the singers you and Bob talk about. The other show my parents never missed was "La Famille Plouffe" – for obvious reasons!

\- No need to have the jitters, Manon, since we definetly won't have to dance the jitterbug! I used to watch "American Bandstand" – so I saw a lot of those dances on TV. There may be a couple where we'll have to wing it, but I'm counting on the bonus points you get for correctly identifying the singer of the dance song. Everybody knows Chubby Checker, but some of the other artists won't be that obvious to the Club regulars. Did you know that the "twist maestro" was inspired to use that name by Fats Domino – you know – checkers and dominoes!

The Romans had this knucklebones game where they would roll the dice. That's where Caesar's expression "the die is cast" comes from! Good old Fats Domino! I found my thrill…'cause I'm loving you still!

\- I thought it was "Blueberry Hill"! Although I think now it's my mother's blueberry pie that thrills you!! But there are contestants coming from Montreal, Denys. Have you ever been to New York?

\- We went on a school trip when I was at St. Xavier's. I didn't appreciate our visit to the Metropolitan Museum of Fine Art as much as I would today. But our afternoon at Yankee Stadium was great! I got to see my idol Mickey Mantle hit two home runs! People are starting to fill up the tables, and there's that New York disc jockey. You can tell it's him because of his T-shirt with the picture of the Statue of Liberty on it! You know, this is the first time I'll have a number on my back since I played football at St. Xavier High. Too bad Bob's out of town, he and your sister would have enjoyed this contest. Have you ever had to wear a number, Manon?

-	Only when I applied for the job at Veterans Affairs. We didn't wear a number at the interviews, but I had to hold one in my hand. I was number 13.

-	Wow, good thing you aren't superstitious like the Romans! Hey, they're set to play the first song! I guess they are going to get people up with some recent dance moves. This is "Do the Hustle" by Van McCoy. You always dance this one so well!

-	That was fun, Denys! I guess if we have fun all night, it won't matter if we don't win. Hey, it's "The Twist" by Chubby Checker. They will probably play his other dance songs, "Let's Twist Again" and "Limbo Rock".

-	I bet you they'll play some of his hits that are not as well-known, like "The Hucklebuck", which I promise not to do like Ed Norton on the old "Honeymooners" show! Then there's "The Pony" and "Slow Twistin'" that he did with Dee Dee Sharp, and he also recorded a song called "The Fly".

-	I'm all twisted out, Denys, especially since they played "The Peppermint Twist", by a singer you were able to identify – Joey Dee.

-	And you knew the name of that last song – "Douliou, Douliou". The name of the singer you identified, Jenny Rock, was familiar from my Quebec music course at McGill. But talk about your "French twist" – and I'm not talking pastry! Now they are playing "The Stroll" by The Diamonds. I saw this on a TV show – just follow me .

-	So far you've named all the singers, Denys. Frank has just announced that our number – number two - is in first place!

-	Of course, Manon, when you're number two, you try harder! Listen, that's Smokey Robinson and The Miracles. Frank's playing "Going To a Go-Go". We won't be able to sit down for a while, because they just announced four non-stop dance tunes in a row. I'll have to remember them so I can write down the singers after we finish dancing.

-	Where did you learn those fancy moves, Denys? I could barely keep up! Did you get the names of all the artists?

-	I sure did, Manon! "C'mon and Swim" is by Bobby Freeman, and then they played The Olympics doing the "Hully Gully" – that one was tricky, since there are a lot of versions of that song. I heard it in Germany, and they called it "Hali Gali"! Next was The Capitols version of the "Cool Jerk". The fourth dance song was "The Harlem Shuffle" by The Foundations. But the best "Harlem shuffle" I've seen is by the Harlem Globetrotters!

- Oh yeah, Bob took Maggie to see them. Now she almost likes basketball! We barely have time to finish our drinks! Good thing the judges have to stop every once and a while to tabulate the points.That sounds like a dance I know - the Bossa Nova!

- It's Eydie Gorme's song "Blame it on the Bossa Nova". While we dance, I'll pretend I'm her husband, the singer Steve Lawrence! Be ready for a few songs right after that one. Have you noticed that there are fewer couples getting up to dance. We're putting too much pressure on them, Manon!

- They played some dance songs I've never heard before. I'm surprised that you knew them, Denys!

- Well, that first one is called "The Madison". Why I know that version by Al Brown's Tune Toppers is because it was created in Ohio – in our capital city, Columbus. Then Frank played that strange "Time Warp" dance from the "Rocky Horror Show" movie. The song after that was "The Crawl" by Guitar Jr. Finally we danced the jerk to the Miracles singing "Come On Do the Jerk". That's not the original version, but hey, we got to hear the Miracles again!

- Frank announced he was going to play a couple of French tunes – I think to encourage some of the local couples. There are some couples from Montreal who are ahead of everybody except us. I recognize that song – it's Les Baronets singing "The Freddie".

- Wasn't that a surprise! Frank played *Manon, viens danser le ska*, and he was looking right at you! Not many people recognized "The Ska" in its Caribbean Reggae version that he played right after. You remembered *Les Habits Jaunes* and "*Miss Boney Maronie*"!

Everybody had fun dancing to "Do the Funky Chicken", but I think I may have been the only one who knew that it was Rufus Thomas singing! They played another Rufus Thomas song next called "Walking the Dog", but this was a version recorded by the Rolling Stones. How about that song "Tighten Up" by Archie Bell and the Drells! I guess they do that dance all the time in Houston, Texas, because in the song he says that's where they're from! The next dance tune was also by them, and is called "The Soul City Walk". And it was great to hear "See You Later, Alligator" by Bill Haley and the Comets! You 've heard the friendly exchange that goes "see you later alligator – in a while crocodile"? Well, I have another comeback line - "won't be too soon, you old baboon"! Just "aping" Mickey's "monkey", I guess – you know, like the song by The Miracles! But "Dance the Boomerang" was new to me. I didn't know that group, The Canjoes. I should have had my Australian friend teach it to me in Greece! But unlike a boomerang, he won't be coming back – he owes me money! But everybody knew "At the Hop" by Danny and the Juniors! Thanks to me, my sister's boyfriend, Danny, loves that song – or not! You must have recognized The Beach Boys singing "Surfin' U.S.A."

- Yes, Denys, it's one of the few songs I knew. But it was fun dancing to a beach dance!

- Too bad you weren't in your bikini – we might have gotten bonus points! And if you were Gidget like in the movie, I could be The Big Kahuna, like Cliff Robertson - or should I leave that role for Frankie Avalon, since he sings a lot better than I do, and could definitely fit that image better than I can? Fantastic Frank has just announced the last set. The judges announced that we are leading the contest, so here we go for all the marbles. Jeremy used to complain sometimes that I had lost mine, but I was always the saner of the two – in mind and in body! The music's starting – it's "Kung Fu Fighting"!

- Wouldn't you know it, Denys, Frank saved his best songs for the end. I knew all those songs, but I don't know the artists.

- Tonight's been really a lot of fun. I got to make a lot of crazy moves, and you were able to follow – a perfect partner! At least we didn't have to do the Charleston! They didn't play any "bump" songs either. Maybe we can do that dance in Paris this summer! I handed in all the names of the singers for that last set. They played two songs by Carl Douglas. The second one just came out, and is called "Dance the Kung Fu". There was Bill Haley's "Rock Around the Clock", The Orlons with their hit, "The Wah Watusi", "The Loco-Motion" by Little Eva, and finally, Dee Dee Sharp singing "The Mashed Potato". That last song made me hungry. After they announce the winners, we should go for a late snack at Le Marie Antoinette.

- Look, Denys! Frank is pointing at us. He's announcing that we are the winners.

We've won a trip to New York – and a trophy!

- That's great, Manon! Since the word "trophy" is derived from the Greek word *tropaion*, which itself comes from *tropaios*, meaning a "turning" – or, in dance terminology, a "twist" – we'll both have a "turn" keeping the trophy. Did you hear that announcement about a '60's revival party next month? The two or four-person team that names the most songs and singers will win $400! We could ask Bob and Maggie to join us as a going away party, since they will be moving a couple of weeks after the contest. It's not a dance contest, so we'll be able to make whatever moves we want. And between Bob and me, we should be able to do really well on the song titles. You know, Manon, that I have a huge collection of records from the 1960's. I can remember all those songs as if I had heard them yesterday.

-	Knowing you, Denys, you probably did listen to some of them yesterday! I'll feel useful, too, because Frank mentioned that they would play some French songs from the '60's as well. We'll have to arrive early – the contest starts at nine! Fortunately, it will be Spring Break, and you won't have to teach that Friday night.

-	I have a good feeling about that contest, but right now I feel like having a hamburger!

Chapter 107

\-   Good day! Our final author in this course is Ammianus Marcellinus. If he had written his work in his native language, you would be taking this course with Professor Marcoux, since, coming from Syria, he naturally spoke Greek. His *History* covered almost four hundred years from the accession of Nerva in 96 to the death of Valens in 378. But only the years 353 to 378 survive in the last eighteen books. Much less for you to read, Denys! Today we will read part of his account of the Emperor Julian, that pagan revivalist. Ammianus admired him because he himself was a pagan, but he did consider some of Julian's laws a little harsh towards the Christians. Denys, would you read today's text from chapter four of Book 25, and give us your translation?

\-   With pleasure, Professor. After all, although I am not pagan, Roman pagan religion has captivated me for many years!

1.   *Vir profecto heroicis connumerandus ingeniis, claritudine rerum et coalita maiestate conspicuous. cum enim sint, ut sapientes definiunt, virtutes quattuor praecipuae, temperantia prudentia iustitia fortitudo, eisque accedentes extrinsecus aliae, scientia rei militaris, auctoritas felicitas atque liberalitas, intento studio coluit omnes ut singulas.*

2.   *Et primum ita inviolata castitate enituit ut post amissam coniugem nihil umquam venereum agitaret : illud advertens, quod apud Platonem legitur, Sophoclem tragoediarum scriptorem aetate grandaevum interrogatum ecquid adhuc feminis misceretur, negantem id adiecisse, quod gauderet harum rerum amorem ut rabiosum quendam effugisse dominum et crudelem.*

3.   *item ut hoc propositum validius confirmaret, recolebat saepe dictum lyrici Bacchylidis, quem legebat iucunde id adserentem quod ut egregious pictor vultum speciosum effingit, ita pudicitia celsius consurgentem vitam exornat, quam labem in adulto robore iuventutis ita caute vitavit, ut ne suspicione quidem tenus libidinis ullius vel citerioris vitae ministris incusaretur, ut saepe contingit.*

4.   *Hoc autem temperantiae genus crescebat in maius iuvante parsimonia ciborum et somni, quibus domi forisque tenacius utebatur. namque in pace victus eius mensura atque tenuitas erat recte noscentibus admiranda, velut ad pallium mox reversuri, per varios autem procinctus stans interdum more militia cibum brevem vilemque sumere visebatur.*

5.   *ubi vero exigua dormiendi quiete recreasset corpus laboribus induratum, expergefactus explorabat per semet ipsum vigiliarum vices et stationum, post haec serias ad artes confugiens doctrinarum.*

6.   *et si nocturna lumina, inter quae lucubrabat, potuissent voces ullae testari, profecto ostenderant inter hunc et quosdam principes multum interesse , quem norant voluptatibus ne ad necessitatem quidem indulsisse naturae.*

7.   *Dein prudentiae eius indicia fuere vel plurima e quibus explicari sufficiet pauca. armatae rei scientissimus et togatae, civilitati admodum studens, tantum sibi adrogans quantum a contemptu et insolentia distare existimabat : virtute senior quam aetate : studiosus cognitionum omnium et indeclinabilis aliquotiens iudex : censor moribus regendis acerrimus, placidus, opum contemptor, mortalia cuncta despiciens, postremo id praedicabat, turpe esse sapienti cum habeat animum captare laudes ex corpore.*

8.   *Quibus autem iustitiae inclaruit bonis, multae significant, primo quod erat pro rerum et hominum distinctione sine crudelitate terribilis, deinde quod paucorum discrimine vitia cohibebat, tum autem quod minabatur ferro potius quam utebatur.*

9.   *postremo ut multa praeteream, constat eum in apertos aliquos inimicos insidiatores suos ita consurrexisse mitissime, ut poenarum asperitatem genuina lenitudine castigaret.*

Here is my translation. As you have probably noticed during the reading of the Latin text, this section presents a very positive portrait of our Julian the Apostate. It could serve as his *curriculum vitae*! Ammianus will later on his presentation of Julian point out some flaws of character, which the Emperor would not include in his C.V.!

" 1. He was indeed a man to be counted among those of heroic character, conspicuous by the renown of his deeds and his ingrown majesty. For since the wise men define four main virtues – moderation, practical wisdom, justice and courage – and corresponding to these other external qualities, knowledge of military affairs, authority, good fortune, and generosity, he cultivated them with complete devotion, all of them together and individually.

2.   And first of all, he was so conspicuous for his unblemished chastity that, when his wife died, he never considered sexual activity, reminding us of what is said in Plato, that Sophocles, the writer of tragedies, being asked when he was quite old if he still had intercourse with women, saying no, added that he rejoiced at having escaped the love of these things, a mad and cruel master.

3.   Likewise, in order to make this proposition even more valid, he often repeated the saying of the lyric poet Bacchylides, whom he read with pleasure, and who asserted that just as a distinguished painter makes the face beautiful, so chastity decorates a life rising to a higher state; such a disgrace he so cautiously avoided on the mature strength of youth, that he was not even accused of a suspicion of lust even by the ministers of his inner circle, as often happens.

4.   This type of temperance increased even more, aided by his moderation in food and sleep, which he practiced rather tenaciously at home and abroad. For the moderate measure of his food and his simple manner were to be admired by those recognizing correctly such virtues, as if he were to put his cloak back on, and in his various battles, while standing according to the military custom, he was seen to be eating little food, and of an ordinary kind.

5.   And when he had refreshed with a brief period of sleep his body, hardened by labors, having woken up, he examined himself the changes of the watches and of the guards, and after these serious activities, taking refuge in the arts of learning.

6.   And if the night-lamps, among which he worked, could testify as voices, they would certainly have shown that there was a great difference between him and certain emperors, for they knew he did not indulge in pleasures, not even with respect to the necessity of nature.

7.   And then there were so many indications of his practical wisdom, of which it will suffice to name a few. He was very knowledgeable of the arts of war and peace, greatly devoted to civility, appropriating to himself only as much as he thought kept him apart from contempt and insolence: he was older in virtue than in age: he was very interested in all legal matters, and was sometimes a rigid judge: he was a very strict censor in regulating morals, he was quietly contemptuous of wealth, despising all mortal things; finally, he declared that it was shameful for a wise man, since he has a soul, to gain praise because of his body.

8.   Many things indicate by what good characteristics of justice he distinguished himself; first, by distinguishing between situations and people, he was frightening, but without cruelty; and then because he controlled vices by the separating of a few, and that he threatened with a sword more often than he used it.

9.   Finally, in order to pass over many things, it is agreed that towards some openly hostile enemies that plotted against him he was so gentle that he restrained the severity of their punishment with genuine mercy. Julian was indeed to Ammianus "A Well -Respected Man", as The Kinks sang in their song. I also like the French versions by Petula Clark and Renée Martel, *"Un Jeune Homme Bien"*, even if the Emperor wasn't so young!

Chapter 108

\-   Oh, Denys, there are already lots of couples and groups of four seated at tables for the song contest. Frank's two DJ friends are here from Montreal, and they seem to have brought contestants with them from the music metropolis of Quebec. They are speaking English, and so are probably ringers who know all those American songs.

\-   No problem, Manon, we'll draw circles around those ringers! And it's a songs and singers contest. The ringers might not know the singers! Hey, I'm a poet, and I got to show it!

\-   And don't you know it, Menace! But I don't get the rings and circles bit.

\-   How can anybody as round as you be so square, Bob? I was twelve years old when the '60's started, so I was already listening to all these songs. You would have been dancing to a lot of them at sock hops, Bob!

\-   Even so, this contest is no shoe-in! Maggie, I think our future brother-inlaw is a little too confident and cocky, either that or conceited and confused!

\-   Don't take Bob too seriously, Denys. He just wants to embarrass you and Manon!

\-   Well, Maggie, I thought it was because he wanted me to be ready to sing "Mother-in-Law" to your mother. That song by Ernie K-Doe might be in the contest. And with his alliteration and puns tonight, I am taking him seriously! I was the master of word play, but now the shoe is on the other foot!

\-   You're always dangerous with those comebacks, Menace. But you didn't have to pay for the supper at Le Deauville for Maggie and me. That cost you and Manny a pretty penny! Still I don't mind admitting that I'm a little uptight about the contest.

\-   You and Stevie Wonder! Maybe they'll play that song of his tonight. Not to worry – we're going to win back the money! The meal was our going-away gift to you two. This will be the last chance to go dancing all together, since you're moving in two weeks. And when Manon and I come back from Paris at the end of the summer, she'll be with her family in Montreal as well. Of course I could go to Montreal on occasional weekends, and we could go dancing at those great dancing clubs that my friend Jeremy used to take me to. Now they're called *discothèques*. He used to like to spot two girls, and when one girl accepted to dance with me, her friend would feel obliged to dance with Jeremy. He said we made a great team, and I always said that we were like Dean Martin and Jerry Lewis. The first time I said he was

"Jerry Lewis" he got mad, until I explained the logic. Since his name was Jeremy, he would be "Jerry". That made him feel better, but I also mentioned that when we started teaching, he would be "The Nutty Professor"!

- You know, Menace, you could probably do just as well without Maggie and me, and you wouldn't have to split your winnings in two.

- It's part of our gift, Bob. Besides, because of golf I'm comfortable in foursomes! I haven't played too often since I've been here in Quebec, but Professor Marcoux has taken me a couple of times to Club de Golf de Lévis, where he's a member. I always smile on the 116 when we go by St. Romuald. Professor Marcoux is not a great golfer, but he's enthusiastic. He usually ends up hitting his "happy ball" – his mulligan - on the first tee. I try to give him friendly pointers, like keeping his eye on the ball, and keeping his head down, since if he looks up too soon he won't like what he sees! He usually tries to turn my suggestions into advice for a graduate student, like "not taking my eye off the ball" – meaning my dissertation! Heaven forbid, he warns, that I should ever "drop the ball"! But he's quite the good "sport" – although he describes himself as rather my "support"! It reminds me of the claim that my good friend Jeremy made when he referred to us as both being "jocks", since I was an athlete and he was an athletic supporter! It was quite a surprise to hear that, like me, Professor Marcoux had paid his school tuition by caddying at a golf course. He caddied at the Lennoxville Golf Club, where quite a few Americans played. They were big tippers, so he has always appreciated me as an American student! We usually play with two other professors from Laval, and naturally, on the course I call them by their first names, Thomas and Maurice. Professor Marcoux is still called "Professor", because he keeps tabs on everybody's shots and marks the score. He also divides the teams into two *Augusti* and two Caesars, even though the other players are not Classics professors. But his idea of a foursome is a Roman Imperial Tetrarchy! You know it is thought that the Roman ball game of *paganica*, played with a leather ball and a stick, was an early form of golf, and when the Romans invaded *Caledonia*, that is, Scotland, the sticks got bent a little – maybe they were using them as weapons! - and Scotland invented the "modern" game of golf. I've played a few times with guys who finished the round with bent clubs! The Scots refused to engage battle early in the morning, because that's when they had their starting times! The name *paganica* does suggest a connection with *paganus*, meaning "of the countryside", where you would naturally have the best "golf courses"! The word gives us "pagan", a word that identifies people who are not civilized enough for sophisticated Christian worship. I guess being "linked" to the game of golf from earliest times led the Scots to build all those "links" golf courses! My own theory is that the game became very popular in Gaul, and hence the name "Gaulf", eventually becoming "golf", meaning "Gauls only, Latins forbidden"! The PGA did not exist for golf in antiquity, since that was the "Professional Gladiators Association"! Apparently, the "Masters" tournament was not played during the slave rebellion led by Spartacus! He had the original "Arnie's Army"! I suppose if Nero had taken up golf, he would have "burned up" the course! He probably would have forced Christians to caddy for him free of charge! On the other hand, this Christian was appreciated by a club professional in Cincinnati! Probably, the first tournament with "major" – or *maior* – status was inaugurated at the beginning of the Roman Empire, and would have been known as the "Augustus Masters"! After Nero's suicide, there was civil war in a year of four emperors – Galba, Otho, Vitellius and Vespasian. The year was AD 69 – which for some reason is about the only date my Classics friend Jeremy can remember! He has serious trouble with dates – both events in ancient history and outings with members of the opposite sex! As Jeremy himself puts it – they are "opposed to sex" with him! But it seems to me that the four generals vying to be Emperor could have determined the outcome by a match-play golf game. Their handicaps could have been determined by the number of legions they had under their command! Just think – they could have replaced all that red from bloodshed with green – actually, greens! I'm sure Vespasian would have appreciated a golf "triumph". He was probably very handy with a wedge – the military tactic, that is!

-       Stop being so silly, Denys! But tell Bob and Maggie about the "Thomas" you play with.

-       Sure, Manon. I just wanted to show how golf can be a "whole" lot of fun! Well, Thomas is a philosophy professor who, when he was just a little boy, met Antoine de Saint- Exupéry, and he claims that he was the inspiration for *Le Petit Prince*! My mother had given me that book when I was quite young, and I owe it to "The Little Prince" for any imagination I have. Being a Latin student would tend to limit wild dreams, since the Romans themselves had no imagination. But then again, if a boa and an elephant can be inside a hat, and a sheep inside a box, I guess a world of dreams can be inside a Latin book! I did come across a Latin translation of this novel. It's called *Regulus vel pueri soli sapiunt*, "The Little Prince, or only little boys can understand"! I think it would be great to introduce young students to well-known stories translated into Latin. It's wonderful that Nicole will be studying Latin when she starts high school next year! She could eventually read *Alicia in Terra Mirabili*, that is, *Alice in Wonderland!* There are so many other good books translated into Latin, like *Ferdinandus Taurus – Ferdinand the Bull, Insula Thesauria – Treasure Island, Pinoculus liber qui inscribitur – The Book called Pinocchio, Vestes Novae Imperatoris – The Emperor's New Clothes, Fabula de Petro Cuniculo – The Tale of Peter Rabbit, Winnie ille Pu – Winnie the Pooh, Maria Poppina ab A-Z – Mary Poppins A-Z.* If you are wondering if "supercalifragilisticexpialidocius" is a Latin word, it's not, but there are some Latin words within it! There are three Latin versions of *The Adventures of Robinson Crusoe,* and all those Charlie Brown books. There is *Carolini Brown Sapientia – The Wisdom of Charlie Brown.* Why didn't they translate "Brown" by *spadix,* meaning "chestnut brown"? Then there's *Linus de Vita - Linus on Life, Mundus Secundum Luciam – The World According to Lucy,* and *Philosophia Secundum Snoopy – Snoopy's Philosophy.* They could call the Charles Schulz *"Peanuts"* series *Nuges Ciceronis –* not "Cicero's nuts", Bob! But chick-peas - *ciceres* or *pisa* - peas. Adults could also profit from "modern literature" translated into Latin. Shakespeare's *Julius Caesar* has been translated into Latin, as well as Françoise Sagan's *Bonjour Tristesse – Tristitia Salve.* Latin translations exist for Louis Hémon's *Maria Chapdelaine* and Longfellow's poem *Hiawatha.*

- I didn't realize there were so many books available in Latin. Do you think there will be more, Denys?

- For sure, Manon. They have started translating some Astérix books, and will probably continue with the other books. They could do the *Alix* series in Latin, since his adventures take place in Ancient Rome and other places in the ancient world. It would be nice to see *Tintin* in Latin. I guess his name would be "Tintinus". Maybe we'll see Mickey Mouse and Donald Duck in Latin someday – they could be *Michael Musculus* and *Donaldus Anas. Cattus Petasatus* could have many adventures as Dr. Seuss' *Cat in the Hat!* And how about Superman as *Vir Omnipotens* or *Supervir,* but not *Homo Omnipotens* like *Homo Sapiens,* because that would suggest "super men and women". Sorry, ladies! Of course, we could have "Man of Steel" – *Vir Adamantis!* Who do you think *Vir Vespertilio* could be? Why, Batman of course! I think The Joker should be called "Dionysus". Just kidding – you see - I'm a natural fit! No, actually he'd be called *scurra,* a kind of buffoon!

- So, Menace, all those beautiful golf courses in L.A. started the golf craze! Apparently, then, all those years you've been studying Latin you have also been listening to music and collecting records! I quit college after the first year, and started working on the trucks, first as a helper, and then as a driver. It looks glamourous, but it can be tough, especially in the winter, and especially when you don't have an ambidexterous partner helping out.

- Bob, I said golf began in *Caledonia,* not California! Nice Latinate word, though – but I think you wanted to say "right-hand man"! The word you used literally means "having two right hands", and so designates someone equally skilfull with both hands, since *ambi* means "around, on both sides" – like a switch-hitter in baseball. That's why we have "ambiguous" – "going in both directions", based on Latin *agere* – "to move along" and "ambivalent" – "conflicting thoughts or feelings", based on Latin *valens* – "being healthy or energetic", as when you say you could go either way, Bob! Even the word "ambition", based on Latin *ire* –

"to go" - comes to us from the practice of Roman politicians "going around" to canvass votes! My Jesuit Latin teacher once told me that the two raised pulpits on either side of the interior of churches are called "ambos" from that same word *ambi.* The Romans used *dexter* to mean "right" and *sinister* to mean "left"! So, yes, Bob, you would appreciate the help of a dexterous person, but not that of an evil person – which is how the Romans looked upon "lefties"! Even golf maintained this viewpoint until recently. No coincidence that the first syllable of *sinister* is "sin"! And nobody likes being "left-out" or "left behind". You have to be really hungry to eat "left-overs"! So, I take it that on the road you were a "Solitary Man", as in Neil Diamond's song!

Yes, I have a huge record collection – but it's not a Guinness record! So, you were in college, Bob? I didn't know. Did you have a major? What was your favorite course?

-       All that double-talk leaves me of two minds to belt you, Menace! Your head is like a record, – there's a hole in the middle! And don't mention Guinness – they don't sell that beer here! Well, I took this course on Geek Mythology. Sorry, Menace, I guess it was Greek Mythology, but my Frat buddies called it Geek Mythology.

-       You were in a Fraternity, Bob? Which one?

-       It was called PBK.

-       You were in Pi Beta Kappa?

-       No, Menace, it was a three-man fraternity named after my best friend, Patrlck Benjamin Kramer - Pat, Bet you're Krappa!

-       I guess the Dean told you to hit the road – even if your name isn't Jack! He probably wasn't referring to trucks either! But you were right, Bob, I listened to my transistor radio all the time. After I had been caddying for Donnie Johnson at Indian Hills for a couple of years, he asked me to help out washing clubs a couple of nights a week - the nights I wasn't working at Pizza Pete's. What I enjoyed was listening to the radio blaring in the back shop where we washed the clubs. The other guys and I would guess the names of the songs. It was fun – but there was no $400 prize! I also got to be night watchman one night a week, when the Monday man, Bones McFarlane, broke his leg. We called him "Broken Bones" for a while! I would spend all night making mental notes about the new songs and who sang them. I was lucky to have the music to keep me awake – that and snacks in the clubhouse kitchen – since I had to make the rounds of the clubhouse and pro shop every hour! No cheating possible, because there were time-clocks I had to punch. A job I liked was weekend starter. I would work in the starter's shack on Saturday and Sunday mornings, and caddy for Donnie in the afternoon. During the summer I had to attend Sunday Mass at six am – I was the altar boy! For the last three years before I came to Montreal, I worked with the ground crew for a few weeks to help get the course ready before the season started. They were a great bunch of guys, but Max, who always made us laugh, had too much of a liquid lunch one day and drove a tractor into the ditch on the third hole. So we didn't have Max around any more to make us laugh! The superintendant "ditched" him! During my year at Xavier University before I left Cincinnati, Donnie hired me to help out during Saturday night parties. I was a busboy, but got to play songs on the juke-box. I loved teasing the barmaids and the waitresses! You'll be able to guess their names when I tell you some of the songs I played. There was "Barbara Ann" by The Beach Boys, "Diana" by Paul Anka, "Sheila" by Tommy Roe, "Donna" by Richie Valens, and "Peggy Sue" by Buddy Holly. Her name was only Peggy, but she still got mad! Because of my name, Holden, they used to call me "Golden Boy"! But one time, Sheila, the older barmaid, told me that my nickname had nothing to do with my real name!

- Well, Menace, with that backround maybe we do have a chance to win tonight. By the way, I've been to Montreal a few times to talk with the folks at the trucking company. It's on Wellington Street in Verdun - you probably know the area. It's near Victoria Bridge. Each time I drove by, there were well-dressed high school students hitch-hiking. I used to give them a ride and they told me they went to a Jesuit high school named Loyola. They made me think of you – clean-cut and polite. One of them said he caddied weekends at The Country Club of Montreal! There's a Jesuit school in Baltimore - Cristo Rey it's called. My cousin attended that school, and now he's a priest. Better get him to the altar, Manny, before it's too late! Otherwise, he'll have a job where he's at the altar every day!

- You keep getting funnier, Bob! I hope you had "Sweet Hitch-Hiker" by Creedence Clearwater Revival on your tape-deck to play for those Loyola boys! I see them around all the time on campus when I go out to teach at Concordia. They're usually staring at the Concordia girls, so maybe no priests there!

- Hey guys, the contest is about to start. With three DJ's it's going to be non-stop music!

- It will have to be, if they want to play all the songs they promised. Hey, the first song isn't in English or French! It's the Japanese song "Sukiyaki" by Kyu Sakamoto, but don't let the title fool you – it isn't about food at all! Obviously we won't be dancing to all of these songs.

-       That's right, Menace – otherwise we wouldn't have time to finish our drinks – and contests make me thirsty!

-       There is a French song playing now, Denys, that we can dance to. It's "Eso Beso", by that cute singer, Robert DeMontigny.

-       Actually, that song was recorded in English by Paul Anka, whom you would probably find even cuter! Yes, let's dance, since the bossa nova and the samba are mentioned in the song. The title of the song is actually Spanish, and it means "that kiss" – hint, hint!

-       We wrote down the name while you two were tripping the light fantastic. What's that song coming on now, Menace? It sounds familiar.

-       One of my all-time favorites, Bob. The title may sound strange since "duke" and "earl" are both terms of nobility. But Earl was actually the name of one of the singers who was in a group with Gene Chandler, who recorded the song, "Duke of Earl". Gene Chandler's real name was Eugene Dixon, but he took his name from the actor Jeff Chandler, the same guy who offered to donate one of his eyes to Sammy Davis, Jr., who had lost one eye in an accident, and thought he might lose the other eye. Then he would have joined that group of great blind singers like Stevie Wonder, Ray Charles, and Jose Feliciano. And there's Bobby Lewis, who sang "Tossin' and Turnin'". He's virtually blind. A great singer who is blind is Al Hibbler, who recorded "Unchained Melody", before it became a hit for The Righteous Brothers. I think Sammy Davis, a member of the Rat Pack, is a great entertainer. They played his song "Candy Man", which a female student of mine in Montreal would like! He had hassles from racists when he was dating white actresses, just like Maxine and I! He also played golf, but admitted he couldn't have had a worse handicap – he was a one-eyed black man who was Jewish! One little golf anecdote from my caddying days at Indian Hills – a golfer in our foursome hit a drive that struck the shoulder of a golfer in the next fairway. The fellow yelled at our golfer that he would sue him for ten thousand dollars. When our member protested that he had yelled "fore", the other golfer yelled back "fine - he would accept four thousand"!

-       I want to say too much information, Menace. While you were telling us all that they played two songs!

-       I heard them, Bob. Jerry Butler – the "Iceman" – sang "Never Give you Up", and that was followed by Andy Williams with "Can't Get Used to Losing You". Now Frank has put on "Bend Me, Shape Me" by The American Breed.

-      I know this one, everybody. It's "Hey Paula" by Paul and Paula. Only my version is "Hey Maggie"! And now it's Dionne Warwick with "Walk on By" and "Do You Know the Way to San Jose". I'm on a roll! Oh! Oh! Spoke too soon – now there's another French song.

-      I have this one, Bob. Guy Boucher and Ginette Sage are singing *Devant le Juke Box*". It could have been your theme song, Denys! It's funny – we hear some of the same songs every time we go dancing.

-      Right you are, Manon! But you can never get too much of such good music! Now let's dance to this song by *Les Classels*, "*Avant de me dire adieu*"!

-      You two were up there for another five songs! I wrote down Jerry Butler and Betty Everett singing "Let it Be Me". But I didn't get titles or singers for the other songs.

-      That's because we were in the "slow zone", right, Manon? As a truck driver, Bob, maybe you don't know that zone! But the songs were Skeeter Davis singing "The End of the World", and two songs by Sergio Mendes and Brazil '66 – "The Look of Love" and "The Fool on the Hill". There's another slow song for you and Maggie – "Turn Around, Look At Me" by The Vogues.

-      It's going to be difficult not dancing with you every weekend, when we move next August. My parents found a nice house in a quiet area of St. Lambert on Maple Street. In fact many of the streets have tree names.

-      Shouldn't they have only ONE name? Just teasing you, Manon! Actually, you'll discover that the whole town is pretty much a quiet area. Yes, I remember Oak Street and Birch Street, but I would have been very surprised if you had been moving to a "eucalyptus street"!

It's nice that Nicole will be able to walk to school, and that Michel and Antoine can take the metro together to UQAM. Since you'll be driving your father's car to work, you'll be taking the Champlain Bridge, which will bring you to the Decarie Autoroute and up to the Queen Mary exit, which is the street your office is located on. Unfortunately, you'll have to pay a toll on the bridge, but it's a simpler route to work than taking Victoria Bridge. Let's join Bob and Maggie on the dance floor for that song by The Intruders – "I'll Always Love My Mama". I know you and I say "Amen" to that! Another song will be starting soon. Here it is – The Ohio Express and "Yummy, Yummy, Yummy" – I can see Bob's tummy!

-      I heard that, Menace! Good thing our team needs you or else... what's this song?

-       That's my girl Dusty Springfield – I mean my singer, of course, Manon! This song is "Wishin' and Hopin'", which describes the way Bob is feeling about winning this contest! Before that we heard "Gimme Little Sign" by Brenton Wood. The Emperor Constantine would likely have played it before the Battle of The Milvian Bridge!

-       You two were lucky to find that bungalow on Gardenville Street in Longueuil, Maggie. In the picture it looks cute. You'll be able to eat and dance at a terrific place on the main strip called Taschereau Boulevard. It's Claude St Jean Restaurant – named for the owner. Jeremy and I ate there once. We actually walked there from his house. It's not as fancy as Le Deauville, but the food is just as good! Let's all dance to this song by The Occasions called "Girl Watcher".

-       With three DJ's the music is non-stop. While we all had a drink, they played six songs. Did you get some of them, Denys?

-       No, Manon. I got ALL of them! The Rascals started it off wth "A Beautiful Morning". After that there was "Everybody Loves a Clown" by Gary Lewis and The Playboys, followed by The Lemon Pipers and "Green Tambourine". The next record was Jan and Dean singing "Little Old Lady From Pasedana". Finally, there was Mason Williams on that guitar solo, "Classical Gas". Now that we're all rested we can hit the dance floor for a few songs. This one is going to be fun, Manon. It's "The Girl From Ipanema" by The Stan Goetz Orchestra, and that's Astrud Gilberto singing.

-       Those songs were all fun, Denys. Could you tell me the names. I know the French songs were "*Tu n'as pas de coeur*" by Pierre Lalonde – he's so handsome! And "*Ne me quitte pas*" by *Les Gendarmes* – I guess we'll be seeing a lot of "*gendarmes*" in Paris!

-       Not if you behave yourself, Manon! Although, after that remark about Pierre Lalonde, I'm not so sure! Well, after those songs we danced to Bobby Goldsboro singing "Honey" – kind of sad, since it's about his wife who died. The Reflections were next with "Just like Romeo and Juliet". That could be us, except for the dying part. Frank is trying to fool the contestants, because he played two songs in a row by the same artist. We heard Spanky & Our Gang sing "Sunday Will Never Be The Same" – maybe because of fewer people going to Church! - and "I'd Like To Get To Know You". That group is named after the "Our Gang" kids from old movies ! The leader of this group of waifs was Spanky, and other members included Alfalfa and Buckwheat. Sounds like a breakfast commercial! There was a member named Froggy, because he spoke as if he had a frog in his throat – but I'm not so sure a character with that name would be well-received in Quebec! But the contest is really just beginning. I guess some couples wanted to give everybody else a head start – they're just arriving at their tables now! Let's go and see what your sister and her beau are up to.

-	Okay, Menace. We sat down for the last song so that we could order you and Manny drinks. We owe you! They're in extra large glasses, and you can take your time, Mr. Music, writing down the songs and singers you might recognize. I haven't seen you miss one yet - if the names you have been giving us are all the right ones!

-	You and Maggie made a nice couple on the dance floor, Bob. Here are the songs you danced to. And don't worry - if I don't know the song title or the artist, I'll just leave it blank. But it hasn't happened yet. Besides, I have all the records Frank and Friends have played.

Say, that would be a good name for our DJ trio. I'll have to tell Frank! The first song you danced to was "Along Comes Mary" by The Association. Don't worry, Bob – I won't sacrifice the points by writing "Along Comes Manon" by "Our Association"! Next, you danced to Johnny Rivers singing "Memphis" and "Summer Rain" and then there was "Georgy Girl" by The Seekers, then another Gary Lewis and The Playboys song – "Count Me In". Could it be that Frank thinks you and I are a couple of ''playboys'', Bob? And Frank did it again – he played three songs in a row by the same group. We heard "Because", "Glad All Over" and "Bits and Pieces" – all by The Dave Clark Five! Trivia question, Bob, how many members are in that group?

-	Again, Menace, only because we need you! You said once something about the word trivia coming from Latin, but it seemed too trivial to take note of!

-	Either the drinks are starting to take effect, Bob, or you really are a witty guy. The word "trivia" indicates the crossing of three roads. People would naturally meet there and exchange news or gossip – often of the trivial kind! It reminds me of when Yogi Berra said "if you come to a fork in the road, take it!". Of course, he also said nobody goes to crowded restaurants because there are too many people in them!

-	Somebody ought to invent a trivia game for you with a category on music. That way you could pursue your passion without bothering innocent bystanders like me! What songs did they just play? And don't be too quick to call me a wit, Menace, because Maggie will say you're only half right! Or that you're nit-picking!

-	Which would make you a nit... you get the picture! I guess Maggie really is your "better half"! The last songs we heard were "The Rhythm of the Falling Rain" by The Cascades – interesting name for a song by a group whose name means waterfall, "One Fine Day" by The

Chiffons, "Suspicion" by Terry Stafford – I bet you some people wrote down Elvis for that song!, "Hello Dolly" by Louis Armstrong, and "You Keep Me Hanging On" by Vanilla Fudge – much slower than the version by The Supremes. And speaking of suspicion, I think we'll hear another song on that theme tonight. Next came "Green Grass", once again by Gary Lewis and The Playboys – Gary is Jerry's son! - and finally "*Tu te souviendras de moi*". Manon confirmed that it is sung by Marc Gélinas.

-        There will probably be some slow songs now, Bob. Let's dance and leave them some "couple time" to talk.

-        Thanks, Maggie. I guess our plans for Toronto and Cincinnati are all set, Manon. Talk about timing! Phoebe's wedding is the day after the ACL meetings finish, and the St. Xavier reunion is a few days before the Conference starts. We get to fly back to Montreal to catch the plane for our weekend in New York. Then it's back to Quebec for your farewell party at Veterans Affairs. When we get back from France you'll be heading off to your new home and your new job in Montreal. I'm reminded of two Pierre Lalonde songs we heard in my class at McGill – "*Revenez à Montréal*" and "*Quand Tu Reviendras à Montréal*" - and will you now be singing them "in the windmills of your mind", Manon? At least you'll still be in the same country! I say that, but with the way things are going, perhaps you will be in a different country! Perhaps "O Canada" will become "Oh Canada"! You know, we'll be able to have dinner downtown on Tuesdays next year when I teach at Concordia. I only have two courses at Laval next year, and none on Wednesday, so I can take a later bus back to Quebec on Tuesday nights. I'm going to have to spend a lot of time finishing off my dissertation for March. I'll be sending off my job applications after Christmas, since universities interview in April for July hirings. I won't be applying to Laval since Professor Marcoux has already told me there will only be a one-year replacement opening for Professor Saucier who will be on sabbatical. Besides, it might feel strange being on Faculty where I've been a student for four years. Keep this under your hat, but he told me he wants to hire a female professor in order to make sure Professor Giguère behaves herself!

-        I guess it will have to be *carpe diem*, Denys! I know Ma is happy that she and I will be spending a lot of time together. And my father is glad his boys will be with us. He doesn't really talk about you and me. When it comes to us, he pretty well plays his cards close to his chest.

-        When it comes to you, Manon, I think his cards are close to his heart! I've been writing down the song titles and singers of the songs Frank has been playing while we talked. I've got them right here. There was yet another medley by the same artist, this time Bobby Vee.

The songs were "Take Good Care of My Baby", "Run to Him", and "Devil or Angel" - just another version of that song. By the way, his family name is Velline – so it does start with "V" (pronounced "Vee"!)! You still tease me when I pronounce the last letter of the alphabet "Zee"! I may be out of America, but not all of the "American" is out of me! Then followed "Calcutta" by Lawrence Welk & Orchestra. I glanced at the dance floor to see how Bob was making out with that one! Next was "Surf City" by Jan and Dean, "Lady Madonna" by the Beatles, "It's My Party" by Leslie Gore, "Jumping Jack Flash" by the Rolling Stones, and "I Will Follow Him" by Little Peggy March.

-       I like this next song – "So Much in Love" by The Tymes. I hope they are singing about us! Shall we dance? Remember the first "time" we danced to it, Manon?

-       You guys were really into those slow songs – again! I guess you can name them for us, Menace. I know it started off with "Running Scared" by Roy Orbison. But then there was this piano song.

-       That was Ferrante and Teicher playing "Exodus". I saw the movie with Paul Newman. Don't ask, but that actor and I are strangely connected! Then there was Ray Charles and "I Can't Stop Loving You", "Stranger on the Shore" by Acker Bilk – I guess you recognized the clarinet, Bob! After that, we heard "McArthur Park" by Richard Harris. Two things I would never leave out in the rain – a cake and my Latin books! I prefer to have my cake and eat it! I'm also partial to lemon pie, Bob! The last two "slows" were "She Cried" by Jay and the Americans and "Don't Let the Sun Catch You Crying" by Gerry Marsden and The Pacemakers. I guess all those "tears" will be for those who don't win the contest!

-       I like this song, Denys – "Light My Fire" by Jose Feliciano. It's our turn to buy drinks for Bob and my sister. I wonder if there will be more French songs.

-       Definitely! Frank's got to keep the regulars happy. When the contests are over, we still have to like him. Hey, I almost thought they were about to play The Righteous Brothers, but it's the French version of "Unchained Melody" by *César et ses Romains!* The title is *"Mon seul amour"*. The drinks are here. Enjoy, guys! Manon and I are off to dance.

-       You were right, Denys. Frank played a bunch of French songs. Some really cool songs! *"Québécois"* by *La Révolution Française*, "Penny Lane" by *Les Sinners*, and *"Rendez-vous à Montréal"* by Marc Gélinas. Again, Manon, is Montreal calling me back?

-       Manon knew all the songs and singers of that last set – I'm so proud of her!

-       Well, someone has to carry the team, Menace! Thanks for the drinks, you two!

We can enjoy them as Menace writes down the next song titles and artists. Tell you what, Menace, if we win the contest tonight I'm going to call you by your real name!

- My English or French name, Bob?

- We'll flip a coin to decide who chooses. Heads I win, tails you lose! What songs have we been missing – they sounded pretty lively!

- There was "Pipeline" by The Chantrys, "Wipe Out" by The Surfaris, "Midnight in Moscow" by Kenny Ball and his Orchestra, "Grazing in the Grass"by Hugh Masekela and "The Stripper" by David Rose & Orchestra. And I'll bet you know the words to all those songs!

- Only the French versions, funny boy! But instrumentals are a good change of pace. I bet you were worried when I took off my jacket as they started playing that last song! But it's getting hot in here!

- When I was at St. Xavier High, we were never allowed to remove our jackets, no matter how hot it got! Something about the classroom not looking like a pool hall!

- They just played some really nice songs – "Where the Boys Are" by Connie Francis, "Puff the Magic Dragon" by Peter, Paul and Mary, and "Travelin'Man" by Ricky Nelson - that song could be my summer theme song! – and finally, speaking of a theme song for my summers, they played "Theme From a Summer Place" by Percy Faith and his Orchestra."Hey, Baby"...

- What did you call me, Menace?

- No, it's the song they're playing by Bruce Channel. You know what you wouldn't like to be transporting in your truck, Bob? Listen to this next song... "100 Pounds of Clay"! That's Gene McDaniels singing.

- You missed your calling, Menace. You were born to be a disc jockey!

- And you were born to be a gas jockey, Bob! No, just like you need gasoline for your passion, trucks, I need records for my passion, listening to music! I bet you thought I was going to say Latin. No Latin is my life! Oh, and Manon here means more than life to me!

- Are you really that romantic, Menace, or is it the drink talking?

- No, he really is that romantic, Bob! And I don't drink much, so you know it's true!

-	And you really are that sweet, Manon! They've played some other songs – "Wolverton Mountain" by Claude King, "Palisades Park" by Freddy Cannon, "Let Me In" by the Sensations, The Doors' version of "Light My Fire" and two songs by Tommy James and the Shondells – "Hanky Panky" and "I Think We're Alone Now". I wonder how many people here think that they were songs by two different groups? Some of the songs they are playing tonight, I haven't heard in a few years, but they are either in my record collection, or I heard them dozens of times on the radio when I worked at Indian Hills Golf Club, or I played them over and over on the juke-box at Pizza Pete's. Now they're playing "That Sunday, That Summer" by Nat King Cole – my mother loves him!

-	Maggie and I have to get back out on the dance floor. You sweet and romantic things can whisper sweet nothings in each other's ear until we come back to the table! But don't forget about the songs, Menace!

-	I get the feeling tonight that I'm the designated Tiro – you know – Cicero's secretary. Bob says that if we win tonight, I should aim for bigger things, like "The Price is Right"! Well, I came on down – from Cincinnati - er, make that UP, since I came north! – and I've won big – you! But Bob is a real card! You gotta like him!

-	My sister sure does, Denys! But what songs have they just played?

-	"Little Bit O'Soul" by The Music Explosion, "Groovin'" by The Young Rascals, "I'm a "Believer" by The Monkees, "Be My Baby" by The Ronettes, and "The Letter" by The Box Tops. That song always reminds me of my mother – something about letters! Bob and Maggie have been dancing for a while. The songs they started off with were "Mountain of Love" by Johnny Rivers, "For What It's Worth" by Buffalo Springfield, "Love Is Here and Now You're Gone" by The Supremes, "It Must Be Him" by Vikki Carr," Ruby Tuesday" by the Rolling Stones , and then a one-hit wonder – we'll hear a lot of those tonight – "Incense and Peppermints" by Strawberry Alarm Clock – I mean really! When we're in Toronto, you'll finally get to meet Jeremy. I think you'll like him – especially since he'll be on his best behavior! We'll only be in Toronto a few days – some people from Quebec would say that's a few too many! Yet quite a few Anglophones from Montreal have been moving to Toronto lately, and even further west to Alberta. I like Quebec – the language and the culture! I love Quebec City – it's so charming! But I have to admit that Montreal has more to offer in terms of diversity. I can go into different parts of the city and speak Italian or German or Spanish or Greek! Once Jeremy tried to impress a girl by telling her he spoke every language except Greek. Her name was Tatiana, and when she asked him to speak Russian, he said that Russian was "Greek" to him! I can go into Chinatown and speak…English or French! You love Chinese food! Remember that really young waitress we had once? I tried to tell her she's too young, but she understood we wanted egg foo yung! Jeremy will be giving us a tour of U. of T. and we'll get to visit the Royal Ontario Museum and the CN Tower. Thankfully, the hockey season will be over, and he won't be dragging us to Maple Leaf Gardens to watch the Maple Leafs. If it had been autumn, we could have gone to see a CFL football game. I like the team name – the Argonauts. Forty heroes on a quest – just like Jason and the Greek heroes in search of the Golden Fleece. But from what I hear of prices in Toronto, it isn't a ram that's getting "fleeced"! It's ironic, isn't it, Manon? You and your family will be living in the town next to Jeremy's hometown of Greenfield Park! Jeremy will be finishing his doctoral programme next year too, and so we will both be on the job market at the same time. Professor Watson, whom I meet with every Tuesday, says my dissertation is looking very good. But he was very candid in telling me that there would be no full-time openings at McGill in the foreseeable future. I can imagine him saying "This Department ain't big enough for the two of us!", since we both specialize in Roman religion! However, to my surprise, but genuine gratitude, he told me that I would be officially co-author of his new book that will soon be published called *Roman Religion: A Reference Guide of Primary and Secondary Sources*. Since I did most of the spade work for the primary sources, I imagine he decided to "call a spade a spade"! I guess you suspected that I would be applying to the University of Cincinnati and Xavier University in Cincinnati, but I'll be applying to other American universities – the University of Vermont is not far from Montreal. I will also be sending applications to universities across Canada, although Jeremy has told me that there is a two-year moratorium on hirings in Classics at the University of Toronto. Even though that is a Latin word, it doesn't paint a pretty picture!

There is no Classics Department at UQAM, and I don't know what the situation is at the Université de Montréal. I did visit them once, and remember meeting some very nice people.

\-   I prefer not to think of the possibility of being hundreds or thousands of miles away, Denys! At least we'll still be able to see each other on a regular basis this coming year.

\-   Like the song says, I'm not "A Thousand Miles Away". It was recorded by The Heartbeats, and Manon, you know my heart beats for you! Shep & The Limelights did another version of that song called "Daddy's Home", so you could have your own version called "Denys' Home"! Since we're talking about songs, I've jotted down the names of all the songs that played while we were having our conversation. Now I can write down the artists' names. They started off with another one-hit wonder –"A Lover's Concerto" by The Toys. I'm sure Fantastic Frank himself doesn't know all these songs, and that many of them were brought by the Montreal DJ's. The other songs were "Expressway to Your Heart" by The Soul Survivors, "Sweet Soul Music" by Arthur Conley, "Kind of a Drag" by The Buckinghams, "Indian

Reservation" by Paul Revere and the Raiders. Paul Revere was a legendary American hero, but those who confined Indians – or Native Americans as we now call them - to reservations, not so much! Then a double Beatles play – "Help" and "All You Need is Love", and Sam The Sham and The Pharaohs with "Wooly Bully". Did you see Bob dancing to that song? Ain't no shame in his "sham"!

- Hi, guys! We danced our legs off! We need a breather!

- Great moves, Bob, and I'm not talking about your move to Montreal! Did you deliberately choose to move on April 21? That's the date marking the founding of Rome in 753 B.C. So you've picked an auspicious date – that's a good thing, Bob! – to found your "new home"! Like the poetry, Bob, "Rome and home"? Not like calling your truck "chrome dome".

-        I recall a song called "Poetry in Motion" - by Johnny Tillotson, I think. So you'd better put your "poetry" in motion right now, Menace, or remember that song we just heard - "Bend Me, Shape Me" !

-        Yeah, it's our turn to "leg it" – but not far – just over to the dance floor! Besides, there's a beautiful slow song starting by Barbara Mason

-        "Yes, I'm Ready". Bob doesn't EVEN know how to dance… but he's ready, yes he's ready, to break my arm, to break my arm…

-        Are you actually singing the song, Menace? I thought I heard my name.

-        We'll be dancing for a while, Maggie, if for no other reason than for self-defense! Let's enjoy these next songs, Manon!

***

-        Did you miss me, Bob?

-        Like a hole in the head - or a hole in my den – Holden! They played a whole lot of songs while you guys were dancing. I got some titles, and the odd singer – maybe we can compare notes.

-        You used my real name, Bob. Does that mean you think we're going to win?

-        No, I said " the head", not "ahead"! And I didn't want to say "like a hole in my doughnut"! So what did you come up with?

-       My guys, The Four Tops, sang "I Can't Help Myself", then The Byrds with "Mr. Tambourine Man", and Herman's Hermits with "Mrs. Brown You've Got a Lovely Daughter". Of course when I sing it, it's Mrs. Plouffe! Another song with Peter "Herman" Noone and the Hermits followed – "Can't You Hear My Heart Beat". And I always add Manon to that question!

Someone once said that "Herman" looked like JFK. Maybe Ed Sullivan was thinking of President Kennedy's goal of putting a man on the moon when he referred to the group's singer, Peter Noone, as "Peter Herman Moon"! Of course, when the President was shot, I would have sung their song "There's a Kind of Hush"! Next came Gary Lewis again with "This Diamond Ring" – a song which has me thinking – but don't ask! Then there was the ever-so dramatic Mel Carter singing "Hold Me, Thrill Me, Kiss Me" – I know I had you at "HOLD me", Bob! They played "The Birds and the Bees" by Jewel Aikens, and "You Were on My Mind" by We Five. Again, Bob, how many… naw, forget it! Manon, when I woke up this morning, you were on my mind! Since you're on my mind every morning when I wake up, I hope "woke" never takes on another meaning – even though, society has to "wake up" to social injustice – just like the plea in the song "Easy To Be Hard" to fight evil and social injustice, which I think is our greatest evil, since it impacts the most people around the world! I remember Martin Luther King saying that if people adopt "an eye for an eye" system of justice, we will all be "blinded" to true justice! You two were still in deep conversation, so Manon and I kept dancing – especially since Frank played "Keep on Dancing" by The Gentrys! And we couldn't stop during a Supremes medley – even though they began with " Nothing but Heartaches"! The other two songs by those Queens of Motown – no, Bob, Aretha Franklin is the "Queen of Soul"! Just like my favorite Latin author, Seneca, should be the "King of Soul", since he has wtitten so much about the "soul"! – were "You Can't Hurry Love" and "My World is Empty Without You". We finished dancing to "Crimson and Clover" by Tommy James and The Shondells – yes, Bob, we heard him before, but not the same song! This is exactly what the DJ's want – for everybody to start second-guessing themselves! Did you see my moves on "Higher and Higher"? Almost as good as those of the singer, Jackie Wilson! As we came to sit down, they started playing "A Boy Named Sue" by Johnny Cash. Now we all have to get back up – it's "When a Man Loves a Woman" by Percy Sledge.

-       I'm glad we all stayed on the dance floor for those two Frank Sinatra songs, "All the Way" and "The Way You Look Tonight". Now they're playing "Shout" by the Isley Brothers. Interesting – because it's my shout! What are you having to drink, Bob? And you, Maggie? About this time Manon starts drinking Shirley Temples – even though she's cuter than Shirley Temple!

-        Denys, you're going to make me blush, and you always say you wish I could dance like Shirley Temple!

-        And that I could dance like Bojangles! Bob, your face is starting to turn a little red – are you blushing too? Oh no, that's the Bloody Mary!

-        Stop trying to "Colour My World", Menace, and tell us the names of the songs they've been playing!

-        Good plug for the group Chicago, Bob, but their hits like "Make Me Smile" and "Beginnings" came only at the "beginning" – did you catch that? – of the'70's – so we won't hear them tonight. And we won't hear "Tonight, Tonight" by The Mello Kings, because that's a '50's song! But the songs we did just hear were "In-AGodda-Da-Vida" by Iron Butterfly and "Paint it Black" by the Rolling Stones . Bob, I bet you thought you could hear them singing "In the Garden of Eden" on that first song! When we're in Paris, Manon we'll probably hear *"Noir C'est Noir"* by Johnny Hallyday. I know – that's not his real name. Like me, a lot of these singers don't use their real name! And his song is not the Stones song we just heard, but the song by Los Bravos, "Black is Black". Speaking of French songs, they played *"Je vais à Londres"* by Renée Martel, who I think is the prettiest girl in Quebec – after Manon and Maggie! They played *"Comme un Garçon"* by Chantal Renaud and *"Toi et Moi"* by *César et ses Romains*. I wonder if Caesar actually sang that song to Cleopatra? We heard two Claude Dubois songs – *"Femme de rêve"* and *"Besoin pour vivre"*. Ironic, isn't it, since I need dreams to live - and I live for one woman! I think it was a coincidence that the Eddie Floyd song "Knock on Wood" followed Claude Dubois – Frank isn't that clever! And he probably doesn't know that it was written in the Lorraine Motel where Martin Luther King was assassinated! Sad memories! The last song I heard was "Sweet Caroline" by Neil Diamond. I'm pretty sure Pierre Lalonde did a French version of that song. Now they're playing "Blue Moon" by The Marcels. I wonder if this is the beginning of a Doo Wop tribute from the early sixties. Doo Wop was more '50's I know, but some artists recorded into the '60's. And many are still performing – I think we'll be watching some of them on TV for another thirty or forty years! Imagine listening to Fred Parris or Jay Black when they're in their sixties! It seems that Frank - or his Montreal buddies – had decided to pay tribute to the Drifters. They just played three of their songs – "Save the Last Dance for Me" – did you hear, Manon? – "On Broadway" – that will be us in New York, Manon! – and "Under the Boardwalk".

Imagine being drunk and singing "On Boardwalk" and "Under the Broadway!" Oh, time for a slow dance, everybody! It's Louis Armstrong with "What a Wonderful World".

\-   You and Manny outlasted us again, Menace. But then you two are younger than we are! But even sitting here, I didn't recognize all those songs. We gave up after "96 Tears" by Question Mark and The Mysterians.

\-   Bob, you and Maggie are only three years older – hardly nursing home material!

They just played some classic songs. They were "Crying " by Roy Orbison, "Lonely Teenager" by Dion, , "Breaking Up is Hard to Do", by Neil Sedaka, and "I Got You Babe"by Cher and Sonny...

\-   That's Sonny and Cher, Menace!

\-   I know, Bob – I just wanted to see if you were paying attention! Well, the other songs were "I Got You (I Feel Good)" by James Brown, "You Really Got Me" by The Kinks, and "My Boyfriend's Back" by The Angels. It's amazing how all these songs are still so familiar to me! But then these songs don't go back further than fourteen years, and many of them are barely five years old. I still listen to songs even from the '50's . And of course, the current songs of the 1970's. I think Disco is really catching on. Frank just played one of my favorite bands – Creedence Clearwater Revival and their song "Down on the Corner". You know, Bob, their name comes partially from a beer commercial, but "clear water" couldn't have been the only ingredient in that beer! I know you liked that fun band, Cannibal & The Head hunters, singing "Land of 1,000 Dances! I like the next song they played by The Stone Poneys – "Different Drum". Their singer, Linda Ronstadt, was too good to be in a group, and is now a solo star.

\-   Sometimes I wished you played the drums, Menace, so I could tell you to beat it!

\-   Well you know I play the guitar, but don't think I'm always stringing you along!

While we were having this serious conversation, they played a few more songs – "I Fought the Law" by the Bobby Fuller Four – Bob, guess how many – no, forget that!, and my favorite country singer, Glen Campbell, and his song "Wichita Lineman". He's my favorite country singer because he's really a cross-over pop singer! After that came "Everybody's Talkin' " by Harry Nilsson.

\-   A slow song is starting, so that's the cue for Manon and I to get up and dance.

It's "You've Lost That Loving Feeling" by The Righteous Brothers. We'll see you guys after a few dances – or maybe more!

\-   Hey Menace, I saw how you "sealed the deal" with Manon while dancing to that song "Sealed with a Kiss" !

-        Just think, Bob, if Bryan Hyland had been with us at Marineland when you and I were there while stopping at Niagara Falls, he could have sung "Kissed with a Seal"! Good thing we stopped overnight, because the fish weren't the only creatures tanked! As we headed for supper, you said something about being on a sea-food diet, and then started gobbling down all the food you could see! I guess it was the drink talking, or in your case – singing – when you broke into a few bars of "Ol'Man River". Bob, no hard feelings, but I prefer the Paul Robeson version from the movie. Still, it brought a tear to my eye, thinking about the struggles of Afro-Americans throughout American history. But nobody could have accused you of being a "Show Boat" when you tried to hum the opening lines of "The Fishin' Hole". I don't think you realized that it was the theme song for The Andy Griffith Show on TV! I couldn't concentrate on the movie playing on TV – which happened to be *Ocean's Eleven*! – because you started bragging about the first car you owned – a Barracuda that you bought with money borrowed from a loan shark! I thought it was kind of fishy when you insisted that it was salmon-coloured! In our condition, watching the late feature – *Moby Dick* – was out of the question! At that point, I was starting to catch up in beers, and began singing "Green River" by Creedence Clearwater Revival - but I was no John Fogerty! I think I did a better job on Simon and Garfunkel's "Bridge Over Troubled Waters". Then, Bob, you started singing Mel Torme's "I'm Gonna Go Fishin'" and Bing Crosby's "Gone Fishin'". But I couldn't do the Louis Armstrong part to the song! Our room was quite small – the cheapest we could find! But all of a sudden you started complaining about being claustrophobic. I thought you were being sarcastic, since by then we had become a couple of "sardonic sardines"! I casually mentioned that we were really drinking up "marine humour".

You got mad, threatening to "throw me in the drink" until I explained that I wasn't insulting the U. S. Marines! We actually were having a whale of a time trying to play "Go fish" with your playing cards! But when you mumbled "hey, little guppy, why don't we sing 'aquarium' by the 'fifth dementia'", and I referred to Manon as "minnow", I realized that our duo of "Pike and Tuna Turner" was due to hit the sack. I'm sure glad it wasn't a water bed! But that's all water under the bridge, isn't it, Bob?

-        I'll drink to that, Menace! Since those aren't fins but dancing shoes you're wearing, you and Minnie – sorry, I mean Manny - can head back to the dance floor!

***

-        Maggie and I thought you were never coming back! You probably can't remember all the songs you just danced to, Menace.

439

-        Oh yes I can, Bob! My feet are dancing, my heart is beating – no, throbbing! - for Manon, and my mind is registering those songs! Here they are, and in order of course, since we have to record the song and singers beside the correct number. Notice my use of "record", Bob! One of those words that has two pronunciations depending on whether it's noun or a verb.

Do I hear a protest, Bob? Manon, methinks he doth protest too much!

-        I think I need a little wine, Maggie!

-        But you've already done a lot of "whining", Bob! Well, here are those songs – "Wouldn't It be Nice" by The Beach Boys, "Mustang Sally" by Wilson Pickett, "Sugar, Sugar", by The Archies, "Everybody Loves Somebody", by Dean Martin, and finally two Beatles songs – "Hey Jude" and "Something". I think I'll order another Budweiser! I always drink Buds in memory of Pizza Pete.

-        I know you only drink beer when we go dancing, Menace, but I usually mix drinks since Maggie is my designated driver. But I'm not particularly patriotic when it comes to drinking beer. I kind of like those Canadian beers – Molson and Labatt and O'Keefe. Didn't they just play another Brian Hyland song – "Itsy Bitsy Teeny Weeny Yellow Polka-Dot Bikini"? I know that song because I recently bought a two-piece bikini for Maggie!

-        I do drink wine at Le Deauville, or as I sometimes call it - "Le Showville"! And I am accustomed to drinking wine at the "civilized" receptions hosted by the Classics Department.

It's ironic that the wine-drinking Romans considered the beer-drinking Germanic tribes uncivilized, since modern-day German scholarship has revealed so much to us about the Romans and their civilization! But Bob, you didn't have to repeat yourself – Bikini – from Latin *bis* – already suggests "two" pieces! Just as "bilingual" means two languages and "bicultural" means two cultures. They are derived from Latin *lingua* and *cultus,* meaning "language" and "culture". Likewise, a "bilateral" agreement is made with the assent of both sides, since *latus* is Latin for "side". A bicycle has two wheels – not like those 8-wheelers that you drive, Bob! But for what it's worth, "cycle" is a Greek word – *kuklos*. Bi-weekly means every two weeks, while bi- monthly and bi-annually – well I think everyone gets the picture!

-        Why don't you boys "Bite" your tongues! Manon and I both know that the French named the bikini after the Bikini Atoll for the "atomic" explosion it caused in the fashion world!

-        Okay, I'll "bide" my time! Haven't you ladies noticed that dinner and dancing with Menace inevitably turns into a Latin lesson? So, Menace, you BUY us TWO drinks!

- Ladies, is it just me, or does Bob hope to be funny some day? Sure, big guy, the next drinks are on me – as long as you don't pour them on me! But while you and Maggie dance to the next songs, I have to talk to Manon about our summer plans. Since I will be spending plenty of weekends apart from you, Manon, two records that I'll be playing often are "Mr. Lonely" by Bobby Vinton and "Only the Lonely" by Roy Orbison. But to cheer you up – and I've been meaning to tell you this all night – I've made some arrangements for us while we are in Europe this summer. Notice I didn't specifically say France! You were wondering what we would do in France for three weeks after the six-week course finished. Wonder no more! After travelling in *Gallia* for a week, we will spend two days in *Gallia Belgica*, and then head for *Britannia*! We'll spend two weeks visiting the land of Oxford and Cambridge, as well as *Cambria*, *Caledonia*, and *Hibernia*.

- What are you saying, Denys? I think you were just talking about the Roman Empire.

- Manon, I've managed to save quite a bit of money from the teaching I have been doing for the last five years. I also have money from the Parker Grant that I don't spend. So I made plans for us to travel around France, and then to stop over in Belgium before going on to England, Wales, Scotland and Ireland. We return to Paris for the flight home, since my grant covers my ticket from Paris to Montreal. We'll be home in time for you to catch your breath before you move to St. Lambert and take up your new position with Veterans Affairs in Montreal. And isn't it wonderful that you are getting a promotion! You'll be able to purchase that car you want sooner than later!

- Well, you sure put a smile on Manny's face, Menace! What did you put in her drink? Put some in mine! Better still – tell me you wrote down all the titles of the songs they just played!

- And I did it without the song "Smile", which was written by Charlie Chaplin. The "Little Tramp" was quite talented, since he also wrote "This Is My Song", which Petula Clark recorded in French and English – as she does with many of her songs! Being bilingual doesn't hurt her popularity in Quebec! And did you guys know that her first name is actually Sally? Well, after all, she did "sally forth" from England to France! But never fear – Alan Freed is here!

Remember that disc jockey who got rock and roll going, Bob? Maggie, I told Manon about the summer travel arrangements. Now you have one very happy sister! And for you, Bob, songs and singers! Say, it sounds like I'm introducing Homeric bards! A Greek singer of tales was rumored to have tried to enter Troy to sing for King Priam, but he was "barred"! I won't even ask if you got that, Bob, because I'm writing down the song Frank is playing. It's *"C'est toujours comme ça la première fois*" by Pierre Lalonde. I didn't know how useful being bilingual in Quebec was before my friend Jeremy told me his cousin got a summer job as a lifeguard without knowing how to swim, but had written bilingual on his application form! Of course, Jeremy sometimes exaggerated. The previous songs were - and there were quite a few of them - "Twenty-five Miles" by Edwin Starr – that's almost two marathons! - "Satisfaction" by the Rolling Stones, "Purple Haze" by Jimi Hendrix, "Teen Angel" by Mark Dinning, "Running Bear" by Johnny Preston, "Cathy's Clown" by The Everly Brothers, "Rescue Me" by Fontella Bass, and then the beautiful "Stand By Me" by Ben E. King. I remember one night when Pizza Pete was with us at the bar next door to his place. As usual, the always obnoxious Stanley Huber was bothering us. This time he was drunk, and dared Pete to put the next song that played on the juke-box into a sentence. It was "Stand By Me". And Pete's sentence: "Stan, buy me a beer, will ya"! Pete got a beer out of it! The next song was "Good Vibrations" by the Beach Boys. When I heard that Brian Wilson's mother had told him that dogs bark in response to "bad vibrations", I made sure my dog Vergil Cane always heard "good vibrations"! In a sense, Vergil Cane didn't "'live a dog's life", because my family treated him so well. But doggone it, he was a source of inspiration for me to maintain a "dogged determination" in this "dog-eat-dog world"! And that expression is unfair to dogs, since only savage – I would say "uncivilized" dogs - would attack their own species! It is the tragic nature of man, however, to do just that! Jeremy brought me to watch a disturbing Italian documentary film called *Mondo Cane* – meaning "A Dog's World". When I saw the title of the film for the American audiences, it left me flabbergasted, since it would have made a good title for my doctoral dissertation on Roman Religion! It was *Tales of the Bizarre: Rites, Rituals, and Superstitions*"! Two songs by the Beatles were next – "I Want To Hold Your Hand" and "She Loves You"- we could have had a contest just for songs by the Beatles! After those songs, we heard "You Really Got Me" by The Kinks, "Wild One" by Bobby Rydell – the name he chose for himself would make a great name for a high school! – "What in the World's Come Over You" by Jack Scott, "Tell Laura I Love Her" by Ray Peterson, "El Paso" by Marty Robbins, and finally a double by King Elvis – "Suspicious Minds" and "It's Now or Never". Remember earlier tonight when we heard a song about suspicion – well this one really is by Elvis Presley. I just realized that we are saving a few bucks tonight because we can't buy Frank drinks like we usually do – that would be considered bribery!

-       Is it bribery when we buy you drinks, Menace, if it helps us to win? They're playing a slow song now, so as part of our bribe, we'll let you and Manon do us proud on the dance floor, as we get the drinks in. But if they continue with slow songs, Maggie and I will be joining you! "I'm Sorry" – that's not an apology, Menace – it's the song by Brenda Lee!

- 	Well , Denys, Frank really slowed things down there. He's never played so many slow songs in a row!

- 	Unless he had some single friends he was trying to match! He played "At Last" by Etta James, "Let It be Me" by The Everly Brothers, and "Greenfields" by The Brothers Four.

They weren't blood brothers like the Everly Brothers, Bob, but frat brothers. Legitimate ones – not like you and your buddies during your one year at college! Then there was "Will You Love Me Tomorrow" by The Shirelles - that's with Shirley Alston, hence the name! There followed "Why" by Frankie Avalon, "You're the One" by The Vogues, and the Chairman of the Board with "My Way". That song is actually sung to the music composed for the French song "*Comme d'habitude*", but the English lyrics were composed by Paul Anka! Naturally, Frank Sinatra sang it "his way"!

- 	You know, Menace, you remind me of Frank Sinatra.

- 	Because I can sing and dance and even act?

- 	Hell no – because you both have blue eyes! If you weren't in love before those songs, you sure were when you finished dancing! I'll go get drinks from the bar for everybody – the waiters look really busy. Don't miss any songs, Menace!

- 	"Walk, Don't Run"

- 	I'm not running, Menace. I'm not even dancing! And you can't call me a "running bear" - that song was played all ready!

- 	No, Bob, they're playing the song by The Ventures – maybe later we'll hear "Walk Don't Run '64". Thanks for the drinks, Bob! I've never danced so much – this is the first time we ever started dancing at seven o'clock! Compared to this, that dance contest was a piece of cake!

- 	Don't mention food, Menace, I'm getting hungry – and we can't go for a midnight snack, the contest won't be over!

- 	And they haven't played "In the Midnight Hour" by Wilson Pickett, or "The Midnight Special" by Johnny Rivers! You won't hear "Midnight at the Oasis" by Maria Muldaur because that's a '70's song. They just played "Being With You" by my man Smokey Robinson and The Miracles and "Everybody's Somebody's Fool" by Connie Francis. Get ready for "chapter and verse", Bob! You've heard of "made-for-TV movies". Well, The Monkees were a "made-for-TV Band" with Davey Jones – he was once on that television show I watch called "Coronation

Street", as was Peter Noone of Herman's Hermits! The other "Monkees" were Mickey Dolenz, Peter Tork, and Mike Neysmith.They played two songs by them – "Day Dream Believer" and "Last Train to Clarksville". Then they played "Go Now" by The Moody Blues, "Time of the Season" by The Zombies, and "Touch Me" by The Doors, with of course Jim Morrison! I have to hand in our answer sheets to Fantastic Frank so that they can start tabulating the points each team has earned so far. But I know for a fact that we have the maximum number of points up to now, since they haven't played a single song that I didn't know. It's funny how they say if you remember the sixties you weren't there. It would be a tragedy if you missed out on all those great songs! They were my high school and university undergraduate years. I was a Latin student then, and I'm a Latin student now! But you don't have to be a musicologist to remember song titles, or even the artists that recorded those songs. Most of those songs I listened to at home.

Some I saw on "American Bandstand", and others were on the juke-box at Pizza Pete's. It's a question of interest, not memory. I could recall Latin vocabulary at St. Xavier High, but I couldn't retain formulas in chemistry or periodic tables.

- That makes sense, Denys. People are surprised that I can produce shorthand so quickly, but I was determined to master those symbols, and I succeeded. I don't know too many American song titles, but I know the French songs they just played. They were "*A t'aimer*" by Michel Pagliaro, "*Alléluia*" and "*Le Jour du Dernier Jour*" by Donald Lautrec. That's the French version of "A Whiter Shade of Pale" – that song by Procol Harum that you're always playing! - and "Oh! Lady Mary" by Jean Nichol. They also played his song "*Sans Toi*" – a situation, I never want to be in! Before you say anything, Denys, no that's not his real name! But then they played some songs in English – did you get them?

- Thanks for the French titles, Manon! – and that romantic sentiment! Yes, I have the English song titles. There was "These Eyes" by The Guess Who, and then "Put a Little Love in Your Heart" by Jackie De Shannon, "More Today Than Yesterday" – I love you more today than yesterday – sorry I was singing out loud to Manon. That song is by The Spiral Staircase. That group will probably have its ups and downs! Then we heard The Grass Roots with "I'd Wait a Million Years", "Lay, Lady, Lay" by Bob Dylan – he mentions a big brass bed, unfortunately, because I can see Bob getting a little sleepy! Dennis Yost and The Classics IV sang "Traces" – which would make a good theme song for classical archaeology! I mean I could dig it!

- Are those jokes meant to keep me awake, Menace? Maybe a trip to the dance floor will help. C'mon Maggie!

-	That first song by Blood, Sweat and Tears, "Spinning Wheel", must have helped to wake up! The second one as well – "You've Made Me So Very Happy". The Ventures playing "Hawaii Five-O" must have gotten his adrenalin going! Next they played "Smile a Little Smile for Me" by The Flying Machine and "Galveston" by Glen Campell. I guess they'll sit down after this slow dance – "Worst That Could Happen" by The Brooklyn Bridge. Before Bob gets here, Manon, I just want to mention that the lead singer is Johnny Maestro. Maybe when Crest toothpaste came out he had to smile too much with his old group, The Crests!

-	I know you got all those song titles, Menace, so as a reward , Maggie and I are vacating the dance floor to give you and Manon a little more room! There aren't too many songs left. I'm getting nervous!

-	You're back! What song titles are in your head, Menace? We'll write them down.

-	Bob, Frank just played "Frank's Feature Four" – four songs by the same group. So many points on the line because for this special occasion contestants have to name the lead singer in the group in order to be awarded the points for those songs. This medley will definitely be a game-changer! But guess what - not only do I know that the group is Three Dog Night and the lead singer is Chuck Negron, I was able to identify all four songs. They were "Easy To Be Hard" - you know that song about social injustice that I talked about – followed by "One", "Joy To The World", and "An Old Fashioned Love Song". The group had some other hits like "Celebrate", "Eli's Coming", and "Never Been To Spain", but different band members sang lead on those songs. That's why they were "Three" Dog Night, Bob! Besides, I HAVE been to Spain! The other songs they played while Manon and I were dancing were "Gimme Gimme Good Lovin' " by Crazy Elephant, "People Got to be Free" by The Rascals, "Words of Love" by The Mamas and The Papas, "Laughing" by The Guess Who - notice how they are really mixing them up as we approach the end of the contest. Then there was "Eve of Destruction" by Barry McGuire and "Cry Like a Baby" by The Box Tops. That's what I'm afraid Bob will do if we don't win!

-	I'm a good loser, Menace – I've had lots of practice! I have to admit, though, win or tie, it's been fun! I'm just joking, Maggie! Seriously, this is probably the last time the four of us will get together here in Quebec City. But when Menace here comes to visit Manny in Montreal, or, I should say, on the South Shore of Montreal, we can all go out to eat, drink, and be merry – that is, go dancing!

-	Very Epicurean of you, Bob! That makes a good contrast to the Stoic attitude I'll have to maintain while Manon and I are apart. But I've had some practice the last few summers while

I have been taking those courses in Europe. By the way, here are the songs they just finished playing. First, there was "Five O'Clock World" by The Vogues, then "Born Free" by pianist Roger Williams, Stevie Wonder singing "My *Chérie Amour*", "Grazing inThe Grass" by The Friends of Distinction, and "Sunshine of Your Love" by Cream. Then Frank and Company played another "foursome" - all by The Duprees, who actually were a group of four! The songs were "Have you Heard", "My Own True Love", "Why Don't You Believe Me", and "You Belong To Me". Right after that, we heard Frankie Valli and The Four Seasons singing "Working My Way Back To You". Frank must be afraid of a tie because he is awarding ten bonus points to the team that identifies what the last two groups have in common – besides having four members, Bob!

The answer is – wait for it, gang! – both groups come from New Jersey. Imagine making a movie about one of the groups and calling it "Jersey Boys"! I wonder if we could get more points if I wrote down that the name "The Four Seasons" didn't come from a hotel, but from a bowling alley!

-       Look, Denys, Frank is indicating that there are two songs left. If he follows his usual practice, they will all be slows. So let's dance, everybody!

-       You called it, Manon. Two final songs with you in my arms. Those beautiful songs were "Somewhere My Love" by The Ray Coniff Singers, and "The Impossible Dream" by Jack Jones. I'll hand in our final list. Then we'll know who won .

***

Frank and his DJ pals are coming over to our table. We won, Bob!

-       No dream is impossible with you, Den! My share was the easiest hundred dollars I ever made! Well, except for the arm-wrestling contest I won that was organized by a gang of truckers. Let's say, they didn't have to "twist my arm" to get me to participate. I didn't have the "finger of fate" helping me - I won fair and square!

-       Wow, Bob, the win has you "elbowing" me out of top word play man! Got to HAND it to you!

-       So, Holden, what are you going to do with all your vinyl records, now that cassettes are popular, and technology will probably produce even more sophisticated devices for listening to music, making your records obsolete?

-	Bob, vinyls will eventually make a comeback – people will want to enjoy the precious past! For the same reason, we will also witness a renewed popularity in Latin studies. What's more, I intend on being an instrument in that movement!

-	Well, different strokes for different folks, but good on you for keeping the faith!

-	And hope and love, Bob!

Chapter 109

- Your presentation on that reading method of learning Latin was extremely interesting and informative, Hold On! If I'm teaching Latin in two years – and I hope I'll be teaching – I would seriously consider using *Lingua Romanorum*. I'd love to teach in Montreal, but my dissertation director has told me that McGill is unlikely to be hiring, so that leaves Concordia. But you've been teaching there for a few years, so they will most likely hire you, if they have an opening. I was following the story of one of the main characters in your Latin book, not the one who becomes a teacher, but the young man who has left his native Tarentum to go north to Rome to study. He somehow becomes a chariot racer, turning aside a military command, and ends up in *Hispania*, where he meets Seneca – I guess you're jealous of that character! His name is Dionysius – probably because he was born in *Magna Graecia*, right? The philosopher is impressed with this academic/athlete, and brings him back to Rome in his entourage. Seneca and Dionysius discuss the works of Caesar, Livy, Vergil, Horace, and Catullus – and the texts are in the later volumes of *Lingua Romanorum* to prove it! Eventually, Seneca sends his young protégé to study and report on religious practices in different parts of the Empire – first to Pompeii, and then further afield to *Gallia, Germania, Graecia,* and *Britannia.* In Greece, Dionysius meets St. Paul, and becomes a Christian – a very fervent one. This doesn't prevent him from producing a thorough account of the pagan religious practices he finds. He also reports to Seneca on the religious practices in Rome and throughout Italy. Seneca shares with Dionysius the texts of his essays and some of his letters to Lucilius, as well as excerpts from the writings of his nephew Lucan and of Petronius – yes, those texts are in the last of the three volumes of this Latin manual. Don't you see, Hold On, this is your story! What are the odds? Of course there is a love story in this narrative. Dionysius falls in love with a dark-skinned noble woman in Hispania – probably of Carthaginian descent! However, her father marries her off to someone in the Spanish aristocracy. He has to fight off the advances of women married to Roman senators, but it is in Gaul that he finds his true love - a Christian woman! This story couldn't have been more about you if the character's name had been Holden Hainsworth! I'm a little put out that I'm not in the story!

- Gosh, Jeremy, I hadn't seen that connection, other than the fact that like me, my namesake was a keen student of the Latin language and of Roman religion. In this case, then, "fiction is stranger than fact"! Seneca's "agent" would have appreciated the Johnny Rivers song "Secret Agent Man"! With that name – maybe being called *Fluvii* – you know "rivers"! - the singer could have serenaded lovers by the Tiber or along the Nile! Do you remember that French-Canadian student in Classics who said that Mark Antony refused to believe that young

Octavian would defeat Egypt because Antony was in "de Nile"? Thanks, by the way, for taking us to the Royal Ontario Museum. Manon has really enjoyed meeting you, and says you are a lot nicer than I had described you! What happened to "the truth will set you free"? She's getting ready for our bus ride to Cincinnati. She's been there before, but not for a high school reunion or a wedding! And attending a second conference – this time the American Classical League annual meeting – is a real test of stamina for a non-classicist! I'm glad we weren't in Cincinnati last year when those devastating tornadoes hit the city and neighbouring county. The city of Xenia was almost wiped out, and there were over thirty deaths reported!

There had been serious tornadoes in that area as well back in 1969, but all the attention in *The Cincinnati Enquirer* went to the Sharon Tate murder. No, I'm glad the only "twister" Manon will witness is yours truly on the dance floor when they play Chubby Checker records! I seem to recall a certain Classics student who was going to take the Toronto social scene by storm, referring to himself as the "Toronto Tornado"! When you invited me to take up studies at the University of Toronto, you had suggested that I could be "Hurricane Holden"! Somehow I think the only "big wind" in the Queen City was a certain Jeremy Bain! By the way, shouldn't Regina be called the "Queen City", since that is the Latin word for "queen"! I'm sure you'll get a teaching job. In fact, with Master's degrees, we could teach at a Cegep. It's one of the reforms Quebec introduced in the field of education. The word stands for *Collège d'enseignement générale et professionelle*, and is a compulsory two-year programme for students going on to university, or, for students not going on to university, a three-year professional training programme. You won't see this in Toronto – this college instruction is unique to Quebec. Even American junior colleges aren't really equivalent. The Cegeps are just opening up, so everyone is anxious to see how they will work out.

- I'm glad you finally met a real keeper, Hold On! She's nice too, and really smart – which makes me wonder what she sees in you! Just kidding, pal – there are worse things she could do than hang around with a Latin student! And she's going to be living in St. Lambert! You know I really do admire you! I bet you were the quintessential all-American boy growing up. I'm talking about all those television shows where the people who knew you could recognize Holden Hainsworth in those wholesome characters. Like you would be Ricky Nelson in "Ozzie and Harriet" – especially since you can sing and play the guitar! You would be Johnny Crawford, who played The Rifleman's son, and Rusty on the "Rin Tin Tin" show - again, especially since you had a dog. Likewise, you could have been Timmy on the "Lassie" show. You'd have been son Bud – no reference to the beer you used to drink! - in "Father Knows Best". And I can see you becoming Jim Anderson, the "perfect" father some day. You'd be Wally to little brother Theodore Cleaver on the "Leave it to Beaver" show. Say, I could have been that wise-guy weasel, Eddie Haskell, who was Wally's buddy! After all, the beaver is Canada's national animal!

I guess Canadians are meant to be hard-working! Dam(n)! You get my pun, Hold On? You could have been Jeff Stone, the son on "The Donna Reed" show. I'm not talking about that guy you told me about, Jeff the Stoner, who worked at Pizza Pete's! As a little kid, I'm sure you "were" Opie, Sherrif Andy Taylor's son on The Andy Griffith Show. Don't you dare say I would have made a good Barney Fife! Well Opie grew up, as did the actor. So you would eventually be Richie Cunningham on that new show, "Happy Days". Have you seen it? Not "Have you Seen Her" by The Chi-Lites – I know music is always on your mind! Of course if you had borrowed your priest's motorcycle, you could be the Fonz. Because, you really are a cool guy! And I remember you telling me that you sometimes had to bang on the jukebox with your fist to get the music playing at Pizza Pete's! Kind of weird, don't you think, that the theme song for The Donna Reed Show was "Happy Days"? Could I have been on T.V.? Sure! I would have been "Howdy Doody" – obviously, not the American original with Buffalo Bob, but the Canadian version with Timber Tom. Maybe - "reaching new heights"! - I could have been "The Friendly Giant"! – he wasn't really that tall! All this reminiscence about T.V. shows makes me wonder if I won't end up being a Johnny Jellybean replica! But Ted Zeigler had a PhD, and the segment on his show, "Lunchtime Little Theater", was very entertaining! He was an American, from Chicago, I think – again, not the music group! Enjoy your stay in Cincinnati, and I envy you two – nine weeks in Europe! You have always been able to "seize the right moment", and now you've managed to "seize the right girl"! I always knew your "Miss Right" would never be "Miss Behaving"! Whereas I'll probably have to settle for "Miss Take"! And, of course, Hold On, you have maintained your "hold on" Latin!

-      You forgot to mention "Miss Informed" and "Miss Construed"! No, you are going to be lucky in love some day, Jeremy, and I think, in your own way, you were trying to compliment me. Actually, you're "spot on", as they say in England! I wouldn't have been a good hippie, since although I "tuned in" and "turned on" to Latin, I would never dream of "dropping out" of my Latin studies – and not only because I'm too busy "dreaming" of other things! I believe in society, and working towards social justice, but I have always "done my own thing". In that sense, I am a bit of a lone wolf. I guess, thinking about the she-wolf that saved Romulus and Remus, and thereby making it possible for the Latin language to come into being, the "lupine"connection - I'm tempted to say "wolverine"- makes sense! Manon and I are off to that restaurant you suggested. I'll try not to "wolf down" my food!

Chapter 110

\-   That was a busy ten days, Denys – but well worth it for you, I'm sure. Didn't Phoebe look beautiful in her wedding dress! It was such a lovely ceremony at St. Joseph's Church, and the priest – wasn't his name Father Brendan? – was very amusing – in a spiritual kind of way! He even teased the groom by playing the song "Wedding Bell Blues", which you said is sung by Marilyn McCoo and Billy Davis, who are actually a married couple.

\-   Yes, but Danny took the friendly ribbing with good humour. If truth be told, I've always found Feeb to be a beautiful girl, but I had never got around to telling her before her wedding day. It seems like yesterday that I used to tease her about me having two pets – Vergil Cane and her – my "pet peeve"! Did you notice my parents crying? I told my Dad the last time I saw him with tears in his eyes was when I beat him on every hole in a golf match! I'm glad he and I got to play a few times during our stay in Cincy, Manon, including once with my old boss, who is still the Club Pro at Indian Hills. Strange, I still knew what club he was going to hit on almost every shot! My Dad's scores were very close to mine. He's improved, and I'm a little rusty! And you're right – Father Brendan isn't your run of the mill priest! I always enjoyed serving Mass for him. I was glad to see some of the Jesuit priests at the reunion. I finally got to officially call Mr. James "Father James". It was kind of sad that Father McNeil had passed away – he had always been my favorite teacher. And it's thanks to him that I am still doing daily spiritual readings. Whenever you refer to me as your "Latin Superstar", I think of him, since he was always saying I was a "brilliant" Latin student - but not in a "starry" way! Father McNeil taught us that the study of Latin could teach us a lot – even about life, but that the best way to learn about life was to live it. *Experientia docet* he kept reminding us! He always added that he hoped our experience would lead us to embrace life. I'll never forget his devotion to "his boys". When I called him "Father", I sometimes thought that in the classroom, he was like a real "father" to me! He sure took his duty of "*in loco parentis*" seriously – the ideal surrogate parent! His sense of humour was uplifting – laughter can really become the "best medicine"! He even made Tommy Nelson laugh. Whenever Tommy asked him if he had a chance to pass a Latin test, Father McNeil would tell him it depended on the weather. As Tommy would turn to look out the window, Father would add "whether you studied or not"! Everyone was very nice to you, Manon, and you didn't seem to mind when they all kept referring to me as "The Latin Student".

It is surprising though that no one else from my year went on to study Classics. Father McNeil had said few would be called to a "life of Latin", but that we are all called *ad vitam aeternam* -

to eternal life! But the two classmates that became lawyers admit to using Latin almost daily. And Harris says he sells quite a few books on Roman and Greek history and culture at his bookstore.

We bowed our heads for a moment in tribute to Tommy Nelson – my best friend at St. Xavier – who was killed in Vietnam. It brought back to mind what Father McNeil said to our Latin class. Being Catholics doesn't make us the "sole" survivors of an eternal death, but all human beings are "soul survivors"! Some of the guys were surprised that I didn't continue playing football, but were genuinely pleased that I was able to continue my studies to the doctoral level.

They felt I was the ideal person to represent America outside the country. Most of my former classmates are doing well, and many of them are in corporate affairs. It sounded strange to my American ear when *Monsieur* Dubois, informing me that his wife was visiting friends in France, said his wife was now abroad! I know you had a nice time talking to *Monsieur* Dubois. He told me he hadn't spoken so much French since he left Montreal.

- Your presentation was well received at the conference, as it was in Toronto. But they asked even more questions this time. Wasn't it nice that your mother got to attend?

- It was, Manon. And while I was attending the sessions on Roman religion and Latin poetry, you had a chance to take my mother for coffee, and catch her up to speed on all that's been happening with you – moving to Montreal and a new position at work. She must have been overwhelmed on hearing of all our plans for travelling this summer. I assume you gave her all the details about the weekend in New York, which starts when we land in Montreal and then hop on the plane and head out to The Big Apple! Did you tell her I graciously accepted the option of attending a Broadway play instead of a Yankees game? I know we have scheduled in time to see two blockbuster disaster films - "Earthquake" and "Towering Inferno" – but we could have saved some time if Hollywood had combined those two stories into one film, and, I don't know, maybe called it "Shake and Bake"! But I guess producers are happy when their films are not "disasters" at the box-office! For me the worst disasters have been the plane crashes that have killed so many great singers like Buddy Holly, Ritchie Vallens, the Big Bopper, Jim Croce, country singer Jim Reeves, Otis Redding and his band The Bar Kays – and many others!

Sadly, I think there will be more! I sure hope no terrible tragedy – worse than what was shown in other disaster films we've seen – ever hits America! Could you imagine a catastrophe involving the Twin Towers at the World Trade Center in New York? I confess that I have this awful feeling – something like a terrible premonition – when I hear that Buddy Guy song "Hold That Plane"! I think my mother - and my Dad - have resigned themselves to the fact that I will probably never be able to call Cincinnati home again. At this point I don't know where home will be two years from now, but I do hope, Manon, that you will be close by! But soon "home" for us will be in Paris and then in other wonderful places for nine glorious weeks! Our residence while at the Sorbonne will be a short walk to the campus. I'll have three classes a day from 9 A.M. to 1 P.M. Your film class goes from 10 A.M. to 1 P.M., but that includes watching two whole films!

After lunch, I'll have to spend the afternoon preparing my classes, but I will be free to visit the "City of Lights" with you in the evening. Some days we'll want to switch the routine to afternoon relaxing and evening study. And of course we'll have the weekends. I'm anxious to see what the dancing is like in Paris!

Chapter 111

- I'm so glad we are in the programme at Paris IV – Sorbonne, Manon. There's a certain pride in studying at an institution that's been around since the Middle Ages! But Paris - the "City of Lights"- has thirteen universities! It could just as easily be called the "City of Enlightenment" – the "City that lights up your mind" - not just your evening! Fortunately we'll be here for six weeks - there's so much to see! The accommodations are great at our international students residence, and the cost is quite reasonable – the administrators at the Parker Foundation will be pleased. We'll be able to try the different *cafés* for breakfast – there are so many of them. I enjoy having lunch at *Café de Flore* and here at *Les Deux Magots* – even though neither of us are ugly like the name suggests! Don't you feel kind of Bohemian knowing that many of the French intellectuals used to exchange ideas here, people like Jean-Paul Sartre, Simone de Beauvoir, Marcel Proust, and André Gide?

- Well, I'm not a classics scholar like you, Denys, but I can imagine the *"artistes"* from the world of film like Yves Montand, Jean-Paul Belmondo, Catherine Deneuve, and so many others, chatting at these tables – on the same terrace - as well as painters like Picasso, Salvador Dali, Renoir, and Paul Cézanne.

- "Scholar" is an exaggeration, Manon! It's true you do some painting – you like still life. You're always saying you could never paint me because I'm never still long enough!

You've discovered that my major fault is impatience – my priest friends would call it a sin! Being together for nine weeks will help us really get to know each other! I'm at "spiritual peace" making love to you. I believe God wants us to be happy – even here on earth. In fact, I feel that God wants us to be pure, that is, "pure of heart". That's my favorite Beatitude – "Blessed are the pure of heart"! The purest of hearts is Jesus – that's why we pray to the "Sacred Heart of Jesus".

My Mom used to listen to a song on the radio that was called "Dear Hearts and Gentle People". Many artists have recorded it, but I like the Dinah Shore version. It's partly because she loves golf – she even has her own tournament for lady professionels! So life is about being nice to everybody – and teaching Latin – yes, I admit – not to everybody! As a "Classics scholar", as you put it, or in reality, a student of Classics, I've wrestled with the notions of fate and destiny, including finding true love. I have reached the conclusion that the two are different – even though the Latin word *fatum* implied both ideas. Perhaps they both are inevitable, but I rather believe that one can react to what fate brings you, and you can then control your destiny by your response to events happening by fate or chance. Aeneas was fated to meet Dido, but realized his destiny was not to remain with her, but to move on to his new home which was Italy. If he had accepted his fateful meeting with the Queen of Carthage as his final destiny, people would be calling me "the Carthaginian student" instead of "the Latin student"!

The same distinction between fate and destiny pushed Odysseus to return to his wife Penelope despite all his fateful meetings with women who desired him as a permanent companion. Even Seneca, in accepting the request of Nero's mother to tutor her son, recognized this as his destiny! Likewise, Manon, after we met on that fateful day in that crowded restaurant – and I'm not using "fateful" in its negative sense, but meaning " fated", bound to happen – we followed up on it, we began to plot our destiny – I guess we are still working on it! I have to discover your major fault, Manon – if you have one! Say, do you want to pretend we're Sartre and Simone de Beauvoir? Or maybe Belmondo and Bardot?

-        You would like to be here with Brigitte Bardot, wouldn't you? How about Deneuve and Alain Delon?

-        That wouldn't require too much pretending for me, since you look so much like Catherine Deneuve. I think I may have detected your flaw – are you a little jealous, my love? Speaking of films, you seem to be enjoying your course quite a bit. I admit I haven't seen many films made in France. I know the film *Le Salaire de la peur*, because Jeremy told me about a book he read in his high school French course called *La Dynamite*, that was adapted from that novel and movie. Four down-and-outs in South America transport a cargo of explosives over a rough terrain to combat a fire in an oil refinery. Three of them die, but Yves Montand's character collects all the money paid to the drivers. The book is a study in fear – the Greeks would have said their *phobias* – but the one driver who survives the explosions dies driving over a cliff, having sped along the road with too much confidence. Fear gave way to brash boldness. What ever happened to the Roman virtue of prudence? I have also seen one of the movies you saw in your first class – *Un Homme et une Femme*. It's a love story I liked, because fate brought together two people whose partners had died, and they went on to unite their destinies together. I could reference it if ever I write a book about my theory on fate and destiny! I remember that the film starred Jean-Louis Trintignant and Anouk Aimée – I don't think it's her real name. What I really like about that film is the music by Francis Lai... ba da ba da da da da da da! A bit like "Strangers in the Night" when Frank Sinatra sings "doo bee doo bee doo"! Only in the French movie they were "strangers in the day" – meeting at their children's school! Pizza Pete used to paraphrase that song with his own rendition – "Strangers With My Wife"!

Jeremy once paraphrased the end of the Sinatra song with "any girl will do"! Don't laugh, Manon, he was serious! I am also serious about writing a book someday. It will be called "Popular Religion in Republican Rome". Obviously it will be based on my doctoral dissertation that proposes the Roman masses were responsible for the Senate's implementation of cult practices, and not the other way round. I'll even have a chapter entitled "SPQR"- "Some Pertinent Questions about Religion"! I would also like to write a book about the genuineness of Seneca's moral philosophy. I feel he needs to be redeemed from the accusations of hypocrisy and profiteering that he is often accused of. I only know the Quebec films, not the ones made here in France, but I like movies! I like watching old westerns on TV, and comedies – including musical comedies. The first rainy day, I'm going to grab an umbrella and perform "Singing in the Rain" for you, Manon! You know, from the movie of the same name. And if you can really picture me as "Gene Kelly", then I will truly be your "American in Paris", which was another of his films! Gene Kelly is my favorite dancer, but I also like Fred Astaire and Donald O'Connor. And I've talked to you enough about all those movies made about Greece and Rome that you are quite aware of my interest in those films. Although I haven't really talked to you about my new course at Concordia, my proposal of a course, "Films on Ancient Greece and Rome", was accepted, and I'll be teaching it this year along with a course on Horace. It will be crosslisted with the Communication Arts Department course offerings. What are the films you've seen in your course so far, Manon?

-       First of all, you shouldn't be so hung up on real names, Holden-Denys! Actors and singers change their names all the time – like Dalida, whose songs *"Paroles, Paroles"* and *"Gigi L'Amoroso"* you like so much, and Mike Brant, whose song *"Laisse-moi t'aimer"* you whisper in my ear when we dance to it! Oh, and I have to tell you – there is a girl in my class from Montreal! Her name is Josiane, and she is studying Film and Theater Arts at UQAM. She and I both like and dislike the same films! She is here alone, and so I've invited her to come dancing with us next Saturday. I hope you don't mind, Denys. She actually looks a little bit like Brigitte Bardot – so you see, I'm not jealous! She split up with her boyfriend – I think that's why she decided to come to Paris this summer – for the therapeutic effect! I told her you acted in plays, but I didn't specify that they were in Greek and Latin! The really surprising thing I learned about Josiane is that her mother works for Veterans Affairs in Montreal! I'll be working with her mother next September! To quote your friend Jeremy – "what are the odds"? Professor Montand – no, not the actor –showed us two films with Louis de Funès. The first film, which also stars Bourvil, was called *La Grande Vadrouille*, and is about British pilots who are saved by Resistance fighters in Paris. I won't tell you the plot of the other film, *Les Aventures de Rabbi Jacob*, because it just came out, and you'll probably want to see it. We''ll be watching another movie soon with Louis de Funès – *Le Gendarme se marie*. How about your courses, Denys, are you enjoying them?

-        Very much so, Manon! We are spending ten days reading the myths recounted in a work called *The Library*. It is attributed to an Athenian grammarian named Apollodorus, but our Professor pointed out a few reasons why that writer could not be the author. That Apollodorus wrote a treatise in twenty-four books called *On the Gods*, which has been lost. What a pity! The tales in the *Bibliotheke* - you see how the French word is really a Greek word meaning "a case for books" - are collected in Three Books and an Epitome, beginning with a "Theogony" - like Hesiod's work – of the Olympian gods and ending with the return of Odysseus to Ithaca. Right now we are reading about the twelve labours of Herakles in Book Two. After reading this Greek text, we will spend ten days reading the Latin poet Statius and ten days reading the poet Claudian. My second class each day is spent reading the compendium of Greek philosophers by Diogenes Laertius – not the Cynic philosopher Diogenes, but he's mentioned in the book. We will read about the Pre-Socratics, Socrates, Plato and his Academy, Aristotle and his followers, the Cynics, the Stoics and the Epicureans. This is an ideal companion course for the seminar on Greek and Roman Philosophy that I have each day for two hours. The Seminar is a challenging course for me, since my background is mostly in the fields of religion, history, and literature, although I have read some philosophers in Greek and Latin courses. However, this course will be very valuable for general courses I might have to teach on Greek and Roman civilization. It's true that the specialized courses I have taken in epigraphy, palaeography, papyrology, numismatics, archaeology, and Italic languages provide good background for supervising the research of graduate school students. My research paper for this seminar will most certainly deal with the philosophy of Seneca. I am especially looking forward to discussions on Cicero and Seneca, which will take place towards the end of the course. I guess we should walk over to the campus – my first class starts at nine. I'm glad you're not bored waiting for your class to start at ten. You are reading some books in the University library on classical civilization, including Roman religion. I admire you, Manon - you wouldn't catch me reading books on Canadian government or veterans' benefits – unless we were talking about Caesar's veterans!

-        I'm also taking advantage of my free time to read some classic French novels by Jules Verne, Honoré de Balzac, Victor Hugo and Albert Camus. When I picked up *La Peste*, I thought of you for some reason!

-        Don't tell Bob about that book. He'll start calling me "Pest" as well as "Menace"! While we are walking to class I'd like to talk about something that is important, I think. When I talked about God wanting us to be happy – I believe He wants us to have a meaningful life in both body and soul. A meaningful life is what we do with the life fate has given us. The fate of the poor boy in an African village is different from our life which presents us with opportunities for study and employment and spiritual and religious devotion. Not to pursue those opportunities would remove meaning from our lives, just as if the boy in Africa were to refuse his tribal customs. Even if some contexts are simpler or at least different, they all provide an environment for accomplishing a destiny. All that to say we both share a common religion, and even a devotion. You are very close to your mother, Manon, and that is probably why you have a spiritual connection with the Blessed Virgin Mary – in Her role as Mother. I became devoted to Mary in elementary school. At first I thought it was the result of the teaching of the nuns who taught me, but as I grew older, I realized that I had a deep fondness for my mother as well. I've always felt that Mary is looking over me and my loved ones – and that includes you! I guess we kind of look to Mary in the same way. That's probably why we always light candles and say prayers in front of Her statue when we are in church. And fate again – you will be working on Queen Mary Road! We will certainly be lighting candles when we visit Notre Dame Cathedral. I also like reading the beautiful prayers to Mary in Latin, like the *Ave Maria*, the *Hodie, gloriosa caeli Regina* - "This day, the glorious Queen of Heaven", the *Salve, Regina, mater misericordiae* – "Hail, Queen, mother of mercy", and the *Ave, Regina Caelorum,* the "Hail, Queen of heaven" that I know by heart.

Ave, Regina caelorum	Hail , Queen of heaven,
ave, Domina angelorum,	Hail, Mistress of angels,
salve, radix, salve, porta,	Hail, O root, hail, O gate,
ex qua mundo lux est orta.	From whom the light for the world arose.
Gaude, virgo gloriosa,	Rejoice, Glorious Virgin
super omnes speciosa;	Lovely above all,
vale, o valde decora,	Farewell, O exceedingly beautiful,
et pro nobis Christum exora.	Plead with Christ on our behalf.

I'll meet you at the usual place after class and we can walk back for lunch. For dinner I'd like to try a new restaurant. I know you want to go see a movie outside of your course content. You say the French version of a new American movie is playing here in Paris, and is called *Les Dents de la Mer*. Okay – I'll bite! What's the name of the original, Manon?

-       *Jaws*! It's about a shark.

-       So, I'm guessing, not a pool shark, but a shark in a big pool!

Chapter 112

- Good-day, ladies and gentlemen! I'd like to bid a special welcome to the students who are joining us for the Latin segments of our course beginning with the poet Statius. He is most known for the *Thebaid* – an epic poem based on the Greek story of the Seven against Thebes. As you know, seven is a significant number in Roman history as well – seven hills and seven kings! However we shall be reading from his collection of poems known as *Silvae*. Today we start with Poem V. 4. Although published after the death of Statius, it is probably his best-liked poem. We have in our midst one student from across the sea – I mean the Atlantic Ocean and not the English Channel! He can truly represent the New World, since he was born and raised in the land of the British colonies – in the United States of America, which once upon a time accepted our gift of the famous Lady of Liberty – but he has studied most extensively in the land of our French colonies in Quebec, Canada with Professor Saucier, a distinguished alumnus of this Institution! We ask you then, Mr. Hainsworth, to please read and translate this poem nobly addressed to Sleep. It is in the hexameter meter. Please take note, everyone, of the alliteration in *curuata cacumina* and of the rhyme in fessos…sommos. *Oetaeae Paphiaeque* refer to the morning and evening stars. The former is a mountain range between Thessaly and Aetolia where Hercules ascended the funeral pyre, as told in the play by Seneca. The latter is an allusion to the planet of Venus of Paphos. Tithonia is Aurora, the Dawn, who uses a whip to chase the stars from heaven; from it dewdrops fall on the poet. Argus is called *sacer* – sacred – because he was sent by the Queen of the heavens, Juno.

- Thank you for that lengthy introduction, Professor, but it risked inducing sleep in my classmates, which, ironically, would have brought great pleasure to our poet, if he had been physically, and not merely metaphorically, present in their number! Another instance of irony which may or may not interest the group here is the fact that my home-town is Cincinnati, which is also sometimes referred to as the "City of Seven Hills" – Mount Adams, Walnut Hills, Mount Auburn, Vine Street Hill, College Hill, Fairmount and Price Hill. Actually, though, there are many more such hills in Cincinnati, and - full disclosure – they are really more like plateaus than hills. I believe the association with the number seven in talking about the "hills" of Cincinnati is because of the Roman hero, Cincinnatus, for whom the city is named. So I was born in the "new Rome". This fateful birth led me to contemplate and pursue my destiny as a Latin student – if my theory about fate and destiny is correct! One thing is certain – the "hills of Cincinnati", as in the film with Julie Andrews, are "alive with the sound of music" whenever the Cincinnati

Symphony Orchestra plays the *Carmina Burana*!

Crimine quo merui, iuvenis placidissime divum,

quoue errore miser, donis ut solus egerem,

Somne, tuis? tacet omne pecus volucresque feraeque

et simulant fessos curuata cacumina somnos,

nec trucibus fluuiis idem sonus; occidit horror

aequoris, et terris maria adclinata quiescunt.

septima iam rediens Phoebe mihi respicit aegras

stare genas; totidem Oetaeae Paphiaeque reuisunt

lampades et totiens nostros Tithonia questus

praeterit et gelido spargit miserata flagello.

unde ego sufficiam? non si mihi lumina mille

quae sacer alterna tantum *statione tenebat*

Argus et haud umquam uigilabat corpore toto.

at nunc heu! si aliquis longa sub nocte puellae

bracchia nexa tenens ultro te, Somne, repellit,

inde veni nec te totas infundere pennas

luminibus compello meis (hoc turba precetur

laetior) : extremo me tange cacumine virgae,

sufficit, aut leuiter suspenso poplite transi.

Please excuse the tear I shed at one point during my reading; it was not because I share in
the sadness of the poet, but rather at the mention of the name of the Moon goddess. My
sister's name is Phoebe, and I don't see her very often!

My translation is as follows: "Gentlest of the gods, youthful Sleep, by what crime or error have I alone so miserably deserved to be lacking your gifts? All the cattle are silent, and the birds and the wild beasts and the curved mountain tops feign weary sleep, nor is the sound of savage rivers the same; the horror of the sea-surface has sunk, and the seas are quiet as they lean on the earth. Returning seven times the Moon goddess looks at my weary eyes that are still; just as often the Oetaean and Paphian lights return to visit, and so often Tithonia bypasses my groans and out of pity sprinkles me with her cold whip. With what resource can I survive? Not even if there were for me the thousand eyes that sacred Argus held only in alternate watches, and was never awake in his whole body. But now – alas! If anyone holding the entwining arms of a girl during the long night drives you away, Sleep, come here, but I do not compel you to pour your wings completely over my eyes (a happier crowd prays for this): touch me with your wand's furthest tip, that suffices, or pass over with your knee but slightly bent."

I'm delighted, Professor, that with the time we have left today you have allowed me to share my passion for music and my interest in film to compile a list of songs and films that Statius – if he were with us today – could consult for better or for worse! There is the French movie *Le Grand Sommeil*, and many movies in English, including the American crime thriller *The Big Sleep* and the sub-titled Japanese movie *The Bad Sleep Well*. Others are *The Black Sleep*, a couple of silent movies perhaps conducive to sleep – *Luke's Shattered Sleep* and *We Never Sleep* - , *So You Think You Can't Sleep* – which speaks directly to our poet! – *Eve Wants To Sleep*, *While Parents Sleep*, *No Sleep on the Deep*, *Night Without Sleep*, and *Miles to go Before I Sleep* – which reminds me of a poem by Robert Frost! The songs are numerous. There is the instrumental by the brothers Santo and Johnny called "Sleep Walk". They apparently wrote this song at two o'clock in the morning – maybe Statius could write his poetry after midnight! The song "Sleepy Joe", by Herman's Hermits, was also recorded in French by Quebec's Pierre Lalonde – with the same title. Little Willie John sang "Sleep", The Everly Brothers recorded "Sleepless Nights", Black Sabbath sang "Sleeping Village", Jody Reynolds sang "Endless Sleep", Cream recorded "Sleep Time", the Beatles had a song called "I'm Only Sleeping", Cher recorded "I Hate to Sleep Alone", Kenny Rogers and The First Edition sang "Sleep Comes Easy" – definitely not addressed to Statius! – and Canadian - turned- American singer Paul Anka has recently recorded "I Don't Like to Sleep Alone" – maybe he should get together with Cher! Ultimately, Statius should probably content himself with the advice Julie Andrews gives in the film Mary Poppins, when she sings "Stay Awake"!

-      I'm not so sure Statius would find the advice in many of those songs helpful. He would probably want to sleep on it! You did such a masterful translation, Mr. Hainsworth, that there is still time left in today's session.

-      Fate at work once more, Professor! I have been working on a poem about time - written, I believe, by Seneca – although not everybody is convinced. It is from the *Anthologia Latina*, and I am prepared to share it with the group. It is going to be a critical work for my paper in the Philosophy Seminar. Here is the Latin text, whose meter is the elegiac couplet.

Omnia tempus edax depascitur, omnia carpit,

omnia sede movet, nil sinit esse diu.

flumina deficiunt, profugum mare litora siccant,

subsidunt montes et iuga celsa ruunt.

quid tam parva loquor? moles pulccherrima caeli

ardebit flammis tota repente suis.

omnia mors poscit. lex est, non poena, perire :

hic aliquo mundus tempore nullus erit.

"Gluttonous time devours everything, grabs hold of everything,

Moves everything from its place, permits nothing to exist for long.

The rivers fail, the shores drain the fleeing sea,

Mountains sink and lofty peaks crumble.

Why do I speak so few words? The beautiful mound of the sky

Will suddenly burn completely in its own flames.

Death demands everything. It is the law, not punishment, to perish:

In time there will be no world here."

Seneca portrays in this poem the Stoic belief that fire is the source of the material world which is destroyed in conflagrations, and then reproduced from fire in recurring cycles. I will be exploring this concept that suggests "it's just a matter of time". I will be going dancing tonight, so I think I'll return to the residence and take a nap!

Chapter 113

-       Josiane should be here soon, Denys. This *discothèque* which she suggested seems very trendy – too trendy if I go by the prices we were charged for our drinks! This place must be full of jet-setters - not the usual crowd for a simple girl from Quebec! We may have to try other clubs during our stay in Paris – otherwise you will have to apply for another Parker Grant! Here's Josiane now!

-       Hello you two. Nice to meet you Denys. You are the patron saint of Paris!

-       Pleasure to meet you Brig – I mean Josiane! Manon wasn't kidding – you do have a striking resemblance to a young B.B.!

-       Are you talking about Catherine Deneuve here? And you look a lot like Robert Redford! How do you like the *décor* here?

-       It's very nice. I think I'll be spending a lot of time admiring it instead of buying drinks! But, of course, Manon and I would like to buy you a drink – what's your poison? You can call me R.R., even though my real initials are H.H. But if you call me Denys, my initials are D.H. – in baseball I'd be a designated hitter, but for Manon, I'm her designated hero! And I'm not the patron OF Paris, just a humble patron at this club IN Paris! But we really are enjoying our stay in Paris. In fact, I gave Manon a Parisian love potion – and she has fallen in love... with Paris!

-       Such a sense of humour! Yes, some of the people here tend to be snobs – unlike yourselves. You seem to be as nice as Manon described you, Denys. The young people here tend to become intoxicated at some point in the evening, and tend to let their imaginations run wild!

-       To prove that I am a Classics student, ladies, may I point out that the word "snob" comes from the Latin *sine nobilitate*, meaning without the actual pedigree of nobility. It refers to people who imitate those with a higher station in life. They may have money, but they're not actually "bluebloods". I read that the word once referred to cobblers, therefore to people of the lower echelons of society. So, if the shoe fits...but don't act like a heel!

-       Hard to believe, isn't it Josiane, that a guy who talks like that is my "hero", as he puts it? But let me tell you about a not so expensive concert we attended last night. A young singer named Shake was giving a one-man show to introduce him to the French public. He was gorgeous – no wait – Denys is gorgeous – but Shake is so cute! Sorry I couldn't get his phone number for you, Josiane! There was a short programme given to us, which mentioned that he was from Malaysia, where he had won a singing contest. His real name is Sheikh Abdullal Ahmad, so that explains "Shake". He sang some beautiful songs like "*Tu sais que je t'aime – You Know That I Love You*". That's right - bilingual refrains! So he could eventually come to North America and make lots of money! When he sang "*Rien n'est plus beau que l'amour*" and "*Soleil, Aide-moi*", the small but enthusiastic crowd started waving their hands in the air. Denys said that will probably become known as the "Hand – Shake"! Naturally, my "music master" mentioned a song that could be a perfect intro for Shake – "Shakin'All Over" by Chad Allan and The Expressions. Since they are from Winnipeg, this Québécoise hadn't heard of them. True to his nature, Denys "informed" me that the song was originally recorded in England by Johnny Kidd and the Pirates. Then Denys started "kidding around" by saying that maybe The Expressions "pirated" the song! Moreover, they didn't want anyone to recognize them, so the record label had Guess Who as the artists! But even I know that the Guess Who with Burton Cummings is one of the top bands in Canada. He also said he would buy a Shake album once those songs were marketed on records. Especially since that song about the sun reminded him of Bobby Hebb's song "Sunny", and, naturally, of me! The student of Roman history that Denys is pointed out to me that Shake's slightly dark skin would have made him an "exotic" performer in Ancient Rome, and so, very appreciated. He added that he wasn't sure, though, that Nero would be willing to share top billing with him! Oh, some disco songs – let's dance, Denys! Excuse us, Josiane.

- Did you notice some people staring at us, Denys, as we came back to our table? Maybe it was your great moves to that music!

- I love those songs, Manon! I guess, Josiane, you are familiar with them. You can't beat The Bee Gees with "Jive Talkin'" and "Kung Fu Fighting" by Carl Douglas, and especially KC and The Sunshine Band with "Get Down Tonight". The name of the band comes from the fact that they are from the "Sunshine State" – Florida. I know Manon was happy to hear them play some slow songs to dance "cheek to cheek – Frankie Valli with "My Eyes Adored You" and Morris Albert with "Feelings". I love that next song we heard – "I'll Take You There", by The Staple Singers. You both realize that music is a "staple" for me! We also heard Patsy Gallant singing "Sugar Daddy". Isn't she from Quebec? And then we heard one of my favorite songs – "Your So Vain" by Carly Simon.

- You're so humble, my love, that maybe that song was FOR you – but not ABOUT you! Actually, Patsy Gallant is from New Brunswick. Like me, I'm sure Josiane studied in high school about the Acadians, those French-Canadians who were deported and settled in

Louisiana. You Americans call them Cajuns! Did I tell you, Josiane, that Denys is really into music?

-       No, but I can see already that he's really into you!

-       Well, Josiane, that's because, as Gary Lewis sings, "She's Just My Style"!

-       You won't mind, though, if I steal Manon away to dance !

***

-       That was fun, Josiane, it was like dancing with my sister Maggie – remember I told you about her? I love that song "Lady Marmelade"! What were the names of the other songs Josiane and I danced to, Denys?

-       I think some of the patrons are already under the influence of too much alcohol, or maybe other substances! A young lady came over to the table and said *Voulez-vous coucher avec moi?*". When I tried to tell her the name of the song is "Lady Marmelade", and before I could tell her it was by Patti LaBelle, she said she wasn't talking about the song! I wasn't about to ask her if she was related to a certain female Latin professor in Quebec, who would probably make the same move on me on hearing Nanette Workman's version! You girls had fun dancing to "Doctor's Orders" by Carol Douglas, "I Will Survive" by Gloria Gaynor, "Rhinestone Cowboy" by Glen Campbell, and "When Will I See You Again" by The Three Degrees, which is exactly what I was thinking at that point, Manon! Fun fact – Gloria Gaynor won a Grammy for her song – the only singer to win a Grammy for Disco, since they removed that category the following year! If we go and dance, I'm sure they'll be lining up to dance with Josiane.

-       They played some nice songs that time, Denys. I'm sure you can name them for me!

-       Yes, but only if you promise to tell me about some of the films you've seen lately in your course.

-       We saw a few films that weren't that great. They basically are part of the programme because they take place in Paris. The films were *Les Parisiennes* - but Catherine Deneuve was delightful! -, *Les Mystères de Paris, Bonsoir Paris, bonjour l'amour, L'Air de Paris, Moineaux de Paris, Quatre Jours à Paris*, and *Si Paris nous était conté*. The last film in that series – *Paris brûle-t-il?* – was actually okay, and I know the title will make you think of Troy! We saw *Le Bal des Vampires* with Roman Polanski and Sharon Tate. The Professor then recounted that horrible murder of Sharon Tate and the others by that monster Charles

Manson. We saw a few films that I liked very much - *Et Dieu…créa la femme*, *Le Mépris,* and *Viva Maria* – all with Brigitte Bardot! – and some films that Josiane enjoyed very much – *Belle de Jour, La Vérité, Répulsion*, and *Les Parapluies de Cherbourg*, all of which starred Catherine Deneuve.

-        I will be showing a film with Brigitte Bardot in my film course at Concordia. She plays a slave girl who helps her mistress Helen in the film *Helen of Troy*. I guess B.B. is popular IN Paris, but less so WITH Paris! – who was also known in antiquity as Alexander, but he was never the soldier that the conqueror from Macedonia was! Okay, the last songs we heard were "I'm not in Love" by 10cc, "Love Will Keep Us Together" by Captain and Tenille, "The Hustle" by Van McCoy and The Soul City Symphony – Manon, you always dance so well to that song!

Finally, we heard "Mandy" by Barry Manilow, and Barry White singing "You're the First, the Last, My Everything". I always chuckle at the fact that Barry White is a black singer and Jay Black is a white singer! No, Al Green isn't…!

-        Josiane and I have to go to the little girls' room, Denys. Try not to be too lonely while we're gone!

***

-        Who were those people at our table, Denys?

-        It seems that these groupies may also have thought I was Robert Redford! They asked me if I was an American actor, and I said yes! That's not a lie since I am an American, and I acted in some Latin and Greek plays! Besides I was Paul Newman at a party once, and he was Robert Redford's sidekick in *Butch Cassidy and The Sundance Kid* and *The Sting*. My old sidekick Tommy Nelson used to call me the "Dance Kid", so that's close enough! I remember when I arrived at McGill, my friend Jeremy would sometimes call me "The Cincinnati Kid" – do you know that movie with Steve McQeen? But I could never have enough of a poker face to be the real "Cincinnati Kid"! When I went to a couple of clubs with Jeremy, I was asked if I was Jim Morrison! Fortunately I wasn't asked that here, since he died a few years ago, and right here in Paris! But since they asked me for my autograph, I scribbled something down.

-        You naughty boy, Denys, what did you write?

-        I scribbled "*Iani Tor*". It was for the Latin word *ianitor,* which designates the one who takes care of the doors, from the Latin word for "door", *ianua.* Yes, it's the origin of the word "janitor". So if I had been Jim Morrison, I would be taking care of The Doors, making sure they "cleaned up" – money-wise, that is! "Scribble" is Latin "writing", since it comes from the Latin verb *scribere*, meaning "to write"!

-	You see, Josiane, you can take the Latin student out of the Latin class, but you can't take the Latin class out of the Latin student! Just another one of his "Latin lessons" I have to put up with!

-	And you seem prepared to put up with them for a long time, Manon! What songs did they play, while we were in the powder room, Denys – or Robert Redford or Paul Newman or Roman doorman or whoever you are?

-	While I was entertaining those hangers-on, I was listening to "I Can Help" by Billy Swan, "Walking in Rhythm" by The Blackbyrds, and "Swearin'to God" by Frankie Valli. I think we should head back to the residence, Manon, before God starts swearing at us!

Chapter 114

- Denys, we've seen so much here in Paris in the last few weeks. We really needed the whole weekend we had set aside to visit Le Louvre. You were just as thrilled as I was to see the actual Mona Lisa, although I know you were enthralled at the sight of the Greek and Roman art. I enjoyed our visit to *Le Pantheon* and *l'Arc de Triomphe*. It was fun walking through *Le Champ de Mars* and *Les Champs Élysées*. It was as if Joe Dassin were singing to us! You seemed so enchanted in Montparnasse, the "original Quartier Latin", as you called it. So interesting to hear how this neighbourhood owes its artistic tradition to the time of Pierre Abélard in the Middle Ages – all those philosophers speaking in Latin to each other! Did that "French Parnassus" give you poetic inspiration?

- Yes, Manon, "climbing Parnassus"- even though it wasn't such a lofty leap - made me feel like a real singer and a real poet – and a real writer! Maybe some day I'll be a "Paperback Writer" – like in the Beatles song! Or at least "A Fool on the Hill"! Everything seems so Roman. If *Elysion* was the Greek heaven, which the Romans referred to as *Elysium*, I've certainly felt like I was in Paradise here with you, Manon! It was so invigorating up on Montmartre - all the hills together in Cincinnati pale in comparison! Thinking about those hills, though, reminds me of the struggle in America for racial equality. I imagine that peace is to be found at the top of a hill – not a high mountain – so it's not unattainable. However, we all have to climb the hill together. I wish I could express those feelings more poetically, but someday a real poet will find the right words to inspire the whole country! Wouldn't it be awesome, Manon, if that poet turned out to be an Afro-American? We got to light candles in *La Basilique Du Sacre Coeur*, and I also imagined a singer serenading us – Charles Aznavour, who sings about Montmartre in "*La Bohème!*" I know it is officially "The Mount of Martyrs", and St. Denis was martyred here. I always feel strange when I hear my name preceded by the word "saint!" Yet I like to think of the etymology making it "the mountain of Mars!" And wasn't The Cathredal of Notre Dame mindboggling. I would want to be Catholic just to be able to claim an affinity with this monumental construction erected in Mary's name! I sensed a rush of spirituality when we lit our candles there. But it didn't prevent me from reflecting on my belief that God has a - how should I put it it – "divine" sense of humor. You mentioned that one of the Victor Hugo novels you are reading is *The Hunchback of Notre Dame*. I saw the movie on television when I was in high school. Although likeable, and certainly someone you would feel sorry for – just like the motif in *Beauty and the Beast* and *King Kong* – Quasimodo was really ugly! Did you know that his name comes from the fact that in the story, he was found on Low Sunday – you know, the first Sunday after Easter. That day is sometimes called "*Quasimodo*

Sunday" because the first two words in the Latin entrance prayer – called *Introit* in Latin, that is, "he enters" - are *quasi modo* – meaning "as if in this manner". Thus Quasimodo was a creature who was a human – "in a manner of speaking" - but not totally, of course, since he was deformed. I hope you appreciate all that serious information, Manon, because there is a lesser known anecdote about Notre Dame which talks about a pious worker who would leave his lunch for the poor every day on the steps of this beautiful church. Each day the caretaker would pick up the brown paper bag. One day, a tourist asked him what that was, and the caretaker replied that it was the "lunchbag of Notre Dame!"

-       You are so mischievous, Denys! But I am impressed by your choice of restaurant. *La Tour d'Argent* is beautiful, and the menu so inviting! Is there a special occasion you want to celebrate? And to think that after dinner we will be visiting the most beautiful spot in all of France – *La Tour Eiffel*!

-       Well the Eiffel Tower at night will give us a magnificent view, Manon, and that is something to celebrate. We'll be going to the highest point that visitors can reach – it's 906 feet above ground, but I suppose someone like Quasimodo would have gone to the very top of the 1,063 feet! It's a good thing we don't have acrophobia – like Jimmy Stewart in the film *Vertigo*! Actually, that Hitchcock film was more about fright than height! I've seen quite a few films with Jimmy Stewart – such a recognizable voice and manner of speaking he has! You could take a course just on his films – *Mr. Smith Goes to Washington*, *The Philadelphia Story*, that Christmas classic - *It's a Wonderful Life* -, *Rope*, *Rear Window*, *The Glenn Miller Story* – we've got to dance to "Moonlight Serenade" some day! There are also a couple of westerns – Stewart is a versatile actor! – *The Man from Laramie* and *The Man Who Shot Liberty Valance*. The title songs for those movies were sung, respectively, by Jimmy Young and Gene Pitney, who sang the song for the film *Town Without Pity*, and who wrote the songs "Rubber Ball" for Bobby Vee, "Hello, Mary Lou" for Ricky Nelson, and" "He's a Rebel" for The Crystals. Say, weren't you going to tell me about some of the films you've seen recently in your course?

-       Denys, I don't know if I can compete with your filmorama, but my favorite films were *A Bout de Souffle*, *Z* – even though I usually don't like movies about politics -, *La Religieuse*, *Jules et Jim*, *Le Vieil Homme et L'Enfant*, *Les Quatre Cents Coups*, *La Guerre est Finie*, and a beautiful love story called *Hiroshima Mon Amour*. This week, as the course is coming to a close, we will be watching *Le Procès de Jeanne D'Arc*, *Sous le Signe de Monte Cristo* and *Le Tour du Monde en 80 Jours*, which will take us two whole classes to watch! But I have been reading the novel in the library.

- *Le Tour du Monde en 80 Jours* is one of my favorite novels! Most people read it as an adventure story, or even as an archaic lesson in world geography. However, it's a great love story! How could it not be? The hero's name - Phileas – is from the Greek word for "love" – *philia*. His surname Fogg just reflects the fact that he is from "foggy" London. The names of the other characters are very telling as well. Passepartout "goes everywhere" – just as his name suggests, and Fix is very determined – he has a "fixed" goal – to bring Fogg to justice. He could have used help from Obélix's dog, Idéfix! Fortunately, Fogg eludes him, thereby avoiding being in quite "a fix"! Mrs. Aouda makes the romance happen. Fate places her in Fogg's path, but his choice to be with her is his decision to determine his – and her - destiny! It has been suggested that the name Aouda means "gift of God", and that is good enough for me. It was for our friend Phileas! Manon, does this story of a man of principle, who is disciplined and passionate about his interests, a creature of habit, yet not afraid to travel, and who ultimately – even if unexpectedly - finds true love, remind you of anyone you know – and love?

- I haven't the foggiest idea! Just kidding, you "Romantic Roman!" Or do you still want R.R. to stand for Robert Redford? The meal was delicious, Denys! Bringing me to a chic restaurant and then off to the Eiffel Tower. You're such a romantic – and so full of surprises! While we are en route, I'll tell you about some of the other films I liked. We saw the film *Le Voleur* with the Canadian actress Geneviève Bujold – Josiane has actually met her. Other films were *Les Biches*, *La Piscine*, *Les Amants*, and *Les Grandes Vacances* – which sets the mood for the wonderful weeks of vacation that we will be beginning soon! Well, here we are at the top of the world! And you were right – the view is beautiful!

- I agree – the view is beautiful – and I haven't even looked out over the city! They say the nine Muses are atop Mt. Helicon in Greece. Well, the name of that mountain comes from the Greek verb *elissein*, meaning to "whirl around". So I can picture all those Muses dancing around, probably to the music of my favorite dee-jay – Dionysos, the "dancing dandy"!

That image always makes me think of us – whirling and dancing on the dance floor! I'm Denys the dancer, spinning around with the only "muse" I need – Manon, My Maenad Muse of Melodious Movement – and, so it seems, of alliteration! You're so inspiring, Manon, that you give wings to my feet, and levers to my legs, inspiring me to dance not with mechanical motion, but with spontaneous symmetry! You always transform my energetic emotion into dancing devotion! Perhaps I'm not making too much sense right now, Manon, so I had better give you this – please accept it and say you will marry me!

- 	An engagement ring! Oh, Denys, I'm at a loss for words – except for one little one – yes! Now I understand the celebration meal!

- 	And the two-week trip is an "engagement honeymoon!" I know you are anxious to find out if I'll obtain a teaching position at a university, and where that would be. There is no rush – I don't want to put pressure on you, since you are moving to a new city and starting a new job. I am just so happy that you want to make the same commitment as I do. If fate has indeed put me on the right path – a path I have freely chosen to follow towards fulfilling my destiny - I will be starting a career a year from now. We could eventually make formal wedding plans and set a date two summers from now. That's the Denys you know, Manon – planning everything well in advance! But with that ring on your finger, I won't have to go to Montreal and fight off suitors! I'm not sure I can manage a tightly stringed bow like Odysseus, or even heroically slay a Turnus like Aeneas!

- 	I love you, Denys!

- 	And I love you, Manon! I believe – no I'm not about to sing that Frankie Lane song – but I truly believe that the only thing that lasts forever is love – if you really want it to!

- 	I know they say falling in love is easier than staying in love, Denys, but I really do want to spend the rest of my life with you!

- 	Well, I guess "We'll always have Paris", Manon. That line is taken from the movie *Casablanca*. It's a film classic that the cinematic connoisseur that you have now become would appreciate! In fact, when we first started seeing each other in Quebec, I thought of another line from the film – "I think this is the beginning of a beautiful friendship!" We've come a long way, haven't we, since that day four years ago in the crowded Marie Antoinette – but when is that restaurant not crowded? We could be Humphrey Bogart and Ingrid Bergman – so "Here's looking at you kid!" I'm really on a roll with memories from that movie. One of the songs in the movie was "Knock on Wood" – but a completely different song from the one we used to dance to in Quebec.

- 	With you as my partner, Denys, I could dance all night!

Chapter 115

\-   In this, our final class, I have asked Mr. Hainsworth to read Claudian's *Epigram XX* in its elegiac couplet meter, and to give us his translation. I have deliberately called upon our American friend because his journey from his native city to cities in a different country with stops on a different continent are in stark contrast to the one considered fortunate by our poet, who obviously equates happiness with the sedentary life.

\-   Thank you, Professor! The one common denominator that I have found in my travels is the study – and indeed, the love – of Latin. After reading mostly Republican and early Empire poets, it has been delightful to read works from a late fourth century poet, all the more so since Claudian switched from Greek to Latin.

Felix, qui patriis aevum transegit in agris,

ipsa domus puerum quem videt, ipsa senem :

qui baculo nitens, in qua reptavit harena,

unius numerat saecula longa casae.

illum non vario traxit fortuna tumultu,

nec bibit ignotas mobilis hospes aquas.

non freta mercator tremuit, non classica miles :

non rauci lites pertulit ille fori.

indocilis rerum, vicinae nescius urbis,

adspectu fruitur liberiore poli.

frugibus alternis, non consule, computat annum :

autumnum pomis, ver sibi flore notat.

idem condit ager soles idemque reducit,

metiturque suo rusticus orbe diem;

ingentem meminit parvo qui germine quercum,

aequaevumque videt consenuisse nemus :

proxima cui nigris Verona remotior Indis,

Benacumque putat litora rubra lacum;

sed tamen indomitae vires, firmisque lacertis

aetas robustum tertia cernit avum.

erret, et extremos alter scrutetur Hiberos;

plus habet hic vitae, plus habet ille viae.

This poem is about an old man of Verona who has always lived at home.

"Happy is the one who has spent his whole life in his ancestral fields, whose very house saw him as a boy and an old man: who reckons a long time in one house.

Fortune has not bothered him with contrary disturbances, he never drank unknown waters as a stranger on the move.

He never feared the seas as a merchant nor the trumpet calls as a soldier: nor did he endure the legal suits of the noisy forum.

Inexperienced in business matters, ignorant of the neighbouring city, he enjoys a freer view of the sky.

He counts the year by the recurring fruits of the earth, not by the consuls: he knows autumn by its fruits and spring by its flowers.

 The same field removes and brings back the sun, and the farmer measures the day with his own cycle; he recalls the huge oak from a little acorn, he sees that the pasture land of his same age grows old with him: neighbouring Verona is further away from him than the dark Indians, he considers Lake Benacus the Red Sea; nevertheless his strength is unrestrained , and the third generation discern in him a robust grandfather with sturdy muscles.

Let someone else wander, and explore farthest Spain; that one has more of a journey, but this one has more of a life."

I like the play on *vitae* and *viae*! Obviously, our old man would not have been one of Shakespeare's *"Two" Gentlemen of Verona*! Nor would he have had the energy to become a would-be Romeo chasing Juliet around Verona! Too bad he didn't find a simple little

"Veronica" to help him pass the time! I think I would like to be a healthy and doting grandfather one day, but one who has been away from his back porch! And I have "explored" Spain! Yet, no matter how far I roam, yet finish my days at home, a part of me will forever be in Rome!

-	Amusingly poetic, Mr. Hainsworth! Enjoy your travels through France – even though our *felix* Veronian would hardly approve!

Chapter 116

-     Denys, how did you know there would be a '50's revival night at this club?

-     I saw it advertised in our residence lobby, Manon. I can just imagine the Parisian beatniks sitting in a bistro back in the 1950's, wearing their blue and black berets, and listening to these American songs to prove how cool they were because they were into American culture!

At least they were more docile than America's Green Berets! What were the last films you saw in your course?

-     There were a lot of films about women. Professor Montand seemed to enjoy them! We saw *Le Journal d'une Femme de Chambre*, *Une Femme Douce*, *Une Femme est une Femme*, *Les Valseuses*, and my favorite – *Le Genou de Claire*. And we saw a few films you would have enjoyed, Denys – *Orphée* and *Le Testament d'Orphée* with Jean Marais – I know you like Greek mythology, especially when it involves a musician! You would also have appreciated *L'Année dernière à Marienbad* and *La Route de Corinthe*. How did your seminar presentation go?

-     Well, I presented that poem by Seneca that I showed you as evidence of the Stoic belief in cyclical time. I pointed out, though, that Seneca himself advised the proper use of the time at our disposal in *De Brevitate Vitae* – *On the Shortness of Life* and in *De Otio* – *On Leisure Time*. I believe that if everyone took Seneca's advice to heart, they would all become classicists! The Greek Stoic Chrysippus taught that time comes to an end, as is mentioned in Seneca's poem, and then repeats itself endlessly. Aristotle also believed that time involves change and was continuous. As time starts over, we actually can conclude that it is continuous.

In a sense, and we know that St. Augustine and St. Thomas Aquinas were eager to find "truth" in the teachings of Aristotle, the Christian belief that after our time ends here on earth but continues eternally in an afterlife which we hope will be "heaven" suggests a continuity of time – a "renewal of time", as the Stoics suggest! Did you hear those great songs playing, Manon? It was about time! They started with Dion and The Belmonts singing "Runaround Sue". Then there was Fats Domino with "Ain't That a Shame" and "Blueberry Hill" – a song that even I sing! Then there was The Dells with "Oh What a Night" followed by Dinah Washington singing "What a Difference a Day Makes". I love that song by Tommy Edwards –

"It's All In The Game". I noticed, Manon, that when The Orioles sang "Crying in the Chapel", someone else was crying! Finally we heard Johnny Ray singing "Cry". Which is what I'm going to do if you don't come dance these next songs with me! They're starting with one of my sentimental favorites – "In the Still of the Night" by The Five Satins.

- Oh, Denys how did you know that we'd be dancing to so many slow songs? There was Frank Sinatra and Nat King Cole – I don't know the song titles like you do – and who sang "Tennessee Waltz"?

- The songs were "I've Got You under my Skin" and "When I Fall in Love". Sinatra and Nat King Cole are very popular in France! Patti Page sang that beautiful waltz – I hope they play her song "Old Cape Cod"! It's always fun to dance to The Platters. They sang "Only You" and "The Great Pretender". Did you know that the girl vocalist in that group was married to Frankie Lymon, whose song with The Teenagers – "Why Do Fools Fall in Love?" was played next. I don't know the answer to that question since I'm not a fool! Of course you recognized the Elvis Presley songs – "Houndog", "Teddy Bear", and "Heartbreak Hotel". He's popular here too! That song "Sh-Boom" was by a group called the Crew-Cuts. Don't laugh – that was my hair-style in high school! We can finish our drinks as we listen to a few songs. You know I'm really anxious to start our "engagement celebration" trip! The song "Butterfly" was originally recorded by a singer from Philadelphia, Charlie Gracie - before the "Philly Soul" sound came along! But I prefer the version they just played by Andy Williams. I remember watching his television show and seeing him sitting there in his perennial cardigan sweater. Of course, his song, "Music to Watch Girls By", is no longer in my collection, Manon! Still, my favorite song at Christmas is Andy Williams singing "It's The Most Wonderful Time of the Year". As it is for you, Christmas has always been my "most favorite time of the year" Especially since, as you know, my mother's birthday is on Christmas Day. In fact, Mom is so "wonderful", we always give her double presents! But Andy Williams sings so many love songs, that I always have the impression while listening to him that "love is in the air". Say, that would be a great song title!

- Denys, you're not on TV, but you also have a trademark sweater. You are almost always wearing a turtleneck. The only time I ever saw you wearing a tie was at your sister's wedding – and wasn't it rented along with your tuxedo? I still remember the blue turtleneck you were wearing the day we met!

- So blue is not only my favorite color – it's my lucky color! When I was in high school, I had to wear a tie every day. So when I started university, I enjoyed the academic freedom, but also "sartorial" freedom. A fancy word, I know, Manon, but I felt "fancy-free" In fact, I really began to appreciate that song written by Bobby Darin called "Simple Song of Freedom"!

-        At least you always compliment me on what I'm wearing, Denys!

-        Maybe because you "complement" me! Two similar but different words to describe our union, Manon! Now they are playing "Earth Angel" by The Penguins, a group from Los Angeles, believe it or not! Kind of hot for penguins in California – except in zoos! Penguins may "walk" funny, but these guys sure don't "sing" funny!

Chapter 117

-      Hi Mom, I hope everyone is well at home. Great news! The next time you see Manon, she will be wearing an engagement ring! I proposed at the top of the Eiffel Tower – and tell Dad it was not because I was going to jump off if she had said no! I like Seneca, but suicide is not one of the Stoic principles I espouse – say, I just made a play on words! No, I didn't bend down on one knee, because that conjures up images of slavery in Ancient Rome! Besides, we had just visited *Notre Dame de Paris*, and I didn't want Manon to confuse me with Quasimodo!

We are planning a wedding for the summer of 1977 – so lots of time to find a dress, Mom! You can tell Dad it was a "not so modest proposal"! He'll understand, since he talked to me one day about a satire called *A Modest Proposal*, written by Jonathan Swift. Something about having children for dinner – not as guests, but as part of the menu! Consequently, a totally absurd idea, and a relief to Feeb and me! I've since learned that the essay was an example of Juvenalian satire, because it was a bitter and ironic criticism of contemporary society. The "bread and circuses" poet was able in elegant Latin to pass on the message that "society sucks!" And speaking of Dad, I hope his golf game is up to par – another pun! Actually, Dad's scores will have to go DOWN to reach par! Manon had mentioned the film – *Is Paris Burning*? I had heard of the novel, and was able to confirm a negative answer to that question. I reminded Manon that Nero was not the head of the French government, and that I was not accompanied by the destructive Greek army that had burned Troy – since I was a LATIN student! Nor did she have to be suspicious of any gifts I might "shower" on her. Come to think of it, a little rain could go a long way in dousing a fire! Nevertheless, in the heat of the moment, I couldn't help thinking of Elvis' song, "Burning Love" I guess Phoebe is getting used to married life. How does she like working in the District Prosecutor's Office? Did she follow my advice and read Cicero's prosecution speeches against Catiline and against Verres – they're "Very" good! Am I making you sick, Mom? Manon and I are getting ready to fly back to Paris for our return flight to Montreal. We saw such lovely sites in the rest of France! We visited Strasbourg and Lyon – one of my Laval professors is from there. The city was called *Lugdunum* by the Romans, and we visited a Roman Theater and a beautiful church – *Notre Dame de Fourvière*. Yes, Mom, I lit a candle for you! We looked for the little village with Astérix and Obélix, but we didn't find it! But the Maître D' and our waiter at the restaurant were very suspicious-looking. One was a very heavy-set man and the other was very short – and they both had thick moustaches! We travelled on to Provence, where in Nîmes we saw the *Pont du Gard* and the *Maison Carrée*, the best preserved Roman temple anywhere! We visited Alesia, where Julius Caesar captured Vercingetorix. Come to think of it, the bus-boy at the restaurant in Lyon also had long hair and a moustache, and a gold chain around his neck engraved with a large V! We visited an art gallery in Toulouse. Manon loves art, so I figured we had nothing "to lose" – you see, Mom, I still have it! That line works every time! Manon told me about a group of three female singers in Quebec called Toulouse! We then spent some time on the French Riviera at Nice and Marseilles – which the Romans called *Massilia,* and which gave its name to the French National Anthem – "*La Marseillaise*". After that, Manon and I "headed for the coast" – like the "sixteen vestal virgins" that Gary Brooker sings about with Procol Harum in "A Whiter Shade of Pale". Except we were only two, and we are not vestal virgins – in fact, we aren't even – well, I think you get the picture, Mom! We visited the ports of La Rochelle and St. Malo, from which the French explorers sailed to the New World. And we got to see the White Cliffs of Dover! Before heading across the Channel, we spent a couple of days in Belgium, visiting Brussels – yes we ate some sprouts! – Antwerp and Bruges, where we saw the Basilica of The Holy Blood. Again, for you, Mom, a candle! Finally, we toured Flanders. These were very touching moments for Manon, since she works for Veterans Affairs! Then it was off to jolly old England, where we spent time in *Londinium* – well, that's what the Romans called London! We saw all the major sites like Piccadilly Circus and Trafalgar Square, Big Ben – I could have used a photo of that for my seminar presentation on "time" – and Buckingham Palace. We didn't get to see the Queen, but we were very impressed by the "Changing of the Guard". We saw Westminster Abbey, and I got to show off my knowledge of The British Museum to Manon. I really dazzled her during our tours of Oxford and Cambridge! We stopped briefly in Liverpool – we had to leave because I was driving Manon crazy by singing all the Beatles' songs. When I got to "Hello, Good-by", she was about to take me literally! Our final stop in England was extremely interesting - more so for me than Manon! In a quaint little pub we got to celebrate the victory of Manchester City over Manchester United – although I would have celebrated just as much if United had won! Manon was a little confused since they were talking about a football match, but it didn't fit the description of the football games I told her about that I had played at St. Xavier High. So I explained why her brothers call it soccer. A memorable moment occurred when we visited the set of "Coronation Street", and had a pint in the "Rover's Return". I shook hands with Ken Barlow – well, actually the actor Bill Roache! He was genuinely impressed with the fact that I was a graduate student in Classics – I don't know if it was Bill or Ken who was impressed! I casually mentioned that I was looking forward to a teaching and research career of forty years, after having spent fifteen years studying Greek and Latin. Bill Roache told me he had been in "Coronation Street" for fifteen years – since December, 1960 – and that he and so, Ken Barlow – would probably be still on "The Street" for at least another forty-five years! He

481

and the "old man from Verona" in the poem by Claudian would have gotten along just great! I was kind of relieved Mike Baldwin – really, Johnny Briggs – wasn't around. I don't know if I could have protected Manon from that womanizer! We spent a couple of days in Wales – in Cardiff and Swansea – and then travelled to Scotland. Tell Dad I got to play a round of golf at St. Andrew's! I didn't actually "find my game" there – more like I lost it! We spent a few days in Edinburgh and Glasgow, and then visited the very pastoral Hebrides – shades of the bucolic poetry of Vergil! The "sleepless suppliant" – beautiful alliteration, don't you think? – in the poem by Statius might have found consolation and relief here – there were plenty of sheep to count! We got to see Belfast in Northern Ireland, but I had the impression I was in another "sort of Quebec" in a political sense. We really enjoyed the capital city of Ireland, but didn't find Dublin as "rich" as Professor Watson had said it was! He had been using a bit of Orwell's "Dubl- speak" – "Doublespeak", Mom! We visited Galway and Cork, where I got to kiss the Blarney Stone!

Manon was only mildly impressed when I told her I much preferred kissing her! Our final stop in Ireland was in Limerick. I love reading those clever little poems, and this one by Rudyard Kipling caught my attention. It's called "There was a small boy of Quebec" and goes like this :

> "There was a small boy of Quebec
>
> Who was buried in snow to his neck.
>
> When they said "Are you friz'?"
>
> He replied "Yes, I is –
>
> But we don't call this cold in Quebec!".

I don't know how Mowgli in Kipling's Jungle Book would have coped! When we get back to Montreal, Manon and I will take the bus to Quebec – yeah, I guess I'm that "small boy of Quebec" - and we'll have a few days together before I start my final year of doctoral studies at Laval, and Manon heads to Montreal to join her family, who have just moved to St. Lambert, and to start her new job in the Montreal offices of Veterans Affairs. I'll be spending Christmas with you guys and New Year's with Manon's family. For sure Manon and I will be in Cincinnati to celebrate America's Bicentennial!

Chapter 118

- Hi, Denys. I trust you had a wonderful time in Europe with Manon, who is now, I understand, your fiancée. Congratulations! We should mention it at our first wine and cheese reception so that our female students – and maybe a certain female professor! – will know that you are officially off-limits! This is your last year with us. You mentioned you were not interested in post-doctoral research – neither here nor in Europe! Not even in an American university! It's understandable that you would be anxious to obtain a teaching position. Besides, you spent all your summers doing graduate seminars. Moreover, I don't think Manon envisages introducing her husband-to-be as "that Latin student"! As you know, you will be taking my Greek course on Callimachus and Theophrastus. You will also be in the Latin course with Professor Saucier, in which you will be reading Lucan, Silius Italicus and Valerius Flaccus. He's anxious to read your paper on Seneca from last summer's Philosophy Seminar. I'm so glad you've accepted the role of Sostratus in our Greek play, Menander's *Dyskolus*! Was it because the beginning of his name sounds like "Disco"? I know you have a quasi "disco – lus-t"! To think I will have to replace you as the Department "jester"! Sostratus is a young Athenian who falls in love with the daughter of the grouch for whom the play is named. This will be your fifth play with our group, going back to that first play we performed at McGill, where you did a few Latin plays as well, and no one else comes close to matching that number. Professor Marois has informed me that your dissertation is coming along very well. I know you want to discuss a couple of issues with Professor Watson.

You will certainly be armed with a number of very positive reference letters from Laval and McGill professors to accompany your applications for a teaching position, and I can't recall having seen such impressive transcripts! I would like to thank you for single-handedly fulfilling our commitment to the Faculty by teaching the Classical Civilization courses to the general public. The fourth and final course is Greek and Roman History. The next series will be given jointly by the History and Comparative Literature Departments, and they will present courses on Medieval and Renaissance History and Literature. Ironically, we have posters from those Departments announcing a session next summer at the American Academy in Rome, which you know well. It's a six-week seminar on Medieval and Renaissance Latin. One hundred and twenty hours of Latin – I don't think you can resist! I am aware that you are eligible for a final summer grant from the Parker Foundation. I imagine the organization which recruited you to teach Latin and Greek to the public will be sorry to see you leave – as will the students at the Seminary. Concordia is certainly making good use of your services. You will be giving an Advanced Latin Reading course on Horace. It's an ambitious syllabus, which will offer selections from the *Epodes*, *Satires*, *Odes*, including the *Carmen Saeculare*, and *Epistles,* including the *Ars Poetica.* And you will be introducing your course on films based on Ancient Greece and Rome. You are – and have always been – a very busy young man, Denys, and it has been a pleasure to have you here as a student at Laval! I must add that what I find truly remarkable about you is that despite being a student of such a serious and sophisticated subject of studies, you are capable of communicating with all and sundry without any complex or complicated conversation. If I may substitute "seasons" for the various social strata of society, your register of language and your range of interests indeed make you "a man for all seasons"!

-        Thank you for the compliment, Professor! But I guess "to every season there is a reason"! That may sound somewhat familiar, but what I mean is that I try to see something worthwhile in everyone I meet, no matter what their station in life is. I have been as comfortable behind a pizza counter as behind a desk in a graduate seminar! It has been a pleasure for me, Professor Marcoux, to have been a student here at Laval. I have indeed enjoyed the plays. Maybe in the *Dyskolus* we can have the grumpy father wear a green tunic, and call him the Grinch! The Professors here have always inspired me, including those I didn't take courses with like Professor Mayrand, the Department's other archaeologist, and Professor Michaud, with whom I got to speak about Hellenistic history and religion. They have all helped me pursue some enriching opportunities. I am so glad Martin is back on track to finish his Master's degree. In fact, I have approached him about replacing me for the Greek and Latin courses given at *Cégep* Ste-Foy, and he is very open to the idea. For obvious reasons, he is less keen on teaching the classes at the Seminary, but a couple of the Seminarians will be completing their fourth course this year, and will be able to teach beginning and intermediate courses. I am interested in the summer programme in Rome, which means I will miss the Summer Olympics in Montreal, but the Games have been around since Pierre De Coubertin's revival of the Olympics in Athens in 1896, and are sure to continue! I would have liked to have been a spectator – no, a participant! – at the first contest in 776 B.C.! I am a little ashamed that they were halted during the Roman Empire in AD 394. Theodosius was adamant in removing all vestiges of pagan antiquity in order to establish Christianity as the religion of the Empire. But I think he just wasn't being a good sport! If he had been around for the Berlin Games of 1936, he would have realized that the Olympics are above race, color and religion, as America's Jesse Owens went on to prove! The film course developed out of a project I did in one of my summer courses at the American Academy in Rome. Now that Manon is in Montreal, my phone bill is sure to be higher!

Chapter 119

-     Welcome to our first class on Lucan! Before we look at his *De bello civili* – sometimes called *Pharsalia*, but I think it unjustified as a title for the whole work - I would like to talk about monsters – no, not about professors who assign too much reading! In the nineteenth century a young lady who was fond of reading Latin, including Lucan, wrote a novel entitled *Frankenstein*. I am speaking of Mary Shelley, the bride – no, not of Frankenstein! – some of you may be fans of those two movies with Boris Karlof – but of the poet Percy Bysshe Shelley. She gave another title to her novel as well – *The Modern Prometheus* – suggesting that she considered Prometheus to be a monster. For Mary Shelley, Prometheus did not liberate man, but rather condemned him to the role of savage meat-eater by returning to mankind the gift of fire, which Zeus had removed when he discovered he was receiving the inferior part of the burnt offerings made by man. Prometheus was chained to a rock, where his liver would be devoured daily and then grow back. Perhaps this chronic liver pain suggests a drinking problem, but medical science has allowed for liver transplants, giving recipients a life expectancy of up to five years. So perhaps Prometheus suffered for only five years! As a Pythagorean, Mary Shelley shunned meat! Today we would call her a vegetarian! It is interesting to consider the influence Latin had – and can still have – on literature, and perhaps even on life itself! The narrator in the novel – a certain Captain Walton – is determined to face death with "the lessons learned from Seneca", obviously a reference to the Stoic philosophy. I myself admit to having learned many lessons from Seneca, but, fortunately, not the lesson of death! The monster Frankenstein actually educates himself with a copy of Plutarch's *Lives*. Dr. Victor Frankenstein, who created the monster, liked Latin, because his creator, Mary Shelley, was fond of Latin!

In Book Six of Lucan's epic, a Thessalian witch by the name of Erichtho resurrects a corpse through necromancy. This reanimation episode, I believe, influenced Shelley in her description of Dr. Frankenstein's "giving life" to his creation. You may recall Ovid's account of Pygmalion's creation coming to life, but I am sure Galatea was much better-looking than Boris Karlof!

Denys, here, is taking his last Latin course with us at Laval, but I think it is safe to say that his well-documented fondness of Latin has not made him a monster! He is soon to be Dr. Hainsworth – not Dr. Frankenstein! Please read today's text from Book One, Denys, and give us your translation, just as Mary Shelley went on to proudly share her translations of Livy, Apuleius and other Latin poets.

485

-    Yes, Professor Saucier. I believe the awkward movements we see Boris Karlof, a.k.a Frankenstein, making are his attempt to dance the "Monster Mash", sung by another Boris – Bobby "Boris" Pickett! I also once saw on TV Herman Munster – the "friendly monster" – trying to dance in a video of the song "Land of a 1000 Dances"! Here are lines 183-212 of Lucan's account of the war between Caesar and Pompey, which tore the Republic apart, just as the American Civil War "disunited" the "United" States! The alternate title was most likely due to the fact that the decisive battle was fought at Pharsalus. Lucan would naturally be philosophical about his own death, ordered by Nero, since he was the nephew of Seneca. Like his uncle, he spilled much ink and, ultimately, some blood!

-    *iam gelidas Caesar cursu superaverat Alpe*

ingentisque animo motus bellumque futurum

ceperat. ut ventum est parvi Rubiconis ad undas,

ingens visa duci patriae trepidantis imago

clara per obscuram voltu maestissima noctem

turrigero canos effundens vertice crines

caesarie lacera nudisque adstare lacertis

et gemitu permixta loqui : " quo tenditis ultra?

quo fertis mea signa, viri? si iure venitis,

si cives, huc usque licet." tum perculit horror

membra ducis, riguere comae gressumque coercens

languor in extrema tenuit vestigia ripa.

mox ait "o magnae qui moenia prospicis urbis

Tarpeia de rupe Tonans Phrygiique penates

gentis Iuleae et rapti secreta Quirini

et residens celsa Latiaris Iuppiter Alba

Vestalesque foci summique o numinis instar

Roma, fave coeptis non te furialibus armis

persequor : en, adsum victor terraque marique

Caesar, ubique tuus (liceat modo, nunc quoque) miles

ille erit ille nocens, qui me tibi fecerit hostem."

inde moras soluit belli tumidumque per amnem

signa tulit propere : sicut squalentibus arvis

aestiferae Libyes viso leo comminus hoste

subsedit dubius, totam dum colligit iram;

mox, ubi se saevae stimulant verbere caudae

erexitque iubam et vasto grave murmur hiatu

infremuit, tum torta levis si lancea Mauri

haereat aut latum subeant venabula pectus,

per ferrum tanti securus volneris exit.

'' By his crossing, Caesar had conquered the icy Alps, and moved by his mind and soul, undertook the future war.

As he arrived at the waves of the little Rubicon the huge image of the trembling fatherland appeared to the general, clear and very sad in features through the dark night, shedding grey hair from a tower-bearing crown. With torn hair and bare arms she stood, and with broken groans she spoke: 'to what point are you advancing?

And where are you carrying my standards, soldiers? If you come by right, if as citizens, it is permitted to come here up to this point.' Then horror struck the general's limbs, his hair stiffened, and weakness, holding back his step, restrained his footsteps on the further shore.

Presently he said: ' O Thunderer, who sees the walls of the great city from the Tarpeian rock, and Phrygian gods of the Julian clan who see the secret rites of Quirinus, who was carried off, and Jupiter Latiaris, residing in the Alban heights, and Vestals and the lofty fires, O Rome in god's image, favor my undertakings, for I do not pursue you with furious arms, behold I,

Caesar, victorious on land and sea, everywhere your soldier (here and wherever it it is permitted), that one, who will have made me your enemy, that one will be guilty.'

Then he ended the delays, and quickly bore the standards of war across the swollen stream.

Just as in the uncultivated fields of scorching Libya the lion, when the enemy is seen nearby, he crouches down uncertain, while he gathers all his anger; soon, when his savage tail arouses him with its swooshing, he has raised his mane, and from his deep jaws a heavy roar has sounded, then if the twisted light lance of the African clings to his side or the hunting-spears reach his chest, he runs off, unconcerned by the cruelty of such a wound."

The lion simile was very apt, I believe, since at the end of this war, Caesar certainly got the lion's share of the spoils!

Chapter 120

\-   Hello, everybody. I spent some time thinking about how we could begin this course on Horace besides simply giving you the course syllabus and sending you on your way. Especially since I once worked on a whole module on the presentation of the first class! The syllabus is important for sure, since it provides the list of works we will be reading and translating, as well as guidelines for reading the poetic meters in Horace's poems and a description of the literary devices in the poems we shall be studying. I noticed some of you scanning down the page. Actually, you will find the evaluation *schemata* – a nice German word borrowed from the Greek – on page two! As you will notice, only the three best of the five translation tests will be calculated towards your final mark. In lieu of a final exam, you may opt to write a paper on the material we will have read in the various works of Horace – the background, subject matter, etc. I guess I should mention that I also completed a teaching module on evaluation procedures! You may be wondering why I opened our session with Bobby Gentry's song, "Ode to Billie Joe". Well it certainly wasn't to suggest we all jump off a bridge like poor Billie Joe MacAllister in the song, nor that you do something drastically heroic near a bridge like the legendary Roman hero Horatius, albeit the fact he bears our poet's name! I am endeavouring rather to build a bridge between odes from the time of Horace to the present. I think I "owed" you as much! Those of you who have had courses with me before – and I see that there are a number of you – can explain my sense of humour to the newcomers. Likewise, those of you who were in my Roman religion course will remember the *pontifices* – the religious officials who "built bridges" between the people and their gods. The word "ode" is, in fact, from the Greek word for "song", and therefore has always been a tribute in poetry or song to someone or something. You will recall that the Latin word *carmen* means song or poem. The other song I played for you was an introduction to words derived from the word "ode". If you are a Lou Christie fan, as I am, you will have recognized his song "Rhapsody in the Rain"! Of course, for the effects of a terrible rainstorm, you will have to listen to his hit song "Lightning Strikes"! A rhapsody was a sort of "song weaver", from the Greek verb *rhaptein*, meaning "to stitch together". There was even a singing group called The Weavers! If there are any jazz music fans among you, George Gershwin's composition "Rhapsody in Blue" comes to mind. Gershwin claimed this song was a "musical kaleidoscope of America", but there are those who suggest that it is a tribute to New York. Before you protest that it's always about New York, consider the 1940's movie *On the Town*, where three sailors on leave – Gene Kelly, Frank Sinatra, and Jules Munshin - sing and dance their way through New York. The song "New York, New York" is featured in that movie, but I have heard a more modern look at New York is being filmed, and Frank Sinatra is anxious to add a more contemporary song about New York to his repertoire!

Other derivatives of the word "ode" include "episode", an incident in a continuous narrative, and "eisodion", an "addition" or "entrance". Actually it's a Greek word synonymous for "prologue", which is itself a Greek word! There is the word "parody", a work that makes fun of another work. The word "melody" comes from the Greek *melos* meaning "tune" and suggests "sweet music". Even the word "yodel" is ultimately derived from "ode", but if I attempt to demonstrate that sound, you will not find it so sweet! The melodeon instrument also owes its name to the "ode" – that play on words is coming back to haunt me! I would like to mention the Odeon – that ancient Greek and Roman "music hall" – the original Place des Arts, the ancient Carnegie Hall! The name has been incorporated into a very successful chain of movie theaters in Great Britain. The "*septième art*" now uses this Greek name, even though there is no Greek "Muse" for motion pictures! Perhaps this is a good time to mention the course I am teaching this year on Greece and Rome in the movies! I believe it is still possible to register for this course, if you are interested. Since a number of you are English majors, I thought we could spend the last part of our first class looking at a few English authors of centuries past who had a particular interest in Horace and in the writing of odes. You will all no doubt be familiar with the 19th century poet John Keats and his "Ode to a Nightingale", which might make you think of Catullus and the sparrow – the *passer* - of his beloved Lesbia, and "Ode on a Grecian Urn". If you should be asked "what's a Grecian urn?" I'm told about ten dollars an hour! Ah, humour – where is thy sting? We will now look at translations and a satirical parody of some Horatian Odes. John Milton, the seventeenth century English poet, and polyglot – he knew English, Latin, Greek, Italian, Hebrew Spanish and Dutch – celebrated for his poem "Paradise Lost", and also for "Paradise Regained" - had a keen interest in classical authors, and was influenced by Homer and Vergil in writing his own poetry. I shall read *Ode 5* from Book One in the meter known as Fourth Asclepiadean, and then we will look at Miton's translation.

Quis multa gracilis te puer in rosa

perfusus liquidis urget odoribus

grato, Pyrrha, sub antro?

cui flavam religas comam,

simplex munditiis? heu quotiens fidem

mutatosque deos flebit et aspera

nigris aequora ventis

emirabitur insolens,

qui nunc te fruitur credulus aurea,

qui semper vacuam, semper amabilem

sperat, nescius aurae

fallacis! miseri, quibus

intemptata nites. me tabula sacer

votiva paries indicat uvida

suspendisse potenti

vestimenta maris deo.

"What slender youth, bedewed with liquid odours,

Courts thee on roses in some pleasant cave,

    Pyrrha? For whom bind'st thou

      In wreaths thy golden hair,

Plain in thy neatness ? Oh, how oft shall he

On faith and changed gods complain, and seas

    Rough with black winds and storms

      Unwonted shall admire,

Who now enjoys thee credulous, all gold;

Who always vacant, always amiable,

    Hopes thee, of fluttering gales

        Unmindful! Hapless they

To whom thou untried seem'st fair! Me, in my vowed

Picture, the sacred wall declare t' have hung

    My dank and dripping weeds

        To the stern God of Sea."

John Dryden, the seventeenth century English poet – England's first Poet Laureate – wrote "Epigram on Milton", "The Works of Virgil", "Alexander's Feast", "Amphitryon", "Oedipus" and a number of works with Latin titles – *Religio Laici* – "The Layman's Faith", *Astraea Redux* – "The Return of Justice", Astraea being the goddess of Justice, *Annus Mirabilis* – "A Wonderful Year", and *Threnodia Augustalis*. A threnody – another derivative of "ode" – is a poem of mourning, from the Greek word *threnos* meaning "lament". You American literature fans have probably read Eugene O'Neil's play – *Mourning Becomes Electra*. I shall now read Horace's *Ode 9* from Book One in its Alcaic Stanza meter, the name derived from the Greek lyric poet Alcaeus. We shall then look at Dryden's translation.

Vides ut alta stet nive candidum

Soracte, nec iam sustineant onus

silvae laborantes, geluque

flumina constiterint acuto.

dissolve frigus ligna super foco

large reponens atque benignius

deprome quadrimum Sabina,

O Thaliarche, merum diota:

permitte divis cetera, qui simul

stravere ventos aequore fervido

deproeliantis, nec cupressi

nec veteres agitantur orni.

quid sit futurum cras fuge quaerere et

quem Fors dierum cumque dabit lucro

appone, nec dulcis amores

sperne puer neque tu choreas,

donec virenti canities abest

morosa, nunc et campus et areae

lenesque sub noctem susurri

composita repelantur hora,

nunc et latentis proditor intimo

gratus puellae risus ab angulo

pignusque dereptum lacertis

aut digito male pertinaci.

''Behold yon' Mountains hoary height

Made higher with new Mounts of Snow;

Again behold the Winters weight

Oppress the lab'ring Woods below:

And streams with Icy fetters bound,

Benum'd and crampt to solid ground.

With well heap'd Logs dissolve the cold,

And feed the genial heat with fires;

Produce the wine, that makes us bold ,

And sprightly Wit and Love inspires:

For what hereafter shall betide,

God, if 't is worth his care, provide.

Let him alone with what he made ,

To toss and turn the World below,

At his command the storms invade;

The winds by his Commision blow;

Till with a Nod he bids 'em cease,

And then the Calm returns, and all is peace.

To morrow and her works defie,

Lay hold upon the present hour, And snatch the pleasures passing by.

To put them out of Fortunes pow'r.

Nor love, nor love's delights disdain,

What e're thou get 'st to day is gain,

Secure those golden early joys,

That Youth unsowr'd with sorrow bears,

E 're with 'ring time the taste destroyes,

With sickness and unwieldy years!

For active sports, for pleasing rest,

This is the time to be possest;

The best is but in season best.

The pointed hour of promis'd Bliss,

The pleasing whisper in the dark;

The half unwilling willing kiss,

The laugh that guides thee to the mark,

When the kind Nymph wou 'd coyness feign,

And hides but to be found again,

These, these are joyes the Gods for Youth ordain."

William Cowper was an eighteenth century English poet who wrote many religious hymns, and is also known for his poem which argued against slavery, and is entitled "The Negro's Complaint". Dr. Martin Luther King often quoted this poem, as did a young girl I had no complaints with!

However, it would not have been too popular in Ancient Rome, except with a few enlightened minds like Seneca! There are some lines penned by Cowper that I would like to share with you.

"There is a pleasure in poetic pain, Which only poets know."

"God moves in a mysterious way. Oh, for a closer walk with God."

I shall read Horace's *Ode 38* from Book One. The meter is Sapphic Stanza. We will then look at Cowper's rendering of the poem.

Persicos odi, puer, apparatus,

displicent nexae philyra coronae;

mitte sectari, rosa quo locorum

    sera moretur.

simplici myrto nihil allabores

sedulus curo; neque te ministrum

dedecet myrtus neque me sub arta

    vite bibentem.

Now for Cowper's translation.

"Boy, I hate their empty shows,

   Persian garlands I detest,

Bring me not the late-blown rose

   Ling'ring after all the rest;

Plainer myrtle pleases me

   Thus out-stretch'd beneath my vine,

Myrtle more becoming thee,

Waiting with thy master's wine."

William Makepeace Thackeray was a nineteenth century British satirist and novelist born in India. Let's read his parodic paraphrase – I was hoping to get in some eccentric example of alliteration today! – of the poem we just read.

"Dear Lucy, You know what my wish is, I hate all your Frenchified fuss, Your silly entrees and made dishes Were never intended for us.

Persicos odi, puer, apparatus, Bring me a chop and a couple of potatoes!" Hardly the same poem you might say. I guess both Williams were aiming for top "BILLing!"

My office hours are listed in the syllabus. As most of you already know, I am only on campus on Tuesdays. See you next week.

Chapter 121

\-   Hi Professor Watson. I've brought a draft of my dissertation, but there are some points I would like to discuss with you.

\-   I'm also anxious to clarify a few of your conclusions. Thank you for leaving a copy of your syllabus for the film course that you are teaching at Concordia. You and your courses are as popular as ever, and Professor Jones is hopeful you will accept a full-time position in their Department next year. There are some interesting selections here. I recognized the films you had presented in your course at the Academy in Rome, but with a full-year course you have the luxury of numerous additions. You mentioned that you used all the money from the stipend for new courses to purchase the films rather than budget research time and course development. Most professors would have taken the money and run! But, as you say, Mr. Hainsworth, you're not a professor yet! If you don't mind, we can spend a few minutes looking at the list before we discuss Roman religion. *Alexander the Great* with Richard Burton – good choice! *Androcles and the Lion* – nice change from blood and gore! *Antony and Cleopatra* and *Caesar and Cleopatra*. The Egyptian Queen is so prominent in your course, she could almost be your T.A.! I wondered why you included *The Silver Chalice*, but in your notes you mention that it was Paul Newman's first film, and that he took out an ad in the newspaper discouraging people from going to see the movie. But his adverse publicity had the opposite effect! *The Colossus of Rhodes* sounds interesting, as does *Brennus, Enemy of Rome*. *The Last Roman* has an all-star cast – Laurence Harvey, Orson Welles, Honor Blackman. *Carry on Cleo* is an interesting choice – did you know that the Cleopatra in that film, Amanda Barrie, stars in "Coronation Street"? *The Robe* is an excellent choice. I know you like to include films based on novels, and the book by Lloyd C. Douglas was a best-seller. I believe the movie you listed next, *Demetrius and the Gladiators* was some kind of sequel. Both films starred Victor Mature. Where did you find *Duel of the Titans*, which has a more revealing alternate title – *Romulus and Remus*? You mention that the authentic "Titans" will probably "clash" in movies sometime in the future! Do you have an oracle in Hollywood that you consult? Your students will probably like the movie *The Minotaur*. It's interesting how many of these films have more than one title. The film *The Centurion* is also listed as The *Conqueror of Corinth*, but you mention in your notes that the title depended on which country the film was being released in. Another example you have is *Damon and Pythias*, which was also released as *The Tyrant of Syracuse*. Is it true you are showing *Helen of Troy* because Brigitte Bardot is in the cast? Of course, *Julius Caesar* with Marlon Brando was a must – and he had to be Mark Antony, not the short-lived Julius Caesar in that movie! *Gladiator of Messalina* is intriguing, although it too has another title – *Messalina Against the Son of Hercules*. I see you have another film with Brigitte Bardot – *Nero's Mistress*. Has your fiancée seen your film list? But I guess you can justify this film because Seneca appears in it, played by Vittorio de Sica. It's sad that de Sica passed away not that long ago. *Romulus and the Sabines* starred Roger Moore as Romulus. You mentioned in your notes that he was "The Saint" on TV, but you would hardly call him a saint for carrying off those helpless women! You note he has been in a couple of movies as James Bond. I imagine he was Agent 753 ... B.C. (behind Connery!). But I prefer your notation – Agent 007...Oh Oh 7 Kings!

You list the film *Hercules in New York* – Arnold Schwarzenegger's first feature film - and have *The Three Stooges Meet Hercules* marked with an asterisk. I guess it would be shown only as a filler. No sense giving Hercules three more labours! With movies like that, it's no wonder Hercules went mad! *Spartacus and the Ten Gladiators* is a good follow-up to the blockbuster *Spartacus* from your project days in Rome. *The Siege of Syracuse* is most interesting, according to your notes, because it stars Tina Louise, "the movie star" from TV's "Gilligan's Island". They could have escaped that island if they had had Daedalus with them! You are also showing the film version of *Trojan Women*, which stars three excellent actresses - Katherine Hepburn, Irene Pappas, and Vanessa Redgrave. As well, you plan on showing *The Bacchantes*, based on the play you yourself starred in, *The Bacchae*! I noted that your tribute film to early Christian martyrs, *Revolt of the Slaves*, features the actress Rhonda Fleming. I'm sure this course will be well-received and there will be no "revolt" by the students!

-       The final section in my dissertation deals with the proliferation of philosophical ideas in the Roman world, originating basically in Greece and in the "Greek thinking" East. These ideas would have made the educated elite in Rome ambivalent towards the beliefs and even practices of traditional Roman religion, practices which "dyed-in-wool" Romans like Marcus Cato wished to maintain at all costs. Varro and Cicero were conscious of the need to preoccupy – and occupy! – the Roman proletariat with the correct practice of *religio*, in order to assure their loyalty to the Republic. Roman religion was very much a civic religion, and the practice of religious devotion was very public, indeed an integral part of the *res publica*! Cicero undoubtedly believed that good "church-goers" made good citizens. This is borne out by the religious code he introduced in his *De legibus*. There he states "no one shall have gods to himself, either new or foreign gods, unless recognized by the State. Privately they shall worship only the gods they have received from their ancestors." Professor Marois has warned me about transferring Judaeo-Christian doctrines and traditions to the Roman world. But I can't help seeing a bit of The Ten Commandments – "thou shalt have no other gods" - in this stipulation by Cicero. In any event, transfers of religious practice seem, in some instances, to have gone the other way, with, for example, the religious symbolism of the Christian halo being probably influenced by the representation of the pagan *Sol Invictus*. Cicero goes on to say "the various gods shall have their different priests, the gods together their pontiffs, and individual gods their *flamens*." Again, this is an appeal to traditional practice and the proper procedure in carrying out the rites - prayers, sacrifices, etc. – to the gods. This tactic – I believe this is is what the efforts of Cicero and others underlay – dated back to Numa, who realized that, since Rome had become powerful, *metus hostilis* – fear of the enemy – was no longer an element that could maintain the loyalty of Rome's citizen body, and he replaced this with *metus deorum* – fear of the gods. While the earliest rituals had to be attached to some kind of belief system – a pantheon of gods – what emerged as really essential for the *pax deorum* – and for a sort of domestic *pax Romana* – was a blind devotion to custom and conformity. The rules and regulations for correct practice of *religio* would be the domain of the government. So, as Varro would say, "necessity makes good prayers"!

-       Therefore, religion – or the practice of religion – would keep the citizen body docile, which is in line with your contention that religious practices were ultimately dictated by the masses, and not by the state or ruling class of elites. My own study of the Roman gods has confirmed – what others had already suggested – that the traditional gods of Rome were more popular in the West than in Greece and the eastern provinces. What do you make of the rise in popularity of these oriental gods, and of the philosophical ideas arriving in Rome from the Greek world?

-       Firstly, Professor, we must remember that from earliest times Rome was in contact with Etruscan and Greek deities and practices of worship. It is true that the philosophical teachings of Epicureans, Stoics, and others, such as Skeptics, Cynics, as well as adherents to Egyptian and Near Eastern cults such as Isis, *Magna Mater*, and Mithras, and we musn't forget good old Bacchus, would come to serve as some kind of theology for an educated elite searching for invigorating change. Likewise, the whole "poetic religion", introducing a "new and improved" mythology, would tend to make the old observances dull and even obsolete. However, with so many claims to "truth", it was, as Varro would suggest – with the approval of Cicero – expedient to remind the vastly non-educated majority that "truth" lay in tradition. Varro would even declare that the ordinary Roman would be incapable of comprehending the new religious ideas.

For those wishing to have the State continue to benefit from the faithful loyalty of its citizens, it was necessary to equate *pietas* and *fides* in civic matters to those in religious matters.

"Truth" would be as it had always been – from the time of *pius Aeneas*, who had rescued the true gods from the fires of Troy. His *penates* – his family gods –would become the gods of Rome. At this point, belief was less important than ritual – the Roman rites – of religion. The "proof was in the pudding" so to speak! So Latin *do* – "I give" - meant I am offering the proper sacrifices and prayers in the proper way – *ut des* – so that you, almighty gods, will be happy and keep us safe. One might call this a "management of religion based on orthopraxy rather than orthodoxy"! Consequently, religious fervor did not need inspiration! Nonetheless, when disasters did occur, such as the defeats that threatened Rome during the Second Punic War, the man on the street would have felt the need to "spend a few more hours in church" in order to appease the gods! These circumstances remind me of a short story by Gabrielle Roy that I read a few years ago. You remember that I have admired her since I studied *Bonheur d'Occasion* in my course at McGill, and since our visit with Mrs. Watson to "Lower Westmount", as you called it. As a matter of fact, after our weekly dinner tonight, Manon and I are going to take a little walk through "Florentine's old neighbourhood" in St. Henri. Well, in "Le Puits de Dunrea", a huge fire is about to destroy a village of religiously fervent believers. As such, they think the fire has been sent by God to punish them. When one of the villagers attempts to appease God's anger by entering a burning building holding a religious icon, he becomes a sad victim of the fire. The villagers then realize that the more practical step to take is to flee the burning village.

Fortunately for the Roman worshippers, the incense for the gods would be burning, but not the altar or temple they would be approaching! But appease the gods they must! They wouldn't have realized that it was not the gods who were punishing them, but Hannibal! Roy's short story about the fire might even have "sparked" some interest – no pun intended, I'm just fired up! - among the Stoics who believed that fire would end the world! Perhaps some of them even thought that the great fire under Nero announced that Doomsday had arrived! To come back to your query, Professor Watson, there is no indication that the Roman masses turned *en masse* – this time the pun is deliberate! – to the "new religions". Many of these "secret rites" remained just that. Even the government elite – polytheists that they were - would not presume to offend gods, even those on visit to Rome from abroad! Evidence that practice, not belief, guided the Roman lawmakers and religious hierarchy was the decree against the *Bacchanalia*. But as far as eradicating the notions of individual freedom and the enlightenment of ideas that arrived from the Hellenistic world, the efforts of Cato were doomed to failure, especially since the ultimate patriot – the "father of his country", Cicero - recognized, as he says in his *De re publica*, that Hellenism "was a mighty river of culture and learning". In researching the reaction to religious ideas from the Greek world, one of my sources, Valerius Maximus, had this to say about Roman "resistance" in matters referring to preserving the Latin language. The situation reminded me in some ways of the language debate here in Quebec! In Book Two of his *Memorable Deeds and Sayings*, Valerius Maximus tells us that "there was this practice which the Romans observed with great earnest, never to answer the Greeks except in Latin." I suppose, Professor, a bit like "potato, potater" – you say Zeus, I say Jupiter! Valerius Maximus goes on to say that "separating them from the fluency of speech in which they excel, they forced them to speak through an interpreter, not only in our city, but also in Greece and Asia, in order to spread the Latin language among all peoples and to make it more respectable." I wonder if we will ever see language laws of that nature here in Quebec!

- Would you say, Mr. Hainsworth, that religious policy dominated the politics of the Republic? Did the people willingly and sincerely adhere to a faithful obedience to what we might call Roman religion?

- Well, the plebeians joined demands for religious authority to their increasing insistence on the right to political representation. The patrician elite could not separate church and state, that is to say, *religio* and the civic practice of the state religion. Plebeians did indeed attain to priesthods and other positions in the religious hierarchy. Again, I believe that these concessions are another instance of the the people dictating to the ruling elite in the sphere of religious affairs. By the end of the Republic, the situation of political factions required politicians and political leaders to observe religion "religiously". We know that the position of *pontifex maximus* was sought after for political reasons, and not as a substitution for the "spiritual exercises of St. Ignatius"! Cicero had insisted that only the best men could be entrusted with the maintenance of religion, and, by extension, with the maintenance of the state. In fact, the political elite had not simply abdicated religious authority to the masses. They still controlled the "organization" of religious practice. Varro had warned that citizens must not be allowed to become indifferent to religion. But when political heavyweights like Julius Caesar began to show just such an indifference – and even a disregard – for traditional Roman religious rules and ritual, the placebo that was Roman religion began to wear off – and the masses began to misbehave! Only the strong-arm measures of authority – ultimately, military authority – would bring the populace back in check. I would humbly suggest, Professor, that the abandonment of the conditions of agreement between the rulers and the ruled in matters of religion were instrumental in the demise of the Roman Republic. Augustus will restore political and social order. How? With a return to the traditional religion of Rome's ancestors, a restoration of the great temples, Vergil's epic on the religious foundation of Rome, Livy's account of the earliest religious traditions, etc. The Roman people were given back the "what" and "how" of *religio,* with a version of the "why" provided by Augustus himself! But someone else will have to write a dissertation on what happens to Roman religion in the Roman Empire!

-       It seems to me that you have been consistent in your approach to the different aspects of your thesis on Roman religion, to wit, that it was largely dictated by the needs and wants of the common people of Rome, especially insofar as those wants and needs were useful to the governing bodies of Rome. It is most likely that you will be able to submit a completed final version of your dissertation to both Professor Marois and myself in February, which will allow me to organize a defense of your dissertation before the Examining Committee in March.

Chapter 122

-        It was certainly different eating in that little *"binerie"* in St. Henri, Denys. I've never been to this part of Montreal. To tell you the truth, I haven't even gotten the chance to visit much of the South Shore yet, and I basically just know my way to and from work on Queen Mary. Thanks for agreeing to speak only in English, since I have to practice. If I pass the language exam at work, I'll receive the bilingual bonus that is given to Federal Government employees. But what is the special occasion for coming here?

-        The food here is perhaps a little pedestrian for someone like you, Manon, because you never cease to amaze me with your delicious variety of delicacies that I always look forward to! And I must compliment your parents' cooking, since you turned out to be quite a dish! You are truly a young woman of many recipes, but my favorite is your "recipe" for happiness – yours and mine! I'm no great chef, but I believe I have managed to concoct a "recipe" for success – the main ingredients being determination and hard work! I guess a clearly defined goal would be a kind of seasoning! I realize it's kind of ironic to be practicing your English in an area where they only speak French. Once you're fully bilingual, we'll work on Latin and Greek! I'm just kidding, Manon, but the Greeks and Romans were the first truly bilingual – and bicultural - peoples. Your Prime Minister Trudeau would be proud of them! The Romans were the first to study comparative literature and comparative religion. For my dissertation, I relied on numerous literary sources, including a substantial number of Greek texts. Since my comprehensive reading and foreign language proficiency requirements in French and German have been fulfilled, it remains for me to defend my dissertation in March – I'll be writing application letters at the same time! The Examining Committee will be composed of professors from McGill's Faculty of Religious Studies and Laval's Department of History. Fortunately, the outside examiner is from the University of Ottawa's Classics Department, and so he won't have to travel too far. You asked me what the occasion was. It's actually a *"Bonheur d'Occasion"*! This year is the thirtieth anniversary of the publication of Gabrielle's Roy's novel. It's a classic of French-Canadian literature…like *La Famille Plouffe*! I know you are waiting for a film version of that novel, now that you have become addicted to the big screen! I thought we could take a little walk through the streets where the fictional Lacasse family spent their days. But I'm warning you, if I see Jean Lévesque, I'm going to throw a rock at him! Speaking of throwing rocks, some of the students at Laval wanted to form an association called *"La Fédération des Latinistes du Québec"*. When I pointed out that this name would produce the logo "FLQ", they decided to have a rethink!

-       You're right, Denys, it is kind of romantic! And I'm much luckier than Florentine! Maybe I should call you Holden now that we're speaking English! Be careful about using the name Lévesque the wrong way. René Lévesque is a hero around here. You also have to be careful about using the name Jean as well, since Jean Drapeau is still the Mayor of Montreal, and people are proud of the fact that Montreal will be hosting the Olympics in July. It's really too bad you won't be able to attend, but then how could "the Latin student" miss an opportunity to study Later Latin from the Middle Ages and the Renaissance? Especially since it will be your last opportunity to receive a grant from the Parker Foundation. So – carpe diem! You see, Denys… Holden, I already know Latin! In any event, the following summer will be more exciting than the Olympics or a summer programme in Rome! I know you are anxious for a June wedding, because of Roman traditions.

-       I am for sure, Manon! Juno was after all the goddess associated with weddings, even though her own marriage wasn't exactly blissful! I'm looking forward to carrying you across the threshold of our new home, wherever that might be. The custom of carrying the bride into her new home is a symbolic act of force demonstrating that the wife is accepting the household gods – the *penates* - of her husband. Since we are both Catholics, it won't be much of a struggle! I'll know in June where I will be teaching in September – that is, if I AM teaching!

There were some nice houses in Brossard, weren't there? I hope we get more opportunities to look at neighbourhoods over the next few months – just in case! I saw some pretty houses on Rome Boulevard! And we wouldn't be far from your family's home in St. Lambert. I'm also glad that you agreed to a trilingual ceremony – in French, English and Latin!

-       Regardless of where the wedding takes place, my sister Maggie will be my maid of honor, and Bob will be your best man. My sister Nicole will be a bridesmade, of course, along with Josiane, as well as Lucie from Quebec. Martin has agreed to be an usher along with my brothers Michel and Antoine. You mentioned that Jeremy would also be an usher. That's a lot of details sorted out considering the wedding is a year and a half away! Denys, what is all that smoke down the street?

-       It looks like a fire, Manon, a big one! Let's go!

-       Everybody stay back! The Fire Department is on it's way! You two, back up please!

-       My baby is in the house - my baby!

-       Try to comfort her, Manon, I'll see if I can get in there.

-     You can't, Denys – the fire is out of control. Stay with us, please! Maybe the firemen can get up there with a ladder! Help me with the mother! The police said to stay back!

-     Got to get the baby, if there's a chance! I can't wait! There's a fire escape on the side of the house. God help me!

***

-     You're a hero, young man! You jumped with that bundled blanket just as the fire escape ladder was giving way. The ambulance will be taking you to the Montreal General. I guess you should go with him, young lady. He probably suffered from smoke inhalation. Don't worry about the mother – she's still in shock, but maybe now from the joy of seeing her baby saved. We'll be sending them in the other ambulance, along with a neighbor. The baby seems okay, but will be looked after at the hospital. The Children's Hospital is just up the street.. Just so you'll know, the fire chief says a quick survey of the ruins – the house is a complete loss – suggests arson. Good luck, you two! And thank you, young man!

-     Thank you, officer. Are you okay, Denys? I almost went into shock myself, thinking I had lost you!

-     Excuse my coughing, Manon, but I did swallow some smoke, I guess. When I got to the door at the top of the stairs, I was able to kick it in – the wood was actually rotten! I crawled toward a room where I heard crying. I was able to wrap the baby with the blanket that was in the crib, and then I crawled back to the fire escape – just in time, because flames started flashing in the rooms behind me. Like the officer said, the fire escape started to give way.

Fortunately I wasn't too high up, and was able to jump – I was just worried about protecting the baby. But it had no burns, and was crying – which I guess is a good thing! I heard the policeman say something about arson. During my first year at McGill there was a huge fire set deliberately in a club – I remember the name – The Bluebird Café. Thirty-seven people died, and of course the story was carried on the news back home. My parents and sister were going crazy with worry, until I reached them by telephone to let them know I had never been there. Even Pizza Pete and the guys were relieved. Jeff was probably worried that he'd have to chip in for flowers!

-     Well, Denys, you'll have to call your parents again, because by the time you got down the fire escape, the television cameras were here. They may have caught you running from the house with the baby.

506

-       This wasn't the Great Fire of Rome, so I doubt this got beyond local news. This is nothing like watching President Kennedy being shot in Dallas or even like watching the news as Jack Ruby shot Lee Harvey Oswald. You know, Manon, I've often thought about that tragic assassination and the shooting that covered up part of the investigation. I've always been haunted by the suspicion that the man behind that murder was Lyndon B. Johnson, who was from Texas. As Vice-President, he automatically became President. It's just a hunch, but that thought has always bothered me. In America today people are bringing their grievances into the streets, leading to riots and destructive "fires" of hate! In Ancient Rome, there was killing and rioting in the streets that eventually overturned civil order. When the mobster Clodius was killed in the streets, the angry mob burned the Senate-House in 52 B.C. The government was entrusted to Pompey, as he was named sole consul. However, this made him a de facto dictator. That prompted Julius Caesar to lead his army into Italy, sparking – I'm deliberately using a word associated with fire! – a civil war. This led to the downfall of the Roman Republic!

-       Gee, do you think that could happen in America? There is already only one man at the head of Government – the President!

-       Manon, who knows if the seat of American Government is sacred enough to always avoid the attack of a violent mob?

-       The policeman called you a hero, Denys. You'll always be my hero! You don't have to jump into a fire to prove it. Maybe you should rest. All this nervous excitement made me forget to call you Holden!

-       I don't feel too bad, Manon. It's kind of ironic. Since I don't smoke, this is the most smoke I have ever inhaled! Other than by you, this is the fourth time I have been called a hero, and as I think about the circumstances, I could be a chapter in a literary handbook. The four incidents exemplify the three types of narrative conflict. During that fire I was "man against nature". Fighting off those two would be rapists put me in a situation of "man against man", and dealing with Livio in the bank in Rome was clearly a case of "man against himself"!

Fighting the current of the St Lawrence River to save the drowning man, whose struggling was hindering my efforts, and making me question my decision to dive in, was a combination of conflicts! My use of alliteration just made those situations sound less scary! I know Stoics like Seneca believed a final conflagration would destroy the world, but honestly, Manon, as I crawled on the floor of that burning house, the thought of you told me I would survive! To think I used to sing "Fire and Rain" by James Taylor at student get-togethers! Two songs I won't be asking for at parties are "Ring of Fire" by Johnny Cash and "Light My Fire" by The Doors! And certainly not that song byThe Ink Spots called "I Don't Want To Set The World On Fire" – without being a "flamboyant hero", I just want to "start a flame in your heart"!

-       Maybe you'll have more respect for Smokey the Bear, Holden, and listening to that Platters song your father likes so much – "Smoke Gets in Your Eyes" - will have new meaning!

-       I'll still like Smokey Robinson! And speaking of my Dad, we were into westerns on TV, and his favorite show was "Gunsmoke!" But right now I'm less into westerns and more into "western" civilization! Like The Intruders sing in their song, I've gone "from cowboys to girls"! Well, actually – to one girl!

Chapter 123

- Today we read our first passage from the *Argonautica* of Valerius Flaccus. Are there any questions before we begin? Yes, Denys.

- May I ask two questions, Professor Saucier?

- Certainly, Denys! What is your second question?

- What about my first question?

- Thank you for your two questions!

Would you please read for us from Book Seven, lines 407 to 430, which describe the encounter between Jason and Medea. In case any of you are wondering why we added a third author to this course, it was in keeping with the Department's policy of introducing as many authors as possible to our graduate students, as they work towards completing the comprehensive reading lists. The choice of Valerius Flaccus is justified in that he was contemporary with Lucan and Silius Italicus, and like the other two first-century poets, he wrote a great epic. After reading the Latin text, Denys, please proceed with your translation.

- With a sorcery like that of Medea, Professor, you actually answered my questions, and injected your usual humor! So I will "embark" on my reading of this chapter on the expedition of Jason and his heroic companions aboard the Argo – my turn to introduce a humorous twist!

Ergo ut erat vultu defixus uterque silent

noxque suum peragebat iter, iamiam ora levare

Aesonidem farique cupit Medea priorem.

quam simul effusis pavitantem fletibus heros

flagrantesque genas vidit miserumque pudorem,

has tandem voces dedit et solatus amantem est

"fersne aliquam spem lucis?" ait. "miserata laborem

nempe venis? an et ipsa mea laetabere morte?

ne precor infando similem te, virgo, parenti

gesseris. haud tales dicet inclementia vultus.

hascine nunc grates, haec exspectata laborum

dona dari decuit? sic te sub teste remitti

fas mihi, virgo –tuum- iustas da vocibus aures.

nec pater ille tuus tantis me opponere monstris

(quid meritum?) aut tales voluit cur pendere poenas.

an iacet externa quod nunc mihi cuspide Canthus

quodque meus vestris cecidit pro moenibus Iphis

aut Scythiae tanta inde manus? iussisset abire

perfidus atque suis extemplo cedere regnis.

spem mihi promissam per quae discrimina rursus

et reddat qua lege vides. occumbere tandem

possumus idque sedet quam non quaecumque

subire patris iussa tui. numquam sine vellere abibo

hinc ego, degenerem nec tu me prima videbis.''

Here is my translation.

"Therefore, as each one was motionless in expression and in silence, and night was pursuing her course, Medea desired Jason to lift his face and to speak first. As soon as the hero saw her trembling, with tears pouring out, and her burning cheeks and her wretched shame, he put forth these words and consoled the girl consumed with love. "Do you bring some hope of light?" he asked. "Do you truly come pitying my labor? Or will you yourself rejoice at my death? I beg you, maiden, not to conduct yourself similarly to your abominable father. Cruelty will not describe such features. Was it proper for this gratitude and the expected gifts of my labors to be given? Is it right for me, maiden, to be sent away with you as witness? Give just ears to my words. Why did that father of yours want me to face such monsters (what have I deserved?) or that I pay such penalties? Is it that my Canthus lies dead by a foreign spear, or that my Iphis has died on behalf of your city's walls?

Or so many bands of Scythia? The traitor should have ordered me to leave, and to depart immediately from his kingdom. You see again through what dangers and in what manner he fulfills the hope promised me. I am able ultimately to die, and it is resolved by me not to be subjected to the orders of your father, whatever they may be. For I shall never leave here without the fleece, nor will you first see me unworthy."

Scythia refers of course to Colchis, the kingdom of Aeëtes and his daughter Medea, and Canthus and Iphis were two Argonauts killed in Colchis.

-       Thank you, Denys. I am trying to work you as hard as I can before you leave us in April! Your classmates here will want to attend your dissertation defence in March. By the way, everybody, in addition to Jason and his heroes in the *Argonautica,* we have another hero in our presence – yes, I am still speaking of Mr. Hainsworth. But instead of a fire-breathing dragon, he had to face a fire-breathing house, to rescue not a treasure of fleece, but a tiny treasure in a fleece blanket. He left the site not with the encouragement of a sorceress as his future wife, but that of his bride-to-be, too nice to bring him strife. He did not sail off in a ship with a golden prize, but in a vehicle of much smaller size, of the color yellow – the color of gold or so I am told!

-       Professor, your poetry is bringing everyone to tears! And I am very choked up – much more than when I escaped the smoke of the fire!

Chapter 124

-       I told you that you would like this restaurant, Manon. I came here to Claude St. Jean's once before with Jeremy, and we were able to walk home. But a taxi to your place won't cost too much since we are not too far. I promise to speak English all evening, but I spoke French in front of your family, because I don't know where your father stands on the language question. It was nice of him though to fix up the spare room in your basement for me. I'm ordering the pepper steak, and I guess you'll have the lobster, or will it be shrimp and scampis? We are a real pair of surf and turf gluttons!

-       You are right, Denys – I mean Holden! The service is great! And how nice that you were able to get us one of the two tables by the window. That singer, Patrick Norman, adds a charming ambience as well. My father can become very confrontational on the language question – and it's partly your fault! He says that if an American like you can master French, why can't people who have lived here all their lives learn to communicate in French? Nevertheless, he manages to maintain a certain sense of humour. When he was asked by a neighbor if he had lived in Quebec all his life, he replied "not yet"! It's so convenient that there is a dance floor and bar next to the dining area.

-       If the singer's name were really Patrick Norman, we could have asked the DJ later on to play the song "Norman" by Sue Thomson! That's the beauty of this place, Manon – we can dance all night after dinner, without leaving the building, but as I recall, the disc jockey doesn't play non-stop music. That will give us time to talk. I'd like to continue telling you about the "Advice for Bride and Groom" I read in Plutarch. When I got my Master's degree my parents gave me the works of Plutarch in the original Greek – not just the *Lives*, but also the *Magna Moralia*, including the *Praecepta Coniugalia*. I know you have been reading books on marriage, so you will appreciate his words of wisdom, although I had to censure some of them, since they only applied to the world of his time. Nonetheless, it's amazing to read some of his advice, which sounds like it could have been written yesterday. I will be lending you the English translation of the *Parallel Lives*. My sister Phoebe gave it to me as a present for earning my Master's, and it consists of seven volumes published in 1831! So handle with care!

-       Be careful, Holden, or I won't handle you with care! I am even trying play on words in English! Yes, you brought some old books to Montreal to show me. You say you find some every once in a while in antique bookseller shops – at bargain prices. I remember some of the titles – and they were all published in the nineteenth century! Let me see, there was *Croquis de Grèce et Rome*, *La Destruction de Pompeia*, *Fabiola,* and *Le Signe de la Victoire*. I believe those last three are historic novels, and I wouldn't mind reading them.

\-   I think you mean "historical", Manon, but then again, since they were published in the 1850's, I guess you could call them "historic" too! I also have a copy of Terence's *Andria* published in 1901, an interlinear copy of Xenophon's *Anabasis* published in 1887, a Latin Grammar from 1832, and three other books published in the nineteenth century – Demosthenes' *Philippics*, the poetry of Horace, and a 125-page *History of Rome*, which is like putting the works of Shakespeare on a postage stamp! I also have a 1918 copy of *Latin Epigraphy* by J.E. Sandys, which I purchased in Germany. I'm proud to say I own a copy of *Cato*, a tragedy written in 1712 by Joseph Addison – even though my copy is a modern edition.

\-   I'm glad you're such a bibliophile, Denys – oh, I'm not always going to remember to call you Holden! – I'll always know what to buy you for your birthday, and wedding anniversaries, and – hopefully – Father's Day! And isn't it exciting that Maggie is expecting?

She and Bob are sure to ask us to be godparents! It would have been nice if they had been able to be here with us tonight, though. Restaurant Claude St. Jean Steakhouse isn't fancy like Le Deauville. But you eat just as well, and it's a lot cheaper. Which is a good thing for you, since you don't believe in "going Dutch". Because you don't speak Dutch, you say! I'm lucky we can't "go Greek", or "Italian" or "German" or "Spanish"!

\-   Maybe they will call the baby Manny, if it's a girl. I sure hope Bob doesn't name it Menace, if it's a boy! Why don't you just call me Lover Boy, like Sylvia calls Mickey in the song "Love is Strange"! But I should tell you now, although it's early days, Feeb is also expecting.

So you're going to be a maternal aunt to Maggie's baby, and I'm going to be a maternal uncle to Feeb's baby. When your brothers have children, you'll be their paternal aunt. If I had had a brother, I could have become a paternal uncle. The Romans were really into family relationships, and had names for paternal and maternal uncles – *patruus* - as I would have been had I a brother who fathered a son - and avunculus - as I'll be for Feeb's baby – and for paternal and maternal aunts – *amita* - as Feeb would be for our children – and *matertera* - as you'll be for Maggie's baby. And Feeb would want us as godparents – I know so many prayers for a baptism ceremony! But being godfather to a couple of children – Manon, people are going to start calling me Don Vito Corleone! You saw the movie *The Godfather*, right? Of course, after studying about Marius and Sulla and Caesar, I sort of feel groomed for that Marlon Brando character! Let's look at some of Plutarch's sayings – we know he was a happily married man, if we can judge by a letter of consolation he sent to his wife on the death of one of their children. I still have my notes from the Plutarch course I took last year. Maybe we can find some material for our wedding vows! He says "married people should succeed in attaining their mutual desires by persuasion and not by fighting and quarreling." Makes sense. I like this one –"many newly married women get annoyed at their husbands, and find themselves in like predicament with those who patiently submit to the bees' stings but abandon the honeycomb." No more whispering "SWEET nothings", I guess! Concordia University's sport teams are called Stingers.

Their "A" teams – not their "B" teams! I think I'd like to start calling you "Honey Bee"!

-         As long as you promise to "bee" nice! Let me see the list, Holden. "In the beginning, especially, married people ought to be on their guard against disagreements and clashes." And this one – " keen love between newly married people that blazes up fiercely as the result of physical attractiveness must not be regarded as enduring or constant, unless by being centered about character and by gaining a hold upon the rational faculties, it attains a state of vitality." I couldn't agree more! But say, my husband-to-be, do you ever think of your old girlfriends?

-         No, Manon, they were all my age!

-         Stop teasing, Holden, you know what I mean! I am talking especially about American girls.

-         Well, Manon, I suppose you would like the song composed by that Canadian pair, Randy Bachman and Burton Cummings for their group, the Guess Who. Do you remember "American Woman"? But when they sang "stay away from me…", they may have been talking about the Statue of Liberty. I did, though, use the "statue of liberty" play a couple of times when I was quarterback for St. Xavier High! Well, since we mentioned older women, does the name Mrs. Robinson ring a bell? A hint – I'm not talking about Smokey's wife, or the wife of Jackie Robinson, who was a baseball hero in Montreal before he broke the Major League Baseball color barrier.

-         You're talking about the movie with Dustin Hoffman – *The Graduate*. She wasn't a nice lady, but the music was quite good and upbeat.

-	Unfortunately, the music of Simon and Garfunkel didn't have the "charms to soothe the savage breast"!

-	Didn't Shakespeare say "savage beast"? I've been reading his plays to enrich my English.

-	No, Shakespeare never met Mrs. Robinson! Actually, it was a poet who lived about a hundred years after William Shakespeare, William Congreve, who wrote those lines in his poem "The Mourning Bride". He probably was inspired by the verses written by the Latin poet Lucan in his poem on the Roman civil war which we read last month in my Latin class. The English translation of Lucan reads "whose charming voice and matchless music moved the savage beasts, the stones, and senseless trees". But maybe Congreve had Mrs. Robinson in mind when he used the word "breast"! Once, when I tried to tell some McGill students at a bar that those words were never spoken by The Bard, I almost ended up being barred! Here's an interesting excerpt from Plutarch for a sea-food lover like you, Manon. "Fishing with poison is a quick way to catch fish and an easy method of taking them, but it makes the fish inedible and bad. In the same way women who artfully employ love potions and magic spells upon their husbands, and gain the mastery over them through pleasure, find themselves consorts of dull-witted, degenerate fools. The men bewitched by Circe were of no service to her, nor did she make the least use of them after they had been changed into swine and asses, while for Odysseus, who had sense and showed discretion in her company, she had an exceeding great "love". By the way, did anyone ever tell you that you have a striking resemblance to Elizabeth Montgomery, who starred in the television series "Bewitched"?

-	Yes, Holden, except that in our home we watched it in French, and it was called "*Sorcière Bien-Aimée*"!

-	It would be nice if you could arrange everything as quickly as she did – and just by twitching your nose! Another sorceress who was well-loved – at least at first – was Medea, who helped Jason by rubbing him with a magic ointment. Of course, after they had been married for a while Jason ended up rubbing Medea the wrong way by taking a new bride. To punish him, Medea murdered their children! Manon, I firmly believe there is no worse crime than for a parent to take the life of one's child. I think Medea became Mad-ea! Tragically, people are committing this horrendous crime even today. Faced with this crime, I admit I would find it extremely difficult to forgive, to "turn the other cheek", as it were. We are reading about Jason and Medea presently in our Latin course with the section on the *Argonautica* of Valerius Flaccus, where Jason has told Medea he won't take any "flak" – no not "Flaccus" – from her father Aeëtes.

- 	I would hope you would never turn me aside for another woman, Holden, and, like Odysseus resisting Circe, please never make an ass of yourself! I like this one – "women who prefer to have power over fools rather than to hearken to sensible men are like the persons who prefer to guide the blind on the road rather than to follow persons possessed of knowledge and sight".

- 	To answer with a song – "Never My Love"! I "Cherish" you too much to ever do that ! Those are just a couple of songs by The Association that I like. Nor would I want to be in Aretha Franklin's "Chain of Fools"! If I can't convince you, maybe Stevie Wonder can with his songs – "I was Made To Love Her" - and "her" is you, Manon! "For Once in My Life"' I have someone like you, Manon, - " Signed, Sealed, Delivered, I'm Yours"!

- 	It's amazing, Holden, how you have a song for every occasion and every situation!

- 	I know, Manon. It's as if I had a little juke-box in my head, and people are constantly throwing quarters at me! And I sometimes feel that way with Roman and even Greek figures from history and literature. It's like reading a "whodunit", and the answers are in Ancient Greece and Rome!

- 	Well then, I guess, like Guy Boucher and Ginette Sage in their song, I'll always be "*Devant le juke-box*"! But at least it won't cost me any quarters! I like these words of Plutarch: "Men who through weakness are unable to vault upon their horses teach their horses to kneel of themselves and crouch down. In like manner, some who have won wives of noble birth or wealth, instead of making themselves better, try to humble their wives, with the idea that they shall have more authority over their wives if these are reduced to a state of humility. But as one pays heed to the size of his horse in using the rein, so in using the rein on his wife, he ought to pay heed to her position." And if you call me a horse, Holden Hainsworth, you are a dead man!

- 	Even the "Wild Horses" of the Rolling Stones couldn't get met to do that! In any event, I'm probably going to be a dead man after I read this next excerpt from Plutarch! "A virtuous woman ought to be most visible in her husband's company, and to stay in the house and hide herself when he is away." But Plutarch and I can quickly redeem ourselves with this pronouncement: "Herodotus was not right in saying that a woman lays aside her modesty along with her undergarment. On the contrary, a virtuous woman puts on modesty in its stead, and husband and wife bring into their mutual relations the greatest modesty as a token of the greatest love." Obviously, Herodotus and Plutarch did not hang around with the same crowd!

No, they weren't contemporaries, Manon, but you know what I mean! It's almost as if the wife can get a Master's degree, but only the husband merits a PhD! Plutarch says "every activity in a virtuous household is carried on by both parties in agreement, but discloses the husband's leadership and preferences." He goes on to say "Most women, when their husbands try forcibly to remove their luxury and extravagance, keep up a continual fight and are very cross; but if they are convinced with the help of reason, they peaceably put aside these things and practice moderation." I would REST my case, but I know you would quickly BE on my case!

-	I like this passage, Holden. "Cato expelled from the Senate a man who kissed his own wife in the presence of his daughter." Cato could have been my father's ancestor! Plutarch goes on to say "This perhaps was a little severe". A little? "But if it is a disgrace (as it is)" – so HE says - for a man to caress and kiss and embrace in the presence of others, is it not more of disgrace to air their recriminations and disagreements before others" – I totally agree with that part! "and, granting that his intimacies and pleasures with his wife should be carried on in secret, to indulge in admonition, fault-finding, and plain speaking in the open and without reserve?" So Plutarch, too, believed that you shouldn't wash your dirty laundry in public! I read those crazy things he said about the wife being playful when the husband is playful, and serious when the husband is serious, which would make her a robot, it seems to me, with no feelings of her own! But Plutarch redeems himself when he says " men who do not like to see their wives eat in their company, are teaching them to stuff themselves when alone. So those who are not cheerful in the company of their wives, nor join with them in sportiveness and laughter, are thus teaching them to seek their own pleasures apart from their husbands." That would be totally lame, Holden. Did you notice how I'm picking up idiomatic expressions in English?

-	Plutarch would have been proud of you! He also says "A wife ought not to make friends of her own, but to enjoy her husband's friends in common with him." Well, you passed the test on that one with Jeremy! Then Plutarch says "the gods are the first and most important friends. Wherefore it is becoming for a wife to worship and to know only the gods that her husband believes in. She should not practice secret rites of her own." We're on the same page on that one! Plutarch then says a man and his fiancée should go dancing together as often as possible!

-	What? Where does it say that?

-	In my heart, Manon! I'm evermore anxious for you to become my *uxor* – my wife! If we have daughters - *filiae* - some day, who take after their mother, they will grow up to be fine ladies! Let's go next door and get a cozy little table for two!

-        Oh, Holden, the dance floor is not that big. But it won't be a problem for the slow songs, will it?

-        Not if they play "Come a Little Bit Closer" by Jay and The Americans, or "Close To You" by The Carpenters! But we're too early for the music. I thought we could read some more Plutarch while we have our first drink. The lighting is good here in the corner. Now, let's see…Plutarch says "it is a lovely thing for the wife to sympathize with her husband's concerns and the husband with the wife's, that the co-partnership be preserved through the joint action of both co-partnership in producing a child and in property, both should pour all resources into a common fund, and combine them, and each should not regard one part as his own, and another part as the other's, but all as his own and nothing as the other's." I guess I could arm-wrestle you for the property, Manon – all or nothing! But read these next precepts – you'll like them!

-        "It is the petty, continual daily clashes between man and wife, unnoticed by the great majority, that destroy married life." I'll drink to that! So order me another drink, dearest!

This one is interesting – "a wedded and lawful wife becomes an irresistible thing if she makes everything – dowry, birth, magic charms, and even the magic girdle itself – to be inherent in herself, and by character and virtue succeeds in winning her husband's love." The next one says "marriages ought not to be made by trusting the eyes only, or the fingers either, as is the case with some who take a wife after counting how much she brings with her, but without deciding what kind of helpmate she will be." And "if the ill favored woman is loved for her character, that is something of which she can be very proud, far more than if she were loved for her beauty."

-        That is true, Manon, but with you I got the "trinity" – Character, Personality and Beauty! And if we slip back into French – even though your English is more and more impressive – they are the exact same words! In fact, I should call you "Miss Personality"! Lloyd Price, who sang the song "Personality", became known as "Mr. Personality." But don't call me "Lloyd", Manon – it sounds like a name you would give to a little warrior from the future!

Maybe he can be a "cellu- Lloyd", and be in films! And since I'm always attempting to "woo" you with songs and movies, I could become "Woo" in my old age – or perhaps using the pseudonym "Wu" like "Hu", the name of a Chinese girl back in Cincinnati. But don't ask how "Hu" or why "Wu"! Listen, the music is starting. To get us warmed up - oh, sorry too soon after that fire – but I'm talking about "Shaft" – the DJ is playing that song by Isaac Hayes. I saw the movie with Richard Roundtree on one of my visits home. I was one of the few non Afro-

Americans in the theater. But that was just more *déjà vu* for me! The dance tunes are starting. They would pick "Disco Inferno"! I guess we'll just have to dance away the memories of the fire!

-        There are some really good dance songs that have come out recently. But as usual, I don't know the titles! Except for "More, More, More".

-        The Andrea True Connection sings that song, Manon. Then there was a song by K.C. and the Sunshine Band – "That's The Way I Like It". "Don't Go Breaking My Heart" by Elton John and Kiki Dee was next, followed by an oldie – Jerry Lee Lewis and "Whole Lot of Shakin' Going On". I wonder if the singer Shake listens to that song! After that came "Play That Funky Music", a song by Wild Cherry. I know – but you did ask! Then we danced to "Get Up and Boogie" by Silver Convention, but of course we were already up! The song after that was "Disco Lady" by Johnny Taylor. Boy, I'm glad we both like disco music – it seems to be all the rage these days! Although that "Disco Duck" song by Rick Dees was a bit much! I'm glad they played two French songs for you, Manon. I guess you recognized the angelic voice of René Simard. That first song – *"L'Oiseau"* – was recorded when he was only ten years old! And "Fernando" was recorded when he was fifteen! He is such an entertainer with a great personality – I guess that makes two of us, right, Manon? He is sure to become a star for many years to come! Didn't you love those slow dances at the end? I can still name the songs, even though my eyes were shut! – "If You Leave Me Now" by Chicago, "You'll Never Find a Love Like Mine" by Lou Rawls, "Love Hurts" by Nazareth and "All By Myself" by Eric Carmen. Okay, while the DJ is resting – why, I don't know – we were the ones moving all around! - we can look at some more advice from Plutarch.

-        Maybe you made the DJ dizzy with your dazzling disco dexterity! I'll order the drinks. What's your poison?

-        Beautiful alliteration – you're English is becoming "letter-perfect"! And nice idiomatic expression, Manon, but the timing is bad. I just finished reading a book about Nero and his mother! Nero had tried to kill her at sea, but his mother must have been listening to "Don't Rock the Boat" by Hues Corporation! Poison mushrooms always do the trick, and those that are past "sell-by-date" sometimes even without the poison! Keep up the clever alliteration!

Your words rock…and roll off your tongue! I think Plutarch wrote this for you, Manon! "That adorns a woman which makes her more decorous. It is not gold or precious stones or scarlet that makes her such, but whatever invests her with that something which betokens dignity, good behavior and modesty". There are a few bits of advice that follow, which I don't agree with, since they all suggest that the wife should be seen and not heard, or even worse, not seen at all! I suppose that's better than being "obscene" and heard! Plutarch gives a little too much leeway to control freaks. Plutarch would need a reality check today when some of his advice invites the wife to always be "nice and pretty" as well as "pretty and nice"! But I do agree with Plutarch when he says "bitterness and anger ought never to find a place in married life." But read this next one, Manon.

-        "The marriage of a couple in love with each other is an intimate union; of those who marry for dowry or children, of persons joined together; of those who merely sleep in the same bed, as of separate persons who are cohabiting but not really living together. The Roman law-giver who prohibited the giving and receiving of presents between man and wife, was not aiming to prevent sharing in anything, but insuring that they shared all things in common."

Holden, "You Should Be Dancing"! It's The Bee Gees – let's follow THEIR advice!

-        It's like Leo Sayer can read my mind with his song "You Make Me Feel Like Dancing"! The song after that - "Love Rollercoaster" by The Ohio Players – you can guess why I like that group! – sort of summarizes the rest of the 48 precepts Plutarch espouses on marriage.

That was one of my better puns, Manon. I hope you got it. But Plutarch does talk about mothers-in-law, and about inviting Aphrodite into our bed if we're in a bad mood. Plutarch is all for kissing and making-up! So am I – even if we don't have anything to make up about! It was special dancing to the songs "Boogie Nights" and "Always and Forever" by Heatwave. That group was founded by two brothers from Dayton, Ohio – Johnny and Keith Wilder. Since that city is only an hour away from Cincinnati, maybe I'll have an attachment to my hometown "always and forever"! The group's name also reminds me how you find Cincinnati so hot compared to Quebec when we visit my parents at Christmas. The absence of snow and a 60 degree difference in temperature will do that to you! The songs that we danced to were "Let Your Love Flow" by The Bellamy Brothers, "December 1963 (Oh What a Night)" by Frankie Valli and The Four Seasons, "Right Back Where We Started From" by Maxine Nightingale, then "You Sexy Thing" by Hot Chocolate – I didn't know there was a song about me! After that we heard "Turn the Beat Around" by Vicki Sue Robinson, "Island Girl" by Elton John, "Love to Love You" by Donna Summer, "Heaven Must Be Missing an Angel" by Tavares, and "I Love Music" by The O'Jays.

-        I didn't need The O'Jays to tell me that, Holden! We should come back here again. –

-        To the restaurant or the *discothèque,* Manon?

-	Both! Don't you want to have your cake and eat it, Holden?

-	You're really starting to master English expressions! But you're right – wine and dine until nine, and then dance while you get the chance!

Chapter 125

-       Hi Mom, "It was the best of times. It was the worst of times." I know you recognize those opening words from Charles Dickens' *Tale of Two Cities*. I recently re-read that novel, and, quite honestly, those opening lines don't apply to me – or rather only the first sentence does. As you recall, the novel is about two men who love the same woman, but one gives up his life for the other, and lets him live to be with the woman. Letting your imagination run a little, I'm two men - an American and a Quebecer (sort of). I've given up America to be with Manon. Montreal and Quebec – a "tale of two cities"! But there haven't been bad times – not really! And so no "worst times"! All "the times" have been good – and the "best times" are yet to come! I mean marriage to Manon, and (fingers crossed) a university professorship! The "best" in Latin is *optimus*, and the "worst" is *pessimus*. As you know, Mom, this gives us the words "optimist" and "pessimist". You've always called me the "eternal optimist" – I get my positive outlook from you, Mom! I mean, when my glass is half empty, I'm happy knowing that I drank the other half! No - an optimist invented the airplane, and a pessimist invented the parachute! Manon and I really enjoyed our time at Christmas with you guys! As usual, your supper was delicious! I guess Dad thought he was funny when I went into the kitchen and he said there were now two turkeys in the room! I think he is still trying to figure out what I meant when I said I was half-ambidextrous! Are you and Dad looking forward to becoming grand-parents? Feeb was radiant! How about having a daughter-in-law a year-and-a-half from now?

Manon's parents seem to be treating me as if I were already part of the family. Even her father smiles when he talks to me! Actually, just having him talk to me with more than a couple of words brought me to the next plateau! New Year's with the Plouffe family was a lot of fun!

I've finally sent off the last of my application letters. I sent letters to about a dozen Canadian universities, and almost as many American ones. I wrote letters to UC and Xavier, and other universities near Cincinnati like Miami in Oxford and Dayton. A few American and a couple of Canadian universities have already written back to me to say they had no openings at present, and consequently would not be conducting interviews. They informed me that they would keep my *curriculum vitae* on file. I was even told by some of them that they found my CV impressive – "out of the ordinary", one department chair wrote! I am busy putting the final touches to my dissertation, and doing the preparations for my teaching at Concordia and for my Latin and Greek courses for the Quebec public – am I, like Julius Caesar, a "man of the people"?!

What I like the most about my Tuesdays in Montreal is spending some time at the end of the day with Manon. The rest of the week, and especially weekends, leave me with a feeling of loneliness. I think about her when I jog through the streets of Ste-Foy and Sillery. Lately, since I have time on my hands, I spend time thinking about time! At least I look for things to do besides reading Time magazine! It's amazing how we are warned so often about taking advantage of the time at our disposal. Chaucer said "Time and tide wait for no man"! And then there is Shakespeare telling us "to make use of time and not let advantage slip" and "let every man be master of his time"! These are simply invitations to *carpe diem*! Julius Caesar's motto would surely be "there's no time like the present", since he wrote his great *Commentaries* in the present tense. I don't think he did that so that Tommy Nelson wouldn't give Fr. McNeil a hard time! Father sometimes quoted Shakespeare for Tommy's benefit, saying "I wasted time, and now time doth waste me"! That quote is timeless! I have even had a few chats with the guy in the next apartment who up to now wouldn't even give me the time of day! He's quite a bit older than I am, and must have studied Latin, because whenever he sees me he mutters, quoting Cicero "These times, these behaviors" - *O tempora, O mores* – as if I were responsible for the way people act today! He seems convinced that we are living in "troubled times"! I should probably have countered with these expressions: *tempori parendum* – "you have to move with the times" or *tempora mutantur et nos mutamur in illis* – "times change, and we change with them" or *tempore cuncta mitiora* – "all things become mellower with time". Or maybe even this quote from Dionysius Cato: *temporibus mores sapiens sine crimine mutat* – "the wise man is without crime in changing his habits with the times". Naturally, if you do commit a crime, you do the time! But Cicero he is not! He didn't react to the Latin expressions I quoted – quite timely they were, since they are all about time! You have probably heard me mention some of them already, Mom. Ovid says *tempora labuntur, tacitisque senescimus annis; et fugiunt fraeno non remorante dies.* Of course I will translate them for you, Mom. That one means "time glides away and we grow older through the silent years; the days flee away and are restrained by no rein".

Here's one from Horace – *tempus abire tibi est, ne rideat et pulset lasciva decentius aetas* – "it is time for you to leave, so that the age more decent in its wantonness doesn't laugh at you and drive you off the stage". I'm glad that in all the plays I performed in or the public readings of ancient authors I presented, no one ever yelled "get off the stage"! Vergil wrote *tempus erat quo prima quies mortalibus aegris incipit et dono divum gratissima serpit.* It means "it was the time when first sleep begins for weary mortals and, by the gift of the gods, creeps over them most pleasingly". Strangely, it reminds me of Jeff at Pizza Pete's when he was sleeping off a hang-over in the back room! Leave it to Cicero to put time in perspective when he said *tempus est quaedam pars aeternitatis* – "time is a certain fraction of eternity". And Ovid again, who spent forced time away from Rome for allegedly giving the Imperial family a hard time!, *tempus ferax, tempus edax rerum* – "time the producer, time the devourer of things", and *tempus in agrorum cultu consumere dulce est* – "it is delightful to spend one's time in the tilling of the fields". Time is also a mainstay of truisms about life, as in *tempus anima rei* – "time is the essence of the matter", *tempus et patientia* – "time and patience" – as you know, Mom, I have plenty of one, not so much of the other! The teaching of Seneca is echoed in *tempus omnia terminat* – "time ends all things". *Tempus omnia revelat* – "time reveals all things" – reminds me of Dad, who often advised me "to just give it time". More and more, I'm beginning to believe that *tempus rerum imperator* – "time is ruler over all things"! The Romans believed that "time flies through the world" – *volat hora per orbem* and that "time is practically a healing art" – *temporis ars medicina fere est* is how Ovid put it. They also believed that "time reveals the truth" – *veritatem dies aperit*, but also that "time is the greatest innovator" – *maximus novator tempus*. Ovid shared many thoughts on time. For example – *tempus erit quo vos speculum vidisse pigebit*, meaning "the time will come when it will disgust you to look in a mirror". I'm wondering, Mom, if for me that ship has already sailed! Ovid also said *tempore ruricolae patiens fit taurus aratri*, meaning "in time the bull bears the yoke", *tempora si fuerit nubila, solus eris*, meaning "if unfavorable times come along, you will be alone". We know, don't we, when the going gets tough, the tough get going, but also that everyone else is seen going! Maybe a friend in need is a friend indeed, but when you need a friend… well…this is what Ovid says: *tempore felici multi numerantur amici; si fortuna perit, nullus amicus erit* – "in happy times many friends are numbered, but if fortune fails, there will be no friend". That person would need to listen to Carole King singing "You've Got a Friend"! By the way, her album *Tapestry* is so good, she won't have to unravel it like Penelope unravelled hers! I know, Mom, there was a reason, but I really don't have time – Penelope had ten years! Ovid seems to have been convinced of the positive power of time. He says *tempore ducetur longo fortasse cicatrix; horrent admotas vulnera cruda* meaning "a wound may, perhaps, in time be closed, but, when fresh, wounds shrink from approaching hands", and *tempore difficiles veniunt ad aratra iuvenci; tempore lenta pati frena docentur equi,* meaning "in time the unmanageable young oxen come to the plow; in time horses are taught to endure the restraining bit". Mom, I've had so much time to think about time since Manon moved to the Montreal area that I made a compilation from my record collection on the theme of time. You may remember hearing some of these songs when I was living back home. Many of the songs are love songs, happy and not, some are songs of loneliness, and a few are protest songs with a political motivation. But I have concentrated on the lyrics that enable me to recall fond memories of the past, to enjoy meaningful moments in the present, and to look forward to rewarding experiences in the future. I thought I'd share them with you. In the song by

Chicago, "Does Anybody Really Know What Time It Is", the lyrics read "Does anybody really know what time it is (I don't)…Does anybody really care (care about time)…we've all got time enough to cry". I think we shouldn't be in a hurry to be sad! That Civil Rights Movement song by Bob Dylan, "The Times They Are a Changin'", has these lyrics "If your time to you is worth savin' …then you better start swimmin'…Or you'll sink like a stone… For the times they are a changin' ". Changing for the better, I hope! In their song "No Time", The Guess Who remind us that time can be a real changer – perhaps, I think, a life-changer! The lyrics are "On my way to better things… (No time left for you) I found myself some wings…No time left for you…Distant roads are callin' me… (No time left for you)… Time, time, time, time, time". Willie Nelson sings these words in "Funny How Time Slips Away" – "I heard you told him that you'd love him…till the end of time… Gee, ain't it funny how time slips away". Well, we can't take time for granted. I also have Al Green's recording of that song. I found one of my Beach Boy records – "Time To Get Alone". The lyrics go "And now we know it's time … time to get alone… to get alone and just be… together". It makes sense when you listen to the whole song! Jim Croce is a real poet, and in "Time In a Bottle", he sings "If I could save time in a bottle … The first thing that I'd like to do… Is to save every day… 'Til eternity passes away… Just to spend them with you… But there never seems to be enough time…To do the things you want to do." I've often felt like that, but with Manon far away (like in Carole King's song "So Far Away"), I realize that time is not the only necessary ingredient for "doing things"! Right now I'm thinking about the Time Capsule that was prepared during my first year at McGill. It will be opened in 2067, the year of Canada's Bicentennial! I was asked to deposit something into the Capsule on behalf of the Classics Department. I placed a Latin copy of the New Testament into the Capsule. I sincerely hope that when the Capsule is opened, people will be able to read the book, and will WANT to read that book! In "Sands of Time" – obviously in the image of an hourglass – Fleetwood Mac sing "And the falling sands of time… blow my wind and drifted by… To and fro the trees still bind… we will be free to wander." I also have a Jay and The Americans album called "Sands of Time". The Outsiders are from Cleveland, Mom, and with their charismatic lead singer, Sonny Geraci, they recorded "Time Won't Let Me", with a lyric I find prophetic – "Time won't let me wait too long"! The lyrics in the song "Where Have All the Good Times Gone" by The Kinks are self-explanatory: "Time was on our side and I had everything to gain… Let it be like yesterday…Please let me have happy days… Won't you tell me… Where have all the good times gone?" Tyrone Davis sings of regret in his song "If I Could Turn Back the Hands of Time". That sentiment is echoed in the film *Love Story*, when love is defined as "never having to say you're sorry"! Linda Ronstadt also speaks of love in her song "Long Long Time", where she says "time washes clean love's wounds unseen… and I think I'm gonna love you for a long long time". The Rolling Stones recorded two songs with opposing messages. In "Time Is On My Side", Mick Jagger is proposing patience when he sings "Time is on my side, yes it is". But in "Time Waits For No One", the message is "Time waits for no one, and it won't wait for me". The cycle of time is echoed in the song "Long Time Gone" by Crosby, Stills & Nash. The lyrics are "It's been a long time comin'… It's goin' to be a long time gone". The lyrics in the Jerry Lee Lewis song "Another Place, Another Time" should remind you of me – think "juke-box"! The words are "One by one they're turnin' out the lights… I've been feedin' that ol' juke-box just to hold you tight… I guess it's for the best I just put in my last dime… I heard you whisper 'we'll meet again another place, another time". How come he only had to pay a dime? The Association has recorded many beautiful songs. The lyrics in "Time for livin'" include "Time for livin', groovin' on everything… Life is givin', from now on I'm taking… Time… for life". How Epicurean! The song you always liked by The Platters, Mom - "Twilight Time" - has such a beautiful metaphor for the darkness of night –

"purple colored curtains"! I love listening to the song too. "Heavenly shades of night are falling… It's twilight time… When purple colored curtains… Mark the end of the day… I hear you my dear at twilight time". The Romans reckoned years with the names of the two consuls elected annually, as I've mentioned to you in the past, Mom. Sometimes we don't even count the years, or distinguish one year from the next – except at New Year's and on our birthdays!

Steely Dan sang this in their song "Reelin' In The Years" – "Are you reelin' in the years… Stowin' away the time". Frank Sinatra's song "It Was a Very Good Year" talks about "a very good year… when I was seventeen… when I was twenty-one… when I was thirty-five". When I was seventeen, it was a very good year – I graduated from high school! When I was twenty-one, it was a good year – I was a year away from my B.A. at McGill. When I am thirty-five, I hope to be a tenured professor raising a family! Paul Simon's song, "Still Crazy After All Those Years", reminds me of the good times at Pizza Pete's, with lyrics like these: "We talked about some old times… And we drank ourselves some beers… Still crazy after all those years". The song "100 Years Ago" by The Rolling Stones reminds me of a poem by Robert Frost – you know the one, Mom. The song goes ""Went out walkin' through the wood the other day…And the world was a carpet laid before me… The buds were bursting and the air smelled sweet and strange… Seemed about a hundred years ago". Neil Young is such a good poet. Here are his words in the song "Here We Are In The Years": "Now that the holidays have come… They can relax and watch the sun… Rise above all of the beautiful things they have done." This next part brings a tear to my eye as I remember Vergil Cane! "Go to the country take the dog… Look at the sky without the smog… Here we are in the years… Lives become careers". This next song by The Three Degrees kind of describes my situation. It's called "Year of Decision", and has lyrics like "This is the Year…To make your decision". A group from Montreal called Mashmakhan – don't ask, because the name has something to do with drugs – recorded a song, "As the Years Go By", that describes a beautiful life of love – to love someone as the years go by from childhood to marriage! If that song were sung in Latin, it could be called *Volventibus annis* – "as the years roll by", or, to borrow an expression from Horace, *Fugaces labuntur anni* – "the fleeting years slip by". The last song I listened to is very upbeat – fortunately, because it's called "A Sign of the Times", and was recorded by the effervescent Petula Clark. It's a perfect description of where Manon and I are at right now! "It's a sign of the times that your love for me is getting much stronger… It's a sign of the times and I won't have to wait much longer". Well, I seem to have used up all those time-worn expressions, so I guess it's about time I ended this letter! My, how time flies when you're busy - *Tempus fugit* and all that! Take care, Mom – and take care of Dad (like you always do!). I'll write again soon! – even though I've written more letters to you than the total of letters we have from Cicero and Pliny! Love as always, Holden (your Den! – as in years gone by!).

Chapter 126

\-   Good day, everyone. Today we begin reading our third and final author, Silius Italicus, whose poem, the *Punica*, is the longest Latin poem that we know of. So, Denys, we shall not be reading all 12,000 plus lines! The poem had lost favor since it maintains the gods as characters in the conflict – whereas, as we saw, Lucan did not mention the gods as forces at work in his epic. But I feel that the length of the poem may have discouraged the study of this epic. You have all read – at least in part – Vergil's *Aeneid*, which served as a poetic model for Silius Italicus, and selections from Livy, which provided the historical source for his account of the war against Hannibal. The poet had a distinguished public career in politics before retiring to a quieter life of writing. Hopefully, I will be able to follow his example, and turn to writing after retiring from many years of public service at a university. Again, Denys, I call upon you to lead us in the translation of the beginning of the *Punica*, after reading in Latin the first twenty lines of Book One. And congratulations on the publication of your article on Seneca. You were gracious enough to cite me as a reference in your philosophical discussion. But this is the second article on Seneca that you have had published. You may have been called "The Latin Student" at McGill, but here at Laval perhaps we should be addressing you as "The Latin Scholar"!

\-   Perish the thought, Professor Saucier! Although I realize I will have to continue publishing in order not to "perish"! Here is the Latin text.

Ordior arma, quibus caelo se gloria tollit

Aeneadum patiturque ferox Oenotria iura

Carthago. da, Musa, decus memorare laborum

antiquae Hesperiae, quantosque ad bella creavit

et quot Roma viros, sacri cum perfida pacti

gens Cadmea super regno certamina movit,

quaesitumque diu, qua tandem poneret arce

terrarum Fortuna caput. ter Marte sinistro

iuratumque Iovi foedus conventaque patrum

Sidonii fregere duces, atque impius ensis

ter placitam suasit temerando rumpere pacem,

sed medio finem bello excidiumque vicissim

molitae gente, propiusque fuere periclo,

quis superare datum: reseravit Dardanus arces

ductor Agenoreas, obsessa Palatia vallo

Poenorum, ac muris defendit Roma salutem.

Tantarum causas irarum odiumque perenni

servatum studio et mandata nepotibus arma

fas aperire mihi superasque recludere mentes.

iamque adeo magni repetam primordia motus.

Before I begin my translation, I would like to point out to everybody that in the poem the Carthaginians are called by a dozen different names, and the Romans are designated by over thirty other names! *Oenotria* was a Greek name for ancient southern Italy, and so a synonym for all of Italy. Dardanus was the Roman general Scipio *Africanus*, a descendant of Aeneas of Troy and the Dardanians, *Agenoreas* meant Carthaginian, after Agenor, a king of Tyre.

"Sidonians", "Tyrians", and "Cadmea" refer to Carthaginians, after the Phoenician cities of Sidon and Tyre and Cadmus, a son of Agenor. Here is my translation of the opening lines of the *Punica*, in which the poet introduces his subject, namely the Second Punic War.

"I begin the story of arms, by which the glory of the *Aeneadae* is raised to heaven, and proud Carthage endures Italian laws. Grant me, Muse, to record the glory of the labors of ancient Italy, and how many men Rome produced for the wars, when the Cadmean race, unfaithful towards the sacred bond, initiated the conflict for supreme rule. For a long time it remained uncertain on which citadel Fortune would finally place the capital of the world. Three times with unholy warfare did the Sidonian leaders violate the treaty sworn to Jupiter and the agreement with the senatorial fathers, and three times the godless sword persuaded them to brashly break an agreeable peace. But in the middle war" – the Second Punic War – "and the peoples in turn striving for the end and destruction, and those to whom it was granted to prevail were nearer to disaster, and the Roman general laid open the Carthaginian citadels, the general of the Carthaginians" – that is, Hannibal – "besieged the Palatine with a surrounding rampart, and Rome protected her security with her walls.

It is right for me to reveal the causes of such great anger and the hatred preserved with lasting zeal, the war passed on to grandchildren, and to reveal the plans of those above. Now I shall trace the beginnings of this great upheaval."

As you mentioned, Professor, the gods are involved in this poet's account of causes and results.

In the passage I read there is mention of the *superas mentes* – "the will of heaven", as it were.

I imagine that in a different time both Romans and Carthaginians would be listening to the song "War" by Edwin Starr! Perhaps, as they huddled behind their walls, the Romans would be playing the song "West of the Wall" by Toni Fisher - even though the "wall" in her song referred to the Berlin Wall!

-       Thank you, Denys, for your translation and explanatory comments. And for the musical addenda. I can imagine how unorthodox your annotated editions of Latin texts would be! And I wonder if the courses you will eventually teach in Classics will be cross-listed for credit with the Music Department!

Chapter 127

\-   Nice to see you again, Professor Gingras! I don't know if you remember me, but I met you a few years ago, when I visited your Department with Claire Talbot.

\-   But of course, Mr. Hainsworth! Claire was a special girl, so pleasant with everybody. I understand she joined a convent. I guess she was more special than we realized!

And, as I recall, she considered you very special, since she referred to you as "the Latin student". I remember that because all Classics students study Latin, and at the time it was a bit perplexing.

But having read through your *curriculum vitae*, I can now understand the significance of that appellation.The other members of the Committee, Professor Pelletier, Professor Micone, and Professor Vlassos, are also very impressed with your credentials. Your transcripts indicate that you are familiar with all the major Greek and Latin authors, and that you have studied in all the different disciplines in the field of Classics. You even have a background in numismatics, which would be an asset, as we will soon be receiving a gift of ancient Roman coins which have not been catalogued. Equally impressive is your summer study experience - Rome, England, Spain, Paris, Pompeii, Germany, and memorable moments in Greece at Pylos, Athens and Thessaloniki!

And you don't seem a bit *fessus de via*. Obviously no one imposed on you a *caveat viator*! Your academic path brought you along an interesting itinerary – I am deliberately using alliteration since it is listed as one of your trademarks by one of your referees – Cincinnati to Montreal to Quebec and perhaps back to Montreal!

\-   No, Professor Gingras, I never became travel weary, and far from being warned off with a *caveat*, I was actually encouraged by my professors to take advantage of those summer programmes. Since I was in the fortunate position of being the recipient of a generous and renewable study grant, I was able to profit from some specialized seminars and international study programmes. Adopting a *carpe diem* philosophy, I was able to expand my horizons in Classical Studies.

\-   I am Professor Micone, and we met briefly once at a SEGELQ conference. I know you are a member of their *Conseil administratif*, and I commend you on your contribution to Classics in Quebec by your service in the provincial association. This contribution is to your credit – *hoc tibi est honori*, as we say! Since you are perfectly bilingual, would you envisage serving at some point on the Council of the Classical Association of Canada?

-       I remember your presentation on the evolution of meaning in words from historico-linguistic contexts to contemporary usage – how words change meaning over time, and lose their original Latin or Roman sense. I can still recall one example that struck me at the time. You talked about a relative of *Tarquinius Superbus*, Junius Brutus, who feigned idiocy, to appear harmless, and to be able to overthrow the last king of Rome. You used the example of a harmless thunderbolt – *fulmen brutum* – to express the idea of an empty threat, whereas today the word "brutal" describes someone who is hardly harmless. The Emperor Claudius also feigned illness and incapacity to protect himself. Yet, once Emperor, HE was hardly harmless! He could truly say with Horace *non sum qualis eram* – "I am not the man I once was" - but with an ironic twist, since he was now powerful! As far as serving on committees, even at a national level, I suppose *nunquam non paratus* – I am always ready to serve – if necessary!

-       You seem to be *natus ad gloriam*, Mr. Hainsworth, definitely destined for great things! I am Professor Pelletier, and I am amazed at your scholarship at such a young age. I know Professor Gingras has read your Master's thesis on the differentiation between the Greek god Dionysos and the Roman Liber, and found it innovative in its analysis. We have all looked at your scholarly journal publications, and your contributions to academic research are promising indeed. As did the others, I read in their entirety your articles in French – "Plebeians and Roman Religion" and "Senecan Tragedy: Why These Plays?", as well as your English-language articles – "Hercules: Star of Myth and Film", "The Pastoral Poetry of Robert Frost in the Context of Latin Pastoral Poetry", and "Worship in the Ghettoes: The Cult of Bacchus in Rome". I was able to read your article in Spanish, "The Language of Religion in Republican Rome", and defer to the excellent comments of my colleagues, Professor Micone, who read your Italian article , "Sincerity in Seneca", Professor Gingras, who read the article you published in German, "Seneca on Time", and Professor Vlassos, who read the article published in Greek, "Religious Sentiment in the *Hippolytus* of Euripides", which I understand is a reworking of a paper you presented at the CAC at Laval a few years ago. With so many publications in foreign journals, you risk becoming more of a household name than the *penates*! As well, your doctoral dissertation on popular religion in Rome during the Republic sounds intriguing. Professor Gingras, who has had access with your permission to the pre-finalized draft, tells us that the argumentation is intricate, but refreshing! Tell me, Mr. Hainsworth, do you have a book project in mind? Do you envisage becoming wealthy with a string of popular books?

- To that question, Professor Pelletier, I am tempted to respond *labor ipse voluptas*, that writing books would be a labor of love, regardless of any pecuniary reward. I would like to pursue certain research interests, notably in Roman religion and the philosophy of Seneca. But I am also interested in the portrayal of Ancient Greece and Rome on the big screen!

I am indeed interested in Latin language and literature in general, and in the contemporary reception of ancient Greek and Latin literature. I know you were just joking in comparing me to the household gods of Ancient Rome, but your comment, even though *per iocum*, was flattering!

- Mr. Hainsworth - Professor Vlassos, nice to meet you! I was afraid our female colleague here would use up all the time at our disposal! Dr. Pelletier knows I am also speaking *per iocum*! You are obviously and foremost a Latinist. But would you feel comfortable and well-disposed to teaching courses in Greek language and civilization?

- Professor Vlassos, I consider myself *ante omnia* a teacher. I specifically took the course on university teaching at McGill with the view to becoming first and foremost a teacher. I must say that I have enjoyed my teaching experience at Concordia immensely. And I say this *ex animo* – quite sincerely! I would therefore not be adverse to teaching Homer or Euripides or Greek history, to mention but a few possibilities. To say that I have a preference for Latin would not be an exaggeration – *praesto et persto* - I stand before this committee in firm admission to this fact. Nonetheless, if I were asked to teach primarily Greek courses, I would welcome that opportunity. My primary mission, I believe, is teaching. I am determined, you will say, *infixum est mihi*! Consequently, I am prepared for either situation – *ad utrumque paratus – Linguam Latinam vel Graecam docere* – to teach Latin or Greek! After all, I would merely be going the same way, but by different steps – *gradu diverso, una via!* Of course, my field of expertise – Latin language and civilization, especially Roman religion – would be more fitting if I were to direct graduate student research.

- You mentioned your experience at Concordia, Mr. Hainsworth. Professor Gingras has informed the Committee members that Concordia would like to hire you. This is of course *inter amicos*, since I am not attempting to prejudice the hiring process in other universities. Unfortunately, however, this interference does occur - I speak from experience – *expertus dico!* But tell us briefly – *paucis verbis* - if and why you would prefer a position here at l'Université de Montréal.

- *Me libente*, Professor Micone, with pleasure! I could quote Cicero and reply *spero meliora*. But to say I am "looking for something better" would be unfair to Professor Jones and the students at Concordia! But to express it in Latin – *Latine dicere* - there is an aspect *ad gustum involved*. What I mean by a "question of taste" is that, although I have derived a certain satisfaction from the courses I have taught at Concordia, I would very much like to teach graduate courses and direct graduate student research. And, having done my doctorate at Laval, in a completely French milieu, I would like to continue working here in a French environment. Finally, even had all other considerations been of equal merit – *ceteris paribus*, as we would say – the beautiful location of this University on the mountainside with its majestic view would easily induce me with an image-filled impression that, as a teacher of Greek and Roman Studies, I was interpreting oracles from the summit of Mt. Parnassus, or possibly reciting Latin poetry among the hills of Ancient Rome!

- We appreciate your frank honesty, Mr Hainsworth. And yes, I believe we sometimes fail to appreciate this geographical position which allows us to "shine" over this great city of Montreal! Professor Micone most probably raised that delicate issue *ex proposito*, on purpose, as it were. He is from the old school which compels him to "seek after truth". You should know that *quaere verum* is his mantra! We all know, Professor Micone, that you are an uncompromising *laudator temporis acti* – a "praiser of past time" who longs for the "good old days"! But, being an American, and having perhaps the opportunity to teach in one of the prestigious American universities, what would attract you to a career here in Montreal? Give us your opinion on life in Montreal, indeed on life in Quebec. *Dic nobis quid sentias*, Mr. - soon to be Dr. - Hainsworth!

- Well, *nihil est ab omni parte beatum* – "there is no perfect happiness", as the saying goes. But I can say from the bottom of my heart – *in meo corde*- I have fallen in love with Montreal! It is a bilingual and cosmopolitan city – where I can speak the different languages I have learned, and partake in the various cultures. True, I could do that, to an extent, in New York, but its motto – *excelsior* – "ever higher" - I personally feel applies more to the Empire State Building than to the quality of life! I feel blessed to have received a grant which brought me to Quebec and to Montreal. On the other hand, as Sallust so elegantly expressed it – *faber est quisque fortunae suae* – "everyone is the architect of his own fortune". I have worked hard to integrate into the fabric of Québécois society, but I have not found it burdensome. Although I have encountered a number of people who seem to have adopted the maxim *disce pati* as their lot in life, I see no need to "learn to endure", but rather a bright future for this city and this province – not to mention this country! But as they say, "to each one's own beauty" – *suum cuique pulchrum*! To them I would pass on Cicero's advice – *tibi seris, tibi metis* – "you reap what you sow"! So, Members of the Committee, a *casus fortuitus* became a *modus vivendi.* This truly wonderful chance is now a way of life for me!

-       Although you say you wouldn't prefer a career in the United States, you certainly seem to put into practice the motto of that great American institution, Harvard, namely truth – *Veritas*! Or maybe it is a case of the truth setting you free – *Veritas Vos Liberabit* – "The truth will set you free", which I believe is the motto of Johns Hopkins University, where I attended an extremely wellorganized conference last year. You have mentioned that you have interviews next week in some Canadian and American universities.

While it is certainly true that auro quaeque ianua panditur - that is to say, "a golden key opens any door", I am quite confident that you will open the door that is meant for you! But as we are on the subject of university mottoes, how do you feel towards our motto *Fide splendet et Scientia?*

-       Well, it certainly is true that this University shines forth in Faith and Science. Yes, the Université de Montréal is a seat of learning, but with a long tradition of education based initially on the Catholic faith of the founders of the territory it served. Faith cannot be taught like knowledge, but can co-exist with learning. Faith does not fear – *fides non timet*, nor should knowledge! In this sense, they both can – and do – shine together! The realization of this was a turning point for me as I embarked on my own quest for knowledge with my faith deeply rooted within me, both calling out together – like an echo, a *vocis imago*. This was truly for me a *magni momenti* – a great moment! Knowing and believing – endeavors of our souls and our hearts and our minds – under the aegis of this great institution of higher learning – can be pursued with united strength – *viribus unitis*! One could imagine this University combining these two beacons of truth – *fides et scientia* - into the expression *lux mundi* – "light of the world", but I have read about another University that has adopted this motto . What's the name - *Non memini* - I can't seem to remember. It's a Christian university in California. Ah yes, it's called Jessup University. Finally, I believe that Thomas Aquinas expressed so sublimely the necessity for the marriage of *fides* and *scientia* when he said *timeo hominem unius libri* – "I fear the man with only one book"!

-       Very insightful, Mr. Hainsworth! Without trying to overdo an obvious word play, since I have heard of your prowess in this domain, you have certainly shed much light on our world! Those who spend their time denigrating those words in our noble banner are "busy doing nothing", to quote the Roman you admire, Seneca, operose nihil *agunt*! And since we know that nothing comes from nothing – *nihil ex nihilo* – they should direct their reflections to more sensible causes, lest we accuse each and every one of them of being *non compos mentis*, yes – not of sound mind! I would like to point out that the referees you asked to write letters for you, Professors Watson, Marcoux, Marois and Saucier, all wrote glowing letters on your behalf!

Nor were they responding to your request *quid pro quo* - in return for some future consideration. They were all adamant in singing your praises. One comment I am still trying to figure out came from Professor Watson, whom I respect very highly! He mentioned in his letter that "praise" was not the only song you knew! Very enigmatic indeed! Was it a *lapsus linguae* on his part – a slip of the tongue? Unless my dear Watson happens to be referring to your uncanny ability to quote song titles as a form of *pseudo-scholia* in translations and discussions. You did mention in your presentation letter that popular music was one of your hobbies. A hobby you extend to performance, having recorded some songs for the "cause of Classics". How noble and inspiring! Comments from your respondents included the notion that even if "necessity were the mother of invention" – *mater artium necessitas* – there would be no need to invent your merits! All concluded that you should be hired *pro meritis* – on your just merits! *Deus avertat* – God forbid that we fail to award you a position - reads one letter.

Professor Pelletier was amused by some of the comments, and uttered at one point during the Committee's preliminary meeting on your application *certe non taedet me* – "I for one am not bored"! A rather poetic appeal on your behalf was a quote to the effect that were we not to bring you on board, an unnatural vacuum would be created here at UdeM – *natura abhorret a vacuo*! You can probably deduce which of your respondents used that line! Another letter suggested that we are to be judged by our actions – *spectemur agendo* - and these actions of course will be based on our decisions! One of your Professors, with an obvious dramatic flair, wrote a small note to accompany his formal letter, in which he stated that if your candidature were not retained, and I quote *actum est de me* – it's all over for me – I shall have to walk barefoot – *pedibus nudis* – like the dregs of society – *faex populi*, a true freak of nature – *lusus naturae*! You are amused, I see, as were we on the Committee, but he goes on to say *nulla ex parte mentem compescere* – there is no way I could control my temper, and you – meaning us – will undergo severe tongue lashings – *linguae verbera,* because after all the law, although harsh, is still the law – *dura lex, sed lex* – referring no doubt to the unwritten principle of avoiding irregularities and possible censure in hiring practices. The author then turns to playful banter as he enjoins the Committee members to consider that *bis pueri senes* – old men are twice children, and as such, we should accept the veracity of his claims since *ex ore parvulorum veritas* – indeed, out of the mouth of little children comes truth! At this point, we on the Committee were ready to say along with Horace *iam satis est* – enough is enough, when Professor Micone reminded us of another passage from Horace – *est modus in rebus* - there is a method in all things - and that probably there was a method beyond the madness of this little note. *Macti animo* – take courage, Professor Micone advised us. We could leave this entreaty as a matter for others – *res inter alios*, or with a grain of salt - *cum grano salis* - take note of as much as we wanted – *quantum libet.* Moreover, the note concluded with a mirthful confession to have been written *fervente die* – in the heat of the day, and that his dramatic plea was but a matter of *lacrimae simulatae* – "crocodile tears", as we might say, and begged our indulgence since he acknowledged that even though art is long (if his words could be considered such!), life is short – words you have no doubt heard often, Mr. Hainsworth – *vita brevis, ars longa*! He added that his colleagues did not sign his "manifesto" under the principle *qui tacet consentit* – consent by silence. He signed off with a pleasant *benedicite* – as that very funny man, Red Skelton, would say – "May God bless"! However, and here we see "the end crowning the work" – *finis coronat opus*, he left us with the question *cui malo* – who would really be losing out if we did not recommend hiring? I would have preferred the query *cui bono* – who would profit? Hopefully, then, the answer would be both parties! The Committee will hold its consultation meeting tomorrow – we are on a deliberate timeline, and do not intend to draw out our deliberations indefinitely, or as you would say, Mr. Hainsworth – *sine die*! Consequently, you will be informed of our recommendation early next week. In the meantime, continue doing what you are doing – *age quod agis*. You are sure to meet your lucky day, your *dies faustus*! But, Mr. Hainsworth, how would you respond to this tongue-in-cheek appeal in one referee's "mirthful missive" - more alliteration for your pleasure?

\-   Often the best reaction, and I learned this from my dog Vergil Cane, is *quieta non movere* – don't move quiet things – just let sleeping dogs lie! I wish to thank all the Committee members for your time, patience, consideration, and most enjoyable interaction!

Chapter 128

-       Welcome to l'Université de Montréal, Mr.Hainsworth! As you may have guessed from the essential message in our phone conversation, I have not invited you back to Montreal to talk about the weather, even though it has improved since last week! I wanted to inform you that the Committee unanimously voted to put your name forward to the Dean as the candidate to fill the position in our Department. Since we did not have any preliminary meetings with you before the full Committee interview, we are ahead of our own usual schedule when hiring, and consequently have finalized our process before the other universities. The fact that we have accelerated procedures and are already offering you a position is proof of our unequivocal interest in having you join our Department! *Res ipsa loquitur* - the very offer is in itself the proof! I thought also that if we were your first choice, you would not have to travel to other cities and undergo the rigors of interviews – although I'm sure you would meet some interesting people! You are naturally at liberty to accept or reject the position here, which is a tenure-track position at the rank of Assistant Professor. And by the way, we were not unduly influenced by the earnest but clearly caricatured entreaty appended to the letters of recommendation from Laval. You should know that Professor Marcoux and myself were classmates for a year in France, and are given to such friendly exchanges when the occasion presents itself!

-       Professor Gingras, I most heartily accept the position here at the Université de Montréal! I can't seem to find the words in any language to express my joy – and my pride - in your vote of confidence! Professor Marcoux was amused to hear that I had referred to him as a "sleeping dog", and wondered if it originated on the occasion on which he was detected with his eyes shut during a lecture being given by Professor Walter! Clearly another case of *res ipsa loquitur*! However, I did point out to him that ultimately "every dog has his day"!

-       Excellent – again welcome to the Department of Classical Studies! Once the Dean's Office has ratified the Departmental recommendation, you will be contacted by the University's Personnel Department to sign all the relevant forms. They will inform you of general employee obligations, salary, health coverage, UdeM working conditions, and other items of protocol. You will be officially a member of the Department as of August 1, but you won't be required to start until August 15. In fact, in the Classics Department our opening meetings are never held before August 20. Of course, you will want to visit the campus before then to get aquainted with the surroundings, including your office, which has been vacant for over a year.

The campus is pretty quiet for most of August, but our Department Secretary, Madame Sylvain, will be in the office beginning August 10, and you will be able to make arrangements to have access to your office after that date. You will become one of the Department's two Latinists – the other one is Professor Micone, whom you met. He was very impressed with the numerous Latin phrases you interjected into the interview last week. He claims that never was so much Latin spoken here outside of the Latin classroom! By the way, he is anxious to converse with you in Italian. Professor Pelletier and myself are Hellenists, my field of predilection being lyric poetry and Greek drama. Professor Pelletier is quite fluent in Spanish and is sure to strike up conversation with you in that language. Professor Vlassos, with whom you will obviously be able to converse in Greek, teaches both Ancient and Modern Greek in the Department. Our introductory Latin and Greek courses are taught by part-time instructors. For German conversation, you will be able to exchange with Professor Geitz of the Philosophy Department, who teaches the Ancient Philosophy courses in our Department. What will you be teaching, you are asking yourself! We are hoping you will inject new life into our Greek and Roman Religion course, which is not offered every year, often alternating with a course on Classical Mythology.

It is felt that these courses really deserve to be taught by someone with a certain expertise in the subject. That course is semestered, as is the course on Greek and Roman Literature, which will also be part of your course load. I think you will be pleased to hear that the advanced Latin reading course you will be teaching is the author Seneca. You will have the opportunity to select course texts and have the book orders placed before the end of June. Your graduate level course, I am happy to announce, will be a seminar on topics in Roman Religion. Our graduate students will be informed of this new course at the end of this session.

-       It all sounds exciting! Professor Gingras, I must tell you that I will be studying Medieval and Renaissance Latin at the American Academy in Rome this summer in June and July. It will be my last programme under the auspices of the Parker Foundation.

Unfortunately, I will be missing the Summer Olympics to be held here in Montreal. But I have no hard feelings just because Montreal beat out the city of Los Angeles for these games! Also, I didn't want to include among my reasons for making the Université de Montréal my first choice an extremely personal situation, but now I can inform you that I didn't only fall in love with Montreal, but also with a young lady now living in Montreal! In fact Manon and I are engaged.

-        I can now fully understand why you are not pursuing an opportunity to teach at an American university. But surely you have mixed feelings about not returning to the United States?

-        No, Professor, even though I do miss my family. But my parents have met Manon on a couple of occasions, and now that I have spent more than a third of my life in Quebec, the possibility of my not returning to America upon completing my studies was very real. I am glad, though, that my sister, who is married and who will very shortly be starting a family, is living in Cincinnati near my parents.

-        You certainly seem very much integrated into life here in Quebec. In the interview, you had mentioned that you were not opposed to teaching Greek. We often offer a summer course on a Greek author. This course is taught in an intensive session during the month of May, but our Hellenists are all off to the islands during the summer – myself to Les Îles-de-la Madeleine, Professor Pelletier to the Caribbean islands, and Professor Vlassos to the Greek islands – he was actually born on the island of Mykonos. So the possibility is there. You are aware that we do not have a theater programme with play productions in Greek and Latin like Laval and McGill. Nonetheless, in alternate years, Professor Micone and Professor Pelletier accompany students to Italy and Greece for a summer programme which usually includes a drama component, including watching plays by the ancient playwrights. You would be the ideal person to join these excursions and lecture on Greek and Roman tragedies and comedies!

-        That sounds very enticing indeed. There are also the public Latin and Greek courses I have been teaching in Quebec. The President of the non-profit group that organizes these courses has approached me about teaching courses in a bilingual programme in Montreal. He had been wondering if I would be interested if I eventually settled in Montreal.

There was also a question of dramatic readings of Greek and Roman authors in both English and French. I had participated in a similar programme of readings when I was at McGill.

-        Teaching Latin and Greek to the general public is an excellent project, and I think we would be in a position to support this outreach programme. We also occasionally participate in the lecture series offered in *Les Belles Histoires*. You lectured in a similar programme at Laval, if I am not mistaken. I realize we are speaking of a number of teaching commitments. And don't be surprised if you are contacted by the Séminaire de Montréal about teaching Ecclesiastical Latin.

-       And I am committed to serving on the SEGELQ executive. Then there is the world of research and writing and conference presentations. I do have a couple of ideas to explore for journal articles and public lectures, and of course, I would like to eventually publish my dissertation in a book. Both Professors Watson and Marois see this as a definite possibility.

-       Yes, now we have three specialists in Roman Religion in Quebec! I can smell an International Conference on the subject in Montreal or Quebec in the not so distant future, organized by the "Triumvirate"!

-       Perhaps we could be known simply as "three men responsible for matters of religion" - the *tresviri de rebus religionis*. References to a dictatorial "triumvirate" risks leaving you with a situation in which what you "smell" is less than pleasant, Professor!

Chapter 129

\-   Holden, I was so excited when you called to tell me the news! Imagine teaching here in Montreal. Your dream come true, isn't it? I know it's mine! I always knew you would succeed. Your PhD can now be explained as "Professor HolDen"! And to try some alliteration under your constant coaching, your secret slogan for success must surely be "Planning and Perseverance"! Did you notice the "s", "p" and "c" combinations?

\-   I'm always thinking of our "dreaming out loud" together under the stars! And speaking of stars, "Planning and Perseverance" sounds like a mission statement for NASA! I've made it to Université de Montréal, but "perseverance" could maybe someday get us all the way to Mars! The letters "s","p" and "c" – would that be "The Society for the Preservation of Classics"? But Manon, you left out the most important "p" in my formula for success – "Plouffe"! Naturally, I'm going to work very hard to obtain tenure. The other Latinist, Professor Micone, will be retiring in a few years, and I'm hoping to move more into graduate level teaching. As students become interested in Roman religion, I will eventually have Master's and doctoral candidates to supervise. I've contacted the people at the universities in Ottawa, Halifax and Winnipeg to let them know that I have accepted the position in Montreal. You probably didn't look forward to the prospect of living in the Maritimes or out West, even though you would have been able to continue working for the Federal Government. The American universities haven't confirmed interviews yet, so if they contact me, I'll inform them of my situation.

\-   You're right, Holden. I was dreading having to leave my family - especially my mother! After all, St. Lambert and Montreal are still very new to them. Even when we are married, I will still want to go out with my mother on occasion. And I want to be able to guide Nicole through her high school years. This restaurant is quite nice. I love the menu!

\-   And I love the FOOD listed in the menu! Now, now, Manon – remember what Plutarch said – no getting mad in public! This restaurant on Côte-des-Neiges is just one of many in our new neighborhood – well, your working neighborhood and my teaching and residential neighborhood, since I've arranged to move into an apartment on August 1. It's just up the street – if we have time, we can visit the building. I'll be able to walk to class, and I can even jog around campus. My *carpe diem* days are working out beautifully, but I don't want to neglect my *mens sana in corpore sano* days!

\-   And you'll be continuing your "Latin student" days – but with a bigger desk!

How did your parents take the news? And have you told Jeremy? He's looking for a position now, isn't he? It seems he took longer than you did to finish his doctorate.

\-   My parents are very happy for me – and for you! They realize that it wouldn't have been easy for you to move away from your family – especially to a place where people didn't speak French or have the same culture. They know I adore Montreal, and we can make Cincinnati a place to visit, and they will have a good reason for visiting Montreal. Of course, we will be visiting my family in June to participate in America's Bicentennial Celebrations – I wonder if the organizers would appreciate the "ABC" slogan I've just created for them! Then, of course, I'll be off to the Academy in Rome for Medieval and Renaissance Latin. You realize, Manon, that in my research on Classical Reception, I will most likely have to consult Latin texts written much later than Cicero and Seneca! I will probably read more Christian writers – actually, in Greek too.

My teaching in Ecclesiastical Latin and Biblical Greek at the Seminary in Quebec has helped prepare me for that eventuality. I've been looking at the *Rotas Sator* Square, which is quite an interesting palindrome. I'm inclined to think it is a Christian code, even though many scholars are not convinced. But I think the encrypted pattern of *pater noster* flanked by the New Testament prophetic symbols of the Greek *Alpha* and *Omega* are too pronounced to be a mere coincidence. I've written to Jeremy to let him know the news. He had to spend an extra year reading some Latin and Greek authors in preparation for comprehensive exams. He successfully defended his dissertation on Greek religion, though, and is awaiting replies from the universities he contacted, including Concordia. I didn't tell Professor Jones, or even the Committee at the Université de Montréal, that one of the reasons I was not leaning towards Concordia was precisely because I know Jeremy would very much like to obtain a position there.

And it is not because I told him about the young secretary in the Classics Department – well, maybe, but that wouldn't be his main reason! Leaving the door open for Jeremy tells me I still have a little bit of "Hans Brinker" in me! Let me explain, Manon. When I was just starting high school back in Cincinnati, I read a book called *Hans Brinker, or The Silver Skates*. It was all about speed-skating in the great outdoors in Holland. I used to pretend I was Hans Brinker while I was skating on the frozen lake – well, artificial lake - in Burnet Woods. I "was" also Hans Brinker when speed-skating on that rink in Ste-Foy! The book was written by an American – Mary Mapes Dodge – in 1865! I remember that date because it was the year the American Civil War ended. Hans had wanted to obtain the silver skates by winning the speed-skating race, but he dropped out to let a friend win. In the present situation, Jeremy is that friend! As a Greek Religion specialist, he could become part of a "tetrarchy" with the Roman Religion "triumvirate"! I'm going to try the *veau parmigiana*, Manon. How about you?

\-   I'll have fish and chips – I took a liking to that meal when we were in England. I am still trying to master Canadian English, and there were all these different terms overseas. A bag of chips is a bag of crisps, chips are our French fries, a fag is a cigarette – but oh gosh, not here in Montreal! A truck is called a lorry over there, and I loved when they referred to a single occurence as a "one-off". I was surprised to hear that "having someone over for tea" was actually an invitation to a complete meal! Tea didn't sound very filling! But, Holden, you haven't told me what you thought of my new car, even though you helped pay for it! I love the color!

\-   A mandarin Pontiac Ventura! I'm pretty sure I'll be able to spot it in a parking lot! I'm glad you took my advice with my *caveat emptor* – you were, in the end, a "careful buyer", and took my advice on negotiating the price. I hope you know that the mph on the dashboard stands for Manon Plouffe Hainsworth! One day we'll head out in your Ventura on the Ventura Highway – listening to the song "Ventura Highway" by that great band America. Yes, in England it would be a motorway! I've always liked the German term – *autobahn*! If the car breaks down, we can look for America's "Horse With No Name"! You talked about strange differences between British and Canadian English. The same goes for the differences between American and Canadian English, and between the French we speak here and the French we heard in France! But language itself is sometimes contradictory. Why do we park in a "drive-way", and drive on a "parkway"? Language – spoken and written – is a peculiar phenomenon. In Latin we call the head of the family – the "father of the family" - *paterfamilias* - even though grammatically the ending for the case showing possession had evolved from '*as*' to '*-ae*'. But "*paterfamiliae*" just wouldn't sound right, given the longstanding use of that term. And speaking of family, Manon, I wanted to say how much I admire you for your affection for and devotion to your own family! You would have made a fine Roman woman!

Chapter 130

\-   That's great news, Jeremy! I guess you weren't to be outdone! You sent me a note a few weeks ago congratulating me for being hired at the Université de Montréal, and now it's my turn to say well done! I think it's wonderful that you'll be teaching at Concordia – so does Manon! Now you have no excuse for not showing up at our wedding! Just think – we'll be able to visit some of our favorite places again – the respectable ones, that is! Right now I'm remembering the crazy times we had together in our student days – or should I say – our "stewed"-ent days! If ever there was a reason for *damnatio memoriae*! No, seriously, all things considered, I really wouldn't want to erase those memories! Strange, isn't it, that the Romans themselves never used that Latin expression, even though they did sometimes "re-write" history! We know that the names of some Roman emperors were removed from official records after their deaths. They were the lucky ones, because some emperors were "removed" from history before their deaths! When I was studying in Germany, Professor Jürgens informed me that a German legal scholar by the name of Christoph Schreiter used that term in a 17th-century thesis. Can't say that I was surprised, considering German scholarship in those days. I believe that, ultimately, if you "damn" history, history will "damn" you! A certain American President learned that lesson when he "removed history" from some tape transcriptions! But I must confess, I've been having flashbacks of all kinds of events from the last dozen years or so! Like when during our intramural football days at McGill you called me "The Flash" because of my speed, and I told you that made me think of the Latin Flash cards from my first year of Latin! I always marvelled at the names you came up with for me – some were almost comical! You weren't so complimentary when we went back to my apartment to celebrate our championship win, and you said you were dying of thirst. You thought I had said "I'll be back in a jiffy", but I had really said "WITH a Jiffy" – I thought the chocolate milk would do you good! However, that drink just left you with hot flashes! I remember one particular episode when you proPOSed a symPOSium at my place, and I supPOSed it would be okay. You were "enthusiastic" about your idea to "toast Dionysos" – an idea which seemed weirdly familiar to me! You arrived with a few bottles of (cheap) wine, and declared "we would get plastered like a wall and wasted like food not eaten at all"! At one point we started talking about the gods, and you mentioned that it was unfair that gods and goddesses like Jupiter and Neptune and Venus and Diana had tributes in song, but not the others. Whereupon you broke into a clever (for you!) play on words to honor the other deities. I could never forget that witty ditty: "JUNO, you get on MINERVAs when you inVESTA lot in your CERES of puns - any VULCAN do that, but we must APOLLOgize with MERCURYal speed because it MARS the will of the Olympians to BACCHUS up"! When I remarked that you had left out Pluto, you said "what the hell", and in your best French chided me for not telling you *plus tôt*! Maybe in this case later would have been better than "sooner"! You started playing my records – "Lightning Strikes" and "Beyond the Sea" and "Venus" and "Diana"! I mentioned that I was "feeling" the omnipresence of the gods, but you said you were experiencing some kind of "ovnipresence"! I had to point out that those "UFO's" were my records that you were flinging through the air! You claimed you were a *discobolos* (I was surprised you remembered the word in your "frenzied" and "ecstatic" state) competing in an "athletic contest" to honor the gods. Since "athletic" comes from the Greek word *athlon,* meaning "contest", you were guilty of using hendiadys – you know, using two words to express one idea! But you were in no frame of mind to recognize "figures of speech", since you were by now having trouble with your own speech! I recall pointing out that technically you were a discus thrower because records are discs, but I had wished I had had frisbees available!

Strangely, I even remembered having read that those "flying plastic saucers" were originally called "Pluto Platters"! So Pluto was being "honored " after all! We've come a long away from those days of goofy gibberish – especially me – since I started out in Cincinnati! I can't forget our bar-hopping – but you insisted on calling it "bar-hoping", since you were always hoping to meet "Miss Right". Most girls, however, called you "Mr. Wrong", but we were known as the "Wright Brothers", because we were occasionally "flying high"! Remember that joke I repeated in reply – there was never a doubt that their airplane would get off the ground because "two Wrights can't make a wrong"! Even when that cute Chinese girl gave you a phone number, it turned out to be a "Wong" number! You must remember Barry, the bartender who called you "the goofy Greek student" – and I was "the loony Latin student"! But we rose to the challenge, and nick-named him "Batty Barry"! And there was his cousin Bart, always over at the end of the bar. We thought ourselves pretty cute when we called them Barry BARtender and his cousin Bart-ENDER! No wonder everyone knew our names at that bar – in a friendly, but funny way, we enjoyed sitting with a beer, bashing our buddies! Whenever you were feeling a "little flushed" you would break into terrible toilet bowl humor – far from our talks about the Super Bowl – and even further from the description of my dog Vergil Cane's supper bowl! My favorite moments were watching you pretending you were cool and trying to warm up to a hot chick, but getting the cold shoulder! Honestly, it was like watching a weather report! Once, when you were in a state of despair, I encouraged you to "keep the faith", and suggested that maybe that American, Oral Roberts, could help. You thought I was talking about a mouthwash! But, now that I think about it, that wouldn't have hurt either! You must recall that evening in a certain bar frequented by so-called intellectuals. You had broken into a few verses of that Lou Rawls song "Lady Love", trying to impress the girls sitting near-by, when this fellow sat down at our table claiming that the girls you were serenading were "amazons". This pseudo-intellectual then tried to impress us with his "knowledge" that the Amazons of Greek mythology were so-called because they had removed one breast in order to have more ability with the bow. He was to learn quickly that he was dealing with two tried and true classicists, as we contradicted him, pointing out that the origin based on the Greek *amazon* was a false etymology deriving from the myth of those fierce fighters, since Greek art never displayed them without both breasts!

When I mentioned that there had been a Persian word – *hamazan* – to describe "warriors", and that it probably referenced those female archers that fought in the wild Scythian armies in the eastern Persian Empire, he was truly perplexed! Besides, as we pointed out to this guy, who obviously wasn't as "abreast" of the realities of the ancient world as he had assumed, the champion female archers of today certainly demonstrate that it would not at all have been necessary to disfigure oneself in order to have superior ability with the bow! We did concede, though, that the word "amazon" would make a super commercial name for a company willing to take on all giant competitors in the fierce world of business, much like the Amazons had fought with Herakles,Theseus, and Achilles! We were so proud to demonstrate our "classical" gravitas – that quality of seriousness the Romans so admired in their leaders! Despite my customary humility, we dealt the "deathblow" to our unfortunate adversary, by "pontificating" that the "law of *gravitas*" was not the same thing as the "law of gravity" – we classicists would never descend from the "level of loftiness" to the "limits of lowliness"! I believe he left with a "grave" inferiority complex! I'm wondering if that same *gravitas* exemplified by those Romans at the top of society and at the head of households could keep me at the "top of my game" on the golf course! Do you remember me telling you that the closest you would come to being a "pro" would be your tendency to "PROcrastinate"! I suggested you look up the word, but you said there was no rush, and that you would look it up later! We will surely want to touch base with our former mentors at McGill. Of course, I will be in touch with Professor Watson on a fairly regular basis on issues of scholarship in the field of Roman religion. Since I had done much of the groundwork on the book he was preparing on sources for Roman religion, he is insisting that I officially co-author the book. He also approached Professor Marois at Laval as well as me about the possibility of joint editorship in a bilingual journal on Ancient Greek and Roman Religion, that would be published annually by McGill University Press. But say, since you'll be in Montreal, you could also be on the editorial board as the respondent for Greek religion! Professor Gingras had talked about the "Big Three" in Ancient Religion here in Quebec, but with you in the fold, there could be a "Big Four" – no I'm not talking football, Jeremy! We could be the *quattuorviri de rebus religionis* – the *viri* just increased by 25%! You remember how Mrs. Watson religiously – sorry, I have that word on my brain – well, anyway, she follows the contemporary trends in music. Professor Watson recently complained to me that his wife is more interested in the Disco Ball than in the Faculty Ball! Personally, I have a soft spot for Lucille Ball! Don't tell me, you "jock" of all trades, you would go with "Play ball"! You have an enviable workload – Greek courses on Homer and Herodotus, as well as Ancient History, and a course on Greek and Roman Religion, that a certain "Latin student" previously taught at Concordia! You will like Professor Jones, the Department Chair who, I guess, was a member of the committee that interviewed you. You will find him very supportive. You told me that my name came up during your interview – probably because of our McGill connection. But the casual remark that a number of students – by coincidence, female students – referred to me as the " Concordia Classics film star", undoubtedly was because of the course on Greece and Rome in Film that I taught there this year! Last year I gave a talk to the Classics students on Graduate Studies. Some students told me afterwards that they had expected the session to be dry and boring, but that I had actually made Graduate Studies sound like fun! Imagine if I had mentioned some of our escapades! You wouldn't just be a film "star"- you would be an "Oscar winner" at Concordia! I wonder if I would get consideration for an "Oscar" in a "supporting role"! Manon and I have been to the Claude St. Jean Steakhouse a couple of times. Dancing there is a lot of fun. You'll be able to join us next year. I imagine you won't want to live on the South Shore because of the commute to Concordia's West End Campus. There are some nice apartments on Cavendish, which is conveniently close to the Loyola Campus. Manon and I are very excited about our wedding, even though it's a whole year away. She asked if you had a special lady in your life, and I said I didn't think so. If that's true, maybe Professor Wilkinson or Mrs. Robinson are still available! Just joshing you! On the other hand, you are in danger of using up your time-outs! So "you better hurry and find a girl that's real purty – before you wake up and say 'gee, I'm already past thirty' "! But I would drop that line you used with one of McGill's T.A.s - " If I asked you to conjugate with me, would you decline?"! I realize that Latin "humor" isn't for everybody, but weren't we surprised that time we were in a bar, and you ordered a martini. The bartender asked if you were sure you wanted a double! I was more sensible, and ordered a "martinus"!

The next day at the delicatessen, you tried ordering a "salamus" sandwich, but the guy at the counter didn't know what you were talking about! It didn't help when you tried telling him that the word "delicatessen" came from Latin *delicatus*, meaning "giving pleasure". I jumped in and explained that the French word "*delicatesse*", which he did know, meant "delicious things". But I lost him again when I pointed out that the word was actually German, since the German verb *Essen* means "to eat"! Fortunately we got him laughing before we left when I said that the

Dalai Lama often ate those sandwiches in New Delhi, and so became the "Deli Lama from Delhi"!

However, I couldn't help recalling the "delicate" situation at Concordia with my student, "Delicate Dido", but she was more "fragile" than "dainty"! I've already mentioned that I'll be taking a course this summer on Medieval and Renaissance Latin – yes, "a Latin student" right to the end! You'll have to be a "good sport" and take notes on the Montreal Olympics for me!

While I'm in Rome, I'll pretend it's 1960, when the Summer Games were held there! At least I'll enjoy the music! Now "that's *amore*"! We'll eventually be attending some conferences together, and I'll be looking forward to articles you write on Greek religion. You know, Jeremy, I think I'd like to write a historical novel. Nor would I need the Catholic Church's permission to have it published - the *imprimatur* of the "old days"! Sounds funny to talk about the "old days" in reference to a historical novel! I wouldn't expect to be the next Robert Graves, but I have an idea for a story set in the time of Seneca. That means Nero would be a character in the book. If I include the Great Fire, do you think the book would become a hot commodity? What's that, you're heading to the *vomitorium*? Or I could write a novel about a young boy who grows up loving Latin. Here we could perhaps speak of the "GOOD old days"! Once again, no worries about the need for a *non obstat* – a confirmation that there was nothing objectionable to the Church. Nevertheless, I would have to be conscious of certain sensitivities in the description of issues and even in the choice of words. I have a feeling that society at large could exercise a "controversial censorsip" that would have ramifications for literature – I would even venture "great literature" – past, present and future! Imagine -the life of a Latin student – I'd be the second classicist to write a "love story"! Manon and I are going to join in the Bicentennial celebrations with my parents – no not their wedding anniversary! - America's two hundredth birthday! With all those candles, talk about your "Great Fire"! So, "Professor", I guess we'll see you at the end of the summer! I hope you're not saying "not if I see you first"! Take care! Your Classics Colleague, Hold On!

Chapter 131

\-   It's been an amazing week, Holden! And I've enjoyed our walks through Burnet Woods! I guess it's kind of a sentimental journey for you. But you look pensive, even a little sad.

\-   Being in Burnet Woods has brought back a lot of memories, and even though I've been a student in Quebec for ten years, I feel that now I'm officially saying good-by to Cincinnati. It's like the song "Then You Can Tell Me Good-by" by The Casinos! It's weird, because they're from Cincinnati! When The Four Lads sang "Down By the Riverside", I'd be listening to my transistor radio along the banks of the Kentucky River. Now I'll be listening to that song beside the shores of the St. Lawrence! I can watch the "Harbor Lights", like in the song by The Platters! I'm lucky, though, that there's a radio station in Montreal that plays oldies hits! One day, I heard the song "Yes, I'm Ready" by Barbara Mason , and, Manon, I really believe I'm ready to start a career in Montreal, and to start our life together there! Just as Renée Claude sings in that song I love – *"C'est le Début d'un Temps Nouveau"*! It has been nice seeing everybody – Mickey, Rick, Jeff – yes even Jeff - from my Pizza Pete days, my teachers at St. Xavier High, Professor Sloan at Xavier University, Donnie Johnson at Indian Hills Golf Club. Even though I saw many of them last year, this year was different. In the context of the Bicentennial celebrations, I saw them as real Americans, all proud and patriotic. And that's a good thing, Manon! It reminds me of Canada's Centennial celebrations when I arrived in Montreal as a student at McGill. There was a high pitch of excitement then too, but I was an outsider – merely a witness. After so many years away, I feel like a spectator to the excitement in America – just a visitor! It was nice, though, to see the Riverfront Park that the City set up.

\-   It was beautiful, Holden! I also found the museum displays and exhibitions very informative. It was like having an interactive lesson on the history of Cincinnati and of Ohio. I've learned so much about the United States in just one week. There isn't any noticeable racial animosity – everyone seems so friendly!

\-   I'm afraid it may only be a temporary situation due to the excitement of the celebrations. Wounds caused by the color barrier are too deep to be healed overnight. Back in 1967, everyone seemed happy and cheerful in Montreal – and across Canada! There was genuine euphoria from coast to coast! But three years later, there was social violence and internecine hatred. If we truly learn from history, then we would be prudent to consider that internecine warfare between Greek states eventually led to a loss of Greek freedom, as their divisions prevented them from opposing a united front against Philip of Macedon! Likewise, conflict over social inequalities ultimately led to the downfall of the Roman Repulican State!

Remember the October Crisis, Manon, and the War Measures Act? The "two solitudes" were again front and center. We are now almost six years beyond those terrible events, and I truly believe that nationalists and separatists - or whatever name they wish to identify themselves by – in some parts of the world they would be called freedom fighters! – are going to try a political answer to their dreams. Think of that TV show that Bob has us watching – "All in the Family". I think that a large part of the French population could probably identify with Edith Bunker, who is always being "stifled" by a husband who has more clout, and takes advantage of her good nature! You know that I'm not really into politics, Manon, but I am almost positive that the Parti Québécois will win the election next Fall. Call it *Zeitgeist*! That's how Germans express the "spirit of the times". For sure, once in power, René Lévesque and his government will be looking for a realistic way of forming a French nation that will allow the language and the culture of the French-speaking majority to benefit fully from "majority rights"!

I like René Lévesque, but in leaving Canada, Quebec would lose more than it would gain. I learned in my history courses on Canada and Quebec that Canada is a great country, and Quebec would be better off as a part OF it and not apart FROM it!

-       Do you really think that would happen, Holden? What would become of Federal Government employees like myself?

-       You might end up working for an expanded provincial-turned-national government bureaucracy, but you could kiss your bilingual bonus good-by! American elections are also taking place next Fall. And I firmly believe that President Ford will be defeated. He's a nice person, and he likes golf, so he's normal! Did you know that he had changed his name to Gerald Ford Jr. after being adopted by his mother's second husband? But he only became President because Nixon resigned. His Republican Party was severely tarnished by recent events, and that translates into a change of government. At least he got to be President during the Bicentennial celebrations. They end on July 4, naturally. But you know, Manon, Washington, Jefferson, Adams, and Ben Franklin are names engraved in American hearts, but Cicero, Caesar, Vergil, Augustus, Horace and Seneca are engraved in my mind! When I think "Republican" now, I think S.P.Q.R.!

-       Of course, Holden, you are much more than a Reds fan or a St. Xavier High alumnus or an Indian Hills caddy or even the best-ever counter-guy at Pizza Pete's! You're a Latin student - the Latin student of my dreams!

-	I wish Pete were still around. He would have treated us to free pizza and all the music we could listen to on the juke-box!

-	Your parents seem to be letting go in their own way. Your mother is already treating me like a daughter-in-law, better – like a daughter! Your father seems genuinely proud of you.

-	When I was in high school, Dad never imagined I'd end up as a Classics professor, much less living in Quebec. But while we were playing golf yesterday – and I'm still the champion, by the way – he kept talking to Donnie Johnson, the Pro and my old boss, about how brilliant I was, a PhD who spoke many languages, a professor at a major Canadian university, and a heroic young man who thwarted a bank robbery by a disoriented young man, who rescued a young woman from a vicious attack, who defied the odds to save a man from drowning, and who had risked his life in a fire to save the life of a baby. And you know what, Manon – he said I was engaged to the most beautiful girl he had ever met besides my mother!

-	Now you have me blushing, Holden! I know your parents were very proud – as was your sister - at the Laval University convocation. When they called your name – the degree of Doctor of Philosophy is awarded to Dr. Holden Denys Hainsworth – I had a lump in my throat. Yours was the first name they called – I didn't have time to be nervous!

-	I was speechless too, Manon when you gave me my graduation gift. I never would have imagined that you could know how valuable having my personal copy of the Oxford Classical Dictionary as a reference book will be! Owning a copy the OCD will make me the envy of many classicists! The diplomas are distributed in alphabetical order. I guess it was a bit exceptional this year that there were no recipients with names beginning from A to G. But there were a number of names beginning with P and Q. Again, Manon, I don't want to appear prophetic, and you can tell me to mind my p's and q's, but the PQ is the political party that will form the next government in Quebec! Don't tell me to "mind my own beeswax", because it's the buzz in Quebec these days! Besides, Honey Bee, I'll be living there with you! Just as long as there is no civil war as there was in America or in Ancient Rome! I think there is still, in a strange way, a shadow of SPQR hovering over us after all these centuries. But there is no *Senatus Romanus* – the government of Rome. Quebec is not Rome, and there is no senate in Quebec. However, for the Romans, PQ meant "and the people". I'm just saying…

-	Awesome, Denys! Have you been reading those Sibylline books you told me about? Your mother will surely be very involved when Phoebe's baby is born. As you said, you don't feel as bad leaving your family, since they'll all be able to concentrate on a newborn child.

And Christmas, Easter, American Thanksgiving, and Spring Break will be wonderful occasions to get together - I know you're thinking of the Beatles song "Come Together"!

- You are starting to read my mind, Manon, and see the songs stored there! I wondered when that would happen while I was listening one day to the Gordon Lightfoot song "If You Could Read My Mind"! We might still want to travel, but yes, Cincinnati or Montreal will be destinations for our families for the next while. I would, though, like to visit Canada in a cross-country train trip. And a road trip across the U.S.A. would be fun!

- I would love to visit the Scandinavian countries, and maybe travel to Japan. But you have to prepare your next trip, Holden. You promise to write often while you are in Rome?

- Right up to the moment I hear Dean Martin singing *Arrivederci Roma*"! It is so nice of your parents to store my clothes and books at your home in St. Lambert – oh, and some records! I'll be moving into my apartment when I get back from my summer programme. Who knows, Manon – if I teach for 44 years like Professor Underhill, we'll be in the year 2021 when I retire. I wonder what Montreal will be like then. There will be changes for sure. I'll bet the Mayor of the City will be a woman! Sorry to say, your father will no longer be with us. Probably a good thing for him, since his beloved Montreal Canadiens won't possibly be able to dominate the league as they do now. Like everything else, hockey will become more about money than "honey" – that's just my way of describing the "sweet pleasure" the sport brought to folks like your father! They dominated the league for so many years – real "lions" during the winter months – but, alas, Montreal – and all Quebec – will have to suffer many winters of discontent!

- I wonder if Quebec will still be in Canada, or even if Canada will still have a Queen. And, Denys, I dread the thought of losing my mother!

- Call me psychic, Manon, but even as an American by birth, I recognize that Queen Elizabeth is quite the lady, and I wouldn't be surprised to see her on the throne in 2021.

She will be the new "Queen Victoria" – but with a better disposition! – and reign, yes even over Canada, including Quebec, until she has spent 70 years on the throne! It's a strange coincidence that Queen Elizabeth's birthday falls on April 21 – the legendary date that Rome began her monarchy! But even powerful Rome moved on from the monarchy. Maybe then Canada also could part – even with "sweet sorrow" – from the monarchy. When I arrived in Montreal back in 1967, you were celebrating your country's Centennial. I have a strong feeling that you're going to be able to celebrate your mother's centennial one day!

Chapter 132

-        Hi there Jeremy, I know I'll see you in Montreal in a few weeks, but I was too excited about the course I just finished here at the American Academy in Rome! Even more exciting is the news about your girlfriend – sounds pretty serious! I couldn't believe it when you told me in your last letter about Michelle - that's her name isn't it? – "Michelle, my belle…" don't get mad – you like the Beatles! But she works for the Federal Government in Toronto – in Veterans Affairs, like Manon! What were the odds? But then, I always found you a bit odd! Just joking! I actually found you very odd! Joking *bis*! You always complained about your love-life – or lack thereof , i.e., "lack of love", just a little poetry, Jeremy, for old times' sake!– and now you have found true romance! I guess Toronto does have its redeeming points! But you're coming to Montreal, and Michelle will be working in Toronto. Well, take it from me, old friend, a long- distance relationship is not only possible – it's more than worth it! Michelle could eventually get a transfer to Montreal, like Manon, and if she stays with Veterans Affairs, she will be working with Manon! Unreal! I guess we could play golf together, since you'll be back in Montreal. But we'll have to find another club besides The Country Club – you're no longer a junior member – so we're talking big bucks! There is a nice little nine hole course in St. Lambert – I think you once referred to it as "The Rock Pile", but I went to play it with my Dad, and it's really okay. Besides, if the rumors are true about low starting salaries for professors, we'll have to be satisfied with going to the driving range! Do you remember that old TV show, "The Honeymooners", when Ed Norton – who was, I think you'll agree, the funniest guy on television - in addressing the ball, says "Hello, ball!"? While teeing off with Dad, I changed it to "So long, ball!" Dad laughed really hard, but not enough to throw him off his game! But now about my exciting Latin course! Before looking at Latin texts from the period, we spent some time on the *Distichs* of Cato – no not Cato the Censor, but a writer of the 3rd or 4th century of our era. Apparently, it was the most popular Latin textbook of the Middle Ages, and was quoted by Geoffrey Chaucer, and even Benjamin Franklin – have you ever read his *Poor Farmer's Almanach*? You probably know that a distich is a two-line verse from the Greek word *distichos*, which was formed from *stichos* – a row or line – and *di*- double, that is, two. Jeremy, there is the Latin word *distichon*, obviously just a transliteration of the Greek word, and not a translation! How many words in English and French – not to mention Italian, Spanish and Portuguese – are mere transliterations of Greek and Latin words? As the kisses Catullus wished to share with Lesbia, they are "countless"! My favorite proverbial saying from this collection is "If you live rightly, do not worry about the words of bad people"! Does it remind you of "sticks and stones may break my bones, but words will never hurt me"? Surely you recall the night we wisely avoided accepting the challenge of five goons on one of our "downtown dallyings". You resented our being called "chickens", but I remarked that I would rather be a "live chicken" than a "dead duck"! You quickly regained your spirits by suggesting I had a "fowl" mouth, and that, at any rate, both those birds would make a fine meal! On a more serious note, I believe that the time is coming when names really will hurt people – call it stereotyping or profiling or systemic racism or whatever – and all that could lead to lots of broken bones! The first session was an introduction to Medieval Latin. Just to be clear, Jeremy, it's not the Vulgar Latin spoken by soldiers and peasants, but a form of literary Latin that is a direct descendant of Classical Latin. It's not a kind of kitchen Latin that some classicists refer to as *infima Latinitas* – you know, the "meanest form of Latin". We studied the morphology and syntax of the Latin of the Middle Ages, and of course, all that new vocabulary. Just to give you one example of the evolution of classical usage, the first word in the Aeneid is the neuter plural *arma*, meaning "arms, military weapons", but also "tools or instruments". Medieval Latin also attests a feminine singular *arma*, a "tool or weapon". But then, my late friend, Tommy Nelson, used to identify *arma* in Vergil as feminine singular back at St. Xavier High! Maybe he could have become a Medieval Latin scholar, if he hadn't been killed in Vietnam, an unfortunate victim of the neuter plural *arma*! Naturally, we looked at the Humanist Latin of the Italian writers, and I learned that there is a distinction between this body of Latin and what I had heard called Neo-Latin, which really encompasses a broader field of works written in Latin. We read some biblical texts and a few scientific treatises, but my favorite Medieval texts, as you can imagine, were the literary works - epic, satire, and drama, just to name a few, much of it Christian in narrative and in tone. We even read Seneca – not really, but I was happy to read the apocryphal correspondence between Seneca and St. Paul, and to "pretend" I was reading my favorite Latin author! We also looked at a category of writing that I had never heard of called Vision Literature, which is exactly what it sounds like – accounts of visions and dreams! And speaking of visions, I found myself imagining sitting in a classroom full of students who spoke different languages outside the classroom, but for whom the instruction was entirely in Latin. In this sense, Latin was a *lingua franca* for many students of different mother-tongues, like some sort of "father-tongue", so to speak! And I am not saying that "tongue-in-cheek"! It reminded me of my Greek courses in the international programme at the Balkan Institute, with many participants only able to communicate with each other in Greek. In the programme in Rome, we didn't all speak in Latin, but I am aware of institutions which offer "conversational Latin" sessions – so, maybe one day, you know, remaining forever "the Latin student"! We read selections from numerous authors – all organized chronologically. Some texts were written in prose, others in verse. From the fourth century, we read, of course, St. Jerome and St. Augustine. The fifth and sixth centuries provided works by Sidonius Appolinaris, Boethius and Gregory of Tours. The seventh and eighth centuries were represented by the poet Venantius Fortunatus and by the Venerable Bede, who wrote the *Ecclesiastical History of the English People*. From the ninth century, we read the poetry of the great teacher Alcuin and of Angelbert – no, he didn't sing "Release Me" – that was ENGLEbert- Englebert Humperdinck! The tenth and eleventh century works were written by Robert the Monk and Hrosvitha of Gandersheim – that name sounds a bit like "Faversham" - the name of the play producer in the "On Stage" episode of "The Honeymooners", who falsely gave Ralph Kramden the illusion that "everybody's favorite bus driver" could act. Yes, I know, like me when I was on stage in those Greek and Latin plays! Thank you, Jeremy "Faversham" from "Gandersheim"! I especially enjoyed reading selections from the plays written by Hrosvitha – *Gallicanus* (in two parts), *Dulcitius, Callimachus Abraham, Paphnutius*, and *Sapientia*. This last play is set in the time of Hadrian. Sapientia is a learned Christian woman – aptly named, isn't she? – who has three daughters, Fides, Spes, and Karitas – Faith, Hope, and Charity! The three girls are martyred for not giving up their Christian religion. Here is a sampling of the play where Hadrian is trying to win over the daughters of Sapientia. *Adrianus: Adhuc mitigate furore. nulla in te moveor indignatione. sed pro tua tuique filiarum salute. paterno solicitor amore. Sapientia: Nolite meae filiae serpentinis huius satanae lenociniis cor apponere. sed meatim fastidite.* Here is my translation – feel free to comment (I replaced the symbolic feminine singular genitive ending with the classical 'ae'). "Hadrian: Soften your anger. I am not moved against you by any indignation. It is with a father's love that I am solicited on behalf of your safety, both that of yourself and of your daughters. Sapientia:" (she would be whispering this!) " Don't take to heart this lewd, snake-like devil. Despise him, as I do." Hrotswitha, as she is sometimes called, the only important Latin playwright after Seneca, was a Saxon nun. Another "connection" between Nero's tutor and the Christians? For the twelfth century, we read from Peter Abelard, Heloise and Geoffrey of Monmouth. We read excerpts from the *Carmina Burana*, composed in the thirteenth century. Finally, from the fourteenth and fifteenth centuries, we read from the works of Petrarch, Boccaccio, Erasmus, and Sir Thomas More – or as I prefer – SAINT Thomas More! We ended the Medieval Latin section of the course rather fittingly with a poem entitled *O Roma Nobilis*, which begins with '*O Roma nobilis, orbis et domina/ cunctarum urbium excellentissima* "O noble Rome, most excellent mistress of the world and of every city". Again, feel free to comment! It's a beautiful sentiment, don't you think, for a "Latin student in Rome"? The Renaissance component of the course would probably have interested you very much, Jeremy. Early on we had a slide lecture on the representation of the Olympian gods in the ancient manner, as it were, or, for us Italian buffs, *all' antica*. The reading list was quite extensive, even if by no means, exhaustive! We started with a transitional Medieval –

Renaissance writer, Francesco Petrarca – we had already seen him in the first section of the course. He wrote *Invectives,* searching to recapture the classical beauty of Cicero. Verifying the accuracy of my translations will make my letter less tedious for you! Petrarch begins with *Quisquis es qui iacentem calamum et sopitum, importunis latratibus ut ita dixerim leonem excitasti, iam senties aliud esse alienam famam prurienti lingua carpere, aliud propriam ratione defendere.* "Whoever you are, with your troublesome barking you have stirred up a discarded pen and, I would say, a sleeping lion, and you will now understand that it is one thing to seize upon another's reputation with a prurient tongue, and another to defend one's own reputation with reason." So Jeremy, *carpe diem, non leonem* – "seize the day, not the lion"! Next we read from Leonardo Bruni's *History of the Florentine People.* In his Seventh Book, he describes the beginning of the Black Death. *Variis tamen morborum generibus laborabatur, et pestilentiae, qua postmodum vastata Italiae est, signa quaedam horrenda tunc primum apparuerunt.* "There was an ongoing struggle with various kinds of diseases, and then certain horrific signs began to appear of the pestilence, by which Italy was afterwards devastated". The text I found the most interesting was the *Platonic Theology* of Marsilio Ficino. He attributes to Plato the belief that we – that is, our souls – can never understand anything without the light – the grace – of God. He praises Plato for his example – for not inviting us to "do as I say, not as I do"! *Neque solum ad id pietatis officium Plato noster ceteros adhortatur, verum etiam ipse maxime praestat.* "Not only does our Plato exhort others to this duty of piety, he himself very much takes the lead". Angelo Poliziano wrote poems in the hexameter meter with the same title as those of Statius – *Silvae.* Here are the opening lines of his poem *Rusticus* – "*The Countryman*" which introduced his lectures on Hesiod and the *Georgics* of Vergil. *Ruris opes saturi gnavoque agitanda colono/ munera et omniferae telluris honorem/ sacrum ludere septena gestit mea fistula canna.* "My seven-reeded pipe is eager to play of the riches of the fertile countryside and the work of the diligent farmer and the sacred honor of the all-producing earth". Shades of Vergil, for sure! We read from another transitional writer Boccaccio, who became very popular by writing in the vernacular Italian, just like Glen Campbell when he crossed over from country to country pop music. He wrote one hundred six biographies of famous women – *De mulieribus claris.* Among them were the goddesses Juno and Venus, famous mythological queens, such as Jocasta, Hecuba, Penelope, and Dido, and also the notorious Cleopatra, and famous Roman women, namely, Lucretia, Agrippina, the mother of Nero, and Pompeia Paulina, the wife of Seneca. An interesting treatise was the one on the education of boys – *De liberorum educatione* – written by Aeneas Silvius Piccolomini. Imagine having "Aeneas" for a teacher! Especially when the curriculum emphasized a sound training for the body and the mind – you can't escape *mens sana in corpore sano*! I quite liked reading from the biographies written by Giannozo Manetti, who wrote "parallel lives" like Plutarch. We read *Vita Socratis* and *Vita Senecae*. He quotes Quintilian who sometimes criticized Seneca, but who nevertheless praised his ''ready and fertile intelligence, his extensive study and his vast knowledge of things" – *ingenium facile et copiosum; plurimi studii, multa rerum cognitio.* Maffeo Vegio wrote a Book Thirteen of Vergil's *Aeneid* – I guess he wasn't superstitious, but then he wasn't in Ancient Rome, nor was he writing about the Stevie Wonder song "Superstition" …"Very superstitious… writing's on the wall…" – oh no, that would be Pompeii and her graffiti! This short epic ends with *De hinc laeta recentem / felicemque animam secum super aera duxit/ immisitque Aenean astris, quem Iulia proles/ indigitem appellat templisque imponit honores.* "Then happily she" – i.e. Venus – ''led the newly blessed soul with her above the air and placed among the stars Aeneas, whom his Julian descendants call *Indiges*" – that is to say, a native god like "indigenous'', Jeremy – ''and she decreed the honors in his temples'' – that is, a cult. All that was missing was Barbara Streisand singing in a "A Star Is Born" – or Earth, Wind & Fire singing "Shining Star"! Speaking of Vergil, we next read *De inventoribus rerum*, a comprehensive account of discoveries and inventions written by one Polydore Vergil. He aimed at praising all those who had been the first to achieve things. We finished the course with three authors - Leon Battista Alberti, who wrote a satirical comedy called *Momus* – the name of his protagonist, a really miserable character; Cyriac of Ancona, who wrote about his travels to Greece and elsewhere and finally, Biondo Flavio, who wrote *Italia illustrata*, which describes the topography of Italy, region by region. Quite the course, wouldn't you agree, Jeremy? During the two days left in Rome/ before my flight to go back home – in case you didn't notice, I just composed a two-line rhyming verse! – I passed the time with two Americans in the course – two young professors. Terry teaches Romance Literature at Penn State, and Warren teaches Medieval History at Ohio State – he grew up just outside of Cincinnati! They had fond memories of their high school studies in Latin, and while enjoying some of Rome's finest wine - I seem to have overcome the demonic effect that *vino* once had on me! - we would invent ways of converting modern expressions into Latin. We weren't bored – just trying to be creative! About someone who was badly dressed, we'd say *condemno virum de criminibus modi.* To someone who looked like he just fell off a truck, we'd say *De autocarro cecidistine?.* How about "Your house is on a building site"? That would go something like *Domus tua in situ aedificandi est.* Walking by the Colosseum, we thought of ''Gladiators were the best athletes", and rendered it by *Gladiatores maximi erant athletae.* If you were feeling lonely, you might be tempted to approach someone with *Cur amicus tuus esse non possum?* – "Why can't I be your friend?" I wish I had thought of this one before – *Quo animo intendis?* – "What do you have in mind?" This one is for my father – *Me patrem vocare potes* – "you can call me Dad"! And again with my Dad, "We saw an awesome game yesterday" would have been *Ludum optimum heri vidimus*. "Can't is not in my dictionary" would be rendered in Latin by *Verbum "non posse" non in thesauro verborum meo est.* Here is one for high school students - *Regulae violandae sunt* – "Rules are made to be broken"! Of course, I don't really subscribe to that advice for the young – or the old! You recall that legal maxim by the third century Roman jurist Ulpian (okay *Domitius Ulpianus*) – *lex dura, sed lex* - the law may be harsh, but it's the law! As I've told you in the past, I believe that disobedience of the law is not the solution – it leads to discord and disorientation. Even if you don't agree with me, Jeremy, you can at least admire my alliteration! No, in a democracy the answer to unjust or unmanageable laws is to change them. That is after all, the literal meaning of "democracy" –"power to the people"! Here's another expression for your typical teenager – *Nunc nobis bibendum est* – "Let's get wasted". Not the best of advice but I seem to recall a couple of McGill students who sometimes swore by it – and were sworn at! Finally, I started thinking about Manon, and this is what I came up with – *Non optima res est emere – sola est!* – "Shopping is not the best activity – it's the only activity!" With apologies to Vince Lombardi! Well, that last expression reminds me I have a little shopping of my own to do – a gift for Manon! See you in a few weeks in Montreal! Your *amicus,* Professor (ahem) Holden Hainsworth!

Chapter 133

\-   Just look at us, Manon – both wearing blue like the first time we met! I heard a new song on the radio by Michel Louvain called *"La Dame en bleu"*. She could be you – wearing my lucky color! It reminds me of that painting you liked at Le Louvre – *"La Dame en bleu"* by Camille Corot. Imagine – that painting is just over one hundred years old! I hope my "lady in blue" lives that long! I know that Van Gogh is your favorite painter, and you told me about his "blue period", and how much you like his still life paintings. You also mentioned "The Blue Boy" painting by Thomas Gainesborough, since I'm often dressed in blue! I recently learned that this painting is hanging in a library in California! Manon, like Al Green sings, this "boy in blue" is "STILL in Love With You"! In my music course at McGill we heard about "The Three L's" – Lautrec, Louvain and Lalonde. We've already danced to Donald Lautrec's *"Manon, viens danser le Ska"*, and Pierre Lalonde's song "Honey, Honey" reminds me of my pet name for you, Honey Bee! Did you know that song was written by Renée Martel? Of course, the "three L's" could apply to me – Latin Language Lover! When those three singers pass away and go to heaven, will they become "L's Angels"?

\-   Denys, now I'm wondering if when I hear you whispering "I'm so in love with you" you are really saying "I'm so in love with blue"! You've already told me that your favorite bird is, naturally, the blue jay. You even said that when we saw one in Toronto, Jeremy mentioned that maybe there would be more of them in that city one day. What I couldn't understand at all was when he said they might hook up with bats! My favorite bird is the beautiful red cardinal!

\-   Gee, Manon, those birds are just like my books – they are all "read"! While we are enjoying an aperitif, Manon, can I share some intriguing reflections with you?

\-   Of course! You haven't stopped being intriguing since we met five years ago!

\-   Well, you remember when we prayed the Stations of the Cross at that beautiful church in St. Romuald? I recently reflected on the fact that I have spent thirteen years in serious study of Latin. I am about to lay to rest my studies in order to take up a fourteenth year of Latin – but now as a professor! Just as Christ's Passion in those fourteen stations narrates a "Labor of Love", my years as a student of Latin are likewise the story of a "labor of love"! And just as the Resurrection is a "fifteenth Station", so our marriage next year will be a "fifteenth station" for me – a "new life'" as is signified by the Resurrection! I had another thought as well. Considering that I was following a university-level Latin course during my senior year in high school I "labored " through twelve years of university Latin! Manon, it's just like the twelve labors of Hercules! And just as that hero's efforts earned him a place on top of Mount Olympus, my efforts have been rewarded with a university professorship on top of the mountain in Montreal at l'Université de Montréal!

- Quite the puzzling parallels indeed! Yet not surprising. After all, you told me that your mother's and father's names destined you for a study of Latin and the Romans!

- That's right, Manon. My mother's name – Patricia – would have made her a noble "patrician" woman in Ancient Rome! My Dad's name is Arnold. When I call him Arnie on the golf course, it is to tease him about not having to worry about being taken for Arnold Palmer! However, his name has the Germanic root *Arn* meaning "eagle". His "eagle power" will not help him eagle a hole on the golf course but connects him to the Roman eagle – symbol of Roman authority!

- The waitress is bringing our meal. It looks delicious, Holden! I know you can't wait for the music to start. I wonder if they will play songs you haven't heard of. I'm looking forward to this '50's and '60's revival night, even though I won't know the names of too many songs. I don't recall music called Doo Wop – maybe I was too young! But I enjoy listening to Motown. I love The Supremes! By the way, you don't mind, do you, if my family continues to call you Denys?

- Well, after all, it is my name – one of my names – as long as they don't wear it out! Speaking of names, Manon, you probably didn't know that The Supremes were originally in a group called The Primettes. Both names suggest "the best", and as far as girl groups go, I'm with you – they are the best! You may be surprised to learn that my favorite "Supreme" has always been Mary Wilson – maybe because she reminds me of my first girlfriend! Well, until I met you, Manon, she had been my only girlfriend! But that was during my high school years in Cincinnati and seems like such a long time ago. Like Dion sang in his song – I was just a "Teenager in Love"! Yes, we always eat well here at Claude St. Jean's. My pepper steak didn't LET me down – as it WENT down! I'm just wondering if they'll play any songs that I don't have in my collection! There is a new song, though, in my collection, that came out last year and that we will be listening to quite often – in fact, we will be living that song! It's sung by Carl Carlton and is called "Everlasting Love"!

- You and I love music, Denys, and that song tells me that music loves us!

- Manon, you would have been eight or nine when Doo Wop started, but that music continued to be popular for at least another ten years – just not on French radio stations in

Quebec! But not to worry, I'll tell you the titles – and the names of the singers. Not all the songs will be dance songs, but nonetheless fun to listen to. Hey, the music is starting!

-        I didn't recognize those songs. I'm glad this isn't a contest! Remember those contests we won – the dance contest – and the '60's song contest? And you won a Motown contest when you were a student at McGill. But, Holden, you'll always be my "winner" – no contest!

-        What a clever play on words, Manon! You are definitely my prize pupil! Or maybe just my "prize"!

-        You always know what to say, Holden, in English or French! Or in those other languages you speak – and especially in Latin! What songs did they just play?

-        I wonder if they will group the songs by style – I guess I should say genre. The songs we heard were all Doo Wop. They started with two songs by Cleveland Still and The Dubs "Could This Be Magic", and "Please Don't Ask Me To Be Lonely". If you listened to the words, it was as if I were talking to you, Manon! By the way, they are "still" singing, and not only in "Cleveland"! Next we heard The Elegants singing "Little Star" and The Excellents with "Coney Island Baby". Were you thinking of our big event when they played "Church Bells Will Ring" by The Willows? After that was "Story Untold" by – don't laugh at the name – The Nutmegs! Then it was The Capris with their big hit "There's a Moon Out Tonight". Once I was out late with Jeremy, and that song came on my transistor radio. I had had a few beers and Jeremy more than a few! Suddenly there were two moons out that night! At that moment, Jeremy began to misquote Shakespeare's Mark Antony, shouting "Friends, Romans, countrymen – show me your rears"! Well, there weren't any Romans – and certainly no friends of ours! As for countrymen, we were lucky not to be exiled – to St. Helen's Island! Just like Napoleon - exiled to St. Helena! Beware of "Helen" – as the Trojans found out! Sad to say, that's only one example of the "nocturnal nonsense" that Jeremy and I got up to – or, rather, that Jeremy put me up to! Nor am I being unfair by "rendering to Caesar…"! The song "Stay" by Maurice Williams and The Zodiacs was next. He wrote that song "Little Darlin'" that you like so much. By the time the Doo Wop songs were over, we managed to finish our drinks. The last songs were "Hushabye" by The Mystics, "Once in a While" by The Chimes, "Silhouettes" by The Rays, "Tears On My Pillow" by Little Anthony and The Imperials, "There Goes My Baby" by The Drifters, and then songs by three popular Doo Wop groups. They started with a group you did recognize – The Platters – and their songs "Great Pretender" and "My Prayer". They were followed by Johnny Maestro and The Crests with "Trouble in Paradise". Then we heard Jimmy Beaumont and The Skyliners with the songs "Since I Don't Have You" and "This I Swear".

- 	You were right, Holden, Doo Wop music is about sincerity and the ups and downs of being in love. As they say, it's easy to fall in love, but harder to stay in love! When you got back from Rome, you couldn't stop talking about the Latin courses you took at the American Academy. You won't be spending all your summers in Europe will you, Holden?

- 	I don't think so, Manon. But Professor Gingras did mention the possibility of accompanying groups to Italy and Greece. These visits wouldn't be as long as my study sessions and ideally we could combine them with your vacation periods, and you could travel with us. In a way, I don't think my days as a "Latin student" are over. Professors never stop learning – there is too much knowledge out there – but from now on, I will be the teacher, not just the student! Hey, there's a Motown song by The Supremes – "Love Is Here And Now You're Gone" – let's dance!

- 	I think you were right about grouping the songs, Holden. They were all Motown songs – and so much fun to dance to! I recognized some of the singers.They followed up with another song by The Supremes – I think it's called "Come See About Me". Then there was Smokey Robinson and The Four Tops, but of course I don't know the song titles, even though I hear them a lot on the radio.

- 	The Miracles' song was "I Second That Emotion" and we heard two songs by The Four Tops – "Bernadette" and "It's The Same Old Song". Then we heard "Don't Mess With Bill" by The Marvelettes and "This Old Heart of Mine" by The Isley Brothers. I could tell you really enjoyed the last songs in that segment– and they were all by The Supremes – I have all their songs at home! They just played "Love Is Like An Itching in My Heart", "I'm Living in Shame" and "Baby Love".

- 	I wanted to tell you how much I like your apartment. It's nice and cozy! And you're so lucky to be able to walk to work! Oh, sorry – you don't want me to call it "work". Are you sure you still don't want to be considered a student? I don't know if I will ever get used to driving across the bridge every day, and it's a pain having to throw a token into the toll booth. I've missed a couple of times. But you cheered me up when you said to just relax during rush hour, since nobody is actually "rushing"!

- 	Manon, the first time I was in Rome, I watched an old 1935 movie on TV at the residence. It was about the life of Saint Don Bosco, the Italian priest who is known as the "Father and teacher of youth". That makes him the patron saint of teachers and learners! Fulfilling my vocation as an educator is a mission of sorts, even if you think I'm a bit crazy for wanting to "spread the good news of Latin"! It was fitting that the modular programme for future professors that I followed at McGill was called "Teaching and Learning"! Well, Manon, if we buy a house in Brossard, as we are hoping to do, I'll be driving across the bridge as well. Since the University is not far from your office, I would have suggested car-pooling, but I may be giving evening courses a couple of nights a week in that Latin and Greek programme for the general public, and lectures for *Les Belles Histoires*. I guess we'll just have to cross that bridge when we come to it! All this talk about bridges reminds me of something I heard Martin Luther King say – "we must build bridges, not walls!" Obviously, he was making a plea for all people in America to reach out to one another, rather than confine each other to ghettoes behind "walls of color"! One could make the same argument about "language walls" in this country! Yet, I'm also reminded of Robert Frost's poem "Mending Wall", where he says "good fences make good neighbors"! We know that fences protect property, and that "mending fences" means repairing broken relationships between neighbours. A wall – in Dr. King's sense – can be exclusive. But in the description given by Frost, a small wall can be protective. I am not a Canadian politician – and not yet a Canadian citizen – but I see" Frost's "fences" – a good name for fences, don't you think, Manon? – as "protecting" the rights of the individual provinces and the "walls" that Martin Luther King is warning us to avoid as "barriers" to cooperative sharing among the provinces. Even the Roman provinces – *provinciae* – shared rights and privileges along with obligations under the eagle of Rome! "Don't fence me in" is tantamount to saying "don't wall me out". It is time, I think, for all of us to "get off the fence", because we know what happened to Humpty Dumpty when he sat too long "on the wall"! We all have to cross Martin Luther King's bridge!

-       My, my Denys – you could be Prime Minister of Canada – or President of The United States! And you'd be sure to maintain good relations with "Latin" America!

-       For sure, I'll never be "King "of England! Manon, if I do decide to buy a car - and I have money saved up from my part-time teaching and from the Parker Foundation – I hope that used two-tone blue Buick is still for sale! We can dance again – they are playing "Two Faces Have I" by Lou Christie. That song could have been a hymn to the Roman god Janus – you know, the two-faced god of entrances and exits, of beginnings and endings, from whom we got the name for January! All of a sudden I'm getting this strange vision of a beginning and an end!

-       True, Denys. For a minute, there, you looked like you were in a trance – like you were somewhere else! Those were very nice songs from the '60's we just heard, Holden. Were they transporting you into the past? I know you can tell me all the song titles. You know that even a year from now, when we are married, this will still be a nice spot to come and eat and to dance. To "wine and un-wined", you brilliantly said! I didn't understand at first, until you wrote "unwind" as "un-wined"!

- Definitely a nice spot! Eventually, Bob and Maggie will start going out again with your mother as official baby sitter. And when Jeremy's girlfriend, Michelle, is in town, maybe they will join us as well. I wonder if you two will ever end up working together. Listening to these songs from the '60's brings back fond memories of Cincinnati and Montreal. People who claim not to remember the '60's missed out on great times – and now great memories! I have to admit, though, that they can't compare with the precious moments of the '70's that I have been sharing with you, Manon! Hopefully some one will produce a TV show about the '70's one day that we will be able to watch and nostalgically recollect these first years spent together! Here's your song list, Manon. It starts with a Ricky Nelson song – "Fools Rush In". Next was "Sherry" by The Four Seasons – no, Manon, they are not a Canadian group, and their name does not refer to Canadian weather. You remember that group whose lead singer is Frankie Valli? Then there were songs by singers that even our parents like – Ray Charles and "Unchain My Heart", Sammy Davis with "What Kind of Fool Am I", Andy Williams singing "More", Frank Sinatra with "You Make Me Feel So Young", Dean Martin with "That's *Amore*", and two songs by Johnny Mathis - "Chances Are" and "Misty". I was wondering why there were some older couples here, but then with that Frank Sinatra song they probably didn't feel so old! If it's not their bed time, I guess they will stay for this last set of songs!

- Don't be cruel, Holden! You know that we are as young as we feel! By the way, when is your meeting at the University next week? –

- You are right about the age thing, Manon! Did you deliberately name that Elvis Presley song? I wouldn't call It a meeting, since only the Department secretary will be there to show me my office. I didn't get a good look at her when I went for my interview, but I gather she is old-school with no nonsense approach to her duties. On the other hand, if she happens to like that Frank Sinatra song…

- Stop, Holden! They are starting the music again. It's the Chuck Berry song "Johhny B.Goode" – it's good advice for you too!

- They did finally play Elvis – "Heartbreak Hotel"! After that came Pat Boone with "April Love", a song by The Beach Boys – "Wouldn't It Be Nice", Tom Jones singing "Delilah" and "Green Grass of Home" and Little Richard with "Tutti Frutti" – they really mixed up that last segment of songs, didn't they? After that we heard Conway Twitty with "It's Only Make Believe" and then a song I haven't heard in ages – "I Remember You" by Frank Ifield - and

"Since I Fell For You" by Lenny Welch. It seems that some of the songs we have heard tonight are highlighting our life together. Like that last song by The Righteous Brothers – "Soul and Inspiration". You are definitely my soul and inspiration, Manon! You can't get more "righteous" than that! And Stevie Wonder's song "Isn't She Lovely" – my answer is "yes", because he's singing about you! You may have recognized the Nat King Cole song that played just before the final song. It describes perfectly for me all the songs we have listened to and danced to since we first met. It's called "Unforgettable"! It's interesting that they ended the evening with the Bobby Vee song "The Night Has a Thousand Eyes". The mythological creature Argus had a thousand eyes, and I would like to have had him around when I did my rounds as night watchman at the Indian Hills Golf Club! On the other hand, Manon, as The Flamingos sang, "I Only Have Eyes For You"!

Epilogue

- I was suddenly startled by a knocking – which sounded like a rapping – on my office door. I soon realized that the light over the city was the artificial glow of electric lights brightening up the night sky. I glanced at my watch – I had been in some kind of cosmic coma for almost ten hours. I could hear The Supremes singing "Reflections" in my head as the hours marched by - that Seneca and time! – and I watched… Cincinnati… Mom, Dad, Feeb…St. Joe's - kneeling at the altar, praying in Latin…St. Xavier High School – conjugating Latin verbs… running with the ball and being chased… taking the pizza out of the oven…putting the coins into the juke-box… Pizza Pete swearing… Vergil Cane…in Burnet Woods…Indian Hills…hitting a five iron… Xavier University…translating Vergil…Montreal… McGill…Concordia…Rome…Quebec City… Marie Antoinette Restaurant…Manon… Laval University….Paris…Manon…all that Latin…Latin student…*mens sana in corpore sano*…jogging up Mount Royal…*carpe diem*…Parker… money…throng of people reciting prayers in Latin behind a hooded flamen standing in front of a temple… Manon…lighting candles in St. Joseph's Oratory…songs…lots of songs…Manon dancing… I was now totally conscious of time and place. As Madame Sylvain approached, I had already looked again around my office and acknowledged that life had brought me here – not just Latin!

- Professor "Ainswort", you had not left your office since your arrival early this morning. I went to eat and came back to see if you were all right.

- I noticed that Madame Sylvain's tightly buttoned blouse was no longer buttoned to the top. Her bun-tied hair was now hanging loose. I then remarked that she had closed the door behind her. As she leaned over my desk, I could see the slight application of blush that had been absent when we talked this morning. Her lips, now coated with an aromatic lipstick, began to part…

- I… want to… show you… something.

Finis